Polly's Angel

A Long and Lonely Road

Katie Flynn

arrow books

This edition published by Arrow Books in 2007

Copyright © Katie Flynn 2007

Katie Flynn has asserted her right under the
Copyright, Designs and Patents Act, 1988 to be identified
as the author of this work

Polly's Angel copyright © Katie Flynn 2000
A Long and Lonely Road © Katie Flynn 2004

Arrow Books
The Random House Group Limited
20 Vauxhall Bridge Road, London SW1V 2SA

www.randomhouse.co.uk

Addresses for companies within The Random House Group Limited
can be found at:
www.randomhouse.co.uk/offices.htm

The Random House Group Limited Reg. No. 954009

A CIP catalogue record for this book
is available from the British Library

ISBN 9780099522768

The Random House Group Limited makes every effort to ensure
that the papers used in its books are made from trees that
have been legally sourced from well-managed and credibly
certified forests. Our paper procurement policy can be found at:
www.randomhouse.co.uk/paper.htm

Printed and bound in Great Britain by
Cox & Wyman Ltd, Reading, Berkshire

Katie Flynn has lived for many years in the Northwest. A compulsive writer, she started with short stories and articles and many of her early stories were broadcast on Radio Mersey. She decided to write her Liverpool series after hearing the reminiscences of family members about life in the city in the early years of the twentieth century. She also writes as Judith Saxton. For the past few years she has had to cope with ME but has continued to write.

POLLY'S ANGEL

For Nell Shepherd, whose lovely letters always make
me laugh and who keeps me up to date
with what's going on in Liverpool.

Acknowledgements

My thanks are due, as usual, to a great many people. First and foremost, Cyril Dodman explained the ramifications of becoming a yeoman signaller, the conditions experienced on the Russian convoys and in general life in the Royal Navy during the Second World War. He also checked the MS for me and corrected a couple of awful errors I had made – thank you, Cyril!

Regarding Liverpool during the Blitz, Rosemarie Hague gave me a child's eye view of this ghastly time and put me right on the transport conditions during early May 1941.

Information about Anglesey during the war came to me via Rhys Bebb Jones of the library service, who put me in touch with John Cave of the Maritime Museum, Holyhead, who, in his turn, told me who could help me most. Life in the WRNS was made explicable to me by Kathleen Roberts of Holyhead, who was actually stationed on the island and was thus able to tell me most of the things I needed to know. The late Captain Pritchard had told me about the ferries in wartime for another book, and his widow, Margaret, refreshed my memory, whilst John Emlyn Williams of Four Mile Bridge was kind enough to tell me of his own experiences on the Irish ferries. Information about RAF Valley was provided by Ken Grey, who also gave me titles of books likely to prove helpful to one wanting to know about Beaufighters.

I spent a good deal of time in the Maritime Museum in Holyhead, talking to people, looking at the exhibits and drinking tea in their excellent little cafe, so I'm very grateful to all the staff there, most of whom are volunteers, for the generous giving of their time. What could be nicer than researching in such surroundings and amongst such company!

Because I'm still suffering from ME this book has taken me nearly twice as long as usual to write and consequently, what with the time-lapse and my highly unreliable memory, I may have left someone helpful out, so I do apologise if I have done so.

Chapter One

1936

It was a warm Sunday afternoon in late October, with the leaves on the trees already turning from green to pale gold, crackly brown and deep, gleaming scarlet. Polly O'Brady and her small brother Ivan, each with a basket at the ready, were picking blackberries whilst the dog Delilah roamed ahead, occasionally raising a leg against a particularly inviting bush to a chorus of objections from both children. Polly, who adored her dog, nevertheless scowled at his scraggy, long-haired body as he pottered around the brambles, inhaling deeply whenever he found a new smell.

'Delly! Oh, Ivan, isn't he the worst dog in the whole world now? Why can't he understand not to widdle on the blackers, when we's still only half filled our baskets?' Polly stamped an imperious foot. 'Come back here at once, you tarble animal, or I'll tie a knot in your penny whistle, so I will!'

Delilah, unmoved by this dreadful threat, turned and grinned at them, gave a perfunctory wag of his undisciplined ginger tail, and suddenly whipped round and broke into an ungainly canter as his large nose caught a whiff of something he hoped might prove to be rabbit. Although he had yet to catch anything – apart from fleas – he was a grand chaser and was hopeful of meeting a rabbit one day which could not run quite as fast as the rest.

'You've got to catch him before you can do anythin' to him,' Ivan observed, watching Delilah's shaggy

1

backside disappear into a likely-looking bush. The children could hear his crashing progress gradually getting fainter as he charged up the hill. 'He's a bad feller, so he is, but we loves him, don't we, Poll? And anyway, Mammy washes the blackers, so it doesn't really matter who—'

'Yes, it does,' Polly interrupted, much shocked. She glanced around her. 'Besides, you shouldn't talk like that. It's rude, so it is. But we've picked the best berries here be now, so we ought to go further up the hill where the bushes haven't been touched yet, 'cos tomorrow's Hallow'een and that's when the girls at school say the devil overlooks the berries an' turns 'em bad, an' they give you bellyache. So if we don't get enough today, that'll be the end of our mammy's blackberry jelly, 'cos you can't pick 'em once the month's turned.'

'That's a lot of nonsense, so it is,' Ivan objected. 'What does the ole devil want wit' blackers, anyhow? I never heared he turned 'em bad in Ireland, so why should he do it here? Not that it matters, 'cos we'll fill our baskets well before teatime.' He sighed deeply and gave his sister a pathetic glance. 'Only me arms is achin' somethin' tarble, an' me basket's only half full.'

'They'll ache worse by the time we get home,' Polly said callously. She picked a couple more berries, popped them into her mouth, then set off up the hill in Delilah's wake. 'Come to think of it, the blackers will be better up there, out o' the trees, because they'll have had more sunshine on 'em.' She glanced back at Ivan, trailing well in her wake. 'Come *on*, will you, Ivan! Aren't you lookin' forward to eatin' Mammy's lovely jelly on a nice round of bread an' butter?'

'Ye-es, but me legs is achin' as well,' Ivan said in what was perilously close to a whine. 'An' don't you say yours is too, Poll, 'cos my legs is only seven, yours is great, twelve-year-old legs – almost a grown-up's. So just you go slower, or – or I'll tell Mammy on you.'

'Call yourself a boy! They say as girls are the weaker sex, but I'm stronger than you, *Ivy*,' Polly said mockingly, using a hated nickname which Ivan had had many a fight over in school. 'Now do stop moanin' an' come along, or it's me what'll be tellin' the mammy a t'ing or two.'

'You called names! Oh, won't Mammy tell you what a bad girl you are, Polly O'Brady!' Ivan said triumphantly. 'An' Daddy won't be too pleased wit' you either. Just wait till we get back to the crossin' cottage.'

Polly, seeing that she had gone too far, slowed and waited until Ivan caught her up, then she took his free hand, saying guiltily: 'It's sorry I am, Ivan – there, isn't that handsome of me now? I shouldn't have teased you, for you've picked like – like Bevin would have. Now I can't say fairer than that, can I?'

'No, you can't say fairer than that,' Ivan agreed, cheering up immediately: such comparison with elder brothers was always welcome. For he admired both of them greatly, as Polly well knew. Now she squeezed his small, grubby paw and smiled down at him. He was a broth of a boy was her little brother, and it was mean to tease him, so it was.

The trouble was, she was missing Grace. Grace Carbery had been her best friend ever since they had come from Dublin to live on the Wirral, and the two girls had been inseparable during holidays, which Grace had spent at the railway crossing cottage. But Polly would never have met Grace, she knew, had it not been for her eldest brother's wife, Sara, who had worked at the Strawberry Field Orphan Home, where

3

Grace had been one of the inmates. Sara had brought Grace to the cottage, and the two girls had become great friends, for all that Grace was some four years the elder. And then Brogan and Sara had married and gone to America, where they had speedily settled down and had a baby boy. They had named him James Peter, after Brogan's father, Peader, though they usually called him Jamie, and the young couple had kept an old promise – they had invited Grace over to America to stay with them and, hopefully, to find herself a better job than had been possible in Liverpool.

So eight months ago, Grace had set sail for the States, where she looked after the baby in the mornings, when Sara was teaching at the small private school where she had worked before Jamie's arrival, and worked at something called a delicatessen in the afternoons and evenings; Polly thought it was some kind of a shop. Grace and Polly exchanged frequent letters, but Polly missed her friend terribly, and found young Ivan a poor substitute, though she did her best never to show it.

But Ivan was a good kid and Polly knew it so she was about to offer to carry his basket for a bit when a shrill, excited bark came from higher up the hill and she and Ivan exchanged anxious glances. 'Come back, you tarble feller,' Polly shrieked, but was not surprised when the dog failed to reappear. Delilah was always chasing rabbits, squirrels and anything else that would oblige him by scuttling ahead, but suppose, just suppose, that he had actually caught something, or was about to do so? Polly knew she would find it hard to forgive Delilah if he killed a fluffy little rabbit – or a squirrel, come to that – but if he half-killed it . . . She closed her eyes tightly for a

4

moment in order to say a quick prayer for the safety of all small animals in the area, then she and Ivan dumped their baskets and set off at a run towards the barking, bursting out of the shade of the trees and into sunshine almost at once.

They saw Delilah immediately, emerging from a bramble patch and dancing across the rough grass and heather towards them, his dark eyes shining with excitement, his mouth open to show what looked like yards of pink tongue and a very capable set of white teeth. To Polly's relief, however, the teeth were his own; the rabbit had clearly escaped.

'Stay wit' us, Delly,' Polly commanded, almost breathless with relief. 'And if you go off after rabbits, me fine boyo, I'll – I'll marmelise you, so I will.' She turned to Ivan. 'Will you stay here, Ivan, while I fetches our baskets? You could pick some blackers to eat, for I've seldom seen bigger berries. Aren't they just great now?'

'You stay here, I'll go for the baskets,' Ivan said. 'And isn't it Delly we ought to be t'ankin', Poll, for bringin' us out o' the wood? 'Cos these are the best blackers I ever did see.'

He turned as he spoke and trotted into the trees and Polly, not to be outdone in helpfulness, followed him. They reclaimed their own baskets – Ivan's had a piece of blue ribbon tied round the handle and Polly's a piece of pink, in order that there should be no squabbles over who had picked what – and returned to the blackberry heaven at the top of the hill where Delilah, still recovering from his earlier pursuit, was lying in a patch of sunlight thoughtfully licking his front paws.

'You're a good feller,' Polly said approvingly, handing the dog one of the larger blackberries.

'Here's a treat I picked specially for you. Now no runnin' off, or Mammy won't let us take you out again.'

Delilah accepted the blackberry and ate it absently, more from politeness, Polly thought, than pleasure. Still, she could see he would stay where he was for a bit, because his sides were heaving from his recent efforts, so she moved away from him and began to pick, telling Ivan that she rather thought another ten or fifteen minutes' work would fill their baskets, so richly berried were the brambles hereabouts.

'Mine's nearly as full as I can carry,' Ivan said after a few moments. 'I'd better stop now, Poll, or I'll be fallin' over goin' down the hill, and blackers aren't so good when they've been scratted up off the ground. How are you doin'?'

'I've got enough as well,' Polly admitted. 'Oh, Ivan, I've only just t'ought but it must be gettin' on for teatime, an' Martin an' that horrible Monica is comin' for tea an' catchin' the last train back to Liverpool. The trouble is, if we're late we'll get in trouble, but if we're on time they'll make us wash an' change an' sit quiet while that Monica talks in her lah-di-dah voice an' Martin agrees wit' every word she utters. So the question is, shall we hurry, or take as long as we can to walk back?'

And this question, Polly could see, taxed her small brother. He frowned down at the toes of his boots, at the blackberry stains on his hands and then at Delilah's coat, sewn thickly with bits of undergrowth where the dog had forced his way into the brambles. After Mass this morning Mammy and Daddy had been talking to the Father and had mentioned Brogan, who lived in America, and Donal, who was a seaman aboard a merchant ship, to say nothing of Niall, who

6

lived in Sydney, Australia. 'You've a far-flung family so you have Mrs O'Brady,' the priest had said, and Polly, having just remembered that Martin and his Monica were coming to tea, had thought to herself, *I only wish that Monica could be far flung – right out of the nearest window!* But she had said nothing aloud. The problem was, as Polly well knew, that none of them, from Daddy and Mammy through Donal and Bevin, right down to Ivan and herself, liked Martin's wife, who was the daughter of a successful baker and thought herself more than a cut above an Irish railway worker and his family. But families stuck together, and despite Martin having made Monica family without so much as a by your leave, family she now was so she must be treated as such.

But amongst themselves, of course, the children could say what they liked. 'If she says one word against me bein' allowed to get meself into a bit of a pickle wit' blackberry juice, I'll stand on her toe be accident,' Polly said disagreeably. '*And* I'll put Lionel in her lap when she isn't lookin', and doesn't she have a good screech when she sees the poor cat now?'

'So'll I, too,' Ivan said. 'I'll tug at her dress wit' my dirty hands, so I will, and then when she says we're mucky, I'll point to the stains on her dress and she'll be sorry.'

Brother and sister giggled together, making their way down the hill. Martin and his Monica were coming to tea, so if she and Ivan were late they would be in trouble and just as Polly made up her mind that it would be best to go home, Ivan turned a sunny face up to hers.

'We'd best stop coddin' and start hurryin' back, Poll,' he said seriously. 'For we do love Martin, don't we? And we wouldn't want to make him sad, because if he knew we didn't like that Monica, he'd be real sad, so he would. Isn't that right, Poll?'

Polly laughed and nodded. 'You're right, so,' she agreed. 'Let's hurry then, me brave feller! Come on, Delly, you can run faster than the pair of us, so let's be gettin' home!'

Deirdre was in the cottage kitchen, cutting bread for sandwiches, when she heard the children coming in. Knowing that they had been blackberrying she was not unduly surprised by the state of them, but she pursed her lips, poured hot water into a tall enamel can and sent the pair of them up the stairs to wash and change before Martin and Monica arrived.

'They're catchin' the three forty,' she said, pushing Polly's red-gold curls back from her forehead and tutting over the stains round the child's mouth and the dirt liberally smearing her hands. 'And you know how Monica will make remarks . . . God above knows why Martin doesn't tell her it's none of her business how I bring up me kids, but he'll not do it, he's still daft about the girl . . . so I'll not have the pair of ye coming in for tea like that.'

'Like what, Mammy?' Ivan said. Deirdre laughed down at him. Her precious little son looked, she told him, like a tinker's brat, and his sister . . . 'Well, words fail me,' she said. 'What a couple! Now, Polly, get those old rags off your little brother and give him a good scrub before you start on yourself; hear me? I'll take a brush to that horrid mongrel of yours . . . I put the cat out half an hour since, so's he'd not jump on Monica's lap like he did last time. Poor girl, she went white as a sheet. She's not a cat-lover, that's for sure.'

'She doesn't know Lionel,' Polly muttered, taking the heavy can of water and heading for the stairs.

'He's no *ordinary* cat I told her when first she came visitin'. But she squealed out anyway, and she'd have t'umped him but for me catchin' him up and takin' him out quick. So it's glad I am that you've put him out of harm's way, Mammy.'

'Ye-es, but it isn't Monica's fault that she doesn't like cats, alanna,' Deirdre felt bound to point out. After all, one must be fair, even to a daughter-in-law. 'It's a feelin' she can't help, like some people don't like spiders and others can't abide rats, or snakes.'

'I'm not too keen on spiders meself,' Polly admitted, turning back on the bottom step and raising her voice so that her mother could hear her. 'But a cat's a lovely t'ing to stroke, and it purrs, and winds round your legs givin' you love. A spider's a different t'ing altogether, wouldn't you say?'

Deirdre, who disliked spiders quite as much as Polly did, would have liked to agree, but it would not do to let Polly blame poor Monica for a dislike of cats which verged on real fear. 'Would you let a spider sit on your hand and gaze up at you with its little squidgy eyes and beg for a dead fly?' she asked. 'Some folk will.'

'Oh,' Polly said, taking this in. 'Right. Poor Monica. I'll keep Lionel away from her, Mammy.'

Deirdre waited until her daughter had thundered up the stairs, then crossed the kitchen and opened the door of the oven beside the fire. She took out a tray of scones, cooked to a turn, and carefully transferred them to a wire rack to cool, then went back to slicing and buttering the brown loaf. Beside her was a plate covered in the ham which Peader had cut for her before he left the house. Deirdre, cutting and buttering the bread and slapping ham between the pieces, reflected that Polly wasn't unreasonable, not

9

when it came right down to it. She had taken her sister-in-law, Sara, to her heart long before Deirdre had realised that Sara was a fine person, and look how attached she had been to Grace Carbery! No two girls had been closer, and though she tried not to feel jealous of their friendship, Deirdre sometimes wished that Polly would hand her Grace's letters so that she could read them for herself, instead of just reading out odd bits. But it was fair enough, the girls confided in each other, she guessed, in a way which they would not want to share with any parent, no matter how sympathetic. In fact if only Monica were not quite so critical, not so demanding, the two of them would probably have got on fine despite the older girl's fear of cats. But there was no getting away from it; Monica was extremely pretty, she dressed fashionably and talked in a very refined sort of way, but you could not blame the O'Brady kids for finding her hard to love. She looked down on them, sneered at their achievements, thought herself superior, even thought Martin fortunate to have won her. And no one, except possibly the saints, Deirdre told herself, could take to someone who treated them like that.

A good deal of their – understandable – dislike of Monica was made worse, Deirdre realised, because back in Dublin Martin had been engaged to a charming girl, Kathleen Delaney, and when the rest of the family had crossed the water to join Peader in Liverpool they had confidently expected that Martin and Kathleen would be married quite soon.

But then Martin had come over to Liverpool for a job interview and had said, briefly, that he and Kathleen had had a 'disagreement', that their engagement was off and that he had decided to take the very good job which had been offered him as assistant to the chief clerk in the Liverpool branch of his bank. Questioning him further, what was more, had got them nowhere. He would not discuss what had taken place between himself and Kathleen, simply saying that they had been mistaken in their feelings, that it had been a mercy they had discovered this before marriage and not after, and had then thrown himself into city life with such enthusiasm that he had met Monica and married her within four months.

Deirdre and Peader, discussing their son's alliance in bed at night, when there was no one about to overhear, had long ago decided that Martin had met and married Monica on the rebound from Kathleen, but there was nothing they could do about it. Martin was hot-tempered and self-willed; he had decided he wanted a smart wife from a well-to-do family and he had got one. Whether he would ever be happy with her was another matter, but it was a matter in which his family had absolutely no say. They could not like his new wife, but they must put up with her for Martin's sake, and hope that, when the babies came, Monica would soften and become more likeable – and easier to live with, for her 'high standards' as she called them meant that every penny of Martin's salary disappeared either on to her back or into the tiny house in Nelson Street.

'And this house won't be good enough for long,' Martin had told his mammy soon after the wedding. He had sounded rather prouder of his wife's ambition than otherwise, Deirdre thought now. 'Soon Monica will be after something detached, out in the real suburbs. Still and all, she's an only child and her parents dote on her. No doubt between us, we'll manage to see that she lives in the style she so desperately wants.'

Deirdre and Peader, terribly worried that their boy would be taken from them by Monica and her parents, were reassured that in this one thing at any rate Martin seemed to be the master. Every other Sunday, the young O'Bradys came out to the crossing cottage, and once in eight weeks the rest of the O'Brady family got into the train on a Saturday and went into the city centre, where they looked at the shops and galleries, had tea with Martin and Monica, and returned – with a sigh of relief – to the cottage on the last train.

But it's no use my worrying over Martin and Monica, Deirdre told herself now as she busily sliced and buttered. He's a man grown and must please himself. As for Monica, she's very young yet. She'll mature, and change, and – and grow nicer, easier to get along with.

'Mammy, where's Daddy gone? Or is he waitin' at the station for the three forty?' Deirdre, with her back to the door, had not heard it open and jumped at the sound of her son's voice and Bevin chuckled and came right into the room. 'Sorry, did I frighten you?' He walked around the table and picked up a scone, bit into it, then hissed in his breath. 'Dear God in heaven, Mammy, that was *hot*!'

'And so I should hope,' Deirdre said severely. 'Wasn't it meself that just took them out of the oven? As for your daddy, he's gone along to the station all right, to have a bit of a crack wit' Mr Devenish. Then he said he'd walk back wit' Martin and Monica so I'm minding the crossing while he's away. And what might you be doing home so early?'

'I remembered you were cooking scones,' Bevin said, 'So I thought I'd come home, give a hand. And anyway, someone's got to stop our Polly going for

12

Monica's throat and stranglin' some sense into her.'

'You're no fonder of Monica than Polly is,' Deirdre said. She began to smear mustard on half the sandwiches; Polly and Ivan hated mustard, even with ham. 'So don't you go pretending to be a peacemaker, Bev! It's your daddy who behaves best, for I'll admit she gets me hackles up so high I'm surprised I don't growl at her, like that misbegotten mongrel your sister's so fond of.'

'Oh, Mammy, we all love Delly,' Bevin said, turning the subject rather neatly, his mother thought. 'Anyway, I'm home now, so I am. What do you want done?'

Deirdre put her knife down and looked up at her tall son. He was getting more like his father every day, she thought affectionately – and more like his elder brother, Brogan, too. All three of them had the same very dark, wavy hair falling across broad, placid foreheads, the same sweet smiles, the same nice natures. For Bevin's offer of help was genuine, as she knew well. The other boys might moan and try to evade household tasks, but Bevin was always ready to give a hand. Just as Polly was, though that, Deirdre told herself, was more upbringing than a family trait, because . . .

'Will I lay the table in the parlour, Mammy? It's a cold tea, isn't it? Sandwiches and cakes and a nice apple pie.' Bevin smacked his lips. 'I dream about your apple pie, Mammy, when I'm slaving away over me books.'

'That's about it,' Deirdre acknowledged. She glanced at the big clock which hung over the dresser and was kept accurate to the second by Peader, for a crossing keeper had to know the exact hour so he could be sure to open and close his gates in good time.'Would you get some eggs out of the pantry, Bev, and hard boil 'em for me? You can lay the table whiles they cook. There's a big bowl of eggs in the pantry.'

'I've got 'em,' Bevin called presently from the big, walk-in pantry by the back door. 'janey, Polly's hens must be laying well, Mammy, the bowl's full.'

'Your sister has a way wit' animals and birds, the same as you've a way wit' figures and examinations,' Deirdre said. 'I swear she goes out and talks to the hens and next day there's an egg or two in each nesting box. Put half a dozen on to boil, Bev; that should do us.'

'Right, Mammy,' Bevin said. 'Then I'll get that table laid.'

For a while mother and son worked contentedly together until a thundering on the stairs heralded the arrival of Ivan, with Polly close on his heels. Ivan was looking distinctly aggrieved.

'Mammy, Mammy, she near on scrubbed me ears off of me head, so she did,' Ivan shouted, hurtling across the kitchen and casting himself at his mother. 'Look how red they are – that wit' bein' pulled out sideways so's she could see the spuds growin' in 'em, she said. I telled her I didn't want lugs restin' on me shoulders and she said: "Shaddup, you, or I'll tie a knot in—"'

'Mammy, don't listen to him, he's tale-clattin', that's what he's doin', and it's wrong to tale-clat, you've telled me so many a time—' Polly was beginning breathlessly when she saw Bevin. Immediately she rushed round the table to hug him, saying: 'Bev! Oh, you're home early for to see that girl – and our Martin, of course. But there's a grand tea, so there is – Mammy always makes a grand tea when . . .'

14

'. . . your penny whistle!' Ivan finished his sentence at the top of his voice, glaring at his sister across the laden board. 'Mammy, she's a bad girl an' she needs a good smackin' for sayin' bad t'ings to her little brother.'

'Well, you shouldn't have kept pullin' away, and me only doin' what Mammy had said, makin' you respectable so that Monica wouldn't get a chance to talk about kids playin' in pigpens and things like that,' Polly said. She cast a guilty glance at her mother, standing with an arm protectively around Ivan's small shoulders. 'Oh, Mammy, I love Ivan, so I do, but he was strugglin' like a fish in me hands . . .'

Bevin held up a hand like a policeman and made shushing noises until both children had ceased their clamour. Then he spoke. 'Polly, the kid's little lugs look like beetroot, so they do. Say you're sorry for mauling the little feller.'

'I'm sorry I heaved at your lug then, Ivan,' Polly said. Deirdre thought she sounded rather half-hearted about it, but refrained from saying so. An apology was an apology, after all, and Ivan was smiling once more.

'That's all right, Poll,' he said with all his customary sunniness. 'I'm sorry I stamped on your toes, then.'

'Truth will out,' Bevin said. He grinned at his mother. 'Best clothes, I see. Was that orders too?'

Deirdre turned and looked properly at her two youngest for the first time. Polly was now wearing a pale green smock dress and white stockings whilst Ivan was in all the beauty of his Sunday suit. Deirdre clutched at her hair. 'Polly! Not your party dress, you silly young wan, nor Ivan's Sunday suit. Just something nice – your dark brown skirt wit' the pink

15

blouse. And Ivan's grey shorts and blue shirt will do perfectly well. It isn't as if we're having the Queen to tea,' she finished.

Polly heaved a sigh and took Ivan's hand. 'Well, there's gratitude, when I put on our bestest t'ings special,' she said as they headed across the kitchen once more. 'I'm sure I don't know why I try so hard, when nothin' I do is ever right.'

'Nor me,' Ivan said in a lugubrious tone. 'You won't have to wash me lugs again, will you, Poll? I does hope not!'

Deirdre waited until they were out of hearing before she and Bevin caught each other's eye and began to laugh. After a moment, however, Bevin heard the eggs boil over and ran to take them half off the fire, and soon enough it was time to drop them into a bowl of cold water, then to crack the shells and peel them off, and to arrange them, each one cut in half on a plate, and to put it down on the big table in the parlour, between the bowls of tomatoes – grown by Peader, in the little lean-to greenhouse against the bicycle shed – and fine, floury potatoes, still hot from the pan.

'I'd best put on a dress,' Deirdre said resignedly, when all the preparations were finished and she had put the kettle on to boil and stood the china teapot patterned with roses near at hand. 'I'll put me pinafore over it, because otherwise I'll spill something down it, so I shall, but I just know Monica will be wearing something new and smart.'

Bevin said he would hold the fort for her whilst she changed, so she slipped up the stairs, meeting Polly and Ivan, now sensibly dressed, on their way down.

'Better, Mammy?' Polly said, holding out her brown skirt and doing a little bobbing curtsey. 'Will she find fault wit' me in this?'

'Oh, you poor lamb, fancy anyone finding fault wit' you,' Deirdre said mockingly, but she pinched her daughter's rosy cheek consolingly. 'You and Ivan both look fine, so you do. Tell you what, the train went past a while ago, why don't you and Ivan take Delly and walk up to the station to meet Daddy and the others? I daresay you'll enjoy that better than sitting quiet in the parlour until they arrive.'

'Oh, yes,' Polly and Ivan chorused at once. They galloped down the rest of the stairs and straight out of the front door, without even thinking about putting on a coat or a hat. Deirdre called after them, but was not surprised to get no reply. Well, it was a warm enough afternoon, they'd come to no harm. And the exercise would mean that they wouldn't fidget so much during tea, nor be so patently eager to make themselves scarce after it.

The train clattered into the small station and Martin stood up and pulled on the leather strap to let the window down. The train was still moving, though slowly, and the crisp, late autumn air came into the carriage, reminding him of the harvest fields, autumn woods, and the cropped grass of meadows where mushrooms grew at this time of year, spangling the grass with their neat white caps. Martin sighed. He loved the country, but he could not imagine Monica ever wanting to live anywhere but in – or near – the city. She was too fond of shopping, people and amusements to take kindly to country living, but privately Martin envied his parents and the young ones their rural home.

'Is anyone waiting? Your da said he might come down and meet us.' Monica squeezed into the window space beside him and they both looked along the platform. It was empty, save for the stationmaster's brown and white terrier and a couple of pigeons, pecking between the big, flat paving stones.

'No one about,' Martin said, and heard her draw in her breath with a little hiss of satisfaction. She had spent most of the journey telling him that his family did not like her, that she did not like them, that this visit, every other Sunday, was nothing but a farce. 'They'd sooner we didn't come, and I'm afraid I don't enjoy being where I'm not really wanted,' she had said in a drawling, self-pitying tone. 'We'll tell them once a month in future, eh, Martin? Then we can go to my parents' occasionally, or spend the day by ourselves.'

Martin had been looking out of the window; for a moment he let his eyes continue to roam over the stubble in the harvest fields, the leaves turning to gold and brown, tumbling down from the high branches, like falling stars from the blue arch of heaven. He had lifted his eyes from the scene beyond the glass and glanced at her briefly. So very pretty! Streaky blonde hair, light blue eyes, the full-lipped red mouth . . .

'We'll come every other Sunday,' he had said. Not as though he were arguing with her, more as though he were agreeing. Yet the words were not the ones she wanted to hear.

'Oh, but Martin, this just isn't fair, they're *your* family, not mine, and they resent me, you know they do. And I'm not used to children, I don't understand them – and they're so *dirty*, and then there's that huge dog, and the cat – you know I'm scared of cats – and all those hens pecking about the place . . .'

They had been alone in the carriage. Martin had said flatly: 'I like seeing them. I'm fond of me family.

As for the kids, you'd better get used to them, so when we have kids of our own—'

She had interrupted him, actually grabbing his arm, pinching it, her face white with temper save for a bright red spot on each cheek. 'Kids! I'm not going to have kids for years and years yet! I *told* you I didn't like kids, didn't want a family, not for years and years and you never said – I'm tellin' you, Martin O'Brady, that I'm norra gal what'll act pleasant if I find meself in the fam'ly way!'

He had looked at her, then smiled. He liked it when she forgot her smart accent, her posh school, and spoke as other Liverpudlians did. 'We're both Catholics, Monica,' he had said gently. 'You didn't think I'd been using rubber johnnies all these weeks, did you? Because I tell you to your head I've done no such t'ing.'

'No, of course not, but—' She had stopped, suddenly seeming to be aware of his sharpened look. She looked down at her feet, catching her full red lower lip with her very small, very white teeth. Then she had looked up at him through her thick, dark lashes. The breath caught in Martin's throat.

'But what, Monica? So why aren't you *in the family way* already, is that what you're going to tell me?' He had caught her hand in his, squeezing the fingers until she squeaked with pain, the pale skin reddening.

'Stop it, Martin! Don't you dare try to knock me about – if that's the sort of wife you wanted I'm telling you here and now—'

'What have you done to make sure we don't have kids, Mon?' His voice had been cooler now, faintly amused even. 'Women's magic, is it? Something us poor, ignorant fellers don't know about?'

She had looked at him doubtfully. 'Well, I – I went

19

to the clinic, and they gave me . . . It's what heaps and heaps of women use if they don't want babies, there's nothing *wrong*, it's not as if . . . It's not like doing bad things to yourself. It – it's just a – a thing, a sort of sponge thing . . . it doesn't *hurt* either of us, it just – just gets in the way, kind of.'

He had nodded. 'I see. But this is no place to talk about birth control and families. We'll discuss it later. And in the meantime, don't let me here any more talk about not visiting my parents. Understand?'

She had nodded, her lower lip trembling, tears misting her eyes. 'All right, Martin. And – and, Martin, don't be angry. I *did* tell you I didn't want babies yet; it was your job to make sure I didn't have them, only I was afraid you wouldn't bother, so I did it myself. I don't see that I've done anything wrong, honest to God I don't.'

Inside himself, Martin had sighed. He had known deep down even before he married her that he was not doing the right thing by her. He liked her looks, her parents' money and her air of fragility. He had not experienced the sharpness of her tongue nor her jealousy until the marriage was a couple of weeks old and then he had been dismayed. She was jealous of his parents and his siblings, of anyone in fact who Martin loved.

As to her not wanting babies, perhaps she was in the right of it after all. Babies need love, and two parents, and . . . He cut the thought off abruptly and jumped down on to the platform. He turned to help her to alight, then the two of them walked slowly, arm in arm, towards the stationmaster's office. It was a good twenty minutes' walk from here to the cottage, Martin told himself rather grimly; they had best spend the time in talking about the things which

20

really mattered and which, to date, they had both avoided. Things like her feelings towards his family, and her reasons for not wanting babies of her own. Things like the money she insisted they put away every month towards a bigger house. For Martin, the only reason for wanting a bigger house was children, who would need more room. Surely, *surely* that must have been Monica's reason too? Why else would she want a bigger house, with a nice garden of its own? It crossed his mind, but fleetingly, that perhaps they ought to discuss their reasons for marrying one another too, but he dismissed it at once. There were some things, he told himself, that were best left unsaid.

'Martin? You said your father was meeting us, didn't you? Not that I mind having you to myself for a while, and the walk's awfully pretty at this time of year, with the trees turning and berries in the hedges.' Martin smiled down at her. She was doing her best, he supposed. 'We'll likely meet Daddy on the way. Come on, best foot forward.'

Polly and Ivan were good at first. Mindful of their decent clothing, they walked sedately along the lane, playing I spy and trying not to stir up too much dust, for they wore their best shoes as well. Delilah bounded ahead of them, not rushing off the lane for once but sniffing placidly at the verge and occasionally stopping to lift his leg. However, such goodness could scarcely last for long. Any time now, as Polly remarked, they would meet up with either Martin and Monica or with Daddy, and that would mean having to behave properly.

'So we might as well play somethin' interestin', whiles we got the chance,' she said brightly, looking all around her. 'Not mud pies – well, it's been so dry there's almost no mud – but something we can do as we're walkin'.'

'Relievio,' Ivan said hopefully. His sister snorted and gave him a glance loaded with scorn.

'That's not a game you can play as you walk, silly, nor wit' only the two of us! How about hide an' seek?'

'That's not a game you can play as you walk either,' Ivan objected, but Polly sighed deeply and shook her head at him.

'Use your imagination, Ivan,' she said. 'Use that – that lump you've got on the end of your neck that you call a head! It just means you have to walk wit' your eyes shut whiles you count to fifty, an' I run ahead like lightnin', and hide. Then you come after me.'

'But we'll take hours to reach the station if we do that,' Ivan pointed out. 'Besides, why's you to hide an' me to seek? T'ain't fair!'

'It doesn't matter how long we take to get to the station, because we're not meetin' the perishin' train,' Polly pointed out briskly. 'It arrived . . . oh, ages ago. Go on then, you run ahead and hide and I'll count to fifty. Slowly,' she added, seeing her brother looking up at her doubtfully. 'Aw, c'mon, Ivan, we'll be bored to death else.'

'Right,' Ivan said. He cantered off in a cloud of dust and Polly shut her eyes and started to count. Presently she shouted: 'Coming, ready or not!' and charged up the lane, scanning the hedgerows, the autumn-tinted trees and any likely hiding place with an eagle eye. She very soon realised, however, that she should have set some sort of limit on the distance away from the lane which the hider could travel, since she could see no sign of her small brother. In fact she was about to give up when a stifled giggle above her head made her glance up into the boughs of the enormous pine tree around which she had been peering. Sure enough, there was her brother's rosy face hanging upside down and laughing at her, whilst the rest of him was laid comfortably along the large, rough-barked branch quite eighteen or twenty feet above the ground.

'Got you!' Polly squeaked, only to be immediately thwarted.

'You haven't,' Ivan said. 'Come up here if you can, an' then you've got me, but I'm safe from you else, Polly O'Brady!'

'Ivan, you're a perishin' liar!' Polly said indignantly after a moment's thought. 'This is hide an' seek, not Relievio. Come on down, or I'll come up and marmelise you, so I will.'

'I know it's hide an' seek,' the tree-dweller said tauntingly. 'But you can't get me, can you? So you've not won.'

'If I come up there I'll . . . I'll . . .'

'If you come up, I'll go higher,' Ivan declared boastfully. 'I'll go right to the top of the tree, an' – an' I'll be able to see the station, an' the crossin' cottage, an' the village . . . Why don't we both go up the tree, Poll?'

'Because I'm wearin' me decent t'ings, an' me best shoes,' Polly said primly, but she was tempted. Boys always thought they could climb better than girls, but in her experience this was not so at all. I can climb like a cat, so I can, she told herself, it's just – just that I'll likely tear me decent skirt and Mammy can't afford to keep buyin' me skirts. T'ings are a tarble price these days, so they are.

'And what am I wearin', Saint Polly?' her brother

23

asked mockingly. 'But I'm up the tree – and never a scratch on me, because I climb so well.'

'Right,' Polly said grimly. She hitched up her skirt, tucked it into her navy-blue knickers and then, after some thought, removed her shiny strap shoes and her white ankle socks. No point in asking for trouble, and she could climb just as well barefoot she was sure.

The difficult part was the beginning, however. For the first dozen feet or so there wasn't a branch to hang on to, you simply had to swarm up the trunk and though she was a good climber, swarming was something she had never tried. But she tried it now, and after a couple of false starts, during which Ivan jeered terribly, she managed to get the hang of it and humped herself, caterpillar-like, up the long, sloping, rough-barked trunk, seizing the first branch with hands which trembled. She hauled herself aboard it, realising with a sinking feeling that now that she was actually on the branch it was possible that neither of them might be able to get down. And it was horribly high, so high that she felt quite giddy when the tree swayed in the wind.

'Grand, isn't it, Poll?' her small brother said complacently. 'Are you comin' up to me or shall we both go higher?'

Polly swallowed. 'This is plenty high enough,' she said, trying to sound calm and matter of fact. 'Let's go down now, eh, Ivan? Me legs is tarble scratched from grippin' the trunk and me hands is *raw*.'

'Oh, well, I'll come down, then,' Ivan said airily. He swung off his branch on to the one below with an insouciance which brought Polly's heart thumping into her mouth. Dear God in heaven, don't let him fall, she prayed inside her head. Oh, it's ever so dangerous up here, so it is – let us get safely down to the ground!

But whether her prayers were answered or whether Ivan simply had no fear of heights she could not have said, for presently he thumped on to her branch, dusted his palms together, and grinned at her. There was a smear of dirt across his right cheek, Polly saw, and bits of bark and pine needles in his thatch of dark hair. His trousers had also attracted quite a lot of bark and the palms of his hands, like hers, were red-raw, but he seemed indifferent to such things. 'There y'are, easy-peasy,' he said non-chalantly. 'I say, Polly, what's that there?'

Polly looked down in the direction of his pointing finger, but could see nothing save for waist-high bracken and a tangle of brambles. 'Where?' she said crossly. 'There's nothin' there except bracken and old bushes, Ivan. Are you goin' down first?'

'If you like,' Ivan said. 'But there was something there, Poll. You can't see it from here, but up where I was—'

'I'm not goin' higher,' Polly said at once. 'It's a long way to the ground from here, so it is. I don't t'ink it'll be easy gettin' down, Ivan.'

'I didn't say to go higher,' Ivan assured her. 'I said from where I was I could see somet'ing glitterin' in the bracken. If I go first, though I'll have to get past you. Can you squeeze against the trunk?'

Not unwillingly, Polly got as close to the trunk of the tree as she could, and was impressed, against her will, by the casual way in which her little brother went past her, swung by his arms on the branch, then gripped the trunk with his knees until he had a good hold and could grab with his arms as well. Then, monkey-like, he descended the trunk until he stood

25

once more on solid ground, looking up at her.

'C'mon, Poll,' he called. 'It's not bad – it's quite easy, so it is.'

Polly nodded, as though she thought it was easy too, then she glanced at the bracken and the brambles, at the pale grass which straggled between them and the beginning of the trees. Just for a moment she, too, saw something gleaming and glittering in the depths of the bracken but then she moved her head and the object disappeared. To distract Ivan, she called down to him. 'I see somet'ing in the bracken, Ive. We'll take a look when I'm down, so we will.'

Ivan nodded and Polly took a deep breath, turned towards the trunk and closed her eyes. Then she launched herself at the tree trunk, hanging on, limpet-like with desperate hands, knees and feet. She felt that, had she been able to do so, she would have hung on to it with her nose and eyelashes as well, but failing that, she decided she would simply stay here for ever – or until someone came along with a good, strong ladder. She dared not move for fear she would lose her nerve – and her grip – and plummet to the uncommonly hard ground far below.

'You've froze, like Bev said some fellers do when they first climb a pine,' a voice from below said with more than a trace of satisfaction. 'Me an' Bev practised climbin' a pine whiles you were goin' shoppin' wit' Mammy last weekend.'

The unfairness of it! He had climbed up and down pine trees before, been taught by Bev to do it, yet here was she, a true beginner, stuck here like a fool, like a monkey on a perishin' stick! Indignation – and a strong desire to clap her small brother's ears until they rang – got Polly's eyes open and, forcing herself not to look down or to remember the drop, she unclamped her hands, one by one, and moved them lower down the trunk, making her legs follow suit. The cheek of that young feller down there, saying that she, Polly, was froze wit' fear, when she was no such t'ing! Determinedly closing her eyes again, she repeated the movements over and over. She would not let him see how terrified she was!

It was Ivan's laughter which made her open her eyes. He was roaring laughing, and when she looked round at him she saw that there were actually tears of laughter on his cheeks. But it wasn't until her foot hit something, and she realised it was the ground, that she knew why he was so amused. She had been so busy concentrating on not looking at the drop that she had reached the foot of the tree whilst still imagining herself up in the air somewhere, above that perilous drop.

However, there was nothing she could do about it now except to act with what dignity she could. She stood up and began to brush bits of bark and pine needles off her clothing and out of her hair. Then, ignoring Ivan's gradually fading mirth she said: 'Where's Delly?'

As she had guessed it would, this took Ivan's mind off her tree-climbing. He looked around him. 'Delly? Oh, janey, he'll be off after rabbits again, Poll. Or else he's gone on ahead to look for Daddy. Shall I give him a yell now?'

Polly was about to agree when the dog burst out of the bushes which lined the lane and hurled himself at Polly, whining and trying to grab at the hem of her skirt. Polly seized his collar and began to try to tow him along the lane in the direction of the station, but Delilah resisted, his whines growing louder. 'What's up, old feller?' Polly said. 'What've you found?'

'It's probably something horrible,' Ivan said with relish. 'Oh, remember that flashing t'ing I told you about? He came from that direction, didn't he? Mebbe we'd best tek a look, Poll.'

'I'm not goin' to have much choice,' Polly panted as Delilah turned round and began to tow her in the opposite direction. 'All right, old feller, what is it, then?'

The children and the dog crossed the road, scrambled through the ditch – dry providentially – and out into a small hazel copse. Delilah, freed from Polly's grip, ran over to a recumbent figure lying face down on the ground and began to bark again, but Polly shushed him.

'Delly, shut your gob, will you?' she said, approaching the figure cautiously. She bent over the man's head, then straightened, her eyes rounding with horror, both hands flying to press against her small, flat chest. 'Oh, Ivan, Ivan, it's Daddy, an' he must have been hurt real bad!'

Despite the shock, neither child panicked. Ivan took one look at his father's white, set countenance and then turned back towards the lane. 'I'll go to the station an' fetch help, so I will,' he said breathlessly. 'I can run like the wind when I want to. You stay here wit' our daddy, Poll. You'd best keep Delly too. He'll give a bark if – if anyone comes near.'

'Well, all right,' Polly said tremulously. 'D-do you t'ink Daddy tripped over something, an' fell, Ivan? Should I try to sit him up, mebbe?'

'No. He's too heavy,' Ivan said simply. 'Shan't be long.'

He disappeared. Polly sat down beside her father and put a tentative hand on his cheek. It was cool, for the sun's rays had little power so late in the day, but it was not cold. No need, then, to try to get him warm. She put her head close to his and listened. To her enormous relief, she could hear his breathing, low and rasping. 'I knew he wasn't dead, so I did,' she whispered to Delilah, who had come and sat beside her on the ground as soon as Ivan had disappeared. 'Me daddy's the best daddy in the whole wide world, so no one would let him die. Not even God . . . because what'ud we do wit'out Daddy, eh, Delly?'

Delilah sighed deeply. Polly leaned over her father once more. She could not help wishing that she and Ivan had been accompanied by someone older – last year at this time it would have been she and Grace – but she would just have to do her best to be sensible and reassure her father. 'Daddy? It's your own little girl, so it is. I'm wit' you, an' Ivan's gone for help. Oh, Daddy, could you say a word or two? Did you fall an' bang your poor head, then? I know I ought to fetch water, like they do in books, to trickle between your lips, only . . . only I don't t'ink there's any water nearby and I don't want to leave you, so I don't.'

Delilah grunted and moved over so that he was leaning against Polly. He looked down at Peader, anxiety written all over his woolly face, and then bent his head and licked the unconscious man's cheek. Polly, despite her fears, chuckled. 'Sure an' isn't it just like our Delly to t'ink a kiss from him will bring you round, Daddy, just as if you were the sleepin' beauty an' Delly was the handsome prince? Oh, don't I wish it would too! But if you've had a bump on your head mebbe it's better for you to lie quiet a whiles. Anyway, Daddy, I'm goin' to hold your hand, so's you know I'm here, an' before you know it they'll come runnin', all the grown-ups from the station, an' you'll be took proper care of, an' better in no time at all, at all.'

It seemed a long while to poor Polly before the adults she longed for actually did arrive, and when they did the men did not waste time in examining the unconscious man or trying to work out what had happened. They lifted him with great care and gentleness on to the door they had brought and took him straight to the crossing cottage. Ivan and Polly had run ahead to alert their mother and a bed had been made up on the sofa, whilst the beautiful Sunday tea had been bundled out of the parlour and waited, unregarded, in the kitchen.

'The doctor's coming,' Martin told Deirdre as soon as they had settled Peader on the sofa bed. 'Mr Devenish telephoned him as soon as Ivan explained what had happened. He'll be able to tell us what's wrong wit' Daddy, Mammy. Maybe he just tripped . . . The doctor will know.'

And the doctor, when he had had a chance to examine Peader, looked grave. He told Deirdre that her man would have to be admitted to hospital and that his condition was serious.

'He's had a stroke, Mrs O'Brady,' he said bluntly. 'He's a very sick man and may not be well for some time.'

'But he will get well, won't he, doctor?' Deirdre said, her voice heavy with pleading. 'He was ill before, when the train near killed him, but he come to himself in the end.'

'He's a strong man,' the doctor said evasively. 'With good nursing he'll probably do well . . . I'll arrange for him to be admitted to the hospital in Liverpool which treated him last time. But strokes are funny things; you'll just have to wait and see.'

Chapter Two

A month later, Polly's entire life had changed completely. It was a Saturday morning and she was strolling along the pavement in Nelson Street, kicking at the scatter of leaves which had been blown along from the trees which lined Great George Square and half-heartedly watching the passing traffic, whilst from the main road ahead of her she could hear the occasional rumble as a tram passed by. She was wondering how she would ever get used to what had happened to them. Her daddy was still in hospital and Polly, her mammy and Ivan were uncomfortably squeezed into the spare room of Martin's little house, whilst Bevin had stayed in the country with his pal. Because Peader's stroke had proved to be a serious matter which would probably affect him for the rest of his life, they had had to agree to the railway company's insistence that they move out of their cottage so that another railwayman could take over the job of crossing keeper.

'I'm sure your married son will take you in until you can find a place of your own, and you'll want to be nearer the hospital,' the official who had come to discuss matters with them had said. 'Something like this is always a shock, but we'll see that you have some money to tide you over, since Mr O'Brady's original injury was a railway matter. What's more, if – I mean when – your husband recovers sufficiently he may be able to take up some sort of desk job in the city, but he's unlikely to be manning a crossing again. The disturbed nights, the importance of a clear head . . . In short, Mrs O'Brady, I'm sure you understand that a less demanding job would be very much better for your husband.'

Polly knew that Deirdre had agreed because in the back of all their minds there had lurked the horrible suspicion that the official did not think Peader would ever recover. And if this was so they would certainly have to leave the cottage. So because of these fears Polly had set off by herself a few days after the accident to visit the church in town and have it out with God.

'Sure and I love me daddy as much as I love me mammy, and that lots and lots,' she told Him earnestly, on her knees in the small Catholic church in which she and her family had worshipped ever since they had left Dublin and come to England to live. 'But me daddy's a special person, so he is, a wonderful feller; everyone says so. Why, if he hadn't dived at Grace Carbery that day and pushed her out of the path of the train, he'd never have been hit himself. And if he'd not been hit the doctors say the clot of blood that gave him the stroke wouldn't have been runnin' around loose in his head, so don't You go makin' me daddy a member of Your heavenly host when he's not had his fair share down here yet.'

She had paused for a moment to consider, and had then proceeded to tell God that much though she would like to do it, she couldn't promise Him that if He let her daddy get well she would be good for the rest of her life because she didn't think she could stick to it. 'But I'll be as good as I can,' she promised. 'And if it means givin' up me hens and me cat Lionel and me pig and me rabbits, and goin' to live in the city wit' that – that Monica, then I'll do that too.' She had glanced consideringly around her. 'I'm tarble fond of Delly, but if you're set on really makin' me suffer for me daddy, then I suppose I'll have to let you take me dog too.' She gave a deep sigh and scrambled to her feet, bobbing a small curtsey at the altar. 'But if you make me leave me pals, and then take me daddy anyway . . . Well, I just wouldn't, if I were You,' she finished on a distinctly threatening note, 'because I can be bad as bad when the fancy takes me, so I can.'

But that had been a while ago, before the move to the city. Now, Polly knew just how much of her offer had been acceptable to God. The hens, the rabbits and the pig had been left behind with the new crossing keeper and his wife, and Lionel, Polly's ginger cat, had not seemed unduly perturbed to find himself left behind as well. And dear Delilah, though he would join them, Mammy promised, as soon as they did have a place of their own, was in the country, with Bevin and his friend Paul.

But now, with a fine Saturday morning at her disposal and no one to play with, for she knew none of the neighbourhood children yet, Polly was simply mooching, passing the time. If Grace had still been living in Liverpool, of course, it would have been very different. The two girls could have looked in the shop windows, discussed the clothes, imagined what they would most like to buy. Naturally, they would have talked too, discussing all their most intimate thoughts – that was one of the things about Grace which Polly missed most, someone in whom she could confide with the complete certainty that Grace would never breathe a word to a soul. And Grace would have made sure that Polly met all her pals, so that games would have been possible – though Grace, at sixteen, would not perhaps have liked games such as Relievio, which Polly still enjoyed. But the girls had been such close friends that Polly knew she would never have been bored in Grace's company.

In Dublin, too, she reflected gloomily, there would have been a *grosh* of things to do, and masses of friends to do them with. She had had her own particular pal, Tad Donoghue, who had seldom left her side and might have got her into all kinds of mischief but was still her best friend. They could have gone to the tuppenny rush at the cinema, or they could have fished in the Royal Canal, or played games with other kids in Phoenix Park, or walked along O'Connell Street looking in the smart shops and choosing what they would have had if they had found a heap of money lying in the gutter.

Because they had only been living with Martin and Monica for ten days or so – it felt more like ten *years*, Polly reflected bitterly – no arrangements had yet been made for Polly and Ivan to attend school. So they were like two little fish out of water, living on sufferance in Monica's spotless house and dreading the moment when Mammy would pile them on to a tram and take them right across the city to the Catholic school of her choice, for plainly she would not let them go to just any old school.

'Education's important,' she had said to Polly one night as the three of them lay squeezed into the inadequate bed in the young O'Bradys' spare room. 'I'll not have you pushed into the nearest school here just because it is the nearest. And anyway, we can't stay here for ever, we're bound to find a place of our own soon, so there's not much point in puttin' the pair of you in school just to take you out of it as you're settlin' in.'

Polly and Ivan agreed fervently with this remark, but realised that Monica did not. She could not wait to see the back of them, though they did their level best to keep out of her way, hanging round the quiet back streets and trekking across to the nearest open space to play games whenever Martin and Monica were at home.

This afternoon, however, Polly and Mammy and her brothers – Bevin too, for he came into the city each Saturday – would visit the hospital. It was no longer as worrying and frightening as it had been at first, for though Daddy could only mumble out of one side of his mouth at least his beautiful eyes looked at his little Polly with recognition and love. At first, when he had not seemed to recognise any of them, Polly had dreaded the visits, but now they were much nicer. She talked a lot and Daddy gave her his peculiar new lopsided smile, and when they went home Mammy always made sure there was something nice for tea because she said Polly did Daddy good, so she did, and never talked about the crossing cottage or her animals but only about cheerful or funny subjects, like the big fat woman in the sweetie shop who always popped an extra piece of toffee into their penny bag because their daddy was in hospital.

But right now Polly wasn't thinking as much about the hospital visit as about her lack of friends. She had always been popular with other kids and it seemed strange to suddenly find herself so alone. When she reached the cross where Nelson Street met St James Street she saw one or two other children, and looked after them a trifle wistfully, but they were all intent on their own affairs and paid no heed to her. Some were running messages, with money in their hands and bags or baskets full of shopping, and others were with their parents, walking along chattering. But none of them looked as though they needed a friend, or were in the slightest bit interested in Polly.

There were never messages for a child to run in Monica's house. 'We're here on sufferance, and don't we know it,' Mammy had sighed on their very first day in Nelson Street when she had bought meat and potatoes and other vegetables and made a big stew for the whole family. Monica had walked into the kitchen, looked at the big pot of stew, and silently taken from her neat little shopping bag two tiny chops, the makings of a salad and a bought sponge cake. A bought cake! 'And she wit' only one man to feed,' Mammy had said later, in the privacy of their own small room. But Monica worked in an office and didn't have the time to make cakes, Martin had said so. Still, she need not have pushed the stew to the back of the stove quite so disdainfully, telling Mammy grimly that she and Martin preferred a light meal, and that Mammy was welcome to make stew for herself and the two children, provided they ate it before Martin came home.

'I didn't understand . . . but surely, just this once . . .' Mammy had faltered, and Monica had heaved an exaggerated sigh and said that on this occasion the family might eat their stew in the kitchen later, since she and Martin intended to go out to the cinema.

'But there's enough stew here for all of us, dear,' Mammy had said, her beautiful eyes filling with tears at the snub. 'Surely just this once . . .'

Monica had not even answered. She had gone over to the stove and had begun to arrange her two little chops in the gleaming new grill-pan, behaving as though she were the only person in the kitchen – in the world, in fact, Polly thought crossly now. And after that, Mammy hadn't liked to cook anything after about four o'clock, since the smell of cooking made Monica wrinkle up her nose and glance around her as though she suspected them of harbouring a pig or worse.

'Polly me love! I thought I might catch up wit' you if I hurried.' It was Mammy, in her brown coat and hat, with her shopping basket in one hand and the other firmly gripping Ivan's small paw. Her cheeks were flushed and she looked bright-eyed and happier than she had done for some time. 'Oh, Poll, you'll never guess what! One of the nurses who's been lookin' after Daddy called round just now, to tell me of a house she's seen which is goin' for a reasonable rent. Me and Ivan's off to take a look at it right away – want to come along, alanna?'

Polly clasped her hands to her breast, just like all the heroines of her favourite storybooks did when they heard wonderful news. 'Oh, Mammy – you never said you'd asked anyone to look out for a house . . . Oh, it 'ud be so grand to have somewhere of our own again! Yes, please, I'd love to come. Where is it? I'm after hopin' it's near a school where me an' Ivan might go – and as far away from Monica as possible,' she added, grinning widely at Ivan, who was hopping up and down and looking every bit as excited as she felt. 'Will it hold the lot of us? Will it suit Daddy when he's better and can come out of hospital? Oh, janey, I'm excited, so I am!'

'I don't know anything about it, alanna, except that it's not far from the Scotland Road, because Nurse Fry had been shopping up there, and cut through Titchfield Street to visit an old aunt who lives thereabouts. That's when she noticed that one of the houses was to let. So now, if you've finished askin' me questions, we'll make our way to the tram stop.'

A couple of hours later, three members of the O'Brady family stood on the pavement outside the new house, for Deirdre, having closely examined every inch of the place, had talked to the landlord. After a little genteel haggling the two of them had agreed a rent and Deirdre had paid a week in advance and meant to move her family in as soon as possible.

'Of course Titchfield Street isn't as smart as Nelson Street, but wit' your Daddy not working and money being tight it's all we can afford,' Deirdre said half-apologetically, looking up at the terraced house which was to be their home. 'But sure and you'd have to look a lot further to find a house so convenient, and wit' room for us all! There's a jigger along the back so's we can reach the yard, and there's a decent Catholic school just up the road, on Silvester Street, right next door to St Sylvester's, so we shan't have far to go of a Sunday, and the best shops for bargains I ever did see are on the Scotland Road, no more than a brisk walk away. Why Monica went and chose to live out on Nelson Street . . . But there, we're all different, praise be to God, and no doubt she prefers the – the quieter side of the city. Now we'll catch a tram back to Nelson Street and tell Martin we're movin' out just as soon as I can arrange it.'

'There's kids next door,' Polly told Ivan joyfully as they crossed Limekiln Lane and dived into Tenterden Street. 'In fact, there's kids everywhere, round here. We're goin' to like livin' here, Ivan me lad!'

'You're right about kids everywhere,' Deirdre said rather dubiously. 'I don't know when I've seen more kids all in one spot,' she said, her voice sinking. 'Or dirtier ones, come to that. Why, that child's wearin' nothing but a petticoat.'

The children, however, treated this remark with the scorn they felt it deserved. 'They's playin' out, Mammy,' Ivan said reproachfully. 'No one wears good clothes when they's playin' out.'

Polly giggled. 'Mammy's got used to country dirt, she's forgettin' city dirt,' she said. 'As for petticoats . . . well, t'ink of Francis Street on a Saturday, Mammy. There was kids playin' around the stalls wit' only a vest to their backs. Remember Swift's Alley, and me pal Tad, and the awful old tenement in Gardiner's Lane that the Donoghues lived in?'

Deirdre laughed. 'Sure and I mustn't forget me past, for there was a deal of poverty in Dublin, particularly in the Liberties. But I'm after forgettin' the bad t'ings, because life's been better since we came over the water and moved into the crossin' cottage. But of course, life's goin' to be hard now, wit' your Daddy ill and me desprit for work. Now look at that, a tram goin' our way on the main road. We could have caught that if we'd walked faster. We'd best hurry.'

'Oh, trams seem to be comin' and goin' all the time,' Polly said, taking Ivan's other hand and beginning to step out. 'We'll not be long gettin' back to Nelson Street and tellin' them the good news. And I'll write to Grace and Tad this very day, so I shall, tellin' them what's been happenin'. I know Grace knows about Daddy, Mammy, because you wrote and told Brogan when Daddy was took bad, but Grace will want to hear all the very latest news, and you can't write every day, to everyone. Grace'll be ever so glad Daddy's gettin' better, because she always says he saved her life and she loves him nearly as much as I do, and even Tad was mortal fond of me daddy, so I'd best let him know what's been happenin',' she finished. But she was not too pleased with Tad. He had been her best, her dearest, pal in Ireland and when the family left the Liberties he had promised faithfully that he would write, and indeed, at rare intervals, had done so. Polly reckoned she wrote four letters to every one of Tad's, and usually the fourth letter had to be full of threats, or he'd not, she feared, have bothered to answer even that. Though his letters usually contained interesting news, they were short and laboriously written on shockingly poor scraps of paper. Several times she had warned him that she would never write to him again unless he mended his ways, but somehow she always gave in.

After all, as she had told her mammy, she and Tad meant to marry one day and that meant she could scarcely stop writing to him. If she did he might move away, or get himself adopted by a rich man and change his name, and then where would they be?

'That's right, you tell your pal what been happenin' to us,' Deirdre said now, as they emerged on to the main road. 'Oh look, there's a tram stop! And a tram goin' in the right direction! Put your hand out, Poll, so's the driver sees us and stops!'

Tad got the letter as he was setting off to take Dougal and Biddy to school, and recognised Polly's writing at once. Not that there would have been any doubt in his mind who had sent the letter, since no one wrote to him bar Polly.

Now Tad took the letter from the postman's hand joyfully and crammed it into his pocket. The postman winked at him. 'Sure and isn't your little Polly a broth

41

of a girl to write so regular to a chiseller like yourself?' he said genially. 'I hope you write back as often, young Tad.'

'Oh well, girls like writin' letters and chisellers amn't so keen. We're more for doin' t'ings,' Tad said rather obscurely. 'Still, I do write.'

'And since when's you taken to bein' a gaoler to that chiseller, then?' the postman enquired next, for Tad had a firm hand on the shoulder of young Dougal. 'Poor feller, what's he done wrong?'

'Sure and he's not so keen on goin' to the brothers to get his schoolin',' Tad explained virtuously. 'I told him he'd need readin' and writin' one of these days, but he t'inks a feller can manage very well wit'out it.'

Dougal, who was seven and regarded school as an unnecessary evil, sniffed. 'You was sellin' newspapers when you was eight, you often told us so,' he pointed out. 'I'll be eight in the summer. And you don't go to school no more. Why can't I—?'

'I'm too old for school, remember?' Tad said smugly. 'Besides, summer's summer, but now winter's comin' and you'll be a deal better off in school than workin' the streets. C'mon, the pair of yiz.' He took Biddy's small hand and, retaining his grip on Dougal's shoulder, set off once more in the direction of the school. When he had delivered his charges Father Mac had given him a fearful, foxy grin, reminding Tad uncomfortably that you learned a lot more than reading, writing and arithmetic when Father Mac was teaching you and he never meant you to forget that. You learned to keep a fair distance from an angry brother and the strap which he wore round his wrist because of the quick temper most of them had on them. You learned to dodge, and to take unfair punishment stoically, and to speak the truth, if you were certain a good lie would be found out. Still, Dougal would thank him one day, if not today, Tad told himself as he turned away. But all the way, the letter had burned in his pocket and as soon as his errand had been accomplished he made for the quays. There was always plenty going on down there, but a feller could usually find a quiet corner out of the bustle, from whence he could keep his eye open for any paid work going, whilst reading a letter. And it was early still, too early to hope for much in the way of running messages or delivery work.

Now that old man Donoghue had left Dublin with the gypsy woman he had taken to hanging around with – and she'll regret it sooner than I will, Tad's downtrodden little mammy had said grimly when she first heard – Tad, Liam and Kevin simply had to do their best to earn what money they could. Tad had a number of jobs; sometimes he sold turves from door to door, or kindling wood when he could get hold of fruit boxes to chop up. At other times he ran messages for anyone who would pay him a penny or so, carried heavy shopping for the elderly, or went round the fish market, collecting odds and ends of fish which he could sell to dog and cat owners for a few pence. His brothers did the best they could, selling newspapers when all else failed, or helping at the cattle market when drovers were scarce and trudging into the countryside in summer to pick potatoes. But being younger than him they were both still in school, so they could not work all day, as he could. However, it was the mammy, Tad knew, who really kept the family going. She cleaned at the big shops and offices on O'Connell Street, took in washing, made neat brack loaves which she sold for a small profit and

43

generally turned her hand to anything. And as she often said, life was not nearly as hard as when Mr Donoghue had been living at home. Mammy kept her wages tucked away from force of habit, but now there was no one crashing into the place drunk as a fish, to burgle Mammy's earnings for his next drinking bout. Now the rent was paid regularly, food appeared on the table each mealtime, no matter how sparse it might seem, and although the children did not own good boots or shoes, they all had a jealously guarded pair of what their mammy called 'rubber runners', which did very well for school and could be handed down to the next child in line when toes were threatening to come out at the end of the shoe.

Tad reached the quays and took up a position behind a large stack of boxes of what, from the smell, he took to be fish. Then, with pleasant anticipation, he opened his letter. He counted the pages before reading a word, though, like a miser checking on his gold. Yes, it was a four-pager, a good, long letter even for Polly, who once she got going tended to tell, in great detail, everything she had done since she last wrote. Grinning happily to himself, and seeing Polly's small, fair face in his mind's eye, Tad settled down to read.

Twenty minutes later, after reading through the letter twice, Tad shoved it back into his pocket and headed for Gardiner's Lane. He was horrified to hear of Peader's stroke and dismayed that the family had had to move from their country cottage – which sounded like heaven to Tad – back into the city, and felt that he must, for once, write back to his little pal immediately. But even in his sorrow for her, a certain excitement could not be altogether denied. They

44

could come home! Back to Dublin! If Peader did not recover then the family would have a pension and would be no worse off – perhaps better off – in Dublin than in Liverpool; and if he did recover – and Tad sincerely and honestly hoped that he would, for Peader had always been good to him – then why should he not take up a desk job, whatever that might mean, in Dublin, where the family had friends and relatives, rather than in Liverpool, where they only had Martin and his snooty wife?

But halfway home, Tad reconsidered. There was no paper at home and probably no pencil, either, and he would have to earn some money to pay for the postage stamp too. Best go and get himself some work, then buy what he needed to write a letter. He turned his footsteps towards the fish market. Old Mrs O'Brien had a stall there, and since her husband's death she had been glad of a hand when she had plenty of customers. Wednesday and Friday were traditional fish days, and today was Wednesday, so Tad turned his footsteps towards the fish market and Mrs O'Brien's stall. He would write back to Polly this very evening, so he would furnish himself with paper, an envelope and a stamp before returning to Gardiner's Lane. And in the meantime he would consider how best to suggest to Polly that this tragedy might, at least, mean a return to Dublin at last.

It was getting dark before Tad left the fish market and headed towards Gardiner's Lane once more, but he did so with a good deal of satisfaction. He had sold a great deal of fish – his hands were raw and chapped from constantly dipping the fillets and steaks into the bucket of increasingly dirty cold water which Mrs O'Brien kept behind the stall – and he had enough in his pocket to buy paper and an envelope, besides his usual contribution to the household expenses. And what was more, he would not need to buy paper; he would nip into Merrick's, on the corner of Mark's Alley and Francis Street, and buy a screw of tea for his mammy. He well knew that if he mentioned he was about to write a letter to Polly, old Mr Thomas Merrick, who weighed out the tea and the sugar and the other dried goods whilst he kept an eye on his staff and other customers, would hand over an envelope. Polly had been a great favourite with the old man, who had beamed down at her over the top of his gold-rimmed glasses and always found a little treat for her – a few raisins, some nuts, or even, if all else failed, one of the strong peppermints which he sucked because he had a dry mouth.

This evening Mr Merrick was in his usual place and as soon as Tad had bought the tea and taken a half-pound of broken biscuits as well, he asked after Polly. 'Sure and wasn't she a grand little lass, and don't we miss her in here?' he enquired, carefully sliding Tad's pennies into the till. 'It was a sad day for us when she left – and her mammy always shopped here, you know . . . Only the best for Mrs O'Brady.'

Tad, who usually shopped round the markets or picked up unconsidered trifles from anyone selling cheap, tried not to look abashed. It was all very well buying the best, he thought crossly, but you'd got to earn the money to do it first. Polly's mammy had been one of the lucky ones; her menfolk didn't drink all the money away and expect the poor woman to manage on thin air, and she had a neat family, not a great big sprawling one, like his mammy. However, he leaned forward with the air of one about to impart a secret, and was amused to see Mr Merrick immediately lean forward too, and cup one thin, bony hand around his long, whiskery ear.

'Well, boy? Have ye news of the little 'un?'

Tad drew the letter out of his pocket. It was a bit crumpled now, and more than a bit dirty, for every time he had been free of customers or errands for a moment he had reread the letter, and in one corner a silvery huddle of fish scales was proof of his activities. But he held the letter out and Mr Merrick, after only the slightest of hesitations, took it, then glanced up at Tad. It was a questioning, almost shy glance, and Tad interpreted it at once.

'Sure you can go ahead and read it,' he said generously. 'See what you t'ink, Mr Merrick, sor.'

Despite the dirt and crumples, to say nothing of the fish scales, Mr Merrick read the letter a good deal more quickly than Tad had been able to do. Practice, I guess, Tad told himself. If I had a job where I had to write out bills and take down orders . . . But he would never rise to that sort of job and he knew it. There were too many bright boys chasing every halfway decent job which came along, he was lucky to be able to make a few bob the way he did.

'There's a Depression on, you know,' was a favourite remark of half Dublin – the rich half, usually. They addressed it to the poor half, Tad thought angrily, whenever anyone asked for a fairer wage, or a day off around Christmas. Still, there you were, it had always been the same. The rich got richer and the poor got poorer – wasn't that a song or something?

But right now, Mr Merrick was folding the letter up and looking enquiringly down at Tad. 'Well, and isn't it a sad t'ing that poor Mr O'Brady's been after goin' into hospital wit' a stroke?' he enquired. 'I scarce

47

knew the feller, but I'm real sorry for him. And they've lost their home . . . though they seem to have another all lined up to be sure. So you're after writing a letter, to tell Polly we're all t'inking of her? Is that it?' Already his hand was reaching into the drawer behind the counter where he kept paper and envelopes, billheads and invoices and so on. 'I'll give ye a nice bit o' lined paper and an envelope, so's you can write properly. And a stamp,' he added. 'And you'll send the family me regards, and tell 'em I'll be putting in a word for Mr O'Brady at Mass on Sunday?'

'Ye-es, Mr Merrick,' Tad replied. 'And aren't I goin' to do just that meself? Only – don't you t'ink they might come home to Dublin now? The O'Bradys, I mean. Polly an' all. 'Cos the cottage has gone, an' they're managin' on a pension . . . Wouldn't it be just as easy to live here? In Dublin.'

Mr Merrick gave this his consideration, which meant that he seized the end of his long, fleshy nose between finger and thumb and then rubbed them up and down for a moment, whilst pursing his lips, bringing his bushy white eyebrows together in a frown and half closing his eyes. Tad, repressing an urge to snigger, continued to look earnestly at him across the counter and was rewarded by Mr Merrick slowly nodding his balding head.

'You could be right so, young feller-me-lad. But they'll manage, because they've sons earning good money, wouldn't you say? Brogan in the United States, Niall in Australia and young whatsisname in the merchant fleet . . .'

Tad knew that Mr Merrick was right; sons always sent money home – daughters too, if you had any. That was why most young people emigrated to

America or went over the water to work; they could earn good money and send a fair amount home. But he also knew that the money would go on arriving whether the recipient lived in Dublin or England, so what difference would that make to whether the O'Bradys came home or stayed away?

'And the t'ing is, young Tad,' Mr Merrick continued, 'who is there in Dublin for them now? The young O'Bradys aren't here any more, they're either overseas or in Liverpool, and jobs are easier to find over the water, so they say.'

Tad could not reply 'They've got me,' because of course he was not family, but he knew he was dear to Polly – wouldn't that count? He sighed and held out his hand for his letter.

'Oh well, 'twas a nice t'ought, Mr Merrick,' he said, carefully folding the four pages and jamming them back into his pocket. He knew he sounded down, and tried to grin up at the older man. 'Mebbe they'll come back for a visit, eh?'

'Or mebbe you'll go over the water yourself one of these days,' Mr Merrick said kindly. 'You're a likely lad, you never know when a chance might come. So don't forget, now, to be after giving me best wishes to the O'Bradys when you write.'

'I will so,' Tad said stoutly. 'And, Mr Merrick, if you've ever a job goin', a job a feller like meself could do, I'd be mortal grateful . . .'

'We'll need an extra delivery boy come Christmas,' Mr Merrick said, and Tad's heart gave a joyful bound. It just went to show, one moment bad news floors you, and the next moment some amazing good news lifts you six feet above the ground. 'If you want to pop back here in a couple o' weeks mebbe we'll manage something. Got a bicycle?'

Tad shook his head, his face falling. Some chance of him having a bicycle – he couldn't even afford a bell!

But Mr Merrick was tutting to himself and frowning. 'No, no, of course not. 'Tis the regular boys who ride the bicycles, you'd have to manage on foot or by tram. Anyway, you call back here around the 15th. I'll not have forgotten.'

So Tad left the shop with his purchases and a light step; it looked as though things were looking up for him, even if Polly and the other O'Bradys would not be on their way home soon!

Halfway back to Gardiner's Lane, however, Tad remembered that if he was going to write to Polly he really should go round to Swift's Alley first and see what news and gossip he could pick up. On the grounds that it made his letters more interesting – and God knew, he found it hard to fill half a page, let alone four – he usually went round to Polly's old home and asked the neighbours if they had any snippets of news for the O'Bradys. Not only did it add interest to his letters, but he hoped that it would keep Swift's Alley, and Dublin, alive in Polly's mind, so that she really would come back here when she was able.

He turned his steps towards Polly's old home and very soon was climbing the first long flight of stairs. Or at least he climbed as far as the first landing, where he stopped because someone was coming down. He glanced up . . . and stayed where he was, with his mouth open and his eyes rounding.

A girl of about his own age was coming down the stairs towards him. She was wearing a blue and white checked dress, white cotton socks and light brown strap shoes, and as she got closer he saw that she had a pale oval face and a pair of very large, light blue eyes. But what really caught his attention was her hair. It was long, thick and shining, and it was the colour of – of moonlight, Tad thought reverently. It must have been recently brushed for it stood out round her head like a halo and indeed, for a moment as he looked up at her, he had a very odd sensation, because it was at this precise spot, long ago, that Polly had seen her guardian angel for the first time.

Tad had been with her though he had not seen the angel, had not believed Polly at first. But Mrs O'Brady had accepted without the flicker of an eyelid that Polly's guardian angel was a fact, and despite loudly pooh-poohing the whole idea of an angel who had nothing better to do than keep an eye on young Polly, Tad had, insensibly, begun to believe that the angel was there all right. He couldn't see it – only Polly said it was a girl, not an it – because chisellers didn't go in much for seeing angels, but Polly was the most honest person he knew, and she saw her angel all the time, so the angel had to exist.

And standing there, pressed back against the chipped and dirty tenement wall, looking up at the vision which seemed almost to float down the stairs, Tad really thought, just for a second, that this was Polly's angel, letting him see her at last so that he wouldn't tease Polly about it any more. Only then the girl caught sight of him and grinned, showing a chipped tooth, and then she swung the basket she was carrying and it caught in the banisters and she said a word – but quietly – which Tad knew full well that no angel would ever allow to pass its lips, and he grinned back, greatly relieved. He didn't mind Polly seeing angels if she was set on it, but he didn't want any truck with the supernatural him-self, be it angelic or devilish. Life was quite tough

51

enough without adding ghoulies and ghosties to the mixture.

But the girl, coming level with him, had stopped. 'Sure an' you don't live around here, or I'd know it,' she stated. 'I've been livin' here ten whole days and I know everyone in the block by sight, just about. What are you doin' here, then? Me family's on the next floor up an' you aren't after seein' me brother Mick, 'cos I know all his pals, so I do. And you're too young to be visitin' the poor girls on the top floor.'

'I was goin' up to see Felicity,' Tad said with dignity. He was not quite sure why she thought him too young to visit the poor girls, since he and Felicity were great pals, so they were, and often had great crack together. Indeed, Felicity was his main source of tenement gossip, for she had lived in this particular block for five years now and knew everyone and was, furthermore, well-liked. Tad knew, vaguely, that the poor girls were thought to be no better than they should be, but he was not at all sure just what this entailed. He only knew that Felicity was sweet and generous, that she sometimes gave him tuppence to run her messages and take her baby boy out for a couple of hours, and that Mrs O'Brady, Polly's mammy, had said that the girls were good girls, or if they weren't good girls then it was not their fault but the fault of their one-time rich employers. So now Tad stuck to his guns, even though the girl grinned more broadly than ever. 'She's a friend of mine, so she is,' Tad said reprovingly. 'And she knows all what's goin' on around here, you bet your life she does! So when I write a letter to me pal Polly, who used to live in the rooms you live in now, I come round here first to find out if there's any news the poor girls t'ink would interest the O'Bradys.'

'I've heard about Polly,' the pale-haired girl said. 'She sounds a great gun, so she does. I wish she was still here. There's no one my age livin' in this block. What's your name, eh?'

'I'm Tad Donoghue,' Tad said readily. 'I'm fourteen, I've left school. Who's you?'

'Angela Machin. Wish I were fourteen, but I shall be, come next summer,' the blonde girl said. 'Where d'you live?'

'Gardiner's Lane,' Tad said. 'I've got a tree growin' out of me bedroom chimney, so I have, an' – an' a huge brown an' yellow fungus on the wall above me bed. It smells somethin' tarble at this time o' year,' he added with pride.

'Truly? Cut your t'roat an' hope to die?' Angela asked. 'Can I come an' see it for meself?'

''Course, when I've been up an' talked to Felicity,' Tad said. 'Do you only have the one brother? No sisters?'

'That's right,' Angela said. 'I'll come up wit' you; I like the poor girls.'

She fell into step beside him and the two of them climbed the stairs together, passed the door behind which the O'Bradys had once lived, and up the next flight to the attic rooms rented by the poor girls. Tad kept giving quick little sideways looks at his companion. What a pretty creature she was! He just hoped that some of the fellers who'd been to school with him would see him with this girl, who was more like a film star than anyone else he had ever met. He decided, as they climbed the stairs side by side, that he would take her home and show her the tree growing in the crooked little fireplace in his bedroom, and the huge, evil-smelling fungus, and that he would tell her all about his daddy's defection and his mammy's hard work and his large family of younger brothers and sisters. If, after that, she decided that she no longer wanted to be pals, that was that. But if she decided he was worthy of being a friend . . . Tad decided that when he next had some money he would take Angela Machin to the flicks, or to some other place of entertainment. She would be his as Polly had once been his – but was, he supposed sadly, his no longer. She was too far away, she would never come back to Dublin . . . And what was more, a description of Angela could easily fill up half a page of anyone's letter.

Thoroughly pleased with himself, Tad reached the attic landing, beat a tattoo on the door with one fist, and flung it open. Felicity was stirring something in a big black cauldron over a rather small and smoky fire.

'Hello, Tad,' Felicity said, looking round. Her smile included Angela. 'So you've met up wit' our Angel, have you? Isn't she a picture, then?'

Tad wanted to make some manly, disclaiming remark, but his traitorous mouth had its own ideas. 'Aye, she's as pretty as Polly,' he said rather thickly. 'Prettier.'

To the old Tad, this would have been almost blasphemy since he had made no secret of the fact that he thought Polly the prettiest girl in the whole of Dublin, if not the world, but Felicity just raised an eyebrow and then turned back to her pot-stirring. 'She's pretty in a different way, so she is,' she corrected in her calm, country voice. 'If you go to the crock on the sideboard, young feller, you'll find some oatcakes. Help yourselves. Now, Tad,' she went on as the two children settled themselves on the wooden table, swinging their legs and munching oatcakes, 'what can I do for you?'

*

By the time Tad and Angela parted company, Tad knew as much about Angela as she did about him, which was a good deal. Her elder brother, Mick, was a young man of twenty and worked in a shoe shop. He was courting, Angie said – she told Tad to call her Angie since everyone else did – and very much disliked being parted from his young lady, who was still in Limerick, but who intended to come to Dublin just as soon as she could. The Machins had come over from Limerick because Mr Machin had been offered the job of head sales assistant in the men's department of Switzers on Grafton Street. Mick, who had been working as a clerk in a solicitor's office, had been glad to leave and take his chance of a job in the capital city, for the wages in Limerick had been poor and the hours long, and sure enough he had been taken on by the shoe shop within a couple of days of arriving here. Mrs Machin, it seemed, was a dab hand with her needle and at home in Limerick had worked as a dressmaker, but her sight was failing, so they had seized the chance of a better paid job in order that they could manage on one less salary.

'I was a lovely surprise to me mammy an' daddy so I was,' Angela told him complacently as they sauntered towards Gardiner's Lane. 'Mammy had given up all hopes of another baby before I was born, so I were a lovely surprise and now they've got me, they want to see I'm brought up right. Which is why they're sendin' me to the convent school, though I dare say there's a lot of t'ings they'd rather do wit' the fee money.'

'I went to the national school; you don't have to pay there,' Tad said. 'Now me brothers go there. Ain't all schools the same, then?'

55

But he knew they weren't, not really. Polly had gone to private school, though she had grumbled about her eckers and the nuns just as much as Tad's sisters, who went to the free school, had done. But Angela was shrugging.

'I don't think it matters. I'm not clever, like some, but I keep me end up. I get good enough marks. And Mammy and Daddy think I'll get a good job when I leave, because I've been to private school.'

Tad nodded gloomily. He remembered Polly saying something of the sort now that he thought back. 'Where's your school, then, Angie? Miles away?'

'Well, I usually take a tram,' Angela said vaguely. 'I suppose I could walk, but it 'ud take me a while. I'm glad you came callin', Tad. I don't know hardly anyone in Dublin yet . . . now I know you!'

'That's the idea. We'll be pals, shall we?' Tad asked eagerly. 'There's all sorts to do in Dublin when there's two of you. Does your mammy give you money for the tuppenny rush at the cinema? I go to the Tiv, on Francis Street; I do love Sat'day flickers.'

'I do too,' Angela said. 'Me mammy used to give me a Peggy's leg or an ounce of rainbow caramels of a Sat'day, so's I don't fade away before me dinner, and I used to see the show and then go round to me cousin Kitty's, an' play Piggy Bed or Shop or skippin' until it were time for tea. But here . . . well, I don't know folk yet.'

Tad understood this completely. If you went to the free school you would meet your pals everywhere, but the small private schools took in children from a much wider area and the chances were that you'd not have a schoolfellow living within two or three streets of you. And Angie and her family hadn't been living in Swift's Alley for long enough to get to know people there, either.

As for Angela finding out about Tad, it wasn't hard to guess most of it once you had visited his home. Small and grubby brothers and sisters had greeted him as he crossed the courtyard and climbed the stairs, and in the kitchen, where the family lived, his sister Annie had been scrubbing a pan of potatoes for their tea whilst Biddy, who was getting to an age when she could be helpful, had been trying to chop cabbage with a knife which was rather too large for her to handle.

'Lemme do that,' Tad said, taking the knife. He put the screw of tea and the brown paper bag of biscuits down on the scrubbed wooden table and turned to Annie. 'Biddy's not old enough to use a knife, alanna. Don't let her chop t'ings or she'll be destroyin' her fingers entirely, so she will.' He saw his small sisters staring and stopped chopping cabbage for a moment to wave the knife towards his companion. 'Oh, Ann, this is me pal Angela Machin, what lives in Swift's Alley, in the O'Bradys' old place. Angie, the big 'un with the spuds is Annie an' the other's our Biddy. They's two of me sisters.' He finished chopping the cabbage, then headed for the door again. 'I'm just goin' to show Angie our tree, an' our fungus,' he added, and picked up a stub of candle and lit it from the lamp.

The boys' room was further along the landing and on the opposite side. It was a tiny room, only about four feet wide though it was a good deal longer. It smelt strongly of damp and the pigeon droppings which came through the missing roof tiles, but Angela, after one somewhat startled glance around her, made no comment. Instead, she admired the tree

57

in the fireplace and the huge, leathery brown fungus with yellow patches, and only looked once at the beds, which were mostly piles of rags and straw, with one thin blanket apiece to pull over each boy.

'Where does your mammy and your sisters sleep?' she enquired, after Tad had pointed out which boy slept in which bed. 'I didn't notice another room.'

'They sleep in the living room,' Tad explained. 'It's a big room. They have to put their beds away before we go off in the mornings, though. Mammy as well.'

'Oh,' Angela said. 'And – and your daddy?'

'Left. He's been gone more than a year, thank the good Lord,' Tad said piously and with some satisfaction. 'Good riddance, Mammy says. He was a docker, and he could drink the Liffey dry, so he could. We's better off now than we was afore, 'cos he used to take Mammy's money off her. And mine too, if he could find it.'

'Oh,' Angela said again. 'But aren't you the lucky one to have all those brothers and sisters – you've always got someone to play wit' when you fancy a game.'

'Ye-es, only I'm the eldest, you see,' Tad explained. 'The eldest does the messages an' helps in the house an' finds firewood to light the fire, you know.'

'I don't, really,' Angela said. 'Micky's the eldest, but he's been workin' as long as I can remember, pretty near. And there aren't many jobs like fetchin' firewood when there's only four of you. But I get the messages for Mammy,' she added, clearly anxious not to appear too different. 'And I put the delft out on the table, and the knives and forks and that, and make my own bed and—' She stopped short. 'Well now, what'll we do next? Your sisters seemed to be managin' the supper wit'out too much fuss, even though they're young.'

Tad considered. He had meant to write to Polly, but he could do that any time, he told himself. 'What would you like to do?' he asked at last. 'You won't want to be too far from home as it's late or your mammy might worry.'

'I'd like to look in the shop windows on O'Connell Street,' Angela said longingly. 'But you're right, it's too late. Mammy's not workin' yet, so she'll be home. Would you like to come back wit' me and stay for a bit?' She added: 'Mammy wouldn't mind.'

'Well, I'll walk you home,' Tad said. 'But after that I'd best be gettin' back home meself. The kids'll see to the supper all right, but Mammy will wonder if I'm not there to give a hand. Only if you tell me where your school is I might meet you out tomorrer an' we could go on to O'Connell Street from there.'

'I t'ought you were workin',' Angela said artlessly. 'Suppose you've got a job tomorrer? No, you come round to Swift's Alley when you finish. If it's too late for window-shoppin' then we can always go up to my house and make ourselves toast before the fire or somethin' of that sort.'

Toast before the fire! Shades of Polly's mammy and the uproarious games the family had sometimes played whilst waiting for toast, or chestnuts to roast, or the cake in the oven to rise flickered temptingly in Tad's mind. He swallowed. 'That 'ud be grand,' he said. They had reached Angela's tenement now and they crossed the cramped little foyer and began to mount the stairs, but on the half-landing Tad paused. 'You can go the rest o' the way,' he said gruffly. 'See you tomorrer, then, Angie.'

But all the way home he thought about her. That

hair, fine as a dandelion clock and almost as pale. And her big blue eyes, and the nice clothes she wore! He wished he could get clothes like that for Biddy and Annie, but there was a world of difference between what two parents and an elder brother in work could afford and what one poor, hardworking mammy with a great many children could manage.

When he reached Gardiner's Lane it occurred to him that if Mrs Machin was a dressmaker she probably made Angela's dresses herself, which would mean they were cheaper than he had supposed. So no one could expect his poor ould wan to compete in the matter of dresses, he told himself, and was vaguely comforted. Besides, Angela had never stuck her nose up in the air and acted superior to him. In fact, she had been very nice. Not a word of reproach had passed her lips over the state of the boys' room, though she had mentioned that she made her own bed each day. He wondered just how one could possibly make a bed like his, though. Knowing Polly and the other O'Bradys had taught him that people with a bit of money had proper beds, with sheets and blankets over a mattress, and pillows on which one laid one's head, but he had supposed that Polly somehow wriggled into her bed without disturbing the neat, tightly tucked-in bedding. Now he realised that Polly – or her mammy, possibly – had had to retuck those sheets and blankets each morning after they got up.

He was just thinking that perhaps he ought to have drawn his blanket up over the pile of straw and rags when someone called his name and, turning, he saw his mammy coming across the courtyard. She was walking slowly, her shoulders drooping, and she carried a large bundle of what looked like bedding

60

under one arm and a string shopping bag hung from the other hand. 'Tad, giz a hand, there's a good feller. These sheets are dry, pretty well, but they'll need ironin' before I can take 'em back to Mount Street tomorrer.'

Tad took the bundle and the string bag from her, tucked the bundle under his right arm and slung the bag on his wrist. Then he put his left hand under his mammy's small, skinny elbow and began to help her along. For the first time it occurred to him that his mammy could not be more than thirty-five or so, yet she was already grey-haired and carried herself like someone very much older. And Angela had said that her own mammy was very smart, with goldy-brown hair and pink cheeks, and didn't look her age. Life, he concluded, helping his mother up the first flight of stairs, was not a very nice business, particularly if you were poor and overworked and managing alone. It wasn't even that, either. His mammy had been knocked about by her bullying hulk of a husband for nigh on thirteen years, to his knowledge. She had had a broken arm, a broken nose, and her lip had been split more times than he cared to remember. Yet she had a lovely grin on her, though it was rather a toothless one, and she could laugh over something the kids did or said as though she hadn't a care in the world.

I believe me mammy's a real heroine, that's what I believe, Tad told himself as they climbed the stained and creaking wooden stairs. When I'm a man growed and earning decent money I'll pay her back all she's done for us, so I will. I won't run out on her like me daddy did, nor I won't let her down. She deserves better than she's had these past few years.

'You're a good boy, Tad,' Mrs Donoghue said

61

breathlessly as they reached the top of the last flight and Tad opened the living-room door for her. 'Oh, me loves, is that kettle just boiled now? And is that a teapot, heatin' up beside the fire? Eh, I'm a lucky woman . . . I'll just sit down for ten minutes and I'll be as good as I ever were. Annie, you're a grand girl to make your mammy a nice cup o' tay and serve it up so spruce, in nice delft!'

Annie, a tiny sprat of a girl with lank brown hair and small, twinkling eyes, grinned, showing that she was just at the age when teeth are neither all gone nor all there. 'There's a biscuit an' all,' she announced with a pronounced lisp, putting the cup down beside her mother, who had collapsed into one of the two sagging armchairs drawn up by the fire. 'Tad buyed some wit' his earnings, didn't you, Tad?'

'That's right. I got 'em from Merricks, 'cos if I send messages to Poll for him, he'll give me envelopes an' paper, so he will. An' today . . . you'll never guess what he said!'

'Have a lollipop? Did he say you could have a lollipop, Tad?' Eileen enquired. She was three and always hungry for something sweet; Tad knew she would already have had the only pink sugar biscuit in the bag but he grinned down at her anyway. She was pretty, round-faced and babyish, though Sammy, a year younger, was the baby now. 'Oh, I does love lollipops, so I does.'

'It were better than that,' Tad informed them. 'Go on, have a guess.'

Obligingly, everyone had a guess but no one was anywhere near, so of course Tad had to tell them, settling himself down on the kitchen table and swinging his legs as he drank the tea Annie poured for him and ate a broken custard cream. 'He said there

62

might be a job for me come Christmas – a delivery job,' he told them proudly. 'I'm to call round once we're into December, an' Mr Merrick says if they need another lad it'll be me!'

'Sure and that's good news enough for a whole year,' his mammy said, clasping her cup with both hands to warm them. 'When I'm makin' me barmbracks for sale I'll buy me dried fruit and me butter and flour from Merrick's, so I will. If they make you a delivery boy, that is,' she finished.

'And Tad brought ever such a pretty lady round to see us earlier,' Biddy said, lifting the lid of the pan on the edge of the fire and gazing critically at its contents. 'She had hair like pure gold, so she did.'

'She's goin' to be me pal,' Tad said contentedly, helping himself to another biscuit. 'She's called Angela Machin, Mammy, an' she's as pretty as Polly was – prettier.'

'No one could possibly be as pretty as Polly, nor as kind and sweet,' Tad's mammy said firmly and the girls nodded approvingly. Polly had a generous spirit and had often brought treats round for her pal's family. 'Still, I don't doubt this girl's a decint girl. Angela – that's not an Irish name, though.'

'No-o, but she's from Limerick,' Tad said, as though folk from Limerick were well known for outlandish names. 'Her fambly live in the O'Bradys' old rooms – ain't that a strange t'ing?'

'Aye, strange enough. And what do they do – the fambly?'

'Well, her daddy's in the men's department of Switzers on Grafton Street, and her brother's in a shoe shop, sellin' shoes. Her mammy's a dressmaker, but I don't think she's dressmakin' here yet. And that's all the fambly,' he ended.

63

'Ah. Well, wit' two of 'em in work they'll be well off,' Tad's mammy said. She heaved herself out of her chair and went towards the fire and the bubbling saucepans. 'You're a good girl, Biddy, to get the food a-goin' afore I'm even through the door. Is it nearly done? Tad, go down and shout the rest o' the kids, then we'll eat, 'cos I want to get this ironin' done this evenin' whiles the fire's hot and I'm not too tired. Then mebbe tomorrer I'll do some bakin'.'

'Sure I will,' Tad said, making for the door. 'Liam an' Kevin will be in soon, I 'spect. I wonder what they'll bring home wit' them?'

Chapter Three

Polly, having despatched her letters, waited in vain for a reply from Tad, and this both surprised and annoyed her. Sure, Tad usually took ages and ages to answer a letter, but she had told him that, in view of her daddy's illness, she expected a reply by return, and had added her customary threat about never writing to him again if he failed her in this matter. And to be fair to Tad, he was a kind-hearted boy and, though he hated writing letters and was a poor hand at it, would, she was sure, have done his best to comfort her in her affliction.

For Daddy's illness was an affliction indeed. Mammy was always off up at the hospital, where children were not allowed to go save with special permission on a Saturday afternoon, and Martin was grumpy.

'Anyone would t'ink he'd enjoyed havin' us to stay and didn't want us to move out to Titchfield Street,' Polly grumbled to Ivan, after an uncomfortable evening during which she and Ivan had done their eckers and then played a game of Snap and tried to ignore the fact that Martin sat in his chair staring at nothing and wouldn't answer when you spoke. 'When you t'ink how his old wife has grumbled and moaned and stopped us havin' meals wit' them and said we eat them out of house and home when Mammy pays for our food and not her or Martin . . . well, he *can't* want us to stay,' she ended.

The two children were in the cramped little spare room, getting ready for bed. Polly, already clean and nightgowned, was watching Ivan as he dabbed at his face with a wet flannel and then hastily rubbed himself dry on the towel which hung beside the washstand. When she saw that he had finished with the water she turned towards the tiny dressing table with its small square of mirror on top and picked up her hairbrush.

'Mebbe he doesn't fancy the t'ought of bein' alone wit' Monica again, when he's had us for her to grumble at,' Ivan said with surprising shrewdness. 'When we're here, she can nag about us. What's she got to nag about when we ain't here but him, eh?'

'They're married, so it's different,' Polly pointed out. She began to brush the tangles out of her curls, wincing and squeaking whenever the brush got stuck, which happened frequently. 'Mart's her husband, so he is, and husbands have to get used to bein' nagged at.'

'Don't call him Mart, he's got a decent Christian name and I like to hear all of it, please,' Ivan squeaked, in a very fair imitation of his sister-in-law's mincing vowels. 'Oh, jeez, Polly, I don't care what Martin wants, I want get to our new house this very minute if it means that Monica will keep whinin' at us.'

'And I've not heard a word from Tad, would you believe?' Polly said, as though her small brother had not spoken. She had got rid of most of the tangles in her hair and now began to brush steadily, counting beneath her breath as she did so. 'Forty-five, forty-six, forty-seven . . . and I told him special to write back at once. Forty-nine, fifty . . .'

'He'll write,' Ivan said comfortably. 'Sure and doesn't he always, in the end?'

'Ye-es, he does,' Polly admitted. 'Ouch! Fifty-three, fifty-four . . . I 'spect he's busy, wit' Christmas comin' up, and them wit'out their daddy to help save up for presents an' that.'

'Their daddy spended all the money, I've heared you say so,' Ivan reminded her briskly. He sat on the bed to remove his last garments – his socks – and then struggled into his striped nightshirt. 'The fellers at the school in the village didn't wear nightshirts, they went to bed in their kecks,' he informed his sister succinctly. 'Wish Mammy would let me do that.'

'They never does!' Polly said, shocked. 'That ain't decent, Ivan.'

'Well, mebbe not, but it's warmer, an' they can dress quick as quick in the mornin's, because they're already in their school t'ings,' Ivan pointed out. He yawned, stretched, then snuggled down. 'Come on, Poll, it ain't fair if I warms the bed an' then you colds it again, comin' into my lovely warm part wit' your cold old feet.'

'Ninety-eight, ninety-nine, a *hundred*,' Polly shouted triumphantly. She threw the brush down on the dressing table and leapt the short distance on to the bed, heaving the covers off Ivan and then disappearing beneath them like a rabbit into its burrow. 'Well, if Mammy knew what those boys at our old school had told you, she'd have took us away from the crossin' cottage anyway,' she said in a voice muffled by blankets. 'I hope the new school's nicer than that.'

'Oh, it'll be grand,' Ivan said. 'Tell you what, Poll, I bet your letter comes tomorrer. I bet you a penny!'

'Haven't got one,' came the muffled reply. 'I'll bet you a ha'penny, though. Mammy gave me a ha'penny

67

to spend for doin' a message for her. She said I could buy sweeties, only I'm savin' it for Christmas instead.'

Ivan began to speak, then his voice unaccountably stopped. And presently, Polly poked her head out of the covers to look at her small brother. As she had guessed, he was sound asleep, his lashes lying on his cheeks, his pink mouth a little open and tiny snores escaping from him now and then.

Lucky chiseller, to be able to sleep like that, between one word an' the next, Polly thought . . . and was asleep herself before Deirdre came stealing in to turn out the light.

If Ivan had remembered the bet next morning he would have been a ha'penny the richer, but as so often happened he had no recollection of what he had been saying just before he slept, so Polly, who wanted all the ha'pennies she could get to buy her daddy a Christmas present, kept her mouth shut on the subject.

'Me letter's arrived,' she said triumphantly, however, thinking that it was only fair to give Ivan a chance to get his money, but Ivan, up to his eyebrows in porridge and making a pathway across it which he promptly filled with buttermilk, merely grunted. Deirdre, who had put the letter down by Polly's plate, was more interested.

'You can read it when you've et your breakfast,' she said, eating her own porridge neatly, and not playing swamps and dinosaurs, as the children did. 'And come to t'ink, 'tis a lucky t'ing indeed that the letter's come today because we're movin' tomorrer.'

Polly started to speak with her mouth full, spluttered, and Ivan ducked as porridge flew everywhere. Fortunately Martin and Monica had departed for

68

their respective places of work some time before so Deirdre, clucking, went and got a cloth from the sink to clean up the mess whilst Polly and Ivan clutched each other and jigged around the table, their breakfast forgotten.

'Tomorrer! We're movin' out of here tomorrer!' Polly squeaked, picking up the envelope with Tad's writing – and a good deal of porridge – on it and waving it in the air. 'Aren't I just so glad, Ivan! Oh, a house of our own again, an' me darlin' Delilah an' me dearest Lionel back in me arms where they belong! An' school, instead of bein' stuck here all day tryin' to be tidy an' not make a mess or a muddle!'

'I didn't mind missin' school that much,' Ivan observed, taking his place at the table once more and beginning to spoon porridge furiously. 'But it'll be good to have Bev back, I agree wit' you there.'

'Oh, Bev's nice, but he's not like dear Delly. And now I'm goin' to read me letter,' Polly announced, putting a finger under the flap. 'You said I could, didn't you, Mammy?'

'I said after breakfast, so have you finished? Then you can wash the dishes, Polly, and Ivan can wipe them. And then you can read your letter, alanna, but not before.'

Polly heaved a huge, exaggerated sigh but obediently began to carry the dishes over to the sink. And presently Deirdre went up to tidy the bedroom and get their outdoor things and Polly and Ivan began to play a vigorous game in which the porridge spoons waged war on the delft, and a good deal of water got scattered on the floor and splashes appeared on Ivan's flannel shirt and on Polly's grey skirt.

But the game was over and all the washing-up done and put away by the time Deirdre came downstairs. She flicked a quick glance over the room, tightened her lips a little over the splashes, and then held out their coats. 'Play out for an hour whilst I do the floor in here, kids,' she said briskly. ''Tis chilly out, so keep movin' . . . Oh, if you want to read your letter first, alanna, take it through to the parlour. Monica won't mind you readin' it in there – well, she won't know. Off wit' you now.'

Almost reluctantly, Polly trailed through into the parlour where she sat in the window, slit open the envelope, pulled out the single sheet of paper it contained, and began to read.

Deirdre had washed the kitchen floor when Polly re-entered the room and was just polishing the taps over the sink with a wash-leather. She looked round and smiled as Polly tiptoed across the wet linoleum. She thought her daughter looked rather pink and wondered what Tad had said to upset her; clearly there was something wrong. 'Well, alanna,' she said carefully, 'what's Tad got to say, then? Any interestin' news?'

'He's got a new pal called Angie. She's got yellow hair – he doesn't say that, but that's what he means – and all he talks about is her,' Polly said in an injured tone. 'Mammy, Tad's *my* pal, what does he want this Angie girl for?'

'I guess he misses you, and is lonely for company,' Deirdre said gently. 'You had plenty of pals when you lived in the crossin' cottage, and you'll have friends again once you're in school and we're in our own house. You mustn't grudge poor Tad wantin' a pal too.'

'Ye-es, but when I write letters to Tad I don't go on about me other pals,' Polly said, pouting. 'Honest to

70

God, Mammy, you'd t'ink there never was a girl born like this Angela! She's come from Limerick because her daddy's got a job on Grafton Street and would you believe, the spalpeen lives in our old house in Swift's Alley, in the very rooms we had, Mammy, when we lived in Dublin!'

Deirdre turned away to hide a smile, then turned back to take both Polly's small hands in hers. 'Me darlin' child, what could be more natural than that Tad would make a pal of a child who lived where his best friend ever had lived?' she asked. 'I expect this Angie was lonely too, if she'd not lived in Dublin long, and was glad of Tad's company. Why, I daresay she's like yourself, and not even in school yet.'

'She's in school all right,' Polly said broodingly. 'She's at the convent, like I was . . . I guess she's probably Sister Andorra's favourite too, the same as me. Only – only she isn't me, Mammy, and – and I don't want Tad lovin' anyone else!'

'I don't suppose he loves her like he loves you,' Deirdre said rather helplessly. What could she say to comfort her little girl, who was taking her pal's defection so very hard? 'But she's a new friend, and he t'ought you'd be interested . . .'

'Huh!' Polly said crisply, but with a curling lip. 'He goes on about her yellow hair, an' her big blue eyes, an' her pretty dress . . . Mammy, he says when he first saw her he t'ought she was me guardian angel!'

The last words came out as a wail and Deirdre hid her involuntary smile by taking Polly into her arms and hugging her. 'Alanna, you're jealous! You should know better – you know what Tad's like wit' the letter-writin', he simply can't t'ink what else to say once he's said *Dear Polly, how are you, I am doing awright but missing you,*' she reminded her daughter.

71

'He's talkin' about this Angie for something new to say, not because he's t'inkin' much about her.'

For answer Polly wriggled out of her arms and thrust the letter into her hand. 'Read it,' she demanded. 'Just you read that letter, Mammy, an' then you can see if the eejit's in love wit' Angie Machin or not! And I'm goin' out to play wit' Ivan, an' *Mr Donoghue* can whistle for a letter from me, I'm tellin' you!'

And with that Polly grabbed up her navy coat and her pixie hood and slammed out of the house and could be seen running down the pavement and struggling into coat and hat as she went.

Deirdre sat down at the table and began to read the ill-spelt and extremely ill-written letter.

Dear Polly,

How are you, I'm doing awright but missing you. I's real sorry your Daddy's Ill, but glad he's Better an he Was. The ~~noo~~ new House sounds fine – is it a whole House, Poll, like the Cotage was a whole House? They's lucky in Liverpool to have whole Houses and not just bits, like we has over here.

When your letter come I went round to Swifts Alley for ~~noos~~ niws. And you'll never Gess! I were halfway up the Stairs, around where you saw your Guarjan Angel that Christmas, when I tought I saw One as well. It came down the stairs, it had a haylo of gold hair an very blue eyes. Well, Poll, it weren't a Angel at all. She's called Angie Machin an she lives in yore rooms!!! She's real nice, you'd like Her so you would. Her Daddy an Mammy brung her from Limerick – she told me how to Spell that, Poll – cos her Daddy's got a job on O'Connell. I'm that glad she's here, she's goin to be me pal, we're goin to the Satday Rush nex week, we went an watched the Big Fellers playin Pitch an Toss, She liked that.

Mr Merrick give me the stamp for the Letter when I bought Tea and Biskits, an he said if I come back soon I might be a Christmas Delivery Boy. I'll have Good Money then an me an Angie will go to the panto and mebbe more tings.

Well goodby for now, Polly, you are still me Best Pal an I wish you was still in Dublin.

Your friend Tad Donoghue

After she had read it through twice, Deirdre leaned her elbows on the table and seriously considered the letter. Tad was clearly smitten with this Angie, and Polly was obviously both upset and furious because of it. Deirdre admired many things about Tad and liked the boy too, but she had never taken the friendship as seriously as her daughter had. Polly was still a child so time, and distance, she had always believed, would mean that in a few more years the two would think of each other as old playmates rather than as the future bride and groom. But then she had never believed that Polly and Tad would continue to correspond for two and a half years, so perhaps the sudden advent of Angela Machin – he spelt that right as well, she thought inconsequentially – might be a very good thing, even if Polly found her old pal's sudden defection painful at first.

Having made up her mind on that point, Deirdre folded the page, put it back into the envelope, and got her own coat off the back of the kitchen door. She got her big marketing basket and her handbag and her hat, for it was still very cold out, and set off down the short garden path. Once in Nelson Street, she could see Polly and Ivan playing Piggy beds with a round tin filled with garden earth as the Piggy, the beds marked out in chalk on the paving stones. Even from a distance, Deirdre could see the dogged, mulish way that Polly kicked the Piggy along; she was still cross, then.

But when she reached them, Polly took her hand and gave a couple of skips before announcing: 'Well, I've made up me mind, Mammy! *I'm* goin' to have a pal of me own just as soon as I get to school – not a girl-pal, Mammy, but a boy-pal, because there's boys go to St Sylvester's school as well, in the boys' half – and I'm goin' to write to Tad an' tell him he needn't write back no more if he don't want to, because we'll mebbe never meet each other again in this life, so what's the point?'

Deirdre, who had been hoping for something like this, was startled at the sudden seriousness in her small daughter's face and said: 'Well now, alanna, you needn't go that far! But you can tell him you'll just be pals. How about that, eh? You wouldn't want to hurt his feelings, would you?'

'Yes I would,' Polly said emphatically. 'I'd like to give him a clout round the lug, so I would. Still, a letter will have to do. And won't I tell him all about me new pal when I've chose one,' she added dreamily. 'I'll teach the wicked chiseller! Oh yes, I'll show Tad Donoghue that he isn't the only one wit' a special pal!'

On Sunday, Polly, Ivan and Bevin all went to the hospital to see their father, though they were only allowed to stay on the ward for ten minutes apiece and then had to wait in the corridor for their mother.

Deirdre thought that Peader was looking a great deal better. There was colour in his face now, and when Polly began to chatter about the new house, and

74

about Tad's letter and the wonderful golden-haired Angela girl, he actually smiled.

'Tad's a good lad,' he said dreamily. 'You won't go far wrong wit' Tad.'

'The nurse says you can come home for Christmas Day,' Deirdre told him, hoping to get him off the subject, for she did not want Peader encouraging Polly to forgive Tad for his behaviour over Angela Machin. 'They'll want you back by evening, they say, but sure an' you'll have had enough excitement by then. And you'll enjoy a day wit' us, won't you, me darlin'?'

Peader nodded, then said slowly: 'Yes, I'll enjoy that.' His voice was slurred, but stronger than it had been since the stroke and Deirdre beamed at him, grateful for every small improvement.

'We're havin' a real waggon to move our t'ings from the storage place to the new house, aren't we, Mammy?' Polly said excitedly. She did not seem to notice her father's halting speech, nor the effort it cost him to turn his cheek towards her for a kiss. 'Oh, Daddy, I'm longin' to see Lionel and Delly again, so I am. Mammy's afraid they may not like the city, but they will, I'm sure they will – they were happy in the Liberties, weren't they, Daddy?'

She would probably have enlarged on the topic, Deirdre thought, but at that moment Bev came in, accompanied by a nurse, who shooed Polly out whilst Bev told Peader how his exams had gone and assured his father that he was looking forward to moving back in with his family, even though it meant leaving the village behind.

'Sure an' no woman ever had better children, me darlin',' Deirdre told her husband as soon as they were alone. 'And when you're back home wit' us . . .

75

Oh, I can't tell you how I'm lookin' forward to havin' you home!'

But later, when she left the ward and went into Sister's office, that lady told her that Peader would be needing treatment for several months. 'He will need to be kept quiet once he goes home,' she told Deirdre. 'Will you be able to manage that, with the youngsters around him all day?'

'We've a front parlour; I'm t'inking he can spend most of the day in there, whilst the kids will be in the kitchen,' Deirdre said. 'But they're good kids, and if I tell them their daddy needs peace and quiet I'm after thinkin' they'd be the last to make a noise or worry him.'

'Oh, I'm sure. But . . . children can't help tiring an invalid, Mrs O'Brady. However, if you can see that he spends most of the day quietly, in your parlour, then I'm sure things will work out all right,' the sister said. 'He's beginning to fret over hospital routine, and that's a sure sign he's on the mend. I don't think it will be too long before the doctors discharge him.'

Walking home with her hand in her mammy's, with Ivan clinging on to her other hand, Polly was happier than she had been since Tad's letter had arrived. Daddy liked Tad, so perhaps she was wrong, perhaps Tad was not trying to give her the brush-off, but was merely being Tad. Probably by the next time he wrote the girl Angela would have gone from his mind and he would be boasting about his job of delivering for Merrick's.

And in the meantime there was a great deal to look forward to: the move, the reunion with Delilah and Lionel, neighbours to meet, friends to make, a new school to tackle, and best of all, Daddy back with

76

them for good. Polly saw the future as bright once more, and danced along beside her mother, chattering like a starling and pushing Tad's defection to the back of her mind. It would all work out all right; things always did. So she might as well enjoy living here, and remember her time in the crossing cottage like a lovely holiday which had come to an end, as lovely holidays always do.

The move went like clockwork and almost before they knew it the family found themselves settled into the Titchfield Street house, with Bevin and his bicycle installed amongst them and Delilah accompanying Polly wherever she went – except to school, of course.

'But Lionel's better off wit' the Templetons, alanna,' Deirdre said sincerely. She hated to disappoint Polly, but she had thought the matter over and believed that the child would understand, given time. 'Cats like people all right, but 'tis places they become attached to, and Lionel knows every inch of the country around the crossin' cottage. I know he was a city cat once, and I know you t'ink he could be a city cat again, but, Polly me darlin', it wouldn't be kind to take him from the place he knows.'

Polly was a fair-minded child. She knew, really, that Lionel had infinitely preferred the country to the city, and feared that, should she insist that he come back, he would be run over by a tram or a horse and cart, having grown unused to such conveyances. Besides, at home in Dublin she had done her best to keep him in the flat. Now that he was older and knew the joys of the outdoors, she guessed he would slip out of the house the first chance he got. So she agreed, if rather sadly, that the Templetons should keep Lionel and threw herself, with considerable enthusiasm, into the life of the neighbourhood. She had always made friends easily, and knew that she would soon have plenty of pals and the sort of social life which she had enjoyed both in the village and in Dublin.

'There's a girl up the road the same age as me, in the same class,' she told her mother excitedly on her first morning at the new school. 'She's got a brother Ivan's age an' all. We're goin' to school together, the four of us, so you needn't fret we'll get lost or anythin' bad, Mammy. And we'll come home together too . . . Mebbe we'll be best friends by the time we come home,' she added hopefully. 'Her name's Alice and she has dear little red mittens to keep her hands warm, an' she takes a white bread roll for her carry-out at break-time each mornin' too.'

'Well, you can have two biscuits, because what wit' the move an' all I've not had time to bake this week,' Deirdre said. 'As for red mittens, won't your green ones do?'

Polly said they would do just fine and Deirdre decided to buy some red wool when she went marketing that morning. They're good kids, she told herself as she looked round her spruce new kitchen, with the furniture which they had brought all the way from Dublin in place round the walls, and a roll of cheap but colourful linoleum on the floor. Many a child would have insisted on her mother taking her to a new school for the first time, but not Polly. She's bright, brave and independent – aren't I a lucky woman to have her!

She left the house, abandoning Delilah to roam the new premises, trusting that he would know better than to splash his mark all over the interior of her home, and walked through to the Scotland Road. It was a good road, she decided contentedly, walking along in the pale, wintry sunshine with her good brown coat buttoned right up to the neck, for it was getting near Christmas and despite the sun it was bitterly cold. It wasn't as smart as Nelson Street, of course. Monica had definitely sneered at the idea of Titchfield Street but money was going to be tight now. Deirdre knew she would have to get a job as soon as she could but this was a good area if you had little money to spare. There were a grosh of shops, most of them selling goods reasonably priced, and if she went further to her right, to where the road divided, there was Byrom Street, with market stalls selling their goods even more cheaply than the shops could.

She found a bakery which looked respectable and went in and bought four large loaves and took a good look round whilst the shop assistant was wrapping them for her. Their new house did not have a baking oven so she would be taking her bread, cakes and pies to a local bakery once or twice a week to be properly cooked and she wanted to make sure the place she chose was clean. This one certainly seemed so, and the assistants were quick and smiled when they spoke, and what was more the shop was crowded, always a good sign. Yes, next week I'll bring me baking here to be done, Deirdre decided, though she could not help thinking wistfully of the bake-oven in the crossing cottage with its two bright metal shelves and the fire blazing up beside it so that it was the work of a moment to rake red-hot coals into position beneath it. The new house had a good closed-in fire on which pans, kettles of water and other such things could be cooked, but there was nothing quite so good as being able to do your own baking. Deirdre had heard about the new free-standing gas and electric stoves, of course, but with Peader still in hospital and only his pension coming in at present, she did not see them acquiring such a wonderful contrivance yet awhile.

Leaving the bakery, she continued down the road, looking in the shop windows as she passed. Christmas this year, she reflected, was going to be a lean one, but she had good kids, they would make the best of whatever she could provide. So she continued to look wistfully into each window as she passed, which was how she came to see the notice. It was not a large notice, and it was tucked into the frame of a window displaying some beautiful clothes, so when it caught her eye she stopped and looked at it more closely. *Wanted, sales assistant*, it read. *Extra help needed up to Christmas and until January Sales finish. Apply within.*

Deirdre had done a number of jobs in her time, but she had never sold dresses, and yet . . . You only got cleaning jobs when you were in the know, she reminded herself. And with the kids still at home she could scarcely tie herself up full-time, but for a month over the Christmas period, surely they could manage? It would make a world of difference to their Christmas if she was earning, and she knew that Peader would begin to worry once he was well enough to realise that his full wage was no longer coming in. She had worked hard in Dublin, until Peader and the boys had been earning enough to make it unnecessary for her to take a job, and she rather enjoyed work. What was more, the dresses in this window were beautiful, it would be nice even to be in the same shop with them – surely they would be easy to sell? Anyway, applying did not mean she would get the job. The proprietor might not want her, might need someone younger, or more experienced, might not like her Irish brogue – but she could at least try!

Deirdre pushed open the door of the shop and went in.

The shop was not a very big one, but it was absolutely full of racks of clothing, so that Deirdre did not at first see the small, skinny, black-clad woman behind the counter. The woman was putting blouses on to hangers – pink ones, yellow ones, white ones – whilst at the same time pinning small price tickets on each. She did not look up as the bell tinged for Deirdre's entrance, then as Deirdre neared the counter she did so, and smiled. Since she had been holding the price tickets in her teeth, this presented an odd appearance and Deirdre's returning smile was full of amusement.

'Don't stop work, sure an' I'm not a customer,' she said quickly, seeing the woman about to put down the blouse she was holding. 'There's a notice in the window . . .'

The woman's gaze sharpened. 'Oh aye, the notice,' she said. 'Done shop work before? In a dress shop, I mean.'

'No,' Deirdre said. 'But I'm a quick learner so I am. Me mental arithmetic's good, and I'm not afraid of hard work.' She paused, desperate for the job but aware that Peader had to come first. 'Only me husband's in hospital and I visit each evenin', so I'm real sorry but I couldn't work much after six o'clock.'

'Oh. Well, you've a nice appearance,' the woman said slowly, taking the tickets and arranging them in a fan shape on the counter, facing Deirdre. 'Can ye add them up and tell us what them prices come to?'

Deirdre did the sum in her head and announced

her conclusion. The woman looked pleased and a little surprised too.

'Quite right. Not that you'll be needin' to go to the till, queen, because that's me own job. I don't believe in purrin' temptation in young people's way.'

Deirdre would have liked to ruffle up – she knew she coloured – but the older woman was smiling at her as though she knew very well how she felt, and sympathised, but would nevertheless stick to her guns. So Deirdre just said, rather stiffly: 'That's all right, then. Is it a six day a week job?'

'No, I shan't be needin' you weekends, nor after six, because I've gorra schoolgirl comin' in each day after six, and all day Saturday. You'll work from nine in the morning till six, and you can eat your carry-out when we're quiet. You should be takin' home between eighteen and twenty-two shillin' a week for six or eight weeks, I suppose. It's more than I'd pay a permanent girl, but I expect to pay more for seasonal work. Would that suit?'

'Oh, yes indeed,' Deirdre said, relieved and delighted. The money would make the difference between a poor thin Christmas and a decent one. Perhaps they could even run to a bird. 'When do I start?'

'Monday, and you'd best come in at eight, your first day,' the woman said. She came round the counter and held her hand out. 'I'm Mrs Bechstein, I own the shop. And you are . . .?'

'Oh, sorry, I'm Deirdre O'Brady,' Deirdre said, feeling her colour rising once more. 'Thanks very much, Mrs Bechstein; I hope I give satisfaction.'

'If you don't, I give the sack,' Mrs Bechstein said, but Deirdre could see she was laughing. 'Shall we say a week's trial on both sides, O'Brady? If we don't get along I'll pay you off at the end of the week and no hard feelings. How about that, eh?'

'That's fine,' Deirdre said. She turned back towards the door of the shop. 'See you on Monday morning, on the dot of eight, Mrs Bechstein!'

The children were cautiously pleased about the job, though Polly, who had once been left in charge in Dublin whilst her mother was away, said mutinously that she did not intend to do all the work in Mammy's absence.

'Ivan's seven, he can flamin' well help,' she said, wagging an admonitory finger at her small brother. 'And Bevin, too. I don't mind puttin' the tea on, if you tell me what to cook, Mammy, but they can wash up an' clear away. I know they's boys an' I'm a girl, but fair's fair. Daddy wouldn't let them bully me.'

'Nor shall I, sweetheart,' Deirdre said stoutly. She did not add that she could never forget the state of affairs she had found when she had returned after her enforced absence. It had not, after all, been Polly's fault; a ten-year-old was not a woman grown and Polly, she acknowledged guiltily, had always been rather spoilt. 'I'll leave you a nice list written out of anything I want done. Will that help?'

'If you put what I'm to do and what Ivan an' Bev's to do as well,' Polly said cautiously. 'Why do you want to go to work, Mammy? Why can't you stay here, wit' Delly an' us?'

'Because though the boys are very good and send home every penny they can spare, and though Daddy's got a little pension, money is goin' to be tight until Daddy's better and can earn a proper wage again,' Deirdre said carefully. She did not want to frighten the kids into believing them to be paupers,

83

but she wanted them to realise that things might be difficult for a while. 'This job is only over Christmas and up until the end of the January sales, so by the time Daddy comes out of hospital for good I'll be out of work again.'

'Oh, well, all right,' Polly said, leaning forward to take a piece of raw potato and beginning to crunch it up. Deirdre, who was scrubbing the potatoes and cutting up a large winter cabbage, swallowed. The things the young ate! 'I'm glad you isn't workin' for always though, Mammy. I like to have you home even when I'm not here meself.'

'I'm sure that's very nice of you,' Deirdre said. She finished the vegetables, tipped the potatoes into a pan and began to push the sliced cabbage into the steamer which she would balance on top of the potato saucepan as soon as the water boiled. 'Now then, I'm goin' to the hospital as soon as we've ate our tea so d'you want to come wit' me, for the walk, like, or do you want to take Delly for an airin' right now?'

'Both,' Polly said promptly. She missed the long country walks which had been a part of her life at the crossing cottage, Deirdre knew. 'And you've not asked me how I got on at school today,' she added accusingly.

'How did you get on?' Deirdre asked obediently, as Polly fastened her length of rope to Delilah's collar. Normally, none of them would have dreamed of putting the dog on a lead but Polly was mortally afraid that if not attached to her person Delly might leap on a tram bound for Lime Street, then get off it and leap on a train, and reunite himself with the crossing cottage.

'Oh, I got on fine,' Polly said airily. 'Me teacher's a great love, so she is, and she says I'm ahead of the

84

whole class – the whole *class*, Mammy – in arithmetic an' history. She pinned me essay on "Nature's Ways" – I did from jelly in a ditch to frog – up on the board and she said that Maisie Lightfoot – she's got the longest hair, she can sit on it! – ought to try to copy my writin', because I'm so neat. And after dinner Father Ignatius came round to talk to us, and I asked him about his choir, and I'm goin' to do a – a audy-something-or-other on Sunday, after Sunday school.'

'Audition?' Deirdre suggested. 'What about Ivan?'

'Him too,' Polly admitted. 'I told the father about him bein' new too, an' he's goin' to audy-what's-it as well. And Ivan can sing in tune, Mammy, everyone can. He just doesn't because he's a bad boy, so he is.'

'He's tone deaf, alanna,' Deirdre said reproach-fully. 'No one can help being tone deaf. But mebbe the priest wants a growler wit' the face of an angel in his choir, you never know.'

'Oh, that reminds me! Mammy, you know I said I'd not seen me angel all the time we were in Martin's house? Well, she were in me room last night, just before I went to sleep. Smilin' at me, she was . . . She looked so beautiful!'

'Good,' Deirdre said. She never asked questions about Polly's angel because the child clearly believed she saw the holy creature and who was she, Deirdre O'Brady, to doubt her little girl, who had never, to Deirdre's knowledge, told a deliberate lie in her life? 'Off you go, then, alanna, or it'll be time for tea. And if you see Ivan outside, tell him tea in twenty minutes, would you?'

'Right, Mammy,' Polly said cheerfully. She let herself out of the kitchen door and banged it shut behind her. Smiling to herself, Deirdre finished off the potatoes, put them on the fire, and began to lay the table. What a lot I'll have to tell Peader when I reach the hospital tonight, she told herself as she worked. I'll say one thing for having kids; there's never a dull moment!

Sunday saw Polly and Ivan, neatly clad in clean clothes and hand in hand, making their way up to St Sylvester's church, where they would first attend Sunday school and then audition for Father Ignatius's choir. Polly, with her curls brushed till they shone and a red ribbon nestling amongst them, was looking forward to everything, but Ivan was frankly rebellious.

'You never should ha' mentioned me to the father, you bad gorl, you,' he grumbled, as they neared the huge bulk of the red-brick church and headed for the steps which led to the side door. 'I doesn't *want* to be in the choir; I'll only get shouted at 'cos me voice won't get up off the floor the way yours does.'

'Well, if you sing like you always does you won't get into the choir,' Polly said with all her usual frankness. 'So why grumble at me, Ive? Anyway, you'll like Sunday school.'

'I shall not,' Ivan said mutinously. 'The fellers in my class don't go to Sunday school, they say it's for girls and cissies, and I ain't either. When's we to play, anyway, if we go to the hospital to see our daddy after this lot's over?'

'After that,' Polly said, undisturbed. 'Sunday school's two to three, visitin' at the hospital's three to four, and we can play out four to six. Then it's tea. And after that I'm goin' to meet Alice Eccles and she's goin' to show me how to play a new skippin' game, and then we'll see if there's a game of Tag or Relievio goin' on that we could join.'

'Alice Eccles? Is her brother called Teddy? Teddy Eccles is in my class at school.'

'I expect so, and he'll be at Sunday school as well, I daresay. If you like, we could all play together when we come back from the hospital,' Polly said craftily, and was rewarded by a beam from her small brother.

'Could we? That 'ud be grand, so it would.' Ivan's footsteps, which had been lagging, quickened up. 'Come *on*, Poll, or we'll be late!'

Polly had always enjoyed Sunday school, but something happened to her just as she and Ivan were about to enter the building which, she later decided, had probably changed her entire life. A group of big boys was standing about on the corner of Rayner Street which led, Polly knew, between Silvester and Ashfield Streets. They did not look like good boys, she decided, after a long stare. For a start, they were all grouped round something on the ground, and when she looked more closely, she could see that they were playing cards . . . and that there were ha'pennies and farthings in little piles on the paving stones.

Gambling! Gambling, Polly knew, was bad, but gambling on a Sunday, right outside a church! That was so bad that the little soft hairs on her neck stood upright with outrage. Those boys would go to hell, so they would, and it would serve them right! But then one of the boys turned round and caught her eye and when he did he grinned, and Polly's heart did a most peculiar double somersault.

'Hello, blondie,' the boy said. Which was pretty good coming from him, Polly thought, since his own straight, shining hair was as yellow as – as a primrose petal. He looked her up and down, then turned back to his companions, and Polly, dragging Ivan by one hand, began to ascend the steps at the side of the church which led into the Sunday school.

'Who was that, Poll?' Ivan asked as soon as they were inside the church. 'He were playin' cards . . . and smokin' a cigarette. Mammy would say he wasn't a nice sort o' feller, wouldn't she?'

'I dunno who he was, but you're right, he's probably not a nice feller,' Polly said automatically. She spied Alice in the crowd of children already gathered, and went over to her. Alice, like Polly, had a number of brothers, one of whom, Teddy, was with her now. Teddy and Ivan immediately gravitated to one another and Alice and Polly sat on one of the long wooden benches and talked about school . . . and Polly thought about the boy with the yellow hair. He had the sort of face that is so guileless and innocent that you just know he's a real devil, and the sort of smile, unfortunately, which makes it a matter of indifference to most girls whether he's a devil or not. He was also tall, and though his clothes were ragged and his runners had holes in the toes he still had an air of being *right*, as though because he was wearing such things they were automatically fashionable.

'So I told Sister that I'd done me best, only we're a big fambly, chuck, an' it ain't easy to get peace an' quiet when you've got bleedin' brothers banging about—'

'Alice,' Polly interrupted. 'There's a feller outside shouted out to me . . . He's got yellow hair. D'you know who he is?'

'Yaller hair? Oh aye, that'll be Sunny Andersen. His dad's Swedish or summat.' Alice touched her hair, pushing back one richly dark, heavy lock, then glanced towards the church door as though she thought that Sunny Andersen might come through it at any moment. 'Ain't he just the best-lookin' feller you ever saw? Everyone's crazy for Sunny.'

'Well, I'm not,' Polly said stoutly. 'He gambles, and he was smokin' too. My mammy says I shouldn't talk to fellers what gamble or smoke.'

Alice laughed. 'If you don't talk to fellers what gamble or smoke you won't be doin' much talkin' round here,' she said. 'Pitch an' toss is a fav'rite game, an' most of the fellers smoke when they gets work. Still, Sunny wouldn't tek no notice of *you*; you're too young by half.'

'Well, good,' Polly was beginning, when the teacher came in. She was young and pretty, and when she took off her long, fur-trimmed coat Polly saw she was wearing a fashionable dress with a fringed hem and a scalloped neckline. Around her slender white throat hung a necklace of gold beads, interspersed with tiny pearls. Polly decided that she was not only pretty, she looked nice, and her smile, as she turned to her class, was both open and friendly.

'That's Miss Rawlins,' Alice hissed. 'She's me fav'rite teacher – I'm goin' to be just like her when I grow up.'

'She looks lovely,' Polly said fervently. She decided to think about Miss Rawlins and her beautiful clothes and just hope that dreadful, gambling Sunny Andersen would get out of her head and stay out.

'Good afternoon, children,' Miss Rawlins said, having hung her coat and hat on the hook provided. She came and stood before the class, smiling at them all. 'Now I'm going to read you a story . . .'

Polly enjoyed the Sunday school class and came out with a coloured picture of Saint Elizabeth with her basket full of roses, given by the teacher to all who could correctly answer questions when her story had been read. The priest had come and given them a short audition and Polly was now a member of his choir, which would cut down her free time on a Sunday to almost nothing, as Ivan insisted on explaining to her. But Polly, who loved singing, said that it was worth it, and emerged from the church with a light heart. She had been immensely gratified to receive the Holy picture and had assured Miss Rawlins that she would take great care of it and would try very hard to win another, and as she and Ivan walked down the steps she told herself that she had forgotten all about the boy Sunny, but nevertheless when she glanced round and saw that the card school had scattered she felt a little pang of disappointment. However, she reminded Alice that she, Polly, would call at the Eccles' place when she was back from the hospital, waved a cheery goodbye to the children she had met that afternoon and set off in the direction of home, for Mammy and Bevin would be walking towards them, since they all liked to go to the hospital together.

Presently, they met Mammy and Bevin and the picture was shown and Miss Rawlins's charm and person described in minute detail whilst Ivan, looking bored, kicked a stone along ahead of them and occasionally broke into a gruff one-note song which only an experienced parent could have recognised as 'Pack up your Troubles'.

'So you got into the choir, alanna, but Ivan didn't?' Deirdre asked as they hurried along the pavement. 'I can't t'ink even the most desperate priest would put up wit' Ivan's flat notes.'

'I'm in,' Polly admitted. And chattered on, retelling Miss Rawlins's story and flourishing the Holy picture which she had won for her good answers. But presently, as they continued to walk towards the hospital, she began to feel she was being watched – perhaps followed. Out of the corner of her eye she seemed to see someone lurking, though the street was by no means empty and they were meeting other people, now, also heading for the hospital. So presently, she stopped to tie her shoelace, and glanced back and upside down though she was, she saw a boy with an unforgettably yellow head dodging into a shop doorway behind them.

Polly straightened, feeling puzzled. That Sunny boy was following them; he could have walked along the pavement in their wake without anyone minding, he could have caught them up and overtaken them . . . What on earth was he playing at?

But presently they arrived at the hospital and Polly pushed Sunny Andersen and his odd ways resolutely out of her mind. He would soon get fed up with hanging around the hospital and go home and leave her alone. She still thought him very handsome, but she did not like being followed one bit. It was stupid, so it was, and he was an eejit to play silly games and him at least three years her senior.

Peader was delighted to see them and he was looking better, sitting up in bed and smiling a lot, even speaking now and then, and obviously looking forward to emerging from the hospital for Christmas Day, even if he did have to go back in by evening.

When the visit was over Polly truly did forget Sunny Andersen and did not so much as glance round when the family emerged on to the pavement once more. They hurried home, because darkness had fallen and the cold was really beginning to bite, and went indoors to start making the tea.

91

'I'm goin' to call for Alice when me tea's ate, though,' Polly announced as she put the delft on the table and began to fish knives and forks out of the dresser drawer. 'We might play at her house . . . unless you'd rather we played here, Mammy?'

'I don't like you being out after dark, alanna,' Deirdre admitted. 'What does Alice's mammy t'ink?'

'Oh, Alice can play wit' me,' Polly said cheerfully. 'There's ten kids, only two growed, so her mammy won't mind at all if she comes round here. I'll ask her then, Mammy.'

But when she went outside, with her warm coat and scarf on and the heels of her best shoes ringing on the icy pavement, the first thing she saw, leaning idly against the wall of the house opposite, was a tall figure topped with that exceedingly yellow hair.

Polly gaped, then hesitated. What would he say if she asked him what he thought he was doing, following her around? Would he deny it, or give her cheek? But the only way to find out was to ask him, so she marched across the road until she was only a couple of feet away from him and then spoke. 'What are you doin' here, feller? Why's you been followin' me?'

He looked down at her from his superior height and grinned. It was a nice grin. It warmed his whole face and made his eyes, which looked unfathomably dark in the hissing gaslight, sparkle like diamonds. 'Oh, I just thought I'd see where you lived, blondie,' he said in a light drawl. 'Nice place!'

'Me name isn't blondie,' Polly said coldly, but with a fast-beating heart. 'Sure and no one's called that, except in the comic strips!'

'Ah, an Irish colleen,' the boy said, his eyes dancing. 'Now who'd ha' thought it! Well, queen, if you aren't called blondie, what are you called?'

'I'm Polly O'Brady,' Polly said at once. 'And I know who *you* are an' all. Me pal told me in Sunday school. You're Sunny Andersen.'

He raised a hand in a sort of half-salute, acknowledging a hit. 'Right on the nail, Polly O'Brady. And what else did your pal tell you?'

'Nothin',' Polly said shortly. She certainly did not intend to tell this self-possessed but wicked boy that Alice thought him handsome!

'Nothin'? She didn't mention that I were the best footie player the Scottie ever spawned? Nor that I can ride a leckie wi' the conductor tryin' to knock me off, an' stay fixed on for miles like a bleedin' limpet on a rock? Nor that I—'

'Were the biggest boaster in the whole of Liverpool? No, she only said you were called Sunny Andersen,' Polly cut in waspishly. She would teach this boy not to play games with her!

'Oh-oh, who's gorra tongue on her like an adder, then?' Sunny Andersen said softly. 'Me little Irish colleen can snap like a bleedin' crocodile, I see. Well, I'm norra feller to take agin a girl wi' spirit, so let's you an' me have a chat, eh?'

'No, I don't t'ink so,' Polly said at once. 'You're older'n me, and – and me mammy doesn't like me talkin' to strangers. I'm off to me pal's house.'

She half-expected him to follow her, or to try to change her mind for her, but he did no such thing. She walked away and he continued to lean against the house wall, though she was fairly sure that he turned to gaze after her. She went round to Alice's house, which was not far away, and then the two of them came back along Titchfield Street, intending to play at number 8. As they came within sight of it, Polly automatically glanced across the road, to where Sunny had stood under the gaslight, but the roadway was empty. Sunny Andersen had gone.

'Good riddance,' Polly said savagely under her breath. But deeper inside her, where only she could hear, a little voice said: *What's the matter wit' you, Polly O'Brady? You liked that feller, you know very well you did. And you didn't have to be* quite *so nasty to him, did you?*

'What'll we play, Poll?' Alice said when the two of them were in the small bedroom which was Polly's very own. She looked enviously round at the white muslin curtains, the pink and white counterpane, at the curtained-off alcove where Polly kept her clothes. 'Ain't this just fine, though, queen? Wish I had a room all to meself like this.'

'Well, we'll start by pullin' the curtains, 'cos you never know who's out there, watchin',' Polly said darkly, suiting action to words. But though she stared very hard, the road outside remained empty. Sunny Andersen, despite his outward appearance of brash self-confidence, had clearly taken his dismissal well. And much later that night, when Polly was getting ready for bed and Alice had long gone, she pulled the curtain aside again to have, she told herself, one last look at the stars.

They were all there, twinkling in the heavens. But the roadway below Polly's window remained disappointingly empty of a tall, yellow-haired figure lounging against the opposite wall.

Well, that's a good t'ing, so it is, Polly told herself as she began to fold her clothes neatly over her chair. Still, it'll give me something to tell Grace when I write next. For Grace was growing up and enlivened her letters with talk of clothes, young men, and the fact that her bosoms, as she called them, refused to grow as quickly as did those of her friend and fellow child-minder, Kate. Grace's letters also mentioned such problems as underarm hair, which did not seem to flourish on her as it did on her more mature companions, and Polly thought that Grace would be the very person to advise on how she should behave should Sunny Andersen continue to haunt her. But it was only because she was new around here, she reminded herself as she climbed into bed and pulled the sheet up round her ears. It was always the same, anyone new in a neighbourhood always came in for extra attention.

So Polly closed her eyes, and began to think about her dear Grace, to wonder about little Jamie her nephew, and to wish fervently that Grace was not quite so far away.

Polly's big brother Brogan had written just as soon as he had got the news of Peader's illness, and had said that Grace had wanted to come home, but had realised, after they had discussed the matter, that her arrival would not make things any easier for the O'Bradys.

For she has a good job here, with us. And though the Depression's biting pretty deep here too, I guess there are still more jobs this side of the Atlantic than there are back home. And Grace isn't just highly regarded by us, the man who owns the delicatessen says he'll take her on full-time just as soon as young Jamie's in school. I guess Sara will go back to her teaching full-time then, but right now . . . well, I reckon we all need Grace, and she's happy here, Mammy, honest to God she is. What's more, Sara's teaching her all about keeping house, cooking and managing the money – some fellow's going to be very lucky to get our Grace. And in the meantime we're all of us thinking about you, so we are, and praying for Daddy.

You couldn't say fairer than that, Polly thought sleepily now. Grace had been an orphan, living in the Salvation Army children's home of Strawberry Field when she and Polly had first got to know each other, and Grace had been very happy to spend all her spare time with the O'Bradys at the crossing cottage. Grace had never complained, she had been happy at Strawberry Field, but she knew she could not stay on there for ever and Polly knew better than most how her pal had longed for a real home of her own, and loving parents. And then Brogan had written, and Grace had gone . . . And from her letters, no one could be happier than she, with a good home, the baby to look after, and Sara and Brogan giving an eye to her and seeing that all was well. What was more, she enjoyed her job and liked meeting people, especially, she told Polly, since they were all intrigued by her accent and this made her feel special. She was beginning to find her feet and to have a circle of friends. The homesickness was not so bad, and she was beginning to appreciate New York and to enjoy her life there.

Coming back to Liverpool to no job and no prospects was not really a good idea. Brogan was right, as usual. So Polly, who had so longed for Grace's companionship, had virtuously not included in her prayers one for Grace's return. Fair was fair; you could not pray for something which would upset your dearest friend, no matter how happy it might make you, personally.

But that doesn't stop me wishing a tiny bit, she thought wistfully, as her eyelids grew heavy.

Chapter Four

At eleven o'clock that evening, climbing wearily up the four flights of stairs, Grace thought that there was not a vast lot of difference, really, between the poor here in New York and the poor back home. The weather had brought extra customers to the soup kitchen; a long line of wet, hopeless men and women took the bowls of nourishing soup and the hunks of bread which accompanied them in hands which shook with cold.

I thought America was a land of opportunity where anyone could rise to be the highest in the land if they had the intelligence, Grace thought. But it was all fairy tales really – there were men in this queue who once had well-paid jobs, motor cars, two or three homes. And there were professors, teachers, engineers, architects . . .

She knew better, however, than to let her depression show; it had been impressed upon her by other Salvationists, that one of the things they could do for the poor down-and-outs they fed was to smile and be cheerful, tell them that better times were bound to come, joke with them if they joked.

So she had worked cheerfully, done her best to cheer everyone up, and had taken heart when Sara had pointed out, in her quiet way, that the faces of those who had been fed and had spent twenty minutes or so in the warmth of the hall were a good deal brighter than those still waiting to come in.

Sara had left before Grace this evening, however. Sometimes they walked home together, but because Sara's job meant an early start, she never stayed later than ten o'clock and this evening the queue had still been waiting at that hour. So Grace had trudged through the emptying streets alone, and had entered their building conscious of enormous tiredness and, strangely enough, a great urge for a cup of tea. She had drunk a cup an hour or so earlier, but it had been weak and though it had quenched her thirst at the time, she was thirsty again now. So it was with considerable pleasure that she heard Sara's voice call: 'Kettle's on!' as she put her key into the front door and opened it. Hanging her damp bonnet, coat and scarf on the small hallstand and kicking off her boots, Grace called back: 'Grand, I'm just about dying of thirst,' and hurried into the kitchen.

Brogan was sitting beside the stove, his heavy boots off, his stockinged feet stretched out before him. He grinned at Grace as she entered. 'My, you've been busy, alanna! I meant to come out and meet you so I did but I fell asleep – bad cess to me – and only woke just this minute when Sara bawled out to you. There's sorry I am that you had to walk through the streets alone, a girl of your age. Was there no one coming your way, dearest?'

Grace shook her head slightly guiltily. 'No, not when I left. But it was all right, there was scarcely a soul about, and the down-and-outs, poor dears, know our uniform. I don't think they'd hurt us, honest to God I don't.'

'That's why they tell us to wear our bonnets when we're going to and fro late at night,' Sara said. She poured three large mugs of tea and handed Grace one, then went and sat in the chair opposite Brogan's,

98

leaving the other chair for Grace. 'Well, it won't be long before I'm in bed, I'm telling you. Jamie decided he didn't want to go to bed, and then when I got him into his cot, he didn't want to go sleep. I wouldn't be surprised if he was cutting another tooth, poor little fellow.'

'What time did he settle?' Grace asked, sipping the hot brew. How good it was to feel warm again, right down to her toes . . . and how she pitied those trying to sleep on the streets tonight! She had done enough of that as a child to remember the way you tried to combat the cold, and the helplessness of it. The thick wads of newspaper underneath you, whatever warm rags you could get over the top of you, and the positioning, carefully thought out, of your makeshift bed so that your back was to the draughts and you had – hopefully – some sort of shelter from rain and snow descending. But then there were the scuffers – they were cops here, she corrected herself hastily – who would move you on if they got half a chance, though there were kindly ones, she knew, who would look the other way. The cops here, she reminded herself, were no better or worse than those in Liverpool. She knew from talking to the destitute there were those who would try to get them into one of the night shelters which had been set up for the vast army of unemployed who had descended on New York in the hope of finding work.

'What time did Jamie settle, Brog?' Sara asked. 'It must have been half past ten, I suppose. Oh well, perhaps he'll wake later in the morning,' she added hopefully. She drained the last of her tea, stood up and took the empty mug over to the sink. Rinsing it in cold water she dried it on a tea-towel and hung it back on its hook. 'Sorry, but I'm really very tired. See you in the morning, Gracie. What shift are you on tomorrow, Brog?'

'It's me day off,' Brogan said lazily, still sipping his tea. 'So mebbe I'll take Jamie out for the day . . . well, I'll bring him back for dinner,' he added hastily, 'Seeing as I'm no sort of a hand wit' the nappy-changing, let alone feeding him that pap you girls hand out. Now when he's on to the steak an' chips, I'm your man so I am.'

Sara, in the doorway, laughed back at him. 'I'm going to teach you to change a nappy if it's the last thing I do,' she declared. 'And it's no good you going green and saying you can't stand the sight of – of what he's just done. These days, with both Grace and myself so busy, you've simply got to have a working knowledge of minding a baby.'

'Oh, I can do it,' Brogan said, finishing his own tea and taking Grace's now empty cup over to the sink. 'But I can't say I like it and the little devil wiggles so I'm scared out of me life that he'll end up on the floor, or wit' a safety pin through his – his—'

Grace, laughing, said she quite understood and dried up the mugs when Brogan had rinsed them. 'Then if you're on a day off tomorrow I'll not wake you,' she said cheerfully. 'As for taking Jamie out, in this sort of weather a rush to the shops is about all he gets – and probably all he needs, what's more, so don't you worry about him. He's no trouble, you know, but a pleasure to be with,' she finished.

'Not when he's teethin' he's not,' Brogan said darkly. 'A bad-tempered spalpeen, that's what he is when he feels the teeth of him comin'. But don't throw me offer back in me face, Jess, or you'll find yourself saddled with him until you go off to work again.'

'I don't mind . . .' Grace was beginning, when she

stopped, a frown descending. 'What did you call me, Brog?'

'Je . . . I mean Grace, I suppose,' Brogan said. He went quite pink Grace saw. 'Now off to bed wit' you, Grace Carbery, or Sara will tell me off for keepin' you chattin'.'

'You called me Jess,' Grace said slowly, ignoring his words. 'And it's not the first time, Brog. Why Jess, though?'

'Oh . . . well, you've a likeness to your sister I suppose,' Brogan said in a mumble. 'Sorry . . . I can't think what made me . . .'

'But it was Sara who knew Jess, and baby Mollie, not you,' Grace said, staring at him. 'I never heard tell you'd met Jess, Brog.'

'You haven't? Well, of course I knew her, alanna,' Brogan said, the pink dying out of his face. He began to get cups, plates and cutlery from the dresser. 'I'll just lay the table for breakfast so I will, since we'll all be takin' it together for once.'

'How did you know Jess?' Grace demanded. She took the cutlery from him and began to arrange it around the table. 'I know Sara met her just – just before she died and – and the baby disappeared, but no one ever said you'd met my sister.'

'I – I guess I saw her hangin' round the railway from time to time,' Brogan said slowly. 'She – she usually had the baby with her – your sister Mollie I mean. She were a good girl were Jess, but I'm sorry I miscalled you, alanna. I think it's because you're gettin' more like her, now you've some flesh on your bones, but it – it doesn't mean anything, you know. Except that I'm liable to forgetfulness. Now off to bed wit' you, or I'll be gettin' a drubbin' from Sara for keepin' you talkin', I keep tellin' you.'

'It isn't the first time you've done it, though,' Grace said thoughtfully, turning towards the kitchen door. 'It isn't the first time you've called me Jess, I mean. Still, it's nice to think I'm even a bit like her; she was one of the best people I ever knew, though I was really almost a baby myself when she died.'

'Aye, four or five, you must have been I suppose,' Brogan said. He was beginning to look hunted, Grace thought, amused. But she was very tired, and what did it matter, after all, that Brogan had called her by her dead sister's name? On previous occasions when Brogan had called her Jess, Sara had always been present and had cut in so quickly that Grace had not liked to comment. But the answer was simple after all – Brogan, as well as Sara, had known her beloved elder sister. So she smiled up at him and opened the kitchen door.

'Do you know, I still miss her, in a way?' Grace said. 'When you think of all the Carberys, the whole great clan of us, and we all somehow lost touch. I don't know whether I've a brother living – or a sister for that matter – and though I'd still love to see Mollie again, if she's alive that is, I've no urge whatever to meet the boys.'

'Better not to meet 'em, from what I've heard,' Brogan said. 'Goodnight now, Gracie; see you in the mornin', and don't hesitate to wake me when you need a hand with the boy.'

Brogan entered the bedroom to find Sara sitting before the mirror, brushing her hair. She had undressed and put on her night-gown, and smiled at him through the mirror.

'I'm sorry, darling,' she said. 'But I was so tired! And then, when I had washed and cleaned my teeth I found I wasn't so tired any longer, so I checked on Jamie – he's sleeping soundly – and then decided to give my hair a really good brushing.'

She continued to attack her hair but Brogan, without preamble, took her shoulders, rested his chin on the top of her head and said flatly, 'I called her Jess again. Grace, I mean.'

'Oh, mercy,' Sara said, her brush suspended for a moment. 'Did she notice?'

'Certainly she did,' Brogan said gloomily. 'She asked me why, too.'

'And what did you say? Oh, Brog, you didn't spill the beans, did you? You know we all agreed not to do so until Polly was older . . . well, until they were both older.'

'Of course I didn't, no more I didn't tell her it was me stole her little sister away after Jess died and sent her to Ireland for me mammy to bring up,' Brogan said indignantly, then spoiled the effect by adding: 'but it was a very close run thing so it was. She asked me why I'd called her Jess and without really thinking I told her the truth – that she sometimes reminded me of Jess now she's growing up.'

'Oh, lor',' Sara said, beginning to brush her hair again. 'What did she say to that?'

'She said she didn't realise I knew her sister, though she was well aware that you did, of course. So I told her the truth, more or less. I said I'd known Jess as well, I used to see her about the railway when I worked in Liverpool.'

'And?'

'And she accepted it. Why not? And it isn't so far from the truth as all that. She does remind me of Jess. Why, she's got a likeness to Polly as well, don't you think?'

'I know what you mean,' Sara said after a pause for thought. 'But it isn't an obvious likeness. Polly's hair is very fair and curly, and Grace has straight brown hair. And Polly's got big blue eyes and dimples; Grace's eyes are grey and she doesn't have Poll's roses and cream complexion, either. I don't think their likeness to each other will ever be remarked on by anyone outside the family. And the family all know better than to say anything, don't they? After all, you stole Mollie and renamed her Polly, and your parents knew, and said nothing because they wanted a baby girl so much. Your mammy is still afraid that the authorities would punish her in some way if anyone ever found out how it was.'

'Aye, that's true,' Brogan said. He moved away from his wife and began to undress, then went over to the washstand and sluiced his hands and face in the water Sara had left. Sara, climbing into bed, giggled.

'I thought you'd not want to bother with fresh water, you horrid thing,' she said affectionately, pulling the sheet up to her chin. 'Now let's hurry up and get some sleep before young Master Jamie decides to start shouting the odds again.'

Tad did well as a delivery boy for Merrick's, because he was not afraid of hard work and was quite willing to continue tramping the streets of Dublin until midnight if necessary, to see that all the deliveries were done before Christmas Day. He was hopeful, of course, that Mr Merrick might see the justice of keeping him on, though his mammy thought this extremely doubtful.

'Just use your head, son,' she said kindly the first time Tad allowed his secret hope to surface. 'Christmas time, everyone eats, no matter how poor.

Well, I know the rich has meat an' pies an' all sorts, and the rest make do wit' whatever they can afford, but one way an' another, we all eat over Christmas. And what happens in January? Why, we all pay for it. Once the 6th of January is over, it's tightenin'-belts time, which is why January an' February are called the hungry months. Folk have spent all their spare cash and after Christmas they know they won't have much of anything until the spring comes again. And there's nothin' goin' free around then, either. No blackers on the brambles, no nuts on the hazels, no apples in the orchards. See?'

'So what?' Tad said, staring. 'D'you mean Merrick's won't sell nothin' after Christmas?'

'No, 'course not. But they won't need extra deliveries, will they? They'll manage wi' the lads they employ all year, so it's no use your gettin' your hopes up. Best start lookin' round for another job come the New Year.'

So when the New Year came and his mammy's prophecy came true, Tad tried very hard indeed to get another job, but he wasn't the only one. All over Dublin, boys who had earned money over the Christmas season were looking for jobs – any job. It was hard enough if you had some sort of training, but when, like Tad and his brothers, you had only sold newspapers, run messages or delivered goods, there were simply too many of you chasing every possible post.

And yet when Tad did get a job, it was largely because of his time with Merrick's, plus the most enormous stroke of luck.

Merrick's not only had delivery boys on bicycles and on foot, they also had an elderly van which did the out-of-town orders. And once or twice in early

December because the deliveries in the countryside were so heavy, Tad had been sent on the van with Mr McGrath, the driver, to help him with his deliveries. Tad had enjoyed the experience immensely; it was fun to sit beside the driver, fun to watch how he actually drove the old van – Tad had not, before, realised that a motor vehicle had gears, he had thought that a brake, a steering wheel and a horn were all that had to be mastered – and because he never complained when asked to carry great heavy baskets of food up long, tree-lined drives which had most town-boys thinking uneasily of ghosts, bulls and fierce dogs, Mr McGrath decided that he pre-ferred 'young Donoghue' to the other delivery boys, and asked for him whenever his workload was heavy.

This, whilst pleasant for Tad, might not have had any repercussions but for the fact that three days before Christmas, when the van was so laden that Mr McGrath had crawled most of the way in second gear, it broke down on a long stretch of country road without any sort of immediate help in sight.

''Tis sorry I am, but you'll have to walk back to the city, young feller,' Mr McGrath said wearily, for it was raining briskly and the sky overhead was grey and lowering. 'It'll be dark soon, and I've no fancy to be stuck out here all night by meself, let alone tryin' to deliver this lot on foot.'

'Let's have a look in the engine before I go,' Tad had said, highly daring. He had discovered that he liked tinkering with motors when a neighbour with an old motorbike had stripped it down one afternoon the previous summer and had instructed Tad in the strange ways of the internal combustion engine. 'You never know, Mr McGrath, it might be somethin' dead simple.'

Mr McGrath had made discouraging noises, but it was cold and wet and as he had said, darkness was coming on. He was a city man himself and really did not like the thought of waiting out here whilst Tad tramped back into Dublin to fetch help. So he walked round to the front of the van, heaved up one side of the creaking bonnet, and surveyed, with a jaundiced eye, the mass of nasty, messy-looking odds and ends which constituted the engine.

'There's no sense in it that I can see,' he grumbled, peering in the fading light at the coils and boxes and pipes. 'I'm thinkin' you'd best be—'

'It's the fan belt. See . . . there,' Tad said coolly, peering into the engine and pointing at something, though Mr McGrath certainly did not know what. 'It's broke, Mr McGrath. If we can just find somethin' to tek its place while we make our way back home . . . there's the belt on me apron, but . . .' He eyed Mr McGrath up and down, then exclaimed: 'Your tie! Sure an' it's a fine tie, but it'll wash! Will ye give me a borrow of it, Mr M?'

Mr McGrath's first impulse was to clutch his tie and refuse to part with it, but as he glanced round he saw that it was already growing darker . . . and the van was still fully laden . . . 'Oh, all right, but don't you ruin it, young Donoghue. Me wife give it me for me birt'day last year,' he said, reluctantly beginning to unknot the tie from around his neck.

Tad had taken the tie, run it round the pulley-wheels, knotted it, and then told his superior to start the engine. Wonderingly, Mr McGrath had climbed back into the cab and watched as Tad went and fetched the starting handle, fitted it into the appro-priate slot in front of the bonnet, and began to crank vigorously. He had very little faith in the ability of a delivery boy to solve the problem, but he had clearly underestimated Tad Donoghue. The engine coughed, stuttered and began to purr like a contented cat. Tad jumped into the cab beside him as soon as he was sure that the engine was really and truly all right and Mr McGrath, with a huge sigh of relief, had put the van into gear and set off once more.

''Tis only a temporary solution,' Tad said when Mr McGrath marvelled at his unusual knowledge. 'But it'll likely get us round and back and then you can get another fan belt – a real one, not just your tie.'

When at last they got back to the shop Mr McGrath took the van to a garage and then told Mr Merrick how 'the temp'rary boy' had got him out of a scrape and Mr Merrick was impressed. However, he thought no more about it until around the middle of January, when he was talking to a customer, a Mr Barnes, who owned a garage on Thomas Street.

'You say you're lookin' for a lad to train up in the trade of mending motors?' he said. 'Well, I may be able to help you there . . .' and he told Mr Barnes about young Tad Donoghue and the broken fan belt.

Mr Barnes screwed up his mouth into a silent whistle; he thought this sounded promising. He got Tad's address from Mr Merrick and when he had paid for the tea he was buying went round to Gardiner's Lane. He found Tad at home, getting a meal ready, and as was his wont, got straight to the point. 'I've been in Merrick's Grocery, and Mr Merrick was tellin' me that you'd got his van driver out of a scrape before Christmas,' he said to Tad's open-mouthed astonishment. 'I've a garage where we mend motor cars, motor bicycles and the like, as well as sellin' the occasional second-hand model, and I'm lookin' for a young feller to train up. There's not a great deal of money in it at first, but if you work hard and do as you're told, you'll find yourself in a good position. Why, I were just a young lad interested in the workin's of cars an' such, yet now I own me own garage!'

Tad would have scrubbed sewers for a chance like this! What was more, the wages of ten shillings a week sounded princely after the sort of money most of his pals earned. He agreed, breathlessly, to all the conditions Mr Barnes laid down – and they were neither many nor unfair – and said he would report at the garage prompt at eight the next morning. Mr Barnes said good, shook Tad's hand and as he was turning away suddenly turned back. 'You'll need overalls,' he said kindly, fishing some money out of his pocket. 'We'll have nothin' to fit you – you're our first boy, see – so buy yourself a stout pair tomorrer, before you come in. So, tomorrer I won't expect you in until nine.'

So by mid-January, Tad had a job he enjoyed and was already beginning to be useful to the garage mechanics who were training him.

'He's a practical lad, so he is,' Mr Barnes told his wife, after Tad's first week. 'What's more, he's willing. He'll make the fellers cups of tea, do messages for them, spend hours under a car trying to discover a broken connection . . . Oh aye, we did all right when we took on young Donoghue.'

And Tad, of course, was very pleased with himself and determined that he would write to Polly and tell her all about his new job just as soon as he could spare the time. He had sent her a Christmas card with some of his earnings from Merrick's, and after much thought had laid out a whole sixpence on a little yellow-haired angel for the top of a Christmas tree. It was a celluloid doll dressed in white cotton, with a halo and gold gauze wings. But what had really attracted him to it was its sweet expression, which had immediately reminded him of Polly herself.

It's the Nearest I could get to your Guarjan Angel, darlin Polly. So you put it on Top of your Xmas Tree an it'll keep you Safe for Me. I tought you might come bak to Dublin for a Visit, perhaps, but I no you can't now, not wit Your Daddy ill, so I've sent the Angel instead.
All Best Wishes from your lovin Tad Donoghue.

He posted off the letter, the card and the little celluloid angel and felt he had done well by Polly. She was, after all, a long way off. Besides, her letter answering the one in which he had told her about his new pal had been very peculiar, not like herself at all. She had asked several questions about Angela Machin – rather stiff, nasty questions, and it had put Tad's back up, so it had. So when it came to Christmas presents, instead of spending all he could afford on Polly he reminded himself that he had to split the money this year, and bought Angela a box of chocolates which also cost sixpence, and a penny card with a picture of the Holy Family on it.

He ignored Polly's questions about Angela too. If she wanted answers then she should have been nice and friendly, the same as he would have been had Polly got a new friend, he told himself. So when, just before Christmas, a letter, card and present had arrived for him – the present was a small dictionary with a faded blue cover and Tad rightly read a touch of criticism into such a gift and was consequently cross – he had opened the letter already prepared for some further nastiness and had read the contents with feelings which were so contradictory and strange that even now he did not fully understand them. Polly had written in her neat, round hand:

Well, Tad, I've met ever such a nice feller, so I have. His name is Sunny Andersen and he's got lovely yellow hair and blue eyes, and he took me to the Saturday Rush last week and bought me a pennorth of popcorn and a Vanilla Ice. So you see I don't mind about That Angela no more, because I know you must of been lonely to turn to a girl like that.

(Like what? Tad thought, and felt even crosser with his Polly.)

Hope the enclosed Dicker is useful to you, because I always have one to hand when I write to you. It isn't Brand New, but it is almost, the feller on the stall said. If you know the first two or three letters it makes spelling a lot easier. My Daddy is better and comin home for Christmas Day so I must go now I have a great deal to do and lots of messages to do.
      Your loving Polly O'Brady.

But it was no use being cross with Polly over the dictionary because he knew very well that he was a poor speller. Mr Barnes, who was taking a great interest in his newest employee, had told him that one day he must learn to fill in job sheets, explaining what had been done to the car, which new parts had had to be fitted, and how much it had cost. At the moment such work was done by others, but one day, if Tad fulfilled his potential and got on as Mr Barnes had got on, he would need to be able to read, write and spell.

So Tad swallowed his indignation because his little

pal had given him such a prissy present and spent an hour or so each evening simply reading the thing. Since he was quite as bright as Mr Barnes thought him, he soon found this an absorbing exercise, for often he met strange and fascinating words with even stranger spellings, and what was more, he began to take pleasure in getting the words by heart. He set himself a target of three new words learned, with the correct spelling, each evening and it was surprising how they mounted up.

What was more, Angela Machin was proving to be a real pal, the sort that seems to want to help you and to spend time with you. Now that he was working he could not meet her out of school, but they usually met at some stage during the evening, either Tad going round to Swift's Alley or she coming round to Gardiner's Lane. She brought her homework and Tad, who had always been top of his class at mathematics as well as actually enjoying the subject, was able to help her a good deal, which gave him a great feeling of superiority. It did not seem to matter so much that he had a poor home and a great many younger brothers and sisters; he could do sums!

So the winter days passed much more pleasantly for Tad than he had ever believed possible with Polly so far away. He and Angela grew easy together. They, too, went to the cinema, though usually in the evening since Tad worked all day Saturday. Because Angela's mammy did not have to struggle to feed her family, with three of them earning, they usually went back to Swift's Alley for meals, and Tad's mammy grew used to Tad coming in late, and fed.

Then Tad had another letter from Polly telling him that her daddy was now at home with them all the time, but would not be working again just yet.

He'll be getting better little by little. But he can't work for a while yet, the doctor says, which means there won't be a special free house, not like the crossing cottage, nor much money coming in, but things should go back to normal in a few months, so they should . . . Mammy says. The boys are very good, and help all they can, and I'm helping to deliver papers so I don't need pocket money no more. And last week I found a poor ole feller of a tomcat, thin and bony wit a horrid patchy coat and his ears so torn they are like lace curtains, and I've called him Tom the Chimney Sweep, like in The Water Babies *– because he's black, of course – and I'm going to keep him instead of dear Lionel, who is very happy with the Templetons. It isn't selfish, because there are mice in this house, and Daddy said a cat was a good idea, so it was.*

I dressed the Christmas tree, as I telled you earlier, and my dear Christmas angel looked a treat, everyone said so. But now the holiday's over and she's come off the tree so I've put her in my bedroom on my dressing table, and every time I look at her I think of you, Tad. You were so good to me. My own real angel is still around, only you mustn't look right at her, only to one side and if you look straight – wham – she goes. I don't tell other people about her, though. Not even Sunny. Going to do my eckers before bedtime so cheerio for now.
Your loving Polly O'Brady.

Tad laughed over the scratty old tomcat – how typical of his Polly! – and nearly cried when he read that she hadn't told anyone else about her guardian angel, not even Sunny. But he knew that Polly was becoming somehow distant in his mind, a memory rather than a real, loving person, and regretted it very much. Only . . . well, he did have Angela now, and she was a great girl, so she was and they got on real good.

113

To be sure he didn't have the same sort of fun with her that he had once had with Polly, but he and Polly had been kids, exploring everything like a pair of inquisitive puppies and frequently getting into trouble for it. He and Angela were verging on being grown-ups, and grown fellers didn't take their girls boxing the fox in the apple orchards outside Dublin, or out to Booterstown to collect cockles on the sands.

The thought made him smile. Angela was beautiful, and kind, and sensible. She had chosen him out of all the fellers she could have had, and that made him a lucky chiseller – if he was still a chiseller, when he was working for his living and taking a pretty girl out to the cinema and – and thinking about her most of the time. But she wasn't his old pal, the one who had known him since he was a scruffy kid trying to keep out of his daddy's way and having a job, most of the time, to stay fed. But he supposed that one's life is divided into little parts, and you hop from one part to another as you grow older. He had hopped out of the chiseller's part, in which Polly had been the only person he really cared for, apart from his own family, and into an almost-grown-up part, in which Angela, who was nearly fourteen, was a more natural companion for him than a child of twelve.

Polly would be thirteen soon, of course. Only the trouble was, Tad couldn't think of her as nearly a woman. He still thought of her as the bright-eyed ten-year-old who had shed such bitter tears when she had been taken away from him, to live over the water with her mammy and daddy. And anyway, she had that Sunny Andersen – ridiculous name – to go about with now.

He – Sunny – was fifteen, according to Polly. Older even than Tad now was, although only by a few months. But he was too old for Polly, that feller, Tad concluded uneasily. Then again it was her business now – she was too far away, and too distant, somehow, for him to meddle in her affairs.

Tad had been reading the letter, and thinking his thoughts, whilst sitting on a broken-down piece of wall in Gardiner's Lane as twilight turned slowly into dusk. Now he stood up. I love Polly like a sister, he told himself, and I'm beginning to love Angela in a – a *different* way. That's all there is to it. And he shoved the letter into his pocket and ran across the court towards his home.

Chapter Five

Sunny Andersen was strolling down the Scotland Road in the beautiful June sunshine, idly kicking a tin can along the paving stones in front of him and wondering what he should do next. He was having a day off; he had a lot of them. Although he was now sixteen years old he was still not in regular employment. However, because of his looks and charm he had had a good many jobs, though he had never stuck to any of them for long. Or perhaps it was not that he had not stuck them, but that they – his employers – had not stuck to him. He did not see why he should work on a sunny day, when he might get out his fishing rod and skip a leckie out to Seaforth and try his luck there. Neither did he see why he should work on a wet day, when it was nicer to stay in bed. Or a snowy day, when considerable fun was to be had making a slide down one of the steep streets which led on to Netherfield Road.

Sunny always pretended to be sorry when employers gave him his cards, but he wasn't really. Of course he enjoyed the wage-packet part of a job and sometimes he quite enjoyed other parts of it too, but this was a rarity, the exception rather than the rule. Ambling along the pavement, he remembered one job that he had enjoyed, though. For a couple of months last summer he had been employed by a firm of ice-cream manufacturers to sell their products in New Brighton. He had been given a stout and reliable bicycle with a cart attached, and all he had to do all day was cycle up and down the New Brighton promenade, stopping whenever he saw a customer.

The job of selling ice cream had been grand, he thought now, whistling a tune beneath his breath as he strolled along the dock road, an eye cocked for anything of interest. But when you ran out of ice cream you had to cycle back to the depot for a refill, and whilst you were doing that you weren't earning. And the bicycle was a heavy old thing, and he had not always enjoyed being at everyone's beck and call. He should have stuck it until the season was over, he realised that, had realised it at the time, but then his mam had come home, having been generously rewarded by someone for something, he did not enquire what, and handed him a big white fiver. That had been the end of the job – a fiver can last a good long time if you're careful and make it work for you. Sunny bought a quantity of powder and lipstick which weren't quite what they should have been from someone he knew on the fringes of the make-up trade, and went round the big offices about once a month, selling the stuff for a nice little profit. But when both the fiver and the make-up ran out, he had not bothered to get another job because Christmas was coming, and a boy with good looks and charm could always find himself a good little job over Christmas.

And then he had met Polly. Sunny had never quite understood what had happened to him upon setting eyes on that small, wide-eyed face surrounded by all those bright, primrose curls. But whatever it was, it had changed things. He wanted to be with her all the time, only she was in school, so it became essential that he get the sort of job which allowed him weekends and evenings free. And he soon realised that he must ingratiate himself with her mam and dad and her brothers, those that were living in the city, anyway, because Polly was still a schoolgirl, although she was only just over two years younger than Sunny, and if he did not have parental approval then he knew instinctively that they would break the friendship up. Polly was very dear to them, and because they loved her they guarded her against anything – or anyone – which they thought might hurt her.

Sunny agreed with this, naturally. He guarded her himself, when they were together. And fortunately, Mrs O'Brady was a nice woman and did not seem to worry unduly that he had not, at present, got a job, particularly when she saw how hard he worked over Christmas – and what nice times he and Polly had together.

'Sure an' you'll get a job when the better weather comes, Sunny,' Mrs O'Brady had said reassuringly when the Christmas job finished. 'Work's always hard to find – harder when there's a Depression, but you're intelligent, always clean and neat . . . Why, you'll be after gettin' a better job than most of your pals, I'll be bound.'

Mr O'Brady, however, had begun to look rather thoughtfully at Sunny lately, so Sunny supposed that he would have to get himself into work again. The trouble was, when his mam was doing well she gave him money and work simply seemed an unnecessary unpleasantness. On the other hand, though, Mr O'Brady had said once or twice, in his deep, slow way, that sure and wasn't Mrs Andersen a fine woman, to keep a lad of Sunny's age and not drive him out to work, and there was something in the way he said it which made Sunny fear that Mr O'Brady

118

had rumbled him. Or worse, had rumbled *them*, for he had no desire for the O'Bradys to look too closely at the way in which Mrs Andersen made her living.

For Sunny had known, ever since he had reached years of discretion, which, in his case, was the age of eight, that his mam earned money from having various gentlemen friends. Now that he was fully grown he knew that this meant she lived on what the priest would have called 'immoral earnings', but he did not put it quite so plainly even to himself; he wrapped it up, telling himself that his mam was 'a theatrical', or, even better, 'a receptionist'. Indeed, she undertook a variety of legitimate jobs when she needed to do so, but he knew, really, that most of the money she made came from men who bought her favours.

And doing such work could be dangerous too. Women who pleased men sometimes had their throats slit as they lay in bed, or were robbed of their takings by other men – shiftless and greedy ones. Some women worked for men called pimps, who took the lion's share of their money, but Cecily Andersen was far too clever to get mixed up with anyone like that. She was a tall, handsome woman, blue-eyed and yellow-haired, but it was from her that Sunny had inherited his casual attitude to the task of earning a living. Cecily liked pretty clothes, cinema and theatre, and her bed. When she was working as an usherette at the cinema – a favourite job, because she met men there – she could have a nice sit-down in the back stalls and a zizz if the film was boring, but when she was doing receptionist duties she had to be – or at least appear to be – alert and ready to help, so although her good appearance and charm might get her into a job, her idleness very soon got her out of it.

However there were always men, she said, when washing her hands of her latest job. Cecily's most regular friend was Sunny's father, Bjorn Berkesmann, a Swedish officer on a timber ship which called every two or three months at the port of Liverpool. He came to the small house close by the Wapping dock whenever his ship was in port, so although Sunny did not have a full-time father in the accepted sense of the words, he saw Bjorn as often as most children of sailors saw their dads.

Bjorn was tall, blond and handsome. He was very like Cecily, so like her that once or twice they had been mistaken for brother and sister, and of course no one who had met Bjorn ever doubted Sunny's paternity. He was proud of his son furthermore, openly acknowledging him, and when Sunny had been small he had helped Cecily financially so that she had not had to work too hard or too often. Now that Sunny was a man grown, however, his father's attitude towards him had hardened somewhat.

'You a good job should hev,' he had said accusingly only a couple of months ago, sitting in the big fireside chair whilst Cecily cooked them a meal and Sunny sorted out his shore lines, for he intended to go fishing next day. 'You should your mudder be helpink to support, not still expectink her to support you.'

'I've had good jobs, but they all get tired of me, an' gi' me me cards,' Sunny had answered, casting his father a mournful look. At least, it was supposed to be a mournful look, but Sunny saw by his father's expression that it had not been mournful enough. 'Now summer's comin' I'll be gettin' somethin', Bjorn,' he said in a wheedling tone. 'You know me, I like a bit of a change, an' a challenge, an' all.'

'You're lazy, like your mudder,' Bjorn had said flatly. 'But it vill not do, Sunny. Why not try the sea? It to me good hes been.'

'It has been good to me,' Sunny had corrected automatically. His father's English was very good, but he sometimes got his sentences the wrong way round and appreciated being reminded. 'I don't think mam would be too pleased if I went off to sea, would you, Mam?'

But to Sunny's astonishment, his mother had let him down. She was stirring something in a large saucepan and her spoon had stopped for a moment whilst she considered the question, then she had replied seriously, as though she had been thinking about it for some time. 'Well, I'd miss you, natural,' she had said thoughtfully. 'But I agree wi' your dad. You'd be better off at sea than idlin' round the docks gettin' into mischief. 'Sides, you've gorra girlfriend, haven't you? Well, she's goin' to expect things like trips to the cinema, an' the seaside, to say nothin' of little gifts when her birthday comes round. Oh, I know I've always done me best for you, but I'm not gerrin' any younger, chuck. It's time you fended for yourself, did your own courtin'.'

Sunny had been so taken aback that for a moment he could only stare disbelievingly at his parent. Then he had said sulkily: 'I don't idle round the docks gettin' into mischief. I've had lots o' jobs and while I'm in 'em I work damn' hard . . . but they bore me after a bit, all of 'em. And as for goin' to sea – what d'you think me young lady would say to that, eh?'

Bjorn, who was always fair, had admitted that a girl liked a feller to be ashore with her, though most girls appreciated that a man must get work in order to keep her. 'So you must a good job find, and soon,' he had insisted. 'Or you will get bad name for unreliability.'

So of course Sunny had promised to mend his ways, and had done so in a manner of speaking. He had kept out of the house during normal working hours and had kept some money jingling in his pocket with a variety of small jobs.

But right now it was a sunny day and yesterday he had worked from dawn until dusk, moving a large houseful of furniture from Rodney Street to South-port for a delivery man he was supposed to be working for, so he had money in his pocket and nothing to do until school came out, when he would be seeing Polly. At the weekend they meant to go over to New Brighton for a day on the funfair and some time on the beach, but today was Wednesday and an evening did not give them sufficient time to go far. Knowing that he would not be working he had suggested last evening that she should sag off school next day, but Polly had frowned on this, reminding him that she would be looking for a job in a year and a good school report was something she could not afford to whistle down the wind.

'But you could say you had a sore throat, queen,' Sunny had said in his most coaxing tone. 'A sore throat's easy to fake . . . An' if them teachers at your school are fussy about such things, I'd write a note for you, pretendin' it were from your mam.'

They had been sitting on the wall which surrounded St Martin's recreation ground, desultorily chatting whilst watching a group of lads playing a forbidden game of football amongst the flower beds. Polly had shaken her head, then turned large, reproachful eyes on him. 'Sunny, you're a divil straight from hell, so y'are, and I'll not risk me immortal soul tellin' huge *lies* just so's you can have someone to mess about wit' when you're out of work. Anyway, what happened to the job on the furniture van?'

Sunny had grinned and caught hold of Polly's small neck, pulling her closer to him so that he might drop a kiss on the end of her nose. Polly who, while she sort-of liked it sometimes, found such behaviour embarrassing in the extreme, gave Sunny a playful punch in the stomach. 'All right, all right,' he had said, laughing. 'There's no need for violence, Poll, it were only to show you how I feel about you. Just a – a lovin' gesture, like.'

'Lovin' gestures aren't needed,' Polly had said sharply. 'Just you remember that if one of the teachers should happen to look out of me school, they'd be starin' straight across at us. And what would they think, eh, if they saw you maulin' me about and kissin' me nose? And the presbytery is even closer . . . Why, if the priests saw what you were doin' they'd probably want you to *marry* me, and what would you be after sayin' then, clever clogs?'

'Can't marry someone of thirteen,' Sunny had said happily. 'Anyway, I don't see why you're so goody-goody. Your Ivan said that in Dublin you were a right hell-raiser, and—'

'What a thing to say!' Polly had gasped, clearly outraged. 'I am *not* a goody-goody, nor I aren't a hell-raiser, neither. Ivan's just cross because when me daddy was ill and me mammy put me in charge of the house, I sometimes made him work a little bit, idle chiseller that he was.'

'He scrubbed the spuds, cleaned the cabbage, mended the fire, brushed the floor . . .' Sunny had muttered beneath his breath, and had turned to grin at Polly, who had grinned back, unrepentant.

'Oh well . . . mebbe I wasn't an angel, Sunny, but I never did tell lies . . . All right, I took apples from orchards an' spuds from the fields . . . Once we sold holly to the big houses round Phoenix Park – and it were their own holly, what we'd robbed from their hedges. But that's just – just mischief, not real badness.'

Sunny, who agreed with her, had still pulled a doubtful face. 'Stealin's stealin', queen, no matter how you try to cover it up. Still, if you won't sag off school I'll call for you when you leave off, and we'll have a ride on the overhead railway down to Seaforth and back. I'll gerra couple o' tickets from somewhere.'

Polly had known, of course, that he was extremely unlikely to pay for the tickets, but apparently her strict code of conduct did not wince at this, so here he was now, walking towards the overhead railway terminus, which was down by the Pier Head. If you were quick, clever and lucky, it was often possible to pick up a ticket which someone had not handed over to the ticket collector, smarten it up, fill in the bit which had been punched out, and use it during the rush hour, when the railway staff were too busy to peruse each ticket separately.

So Sunny strolled on, and thought about getting a part-time job selling ice cream up and down the Pier Head; ices would go down well there on a hot day like this one. He could sell the ha'penny wafers, most folk could afford a ha'penny. In fact, he could make his way to the warehouse now, see if there was a spare bicycle and cart not in use . . . After all, what good was a lovely sunny day when you were alone and hadn't got your fishing rod handy? And he knew Polly – she would enjoy the ride on the docker's umbrella a good deal more if it was accompanied by a bag of popcorn or an orange or two. Sunny jingled the money in his pocket and decided to go down to the ice-cream factory. And if they didn't have a spare bicycle, perhaps they would sell him one of those big metal cases of the stuff; he reckoned he could shift a deal of ice cream on a day like this even without the bike.

Polly sat in the classroom with her books spread out on her desk, her friend Alice on one side of her and her friend Sylvia on the other, regarding Miss Witherspoon seriously with eyes which followed the teacher's every movement as she wrote on the blackboard and turned occasionally to explain something to her class. But despite her apparent deep interest in the lesson, Polly's thoughts were elsewhere.

It was a lovely day, the nicest one of the summer so far, and far from listening to Miss Witherspoon, who was teaching them to analyse a sentence, Polly was thinking wistfully that if only she had not been such a goody-goody, as Sunny had put it, she might at this very moment have been skimming stones across the River Mersey or searching for four-leaved clovers in Princes Park or paddling in the little waves on Seaforth shore.

'Now we need a subject, a verb, an object . . . Which of you would like to come up and mark out this sentence?' Miss Witherspoon said, turning back to her class. 'Polly O'Brady, can you show the class the adjectival clause, please?'

Polly dragged her happy mind, up to its ankles in cool seawater, back to the hot and stuffy classroom with its smell of girls, cabbage and chalk dust. Fortunately the teacher had said her name before the question and not after it, so she stood up, went to the board, and after a short hesitation, during which time subjects, objects, predicates and various other parts of a sentence whirled in her head, she marked the adjectival clause firmly with the piece of white chalk Miss Witherspoon held out.

'Correct. Thank you, Polly,' Miss Witherspoon said. Rightly taking this for dismissal, Polly returned to her seat whilst another girl took her place to find the subject and object of the sentence.

'Considerin' you was half-asleep . . .' Alice whispered as Polly sat down. 'Still, ole Withers don't usually prose on like this. I wish she'd forget all this rubbishy stuff an' let us read *A Tale of Two Cities*. We was up to an excitin' bit when the bell rang last time.'

Miss Witherspoon, despite her nickname, was an energetic young teacher with black hair arranged in the popular pageboy cut and a trim figure clad in grey and white poplin. She was a great favourite with the girls and her lesson, English, was easily Polly's best subject yet somehow, today, even had the class been reading the Dickens classic, it would have seemed a waste of time. But she had refused to sag off school because she wanted a good report at the end of the summer, so she really ought to concentrate on the lesson.

For a few minutes, indeed, she did so, but then her mind began to wander again. What would Sunny be doing? He wasn't working, that much was certain, so he could be doing almost anything, she supposed wistfully. He loved to fish, probably because he usually fished either sitting down or standing still, and he liked the cinema too. Polly remembered trips to the Grand Canal in Dublin, with Tad importantly hefting a hazel wand and carrying a tin filled with a quantity of writhing, bug-eyed maggots which he would examine with masculine pride every five minutes, just so that he could make her squeak with dismay, and that made her wonder what Tad was doing as well. It would be a lovely day in Dublin of course, that went without saying. She could hardly remember any dull days in Dublin, either the sun was shining or the snow was falling in her dreamy recollections of her home town, and now she visualised Tad setting off to catch himself a few minnows in the canal, or maybe going down to the quays to see what he could pull out of the Liffey . . .

'So if we're left with only that phrase . . . Polly, would you like to come up and mark the last words, please?'

Miss Witherspoon was so nice, so polite, Polly thought dismally, making her way to the front through the rows of desks. Other teachers ordered, threatened, shouted, but Miss Witherspoon treated them like the young ladies they thought themselves, and never forgot to say 'please' when she asked one to do something, and 'thank you' when it was done. Now, Polly looked across at the board and saw at once that the unmarked phrase was an adverbial clause . . . as if it mattered! She stopped short, a couple of feet from the board, and turned to face the teacher. She could feel boredom and rebellion rising in her chest like the River Mersey rose when the tide began to come in, and suddenly she did not like school at all, or lessons. Not even Miss Witherspoon seemed worth the waste of this lovely day.

'Well, the t'ing is, Miss Witherspoon – what does it matter? I mean, who's goin' to ask us to analyse a sentence once we've left St Syl's?'

It wasn't a fair question, she realised that as soon as she saw the colour rise up the white neck and invade the face of her favourite teacher, and she was suddenly shocked that she had asked it. But having asked it she did not intend to let such a thing as fairness cause her to back down so she stood there, politely smiling, her eyebrows still raised.

'Well, unless you're intending to be a traveller, Polly, I don't suppose that geography will be of much use to you in your future life, do you?' Miss Witherspoon said with a very slight edge to her voice. 'As for mathematics, well, since you don't intend to become a chartered accountant I suppose one could argue that mathematics, too, has little use for a young person such as yourself.'

No one laughed. The class, to a girl, thought that Polly's question was fair and Miss Witherspoon's answer was not. Polly went on waiting. Miss Witherspoon sighed. She pointed to the board. 'Don't you know the answer, dear? Then I'll ask someone else to come up, so if you'll return to your place—'

'I do know the answer as it happens, but you're not after answerin' me question, Miss Witherspoon,' Polly said obstinately, keeping her eyes fixed on the teacher. If she had been a bad girl, the sort of girl that Sunny would clearly much have preferred, she would not be here at all, on this hot and delightful day, standing in front of the board in a stuffy classroom whilst the teacher tried to evade giving her a straight answer. 'You could say that it's kind o' useful to know that the Chinese grow rice, I suppose, or good to know Paris is the capital of France – for them cross-word puzzles – and even bein' able to add two and two is useful if you're workin' in a shop. But analysin' a sentence . . . well, I don't see the *use* of it, no matter how hard I try.' And in a final burst of bravery she added, 'Which makes this lesson seem a waste of time, so it does.'

Someone giggled. Someone else gave a muffled snort. Miss Witherspoon turned from a delicate shade of rose-pink to the dark red of a boiled beetroot. She pointed her chalk at Polly in a very decided sort of way, though her hand trembled a little. 'In that case, since my lesson's useless to you, you'd best go and call on Miss Rutherford,' she said in a voice which she strove to keep even, but which climbed a trifle. 'No doubt she will be able to convince you that I'm not analysing sentences just to waste either your time or my own,' she finished.

Polly had never been told to go to the headmistress before, but she found that she did not care in the least, and once outside the classroom door, decided that she would *not* go to Miss Rutherford to get told off for asking a perfectly respectable question. Instead, she would go quietly off home . . . No, she would go off to Sunny's home, and see if he still wanted to go to Seaforth for the day.

It was not hard getting out of the school – in fact, she just walked across the playground, through the gate and into the road. And she felt free, and lovely, and not in the least guilty. I'm thirteen years old, so I am, and that's too big for stayin' indoors on a hot day whilst a teacher writes on the board and won't answer questions, she told herself, padding along the pavement. She rather wished she had taken her carry-out with her, but that would have made Miss Witherspoon suspect that something was up. No, she would go round to Sunny's house and he would doubtless find her something to eat – and he would praise her for being sensible for once – and then they could set off for Seaforth, or wherever they decided they most wanted to spend the rest of the day.

Whistling a tune beneath her breath, Polly stepped out.

It took a good deal longer to catch up with Sunny than she had supposed it would, because when she reached his house no one was in at all, but a neighbour, an old lady who spent most of the day sitting on her front steps watching the life of the waterfront go by, had seen Sunny setting off earlier in the morning and had asked him where he was bound.

'He said somethin' about the Pier 'ead,' the old lady said. 'I wondered if he'd tek off to New Brighton, bein' as 'ow he's rare fond o' the seaside. This time a year ago, he were sellin' ice cream over there, wi' a bicycle an' cart.'

So Polly, though a little daunted by the vagueness of the neighbour's suggestions, set off for the Pier Head, and it was here that she found him, leaning on the handlebars of a stop-me-and-buy-one bicycle whilst he studied the goods set out in the window of the small shop which huddled beneath the docker's umbrella.

'Sunny, I'm out o' school,' Polly had shouted, running across the roadway and grabbing his arm. 'Where d'you get the bike?'

'From the factory, of course,' Sunny said. He sounded rather cross. 'Honest to God, Poll, what a girl you are for messin' a feller about! I'd not have hired the bleedin' bike if I'd known you was goin' to sag off school after all – now what'll I do?'

'Whatever it is, I'll do it as well, so I shall,' Polly said peacefully, turning to stare into the shop window which seemed to be interesting Sunny so much. 'What does it matter about the bike, Sunny? You can push instead of ride, when I'm out o' breath wit' runnin'.'

Sunny's frown disappeared and he grinned at Polly, all his annoyance seeming to melt away. Then he turned round and began to wrench open the metal container which was strapped to the rear part of his bicycle. 'It don't matter about pushin', queen,' he said. 'Here, I'll mek you up a wafer. I were goin' to sell this lot round here, where there ain't no one else sellin' it, so I could earn us some spare money for Sat'day . . .' he went on, gesturing to the ice-cream container, which was now open and sending a delicious smell and wreaths of white vapour into the warm air, '. . . only I didn't know they'd mek me hire the bike, so I've no money left. Still, you can have all the ice cream you can eat until I've sold some of the stuff an' made some gelt,' he added with his customary generosity. 'Eh, look, a customer!'

Polly, standing beside him and licking her wafer, saw very soon that Sunny's instinct had been right about selling the ice cream. Within five minutes he had a small queue of people waiting, within ten minutes a long queue. After an hour he was regretfully scraping the bottom of the container and the old leather bag slung round his chest and one shoulder literally bulged with pennies and ha'pennies.

'Come wi' me to tek the bike back,' he suggested presently, having closed the lids of the container and turned the bicycle back towards the main road. 'I'll gi' you a seater; hop on!'

Nothing loth, Polly hopped, and very shortly the two of them, having concluded their business with the ice-cream factory and handed back the hired bicycle, were jumping aboard a tram and heading for the overhead railway.

'Seaforth Sands, here we come,' Sunny said blissfully, as they got off the tram at the Pier Head and went to buy their tickets. 'Eh, you won't regret it, young Poll – and I called you a goody-goody! Yet here you are, saggin' off school wi' the best of 'em.'

'I know,' Polly said. 'And I don't feel at all guilty, I just feel happy.'

'So you ought,' Sunny said decidedly. 'Two returns to Seaforth, please, mister.'

When, tired but happy, Polly got home that evening she waited for Mammy to start asking her just what she had been up to, leaving school in the middle of the morning, but Deirdre said nothing. She had taken Peader in his wheelchair to Princes Park, and the two of them had wandered amongst the flower beds and the lawns, and admired the lake and the ducks, and it had put Peader in mind of the crossing cottage and how he had enjoyed his life there. The two of them, Deirdre told Polly, had spent a wonderful day planning how they would go back to the country when Peader retired and how, until then, Peader would potter about the house and maybe take on a simple little job like stuffing envelopes, or helping someone with their books, whilst she worked outside the home for a while. This meant that they could, she hoped, save up sufficient money for a place in the country again.

'Not to buy,' Deirdre added hastily, seeing her daughter's eyes widen. 'Just to rent . . . but we'll need money to live on, and though the railway pension's a help, we'll need a bit more earned if we're to put anything by for a rainy day.'

'Do – do you really think Daddy will work again?' Polly asked, as Deirdre cleaned lettuce and sliced tomatoes whilst she herself cut and buttered the bread. 'Only his walkin' doesn't seem to get much better, no matter how hard he tries. And sometimes I've wondered whether he could stand bein' in some ticket office all day, so I have.'

Deirdre looked all round her, clearly checking that Peader was still reading his book in the front room and not about to appear in the kitchen, then lowered her voice. 'Sure an' you're a sensible girl, Polly me love, so I don't mind tellin' you that it'll be a long job, if it happens at all. But if he's here, at home, wit' something to take his mind off himself, then I t'ink he'll get better quicker. I don't mind telling you there's days when I don't know which way to turn for the rent, let alone extras. Ivan seems to go through trousers like nobody's business. We managed while me little job lasted but since then . . . If only I could get another job . . . But work's hard to come by.'

So Polly went to bed with a good deal to think about despite not having had to pay for her day's illicit pleasure. She wished that Deirdre did not have to work, but being a practical person, she realised that every family needed a wage-earner. So if Mammy works now, then as soon as I'm fourteen I'll get a job and she can go back to being a housewife again, she told herself, snuggling under the covers. And though it's grand, so it is, that no one at home knows about me day out, tomorrer I'll probably get a good scolding, if nothing worse.

Yet when she went into school next morning she was neither seized upon nor punished. 'Miss Witherspoon said you'd been unwell in class, and had probably gone home rather than risk upsetting the lessons,' her class teacher, Miss Chardwell, had said. She had stopped Polly as the girls were streaming past her after a history lesson, heading for the playground and twenty minutes of comparative freedom.

'But another time, Polly, just tell me you're feeling poorly and want to go home. As your class teacher I'm responsible for your well-being, you know. What exactly was the matter?'

'Sorry, Miss Chardwell,' Polly said. She decided to buy Miss Witherspoon a bunch of roses and bring them in to school the following day. What a sport old Withers was, not to give her away – and she had behaved awful bad, she knew it. 'It was women's troubles, miss,' she added with relish, since her class teacher was still looking at her enquiringly. She knew that there were such things as women's troubles, she had heard her mammy talking about them, but as yet they had not troubled her. But having been bad yesterday, a little lie to keep the stick from her back seemed only sensible.

'Oh . . . I see,' Miss Chardwell remarked, turning away. She went rather red as she did so and Polly, fascinated, wondered what she had said. Mammy and Alice's mam, Dora Eccles, talked about women's troubles in hushed voices when the men were about, but loudly enough in all-female company. Still, Miss Chardwell was a teacher, not entirely a woman, so perhaps that made a difference, Polly decided, returning to the playground and her pals.

Out there, she asked Alice and Sylvia about women's troubles but though they both giggled and said it wasn't something you should talk about to teachers, they seemed to have very little more idea than Polly. 'When you get 'em, you're a woman growed,' Sylvia said, and so not unnaturally Polly thought that it must have something to do with having to wear a bust bodice because your chest bounced about otherwise, and then forgot it. Why should she worry, after all? She had always been

134

taught that badness was always found out and that only goodness was rewarded, but Sunny had laughed this notion to scorn and he had been proved right. She had been downright wicked, now that she thought about it, but she had enjoyed a marvellous day out and was clearly not going to suffer for it. Perhaps, Polly thought, it's just a waste being good. Perhaps a little wickedness now and then added spice to life. Or perhaps she was beginning to grow into a different girl, the sort of girl Sunny liked, but her mammy and daddy – and Tad – might not like at all. As for her guardian angel . . . Polly gave a superstitious little shudder. She decided she would have to think very hard before she risked mitching off school again – her angel might not approve!

Deirdre had decided very soon after Peader got home from hospital that she would have to think about getting another job. She had enjoyed working in the dress shop, but it had been a long day and she knew the children had not liked being left with so much to do. What was more, though the money had been useful, with only four weeks' work it had been impossible to put any money aside, so another job it would have to be, whether she liked it or not. She had always worked as a young woman – until Polly had arrived, that was. Then her menfolk had seen that she had sufficient money to stay at home, and she had been glad to do so, not from laziness, but because she had always felt that children needed at least one parent in the home. So from the moment Polly had arrived Deirdre had concentrated on being as good a mother and housewife as she could possibly be. Oh, she had done small jobs from time to time, taking in washing and ironing to earn something extra towards

Christmas, fruit-picking in summer when she could take the children with her, even 'obliging' a woman in one of the big houses with a few hours' cleaning when Polly and Ivan had both been in school. But that had been casual work, and in a city she knew like the back of her hand. Liverpool was still strange to her; she did not even know in which direction to walk if she wanted to find the sort of houses which would employ staff, and the staff themselves would be strangers to her. She knew herself to be clean, hard-working and of good appearance, but would that be enough? She was in her late forties and thought that was too old to try for shop work. There was, as everyone kept reminding her, a Depression on, and she guessed that shopkeepers would rather employ young girls that they could underpay and overwork rather than a mature woman like herself who would expect at least a show of fairness.

Cleaning in some large private house was the obvious choice, but she was afraid that it might involve taking a long tram ride, which would mean being away from Peader for more hours than she needed to be. Then there was taking in washing, but although she knew some women still did this, the pay was poor, the work incredibly hard, and in winter, Peader would be sitting in a room which was full of the steam of drying sheets half the week, and she was determined not to do anything which might undermine his chances of a complete recovery.

So a couple of weeks after her talk with Polly, when she had despatched the children to school, Deirdre helped Peader to dress and to eat his breakfast, settled him in a chair by the back door with the morning paper, and told him she was going shopping.

'Shan't be long, me darlin',' she assured him, and

he never queried her best hat, a jaunty lilac-pink pill-box with a tiny veil, or her navy coat and skirt with the matching shoes. He just smiled his slow, sweet smile and told her to be as long as she liked, for hadn't he the paper to read now and the good fresh air coming in through the open back door?

'I'll come out with you this afternoon,' he said in his slow, careful voice which had grown, alas, slower and even more careful since the stroke. 'If you'll not mind wheelin' me a way?'

Deirdre dropped a kiss on the top of his head and squeezed his shoulder. 'I love to wheel you, so I do,' she assured him. 'We'll go down to the docks and watch the shipping if the sun goes on shining. You'll enjoy that.'

'I'm not so keen on all them handsome sailors watchin' you, alanna,' Peader said, making her smile. 'I'll peel some spuds for you while you're out gadding.'

Deirdre thanked him, trying to ignore the stab of dismay which went through her. The trouble was, Peader found the knife difficult to handle and sometimes she ended up with what looked more like marbles than spuds. But there you were, trying his hand at small tasks was all part of him getting better, the doctor said so.

'Well, only if you're bored wit' the paper,' she said as she went out through the back door. She crossed the yard with a brisk step, opened the gate into the jigger and turned and waved, only Peader was already holding the paper very close to his eyes and squinting at the headlines and didn't look up. I'll have to get him some spectacles, she told herself as she made her way down Tatlock Street. But I'll leave it until I've fixed meself up wit' some work, then I won't have to worry about the cost.

It was a fine morning, however, and Deirdre, who had a naturally optimistic nature, found it difficult to remember that the family had fallen on hard times, that she had to work. The truth was, she had been rather lonely since moving from the crossing cottage into the city, and had frequently longed for the women friends she had had in Dublin, and in the village on the Wirral. Her conscience had kept her close to Peader's side, but if she worked, and brought in money, then Peader would realise that she was not being selfish at all, at all, but doing no more than her duty. And if working led to her making friends – Deirdre smiled to herself – then that was just a bonus, so to speak, a piece of good luck for her.

So Deirdre made her way to the Scotland Road and browsed along, keeping a weather eye on the windows for any sign that a worker was needed. And she had not gone far before she came level with a large cafe with the legend *Mathilda Ellis's Dining Rooms* written in fancy gold letters across the very large bow window. And beneath it, tucked into a corner of the frame, was a small white card. Heart beating with excitement, Deirdre bent and read it.

Wanted, a reliable Woman to assist with dinners and teas at Busy Times and to Wait on; supply own Overalls but aprons provided. She read it, with some puzzlement. That sounded odd! You had to bring your own overalls, that was clear, but they would provide you with aprons. Yet surely, if you were swathed in overalls, you were not likely to need an apron as well. However, it was the first job she had seen – and that meant the nearest to home, so checking her appearance in the window and finding that she still looked neat, Deirdre took a deep breath, squared her shoulders, and entered the Dining Rooms.

It was mid-morning, so a few women were sitting at the small tables in the window drinking coffee and talking, but the rest of the very large room was empty. However, there was a till behind a glass panel in one corner and a woman in a navy dress with her grey hair pulled back from her face into a neat bun and a pair of small gold spectacles halfway down her thin nose, was sitting there, head bent, writing in a large ledger. When the bell rang to announce Deirdre's entrance she looked up, then looked down at her work again. She thinks I'm a customer, so she does, Deirdre thought with some dismay. Oh dammit, she won't like it when I tell her it's after the job I've come!

But here she wronged the lady at the till. When Deirdre walked across towards the till and stammered that she had come about the card in the window she half-rose to her feet and gave a very thin, lemony smile. 'Ah, the job,' she said, with a world of satisfaction in her tone. She raised her voice. 'Miss Collins, can you come and take over the till for a moment?' she called. 'I'll go through to the office; I'm interviewing.'

In response a thin, harassed-looking woman came out of the swing door to one side of the room, eyebrows raised. She was clad in rather stained white overalls, had a white cloth tied around her head from which stray locks of grey-streaked hair depended, and looked to be about fifty.

'Yes, Mrs Ellis?' she enquired in a voice in which Deirdre unerringly detected a touch of Irish brogue. 'Were you after wanting me? I t'ought I heered me name called.'

Mrs Ellis, for she was clearly the owner of the Dining Rooms, raised her eyes to heaven and said: 'Yes, I did call you, Miss Collins. This – this person has come about the job. Will you keep the till for me whilst I have a few words with her?'

No brogue there, Deirdre thought. Only sharpness and impatience. Oh dear! But the older woman was speaking again. 'Right you are, Mrs Ellis,' she said, wiping her hands down the sides of her overalls. 'But who's to finish making me Yorkshire I don't know, for you're no hand wit' eggs and flour as I've telled you a t'ousand times.'

'I don't pretend to be a cook,' Mrs Ellis said, lowering her voice but not abating the sharpness of it one bit. She jerked her head at Deirdre. 'Follow me.'

Half an hour later Deirdre emerged from the Dining Rooms. Despite some private doubts, she felt on top of the world. She had got the job, which seemed to be just the sort of work she could do. She would go in at eleven thirty each weekday morning and remain there until six thirty, when what Mrs Ellis described rather grandly as the 'evening shift' came on. On a Saturday she had schoolgirls, she said, from the local convent, eager to make some money in their spare time, so Deirdre guessed that the 'evening shift' was probably made up of the same young girls.

Her own work would consist of laying, clearing and wiping down tables and serving the customers, and when not doing this she would assist with the cooking, which was in the capable hands of 'my junior partner, Miss Collins'. The washing-up, she was told, was done by a cheerful, cross-eyed woman, who must have weighed ten stone though she was less than five feet tall. Her name was Naomi, and whenever she caught Deirdre's eye she grinned and winked, which, combined with a squint, was somewhat confusing, though Deirdre realised that it was a friendly overture.

Deirdre had been told that she must provide herself with three overalls, preferably white but Mrs Ellis was willing to accept colours until her new worker had earned enough money to purchase the white ones.

'Skirt and jumper, or a dress, it doesn't matter which provided they are black, clean and in a good state of repair,' Mrs Ellis had told her. 'We provide the aprons. You will wear your black skirt and top with the white frilly apron round your waist when you are waiting on tables and the overalls whilst doing kitchen work.'

Deirdre had agreed meekly to all this, for the money was a little better than she had imagined; she thought that this was probably because she would be doing the work of two or three people, but reasoned that beggars could not be choosers.

'Can you start tomorrow, Deirdre?' her new employer had asked. She pronounced the name English fashion, as though it were spelt 'Deirdree', but Deirdre decided not to correct her. Not yet. Mrs Mathilda Ellis, she had already guessed, was not a woman to take correction lying down. No point in getting her back up before I've even started the job, Deirdre had thought, and was then told by Mrs Ellis that the customers would call her 'miss', and that she was not to tell them she was married.

'We are all referred to as miss, except myself,' she said grandly. 'As the proprietor, I am respected more as a married lady, I feel.'

She had introduced Deirdre to the other waitress too, the one who came in early for the breakfasts and morning coffees and then came back at five thirty to help out with the evening rush. Her name was Trixie and she was a pretty redhead of thirty or so with a roguish twinkle in her green eyes and a ready smile which endeared her immediately to Deirdre.

'Regardin' your clo'es, if you can't find nothin' black, chuck, we're abou' the same size, so you can always borry from me,' Trixie said in a thick Liverpool accent, lowering her voice when Mrs Ellis had returned to the till to take a customer's money. 'It ain't a bad job, if your feet'll stand up to it an' you're strong, 'cos the fellers who come in for dinners tips good, 'specially if you're quick. Of course, ole Ellis is a drawback—' She broke off as Mrs Ellis turned away from the till and came towards them. 'Well, see you in the mornin', queen,' Trixie said cheerfully, raising her voice. 'Don't forget, I live over the greengrocer's three doors along, so pop in tomorrer if you wanna borry some blacks.'

'Trixie's a hard worker, but common, very common,' Mrs Ellis said, as soon as the other girl had disappeared. 'That accent! But she's quick, and the gentlemen like her.' Deirdre must have looked startled for Mrs Ellis went quite pink and immediately began to talk again, faster than before. 'Not that I'd dream of encouraging . . . I mean, my girls must be above reproach . . . It don't do to get a name for employing flighty young pieces . . .' The older woman seemed about to lose herself in a maze of half-sentences, but Miss Collins came to her rescue.

'They're all good gorls, so they are,' she said soothingly. 'You've got to have a way wit' you, though, Deirdre, if you're going to make a good waitress. A ready smile, no offence took if a feller makes a bit of a pass, but he's got to be shown you aren't interested in that sort of t'ing . . . It takes tact, so it does, but you'll know what I mean.'

Deirdre thought she could guess, but simply smiled, agreed to be in at eleven next morning so that Trixie could show her the ropes before going off, and went proudly home to tell Peader that she was now an employee and would be bringing in an extra eighteen and sixpence a week, plus tips, and might sometimes be given leftovers into the bargain.

Polly and Sunny were walking up the Scotland Road, arguing hotly over what they should do that day. Sunny wanted to go fishing at Seaforth Sands but Polly, who had had some of that, said it was boring and why could they not catch the next ferry to Woodside and go into the country for the day? Sunny had a proprietorial arm about Polly's shoulders and Polly was snuggled against him when they stopped for a moment to look into a cake-shop window.

'Do we have enough pennies for a bag of sticky buns?' Polly was saying longingly when a voice which turned the marrow in her bones to ice said: 'Polly O'Brady, what in the good God's name are you doing here in the middle of the morning? I sent you off to school wit' your little brother and what do I find? Don't you try to tell me you aren't mitching, Polly, because I'll not believe you, not if you swear it on a stack of Bibles!'

'Mammy!' Polly gasped, thunderstruck. 'Oh, Mammy!'

'She felt unwell, Mrs O'Brady,' Sunny said at once, giving Deirdre the benefit of his most charming smile. 'Poor kid, I met up wi' her outside her school an' said I'd walk her home, but I thought mebbe she'd feel better wi' some food inside her, so . . .'

Polly might not have been the Saint Polly her

143

brother had called her, nor the goody-goody Sunny had taunted her with, but she was not a liar and she would have been ashamed to shelter behind the lies of another. She pushed Sunny's arm off her shoulders and faced her mother, very pink-cheeked and hot-eyed, but straightly, as was her wont. 'I am mitchin', Mammy,' she said in a very small voice. 'I didn't feel even a little bit ill, only it was such a sunny day, and—'

'It's all my fault, Mrs O'Brady,' Sunny said, charming again. 'I talked her into it, she wasn't at all keen at first . . . If you want to blame anyone, blame me.'

'I do,' Deirdre said steadily. 'She's always been a good girl has my Polly, and would be still if she'd not met yourself. Oh, I know a bad, idle feller when I see one, Sunny Andersen, and I'll t'ank you not to try to turn my good daughter into just such another.' She put her arm around Polly, so that she and Polly faced Sunny across the pavement. 'Leave her alone, d'you hear me, lad?' She swung Polly round, taking her hand in a firm grip. 'You go off home, as Polly and meself will. Then I'll go up to the school and see what the teachers have to say.'

'But it ain't Poll's fault, Mrs O'Brady,' Sunny said, sounding agitated now and almost running along beside them to keep up with Deirdre's fast pace. 'I told her to sag off school, I told her we'd have fun . . . it's all my fault!'

'Oh? You went into the schoolroom, did you, and dragged her out by one arm and a leg?' Deirdre enquired frostily, still keeping up her fast pace and not allowing Polly to hang back. 'And she does what you tell her, eh? When you say mitch, she mitches. Is that the story you're trying to get me to believe? Well, all I can say is, what next will you say to me daughter?

144

Will you tell her to take flowers from the graves in Anfield Cemetery, and sell them around the streets? Will you suggest that she goes into Mrs McKenna's and helps herself to a quarter of aniseed balls and two ounces of liquorice? Oh, go 'way, Polly's not afraid of taking responsibility for the wrong she's done.'

'Oh, but . . . please, Mrs O'Brady, it were all my fault,' Sunny said desperately. 'I just want to explain . . . want to tell you how sorry I am . . .'

Deirdre stopped short and turned to face him. She longed to give him a hard slapping, to march him home to his own mother and tell that lady just what she thought of her good-for-nothing son, but she knew that Sunny was too big, too old for such treatment and anyway, she knew better, she told herself, than to slap another woman's child. But she did not intend to have him trailing along behind them all the way to Titchfield Street. 'Go home, boy,' she said, in a quiet tone which nevertheless had ice in it. 'Go home and don't come near me daughter no more. I'm telling you I mean it, and if I catch you hanging around her it'll be the scuffers who'll come knocking on your door; hear me? Because as God's me witness, I mean to stop you seeing Polly. She's only thirteen still, so I'll have right, and the law, on me side in getting rid of you. I've telled you once, now I'm telling you again. Clear off.'

Sunny scuffled with his feet in the dust, then turned to Polly. 'Ah, I were only sayin' it weren't your fault, queen,' he began, but Deirdre did not wait for any more arguments. Further up the street she could see a policeman, strolling along in the bright sunshine with his helmet tipped back a bit and his white gloves in one hand. She pointed and Sunny, after a startled glance, sighed, shook his head, then turned on his heel. The last Deirdre saw of him was his back view as he hurried away down the pavement.

'Oh, Mam, he was only tryin' to say he was sorry—' Polly began, only to be told to hold her peace until they got indoors.

'For this sort of behaviour has got to stop, and I'm the woman who's after stopping it,' Deirdre said briskly to her daughter's downbent head, for Polly was staring at her sandals as though they were the only interesting things for miles. 'Not another word now, miss, until I've got you indoors.'

It was late before Polly got to bed that night. The row had lasted, on and off, all through the afternoon and into the evening, but at last she had capitulated, and now that she had done so, had agreed not to see Sunny again, she found that she was almost relieved. Ever since she had started her life of sin, things had been going wrong. Her angel, who was usually on the half-landing when she made her way up to bed, had not so much as appeared, no matter how hard she tried to peep out of the corner of her eye. Ivan had realised that something was going on and though he was too good a kid to tell on her, he had begun muttering that she would be in big trouble, so she would, when Mammy found out, and she had known that this was true. What was more her friends, Alice and Sylvia, thought she was being a proper fool, and had begun to count her out of evening entertainments because she was so often with Sunny.

And she had known, with increasing conviction, that what she was doing was really wrong. She had mitched off school whenever he asked her to do so, that was certainly true, but her conscience had begun first to whisper, then to mutter and, this past week, had been positively shouting. She knew it was wrong to mitch, to catch trains and ferries using tickets skilfully 'doctored' by Sunny. Even more wrong was going into shops and picking up any sweets or biscuits handy when the staff were serving someone else. She had refused to do it at first, but then it had seemed awful mean to enjoy the stuff that Sunny prigged in that fashion and never to do her share.

Of course, Mammy hadn't known about the used tickets or the sweeties, but it was almost as if she guessed that such things were a regular part of Sunny's days when he wasn't working. Polly had tried to defend herself against the only known sin, which had been mitching off school, but it hadn't worked.

'You've not got a leg to stand on, Polleen,' her father had said, his voice so sad and so loving all at once that Polly had had hard work not to start crying again. 'You lied to the teachers, you took in false notes to say you'd had a family bereavement, you simply let that young feller lead you round by the nose, so you did. And it isn't as if your mammy wanted to punish you for these t'ings, because she's said a dozen times she won't do so. All she's doing is trying to see that you behave properly in future. And she's doing that by askin' you to promise, on the Bible, that you'll not see that young feller again. After all, alanna, he's t'ree years older than yourself, he should be workin', not idlin' round the streets corruptin' a child still not even in the top class at school.'

So Polly had promised, with her hand on the Bible which Mammy had fetched out of the parlour, that she would not see Sunny again, although she didn't think that Peader's comments about Sunny's age were very fair – he was only a little older than her pal

Tad, and Polly herself would be fourteen next year.

'Only I can't stop him speakin' to me, Mammy, and it's awful rude not to answer, so it is,' she had pointed out in a small and shaking voice, for it had been a gruelling row in which she had done little but cry and protest that Sunny was all right really, so he was, and that she would never mitch off school again.

'I'm afraid you'll have to be rude then, alanna,' Deirdre had said firmly. 'You've made a promise, a serious promise, remember.' She had patted Polly's shoulder, then bent and kissed her tear-streaked face, rumpling the soft, untidy curls. 'Don't worry about it; he'll soon find someone else to go around wit', especially if he gets himself a job.'

So Polly, having given in and agreed not to see Sunny again, had sat down with her parents and her two brothers, eaten a meal, washed up and cleared away, and had then come up to her room, where she sat on the edge of her bed, slowly taking off her clothing, and wondering why, after such a dreadful time, she was actually feeling almost better. A peacefulness which she had not known for weeks and weeks was slowly taking possession of her. She supposed, as she pulled her white cotton nightie over her head and began to brush out her hair, that it was because at last her conscience was clear. She had known all along that Sunny had encouraged her to be a bad girl, she had even known that her guardian angel was so disappointed with her that she – her guardian angel was definitely a she – had taken herself off somewhere. She had stopped saying her prayers before bed each night, not because she wanted to do so but because she was afraid of what God would think if he took a peep at her and saw all the sins weighing down her soul.

And now all that was over. As she had been wearily climbing the stairs she had seen, on the edge of her vision, a shadow, a shade which she had been almost sure was that of her guardian angel, almost visible but not quite, in the very corner where she had always appeared to Polly.

I'm meself again . . . though I'm goin' to miss that Sunny tarble bad, Polly thought drowsily as she said her prayers and then climbed into her little bed. It were fun while it lasted, but I t'ink not seein' Sunny again is for the best.

Just before she fell asleep, she thought of something else too. She thought of the friendship of Tad Donoghue, far away in Dublin, Tad who had taken care of her and given her Lionel as a kitten and teased her and played with her, but had never led her into bad or sinful ways.

It was a pity, she thought, that Sunny was so handsome and Tad so plain. Of course, everyone knew that it wasn't looks which mattered, it was character, but she'd been awful proud to be seen out wit' Sunny, so she had, and now she would have to go around wit' girls again. And write to Tad and tell him . . . Or was it really necessary to tell him anything, save that she still thought about him all the time? She had boasted about Sunny's friendship, of course, but she need not actually admit that she didn't see Sunny any more. She would just write a nice, friendly letter . . . and with Tad she could be a little girl again, because he didn't expect anything else. Sunny's arm round her in the cinema, his habit of kissing her nose and tousling her hair, was something she would not miss at all. It was all a bit worrying and grown-up, and was one of the reasons, she realised now, that she had not been too dreadfully unhappy over her promise not to have anything to do with him in future.

She had not yet dropped off when her bedroom door opened softly and she saw her mammy. Once, she would have feigned sleep but now, because of the guilt she felt, she stirred and opened her eyes to smile at the figure in the doorway.

'Not asleep yet? Well, it's been a long day so it has but it's over now, and forgotten. Tomorrow's a fresh day for a fresh start. All right, acushla?'

'I'm fine, Mammy,' Polly whispered. 'Will you come and give me a butterfly kiss now, and tell me you aren't still in a bate wit' me?'

Deirdre with Peader, hovering behind her came and gave Polly the required butterfly kiss and then a cuddle. 'Oh, Polly, I can never be in a rage wit' you for more than a few minutes,' she said. 'Go to sleep now and forget all about today. As for tomorrow, it's another day as they say in the song. Goodnight, alanna.'

'Goodnight Mammy, Daddy,' Polly whispered. 'I'll sleep good now – I've said me prayers and I saw me guardian angel as I come up the stairs . . . just a shadow, you know, but she's there again so she is.'

Deirdre smiled, then bent and kissed her. 'All's right wit' the world, then,' she said softly. 'Sleep well, me darlin' daughter.'

Chapter Six

DECEMBER 1939

It was a cold day and Polly, emerging from Blackler's with her arms full of packages, paused for a moment on the pavement to put down her burdens whilst she straightened the belt of her navy-blue coat and pulled on her knitted mittens. As she did so her breath fanned out like fog round her and she gave a little shiver, then glanced up at the lowering sky. It wasn't snowing yet, but it was cold enough; they might have a white Christmas.

Someone else came through the swing doors and stopped short just behind Polly's packages. It was Ivan, also heavily laden, saying in a plaintive voice: 'Hey, our Poll, wharrabout that cup o' tea you said we'd have, eh? And them iced buns, an' all? It's hours an' hours since me dinner an now I'm that hungry me belly thinks me throat's been cut!'

Polly turned and surveyed her small brother. He was right, she had promised him tea and a bun if he came Christmas shopping with her, and he had been remarkably patient for a ten-year-old, waiting whilst she searched the big store for suitable presents for everyone. He had not suggested that they tried elsewhere either, knowing as he did that Polly, who worked part-time at Blackler's on a Saturday, got a staff discount which meant that she could buy the best without having to pay top prices. During the week she was an office junior in a very large firm of accountants on Sir Thomas Street, and on a Monday, Wednesday and Friday she went to evening classes to learn shorthand and typewriting, so no one could have said that Polly did not work hard. What was more, she gave Ivan tuppence a week pocket money, so she felt entitled to ask for help from him now and then.

'Oh aye,' she said vaguely now, however. 'But where'll we go, Ivan? It looks to me as if the whole world and his wife are out Christmas shoppin' this afternoon, and I don't fancy fightin' me way into one of the posh teashops and then havin' to wait hours to get served. How about if we go straight home and I make you a nice butty and a cuppa?'

She hefted her parcels again but Ivan was shaking his head. 'No, Poll,' he said obstinately. 'You *said* we'd go to a teashop, an' I've gorra thirst on me that can't wait till we's home. Can't we go to Cooper's, on Church Street? They do lovely cakes an' buns . . . doughnuts, an' all.'

Polly thought about reminding Ivan that there was a war on, but she had had it said to her so often now, that it was beginning to lose a good deal of its menace. Back in September, when war had been declared, they had all been very frightened indeed; Mammy had talked about going back to Dublin and Martin had joined the Navy whilst Bev, who had been about to go back to university, had thrown it all up and joined the Air Force. Only there had been a hold-up – too many young men trying to join the forces all at the same time, Peader had said wisely – and though Martin had got a ship and left his nice new house and Monica – quite quickly – Bev was still mooching around at home, neither one thing nor the other, he said gloomily, waiting for his papers to arrive.

'Poll? Aw, c'mon, it's only fair, I've done what you said, haven't I?'

152

Polly, who fancied a cup of tea herself, capitulated. 'You're right, Ivan me boy,' she said, turning in the direction of Church Street. 'We'll go to Cooper's – why not? Mammy won't be home yet, and Daddy will be havin' a nice sit-down before he puts the kettle over the fire and the spuds on to boil. Anyway, we'll probably have to walk home – look at the tram queues!'

'I don't mind walkin' if I've had me tea first,' Ivan said equably. 'And you're used to walkin', ain't you, Poll? You often walk to work an' back when you want to save your tram fare.'

'That's right,' Polly admitted. 'But I'm not usually all hung about wit' parcels, like a bleedin' Christmas tree. And don't tell the mammy I swore,' she added hastily, 'or you'll not have one iced bun, let alone a doughnut!'

'It's funny how cross the mammy gets over swearin', ain't it, Poll?' Ivan enquired, trudging along beside her. He was wearing a stiff navy coat much too big for him, grey socks which hung wrinkled around his ankles where they tended to end up if he forgot to put on his garters, and a large checked cap. When war was declared Blackler's had decided to do a half-price sale and the O'Bradys had been at the head of the queue which had formed on the first morning, thanks to Polly's advance information, so Ivan was now wearing on his back clothing which, his mammy had said gloomily, might have to last him for several years if the shortages being predicted came to pass.

'Swearing's wrong,' Polly said judiciously. 'Only what with the war, an' all, Ivan, us young folks have to relieve our feelings somehow. Only not in front of mammies and daddies,' she added. 'Come on, best foot forward!'

The pair of them turned into Church Street and headed for Cooper's, but before they had reached that haven of tea and buns, Ivan gave a squeak. 'Polly, you 'member that feller Mammy told you never to go out with again? The feller wi' the yaller hair? That's him, ain't it?'

Polly stopped short and followed the direction of his pointing finger. Ahead of them, a tall figure strode jauntily along the pavement, a figure topped with a good deal of wheat-coloured hair, though some of it was hidden beneath a sailor's hat.

'I think you're right, so I do,' Polly said, suddenly beginning to snatch the parcels from her young brother's arms. 'Yes, I'm sure it's Sunny . . . Oh, give me the stuff you're holdin', Ivan, and then you run and stop him for me! 'Cos I can't get up any real speed wit' all these bleedin' packages in me arms!'

'Oh! But Mammy said—' Ivan began, only to be abruptly cut short.

'When Mammy said that I was only a kid, and there wasn't a war on! He's in uniform – a sailor's uniform – if I don't stop him now I might never see him again! Run, Ivan, there's a good feller!'

Ivan accordingly dumped the rest of his parcels in Polly's arms and set off at a canter along the crowded pavement, dodging the people and shouting apologies as he went. Polly, with bumping heart, leaned against the nearest shop window and prayed that Sunny would not suddenly disappear as abruptly as he had done over two years ago, after the row with her mammy.

He had not disappeared at first, of course. Despite her promises, she could not simply shut her eyes to the tall, yellow-topped figure which lounged outside the school, popped up when she was doing Mammy's messages, appeared in church, head devoutly bent, eyes fixed burningly upon hers. But although she shed many tears over it, she had been true to her promise. Not a word had he got out of her for all his pleadings, and whenever possible she had avoided him altogether. And then one day she realised that she had not seen him for a week . . . two . . . three. She had asked her friend Alice to find out what had happened to Sunny Andersen and after a while, Alice had reported back that he had left the 'Pool. No, she did not know where he had gone, but she had been told that he and his mother had moved out of the old house. Did Polly want Alice to go round and ask the people who lived there where the Andersens had gone?

But Polly's conscience, which had been extremely uneasy over her tentative enquiries, had made it clear that asking for news of his whereabouts from his old school pals was one thing, cross-questioning the neighbours quite another. So Polly said no, it didn't matter, that it was best left, and Alice, greatly relieved – for she had never thought Sunny a good influence on her friend – had put the whole matter of Sunny's whereabouts out of her mind.

But right now Polly could see Ivan haring along the pavement and the yellow head bobbing along, the distance between the two lessening, and it occurred to her that after so long, the feeling between herself and Sunny must have changed. In the time since her mammy had put a stop to their friendship Sunny would undoubtedly have had several other girl-friends. And she had been friendly with several boys, though she knew that none of them had come any-where near being as good a friend as Sunny had once been. So what would happen when they met up again? Would they seem like two strangers, or would they fall immediately into the happy friendship – no, it had been warmer than mere friendship – which they had once shared?

But it seemed she was not to find out, for suddenly she realised that Ivan had turned round and was heading back towards her – and that the yellow head in the jaunty sailor's hat had disappeared.

'The bloody feller must have gone down a side street, or into one of the perishin' shops,' Ivan panted, coming up to her once more and beginning to reclaim his parcels. 'Cripes, I never run so hard before . . . not through a crowd o' people doin' their Christmas shoppin', that is. Sorry, Polly, but I did me best.'

'So you did, Ivan,' Polly said, realising that she was not sure whether to be glad or sorry that her brother had not caught up with her old friend. 'Oh well, mebbe it weren't him, after all. But I've not forgot me promise and after all that runnin' I reckon you deserve an ice as well as a couple o' cakes. Let's get into Cooper's and bag a table before they're all taken.'

But seeing that glimpse of someone who might well have been Sunny Andersen had definitely started something so far as Polly was concerned. She ate an ice and two doughnuts and drank several cups of tea and she laughed and joked with Ivan and marvelled at his ability to eat her under the table, but all the time she was wondering, wondering. She was almost sure that it was Sunny she had seen which meant that he had come back to Liverpool, even though, since he was in uniform, this might well be only a flying visit. And she was fifteen, going on sixteen – surely that was old enough to meet up with a young man who had once been her good friend? She had promised her parents that she would avoid

Sunny, have nothing to do with him, but she had only been thirteen then, and in school. Now she was working, earning her own living. That must mean, surely, that she could choose her own friends?

'Poll, is there another cup o' tea in that pot?' Ivan suddenly shouted, his face only inches from hers. 'Dear God, girl, is it deaf you're goin' now you're gettin' old? Because I've asked you ten times if I've asked you once!'

'Oh . . . sorry, I was just thinkin',' Polly excused herself, reaching for the pot and taking off the round brown lid. 'I'll get the waitress to bring some more water, then we can both have another cup.'

'I t'ought you must be thinkin' about that Sunny feller, moonin' across the table wit' a soppy smile on your 'ole face,' Ivan observed, when the waitress had supplied them with another jug of hot water. 'And I 'membered Mammy hadn't liked him overmuch. Mebbe I shouldn't have chased him for you, Poll.'

'It's ages since Mammy said she didn't like him,' Polly said, pouring tea. 'Anyway, it probably wasn't him at all – you know what it's like when you t'ink you know someone – when you catch them up it's always someone else altogether. Thanks for tryin', though, Ivan. You're a good little feller, so you are.'

'Tha's okay,' Ivan said magnanimously. He smiled hopefully. 'D'you want the last doughnut, Poll? Only there's a chink left in me belly just about the size o' that doughnut!'

Tad was saying goodbye to Dublin and the life he had known there, standing on the station platform and waiting to board the train which would take him across the water to join up. He looked wistfully at Angela as they stood in the pale wintry sunshine, hand in hand and neither far from tears, because their friendship had become a precious thing to them and they both, he thought, dreaded the separation to come. But for him there was the consolation of seeing Polly again – a Polly almost full grown and not the ten-year-old who had left Dublin almost six years ago – whereas for Angela there was nothing like that to look forward to. She would be terribly lonely – though he hoped that she might make more girl-friends, for he had always been aware of her lack of them. Polly, he also remembered, had had a *grosh* of girlfriends as well as a great many young fellers like himself, but that had been Polly the child, of course. He could not imagine her as a young woman, but he reflected that he could once have said the same of Angela, who had only been a kid, really, when they had first met. Now she was a beautiful, rather serious girl, seventeen years old and she had never wavered in her affection for him. Polly, on the other hand, he reminded himself sternly, had not just wavered, she had taken up with some English feller, and though she scarcely ever mentioned him now, Tad had not forgotten Sunny Andersen, even if she had. So he would meet Polly, he hoped, and renew their friend-ship, but it would not – could not – be the same sort of friendship that he shared with Angela, for he and Angela meant to get married one of these fine days, when they were old enough and when he could afford it, of course.

Affording it might not have been all that far away either, had it not been for the war, for in the years since he had joined Barnes's garage Tad had become a first-rate mechanic. What was more, Mr Barnes told anyone who would listen that Tad had flair. 'He ought to be workin' wit' a racin' team, 'cos there's no one in Dublin can mend a puncture faster, and he's the quickest worker I've ever had on the oil changes. But there you are, it's happy he is wit' us, thank the good Lord.'

Only then the war had started, and Tad had got restless. Polly's letters, which had continued to come across the Irish Sea with great regularity, even when Tad's replies were less reliable, constantly referred to the war. They had a blackout over there, and the government said that food would be rationed, though it had not happened yet. But they had closed all the places of entertainment – picture houses, theatres, ballrooms – which seemed uncommonly mean to Tad – and to Polly as well. She had written discontentedly:

There's nothing for me and the mammy to do but knit for the soldiers and sailors and airmen. It's all right for the boys, they've joined up – Bev's going into the Air Force and Martin's in the Navy – but I'm too young for everything that's fun. Mammy says I should be thankful I can't be called up, but I'm not. I'd look nice in the WRN uniform, so I would, except for the horrible hat, which is just like the one they wore at the convent school – ugh! But I'll maybe go for to be a WAAF when I'm old enough; the colour would suit my eyes. Only they want girls on the land and I do love the countryside, so I do – they might let me take Delly!

Tad thought it highly unlikely that anyone would encourage a Land Girl to take a dog along to her place of work but wisely did not voice such thoughts in his next letter. He had learned, the hard way, that a quarrel which takes place in correspondence takes a long time to sort out and can leave lasting scars. Instead, he told Polly that she should come back to

Ireland. *'Your daddy's been poorly for a long while and would be better here,'* he wrote. *'And you're Irish, Polleen. Why should you stay over there and talk about fightin their war? We don't have this here blackout, nor we haven't closed cinemas. Come back, an bring your family.'*

But this had apparently been defeatist talk. Polly wrote back indignantly to say that only a coward would run away when the country she lived in was in trouble, and whatever she might be she was no coward, as she hoped Tad would acknowledge. Even Angela, to Tad's dismay, talked wistfully of uniforms, and she had a good job now working as a secretarial assistant in the Pensions Office. She constantly reminded Tad that one day she would be a secretary, earning even better money, so he considered that she should not be thinking of uniforms, and a war which was not her country's own. Advancement, for Angela, meant staying just where she was, whereas for himself . . .

'I dunno about this blackout, an' rationin',' Tad's mammy said when he read her bits out of Polly's letters. 'But I don't see how wc'll be after managin' to stay out of the war once it gets goin', for sure an' if enemy ships blockade British ports to starve 'em out, how will the food get to us? I'm after tellin' you, son, that t'ings won't be no easier here than over there, once the Germans get theirselves organised.'

But Tad did not believe it. The Irish and the Germans were *friends*, weren't they? Ireland and Britain had been at loggerheads for ever, so why should anyone expect Ireland to make things difficult for themselves just to please the ould enemy? Only . . . well, Polly was there, and several other O'Bradys, and he had a good few pals who had gone over to join up and fight against the Jerries. In the last war they had

called them Huns, Tad had thought inconsequentially, but now they were usually referred to as Jerries.
Like the pot under the bed was called a jerry, though
Tad had no idea why this should be so. But he
supposed that to each generation their own enemy,
and what had sounded right in 1914 was not quite
right in 1939.

He might have stayed in Dublin, enjoying his work
at Barnes's Garage, taking Angela to the cinema or the
theatre, going dancing on a Saturday, but for Phil,
who also worked in the garage.

'Me big brother Albert's joined the English Air Force,
an' it's desperate keen they are to get more fellers what
know a t'ing or two about engines an' the like,' he told
Tad eagerly one freezing afternoon when the two of
them were down in the inspection pit, trying to change
a shattered exhaust system for a new one. 'And the
engines in aircrafts is just like cars. Some of them are
even made by the same firms. They need mechanics –
fellers they can train to work on the aircraft engines an'
make sure they run sweet. Fellers like us, Tad.'

Tad stood up and banged his head against the old
exhaust which was covered in rust and mud yet
refused to budge. It was one hell of an impact, and a
good part of the exhaust shifted, covering Tad's hair
in rust. Tad cursed and gave the exhaust another
heave, causing it to wobble hopefully, then repeated
the remark. 'Aircraft engines? But we don't know
anything about 'em, Phil.'

'No, but nor do most fellers; that's why the Air Force
is willin' to teach you, if you join up and put down for
to work as a mechanic,' Phil said eagerly. 'I tell you
what, Tad, it'll help us in our trade when the war's
over, if we know a t'ing or two about aeroengines. I
t'ought if you'd be willin' to go, I'd go too.'

161

'To England?' Tad said doubtfully. He could not personally remember the Tans when they had rampaged through Ireland, but he could remember the stories about them all too clearly. They had killed this one and hung that one, fired buildings, raped women . . . But that had been a long while ago, and to wear a smart uniform and yet still work with engines was an ambition which burned in most of the mechanics who toiled in garages. And I've nothin' against the English now, Tad had reminded himself magnanimously as he and Phil heaved at the recalcitrant exhaust system. Some of them are grand, Polly says so and she should know. She's lived amongst 'em now for years and she's a girl what knows a bad 'un when she sees him. Oh aye, you can't pull the wool over our Polly's eyes!

So the long and the short of it had been that he and Phil had taken a day off and bought themselves train tickets to Belfast, where they had gone into a recruiting office to join the Royal Air Force. Time passed, and then on the very same day they both got letters telling them to make their way to England and to appear at Cardington, where they would be kitted out and sent for further training. So they gave in their notice to Mr Barnes and packed their bags and now here they were, Phil with his family clustered round, Tad with his hand warm in Angela's, having positively forbidden the Donoghue clan to come down to the station to see him off, for they had to make their way to England via Dundalk and Belfast, where they had been accepted by the RAF.

'It'll be hard enough sayin' goodbye to Angela,' he had told his mother and his younger brothers and sisters. 'But sayin' goodbye to you, wit' half Dublin lookin' on – well, I couldn't do it, I'd be blubberin' like a five-year-old. So I'll say goodbye at home and save me blushes.'

They had agreed, therefore, not to come, and he was glad, yet when departure time arrived and Phil's family surrounded him, he realised that he was also a little sorry. However, he hugged Angela, kissed her, and then told her to go; no point, he said, in hanging around, it would only make it harder for both of them.

He slogged his way on to the train and into a crowded carriage beside Phil, lugging his canvas bag. It held all his worldly goods and was, Tad reflected with grim humour, uncommonly light. Once he had slung his bag on to a seat he stood up and looked out of the window to give one last wave to Angela and one last look at as much as he could see of Dublin – and saw a small group of people coming on to the platform where they stood in a bunch, staring towards the train and waving desperately. He stared again, and all in a moment he realised that it was the kids – Liam, Kevin, Dougal, Annie clutching Sammy's dirty little paw, and Biddy, Meg and Eileen. Angela had not seen them, she was still gazing up at him where he stood, waving . . . he could see tears running down her cheeks. But somehow, at that moment what really mattered was that despite his strictures the kids had come to wave him off – and the mammy! She stood a little apart from the kids and she waved and waved . . . and now and then put up a hand to her cheek. And Phil, beside him, was shouting something, and the porters were running along the train slamming doors, someone was waving a green flag, Angela was standing back, dabbing at her eyes . . . and Tad felt tears on his own cheeks and waved and waved and waved, and didn't care that he

163

was crying – so was Phil, so was everyone within eyeshot. And presently the train gave a long, sad-sounding whistle and began to move and then the station began to recede, Dublin grew smaller and smaller, the people could no longer be distinguished, one from another . . . and the train whistled again as it picked up speed and the little houses they were passing became fewer and fewer, further and further apart. Tad and Phil were on their way to war!

They didn't talk much as the train ambled its slow way across the Irish countryside. When they reached Dundalk however they had to leave the train and queue up for customs and for the first time a nagging doubt assailed Tad that the customs officers might guess they were leaving Eire for the war.

'What'll we do if they turn us back,' he muttered to his friend as they shuffled forwards. 'We'd never live it down, so we wouldn't.'

'We'd have to try again tomorrow,' Phil said philosophically. 'Oh janey, I wish I didn't have this old suitcase. Suppose they make me open it?' However such doubts soon proved groundless. There were a great many young men crossing over, mostly armed with bags or suitcases, and though Tad and Phil both told the official that they were taking outgrown clothes to a younger cousin living in south Belfast the officer merely grinned at them, marked their cases with a chalk cross and sent them back to the train to continue their journey across the border.

'Well, that's a relief,' Tad said as he sank once more into his corner seat. 'Another few hours, Phil and we'll be seeing England for the first time. It was hard leavin' me fambly but I know we're doin' the right thing!'

Despite himself, Tad was impressed with Liverpool. Come to that, he told himself, as the ferry passengers began to descend at the Pier Head, he had been impressed by Belfast, which was a larger city than he had expected to find north of the border. But the waterfront, with the huge buildings lining the edge of the River Mersey and the great Liver birds with their half-open wings outlined against the noonday sky, was awe-inspiring. So this is where my Polly lives, Tad thought as he and Phil joined the others making their way down on to dry land once more. I hope I'll be able to find her in this scrimmage – but then I know the address, I can see a grosh of trams waiting alongside the dock . . . I'll find her all right!

'Let's book into a boarding house first, though, Tad,' Phil said when Tad asked him if he could amuse himself whilst he, Tad, went and visited his pal. 'If it's all the same to you I'll come along too. I don't fancy bein' left in a foreign city all by meself.'

'All right,' Tad agreed with assumed reluctance – assumed because he suddenly realised that it could take him quite a time to find this Titchfield Street place of the O'Bradys. They were on the Goree Piazza now, and Tad remembered Polly telling him, in one of her letters, that it had been here that the slaves had been sold long ago. 'Look, there's a pub – the Vaults – see it? We'll try there, most pubs can put a feller up for a night or so.'

'It'll probably be noisy, but it's only for the one night,' Tad said as the two of them went into the beer-smelling, sawdust-floored barroom. The bar was deserted but the two young men could hear voices coming from the back somewhere. Tad dropped his bag on the floor and rapped on the counter, shouting:

'Anybody home? You've got customers!' He lowered his voice again, and addressed his friend. 'Eh, I can't wait to find Poll again – it's been five *years*, Phil. She'll have changed a good deal, I daresay.'

'You've changed a good deal yourself,' Phil said just as a fat, slovenly-looking woman came through from the back and grinned at them, showing a fine array of black and broken teeth. 'Oh, mornin', missus. We're after wantin' a room, just for the night, you understand. And we'll be off early in the mornin', so we will, for we're bound for the station.'

'One betwixt the two of ye?' the woman said. 'I'm the landlady, by the way – Mrs Collett. Folly me, fellers – just off the Irish boat, are ye? I've relatives across the water meself.'

'That's it; we're headed for Cardington, to join the Air Force,' Tad said. 'I expect you can tell us the way to Lime Street Station?'

'Oh aye,' Mrs Collett said. She crossed the bar, her downtrodden slippers scuffing two clear patches in the sawdust on the floor, and headed for a blackened open staircase in a corner of the room. 'The Air Force, is it? Most of 'em's joinin' the Navy, I'd ha' said.'

'We're mechanics,' Tad told her. 'I say, missus, you don't happen to know Titchfield Street, I suppose? It's near St Sylvester's church, I know that much. Can we walk there, d'you suppose? Only I've a pal lives thereabouts – several pals. I thought I'd look 'em up whilst I'm in the city.'

The woman stopped at the head of the stairs to consider the question with a wrinkled brow. 'Titchfield Street. Oh aye, that'll be one of them roads near the Scottie, I don't know exactly which one it is. Well, lads, you could walk but your best bet will be to catch a number 43 or 44 tram from the Pier Head and get off at Burlington Street and then ask again. There's folks which will be able to tell you all right and tight once you get that far.'

'Thanks very much,' Tad said gratefully as she flung open a door and gestured them inside. The room was quite large with a lofty ceiling and a big sash window overlooking the Piazza, and the bed was a double one with a sagging mattress and a darned white sheet folded down on to a faded pink cotton bedspread. The washstand was old-fashioned and marble-topped and the wardrobe looked large enough to house a regiment of soldiers, but despite Mrs Collett's unkempt appearance the room was clean and the bedlinen fresh enough. 'And this looks fine, so it does. What d'you say, Phil?'

'How much?' Phil said immediately and the woman grinned again, then pushed a lock of lank brown hair off her forehead with a fat, pink-palmed hand. 'Half a crown each,' she said, adding hastily: 'There's a war on an' call for me rooms, you see. That includes breakfast, an' I'll do a dinner at seven for one an' six a head.'

'That'll suit us,' Tad said. 'Shall we have a dinner, Phil, or would you rather get some fish an' chips?'

'A dinner,' Phil said at once. He slung his own bag on to the washstand and held out his hand. 'Can we have the key, please?'

'Oh aye, when I've 'ad me five bob,' Mrs Collett said, chuckling. 'I waren't born yesterday, fellers.'

Tad and Phil handed over the money and closed the door behind their landlady, then grinned at each other. 'She's all right,' Tad said. 'But we'd better get a move on, old feller. Are you sure you want to come all the way out to Titchfield Street, though?'

'I won't come all the way, but I've heard about the

167

Scottie – that's the Scotland Road, isn't it?' Phil said, going over to the washstand and pouring water into the blue and white china basin. 'There's shops galore, all sorts . . . I've an uncle in the Navy and he says he never leaves Liverpool without visiting the Scottie – and somewhere called Paddy's Market, an' all. So if we go up together, we can come back separate.'

'Right. And look, Phil, if me luck's in I'll get asked in for me tea, very like, so if I'm not back by six, just explain to Mrs What's-her-name, will you?'

'Sure I will, so,' Phil said peacefully. He began to wash his face, not bothering with soap, ducked his head under the water briefly and then smarmed his hair flat to his scalp with both hands. 'Your turn now, Tad.'

Tad found Titchfield Street without difficulty, but as he had feared, the house was empty. He knocked as hard as he could, and even went round the back, but then, shrugging, he did the only thing he could. He wrote:

Dear all,
    I'm off on the train to Bedford tomorrow morning, early, but thought I'd just nip in and see you whilst I was in Liverpool. Will come back later, and hope there's someone home. All the best,
    Tad Donoghue.

He shoved this brief epistle through the letter box in the front door and then headed back to the Scotland Road, where he met up with Phil almost at once, since he had been such a short while away.

'I'm coming back this evening, around eight,' he

told Phil. 'They're all out so I left 'em a note, but at least this means that Poll can make sure she's in when I come back. Now what'll we do?'

'Take a look around,' Phil said. 'There's a grosh of shops and stuff's cheap compared with home, so it is. We'll ask the way to Paddy's Market presently – that's good, I've heard a thousand fellers say so.'

'Right,' Tad said. He was happy to do anything which would occupy the time between now and eight o'clock. 'There's some dining rooms just up the road, I passed 'em on my way back to you. We might get a meal there, or at least tea and a bun.'

Phil agreed and the two young men began to examine the shop windows.

At a quarter to eight Tad was walking along the Scotland Road once more, anticipation tightening into knots in his stomach. Very soon he would be seeing Polly after rather more than five years, and he found that her old magic was still at work. Angela might be his girlfriend, but he suspected that Polly would always have a special place in his heart.

So Tad trod the pavement with the palms of his hands damp and his heart beating overtime. His hair had been Brylcreemed to his head but because of its tendency to curl, it had not remained fashionably sleek for long. Still, Polly wouldn't mind, she wasn't a girl, Tad knew, to be taken in by appearances. Nevertheless he had done his best. A brand-new tie, checked in red and blue, was definitely eye-catching and the white of his brand-new shirt could have scarcely been surpassed. He had polished his best black shoes until he could see his face in them and despite the cold he had not worn his overcoat, which was a sight too small for him, though he carried it over one arm – no point in getting caught in a downpour and half-freezing to death.

It was very dark in the street now without any shop windows blazing and with what traffic there was showing only the cold, dim blue light of the special lamps the regulations allowed. People, mainly dark-clad, passed him, the pale ovals of their faces just about visible once your eyes got used to the gloom. Good thing there was a moon, Tad reflected, otherwise God knows how folk in cities managed to make their way about. And you took your life in your hands when you crossed the road; bicycles, for the most part, did not bother with lights at all and dashed along at a good old rate, the riders trusting to speed and their ability to swerve to save themselves from becoming killers or corpses.

He was about to cross over himself, in fact, when he saw a small group of people coming towards him. One of them, a girl, had primrose hair of such fairness that you could see it gleaming silver in the moonlight, and although he could only see the blur of her face, there was something familiar . . .

'Sure an' wouldn't I get out early when it's your last leave, me dearest?' the girl said, as she and the young man on whose arm she swung came alongside Tad. 'Nothin' would have made me stay late tonight, not if they'd been willin' to pay me a fortune!'

'Polly?' Tad said uncertainly. 'Is it yourself, Poll?'

The girl half-turned her head. Her face, in the moonlight, was all white and silver, the eyes hidden in the deep shadow, her mouth half-open still in speech. She said: 'Who's you when you're at home?'

The young man on whose arm she hung, however, had no intention of allowing her to stand in the street exchanging small talk with a stranger. He gave her arm a sharp tug, pulling her past Tad. 'She's me girl, an' she don't know you, no more'n I do,' the young man said sharply. 'Wharrer you think you're doin', accostin' a young lady in the street? Come on, Poll,' and he pulled her sharply away.

Tad stood for a moment, sick with horror. His Polly, behaving in such a way! Well, she had changed and no mistake – she'd not recognised him, her old playfellow, for a start off, and wasn't that a dreadful thing, for she should have been expecting him, having, he assumed, read his note when she got home.

For a moment he stood, irresolute, on the edge of the pavement. Then, very slowly, he turned back the way he had come, feeling more miserable than ever before. She had looked at him and not recognised him! She had allowed herself to be pulled away from him by a young feller she must, clearly, think pretty highly of to have treated her old friend so. Well, no point in going round to Titchfield Street now, he might as well take himself back to his lodgings and go to bed. They had an early start in the morning, best get a good night's sleep.

By the time he reached the Vaults, of course, he was beginning to have second thoughts. He sat in the downstairs bar drinking beer and playing poker with Phil and a couple of lads who had just signed on as ratings in the Navy, puzzling over the nasty little encounter. He was no longer at all sure that it had been his Polly – Polly O'Brady – that he had met in the darkened street. There must be a hundred girls called Polly in Liverpool, and probably a good few of them lived on or near the Scotland Road. And as for the hair, there were hundreds of blondes in Dublin which probably meant thousands in this great city. Most of them were bottle blondes, he knew, but he could not always tell the difference between bleached and natural even in daylight, and moonlight was the trickiest light there was, just about.

He had not said too much to Phil, only that he had missed Polly, who had gone out, but now he got to his feet a little uncertainly. 'Could you go on wit'out me, fellers?' he said rather thickly, for he did not normally drink more than a pint in one evening and now his score was at least three. 'I think I'm after going back to Titchfield Street to see if me pal's back yet.'

'You can't do that, Tad,' Phil said. 'It's after ten o'clock, so it is, and the family will be in bed and won't thank you for disturbing them. Besides, after this hand we'd best make our way to bed ourselves. We don't want a black mark against us at the very start because we've missed the bloody train!'

So Tad had sat down again, and presently the game finished, with Tad, oddly enough, four shillings the richer, when you thought how far his mind had been from the game, and the four of them made their way to bed. Tad decided, as he pulled the blankets up round his ears, that he must write to Polly first thing, and make some excuse for not turning up in Titchfield Street. The more he thought about the encounter, the more he became convinced that the girl he had met had not been Polly.

But a letter will explain it all, he thought sleepily, trying to keep to his own half of the bed, for Phil, already snoring, kept kicking and heaving at the covers. I'll write before I have my breakfast tomorrow, so's she'll understand.

'I waited in all evening, so I did, and not a bleedin' sign of the feller did I see,' Polly told her friend Alice

172

next morning as they waited for the tram which would take them into the city centre. 'But something must have come up – Tad's very reliable as a rule. Or he was when we all lived in Dublin. I can't imagine him letting me down, not if he was able to come.'

'Oh well, once they're in the forces their time ain't their own,' Alice agreed cheerfully. 'He'll write and explain, I daresay.'

'Sure to,' Polly agreed, but she was rather cross with Tad no matter how she might excuse him to others. This was the first time they'd been within shouting distance of one another and he had failed to turn up – and he'd missed out on a treat too, so he had. Mammy had cooked a lovely supper and she, Polly, had baked a load of fruit buns. She had cooled them and parcelled them up and had meant to give them to him to eat on the train, and even this morning she'd not had the heart to hand them round to the rest of the family. Who knew, he might have meant this evening, he might yet turn up on their doorstep, stammering and apologetic, explaining how the mistake had happened. She would save the buns for one more day and if he did not come tonight, she and Ivan would eat them, which would show him!

All through the rest of the day, every time the office door opened, Polly glanced up hopefully, but there was no sign of a square figure with close-cropped hair and an anxious expression, so that evening the buns were ceremoniously served after tea and Polly got out a book and began to read, though in fact she was listening so hard for a sound on the doorstep and a knock on their door that she scarcely turned a page all evening.

'You know Tad, he'd not let you down,' Deirdre said comfortably when Polly put aside her book and said she might as well be off to bed. 'He'll write and explain, alanna, never you fret.'

'Oh, it doesn't matter,' Polly said with elaborate casualness which, she suspected, would not deceive her mother in the least. 'There's other times. Tad'll get leaves, I expect. Bedford isn't far away, like Dublin. He'll turn up again, like a bad penny.'

'So he will,' Peader said heartily. 'I must have stepped down to the Post Office when he come knockin' the first time. It's a pity, but there'll be other times.'

Agreeing, Polly trailed up the stairs . . . and saw, out of the corner of her eye, that the slight shape of her angel was not in its usual position at the bend in the stairs. Oh well, I'm growing up, so I am, Polly reminded herself, climbing the rest of the stairs and pushing open her bedroom door. Besides, she can't be there all the time . . . Oh, janey, I can't write to Tad, I've not got an address any more! Still, he'll write to me, I know he will. And with that she began her preparations for bed, pushing Tad's strange behaviour to the back of her mind, or trying to do so. Instead, however, she found herself thinking defiantly that Sunny would not have behaved so; if he had been able to come and see her he would most certainly have done so, even if he had got into the most awful trouble as a result.

Much comforted by this thought, Polly climbed into bed and presently slept.

Chapter Seven

Despite the war, the O'Bradys intended to have a good Christmas, and it certainly began well, Polly thought on Christmas Eve, as she joined the rest of the family round the fire. Peader was roasting chestnuts on the coal shovel, Bevin was whittling a whistle out of a smooth piece of pine, and Polly and her mother were knitting. Polly worked laboriously, Deirdre with precision and speed, so that the wool seemed to spin through her fingers and the needles clicked so rapidly that she sounded like a sewing machine, Polly thought enviously. Her own needles clashed together ever slower and Polly noticed, with annoyance, that she had dropped a stitch at some time or other and the resultant hole had now formed a small ladder which did little to add to the attraction of the khaki scarf she was making.

Sitting comfortably in the living room, Polly could hear an occasional gust of rain hitting the window panes and knew a moment of intense happiness – there is nothing like foul weather outside and a good fire inside to warm the cockles of your heart, she told herself, reaching for a roasted chestnut. Another gust made her think of Martin out on a tossing ocean with no warm fire, no chestnuts and precious little Christmas cheer. I'll write to him later, Polly told herself, and I'll work harder at the knitting. Earlier, she and Ivan had dressed the tree, with Polly's Christmas angel sitting demurely on the topmost bough and candy walking sticks, shiny silver and gold balls and small, gaily-wrapped presents hanging from every branch, and Polly was just covertly admiring it and wondering which of the little presents was for her when someone knocked at the front door. Ivan, who was nearest, pulled a face but got to his feet. 'It'll be bleedin' Alice, for you,' he muttered to his sister, but he kept his voice down, for although Deirdre and Peader both realised the inevitability of their younger son losing his Dublin brogue and picking up the local accent, they did not approve of the local swear words which were frequently on that same son's lips.

'It won't be Alice,' Polly said, but she turned towards the door nevertheless. 'Alice's mam was takin' her to see her gran tonight; they won't be back until ever so late, so they're goin' to Midnight Mass. Then they won't have to mess up Christmas mornin' by goin' to church. I wouldn't mind goin' to Midnight meself, so I wouldn't.'

Peader, fishing hot chestnuts from the ashes, said mildly: 'Communion doesn't mess up your Christmas mornin', alanna, it gives meanin' to it,' but Deirdre, still furiously knitting, looked up and smiled at Polly, though she shook her head a little reprovingly too.

'It's a period of calm in a busy day, so it is,' she said. 'And if you'd cooked as many Christmas dinners as I have, Polleen, you'd appreciate that quiet time more. If it's not Alice . . .'

But any more conjecture was banished by the sound of steps in the hallway, the door opening and Ivan ushering Monica into the room. In the years which had elapsed since they had left the crossing cottage nothing which Monica had said or done had

176

endeared her any further to the family and Polly endeavoured to see as little as possible of her sister-in-law. Furthermore, when Martin had joined up Monica had moved out of their house and back in with her parents, who now lived in Southport, so there was a moment of astonished silence before a babble of conversation broke out.

'Monica, my dear! What in heaven's name are you doin' miles from home at this hour on Christmas Eve? What's happened? Is there – is there news of – of—' That was Deirdre, who had jumped to her feet at the sight of her daughter-in-law. She sat down suddenly, white to the lips. 'Oh my God!'

'Come in and sit down, girl,' Peader said comfortably. He turned to his wife. 'Don't you worry, alanna, Martin's fine; I'm sure that's what Monica's come to tell us, isn't it, eh?'

'What are you doin' here, Monica?' That, of course, was Polly, straight to the point as usual. 'I thought you'd moved back in wit' your mammy an' daddy. I thought you were all in Southport.'

'Sit down, girl, an' have a roast chestnut. Daddy's got a grosh of 'em ready.' That was Bevin, always the most phlegmatic of young men. 'Mart's all right, I'm sure of it. I'll go and put the kettle on, Mammy.'

Monica, who had listened to the babble of talk without uttering a word in reply, shook her head rather feebly when Peader proferred the nut and began to struggle out of her coat, talking as she did so. 'It – it's all right. I'm sorry I frightened you, Mrs O'Brady, I didn't mean to. I – I've heard from Martin and everything's fine. But me mam and dad took it into their heads to go up to Scotland to have Christmas and to see the New Year in with my aunt Pearl and uncle Alfred, and I – I didn't want to be so

far away . . . I got the idea that Martin might be gettin'
home for Christmas, you see, and Southport's a long
way from Liverpool, and so I thought . . . I thought . . .'

'He's written? Oh, thank the dear Lord for that,'
Deirdre said passionately. 'We've not heard . . . but I
know it's difficult when a feller's at sea. When did
you hear?'

'A letter come yesterday,' Monica said, shivering
and holding out her hands to the blazing fire. Polly
saw that her sister-in-law was very pale, without a
trace of make-up for once, and that her usually
smooth, carefully cut hair hung in rats' tails round her
face. 'He s-said it didn't matter that I'd moved out of
the house, he was sure I'd have a good Christmas,
though it was unlikely, even if he got leave, that he
could get all the way to Southport in the time he had
ashore. So I thought . . . if you didn't mind . . . you see
it's much easier for Martin to come to this house . . .'

'Of course we don't mind,' Peader said in his slow,
placid voice. 'You'll have to share wit' Polly, but no
doubt you realised that. And as you say, when Mart
gets home he'll want to see you right away, an' if
you're stayin' wit' us you're a good deal nearer than
if you were wit' your own parents. Did you bring a
few clothes? A bag?'

'It's outside,' Monica muttered. Polly saw that the
colour was beginning to return to her cheeks and that
her trembling hands were lying more quietly in her
lap. 'In case . . . in case you couldn't fit me in, an' I had
to go to a hotel . . . I'll bring it in.'

'I'll gerrit,' Ivan said. He sounded resigned rather
than pleased, and Polly quite understood why. This
would have been the first Christmas since Martin's
marriage that they had not had Monica and Martin to
stay and had had to struggle with Monica's obvious

urge to be anywhere but with her in-laws over the holiday, and they had all been looking forward to it. Of course, Ivan would be very sorry that Monica was in such a taking, but that didn't mean he was any fonder of her now than he had been ten minutes earlier! 'I'll take it up to Polly's room, shall I, Mammy?'

'Yes, please, Ivan. You're a good feller,' Deirdre said. She stood up and took Monica's coat, then frowned. 'It's wet – is it rainin', Monica?'

'It's pouring,' Monica said. She shivered again, and rubbed her hands over her wet face. 'Oh, I feel ever so odd, Mrs O'Brady, I think . . . I think . . .'

'She's goin' to faint,' Peader said, and tried to jump to his feet as Monica sagged sideways in the chair, but his movements were still slow and his wife was before him. She reached Monica in one bound and pushed the younger woman's head between her knees, then shouted to Bevin to make a cup of hot, sweet tea and bring it through as quickly as he could.

'The girl's wore out an' frightened half to death, what wit' the blackout an' the journey from Southport and her parents goin' off wit'out her,' she declared roundly, pushing Monica's wet hair away from her eyes. 'What's more she's soaked to the skin. Polly, go up and fetch down a decent dressin' gown, your red one will be just fine, an' some warm clothes – socks, a jersey, stuff like that. We'll warm her up an' get her right in a moment.'

Polly pulled a face, but knew better than to say what she was thinking. She stomped off up the stairs and by the time she returned to the living room, carrying the clothing her mother had requested, Monica was stripped down to her brassiere and pink, embroidered cami-knickers whilst of Peader, Ivan and Bevin there was no sign. Polly raised her eyebrows at her mother as she handed over the clothing.

'In the kitchen, so's we could make the girl decent,' Deirdre said, reaching for the thick grey jersey which Polly had taken out of Bev's room. 'She's all floppy-like – giz a hand, Polleen, to get her into these warm t'ings.'

In ten minutes Monica, dressed in her borrowed finery, was sitting in the chair nearest the fire, sipping a hot cup of tea and explaining what had happened in a far quieter and more coherent fashion than she had been able to do earlier. 'Me mam and dad didn't realise I were going to try to stay in Southport alone,' she said between sips. 'I said I'd gerra friend in, only I don't know many folk in Southport yet. And – and it's a lonely house, or it seemed lonely once they'd gone. Only I'd ha' been all right, except that Martin's letter arrived. And – and I thought of him gerrin' home, and findin' his way here . . . and me up there in Southport all by me lonesome . . . Oh, Mrs O'Brady . . . Mam, I mean . . . I just couldn't bear it! So I put some things into me Gladstone bag and come as fast as I could, only I forgot me umbrella, and I missed the first bus . . . the feller wouldn't wait, though I waved and shouted . . . and a course I got awful wet an' cold . . .'

'Never mind, alanna, you're here now,' Deirdre cooed. 'Well, you're a lovely Christmas surprise, so you are, and Martin will be pleased as punch to find you here when he gets home. Now don't you worry about a t'ing, darlin', I'll get you a bite o' supper and then it's a warm bed for you, and sleep until mornin'. Polly, go an' make your sister some cheese on toast, wit' me homemade chutney on the side. Are the sheets on your bed clean?'

This was too much! Polly had often thought what fun it would be to have a sister, but Monica? Anyone but Monica! 'The sheets are clean enough for me,' Polly said, shooting a darkling glance at the new arrival. 'Whether they'll be clean enough for Monica I couldn't say, I'm sure. But I'll make the toasted cheese the best I can,' she added hastily, seeing a martial sparkle in her mother's eyes.

'Good. Now come along wit' me, Monica,' Deirdre said. She had dropped her knitting upon Monica's entrance but now she picked it up and put it on her chair, then took Monica's arm. 'Will toasted cheese suit you, me dear?' she enquired solicitously. 'It won't give you nightmares? Cheese can be after causin' nightmares, I forgot that when I telled Polleen to make you some.'

'It'll be just fine, Mrs— Mam,' Monica said, still in the small, faint voice which Polly scarcely recognised. 'Oh, you're so good, and I've been so—' She began to sob and Polly, feeling self-conscious, slipped past her and into the kitchen, closing the door behind her. Once there, she took a long, hard look at her feelings. Sure an' she didn't want Monica sharing her room, no she didn't, but the girl *was* Martin's wife, and she, Polly, was mortal fond of Martin, so she was. And it wouldn't be for long; Monica wouldn't stand being cooped up in the little house for longer than necessary. Then there was her job. Monica had got a good job in an expensive gown shop when she had moved to Southport – she would not want to whistle that down the wind, Polly was sure. Apart from anything else, Monica liked spending money, and Polly knew that the small amount which the Navy sent home to her from Martin's pay would scarcely help towards the rent, let alone provide for such things as stockings, lipstick or a few sweeties.

Much heartened by this thought, Polly set to with a will and very soon she had laid out a tray with an embroidered traycloth and put upon it a mug of hot cocoa, the toasted cheese, some chutney and a little dish of stewed apple and custard. She added a white table napkin in a bright red ring, knife, fork and spoon, and set off up the stairs, mounting each one carefully so that she should not spill anything on the cloth.

She went into her own small room and there was Monica, tucked up in her bed, with her hair now brushed, her face shining with soap and water and a smile back in position. Not that she smiled at Polly – not she! Her smiles, it seemed, were all for her mother-in-law, who she had treated so badly in the past.

'Here's your supper, Monica,' Polly said softly, putting the tray down across her sister-in-law's knees. 'I hope it's all right for you, so I do.'

'It looks very nice,' Monica said. 'Thank you, Polly.'

'It's a pleasure,' Polly said politely if untruthfully. 'Will I be goin' to bed soon, Mammy? Will I be head-to-tailing it wit' Monica, then?'

'No, not tonight,' Deirdre said. 'You can sleep downstairs tonight, on the sofa in the living room. You'll do very well there, just for one night.'

Polly drew in a breath to expostulate. It wasn't fair that she should have to give up her bed, and on Christmas Eve too, when heaven knew what angels and magic might be abroad, for even if she no longer believed in Santa Claus, she believed in the magic of Christmas. Then she let out her breath in a long, quiet sigh. 'Yes, all right, Mammy,' she said. 'What did you do wit' me nightie when you tucked Monica up? I'd best take it downstairs if I'm to sleep in the livin' room.'

'Oh, I feel so guilty, putting you out of your room, Polly,' Monica said, and she sounded almost as though she meant it. 'Oh, and cocoa – just what I like before I go to sleep.'

'Your nightie's here, on the chest of drawers, alanna,' Deirdre said, passing it over. 'Now we'll leave Monica to her supper. Mind you eat it all up, me dear, because you've had a tiring day by the sound of it.'

Oh, so Monica's been telling her what a rotten old day she's had, has she? Polly asked herself grimly as she made her way down the stairs again with her mother close on her heels. Well, she's not done much for my day either, turning up here and putting me out of me bed! But there was no use repining, it was the sofa for her tonight. And it would, Polly reflected, be rather fun to sleep downstairs, and to watch the lovely bright fire gutter and die, and to sneak into the kitchen and let Delly in with her, so that they could cuddle up on the sofa together. Old Tom the cat might like to join them – sleeping downstairs wouldn't be so bad, and she would be first to see the tree in the morning too.

Back in the living room again, she saw her parents exchange a speaking glance and reflected that happy though they would be to have Martin back with them, they, too, were not as thrilled about Monica's unexpected arrival as they had pretended. Indeed, once the boys had gone to bed Mammy came down again on the pretence of checking that the fire was damped down and bent over Polly to give her a kiss.

'I know you must feel a bit put-upon, alanna,' she whispered, carefully tucking the covers in on the makeshift bed. 'But we're doin' it for Martin's sake, remember. May you have sweet dreams, me darlin' girl, and wake to a good Christmas!'

Polly lay awake for a while, enjoying the novelty of being downstairs when the rest of the family were in their rooms, asleep. And presently she began to think how lucky she was, and to wonder how Tad felt, in his barracks or whatever it was, down in Cardington.

He had written, explaining that thanks to a misunderstanding he had been unable to come to the house as his note had promised; the forces, his letter had said vaguely, were like that. And Polly had written back at once, of course, telling him how sorry she was to have missed him and reminding him that the O'Bradys were almost always to be found in Titchfield Street, and he must not hesitate to come and see them if he ever had enough leave to make the journey possible.

He had not replied to the latest letter yet, but a pal of hers, Nobby Taylor, had told her that the first few weeks in any of the armed services were pretty hard, and that Tad would not have much time for letter-writing until he got his first posting, so that was all right.

Grace kept writing, though. She had been horrified when war had been declared and had written at once, to say she was coming home just as soon as she could make the necessary arrangements. '*I don't intend to stay safe over here while my country fights these Huns,*' she had written fiercely – Polly could almost see the frown on her face.

*I'm coming home and I'm going to fight as well, in
whatever way will help most. After all, I'm a Salvationist
and we're all soldiers, fighting evil and trying to do right.
But I can't leave Sara and Jamie in the lurch. I must make
arrangements. As soon as I've got a passage booked,
though, I'll write and tell you, so's I can come to stay. The
Strawb would have me – Matron writes almost as regular
as you, Poll – but I'll come to you first. The O'Bradys have
been as good as family to me, and that's the honest truth.*

At first, Polly had waited daily for the letter to
arrive, telling her when her dearest and best friend
expected to be on British soil once more, but the
weeks had passed and Grace had not been able to
'make arrangements' as easily as she had hoped, so
Polly was still waiting.

I'll be glad when Grace is home, Polly thought
sleepily to herself, eyes shut now but knowing, even
through her closed lids, that the firelight still
flickered. It would be fun if we could both join one of
the services together – but then I'm not old enough,
not yet.

Presently she fell asleep, and presently, too, she
dreamed. She seemed to awaken in the early hours to
find the fire out, the air chilly, and the Christmas tree
looking shadowy and rather frightening in the
darkened room. But she was snug enough in her
blankets and merely looked about the room in a wondering sort of way, until she noticed Tad's present, the
angel on the top of the tree, and it seemed to her that it
would be sensible to climb out of bed and go over to
have a word with her angel, now that it was almost
Christmas morning.

She looked up at the little angel, with its golden
hair, long white gown and gauzy wings. 'Merry

Christmas, angel,' she whispered up to it, and was sure that it smiled down especially for her. 'There's something I'd like to ask you, if you wouldn't mind.'

The little angel inclined her head very graciously, which Polly took to be a nice way of telling her to get on with it, so having thought for a moment she said slowly: 'A long time ago, me mammy and daddy telled me I wasn't to see Sunny again. He was me pal, but he got me to wag off school, so he did, and I did some pretty bad t'ings.'

The angel looked sorrowful yet encouraging, and it suddenly occurred to Polly that though her own guardian angel was neither golden-haired nor clad in gauzy white, the two of them shared, at this moment, very similar expressions. So Polly, who often talked to her guardian angel when she was unhappy or puzzled, went on. 'But that was ages ago, angel, when I were just a kid. Now I'm almost growed, and me and Ivan t'ought we saw Sunny a little while back, in naval uniform, walkin' along Church Street just the way he always did. So Ivan chased after him, but he got away. Now d'you t'ink it would be wrong of me, angel, to try to see him again?'

The angel bent down, lower and lower, and she no longer looked like the little Christmas angel but just exactly like Polly's own guardian angel. She began to answer Polly's question, speaking very low indeed, saying that surely Polly's mammy . . . And Polly reached up and reached up so that she might be near enough to catch every precious word . . . and woke, to find pale sunlight streaming through a crack in the curtains and her mammy softly brushing the piled-up ash off the top of the fire and lifting the coals with a poker to let the air in underneath so that it would blaze once more.

Polly must have stirred or muttered, for her mother turned round and smiled lovingly at her. 'Happy Christmas, Polleen – did you sleep well?' she whispered. 'There's only you an' me awake in the whole house, for I t'ought I'd let the fellers have a lie-in, and Monica's curled up like a dormouse and snorin' like a lion. Do you feel like gettin' up and helpin' me to make some breakfast?'

'Happy Christmas, Mammy,' Polly said, keeping her voice very low. 'You'll never guess what! I woke in the night and me angel leaned over me an' said—' She stopped short. It had been a dream, of course, and now that she thought about it, she had only caught a few of the words that the angel had addressed to her in the dream. Besides, she was fifteen and three-quarters and should be too old for chatting to any angel, either the one on the Christmas tree or the shadowy figure she sometimes saw on the extreme periphery of her vision. She sighed; how difficult it was to know what was real and what wasn't, even if she was fifteen and three-quarters.

'What did your angel say?' Mammy asked. She sometimes looked a bit apprehensive when Polly talked about her angel, but she never even hinted that there was anything odd about a child who conversed with someone no one else could see. 'I trust she gave you good advice, and told you to be kind to Monica?'

Polly giggled. 'I don't know what she was goin' to say, Mammy, but I t'ink what she *meant* to say was that I should tell you about me problem, an' not herself. The truth is, Mammy, Ivan an' me saw Sunny a few days ago. Just in the street, you know, not to speak to at all.'

'Sunny?' Deirdre said as though she did not know what Polly was talking about. 'Sunny what?'

'Sunny Andersen, the feller you said I wasn't to see again, and I haven't,' Polly explained, sitting up in her couch bed and hugging her knees. 'Only I'm old now, Mammy, and Sunny's in the Navy – at least he was wearin' that uniform – and I t'ought, if I bumped into him . . .'

'If you do, bring him home, acushla,' Mammy said gently. 'As you say, that other business was a long time ago, and I wouldn't want you to be upsettin' a feller what's fightin' for his country. Only bring him home, eh, alanna?'

'Oh, Mammy, I do love you!' Polly exclaimed. She hurtled off the sofa and flung herself into her mother's arms. 'I don't suppose he'll mind if I talk to him or not, because he's past eighteen now, and a man growed. But he was nice, and I'd like to bring him home, so I would.'

'Then that's settled,' Deirdre said. She pushed Polly gently towards the doorway. 'Can you wash in the kitchen, alanna, and dress there too? Then we'll make breakfast together once I've cleared this bed away and made the room neat.'

And presently Polly, washed, brushed and dressed, was slicing bread and laying the table and singing a carol as she did so, whilst upstairs various bumps and bangs seemed to intimate that the other members of the family were also getting up. She felt very happy, and at ease with herself in a comfortable sort of way. She *had* liked Sunny, and now that he was in the Navy he could scarcely get her into hot water – come to that, now she was working and not at school, surely the same applied?

So Polly continued to slice bread and sing and think happily about Christmas and wonder about the little packages on the tree, and the memory of Sunny's back vanishing into the Christmas-shopping crowds disappeared from her mind. Time enough to wonder what had been happening to him, time enough to plan how she would bring him home and introduce him to Mammy, Daddy and the rest of the family when they met up once more. For now, it was Christmas, her sister-in-law would be waking up and coming downstairs any time, and she must be really nice to the girl, for Martin's sake.

Oh the holly and the ivy, when they are both full grown
Of all the trees that are in the wood, the holly bears the
*   crown.*

So sang Polly, working happily away in the kitchen, on the first wartime Christmas she had ever lived through. The blackout curtains were pulled back and the thin wintry sunshine streamed into the room and Polly, at peace with the world even if the world itself was not at peace, was suddenly sure that Martin would come home safe and sound and that Sunny and she would meet up again, as friends. Nothing but good could come of such a day as this.

Martin's ship had docked at three on the Christmas afternoon and by four o'clock he was walking across the almost deserted, frosty dockside and thinking peacefully that he and the rest of the crew of the frigate *Campion* had been extremely lucky. Their engine had gone on the blink a couple of weeks back and the captain had turned back to port as soon as he could. So now most of the crew had five days' leave – and over Christmas too.

Martin had been as pleased as anyone when he had been given this break whilst the *Campion* was checked and repaired. He had applied to join the Navy in April, believing, despite Chamberlain's 'Peace in our time', that war would come all too soon, and had comforted Monica over his departure by telling her that at least, when war did come, he would be trained to face it. She had not been pleased, of course, had said that he was too eager to get away from his city job and their small house, had accused him of becoming tired of her, of marriage, of his life in the city. Because she was not so far out he had explosively denied all her accusations and what had started out as a discussion had speedily become a full-blown row, with the result that they had parted awkwardly, both aware, he supposed, that their relationship was less strong, after more than three years of marriage, than it had been when they first met.

But now, knowing that she was safely tucked away in Southport with her parents, he was preparing to reach Titchfield Street with almost boyish excitement. It would be good to see the family, good to hug Mammy and Daddy, to buffet the boys on the shoulder, and to kiss Polleen. Of course he had seen them on a previous leave, but never alone, always with Monica either literally or figuratively clutching his arm, making it plain that he was hers, all hers, and was only on loan to his family.

What was more, the night alone in whatever makeshift bed his mammy could offer him would give him some much-needed thinking time. He knew that he was not being fair to Monica, criticising her because she was so possessive, but he did resent her obvious intention of keeping him away from his family. He had married her knowing that she was possessive and clinging so should not have expected her to suddenly become an independent and generous person. What was more, he had known for two years that she did not want children of their own, yet he was still annoyed by such selfishness – he saw it as selfishness, recognising it as a desire to have all of his affection for herself.

However, this was one Christmas Day, he told himself as his footsteps rang out on the icy pavements, which he would have with his family. He did not want to have to lie to Monica, to pretend that he had not had time to reach Southport that day. Now, it was no lie but a reality; dusk had already fallen and the streets were dark and difficult. A couple of trams had passed him, black, blue-lit ghosts with windows papered over and no headlights, but he had not attempted to hail them. The walk would do him good. He changed his kitbag from one shoulder to the other and stepped out, smelling the city smell of burning coal, cats and the contents of dustbins, almost enjoying it after weeks and weeks of the frowstiness of a small vessel crowded with men who found washing in such confined quarters difficult. Soon be home now! Soon have his mammy's arms round his neck, his daddy's hand in his! Tomorrow would be time enough to face Monica, give her the present he had brought, listen to her various woes.

As he reached Titchfield Street Martin felt his heart give a joyful thump at the sight of number 8 and, guessing that they were in the parlour though no glimmer of light showed through the blackout, he decided to go round the jigger and across the yard, then creep softly through the kitchen and the narrow hall and burst into the parlour, to surprise them.

Accordingly, he went round the back, opened the door and stepped in, basking for a moment in the warmth of the kitchen. The fire glowed, there was the most marvellous smell of roast meat and other good things and, although the lamp in here had not yet been lit, he could see in the firelight that preparations had been made for a high tea. The long wooden table had a checked cloth laid upon it, the cutlery was spread out and the best plates were ready to be piled with food.

As it's Christmas there will be cold ham left over from dinner, Martin thought longingly, taking off his duffel coat and hanging it behind the kitchen door. He began to struggle out of his boots, standing them neatly to one side of the back door, then picked up his ditty bag and slung it on one shoulder. Food on HMS *Campion* was doubtless as good as the Navy could manage in wartime, but it was still pretty dull stuff. For obvious reasons everything – or almost every-thing – was dried or canned, and although the frigate was rarely at sea for longer than a month, the crew had still got extremely tired of corned beef, mashed potatoes and the sort of peas to which you added a fizzy tablet in order to turn them from off-white to a more appetising green. There was the rum ration of course but it scarcely made up for the hardships and constant danger of being on the *Campion*.

As Martin crossed the kitchen he remembered the luscious taste of his mammy's Christmas cake and risked a side trip into the pantry just to reassure himself. There it was, standing on the slate slab, a white and scarlet edifice, as yet uncut. Martin, mouth watering, turned away and opened the door into the passage, his socks soundless on the red linoleum. He paused outside the parlour to adjust the ditty bag, since it contained the small gifts he had brought home for everyone. Right at this very moment, he had never loved his family so well. They were the salt of the earth, so they were; Mammy and Daddy the best parents a feller ever had, Poll and the boys the best sister and brothers. He grabbed the door handle and pushed it wide, grinning from ear to ear, shouting, 'Hello-ello-ello, here's Santy come to bring you what you most wanted at Christmas! And just in time for tea, so he is!'

Someone hurtled across the room and into his arms and Martin, fielding the girl, thought for one startled moment that a total stranger had mistaken him for someone else. Then all in a moment he recognised her. It was Monica, and he had thought her thirty miles away, in Southport!

He should have kept his mouth shut, of course. He meant to, but it wouldn't be silenced. Before he knew what he was saying he had spoken. 'Monica! What in God's name are you doin' here, when I t'ought you safe in Southport?'

His mother had jumped up as he entered, rushing to his side almost as quickly as Monica had, and now she said quietly, gripping his arm warningly: 'Isn't it a wonderful t'ing, me darlin' feller? Monica t'ought you'd likely be home for Christmas so she's come to stay – well, I can see for meself you're thrilled as can be, almost wit'out words!'

'Oh, I am, I am,' Martin said quickly, hugging Monica so hard that she squeaked in protest. 'Darling girl, you're the last person I expected to see here – I – I thought I'd have a quick word wit' me family and – and then mebbe get to Southport tonight, or tomorrow if I couldn't make it. I've got five days' leave – imagine that, five whole days ashore!'

By now Polly was hanging on to his arm and Peader was shaking his shoulder and grinning at him, whilst Bevin and Ivan were on their feet and crowding close, their faces alight with excitement. 'Me boy, it's the best Christmas present any of us could have asked for, to have yourself amongst us,' Peader said in his slow way. 'Come to the fire – we're eatin' in ten minutes or so, but until then sit yourself down and tell us how you come to be here.'

'Oh, we berthed this afternoon, so I got meself ashore as soon as I could and come on home,' Martin said. He still hadn't got over the shock of finding Monica in his parents' parlour, but had himself well in hand now. 'If I'd only had a forty-eight I'd have gone straight to Southport, of course, but since it's five days I thought I'd stop off here first . . . and now I don't need to rush off anywhere,' he added hastily, with Monica still pressed against him, her face hidden in his seaman's jersey. 'Well, I thought I'd give you all a surprise, but you've given me a better one.'

'So we have,' Deirdre said equably. 'Monica, you sit right down by Martin. Boys, go and wash up ready for tea and you, Polly love, go and warm the pot. Your daddy and meself will start slicing ham and buttering bread . . . because these two will have a great deal to say to one another, that I do know.'

Martin obediently sat down in one of the fireside chairs and as soon as his family had left the room Monica came and sat on his knee. Martin put his arms round her and gave her another hug, a gentler, more genuine one this time, and then turned her in his arms so that she faced him. 'Sweetheart – what a wonderful surprise! But you said you were living with your parents . . . I never dared hope to see you today . . . not unless I managed to – to make it back to the station . . .'

Monica heaved a huge sigh and snuggled into his

arms. 'Oh, Martin, I've missed you so! And – and your mam's been really nice to me, though that Polly . . . but never mind that. She's had to give up her room, and . . . well, I suppose I've not tried very hard with her. But I will now, really I will. I'll really try to gerron with your family.'

Martin kissed the side of her face and then bent down and rummaged in his ditty bag. 'Got something for you,' he said. And he pulled out the little square parcel which contained the box with the thin gold chain in it and held it enticingly before her. 'Want it now or later?'

'Oo-ooh,' Monica said longingly. 'Only I'd better purrit under the Christmas tree, Martin, with all the other presents. It wouldn't be fair, else.'

And Martin, saying that he understood, put the parcel under the tree and began to tell his wife about his latest voyage and the course in gunnery which he would take, starting in the New Year. And he tried not to be glad when Polly popped back to tell them to come through to the kitchen for tea.

Grace was going home. As soon as war had been declared she had written to the Admiralty offering her services to the WRNS and had started to enquire about a passage to Britain, but it was not until mid-January that things began to happen.

The Admiralty had not replied, but she had been offered a passage by two Salvationists who were also keen to return to their native country. Mr and Mrs Carewe needed someone to help with their two small children, and who better than Grace? So she had cabled to the O'Bradys that she was coming home and now, with tears running down her cheeks, she stood by the rail of the SS *Queen of the South*, waving to Sara,

Brogan and Jamie, and trying not to wonder whether she would ever see them again, or whether she would see England for that matter, because it would not be an easy voyage, everyone aboard knew that. A great many vessels had fallen victim to the magnetic mines which now infested the seas, though Grace thought they would probably account for as many friends as foes, since no one could tell where they would turn up next. Then there were the U-boats, skulking below the waves, aiming their torpedoes at any ship they did not recognise as one of their own. Civilian ships owned by countries which had no part in the conflict had been sunk, so everyone on board knew the risks, and knew also that the voyage was unlikely to be an entirely peaceful one.

But it was no use dwelling on the dangers ahead. Being a member of the armed forces would not be all smooth sailing, she supposed. So Grace dried her eyes and led her young charges down to their cabin. She was here to do a job so the sooner she started the better.

'Let's have a game of "Happy Families",' she said brightly, getting out the pack of cards. 'Who'll deal, children?'

Because of her mother's words, Polly began to search for Sunny as soon as she could after the Christmas holiday was over, but she did not find him. Remembering what Alice had been told she went to his house, or what had once been his house, feeling very silly indeed and hoping that she would not make a fool of herself. At Sunny's old address she found a stringy, hatchet-faced woman with dyed black hair who told her, in the strangest accent that Polly had ever heard, that the Andersens had moved out some time previously and that she herself had been the tenant for nigh on eighteen months.

'Wh-where did they go, do you know?' Polly quavered. She felt sure the woman thought she was pursuing Sunny like some sort of common Mary-Ellen, but having come this far she was determined to get what information she could. 'Sunny was me pal, only we – we've not seen each other for a while. He was at school wit' me brother,' she added untruthfully, and imagined the woman's sharp black eyes softened a little.

'Oh aye? Well, his pa vas a sailor, so folk hereabouts kind o' thought that the lad vould have follered in his footsteps. Then it vould have been natural that the boy's mother would have headed for Pompey,' the woman said, having given the matter some thought, with her dyed black head cocked to one side like a blackbird, and her little eyes taking Polly in from top to toe. 'Pompey's a good place for sailors, and sailors' vives.'

'Yes, I expect so. I believe Sunny has joined the Navy, so perhaps his mother has gone to this – this Pompey to keep house for him,' Polly said, and was rewarded with an even sharper look, an abrupt crow of laughter – and the door slammed almost in her face, though the woman did have the grace to say: 'Try Pompey,' as she disappeared from sight.

Polly went thoughtfully home and got out the old *Atlas of the World* which countless O'Bradys had turned to for geographical advice from time to time. She found Great Britain with its principal cities, ports and harbours, but she could not find Pompey, no matter how she spelt it. Finally, she concluded that the woman had just been taking a rise out of her, put the atlas away and decided to think no more of

197

Sunny. Indeed, if he no longer lived in the 'Pool, she might as well forget him, because she was unlikely to walk into him again by accident. For by now she was even more certain that the naval back view she and Ivan had seen on Church Street had been Sunny, probably visiting Liverpool en route for somewhere else.

Martin and Monica spent the first two days of his leave at number 8, but then they went off to Southport, and it was not until they came back again, Martin walking into the house to say goodbye to everyone, that it occurred to Polly to ask her elder brother whether he had ever heard of Pompey.

'Yes, 'course I have,' Martin said indignantly. 'So should you, Poll. It's an Italian city out of Roman times, it was buried when one of the Italian volcanoes erupted – Etna, was it? Or was it Vesuvius? Any road, it's an Italian city.'

'Oh,' Polly said, confounded. 'Is it a port, Mart? Only someone told me that there are lots of sailors in Pompey and . . .'

Martin gave a little choke of laughter and put a brotherly arm round her shoulders. 'I thought you meant *Pompeii*, the ancient city,' he said kindly. 'Pompey's another kettle of fish altogether, so it is. It's a sort of nickname that sailors have given to Portsmouth, God alone knows why. And there are certainly a great many sailors in Pompey. All right, alanna? Does that answer your question?'

'It does,' Polly said with great relief. You never knew, if she decided to join the WRNs when she was older she might easily go to Portsmouth one day, though if there were really hundreds and hundreds of sailors there, she had not yet worked out how she might find Sunny and his mammy. But having discovered the possible whereabouts of the family, she decided that she would do nothing, for now – there was little enough that she could do, after all. 'Thanks, Mart.'

So now, knowing that in all probability Sunny was unlikely to be in the city, she decided to put him right out of her mind. Besides, she wasn't at all sure she wanted to join the WRNs; joining the WAAF might be more fun, because Tad was in the Air Force and she kind of liked the thought of meeting up with her old friend again.

So Polly continued to work, and study, and to help her mammy and write letters to anyone, just about, who would write back. And waited for the months to pass until she, too, could help to fight this war which seemed so slow in getting started.

Chapter Eight

Years ago, when it had first happened, Sunny had been deeply upset and angry that Polly had suddenly stopped meeting up with him, but even in his disappointment he knew better than to blame her. It was her stuck-up, stupid parents, that's what it was, and he was fairly sure that if he could just get Polly alone . . .

The trouble was, he could not. He had been baulked at every turn, not by Mr and Mrs O'Brady but by Polly herself. With her blue eyes sad instead of smiling, she had turned away from him, ignored him, moved if he came near her, until he was forced to realise that this was serious. He had done wrong to encourage Polly to mitch off school and now he was being paid out for it. They would not let him see her and since they had clearly abstracted some sort of promise from Polly, he knew that she was far too honourable to break her word and would consequently have nothing at all to do with him.

It was sad, but Sunny was young and on the brink of a new adventure. He was very soon fed up with skiving round Liverpool picking up bits and pieces of jobs when he could, and without Polly, life suddenly seemed dull indeed. So Sunny Andersen, son of a sailor, went and joined the Navy, because he saw a life on the ocean wave as being very much to his taste. He joined the Royal Navy as an ordinary seaman, of course, the lowest of the low, but he was bright and rapidly rose to able seaman and then he was sent on a course to learn to be a signaller, and when he had successfully completed the course he was posted to the sloop *Poppy*, whose home port was Portsmouth.

War was coming; everyone in the armed forces knew it and Sunny was no exception. He also realised that he was likely to be carrying out his duties on various ships anywhere in the world and it was unlikely he would be able to return to Liverpool often, since his ship's home port was in the south of the country. It was sad, because he loved the city, it was his home, the only one he had known until he joined the Navy, but as soon as he had moved away his mam had moved down to Portsmouth, 'to be near your dad,' she had said, though Sunny took that with a pinch of salt. Now when he was ashore it was convenient to move into the small spare room in his mam's warm, untidy little house and he supposed that he would be spending his leaves in Pompey now, so that he could see his mam and, when he was in port, his dad. A pity, because he had lost touch with Polly, and he still thought of her with affection and just a touch of desire, but he had had a good few girlfriends since he joined up and no longer thought of Polly as often as he once had.

He thought of her, however, when he found himself, just before Christmas, with a five-day leave – and a pal, also with five days off, who still lived in the 'Pool. Dempsey was a cheery lad, one of a big family, and when Sunny had explained that he could no longer spend his leaves in the 'Pool because his mam had moved – he did not say where – Dempsey had immediately told him that the entire Dempsey family – especially his three sisters – would be delighted to entertain him.

'Any pal of Reg Dempsey's a pal o' theirs,' he said lavishly. 'You come along o' me, Sunny, an' you can look up your old mates whiles I do the same.'

So Sunny had got himself a rail warrant and arrived in Liverpool on a cold afternoon just before Christmas.

Naturally, Sunny was rather pleased than otherwise to find himself, in all the glory of his uniform, back in Liverpool for a short spell. His first thought was that now he should get in touch with Polly again, since she would be a working girl by this time and no longer quite so much under her parents' thumbs, so at the first opportunity he left the Dempsey household, telling Reg that he was going to look up old friends, and then began to make his way across the city towards Titchfield Street.

He was nearing the turning he wanted when he thought he saw a girl he vaguely remembered from school, Edith something-or-other. He took a long, hard stare before approaching her, however; she was so different from the scruffy kid in her worn plimsolls and ragged clothing he remembered. Yet there is always something about a person which never changes, and there it was, in Edith's sharp, knowing little face despite the smart black coat and matching hat with violets on the brim, the high-heeled shoes on her feet and the liberally made-up face.

'Edie? D'you remember me, queen?'

The girl – only she was no longer a girl but a young lady – turned and smiled coquettishly up at him. 'Sunny! As if anyone could forget you! You ain't changed at all, chuck – you're in the Navy now, then? Eh, I've gorra yen to join the WRNS or the WAAF meself, but I'm makin' guns in a factory on Long

Lane, an' it's too well paid to throw over just 'cos I fancy meself in a uniform!'

'I'm sure you'd look very nice in it, but no nicer than you do now, Edie,' Sunny said, taking her arm. Suddenly he felt he needed time, and a bit more information, before he approached the house in Titchfield Street. 'Tell you what, I'm longin' to hear all the news; what say you an' me go an' get some char an' a wad – that's a cake to you, gorgeous – an' you can fill me in on what's been happenin' since I left.'

Edith was willing; clearly she had no objection to being seen with as personable a young man as Sunny. He took her to the nearest cafe, bought her what looked to him like a very sickly cake and a cup of tea, and then settled down opposite her to gather what news he could.

'What's been happenin' to the rest of 'em? Dougie Saunders, Bet O'Flaherty, Sid Smith? Oh, and young Polly O'Brady, what's she been gettin' up to?'

'Oh aye, you went around wi' her at one time, I remember,' Edith said. She took a bite out of her cream cake, then dabbed at her mouth with a paper serviette. It came away red with lip gloss, Sunny saw with mild amusement. He only had one use for lipstick himself – to see how quickly he could kiss it off – but he knew girls liked the stuff and this one clearly put it on with a trowel, judging by the fact that her mouth was still blood red, as was the serviette.

'That was when we were both kids,' Sunny pointed out virtuously. 'Tell me about Dougie, an' Bet, and Sid, then. Polly's a deal younger'n you, I suppose.'

This seemed to catch Edith on the raw. She looked up quickly, a martial sparkle in her eyes. 'Younger'n me? Well, no more than a twelve-month, if that! She don't change much, what's more – her mam an' dad and all them older brothers make sure she don't wear nothin' decent, nor run about wi' the fellers like the rest of us. She's workin', of course – I seen her in Blackler's t'other week – but she still looks like a school kid. No make-up, hair just the same, plain sort o' clothes . . .'

'An' Bet?' Sunny asked. He did not want to rouse Edith's suspicions and have her going round and telling the O'Bradys that he had been asking questions about Polly. Besides, he now knew quite enough to be going on with. Despite the fact that she was now fifteen years old, getting on for sixteen, in fact, it seemed that her parents were still babying – and bossing – his Polly. Better not go to the house then, particularly as he now knew where she worked. Blackler's was a big place but he was here for two more days; he could haunt the store for pretty well the whole of that time.

I'll lay siege to the bleedin' place, he vowed as Edie prattled on beside him. I'll kip down on the bleedin' floor if I have to, but I'll see Polly, and talk to her before me ship sails if it's the last thing I do!

But when the two lads set off back to the *Poppy* once more, Sunny's bright and optimistic hopes had suffered a hard knock. Despite the most exhaustive search, he had failed to run Polly to earth in Blackler's, and assumed that she must have had a couple of days off, possibly for Christmas shopping. Several times he thought he saw her – once, he walked all the way to Titchfield Street and actually hung about near number 8 – but no Polly appeared. It was a Friday, and since he had to return to his ship on the Saturday morning Sunny decided that he had done all he could, and would have to give up the search until his next visit.

I'll write to her, Sunny told himself, and spent the best part of the train journey plotting a letter which would sound like innocuous friendliness to Polly's parents but which would somehow manage to prove to Polly that he still wanted her to be his girl. He wanted Polly's friendship, he was still very fond of the kid, but he did not want anyone, either Polly or her parents, thinking he was . . . well, serious. He wanted her as his girl all right, but had no desire to 'go steady' if it meant cutting out the delightful inter-ludes with other young ladies which he had come to think of as his due. After all, when there were so many pretty girls falling over themselves to be seen with a handsome blond sailor it would be a dull sort of chap who would get tied to a kid. So he decided not to overdo the eagerness, and as the *Poppy* set out for Londonderry and convoy duties in the North Atlantic he began to write the letter.

Grace reached Liverpool as afternoon was turning into dusk on a rainy February day. She looked up at the Liver birds as the big ship passed slowly up the Mersey and felt the sting of tears in her eyes, and then the warmth of them as they ran down her cold, rain-wet cheeks.

Home! New York had been grand, Sara and Brogan wonderful, but this – oh, this was home! But despite these feelings she went down to the cabin she shared with the two Carewe children and began to gather up their baggage. Presently, Mrs Carewe, with her small daughter in her arms, joined her there and soon enough the five of them were on deck, waiting their turn to descend the gangplank.

'I can't tell you what it's meant to us to have you with us, my dear,' Mrs Carewe said as they reached terra firma once more. 'You're efficient and kind and good, and a credit to the Strawberry Field Orphan Home, and we shall all miss you most dreadfully. But we can manage now; we'll get a taxi to Lime Street and book ourselves into a hotel, or a guesthouse, then catch the first train south tomorrow. And don't forget to write to us to tell us how you're going on.'

'I won't,' Grace said. 'Umm . . . some of the hotels near the station . . . well, they aren't very – very nice, you know.' She did not quite know how to tell these good, kind people that Lime Street was frequented by the sort of women that decent people tried to keep away from. 'Some of them . . . there are all sorts come up from the docks, and . . .'

'Don't worry, Grace,' the major said, smiling at her. 'We've not worked amongst the very poorest people in New York without knowing that hard times sometimes produce a desperate reaction. Poor souls, just to keep body and soul together . . . But there, we'll go to a respectable place, don't you fret.'

'Oh, I know you will,' Grace said hastily, hoping she wasn't blushing but knowing that she almost certainly was. 'And don't think I'll ever forget you, because I never could. I'll write as soon as I'm settled . . . but I don't know whether the forces will accept me, if they don't . . .'

'Any of the women's services would be glad to get someone as competent and experienced as yourself, Grace dear,' Mrs Carewe assured her. She took the baby's pudgy fist in her own and flapped it up and down. 'Wave bye-bye to Gracie, dear one.'

Grace watched the little family until they had found themselves a taxi cab, got their luggage and themselves aboard, and set off down the street, then she turned her feet towards the nearest tram stop with a great warmth beginning to flood through her. She would soon be at the house she had never yet entered – number 8, Titchfield Street – yet still felt would be her home. The O'Bradys had assured her, over and over, that since they now lived in the city she must stay with them, and she meant to do so. Until she joined up, that was. For Grace was determined that she would do her duty by her country and right now, her country needed all the help it could get, even if she only scrubbed potatoes or mended the uniforms of those more able to fight.

A tram came clanking up the road and stopped alongside the small queue of people waiting at the stop. In the dusk Grace could not see the destination board clearly but said breathlessly to the short, elderly woman directly in front of her: 'Excuse me, does this tram go along the Scottie, ma'am?'

The slight Americanism of the last word made the woman turn and stare, then she grinned. 'Aye, tharrit does, queen,' she said in the familiar, nasal accent which Grace had once used herself, until the years with Sara had made her almost forget it. 'What stop does you want? I'm gerrin' off at St Martin's Street meself.'

'That'll do me too,' Grace said as they both climbed aboard. She wedged her bulging suitcase in the gap under the stairs and began to push her way further down the vehicle in the small woman's wake, for it was crowded with home-going workers at this hour. 'I'm going to Titchfield Street – that's the best stop for me as well.'

'Right, chuck. When you see me shovin' me way out, jest you folly,' the woman said. She settled herself with her broad bottom wedged against an occupied seat and clung on to the back of the next one with both fat hands. 'Hold very tight, please,' she said in imitation of tram-conductors the world over. 'We're off, queen. You goin' home? In the forces, are you?'

'Not yet,' Grace said, smiling at the other's open curiosity. 'I'm just back from the States, where I've been working for a while. But I've come back to join up, though.'

'Good for you,' her new friend said heartily. 'We'll give old Hitler the runaround, so us will! What'll it be, then? ATS? WAAF? WRNS?'

'Well, I've applied to become a WRN,' Grace said, grabbing for a strap as the tram suddenly lurched to a halt, presumably at another stop. 'I wrote several times, from the States, but I've not had a reply, so I suppose I'll just have to see who wants me.'

'Hmm. Can you drive? Type? Or are you the domestic sort?'

'I can't drive,' Grace said at once. 'Wouldn't mind learning, though.'

'Well, there you are, then,' the woman said as triumphantly as though Grace had just admitted that she could drive, type and also steer battleships through minefields unaided. 'D'you favour brown? Or is navy more your style? Or that sort o' grey-blue?'

'I think I look best in dark colours,' Grace said, wondering where the question was leading and thinking of her Salvation Army uniform, which she secretly thought very becoming.

'Then that's settled,' the woman said. 'You done the best thing when you applied for the WRNs. Their uniform's navy like the fellers. So that's settled.'

Just as she spoke, more passengers began to climb aboard the tram led by a group of girls who, pushing and giggling, got between her and her erstwhile companion making it impossible for them to exchange any further conversation.

Deirdre was still working in the cafe, though her hours had been cut; no one wanted to pop in for a nice high tea when it meant struggling home through the blackout so she only worked, now, until three in the afternoon. Naturally, this affected her wages and made her think of changing her job because it was common knowledge that those working for the war effort were extremely well paid. In a way it was a pity, Deirdre thought as she cleaned down tables and brushed crumbs up off the floor, because she loved the work. The customers were friendly, Mrs Ellis wasn't bad once you got used to her odd little ways, and Miss Collins was all right as well, though despite her cuddly appearance and soft Irish voice she was capable of considerable malice and you always had to take what she said about others with a pinch of salt.

However, it was not war work and Deirdre thought that as soon as it was possible she would apply for a job which would help with the war effort. For the time being, though, she simply spent more time at home, cooking, knitting, and occasionally helping Peader to sort his employer's coupons. Peader, doing his books – or rather his employer's books – in the front room was glad of her occasional help but happier still, she knew, because it meant he had company. He had always worked with other people and found being alone in the house all day dull work.

'All right if I go now, Mrs Ellis?' Deirdre enquired when she had finished cleaning down the dining room. 'Only it's a quarter past three and it's that dull and rainy outside that you're not going to find yourselves rushed off your feet.'

Mrs Ellis, who was counting out the float which she would leave in the till so that next morning they had some change for early customers, nodded silently, her fingers still busy amongst the ha-pennies, pennies and threepenny bits but Miss Collins, polishing glasses with a nice piece of wash-leather, said almost in a whisper: 'Want a sultana cake, luv? Well, most of one, anyway. It'll be too stale to sell tomorrer and I don't hold with using fruit cake in trifles.'

'Thanks very much, if you're sure no one else wants it,' Deirdre said rather nervously. It would be just like Miss Collins to offer her the cake and then to tell Mrs Ellis that Deirdre had asked for it, and with butter and sugar now on ration, making cakes at home was almost impossible. But Mrs Ellis, despite her preoccupation with small change, had obviously heard since she turned round for a moment and said: 'You take it, Deirdre. Rose can have the bit of meat and potato pie that's left over; she's no hand at cooking, I feel downright sorry for that husband of hers sometimes.'

Rose's husband, Dick, had suffered from TB as a young man and though he had been discharged by the sanatorium as cured, he was painfully thin and weedy and had a hollow cough which made the older ladies exchange significant glances. Deirdre could imagine her own mother looking at Dick and saying, in the sepulchral voice she kept for such occasions, 'There's a feller that's not long for this world,' whereas Peader's mammy, well known for her cheery and optimistic nature, would have announced bracingly that creaking gates lasted longer than sound ones.

'Right you are then, Mrs Ellis,' Deirdre said now,

taking the piece of cake and wrapping it in greaseproof paper. She put the small parcel into her capacious handbag, then turned to smile at her employer. 'Peader will be grateful – he dearly loves a piece of cake with his cup of tea. What time shall I come in tomorrer?'

Mrs Ellis cocked her head to one side. 'Well, what with January being one of the coldest months ever, and February not being much better, business doesn't seem to start until nearly mid-morning. Best be in by ten thirty, though, dear.'

'Right,' Deirdre said with unimpaired cheerfulness, though her wage packet at the end of the week, which had been so thin all through January, did not look as though it would improve much now. 'Cheerybye, all.'

She had been putting on her coat, hat and gloves as she spoke and now she went briskly out through the cafe and into the Scotland Road, putting her umbrella up as she came on to the pavement for Miss Collins, who had a superstitious streak, would have announced that the war was as good as lost had Deirdre erected it indoors.

Outside, the rain was falling steadily, and there was a raw chill in the air. Deirdre thought gloomily that if it froze tonight they would all be in a pickle tomorrow, and wondered whether to walk home or go for a tram. But it was growing dusk and the thought of hanging about in the cold waiting for a tram that might take almost as long to arrive as it would take her to walk, settled the matter. She sighed and set off, head down, umbrella lowered against the driving rain, trying to concentrate on what awaited her – the warm fire, the kettle on the hob, and Peader's welcoming smile.

She was almost at the Bevington Arms pub on the corner of St Martin's Street when a tram rattled up behind her and stopped in a shower of spray, decanting several passengers, all of whom either tucked their heads low into their coat collars and set off up the road or erected their umbrellas and followed suit. Deirdre glanced sideways, to see whether a friend or neighbour was aboard, and was struck by something about one of the girls who had alighted last from the tram, carrying a sizeable suitcase and a canvas bag. She had turned her coat collar up and pulled a dark red felt hat well over her face but due to the things she was carrying she could not use an umbrella – indeed, she did not seem to have one. The girl set off ahead of Deirdre, walking purposefully, and there was something about her, something familiar . . .

Deirdre quickened her pace. It was difficult to take in any details in the driving rain but she rather thought she had seen the girl somewhere before. She was overhauling the girl fast and presently they were side by side on the pavement, so Deirdre glanced sideways. A tall girl, and very slim, though her dark coat hid her figure pretty effectively. She had shoulder-length hair darkened by the rain which was probably quite a light brown under normal circumstances, and a pale face with a small straight nose and eyes whose colour was hidden but whose long, light lashes were beaded, now, with raindrops, though the rain itself seemed to have stopped, for the moment at least.

A neighbour? No, not a neighbour. Someone, Deirdre decided, folding down her umbrella, that she had known long ago and so now could not immediately recognise. Someone from Dublin, probably, that was why the girl carried a suitcase. They reached Limekiln Lane where Deirdre had to turn left and she stretched out a hand to stop the other, but the girl turned left as well, and as she did so, glanced at Deirdre. Immediately she stopped short, a smile breaking out.

'Oh, it's Auntie Deirdre, isn't it?' The girl dropped her suitcase and her canvas bag and grabbed Deirdre's hands, causing her to drop her umbrella and to clutch desperately at her handbag. 'You don't recognise me, do you? I can't have changed that much – I'm Grace Carbery, and you're Polly's mam! Why, I'm making my way to your house this moment!'

Deirdre squeaked and stood on tiptoe to give Grace's cheek a hearty kiss, then bent to retrieve her umbrella. She scooped the canvas bag up at the same time and slung her own bag over her shoulder to give her a free hand. 'Grace! Well, and haven't you changed now! You were just a slip of a thing when you left for New York, now you're a woman, and a very pretty one at that! Just wait until Peader sees you, he'll think I'm bringing a visitor to stay, and a very smart one too.'

'How *is* he?' Grace asked, picking up her suitcase. 'Now don't you go carrying my bag, Auntie Deirdre, you've got your own handbag. Let me do it, I'm very strong, you know.'

Deirdre, however, hung on to the canvas bag. 'No, no, my dear, me bag's doing very well hung from me shoulder, it'll do me no harm to give you a hand,' she insisted, beginning to walk forward once more. 'I'm so sorry no one met your ship, but with you not being able to give us any sort of definite landing time . . . My goodness, how thrilled everyone will be to see you at last!'

'I'm thrilled to be home,' Grace said quietly. 'I've had a grand time living with Brogan and Sara, and I dearly love Jamie, but . . . Oh, Auntie Deirdre, England's me home, Liverpool especially. Why, I've been gone years but I can still remember every street, every pub, every shop, just about. Oh, and I've brought you some photographs . . . Brogan's got a pal who takes pictures all the time so he took the apartment, the street, the park, and lots of Jamie. I'll get them out just as soon as we're indoors.'

'It'll be grand to see some snaps,' Deirdre said as they turned into Titchfield Street. 'We've had a shockingly cold winter, so we have, but spring will be on the way soon, and then you'll be able to enjoy being home again.'

'Ye-es, only I'll not be home for very long,' Grace said rather apologetically. 'I didn't come home just to *be* home, you know. I'm going to join one of the women's services, if they'll have me. Brogan thinks that the US will join the war quite soon, but I'm not so sure. There's a strong lobby for neutrality and although they've heard the stories of Nazi atrocities, same as you have no doubt, they're still holding back. And a good many of them have German roots which makes them unwilling to interfere in a war which they still feel needn't touch them.'

Nodding her understanding, Deirdre noted the slight American accent and smiled to herself. No doubt Sara and Brogan had that trace of an accent as well, and little Jamie who she had never met too.

'Right. So maybe we'll have to fight on alone, but judging from the people in the street, they're prepared for that. And you've come back to help us, you good girl, you.'

'Brogan wanted to come back too,' Grace said

quickly. 'But Sara remembers . . .' She hesitated. 'Well, they left because it seemed best and I don't suppose things like that have changed much, have they?'

'No, the feeling would still be strong,' Deirdre admitted. 'Oh, not from the family, nor our good friends. But a good many people don't like mixed marriages, and— Why are you smiling?'

'You sound like some of the folk in the States,' Grace said, smiling down at Deirdre. 'Only over there, mixed marriages don't really mean religion so much as colour. There's a lot of feeling against whites marrying coloureds, and of course you can tell at a glance when a man is black . . . I don't know, Auntie Deirdre, there's a lot of prejudice in this world against people who can't help what colour they are, or what religion they follow.'

Deirdre, who knew very well that anyone who was not a Catholic was doomed to spend eternity regretting the error of their ways, returned some non-committal answer just as they reached number 8 and went down the jigger and round to the back yard. The front door, which would have been the usual way to bring in a visitor, would have meant getting Peader up from his chair and she wanted to surprise him.

'Well now, and won't Peader be delighted to see you safe?' she said as they crossed the back yard. 'For he's known better than any of us the dangers of sea voyages in such times as these. I wonder if he'll recognise you? You've grown into a really pretty young lady, that's what, our Grace! And just wait till Polly sees you! She'll be tickled pink, so she will.'

Polly came in from work in the best of spirits, full of stories of what had happened to her during the day. She burst into the kitchen in her usual impetuous manner and for a moment did not recognise the tall young woman with the bun of light brown hair on top of her head who sat opposite Peader beside the fire and turned a smiling face towards her.

'Hello, Polly,' the girl said, getting to her feet and holding out her arms. 'Haven't you a hug for me, then?' And all in a moment Polly knew her and with a squeak of excitement hurled herself across the kitchen and into Grace's arms.

'Oh, Gracie, Gracie, aren't you smart and lovely? Oh, and you're a real grown-up lady, just like Mammy said you would be, only I couldn't believe . . . I love your hair done like that, and isn't it smooth as satin now, and you've not a spot to your face – wish I didn't have spots – and that dress . . . Oh it's lovely, so it is.' Polly began to drag her own coat and hat off, dancing across to the back door and hanging them on the hooks before turning back to her friend. 'How long have you been here, me darlin'? Did Mammy meet you off the boat? Have you had your tea yet? How's Brogan, Sara and Jamie? I've a million questions to ask you, I don't know where to begin.'

'Glory be, Poll. Glory be, Poll,' Grace said, picking up the scarf which had slid to the floor, handing it to the younger girl. 'You've grown up a good bit yourself but you haven't changed in other ways; you're still my dear little Polly. Don't you ever stop asking questions, honey?'

'Honey! That makes you sound like a real American,' Polly said, flinging the scarf on to the nearest chair regardless of the fact that it contained her father. Peader unwrapped the scarf from around his head and smiled across at Deirdre, who was quietly laying the table for tea.

'What a terrible girl she is,' he said fondly,

indicating his daughter. 'Now, stop motherin' Grace, Polly. Or she'll up and leave before she's arrived, so she will. And stop shootin' questions at her like a machine gun.' He turned to his wife. 'If tea won't be ready just yet, Deirdre, should the girls take a jug of water and go up to their room to wash? They'll be head to tailin' it same as they always did, though I daresay it'll be a bit of a squeeze because both of 'ems tall and neither of 'ems skinny.' He turned back to Polly. 'An' while you're up there, alanna, Grace'll tell you all about your brother and sister and the little lads and you can catch her up with our news. Grace took her case up earlier so she knows where she's headin'.'

'That's a grand idea, so it is,' Deirdre said. She went over to the stove and began to pour hot water from the kettle into a white enamel jug. She handed the jug to Polly who had begun to chatter again and pointed sternly to the stairs. 'Off wit' you,' she said with eyes that smiled though her mouth was grave, 'and be sure to be down in half an hour with all your questions answered and all your news given so we can enjoy our tea without bein' driven crazy by your brangling.'

Polly took the jug and headed for the stairs with Grace close on her heels. 'Thanks, Mammy,' she called over her shoulder, 'but half an hour's not long enough for all my questions! Still, we've got all night, once tea's done.'

It was true that the two girls had had a good deal of catching up to do, Polly reflected next morning as she crept out of the bedroom, having washed and dressed in almost total silence, without once causing Grace so much as to stir in her sleep. But despite having talked non-stop from ten o'clock or so until well after three, there was still a good deal she wanted to know. Oh, Grace had told her all about Sara, Brogan and Jamie. Sara and Brogan, she had said, were as eager to come home and help with the war effort as she, but they felt it would be deserting their adopted country. 'If America enters the war, however, they'll come back,' she assured Polly. 'Poor Brogan really envied me, I know it.' But she had not said a great deal about her own social life or what her plans were, apart from the fact that she had come home to join up.

'Which service will you join?' Polly had asked eagerly, and Grace had not been evasive – but not too keen to decide either.

'I wrote to the WRNs,' Grace had said rather crossly. 'I wrote two or three times – maybe four – but I never once got an answer. Oh, I'd like to be one of them, all right, but someone on the boat said they're the senior service and not nearly so keen on recruiting as the younger services. So I'll have to see.'

'But you'll try the WRNs first, won't you?' Polly had said eagerly. 'I'm goin' to join them, Gracie, just as soon as I'm old enough. And it 'ud be nice if we was both in the same service, don't you think?'

'Yes, it would,' Grace had said. 'Only they won't let the girls go to sea, will they? Did I tell you, Poll, that when there was a storm I was just about the only person on the ship that wasn't sick?'

'You did mention it,' Polly admitted, smiling to herself in the dark. 'Monica – she's Martin's wife, me sister-in-law – said she'd join the WRNs if only they'd let her go to sea wi' Martin. But she's ever so wet, not a bit like us. I mean, we'd like to go to sea all right but not so's we could be with our relatives!'

'No-oo,' Grace said cautiously. 'But some of the

sailors are awful nice, our Poll. Ever so friendly. One of 'em asked me if I'd like to go to the flicks with him one afternoon.'

'Did they have a cinema on the ship?' Polly had asked, wide-eyed at the thought, only Grace told her that Sam – that was the sailor's name – had actually meant her to go to the cinema in Liverpool, before the ship sailed again.

'Oh, I see,' Polly said, rather disappointed. 'Well, you could go, of course. When the war first started they shut all the cinemas and theatres and that, but they soon opened 'em again. I expect I told you in one of me letters.'

'You did mention it,' Grace said. She chuckled. 'Sara said if anything persuaded you to go to America it would be the cinemas shutting, I remember. But they changed their minds in time to keep you, I guess.'

'That's right,' Polly said. She laughed too. 'I were that mad – oh I *do* love the flicks, Gracie – that I'd have blowed up the houses of parliament if I'd had the chance. I love dancing, and going on walks wi' me pals, and going to the theatre now and then, but the flicks is best.'

'Why? Because you can hold hands without anyone knowing?' Grace asked curiously. 'Or because of the stories?'

'We-ell, it's a good place to go with a feller, all right,' Polly admitted after a moment's thought. Over the past four or five months she had gone about with a good many boys, though none of them had been particularly important to her. She was saving her real affection for her old friends, she told herself virtuously – friends like Sunny, or maybe even Tad – but the other fellers were great fun, and good company

219

after a day spent dancing attendance on customers in the shop or taking dictation from dull old men, because all the young ones had been whipped into the armed forces. 'But it's the stories really, Gracie. And – and the acting, and all the girls so beautiful and all the fellers handsome . . . Oh, I don't know. It's me best thing, anyhow.'

'Yes, I know how you feel, 'cos I'm fond of a good film myself,' Grace acknowledged. 'But . . . well, with so much – well, reality going on, it seems a bit daft to go meeting guys at the cinema. And besides, I scarcely know Sam, not really. So I said I didn't think I'd have time, because I meant to join the forces at once, so that means I should really go along to the recruiting place first thing tomorrow, I suppose.'

'Guys? And first thing *tomorrer*?' Polly almost wailed. 'Oh, but they might send you away from the 'Pool right away and then what 'ud I do? I've been looking forward to you coming home so much, Gracie! I've a heap o' pals you've not met yet, girls and fe— guys, I mean, I've told them all about you and they're really looking forward to meeting you. Don't go away too soon, there's a luv!'

But Grace, though tired, was adamant. 'I think I ought to go along to try to join up tomorrow,' she said obstinately. 'They won't take me at once, Poll, that much I do know, so you'll have plenty of time to introduce me to your pals.'

So now, with this in mind, Polly did wonder whether to wake Grace up. Might it not be kinder, perhaps, to do so? But Grace looked so tired, and was sleeping so soundly, that eventually she decided that like it or not, Grace should lie in this morning, and went quietly down the stairs.

In the kitchen, Deirdre smiled at her daughter and

put a large plate of porridge down in front of her place, then poured her a mug of steaming tea. 'They've mebbe rationed bacon and butter and sugar but you can still have a nice plate o' porridge and a big mug o' tea,' she said, 'to say nothing of a pile of toast and margarine. Now get eating, or you'll be late for work, and that 'ud never do. Where's our Grace? Comin' down in a moment?'

'No. I've left her to sleep,' Polly said, sitting down and beginning to spoon porridge. 'She wants to join up today, Mammy, but I said she should get used to being home a bit first. Only you know what? She's that determined she'll probably take no notice of what I said, and there's me longing for her to meet me new pals, which wouldn't mean a huge delay in her joining up.'

She sounded so injured that her mother laughed. 'Never you mind, alanna,' she said, taking her place opposite her daughter. 'She'll mebbe go to the recruiting office, but I doubt they'll send her straight off to wherever she's to go. They'll have to go into her credentials first. Why, she's just got back from America – she could be a German spy for all they know.'

'Huh, not our Gracie,' Polly said. She finished her porridge and reached for the topmost piece of well-browned toast. 'She sounded ever so American when she first came home, but by the time we fell asleep she were talking just as ordinary and nice as I do!'

'Well, that's all right, then,' her mother said comfortably. 'Now you go off to work, me darlin' daughter, and I'll see that Grace is still around when you get home.'

With breakfast finished, Polly put on her green coat, wrapped her striped blue and fawn scarf around her throat, and set off for a day's work at the Reliant Insurance Company. She did not go willingly – like her mother Polly wanted to do war work – but for the time being Mr Slater of the Reliant would have to do.

She reached Exchange Flags and went slowly through the big oak doorway, up the stairs and in through the door marked *Reliant Insurance Company – Reception; please Enter*, where she found the receptionist, Sadie, already behind her desk, polishing her long, filbert nails with the little wash-leather buffer which was part of her manicure set. Polly envied her the little leather case with her initials – S.P. for Sadie Phelan – on it in gold, but she knew her chances of owning such an object was slight. Sadie was twenty-four and had been earning for years, whereas Polly was very much the office junior and was paid accordingly.

Sadie looked up as Polly entered and smiled. 'All ready for another day of glamour and excitement?' she asked, fitting the buffer into its place on the cream suede which lined the small case and extracting a spade-like object with which, Polly knew, she pushed down her cuticles – cuticles, Sadie had explained, being highly unfashionable this year. 'I don't know how you stand old Slater, chuck. What wi' his bad breath an' his terminal dandruff, to say nothin' of his whiney voice,' Sadie remarked eyeing Polly quizzically. 'I reckon he's old Hitler's secret weapon. Guaranteed to send any halfway pretty girl mad after workin' for him for a week, let alone months an' months.'

Polly took off her coat and scarf and hung them on the coatstand, then perched on the edge of Sadie's desk and eyed Sadie's small telephone exchange enviously. Lucky Sadie, she met all the people who came into reception, sent them to the appropriate departments or offices, and no doubt, knowing Sadie, made eyes and light conversation with any feller who took her fancy, whilst Polly was either stuck in the typing pool, or sat opposite Mr Slater, taking dictation and praying she would be able to read her shorthand outlines when she returned to her own desk. The trouble was, if she got sufficiently bored she simply stopped listening to what Mr Slater was saying, though her obedient hand continued to write neat shorthand across the pages of her notebook. If she had been listening, reading the work back was easy enough, but when she had not been listening, her own shorthand outlines looked more like Chinese characters to her, and she could usually only make a vague stab at their meanings.

'Oh, old Slater isn't that bad,' she said vaguely now. 'Besides, Sadie, I'm waiting for you to move on, so's I can take over in here. Aren't you longin' to join the forces, queen? Me pal Grace came back from America yesterday, docked in the early evening, and she's going to join up just as soon as she possibly can. The WRNs, I guess.'

'I've gorra lorra responsibilities,' Sadie said primly, and winked at Polly. 'To say nothing' of a nice wage packet – they don't pay you much to be a WRN or a WAAF, you know, queen. But tell me about your pal – she's been in America a while, hasn't she? I bet she's as fashionable as anything – how old is she? What about fellers? Don't say she left a feller pinin' for her in America! Oh, it's me dream to go over there some day – I got cousins . . . But the war's purra stop to all that. Bleedin' pity, but there you are.'

'I don't think Grace has any particular feller,' Polly said slowly. 'Which is odd, now I come to think, because she's got rather pretty in an – well, an unusual sort of way. She's got light brown hair which curls under when it reaches her shoulders, and a straight little nose, and really nice blue eyes, as well as a wizard figure, so you'd think she'd have the fellers swarming round her like bees after the honey. But it's a good thing she didn't have one over there, since she's come home now, to where she belongs. I expect she's hoping to meet one when she's in the WRNs – I would, anyway. A sailor . . . Oh, I do like sailors!'

Sadie chuckled. 'Don't we all, queen? Now you'd best get to your desk before old man Slater—' She broke off as the outer door opened. 'Good morning, Mr Slater!'

Polly promptly fled and joined her fellow-workers in the large, chilly room which had once contained eighteen young ladies, and now held only six. The other five were already there – Miss Highes, the senior typist, who worked as secretary to Mr Richards, the managing director, and occasionally unbent enough to go down to Claims and take dictation for the solitary man still working there, and Gladys, Paula, Anita and Jane, who were already clattering away on their elderly typewriters, although Polly knew very well that they could not actually be working yet, because it was only five to nine and none of the men would have sent for a typist yet.

'Where've you been?' Jane asked as Polly heaved the black cover off her old Remington and snatched her shorthand notebook out of its drawer and her pencil from the handleless mug which held an assortment of different writing tools. 'Chatterin' to that Sadie, I daresay?'

'Sadie's all right,' Polly said rather breathlessly. 'Look out, though, old Slater . . .'

The door opened and Mr Slater, coatless now and with his black bowler in one hand, came into the room. He gave them a brief, meaningless smile and then fixed his eyes on Polly. 'Good morning, ladies! Miss O'Brady, bring your notebook through, would you? I have to go to a meeting this afternoon so this morning will be a busy one – we had better start work at once.'

Polly got slowly to her feet and took an extra pencil out of its mug, in case the other one broke. Mr Slater got very cross if she was not prepared for such emergencies. If only he had been a trim, soldierly major with a blond moustache and laughing eyes! Or – or a sailor, with lots of gold braid, or a nice flight lieutenant . . .

'Miss O'Brady, why are you staring into space? Don't say you've forgotten your pencil again! If I've told you once . . .'

Mr Slater's whiney voice brought Polly back to earth with a jolt. She heaved a sigh and flourished her pencils at the old horror, noting with evil satisfaction that despite only just having arrived at the office, Mr Slater's shoulders were already well speckled. Thank the good God I don't have to get near enough to smell his breath, she reminded herself reverently as she took her seat opposite him. Now concentrate, Poll, or you'll regret it later. And anyway, when I join the forces I shan't work in a perishin' office, not me! I'll be something exciting, and outdoors, I'll not . . .

'Miss O'Brady, I said take a letter to Mr French of the Plymouth branch, but I've not seen your pencil so much as touch the paper. Really, if it wasn't for the fact that most of our staff have left to join the armed forces . . .'

'Sorry, sir,' Polly said with another sigh. 'It's just

that me pal – my friend, I mean – came back from America last night and we had a lot of talking to catch up on, so I'm a bit—'

'I'm not interested in your private life, Miss O'Brady, just in getting my letters typed,' Mr Slater said with unnecessary sharpness. He looked spitefully at her and Polly knew that if it had been in his power to do so, he would have sacked her on the spot. But fortunately she was a quick typist and, when she was not dreaming, an accurate one. So he knew he would have to put up with her for a while, anyway.

'Sorry, sir.'

'Right. Now are you attending? Good. Then a letter to Mr French, if you please . . .'

Grace woke late and lay in bed for a few moments, wondering where she was and why the ship seemed suddenly so still. Then she opened her eyes and saw the Sacred Heart on the wall above the bed and the edge of the pink and white checked counterpane which Deirdre had laid lovingly over the pair of them once they had settled, Polly at the foot of the bed and herself at the head, and remembered everything. She also glanced at the alarm clock on Polly's little bedside table, and gave a squeak. Half past eleven, the morning was almost gone and she had done nothing but sleep! But then she remembered the previous day and how very tired she had been and settled back on her pillow. It wouldn't hurt to lie in just this once . . . and although it was getting on towards lunchtime, she could join the WRNs just as well in the afternoon. Indeed, she would get up presently and go down to see if there was any hot water for washing and then she could make her plans. Auntie Deirdre would advise her what was best to do.

But ten minutes later, reaching the kitchen with her blue dressing gown on over her striped pyjamas, Grace realised that quite a lot had changed since she had last been in the O'Brady house. Deirdre had gone to work, Peader told her, pulling the kettle over the fire and getting out the loaf, but he was to be her deputy until his wife came home at around four.

'Your Auntie Dee said you'd have a bowl of porridge and a boiled egg for your breakfast, alanna,' he said, pouring cold water into an enamel jug, adding hot from the kettle, and handing it to her. 'And I t'ought the pair of us would have a couple of kippers at midday. But as you're late up, how about missin' out breakfast and havin' a nice hot bowl of vegetable soup first and then the kippers? Would that suit you?'

'Kippers! I haven't tasted a kipper since I left the 'Pool,' Grace said, her mouth watering at the thought. 'What about me cutting some bread and butter, Uncle Peader, while you put the soup on the stove? When I'm up, that is – and you may depend upon it, I shan't be long, not with kippers waiting.'

And so it was a comfortably full Grace who finally left the house at about half past one, bound for the recruiting offices. Peader had reassured her that she could perfectly well join up without having to leave them immediately; indeed, he said he'd told Polly over and over that it took at least a couple of weeks to get all the paperwork done when a body joined the services. Then she would have to wait until there were sufficient girls ready to undertake their basic training.

'Don't you worry your head that you'll be sent off to somewhere like a little parcel as soon as you sign on the dotted line, Grace me darlin',' he said with a comfortable chuckle. 'You'll be wit' us for a while yet.'

So Grace found herself heading with a quiet mind for Canning Place, where Peader told her she would find the Naval Recruiting Office. She was wearing her best navy-blue coat with a matching velour hat perched at what she hoped was a becoming angle on her smooth and shining hair, a pair of neat, navy lace-up walking shoes on her feet and a bounce of delighted anticipation in her step. As she walked, she glanced around. It was a fine, bright February day, with more than a touch of frost in the air so that her breath fanned out round her like a cloud, but the sunshine, though pale, was cheering and Grace, who had so enjoyed New York, still found herself remarkably glad to be home again. It was odd, she mused as she walked, that she remembered Liverpool with such fondness considering that the first dozen or so years of her life had been spent in this city in poverty and fear. But it had been Liverpudlians who had fed her and given her affection, and there had been pals, a good many of them, amongst other kids ... Oh yes, Liverpool was home all right, and one that still had the power to bring tears of affection to her eyes.

But best of all, the Liverpudlians, she reminded herself as she turned on to the Scottie, were the Salvationists. It had been Sara who had recognised her as Grace Carbery when she had first entered the Strawb, and she was a Salvationist. From then on she had had her own place, and that had been as a loved child of the Strawb. The Army had taken her in, and she had suddenly found herself with two families – the O'Bradys, and the Strawb. From being a child alone, with no brothers or sisters who acknowledged her, she had had a dozen sisters, and as the home grew, so did these wonderful new relatives, until by the time she was sixteen and able to go out into the world and earn her own living, Grace had had confidence, and friends galore.

She was thinking this, telling herself that as soon as she had cleared up the matter of joining the WRNs she must go back to the Strawb and tell them she was home, when a voice hailed her. She glanced across the road and saw a plump, yellow-haired girl heading in her direction, a wide smile spreading across her face.

'Gracie! Well, wharra turn-up for the books, eh, our Gracie! I reckernised you at once, you've not changed at all – where you been these past few years? Ooh, if that ain't the smartest coat I seen . . . You a member of one of the services yet? The coat's awful like a uniform one, only a bit too smart . . . I did hear as you'd gone to America . . . now who told me that, I wonder? . . . But I see I were wrong. Oh, Grace, give your old pal a hug!'

Grace squeaked and threw her arms round the other girl, hugging as tightly as she could, pressing her cheek to the plump, pink one so close to her own.

'Fanny! Oh, Fan, it's so good to see you! You were right, I have been to the States – I mean America – but I'm back now, and on my way to join up! This was my nannying coat – I was a nanny in New York – but I couldn't stay over there when dear old England was at war, and things weren't so good. How about you? What've you been doing all these years?'

Fanny stood back, then caught hold of Grace's hand and began to pull her along the pavement. 'Look, we've gorra deal of talkin' to do, our Gracie, so we might as well do it over a cup of char! There, that's Army slang for you, not that I mean to join the ATS, because I don't like that sludgy-brown uniform – the same colour as a baby's nappy when the baby's been feelin' poorly, I always say.' Fanny threw back her head and laughed uproariously, then continued to drag Grace along the pavement. 'Here, Miss Young's place is all right, we'll catch up a bit and then what say we join up together? Things is always more fun if there's the two of you in it. I've a mind to try the WAAF – what d'you think?'

'Oh . . . but I've applied for the WRNS,' Grace said slowly as they sat themselves down in the small tearoom. 'I – I wrote from the States, but—'

'The WRNS? But they say they've gorra waiting list, believe it or not,' Fanny told her. 'Besides, they don't let the WRNs go to sea, you know, or do anything much other than office work or cookin'. Now if you're a WAAF you can be a driver, or a mechanic, or you can pack parachutes . . . Oh, there's all kinds of thing you can do, queen. And then the WRNS are a bit kind o' snobby about gals from orphan homes, I daresay. Did they answer your letters, eh?'

'No, but—'

'Oh well, we'll talk about it when we've catched up on each other,' Fanny said with all her usual unimpaired cheerfulness. 'Oh, yes, two teas, please, miss, an' a couple of iced buns.'

Grace ate her bun and drank her tea and listened to Fanny telling her the story of her life so far. She had always greatly admired Fanny's easy ways and friendly attitude and when the two girls had become seniors they had shared a small bedroom and talked of all the things sixteen-year-olds talk about – young men, work, their dreams and aspirations. Now it was no hardship to talk to Fanny of her own wishes and dreams, and to listen, too, as Fanny shared hers.

'But I think I'll probably try the WRNS first, all the same,' she said finally, as the two of them prepared to leave the tearoom. 'Why don't we both go to the WRNS recruiting place? You might find you wanted to join them, after all. Think of the black silk stockings!'

'And them 'orrible school prefect hats.' Fanny laughed. 'Still, an' all, I'll give it a go, queen. And when we've done the deed, how about us goin' back to the Strawb, tellin' them all that we've joined up? Come on, we can catch a tram a bit further up the road that'll take us to the Pier Head. It'll save us quite a walk.'

When Polly burst into the little house in Titchfield Street that evening, full of curiosity to know how Grace had spent her day, she found her friend settled in front of the fire with a round of bread on a toasting fork, held out to the flames. Grace turned round and smiled rather guiltily at Polly.

'Oh, you're back, Poll! I've had a grand day, but I did miss you, though I did meet up with an old friend . . . Do you remember me telling you about Fanny Meeson, when we were at the Strawb? We shared a bedroom when we were seniors.'

'Oh, aye, the girl with yaller hair,' Polly said, casting her coat and hat on to the floor and hastily picking them up again as Deirdre turned from the sink to give her a reproachful look. 'Sorry, Mam . . . Well, go on, Gracie! Tell me the most important thing – have you joined up?'

'Yes, I have, and as your dad and mam said, it'll be a week or three before I hear anything further, but I've signed and now I'm . . . well, guess!'

'You're a WRN!' Polly shrieked, diving across the kitchen to give Grace an exuberant hug. 'Oh, aren't you the luckiest girl? Oh, don't I wish I were a bit older, so's I could be a WRN too!'

To Polly's surprise, Grace's cheeks went bright pink and she glanced rather guiltily across the kitchen, to where Deirdre, at the sink, was clearly amused by the conversation.

'Oh . . . well, I did go to the Navy, but . . . and anyhow, they didn't seem at all interested in my letters, said they were being besieged by applicants . . .'

Her voice trailed away and Polly's mother turned away from the sink and began to dry her hands on the roller towel which hung on the back door. 'She's a WAAF, Polly me love,' she said gently. 'Our darlin' Gracie's been and gone and joined the Women's Auxiliary Air Force!'

There was no denying that Polly was delighted to get Sunny's letter, particularly as it proved that she and Ivan had not been imagining things – Sunny had been in Liverpool just before last Christmas. Once she had an address for Sunny, Polly wrote regularly – as regularly as she wrote to Tad, who had joined the Air Force and had trained to be an aero-engine mechanic and was now attached to a squadron based in Lincolnshire. She looked forward to the post each morning, though, once a letter came, she naturally had to reply to it, which was not so easy now that she was working so very hard. 'Me war's passin' in letter-writin',' Polly grumbled to Deirdre one day as she sat at the kitchen table scribbling away, whilst outside the May sunshine fell on the kids playing in the jigger and Ivan and his pal Boz, kicking a bundle of rags up and down and ferociously screaming 'Goal!' every time one or other of them let the 'ball' get past him. 'It's not as if me life was full an' excitin' either, Mammy . . . not like Sunny an' Tad, to say nothin' of our Grace. She's up there, on an airfield full of fellers, payin' them their wages and dancin' with them and all sorts, whereas you don't even let me go to the hops, in case I meet someone interestin' who isn't a Catholic and might . . . well, might be – be interestin',' she finished.

'We're not against you going dancing, provided you go wit' a group of friends,' Deirdre said mildly. 'And what about the letters you get from Sunny and Tad? Both of them young fellers is probably holdin' a torch for you. Yet here's you, wantin' to gad off every night and have an exciting life . . .'

'I don't! It's just . . . well, Sunny says in his letters that he's a signaller now, and not just an ordinary seaman – he wasn't too keen on bein' down in the bowels of a ship, said he were rotten seasick – and Tad's with his squadron, messin' about with the innards of aeroplanes and probably getting covered in grease the way he always liked to be. Not that any of 'em's allowed to write much about what they're doing, because of walls havin' ears, but their letters are more interesting than mine. Once I've said I earned a bonus for typin' Mr Slater's private letters I've said it all, just about.'

'What private letters?' Peader said. He pushed his spectacles down on his nose and looked at Polly over the top of them. 'I didn't hear nothin' about this, not a word did I hear. I t'ought he was such a dull, pernickety old feller, too, but now you tell me he has a private life, and private correspondence, to boot! Not that it can be very private if he lets you into his secrets,' he added thoughtfully.

233

Polly giggled. 'Well, I'd never have thought it, but he's the father of six kids, Daddy, four of 'em in the forces. They write home, so he has to write back, of course, and he suddenly realised that if he paid me a bit extra and worked half an hour late in the evenings he could get 'em typed, which is a whole lot easier than handwriting.' She glared at her own corre-spondence, then rubbed her aching wrist. 'I wonder if I could type my letters in me lunch hour? she enquired plaintively. Not that there's anything much to tell 'em,' she concluded rather bitterly.

'Never you mind, love,' her mother said serenely. She was making bread for the week, pounding the great lump of dough as though it were alive and dangerous, Polly thought with some amusement. 'I dunno about Tad, but I reckon Sunny's life isn't all that easy; life aboard ship never is. I reckon your letters bring him a lot of pleasure.'

'Tad's still got that Angela girl writin' to him,' Polly muttered. She tried to write another word but her pen seemed empty so she shook it and was rewarded with a blot. 'Oh, damn!'

'Language,' Peader said mildly from his place opposite her at the kitchen table. 'If it were me, Polly me darlin', I'd write one letter and then copy it out twice more. After all, alanna, you've only the one life! They're leading their own lives, so why shouldn't you ease your trouble a little? Answer me that now.'

'No, that wouldn't work, Daddy,' Polly said firmly. She frowned over her letter for a moment and then signed off with a flourish and reached for the blotting paper. 'When I write to Grace I write like a girl, and when I write to Sunny . . . Oh well, I think I write a different side of me, so I do, If you see what I mean.'

'I do,' Deirdre said at once, when her husband

234

merely went on with his own work of addressing envelopes, though he did give his daughter a puzzled look before bending once more to his task. 'But never mind, love. Your letters give a lot of pleasure, I can tell you that without ever having read one word of them. You're a good girl, Polly.'

'Oh well,' Polly said. She heaved a sigh and glanced across at her father. 'Could I give you a hand wit' them envelopes, Daddy, seeing as I've finished me letter-writing for this week? I can do it without having to think too much, unlike letters to me pals.'

Chapter Nine

AUGUST 1940

Sunny leaned on the rail and stared towards the outlines of the Devonport dockyard as the ship nosed its way into its berth. The *Poppy* was coming in for repairs, since she had been nipping round a convoy when she had been attacked by Stuka dive bombers and holed just above the waterline, as well as losing some of her superstructure, for the attack had been a vicious one. They had been lucky, however; one of the anti-aircraft gunners had suddenly found one of the diving planes in his sights and had poured enough lead into her for the attacker to suddenly become the victim, as it fell, corkscrewing madly, into the sea. They had been even luckier, Sunny reflected now, that the bloody plane hadn't hit one of the convoy, but although they had managed to get the ships with their precious supplies safely home, they would have to go into dry-dock for repairs.

Which was why they were now steaming slowly into Devonport dockyard but although this might make things difficult for some members of the crew Sunny realised that it did not worry him at all. He was studying hard and knowing he would be given some leave while the ship was undergoing repairs he was considering staying at the sailors' home in Plymouth instead of returning by rail to Portsmouth and his mother.

The truth was that Sunny had begun to find his mothers 'guests' an embarrassment when he returned home unexpectedly, as he so often did. To find a boy of his own age or even younger at the breakfast table was somehow humiliating and though Sunny avoided such encounters whenever possible it did not make his leaves either easy or comfortable. But if he stayed in Devonport he could have some leave and get stuck into his books. He had another exam ahead of him and he was determined to pass, because he was beginning to enjoy his job. Signallers had to do a great many things other than learn how to read and send morse and to use the big Aldis signalling lamps for ship to ship messages. Folk thought it was all done by radio these days, but unless you wanted the enemy to know your every move – and secrecy was particularly important with the slow-moving ships in a convoy – you had to maintain radio silence once you were out of port. This meant that a signal, which could ideally be seen only by the ship to which it was addressed, was of the first importance, and Sunny had begun to realise that he relished the nature of his job and the standing which it gave him amongst the ship's crew. So he had studied on board ship whenever he was not actually on watch, and meant to pass this particular exam with flying colours so that he might, in the fullness of time, become a yeoman signaller, the right-hand man of his captain and someone who would indeed be of vital importance to his ship.

'Hey'up la'! Dreamin' of your sweetheart or a nice cool pint?'

Sunny jumped and turned to face the speaker. 'Dempsey! Warra' you trying to do, give me a bleedin' heart attack? I was just wondering whether to stay on Devonport and get some studying done. I've got an exam coming up and there's too much coming and going in me Mam's house for me to work. She won't know I've docked so there'd be no hurt feelin's although a week or so in the sailors' home ain't much bleedin' fun. If we were still livin' in Liverpool it would be different; I've a heap of pals there what'd let me work in their parlours if I were desperate but I don't know anyone in Pompey apart from me Mam – she's always busy . . .'

'Why not come back wi' me, old feller, same as you did last Christmas an' you can see all your old pals. Jest ask for a warrant to the 'Pool, 'stead of one to Pompey. The skipper won't notice where you're bound unless you're not back in time. What say, old pal?'

It was a generous offer, but Sunny had no doubt that Dempsey meant every word and after only the slightest of hesitations he accepted.

So thus it was that Sunny left the *Poppy* later that day with his old friend Dempsey – both Liverpool bound. It had been a while since he had been to Liverpool and he was looking forward to seeing his old friends, particularly Polly. He had written to her at least once a week and she wrote back with great regularity, though the letters could only be sent and collected when he was in port which made the correspondence a somewhat jerky one, but it wasn't the same as meeting, he reflected now as he and Dempsey strode towards the station. Meeting Polly would be wonderful – he just hoped she could arrange for some time off so that they could see more of each other.

There were his old friends, too. A good few of them had joined up, mostly going in the navy, as he had, so maybe there would be others on leave, too. And he liked the Dempsey family though he appreciated that with the overcrowding in their small house, studying for his exams would be difficult. However, Mr and Mrs O'Brady seemed like the sort of parents who would want a feller to get on. It was quite possible that when he told them he needed somewhere quiet to study, they might offer him the use of their front parlour, which would naturally enable him both to see more of Polly and to win her parents over.

On the station he and Dempsey learned without surprise that their train was running four hours late, so they decided to go back into the town and get themselves a meal – in fact they were on their way out of the station when something else occurred to Sunny. He would send Polly a telegram telling of his imminent arrival so that she might prepare her parents and, possibly, even meet him. He told Dempsey what he meant to do and the two young men went straight to the nearest Post Office where Sunny wrote and discarded half a dozen telegram forms before deciding that brief was best.

'Coming back to Liverpool as ship in dock stop. Arriving tonight stop. Will call tomorrow stop. Sunny.'

'That took you long enough,' grumbled Dempsey as Sunny rejoined him on the pavement. 'You and your girlfriends, old feller! Now let us get ourselves some grub.'

Polly was home from work and making tea when the knock came at the door. Since her mother now did war work, slaving away at Littlewoods, off Hanover Street, making parachutes for the Air Force on a huge commercial sewing machine, Polly and Peader between them quite often made the tea.

'I'm not as young as I was,' Deirdre would say as she came across the kitchen, to drop wearily into a chair and accept the proferred cup of tea which either

239

her husband or her daughter would be sure to make as soon as they heard the latch on the gate click. 'I tell you, war work pays well and we have some fun, the girls and meself, but I'm fair wore out by the time I catch the perishin' tram home.'

So what with the hard work and the tram journey on a vehicle crammed with other tired workers, naturally it was a relief for Polly's mammy to find that the potatoes had been peeled, vegetables such as cabbage or carrots prepared, and some sort of main dish got ready by Polly. Peader was handy about the house and getting handier, but most of the actual cooking was done by Polly. A day sitting behind a typewriter and running messages was not particularly tiring, and besides, she liked to make a meal. The shortages of almost everything unrationed made meals a challenge although Polly was glad she rarely had to do the marketing. If one saw a queue outside a food shop one joined it so Peader was largely responsible for the shopping since he had more time to spare. It gave her a far greater sense of achievement than typing boring letters for old Mr Slater.

So when the knock sounded Polly ran to the door and took the small yellow envelope and found it was addressed to herself. For a moment her heart did a very peculiar tap dance of fear, for did she not have brothers in the forces, and friends, and a mammy who worked the other side of the city and could easily be in some sort of trouble? So without delay she tore the little envelope open whilst behind her, Peader said anxiously: 'What is it, alanna? Not bad news, I hope to God.'

Peader had been sitting in the front parlour, with account books spread around him and his glasses perched on his nose. Naturally, Polly realised, he would have seen the telegram boy through the front window, and would have wondered, as she had.

But right now it was easy to reassure him. 'It's all fine and dandy, Daddy,' she said, popping into the parlour and waving the short telegram in the air as she entered the room. 'It's from me old pal Sunny, so it is. He's coming home on leave, should be in the city tonight, he just dropped me a wire to let me know.'

Peader's anxious look vanished at once and Polly realised that the telegram had done Sunny a good turn, even though he had probably not thought of it in quite that way; because he was so relieved that nothing bad had happened to any of his sons, Peader positively beamed at her.

'And he's goin' to visit us, no doubt,' he said heartily. 'Well, there's a thoughtful way to behave, alanna. And telegrams cost money, so they do. I hope he'll come round and see us as soon as he's able.'

Polly, assuring her father that no doubt Sunny would do so, returned to the kitchen and her work of dipping slices of liver into seasoned flour prior to frying it in the big pan with the onions she had already sliced and wept over; she smiled gleefully to herself.

It would be lovely to see Sunny after all this time. Oh, and Grace might meet him, because she would be arriving back for her leave the day after tomorrow. Polly frowned at the thought. She wondered how long Sunny's leave would be. She was longing to see him again, of course she was, but she could scarcely expect Grace to want to play gooseberry to the pair of them, and Grace was her best friend. If it came to a choice, Polly would plump for Grace every time. Still, what was the point in meeting trouble halfway? Grace had a week's leave but Sunny's was bound to

241

be shorter. They might meet – that would be rather nice – but then Sunny would go back to Portsmouth and she and Grace would be able to enjoy themselves together as they had planned.

Sunny, knowing nothing of Polly's thoughts, however, took his time getting ready to go and see Polly the following evening. He knew from her letters that she worked for the Reliant Insurance Company during the week, which was on Exchange Flags, and had decided that it would be safer to meet her out of work, because you could never tell with parents. They might let bygones be bygones and treat him in a friendly fashion, or they might decide that they still did not want their little girl mixing with the likes of him and treat him coldly. In which case, he thought now, brushing his best bell bottoms with Dempsey's clothes brush, it might be as well to have a word with Polly first. If she gave him the go-ahead he would walk home with her and suggest going to a flick; but if she said her parents were still doubtful of him, they would at least be able to discuss what best to do.

Fortunately, Sunny was so eager to see his young friend that he arrived at the offices at four thirty, believing that she left off work at five, but he underestimated Polly's excitement at the thought of seeing her old pal again. Polly had got special permission to go at four thirty and as he arrived at the statue in the middle of Exchange Flags there was Polly, tripping down the steps of her office, not even looking around for him but heading in the direction of the tram stop.

For a moment Sunny stood staring, taking in the changes. His little Polly had been a lively and affectionate girl; now she was a young woman. She wore a white blouse and a navy skirt and carried a dark jacket of some sort over one arm, for it was a warm afternoon. She was bare headed, but the delightful bouncy curls that he remembered were pulled back from her face and tied into a bun at the nape of her neck with a piece of black velvet ribbon. She did not even glance round her as she crossed the flags so Sunny shouted.

'Hoy, Poll!' he called, and as she turned towards him, it suddenly seemed the most natural thing in the world to fling his arms around her, lift her off her feet, and give her an exuberant hug. 'Oh, Polly, ain't you grown up! And aren't you still the little smasher I remember! Give us a kiss!'

Polly, blushing a most becoming shade of rose-pink, laughed up at him and kissed his cheek, then pushed him back a bit so that she, in her turn, could take a good look at him. 'You're taller,' she said in a rather awed tone. 'And . . . and your hair's even more gold and you're brown as brown . . . Oh, Sunny, it's just wonderful to see you, so it is.'

'It's nice to see you too, beautiful,' Sunny assured her. He took a quick look round, then drew her close again and bent to kiss her mouth, though she wasn't standing too much of that, he realised as she shoved heartily against his chest. 'Oh, Polly, don't keep me at arm's length! It's been so long, and I've thought of no one but you ever since—'

'Liar, liar, kecks on fire.' Polly chanted the old school taunt in a hushed but laughing tone, but she blushed even deeper as she did so, Sunny was pleased to notice. 'I bet you've had twenty or thirty girlfriends since you and me went our separate ways. Not that it matters. It's now that matters, isn't it, Sunny? And you're coming home to tea, of course . . .

Don't worry about Mammy and Daddy, they'll be right pleased to see you, they were so happy when your telegram arrived.'

'Happy?' Sunny said wonderingly. He could not for the life of him see why a telegram from him should have made Polly's parents happy, even if they had quite forgiven him for his previous misconduct.

'Well, yes,' Polly said. She dimpled up at him, mischief clear in her glance. 'You see in wartime, everyone thinks that a telegram would be bad news, and I've brothers in the forces and me pals and all . . . so when I read your telegram out, they were just as pleased as could be. And Daddy said you were thoughtful to have sent it! So you'll come home with me, won't you, and have your tea wit' us?'

'Thanks very much, I'd like to,' Sunny said, really gratified by Polly's words. They weren't bad old sticks, the O'Bradys, he decided, glancing down at Polly's animated face close to his shoulder, and they had the prettiest daughter although he didn't approve of her new hairstyle.

He said as much as they walked towards Tithebarn Street where they would catch a number 16 tram for home. As he spoke he put a hand up and tried to loosen her hair but it felt as though the ribbon had been glued into place and Polly, though she laughed, pushed his hand away and shook her head at him. 'It takes me half an hour to get me hair flattened and tamed,' she said severely. 'I've growed it and growed it but it won't go straight, it just loves to curl and curls aren't right for working in an office, or me boss doesn't think so at any rate.'

'Well, I'm not your boss,' Sunny said as he put his arm round her and squeezed her waist. She really was a cuddlesome armful and the soft blonde hair so near his face smelled of sunshine and primroses. 'Wish I was, though – why don't you join the Navy and come aboard the sloop *Poppy* so's we could be together all the time? You could be me cabin boy when I'm captain of the ship, like I will be one day.'

'Oh you!' Polly said as they crossed Tithebarn Street and headed for the tram stop. 'I *am* goin' to join the Navy – the WRNs, I mean – when I'm old enough but they won't let me go to sea, and well you know it. Oh Holy Mother of God, look at the length of that queue! Still an' all, it's not as bad as it would have been at five o'clock which is why I got out early. I kind of thought you might come round to Titchfield Street this evening and I wanted to get ahead with the tea. Mammy's working at Littlewoods making parachutes and she's dead tired by the time she gets home so I usually gets the tea to save her the work. Or did I mention that in me letters?'

'You may have mentioned it,' Sunny said gloomily, 'but that's one bit the censor would have chopped. Some of your letters come through to me lookin' more like lace doilies than correspondence. Though I love gettin' them,' he added hastily.

'Yes, yours have holes cut in 'em too,' Polly said, having thought the matter over. 'But one of the gals at work – she's a woman really, quite an old one, I reckon she must be thirty at least – she says she and her old feller have worked out a code, so he can tell her where he's going and what he's doing, without the censor – or the bleedin' Huns, come to that – finding out where our Navy is. Although I don't see how letters can fall into enemy hands. I mean, if they torpedo one of our ships letters would be the last thing they'd fish out of the drink, wouldn't you say?'

'I dunno,' Sunny said. 'You'd think so, but there's

gorra be a reason. Anyway, most of your letters wait in Pompey until the *Poppy* docks, though one or two have follered me around,' he finished. 'Hey up, gal, is this 'un ours?'

The tram bearing down upon them was crowded, but the conductor seemed to have a knack of getting his passengers to move up, and presently Polly and Sunny found themselves on the step and then being pushed by the folk behind until they were halfway down the car.

'Reckon that feller used to pack sardines before he started tram conductin',' Sunny said in Polly's ear. 'It's real nice squeezin' *you*, Polly O'Brady, but I dunno as I'm particularly fond of bein' squeezed by a fat mary-ellen! What's more, her basket's diggin' into me best bell bottoms. I hope I don't get caught up on her wickerwork.'

Polly giggled. 'Well, it won't be for long, only half-a-dozen stops,' she told him. 'Oh, what'll we do tomorrer, Sunny? Only I've took a some days off work, and tomorrer's one of 'em. We could go to New Brighton on the train, or over to Eastham on the ferry and walk in the woods. Ivan and me used to do that a lot when we was kids. We could take a picnic – or what about Seaforth? We could go on the docker's umbrella, that's a nice trip, so it is, especially if the day's fine.'

'Anything would be grand,' Sunny said. He was pleased and flattered that Polly had taken some time off, obviously because he was coming home. 'Whatever we don't do tomorrer we can do the next day, though, if you're off work for a bit.'

'Ye-es,' Polly said, with considerable doubt in her tone. Sunny was about to ask her why this should be so when the tram stopped with a jerk which sent all

246

the passengers staggering into one another and somehow the two of them got separated. The mary-ellen
once more jammed her vengeful basket into Sunny
whilst people fought their way out of the crush. Then
the tram started up again and Sunny, staggering in
the other direction, found himself pressed up against
a couple of giggling girls and a thin woman whose
string bag smelled strongly of fish.

Sunny would have liked to reach Polly once more
but when he made the attempt the fat mary-ellen told
him to stop shovin' or she'd end up on someone's lap,
very probably breakin' their bleedin' legs wi' her
weight, and since this was clearly no idle threat he
heaved a sigh but stayed where he was. After all, he
and Polly were going to have almost a week to themselves, ten minutes apart should not bother them.

And presently, they reached the corner of Tatlock
Street and the tram jerked to a stop once more. This
time the mary-ellen, Polly and Sunny joined forces to
squeeze and batter their way off the tram, landing on
the pavement with triumphant grins – and crushed
clothing, Polly said, surveying her once neat jacket
and skirt with some dismay.

'Oh, a bit of a crush don't matter, but is me bum all
scratched?' Sunny asked rather anxiously as he and
Polly began to walk along Tatlock Street. 'Take a look,
there's a good gal. I hope I haven't ruined me best
kecks.'

'You're fine,' Polly said, giggling again. She linked
her arm with his and fell into step beside him. 'Only
. . . well, there's one thing I've not mentioned . . .'

'You must have asked for leave as soon as you got
me telegram,' Sunny said. He squeezed her arm.
'Clever little Polly!'

'We-ell,' Polly said again, and cast him what

seemed to be a conscience-stricken look as she spoke. 'We-ell, the fact is, Sunny, that me old pal Grace is comin' to stay tomorrer, and since she's in the WAAF and has only got a week's leave, and two days of it, almost, will get used up in travelling, I thought it only fair to get some time off.'

'Grace? Who's Grace when she's at home?' Sunny said. 'But anyway, why does she stay at your place, eh? Wharron earth's wrong wi' her livin' at her own home, or wi' one of her other pals?'

Polly shook his arm and pulled him to a halt on the corner of Titchfield Street. He could see her house from here, the neatly painted green gate, the jigger down which he had once run when calling for his little pal. He turned to look searchingly down at her; suppose . . . well, suppose she was going to cast him aside for this Grace person? But she wouldn't, Polly wasn't like that. Only he had rather hoped . . .

'Grace is Grace Carbery, and she's been me pal for years and years – until she went to New York, in fact, to live with me brother Brogan and his wife, Sara. She's an orphan, she was brought up in the Strawb, you know, out Calderstones way, and though I suppose she could stay with them on her leaves, she'd much rather come to us. Sunny, she were like a sister to me when we was kids, I – I couldn't expect her not to come to us.'

'But – but you're me best gal, our Poll, and there's a war on! No one, not even this Grace girl, would expect us to spend our precious time with someone else playin' gooseberry, when all we want is to be together. Together alone, I mean!'

Sunny looked down at her rosy, determined face. She seemed unmoved by his impassioned words, and he sighed inwardly at what might easily be the death of all his bright plans. It had been going to be such a marvellous leave, with he and Polly off by themselves all day and, he had hoped, him catching up on his book work in their front parlour of an evening. He had even indulged in the unlikely dream that Mrs O'Brady would beg him to stay over, to share with Ivan, perhaps, so that he and Polly could be together for his entire leave, even sharing the same roof. And now this – this Grace person was about to spoil it all! But surely he was clever enough to circumvent this in some way? He pulled Polly to a halt and took hold of both her hands, swaying them gently from side to side. Girls, he had discovered, seemed to like this gesture, to consider it romantic. But apparently Polly was not to be numbered amongst them, for she snatched her hands away and addressed him quite crossly.

'Don't, Sunny, you're making me feel seasick! As for Grace playing gooseberry to you and me, it's no such thing! Oh, I like you quite a lot, I suppose, but don't you tell me you've never taken a girl out since we split up all them years ago! It's grand to see you, and I want us to get to know one another all over again, but don't pretend I'm *that* special to you, or you'd have perishin' well come home and seen me before.'

'But I tried! At Christmas I tried! I hung about outside Blackler's because that silly mare – I can't even remember her name, now – said you worked there . . . I came round to your place too, only I didn't have much time and I missed you . . . Oh, Poll, don't pretend you weren't glad to see me, because I saw your face light up, and your eyes sparkle . . .'

Polly tucked her arm in his once again and pulled gently. 'Come along, Sunny, it's daft to quarrel, so it

249

is! I *do* like you, I like you ever so much, but you don't understand about Grace. When we lived in the crossin' cottage she came to stay most weekends and we never had a cross word . . . Anyway, it's no use, because it's all cut and dried. Grace is coming to stay tomorrer evening and the only twosome there after that will be me and her! I can't let her down now.'

Sunny had always known when to back down and accept defeat gracefully, and he knew, instinctively, that if he continued to object he would lose Polly as well as his beautiful dreams of being alone with her. So he said remorsefully: 'Awright, Poll, that's fair enough. We've got tomorrer, after all, and after that I'll have to make do with me own company. Unless that is . . .' Sunny pretended to be struck with a bright idea, clapping his hand to his head and momentarily closing his eyes as if in deep thought and then opening them again to say triumphantly: 'What about this, Poll? Say I bring Dempsey along to make up a foursome? Dempsey's me shipmate and a grand feller – you'd like him and so would Grace. Unless she's got a pal of her own in the 'Pool. How do you know she's not got a feller in the RAF, or someone who she was friendly with at the Strawb? Or d'you know of any feller she seemed to fancy?'

He glanced hopefully at Polly, and was glad to see that the frosty look in her eyes which had warned him not to go too far was beginning to dissipate; instead, she was thoughtful. 'I don't think there was anyone special, not a feller, anyway,' she said after a moment. 'But look. I'll have to think about it and talk to Gracie. After all, she's never met yourself, the poor, unfortunate girl, nor your friend Dempsey! Now, let's forget all that and talk about tomorrer.'

Sunny grinned but made no comment, and

presently, Polly said brightly: 'Well, if there's no one home from the war stayin' at the Strawb, you could always take Ivan so you's got someone to go about with. Don't pull a face, Sunny, or I'll t'ump you one, so I will! But we'll see what Mammy says when she gets in; she's full of good ideas is me mammy! I don't want you to be lonely either. Oh, if only things had been different . . .'

By now, they had reached the jigger and were making their way round the backs of the row of houses. Polly pushed open a tall, green-painted door in the crumbling brick wall, led Sunny across a tiny, brick-paved yard and in through the back door. They stepped into a pleasant kitchen with a table laid for a meal and a kettle steaming on the hob. As they came in Polly said: 'Daddy, here's Sunny come to meet me! Oh, Daddy, was it a little doze you were having? I'm that sorry to waken you!'

But the tall, heavily built man got up out of his chair and limped across to Sunny, holding out one large, work-worn hand. 'Well, and how are you, me dear feller? Isn't it a grand t'ing to see you again, after so long?' He shook Sunny's hand, smiling all the time into Sunny's eyes, clearly bent on making his feelings clear. 'And wasn't it angry we were wit' you, all them years ago? But that's all over, old feller. You're our Polly's good friend and our guest, so sit yourself down and I'll make the tea.'

Sunny was much touched by the generosity of Peader's welcome, but could not find words to show his own feelings. Instead, he took the proferred chair and, presently, the cup of tea, and said he hoped that both Peader and his wife were well, and all the rest of the family, and allowed the talk to turn, as talk usually did these days, to the war.

By the time that his hostess came home, tea was made and Sunny, feeling quite at home, was buttering the bread which Polly sliced. He almost gave Mrs O'Brady a hug, so charming was her welcome to him, but decided against it at the last minute and shook her hand very heartily instead.

'It's grand to be back in Liverpool,' he told her honestly. 'I'm stayin' wi' me pal Dempsey, though it's terrible crowded. Still, they're friendly folk and I'm used to living in a crush. Once the hammocks are slung there isn't much room inside a sloop, I can tell you.'

'How'll you study then, Sunny?' Polly asked, almost as though coming in on her cue, Sunny thought gratefully. 'I know you've got an important exam coming up because you said so in one of your letters.' She twinkled up at him. 'And the censor let it come through too,' she added.

'Oh, I'll manage somehow, Poll,' Sunny said immediately. 'Though it won't be easy. I could go down to the library on William Brown Street, I suppose, but that's a way off. Still, it 'ud be quiet, and—'

'Sure and why shouldn't you use our parlour, Sunny?' Mrs O'Brady said at once, also as though she had learned the script, Sunny thought. 'Peader likes to work on his books wit' them all spread out on the kitchen table, but if you can manage on your knee in the parlour – and there's one or two little tables in there – well, you're very welcome.'

And Sunny, graciously accepting her kind invitation and thanking the O'Bradys for making him feel so at home, reflected that though he clearly could not expect an invitation to stay, not with another guest due late the next evening, at least half of his hopes had been realised, and with his usual optimism Sunny was sure he would not find himself alone – even after Grace's arrival.

Sunny and Polly had a marvellous time the next day. It was another fine, warm one, and they caught the ferry to Eastham and walked, talking constantly of their lives, their work, their friends. They ate their picnic in a little glade with a stream running through it, and later had tea in a farmhouse garden, where Sunny ate enough, Polly told him, to keep a normal feller alive for a week.

It was not until they were making their way back to the ferry in the early evening that the subject of Grace – and the morrow – cropped up again.

'Grace is arriving tonight. She and her pal Fanny have had their posting,' Polly said as they strolled down the road towards the landing stage where the ferry would presently dock. 'But first thing tomorrer we'll go off up to Beaconsfield Lane and see if we can find one of her pals. I know they probably won't be staying at the Strawb,' she added hastily, when Sunny looked doubtful. 'But everyone will go along to see the staff and the kids. Grace will; she said so. And that way, we may discover whether she's any pals in the 'Pool right now.'

'Why can't I come?' Sunny said at once. 'I've never been in the Strawb; I don't see why I can't come. And anyway, poor Grace won't want to spend the first day of her leave trailin' across half Liverpool! No, the three of us can find something to do tomorrer, and then we can all go up to the Strawb the following day.'

'No, Sunny, stop trying to boss me around,' Polly said vehemently, stamping her foot and glaring at him. 'You haven't changed a bit, have you? All those years ago when I was just a kid you told me what to do and got me into big trouble and listen to you now! No, don't shake your head, you're doing it again! I'm tellin' you Grace and me's goin' to the Strawb tomorrer and if you don't watch out you'll find yourself doing a whole lot more studying than you'd planned – and not in our front parlour either! Why, you're as bad as Ivan. He pestered to be taken with us today if you remember and we had to disappoint him. I can't have two people bothering me like that.'

'I'm sorry, Polleen,' Sunny said humbly. 'Honest to God I didn't mean to boss you about. It were only a suggestion and I take it back. If you and Grace are set on goin' to the Strawb tomorrer, *of course* you must go, only I haven't ever been there and I thought . . . I thought . . .'

He did his best to look thoroughly ashamed of himself and must have succeeded, for Polly's face softened as she squeezed his hand remorsefully. 'It's me that should be sorry, shoutin' like a fishwife at you when you're only tryin' to see everyone enjoys their leave. Look, you come round to my house tomorrer about dinnertime. I'll have had a chance to talk to Grace and see how she feels – we might even have been up to the Strawb by then – and I'll be able to tell you how things stand.'

'That'd be grand,' Sunny said, squeezing Polly's hand in his turn. 'I wouldn't spoil your friend's leave for the world. I suppose Dempsey and me could amuse ourselves somehow – we could even take Ivan at a pinch, get him out of your hair – though I'll miss you something awful, Poll, and it'll be harder somehow knowin' you're so near.'

'Let's not talk about it now,' Polly said, smiling up at him. 'Just you come tomorrer like I said and no more shouting or bossing from either of us.'

Agreeing, Sunny felt downright amazed at himself. Here was he, the popular, much in demand Sunny Andersen, who always had a couple of girls yearning for him, suggesting he wanted to see the inside of a children's home just so that he would be constantly with Polly, and then pretending he would take her kid brother around with him just to keep in her good books. What on earth was the matter with him? She was a pretty girl all right, but why should he go to such lengths just for a pretty girl? There were dozens of 'em about, he reminded himself, and most of them were a good deal more willing to let a chap have a bit of a kiss and a cuddle than Polly was. Delightful though the day had been, she had kept him at arm's length from the very start, and no doubt intended to do so for what remained of the day too.

But they were approaching the Mersey, and Sunny remembered that there was a cafe down near the ferry's landing stage where they could get a cup of tea, or a bun, or both, whilst they waited for their craft to arrive.

He reminded Polly of Mrs Jessie O'Brien's Refreshment Rooms and suggested that they should wait there and get themselves some tea instead of hanging about by the water. Polly shook her head, laughing at him, her eyes teasing. 'Sunny Andersen, we had tea – and a good one – just now, so we did. What can you be wantin' with another tea so soon?'

But Sunny, consulting his wristwatch, told her that their farmhouse tea had been two whole hours ago and added that he would murder a cuppa and Polly agreed that she, too, was thirsty.

'So we'll go inside and watch for the ferry from there, and have us tea and cakes,' Sunny said in his most masterful manner. 'And then, whiles you O'Bradys have your own meal, I'll be gettin' back to Dempsey's and studyin' for me exam. I know your mam said I could use your parlour, but I won't do it tonight, not wi' your pal comin' home and all the greetin' to be got over.'

Polly, following him meekly into the refreshment rooms and agreeing to tea and cakes, also agreed that Sunny had best go straight home when they crossed the river. 'For welcome though you'd be, everyone's attention will be on our Grace,' she admitted. 'But – but you'll come at around one o'clock tomorrer, won't you? You see, the three of us will be waitin' for you.'

'Three?' Sunny began, then his brow cleared. 'Oh, I forgot Ivan. Ah, there's a cream doughnut and an eclair. Which one would you like, queen?'

'It may be only mock, but it's still delicious,' Polly said, her hand hovering over the plate of cakes. 'Ooh, I do love doughnuts, but there's chocolate on eclairs. I think I'll just close me eyes and grab. This is a real treat. I don't get cakes like this often.'

This caused a good deal of hilarity, especially since Polly's small hand missed both eclair and doughnut and landed upon the only fairly plain cake on the plate, a Viennese whirl. Sunny tried to persuade her to eat both doughnut and eclair and they ended by cutting the two rich, squishy cakes into four more or less even pieces, and having half a doughnut and half an eclair each.

In fact, so merry was their tea and so happy were they that they missed their ferry and had to hang on for the next one, which meant that Polly fairly tore up to the tram stop and implored him not to waste time by coming all the way to Titchfield Street, but to go straight back to the Dempseys' place.

'If you take me home, Mammy and Daddy will feel they ought to ask you to stay,' she pointed out as the two of them climbed aboard an already heavily laden tram. 'But if you get off this tram and go straight to the Dempseys', then we'll meet up tomorrer, as we'd planned.'

It made sense, Sunny could see that, so he leaned over and gave Polly the only sort of kiss possible when you are both standing up on a crowded tram, and then jumped down, waving until the vehicle was out of sight, though he could see no answering movement from within.

And presently, back home in the Dempseys' crowded little house, he was glad he hadn't gone all the way back to Titchfield Street with Polly. You're makin' a complete fool of yourself, Sunny, he told himself severely as he sat himself down on the window sill in the boys' room and got out his books. Before you know it, she'll be talking about weddin' bells and gettin' engaged. And there's no sense in that, particularly in wartime.

But he knew, really, that there was little chance of Polly doing any such thing. She liked him, but it was a much cooler and more sensible liking than that usually shown him by girls he flirted with and took notice of. He was going to have to play his cards very carefully indeed to retain a place in Polly's affections without committing himself more than he wanted to do – and the thought of losing her still sent such a stab of dismay through him that he could scarcely believe the pain.

Still, all this wouldn't get his exam work learned. Sunny opened a large manual of seamanship and began to con the pages.

*

Grace woke and lay for a moment looking up at a low white ceiling just above her head, on which the sunlight played dappled shadows. She knew where she was, of course, having been looking forward to this leave for a week, but it was still rather nice to wake of one's own accord instead of being shouted out of sleep by reveille, and it was nice to feel the soft warmth of the bed around one, and to know— Good gracious, where was Polly?

The answer to that particular question came smiling into the room even as Grace began to sit up on her elbow. Polly, fully dressed, came through the doorway, a laden tray in her hands. 'Tea, bread and butter an' a lightly boiled egg, Miss Airwoman,' Polly said. 'Mammy thought we should spoil you today, just for once. My, you got in awful late! You must have been perishin' tired – you came up to bed and you were asleep before I'd finished gettin' me clothes off.' She settled the tray comfortably across Grace's knees and then plumped herself down on the foot of the bed, causing the tea to rock none too gently. 'Hey up, drink it quick, Gracie, before I spill it all over Mammy's clean sheets! Oh, but it's good to have you back after so long!'

'It's good to be back,' Grace said gratefully, sipping the tea. 'Well, this is the life, Poll! I'm sorry I was so worn out last night but that journey! It should have taken about four hours and it actually took nearly ten. Well, the engine broke down twice, which didn't help, and then there was a goods train on the line . . . I can't remember all the excuses, but there were lots. I was so tired I nearly wept when a porter told us we'd missed the last tram, but a few of us – all services – clubbed together and took a taxi, or we'd have been later still. What time was it when I finally staggered up to your door?'

'Midnight,' Polly said, satisfyingly round-eyed. Mammy kept trying to send me to bed, but Daddy said I'd a right to wait up for you, bless him. And of course I'd got holiday so I didn't need to get up early for work. Only you know how it is, the sun peeped through the window and I was awake, so I got dressed as quietly as I could and sneaked down to get you some breakfast. And here we both are. Do eat your egg before it goes cold and hard,' she added. 'Daddy's got an allotment, though it's a long way off, but he's got six hens, so we get extra eggs sometimes.'

'We do all right in the WAAF, though most of the eggs we get are dried,' Grace said, beheading the large brown egg and dipping a finger of bread and butter into the orange yolk. 'Oh, this is so good, Poll! I do love a runny egg.'

'So do I—' Polly was beginning, when there was a perfunctory knock on the door and Ivan appeared. He grinned at both girls and then said, all in a rush: 'Hi, Grace! Will you be long? Only that feller of Polly's is downstairs, and Mammy's gone to work so Daddy's put him in the parlour until you come down.'

'I told him dinnertime,' Polly said, her cheeks beginning to flush. 'I told him Grace and me would have things to do this morning. My goodness, I—'

'He says as how he thought you might like him to take me out today,' Ivan said, grinning from ear to ear. 'I don't believe a word of it meself, but that's what he said.'

Polly sighed. 'I forgot – we did say something like that,' she admitted. 'But I didn't really think . . . Oh well. I'll come down in a minute, Ivan, and have a word with him.'

Grace put a hand to her mouth and went to jump out of bed, but Polly pushed her back again. 'Sure an' there's no hurry,' she said breezily. 'It's just me pal Sunny's home on leave an' all, Grace. I did tell him to come round at dinnertime so you and he could meet, so he's only jumped the gun by a couple of hours. The thing is, he's at a loose end so he thought we might like his company if we go along to the Strawb later. He's never seen a children's home, you see, so he was quite curious about it.'

To tell the truth, Grace was more than a little dismayed by this information. She had gathered from Deirdre's letters to her son and daughter-in-law that Sunny had been a bad influence on Polly, had caused her to sag off school and generally misbehave, and did not much enjoy the thought of being forced to spend time with someone she scarcely knew and of whom she could not approve. But on the other hand, she could not expect Polly to cast off her friend for someone who had been out of the country for several years. However, she had no intention of making her feelings known.

'Why don't we go up to the Strawb right now, then, Poll? As soon as I get up, I mean,' she said, busily despatching the egg, the bread and butter, and several cups of tea. 'Come to that, why not let me go up to the Strawb? I could take Ivan, if you like, leave you and – and Sunny a bit of time to yourselves.'

But this Polly would by no means allow. 'Me and Sunny had all day yesterday,' she said, her eyes widening with dismay. 'It's *you* I want to spend time with, Grace, not Sunny. Sunny's a good chap, so he is, but you're me oldest friend and it's you I've been missin'. Oh, I know he's me friend, but he's a *feller*. You can't talk to them the same as you can to your bezzie, and you're me bezzie, honest to God you are.'

Grace laughed. 'You sound a real little scouser,' she

said teasingly. 'Look, you and I will go up to the Strawb this morning, because I do want to see if any of my pals are back on leave as well. And then there's others . . . they may be working in the city, I'd like to get in touch with them again for old time's sake. The staff always know where everyone is – the Army's a small world and you stick by your friends. I've got another six days before I'll have to do that awful journey again – not that it will be the same awful journey, come to think, me and Fanny Meeson will be heading south in a week, we've been posted – so whilst I'm looking up me old pals you can see Sunny. Isn't that fair enough? It means I shan't have to play gooseberry, but we'll both have plenty of time together. What d'you say?'

'That sounds very good to me,' Polly said, going over to the door. 'You get yourself dressed and ready then, Gracie, and I'll go downstairs and tell Sunny to slope off. He and Ivan can go down to the Pier Head or – or off somewhere, and come home here like I said in the first place, for a snack at one o'clock.'

Sunny, with his kitbag slung over one shoulder, was walking to Lime Street Station, on the first stage of his journey back to his ship. He and Dempsey had had a telegram saying that the *Poppy* was due to sail in forty-eight hours and requesting their presence. Or at least, if the telegram had not been worded quite like that, it was what it meant.

Dempsey had set straight off for the station that morning, although they both guessed their train would be late, but Sunny had nipped round to Titchfield Street first, because he wanted to thank the O'Bradys for making his leave such a good one. He had arrived, unfortunately, after Polly and Deirdre had both left for work, for Polly had only taken five days off from her job since that was all the time that Grace had been able to spend with her, but Peader was in. Sunny thanked him with real sincerity and told him that he would be writing to Polly, of course, and hoped that she would write to him too.

'But she's a great hand wi' a pen, unlike meself,' he said cheerfully, shaking Peader's outstretched hand. 'I know she won't let me down, not your Polly.'

'I daresay Polly isn't the only one you'll be gettin' letters from,' Peader said in his slow, amused way. 'The t'ree of you got on so well I'd be amazed if young Grace doesn't write an' all.'

'Well, the more the merrier,' Sunny had said, but he hadn't really believed that Grace would write to him as well. He had left after that, striding along the pavement in the brilliant August sunshine, beginning to remember just how good this particular leave had been – and he had not been exaggerating either – from the first moment that he had met up with Polly to last night, when they had said what they thought was a brief goodbye until next day, he had thoroughly enjoyed himself.

Despite the fact that there were three of them most of the time as well. Oh, at first he had had to be very careful not to get on the wrong side of Polly, but Grace was a real little smasher, for all he hadn't thought so at first. At first he had thought her rather plain, but after a day in her company, he had begun to see that she was a very pretty girl indeed, only beside Polly's bright blonde hair and vivid eyes, her own paler colouring seemed insipid. Grace was tall and slender, with light brown, shining hair which she wore in the popular fashion, curled round a piece of hair ribbon with the front of it swept up. But once

Polly had pointed out severely that she was no longer in uniform and could relax a bit, Grace had let her hair fall from a centre parting into a long, soft page-boy style, which suited her very well indeed. And though her skin was pale and her eyes hazel, that skin was very clear and those eyes very bright. Oh aye, Sunny considered that Grace was a pretty girl, and a pleasant companion too.

There had been one afternoon, furthermore, when he and Grace had gone off together, because Polly had been called back to the office. Grace had announced her intention of going up to the Strawb to say good-bye to Matron and the rest of the staff and Sunny, because he'd never been to the Strawb, had decided to go along. Sunny remembered various institutions he had visited as a youngster, the chill of the places and sheer soullessness that filled them, but the Strawb – well, no wonder Grace liked going back to the Strawb, he told himself now, remembering that visit. The staff were mostly quite young and very friendly, talking and laughing with Grace and himself as though they had known each other all their lives.

The kids had been fun too, swarming all over Grace and not saying a word when she gave the sweets into the care of a member of staff. They all knew that the sweets were meant for them and would be given to them at the appropriate time. One little girl in particular had taken a great shine to Sunny. She was about seven, he guessed from the gaps in her front teeth where the baby ones had fallen out but had not yet been replaced by the grown-up ones, and her name was Suzie, only due to the lack of teeth she called herself 'Thuthie', which amused him very much. Suzie had proved to be very good at Grand-mother's footsteps and when Sunny consented to be

Grandmother (to delighted shrieks from the children and broad smiles from the staff and Grace) she managed to sneak up on him without his once seeing her move, so that her final quick dash, and her climbing all over him and breathing stickily into his face was a great triumph. Cooing like a contented little pigeon, she had pressed her hot little face against his cheek and told him in a breathy whisper that when she was growed up, she meant to marry him. Sunny, laughing, had told her that he would be an ugly old man in his thirties or forties before she was in a marrying mood, but Suzie had just shaken her head and continued to clasp his hand and climb on to his lap whenever she could.

But now he was entering Lime Street Station, and began to look around for Dempsey.

'Sunny! Over here! So you made it, me ole pal – the next one in is supposed to be ours, so look lively, feller! I've kept a place for you by me.'

It was Dempsey of course, in what Sunny now realised was a vast queue. 'Thanks, Demp,' he said. 'It looks like we'll soon be on our way, ole mate.'

'Yeah, this is goodbye to the 'Pool for a time,' Dempsey agreed.

'Hope it still looks as good next time we come home,' Sunny said.

Dempsey, pushing his way ahead shoulder to shoulder with Sunny, turned and grinned. 'You comn' up this way again?' he asked. 'Wharrabout the disturbed nights then, la'? I thought you'd be glad to get some peace, in Pompey.'

There had been fairly constant enemy activity over the city for a couple of nights, but though the docks had been bombed in Wallasey and Birkenhead there had been no actual raids on the city itself. Sunny, battling through the crowd towards an emptying carriage, snorted. 'If you think the jerries are goin' to leave Pompey alone once they get goin', you're a bigger fool than I thought you were, Demp,' he declared. 'I reckon they'll home in on the south of England and start givin' us hell any time now.'

'Only we shan't be there,' Dempsey panted. 'Gerrin this first carriage, Sunny, then at least we're aboard. We can worry about gerrin' seats later.'

Chapter Ten

Grace and Fanny soon settled into their new station, and Grace began to enjoy her new job, for though Fanny was still on cookhouse duties Grace had been promoted. She would be tried out as an RT operator, which meant that she would be working in the control tower, talking the planes off and back, would be doing shiftwork, and would most definitely be learning new skills.

'The jerries were talking about invasion at the time of Dunkirk,' the officer who began to train Grace told her. 'Everyone believes that will be their next move, but before they can carry it out without the risk of being wiped off the board they'll have to gain air supremacy. That means we'll need every plane we've got to fight them off, and every girl with enough intelligence to help in the fight must use her wits and strain every nerve to see our chaps get down safely. Savvy?'

He was probably no more than forty, with a huge blonde moustache and a sprightly way of walking which the girls imitated when he was out of sight, but he was talking sense and Grace knew it, so she threw herself into her training with the greatest enthusiasm and very soon was as useful as any other WAAF RT operators on the station. 'It stands for radio telephone operators,' she said in a letter to Polly. 'I think that's because we hear the chaps over their radio sets, but we talk back to them on a sort of telephone thing which hangs down just by our mouths. I really feel I'm being useful, Poll, at last. This is a million times better than adding up columns of figures and paying a queue of men their wages.'

She wondered whether the censor would start clipping out half of this letter, but did not worry overmuch. She would see Polly when she next got a decent leave and would be able to tell her in person much of what was happening to her.

And what was happening was a great deal more exciting than just being a RT operator. For the first time in her life, Grace had met a young man who really mattered to her, though the fact that he was Polly's boyfriend might have taken the gloss off Grace's feelings for Sunny had she ever considered herself as being in competition with her young friend.

For Grace, who had dreaded meeting the dreadful young man who had set her darling Polly's feet on the road to wickedness, found that she liked Sunny more than any other young man she had met. He was incredibly handsome, she had guessed that he would be, but that he was kind, understanding, sympathetic and good company had come as a total shock to her. Most of the handsome young men she met – and she met a good few now that she was in the WAAF – were not in the least bit interested in a tall, shy, rather plain WAAF, but Sunny had not even seemed to notice that Grace was no looker, that compared to Polly's bubbly prettiness she was plain, gawky and shy. Sunny had simply seen someone who could share in the fun of a brief leave in the city.

But he was Polly's feller. That was understood, and funnily enough it did not worry Grace in the least. After all, she did not have the slightest intention of trying to wrest Sunny from Polly; she knew it would be impossible for a start, and would not have dreamed of doing such an unfriendly thing in any circumstances. What she felt for Sunny, she supposed, was a sort of hero-worship, combined with gratitude because he was so nice to her and never made her feel left out.

She had thought, however, that it was no use her writing to him. He would not reply; she might only make a fool of herself. Nevertheless she had written, just a funny, jokey sort of letter about the journey down from Liverpool to her present station, how she and Fanny had managed in the train and a little bit about her new job. She had sent the letter off immediately on arriving at her new station and had not expected much of a reply, if any, for months, but instead had got one from Sunny within the week which had clearly crossed in the post with hers. It was a nice letter too, telling her of his experiences on the train returning to Devonport and all about the friends who had joined himself and Dempsey before they had gone very far on their journey.

The good old Poppy *is sailing almost at once, so this is just a short note to let you know I got back safely and trust that you did the same, and I hope that one day you'll drop me a line. I expect we all like letters, and though mine are likely to be scrappy – and short – and probably full of holes where the censor has snipped bits out, I hope you'll write to me whenever you've got a spare moment.*

Grace had gone around in a daze of happiness, almost unable to believe her own luck. And oddly enough, it must, she thought, have given her confidence a boost, because next time she, Maria and

Annette, who were all budding RT operators, went off to one of the RAF dances together, she got quite as many partners as they did and, what was more, found it easier to talk and laugh naturally with the young men instead of becoming tongue-tied and awkward.

Next time she wrote to Polly, she told her about Sunny's letter and said how happy it had made her feel that Sunny, who was Polly's feller, still wanted her to write to him as a friend. Polly's reply was warming, too: *Of course Sunny liked you; anyone who doesn't is plain daft*.

Her letter went on to describe the fun she had had, dancing with a very motley assortment of young men at Daulby Hall and making it plain to Grace that much though she liked Sunny, she did not consider the two of them in any way tied to each other.

Not that I've the slightest intention of being serious about Sunny, Grace told herself that evening, as she prepared for bed in the long, blacked-out Nissen hut which was the nearest thing to a home the girls had on the station. He is awful nice, I like him a good deal, but even if he wasn't Polly's – and he is, whatever she may pretend – him and me would never do together. I'm too serious and he's too – well, unserious, I suppose. I'd begin to bore him and I expect he'd go back to his old ways, like when he led Poll astray, and then I wouldn't be able to respect him, and respect's ever so important. You have to respect someone before you can love them . . . not that I'm thinking of loving anyone, not yet . . . And Grace's thoughts broke down in confusion, leaving her with only two really coherent ideas. It was good that she and Sunny could be friends without any strings, and better that she was now finding it easier to mix with people of both sexes.

And then Grace forced her mind back to RT operating and the way the war was going and she thought about the fighter pilots, and the girls who loved them, and the number of planes that she and her fellow-operators saw off as they scrambled from their stations, and the number – quite often less – which came back. And she thought about the dangers which faced sailors, all sailors, and the bombing of Liverpool docks, which had taken place soon after they had left the 'Pool. And she remembered that those dangers were faced every day by Sunny, and she found, suddenly, that she was glad that she was just his pal, that if anything bad happened it would not be her tragedy, her gut-wrenching, pain-filled loss.

She turned over in bed and buried her face in the pillow. She wanted to be friends with fellows, of course she did, but she suddenly realised that real involvement, the sort that poor little Polly had with Sunny, was a cruelly sad business in wartime.

And presently she went to sleep, telling herself firmly that it was better to be uninvolved, fancy-free. And woke in the middle of the night to the terrible knowledge that if anything happened to Sunny – who was just a friend, and Polly's fellow – she would carry the scar of it on her heart to the end of her days.

Tad, up on his Yorkshire bomber station, was as aware as Grace of the loss of life – and the loss of aircraft – which was the sad result of even the most successful bombing raid, but although he knew the crews and the pilots a good deal better than she did, his main preoccupation, at this stage, was with the planes which he serviced. He had been a con-scientious motor mechanic when he worked at

Barnes's garage in Dublin, but now he was obsessional about the engines which he worked on. Men's lives depended on him and he was sharply aware that nothing, absolutely nothing, was more important than sending the fellers off in a machine they could depend on. He could do nothing if they were caught in the flak or gunned down by enemy aircraft, but he could make sure that their engines, their machines, were as perfect as he and his mates could make them.

Once away from his job, however, Tad had other tasks, amongst which was letter-writing. Never too keen on such an occupation, he now found himself with a number of letters to write each week – except that it was usually each month – and in order to ease matters he had taken to writing one letter, sometimes to Angela, sometimes to Polly or his family, and then copying it, with minor alterations, to his other correspondents.

'One of these days you'll be in a rare ole mess, cheatin' on folk the way you do,' his pal Smiffy told him one afternoon when he came into the billet and saw Tad, with four sheets of paper spread out on the table before him, the laborious script already completed upon the first page, whilst he copied it first on to one sheet and then on to the others.

Tad, looking up from his work, grinned. 'This is nothing, old feller. Last month I paid young O'Mara a packet of Woodbines to do the copying for me,' he said. 'Me writing's so bad that he just scribbled 'em down anyhow, and not one squeak from me family or friends did I get to say why was I writin' so fine all of a sudden! I'd do it again,' he added, 'except O'Mara's gone into town and no one else needed fags that badly.'

Smiffy heaved an exaggerated sigh and sat down at

the table, pulling the completed letter towards him. 'What've you said this time?' he asked accusingly. 'Not a great deal, by the looks of this. Dammit, Tad, you've only covered one side of the page, and I've seen the letters that you get back from your girl-friends, they write you sheets and sheets.'

'They've got nothin' better to do, so they haven't,' Tad said righteously. 'Oh, I know they both work, but it's not like our work, Smiffy. No one's life hangs on whether Angie sells some woman a silk dress or Poll makes mistakes when she's typing out an insurance policy. You an' me, now, we can't afford to make a mistake or one of our squadron could pay wit' his life. And put me letter down,' he added. 'Didn't no one ever tell you 'twas rude to read letters not addressed to yourself?'

'You don't write letters, you write round-robins,' Smiffy said absently. He screwed up his eyes, held the letter at arm's length, and read slowly, '"Dear blank, many thanks for your last. Glad you are well, as I am. We're well fed up here, but I miss blank. Last week I went into Lincoln to see a flick, and I wished you could have been with me. Only you couldn't, so I went with one of the lads. After, we had tea and a bit of sawdusty old cake at a little teashop down by the river. It was a sunny day and the sins . . ." No, swans . . . God, Tad, your writing is appalling, to say nothing of your spelling! "The swans were begging for bread and hissing at us if we didn't throw them any . . ."'

He threw the letter back on the table as Tad made a lunge for it. 'How you manage to keep one girlfriend, let alone two, I can't imagine! If they only knew what you did with your letters – but I reckon they must suspect something of the sort. And why the blanks, anyway?'

Tad heaved a sigh. 'Because you can't say exactly the same t'ing to your mammy and your girlfriends,' he said patiently. 'So I leave blanks and fill in the little odds and ends separately. Polly's real keen on animals, so at the end of her letter I'm goin' to put in a bit about Sergeant Smiler, but Angie wouldn't be interested, so at the end of her letter I'll tell her a bit about the fillum I saw last week. And me mammy likes to know I'm being fed right, so I'll tell her what we had for supper last night. See? It's simple if you use your brain.'

'You'll be caught out one day and get what you deserve,' Smiffy announced, having strolled round the table to look at the other pages, almost identical, which Tad had spread out round him. 'One of 'em's in England, isn't she? Why don't you go and see her, instead of all this letter-writing? You're bound to get a decent bit of leave one of these days.'

'Oh, you mean Polly,' Tad said, reaching for the nearest letter. 'She's more like a sister to me than a girlfriend, so she is. We was brought up together, like, when we was just a pair o' kids livin' in the Dublin slums. Now Angie – she's a real girlfriend, the sort you've got, Smiffy. She's pretty as a picture, smart as paint . . .'

'And waiting for you, I suppose, with no thought of any other feller,' Smiffy interposed, grinning. 'Yet you send her the same letters as all the others. Oh, what a peculiar bloke you are, Donoghue!'

But Tad, putting the first letter into its envelope, merely grunted. He could see nothing peculiar about his method of letter-writing and Smiffy, he well knew, did not have a great many younger brothers and sisters who liked a line occasionally, to say nothing of friends back in Ireland. Sometimes, his conscience gave a twinge when he posted off two very nearly identical letters to Angie and Polly, but they would never know and anyway, he reminded himself reasonably, a feller only had one life. He was merely simplifying a task which, had he tried to write individual letters to each one, would have kept him busy from dawn to dusk on any day that he happened not to be working.

Still. The thought of visiting Polly when he had sufficient leave had occurred to him several times, though in a way he felt guilty about even thinking about it. She was his dearest pal, they had shared so much when they were kids, but he had a feeling that she had never fully understood about Angie, that she thought him shallow and in some way fickle for having found himself a girlfriend other than herself. But this was clearly not the case, could not be the case, since she, on her side, had told him that she was seeing a feller by the name of Sunny, wrote to him, went around with him . . . Oh well, Poll would simply have to understand about Angie. What's sauce for the goose is sauce for the gander, Tad thought to himself, but Polly was a darling, he would really love to see her again.

He would, he decided, go to Liverpool the next time he got enough leave and spend a few days getting to know Poll all over again.

Sunny was soon engrossed in life aboard ship once more, though this time he was not aboard the sloop *Poppy* with the men he had sailed with for many months. It had not been possible, it seemed, to finish the repairs to the sloop in the time at their disposal so he had been drafted to the *Felix*, a destroyer. Rather to his dismay Dempsey was not with him but he knew from past experience that he made friends easily so had few worries on that score.

When first he came on board he was met by the ship's coxswain who took his draft documents and called a seaman to take Sunny forward to the starboard fo'c'sle where he would mess. He was told that eighteen men including himself would eat, sleep, stow their gear and live in an area about sixteen feet by twelve, but he was used to the cramped conditions aboard the *Poppy* and thought that this was fair enough. Life in a destroyer was clearly going to be a matter of cramming the maximum number of men into a tiny space as in all warships. On that first day, therefore, he found somewhere to sling his hammock and then followed the seaman back out on deck, and thence to the flag deck below and on either side of the bridge, where he would work when on watch.

'We've been told we're on convoy escort duty,' the leading signaller told Sunny later that same day. 'I hear the slops is full of tropical kit so's I reckon it'll be the arctic but we'll go where we're sent, as usual, and discover our destination when we arrive. That's the navy for you.'

Sunny knew that he would miss his pals aboard the *Poppy*, particularly Dempsey, but a destroyer, he considered, was a ship worth boasting about, and the chances of promotion were possibly even better than they had been aboard the *Poppy*, since he had passed his recent exam with flying colours. And although he had believed himself friendless aboard the *Felix*, he realised when he went below for his first night's sleep that he was not the only scouser aboard.

They were a mixed bunch, he could see that at a glance, and was slinging his hammock and shaking out his blankets when something about the able seaman nearest him caught his attention. The man was putting up his own hammock, frowning in concentration, and when he became aware of Sunny watching him he turned and grinned.

'Hello – you're part of the new draft, aren't you? First time aboard a destroyer?'

'That's right,' Sunny said. 'I was on the sloop *Poppy* before, but she was badly knocked about so they've re-drafted a good few of us, I think. None to the *Felix* except me, though, worse luck. Wharrabout you?'

'I was on the corvette *Campion* before I joined,' the other said. 'They're grand ships, but a bit on the cramped side. Not that I've sailed with a destroyer before, mind, this'll be my first voyage with the *Felix*. But I can tell from your accent that you're a scouser, like me, though Liverpool's my adopted home rather than my birthplace. I'm from Dublin.' The older man glanced at Sunny's arm, but he had stripped to his white top in the heat of the fo'c'sle. 'Do you have a trade? I was made up to able seaman aboard the *Campion*.'

'I'm a signaller. I've just passed me latest exams okay, so mebbe I'll be made up to leading signaller soon,' Sunny said with more than a little false modesty. 'One thing you can say about the war, promotion comes quicker than in the peace. But I reckon you're norra a regular, like me?'

'No, I'm a Hostilities Only man,' the other said, grinning. He held out a square, capable-looking hand. 'O'Brady. And you're . . .?'

Sunny stared, too surprised to hold out his own hand. He stared very hard at the older man and it occurred to him, for the first time, that he had seen him somewhere before – or someone very like him. 'O'Brady?' he repeated. 'I've gorra pal in Liverpool . . .

now I come to think . . . you've gorra look of Peader . .
. an' I reckon you're a bit like Ivan, an' all. Is – is your
first name Martin? Only I've just spent me leave with
the O'Bradys, they've gorra house in Titchfield Street,
and—'

'You wouldn't be Sunny, would you?' the other
man said, his grin widening. 'Dear God, if you are this
is the strangest coincidence! Yes, I'm Martin, and I'd
bet my bottom dollar that you're Sunny, who caused
poor old Polly such grief when she was a little 'un.'

The two men shook hands, Sunny grinning now
with more than a shade of embarrassment. 'Put it
there, Martin,' he said. 'Me mam's always telled me *be
sure your sins will find you out*, and by and large she's
been right. But I'm a welcome visitor in your mam's
house now, honest to God I am, me an' your Polly's
still good friends.'

'Yes, Mammy did say you and Poll exchanged
letters,' Martin admitted. 'I seem to remember Polly
saying that you'd joined up back in '38. I wish I'd
done the same,' he added rather bitterly. 'If I had
done so, I'd have stood a better chance of promotion
myself.'

'But you're an accountant, aren't you?' Sunny
asked. He began once more to shake out his blankets
and Martin, two feet away from him, followed suit. 'I
seem to remember you were in an accounts department somewhere. And you're a married feller – you
wouldn't have wanted to be at sea before the war,
would you?'

'I dunno,' Martin said. He finished making his
bunk and sat down on the Rexine cushion which lay
across his locker and began to pull off his soft-soled
shoes. 'My wife's gone back to live wit' her parents for
the duration, which means that when I do get back for

a forty-eight, I have to muck in wit' her parents. They're nice enough folk,' he added hastily. 'But it's not the same as having your own place.'

'I reckon sailors shouldn't marry too young,' Sunny said, sitting on his own locker. 'When you're fancy-free you can tek your pick, just about.' He was stripped down to underpants and vest and flicked himself into his bunk. 'What's it like being a gunner, anyhow?'

'We're just like everyone else – unless they pipe action stations we do any job that needs doing, just about. What was it like in your sloop?'

'The same, only signallers spend most of their time on watch on the flag deck,' Sunny said. 'Rushing backwards and forwards, reading signals, hauling pennants up the halyards. We aren't as important as the yeoman signaller, of course – he's our chiefie – but no one can afford to make mistakes, especially if they want to get on in the Navy. Still, we clean and scrub and sweep, good training for a housewife, that's wharr I always say.'

'Except that these days,' Martin observed, 'house-wives seem to spend most of their time having fun, going to dances, entertaining the troops you might say.'

Sunny, rightly interpreting this embittered remark to apply to Martin's wife, was silent, having nothing to say, but after a short pause, Martin continued. 'Oh, I shouldn't moan, Monica does write . . . but her letters are so short and mostly she talks about dances, helping in the NAAFI, that sort o' thing. I suppose she doesn't know much about the Navy, so she thinks we're livin' it up in exotic foreign ports, or at least that's how she makes it sound. She actually asked me, in one of her letters, if I ever got a chance to buy pretty materials, because she'd like to make herself a new dance dress!'

'You want to put her right,' Sunny suggested. 'Poor gal, she'd be rare ashamed if she knew what your life was really like. I mean, I reckon the Navy's the hardest of all the services, don't you?'

'Yup,' Martin said briefly. 'Monica's all right, really – I shouldn't have criticised her to you, it wasn't fair. It's – it's just that she's got no relatives in the Navy, no uncles or brothers or anything like that and her daddy wasn't in the last lot so she's got no idea of what it's all about and I suppose I – I underplayed it a bit, so's not to worry her. Given time, she'll work it out and mebbe, when I'm home next, I'll tell her a bit more.'

'Right,' Sunny said equably. 'G'night, Mart. See you in the morning.'

It took several days for the convoy to assemble and during that time Martin and Sunny found that it was comforting to have a pal aboard. They talked a good deal about Polly, the O'Brady family and Sunny's parents and by the time the convoy finally went to sea they were good friends.

'Me dad encouraged me to go to sea,' Sunny told Martin as they prepared dinner for their mess, chopping vegetables and dried beef. 'I joined in '38, so he saw me in me uniform before war was declared. But I can't write to him or anything like that. Or perhaps I could, if I posted the letter when we are in port for refuelling,' he added thoughtfully.

The early part of their voyage was fairly uneventful, apart from a practice attack by the RAF during the course of which bags of flour were dropped on the ships by the attacking 'planes, putting 'out of action' a large number of the escort.

'Good thing it wasn't for real,' Sunny grumbled to Martin. 'The trouble is, Mart, that you couldn't tell if any of your guns hit an aircraft, so it was all a bit one-sided.'

'You say that because you got a flour bag right on the flag-deck,' Martin grinned. 'Did you know we're stopping at Gibraltar? It might give us the chance of an hour or so ashore.'

'It'll give me the chance,' Sunny said smugly. 'I'm the buffer's assistant that day. Of course they might let us all go ashore, but somehow I doubt it. Tell you what, Mart, if I get a chance, shall I get some material for your old woman? You can pay me in "sippers", or in fags if you'd rather.'

All men over twenty got a rum ration each day and it was a common practice to swap goods for either 'sippers' or 'gulpers' of your rum, if you didn't mind losing just about all your ration.

'I'll pay you for the service in fags and for the stuff itself in money,' Martin said promptly. 'Would you really buy it for me, Sunny? It would be kind of you so it would. And just how did you get a cushy job like that, come to think?'

'Oh, I heard the bo'sun sayin' he was going ashore to get fruit and that,' Sunny said airily. 'He said he'd not been ashore in Gib for years, and would like to go again. So I said I knew just the place for fruit and vegetables, good alright, but cheap, too. So he said I could come along if I liked to give him a hand.'

'How come you know the Rock so well?' Martin asked suspiciously. 'The bo'sun's been on the andrew for years.'

'Yes, but not on the med. runs,' Sunny said. 'As for knowing Gibraltar, I've only been there a couple of times meself. But mostly, it's one long street that winds up from the foot of the rock itself to near enough the top of the town, so I reckon we'll find a shop selling fruit along there somewhere.'

'You're a bit of a skate, aren't you?' Martin said, half-admiringly. 'Telling the bo'sun a load of tosh to get yourself a trip ashore. And anyway, we may all get shore leave; you never know.'

'That's true enough, la'. Wi' the Navy you never do know,' Sunny said. 'And I wasn't taking no chances, so do you want me to buy you some silk for your missus or don't you?'

'I'd be grateful, so I would,' Martin said promptly. 'She's not a bad girl, my Monica, just a bit thoughtless. And . . . and I daresay I've not been much of a husband to her in some ways. Will you be able to get some silk, d'you think?'

'Sure to,' Sunny said. He remembered the wonderful, colourful shops on Main Street, with the delicate embroidery, the fashionable gowns and the brilliant jewellery displayed in the shop windows. 'If you knew her size you could get her a dress, come to that. Would she rather have a dress, d'you suppose?'

But Martin, after only a second's thought, shook his head. 'No, she'd rather have material to make one up for herself. She's good wit' her needle, and if I can get enough stuff it'll keep her busy for a night or two.'

Sunny grinned. 'Right you are, ole pal,' he said cheerfully. 'A bolt o' silk it shall be!'

By the time Sunny and the Bo'sun set off on their expedition, Sunny had collected little commissions from a good half of his companions, for their stay in Gibraltar was to be a short one, and most people wanted something which they could not get aboard the *Felix*. On his own account, he decided he would buy a pair of pretty earrings for Polly, or perhaps a necklace; something pretty but inexpensive.

So it was with a light heart that Sunny set off with the Bo'sun, walking up through Irish Town towards the main shopping centre. It was a brilliant day and very hot in the narrow street, however, and presently Sunny began to realise that he felt rather odd. The money in his pockets seemed to be weighing him down, and when he glanced up at the whitewashed buildings, they seemed to dazzle and change shape before his eyes.

However, he said nothing until they entered Main Street and began their shopping, and even then he only told the Bo'sun that he thought he ought to walk on the shady rather than the sunny side of the street, since he was beginning to feel very hot indeed.

The Bo'sun made some joking remark about how odd it was that a feller known as Sunny should want to keep out of the sun and then they went into a shop selling the most marvellous materials, and Sunny began the serious task of choosing, for his pal, something that would both keep his wife indoors and before her sewing machine whilst at the same time making her think of her absent husband with warmth and affection.

In the end he chose a very beautiful cream-coloured silk covered with bronze poppies, which took up almost all Martin's money, and then the two of them went back into the hot and dusty street once more.

Out there, Sunny realised that he felt very peculiar indeed. Now, the buildings did not merely dazzle, they swooped up and down, seeming immense one moment and tiny the next. What was more, his skin felt as though he were being roasted, and also as though he had been attacked by a thousand fleas – his skin actually *crawled*. He had heard people say their skin crawled often enough but had never understood what they meant until this moment.

He turned to the Bo'sun with the intention of suggesting they went into a pub for a drink, but realised he did not even feel capable of speech, so merely continued to trail in the older man's wake, the steepness of the street seeming suddenly like Mount Everest, though the stifling heat gave the lie to this fancy.

Afterwards, Sunny could not remember what they bought or how they arranged things, but he realised they must have done most of their shopping when the Bo'sun steered him into what he dimly realised must be some sort of graveyard, right at the top of the town, and sat him down on a bench beneath a shady tree.

'You're not lookin' so good, young feller-me-lad,' the Bo'sun said. His voice sounded concerned, but not only concerned; it sounded hollow and echoing, and very strange indeed. 'If you don't buck up in the next half-hour I'm thinkin' I'd best get you back . . . Whoa up, hold up, young feller!'

Sunny wondered what on earth the other man was on about, but just then his mind was taken off the Bo'sun and his behaviour by the even odder behaviour of the land around him. It seemed to tip, tilt and slide sideways, so that though he was unaware of moving himself, he presently found that the burning blue sky was above him, and that he was seeing it through what appeared to be large, dark bars.

And then, as he tried to struggle up, to tell the Bo'sun that he would be all right in a minute, he found that everything was rushing away from him very fast, getting smaller and smaller until it disappeared into very unpleasant, roaring blackness.

Sunny came round, groggily, to find himself being carted over the cobblestones of what appeared to be a courtyard. He groaned and the Bo'sun's voice said breathlessly, close to his ear: 'All righty, young feller, soon have you where you belong.'

'Back . . . the ship?' Sunny asked dizzily. He was suddenly aware that he had not bought Polly's earrings – or had he been going to get a necklace? He tried to struggle free, to say he was all right, it was just the heat, and found that his arms were apparently tied to something, that he could scarcely move. He gave a squawk of alarm and forced his eyes open and realised that he was between two sturdy men – the Bo'sun was one, the other was unknown to him – being carried along with his feet trailing, his arms across their shoulders.

'We're takin' you up to the horspital, mate,' someone said. 'You'll be awright there – you seem to 'ave got yourself a touch of fever, you're burnin' hot, so y'are.'

Another sailor, Sunny thought. It's another sailor, from another ship, and he's helping the Bo'sun to carry me . . . where? A hospital? But I don't need a hospital, all I need is – is a nice cool bath and then my own hammock. I'll be fine after a sleep.

He tried to say this but found it was simply too much trouble, and, without remembering how he got there, he found himself being divested of his clothing by what sounded like a couple of girls, dressed in some sort of nightgown, and thrust, gently but firmly, between snowy sheets whose brilliance was so extremely painful to his burning eyes that he shut them with great determination and kept them closed.

He was horribly thirsty now, though, and said so in a cracked, painful voice, and presently the soft-voiced girls brought a cup with a sort of pipe thing which they put between his lips and lovely cool liquid trickled across his parched tongue and down his burning throat.

He had barely finished the drink before a man came to the bed and addressed him in a voice of determined cheerfulness whilst heaving Sunny into a sitting position and beginning to fiddle with whatever garment – if felt like a large shirt – he was now wearing.

'Sorry to maul you about, old fellow,' the man said heartily. 'Dear me! Nurse, have you seen his chest?'

'He's covered in it, doctor,' a girl's voice said. 'His eyes hurt . . . Is it – can it be measles?'

'My own diagnosis exactly,' the doctor said. 'Here's one little rating who won't be sailing with his ship later today.' He turned back to Sunny, gently lowering him down the bed once more. 'Been in contact with any sick children lately, lad? Got younger brothers and sisters, have you?'

Sunny groaned. 'Oh my Gawd,' he mumbled disgustedly. 'I took me girl up to the Strawb, doc, and one of the kids were all over me. I said to me pal she were burning hot – the little gal – and somehow I never did get the measles, as a sprog.'

'Well, you've got 'em now,' the doctor said cheerfully. 'And you'll be in quarantine for two weeks, so you can forget sailing with . . . what is it? Oh yes, the *Felix*. She'll be going on without you, if she hasn't already gone, but the captain sent a message up to say she'd call for you on her way back, when she's taken the convoy to its destination.'

'Gone without me? Oh, but I were buyin' stuff for

me pals, the fellers aboard,' Sunny said, trying to struggle up the bed once more. 'I don't remember much . . . I'd not gorra pair of earrings for my girl . . . there was silk for me pal Martin . . .'

'Don't you worry about a thing, or you'll be here a lot longer than a fortnight,' the doctor said reassuringly. Sunny risked a peep and found that he was a large, cheerful-looking man with very short gingery hair and a pair of amused, grey-green eyes. 'You're going to feel pretty bad for a couple of days – measles once you're fully grown is no light matter – but you'll get excellent nursing and be up and about after a week, you mark my words. You're in a room by yourself because we've no one else with a contagious disease in at present, so make the most of the quiet to have plenty of sleep. Nurse Whitaker had measles when she was young so she will take good care of you, and mind you do what she says. Take your medicine – it's only aspirin dissolved in water, there isn't a great deal else we can give you at this stage – and you'll be fighting fit by the time your ship returns. Good day to you.'

Sunny risked another peep out of his sore and aching eyes. Nurse Whitaker was young, fair-skinned, freckled. Definitely pretty. He tried to smile at her and found, to his own astonishment, that he was tired, really tired. Seconds later, he slept.

The doctor was soon proved right. Sunny thought afterwards that he must have slept a good deal that first week, but at the end of it he was taking notice, eating whatever food was put before him and probably driving the nurses crazy by trying to persuade someone to let him go outside.

'We've no gardens, unfortunately, space being at a

premium on the Rock,' Sister told him when he fretted and fumed over being shut up indoors in his small private room all day. 'And you're still infectious, so we can't let you go wandering about the town or the dockyards. Just be a little patient, young man. And anyway, since you spend your life cooped up on board your ship . . .'

'That's different,' Sunny said, and was then unable to explain why. But the nurses provided him with jigsaws, copies of the English papers several days, or even weeks, old, and as much fruit as he could eat, and at last the doctor pronounced him free from infection and told him he could go to the Royal Naval Barracks and sling his hammock there until the *Felix* came back for him.

'Which shouldn't be long,' Sunny told Nurse Whitaker as she helped him to pack up his personal effects. To Sunny's joy, Martin had thoughtfully sent his shaving kit, clean underwear and various other bits and pieces to the hospital by messenger as soon as he heard what had happened to his pal. He had included a note thanking Sunny for the silk which had eased Sunny's conscience considerably. It was the first real proof that the Bo'sun had got all their shopping back on board the *Felix* before she sailed, and it had comforted him in his illness to know that at least he had not let his shipmates down.

Once in the Naval Barracks, with the companionship of other men, Sunny soon recovered his full health and although he was impatient for the *Felix* to return, he made the best of her absence. He went all over the town, made friends with some of the soldiers stationed there to guard the dockyards and thus got taken round the amazing defences which, long ago, other servicemen had tunnelled and blasted out of the limestone of the great face of the Rock. He also wrote letters to Polly, to Grace, reproaching her for giving him the measles, albeit second-hand, so to speak, and to his mother. He went up to the top of the rock where the Gibraltar apes lived and reassured himself that they were still very much there and in good health, since an old proverb said that when the apes left the Rock then the British would do likewise, and he stared out to sea, to the constantly changing face of the ocean and the various craft making their way into the enormous spread of naval dockyards below him.

But the *Felix* did not come. And one morning he was met by a seaman, also waiting for a ship, who told him that the pair of them had been drafted.

'Drafted? Where to? Why?' Sunny said, astonished. 'But I've gorra stay here, mate. Me ship's comin' back for me!'

'Oh aye?' the other man said, disinterested. He was also from Liverpool and had been brought ashore with a ruptured appendix some three months previously and had almost forgotten the name of his previous frigate. 'Well, we're to report to the *Pursuer*. She's a destroyer, so you'll know your way around.'

So Sunny got his gear together once more and went down to the dock and aboard the *Pursuer*, to find himself hailed with considerable glee by Dempsey, who had been with his present craft ever since Sunny had joined the *Felix*.

'It's grand to see you again, Dempsey,' Sunny said, going below and taking possession of his new locker. 'But why hasn't the *Felix* come back? Have you heard?'

Dempsey shrugged. 'The convoy could have been slower than they thought,' he said. 'Or she could have been sunk.'

288

Sunny stared, his heart sinking into his boots. 'Not – not sunk, surely?' he said incredulously. 'Someone would've told me. Someone would have known!'

Dempsey looked embarrassed. He began to heave Sunny's hammock up on to its hooks and to spread out the palliasse. 'The convoy was about ten days outside Gib when they were attacked,' he mumbled. 'I – I don't reckon they fished anyone out, ole pal. You must have known something was up when she didn't come back for you earlier.'

But Sunny was staring at him, round-eyed. 'Polly's brother was aboard her. He was me bezzie,' he said slowly. 'Are you tellin' me he's drownded? Oh, Jesus, Dempsey, what'll I be telling my Polly?'

Martin had known they were going to have a sticky time as soon as he saw the Fokker-Wolf reconnaissance plane with the black crosses on its wings approaching the convoy. 'Action stations – clear away for battle,' had been piped as soon as the skipper saw the plane, a mere dot in the bright evening sky. The plane he knew could be the forerunner of an attack which they had feared ever since the plane had appeared in the sky the previous day. Then, the first enemy ships had been seen approaching over the horizon converging fast on them. Martin knew the German destroyers had 5-inch guns, heavier than their own 4.7s, but this need not affect the outcome of a battle at sea. Luck, the ability to move fast and to change direction quickly and above all, accuracy of fire, would more drastically affect the outcome.

He climbed into his gun trainer's seat in the turret where the guns were loaded and pointed skywards, ready to fire as soon as the order was given. Settling himself comfortably, he glanced at his companions.

They were standing as steadily as if this were just a practice, but like him they were ready to fire, knowing that everyone's life depended on the speed with which one's guns could retaliate.

Martin settled his anti-flash helmet and tightened the wrist-straps of his gloves. If there was a flash-back from one of the rounds then helmet and gloves, with vaseline liberally smeared on his face, could save him from nasty burns. The gun captain reminded them that they should keep the gun firing once they started, making sure that the ammo was handy.

The order had been given that no one was to leave his position and now Martin settled back in his seat and gripped the training wheel, watching as the two white pointers drew into line. They were on B-gun, and Martin could see through the opening in the gun-shield that the enemy were fast approaching, and that they were approaching, what was more, in force. It was easy to tell oneself that it was the wallowing merchantmen that the slim, deadly destroyers would be aiming for, but it did not take a great deal of intelligence to realise that the merchant fleet would be a good deal easier to attack if the enemy could first sink their defenders.

There was a commotion on deck; Martin could visualise what was happening as the officers watched the approaching destroyers through their binoculars, calculating the moment when they would come within range of the *Felix*'s guns. He risked a quick glance round and saw the crew of B-gun, shells at the ready for the reload. Martin was aware of a sickly sinking sensation in his stomach and a sweat breaking out on his forehead. As always of late, just before they went into battle, he saw Monica in his mind's eye, pretty in a summer dress, her adoring eyes fixed on his, anxious only to please him. He had not been fair to her, he had acknowledged it some time ago. He had tried to turn a little Liverpudlian girl with a head full of nothing but lovemaking and pretty clothes into the sort of woman he had wanted to marry. And when, in despair, she had stopped trying to please him and begun to rebel, he had been angry, hurt . . . but he had not gone about convincing her that he loved her, that their marriage, which had been at least half-play for her, could be real, earnest. And now they were going into battle and he might be killed, might never have the chance to tell her that he did love her, did value her, and was determined to make their marriage work. Why, he might never be able to give her the silk, which was so beautiful, which her clever fingers could make into a dance dress of such beauty that the fellers would vie for her attention – but other fellers would not matter, because she would know, by then, that it was Martin she loved.

He swallowed hard and despite his thoughts the sick feeling began to recede. It would be all right, he would have another chance, get back to Liverpool and see his poor, pretty little wife, show her how he felt about her, talk to her of serious matters. Get her a nice little house somewhere, where they might be together without her parents only a thin wall away so that even their lovemaking was circumscribed.

Fire! The order had been given, Martin's work had started. As he heard the first salvo, heard the clatter of spent shells on the deck and the snap of the closing interceptor, fear receded, thoughts of home became something which might take his whole concentration from the job in hand. Outside, the din of battle was enormous, and in the slight lull between broadsides, Martin risked a peep through the opening in his gun-shield. The light was fading from the sky and the dusk made the bursts of fire from other shipping seem even more brilliant. Screeching shells, whether from friend or enemy he could not tell, were falling all around and the pom-poms on deck, their noses turned to the sky, blended their clatter with the flash and thunder of their own guns.

Martin lined up his pointers and B-gun belched forth fire once more. In the pause, Martin could hear the sobbing breath of the men passing the shells up from the magazine and knew, amazingly, a moment of calm and confidence. They knew their jobs, they all did, so how could they fail to come out of this, to be the victors?

As night came down, the battle continued to rage and the sea grew rougher so that the ships, which had drawn close, were buffeted apart. The guns had blazed constantly until the ammunition in the magazines ran out and only then, when they were more or less defenceless, did the *Felix*, battered but still relatively uninjured, draw back a little from the fight. It was at that moment the explosion came. Martin, in his gun turret still, for they were still at action stations and would be until the battle was resolved, heard a tremendous bang and saw a sheet of flame appear before his eyes, the heat of it so strong that he was flung back, scorched.

He must have lost consciousness for a few moments for the next thing he knew he was out on the open deck, being supported by one of A-gun's crew, a Scots lad called Hamish.

'I think it was a torpedo, it hit us below the water-line and blew up our magazine – good thing it was empty,' he said, managing to give a short crack of laughter despite the conditions, the dark, the flames, the list of the deck which made Martin think for a moment that he was climbing some great hill. 'You got a chunk of metal on the head, we all thought you were a goner, and then, just as I was about to get the hell out o' there, I heard you groan and begin to come round. We should be okay, though we're a good way from the rest of the fleet . . . They're dropping boats, but the sea's very rough . . . You'll not have heard the pipe to abandon ship.'

It was now that Martin realised for the first time that it was quiet; they could hear, distantly, the sound of battle, but their own firearms were silent and apart from the roar of the waves and the hiss of the wind, the *Felix* might have been on her own in the great ocean. He looked around him; men were lining up, an officer was going from group to group, checking that they all wore life jackets, that they knew what to do.

He and Hamish joined one of the queues, and then suddenly it was as though Martin came completely back to life. That was it! They were in the *Felix*, heading for home albeit by a roundabout route, and he was taking Monica home a present of silk – cream-coloured silk covered with bronze poppies. It was the most beautiful thing he'd ever seen or imagined, his pal Sunny had chose it, and he would get it back to Monica if it was the last thing he did. He looked round wildly. A nearby companionway led down into the bowels of the ship – to his fo'c'sle, in fact. It looked very like the descent into hell, but . . .

'Come back . . . Martin, you fool, you can't go down there!'

'I've got to go, there's a present I bought for me wife . . .'

And he had gone, was fighting his way down the

steps into that strange darkness which smelt of gunpowder and charred wood and worse. It was like a vision of hell, and God alone knew how he found his own locker, wrenched it open, seized from it the soft thickness of the material and began to blunder out again, the stuff in his arms. But after only a few paces he realised he would need both his hands free for the clamber back to the deck, up the companionway, so with difficulty he heaved his life jacket away from his chest, pushed the material down the front of it, and struggled on, with water now above his knees. And presently, he heard a rushing and a crash behind him and felt the ship tilt more violently yet, and when he battled his way back along the narrow corridor and reached the companionway water, sizzling like frying sausages and churning and tearing apart anything in its path, roared to meet him. Martin seized the bannisters and for a moment imagined that he would be all right, that he could fight his way out on to the deck once more.

Then another, larger wave roared down upon him, snatching his hands from the rail as though he were a year-old child, and threw him back even as another huge explosion caused the ship to open up like an oyster to the knife. Martin caught a muddled glimpse of a dark sky blazing with stars, flames shooting skywards, and then it was just water, water, everywhere he looked. Heavy, salty, and icy cold it threw him down, overwhelmed him. Snuffed out the stars.

'If you ask me, I'm the only person in this war who's spending it writing bleedin' letters,' Polly said crossly, sitting at the kitchen table with her writing materials set out all around her. She pushed the pad away and stared mournfully across at her father, counting coupons on the opposite side of the table. 'First, I just wrote to me brothers, then it was to Tad, then to Sunny, now it's Grace as well . . . Oh, it isn't fair! If I were in the WRNs people would have to write to *me*, which would be more like it, so it would. Besides, I'd be doing interesting things, which would make letters far easier to write. Still, Grace writes pretty regular, and her letters are really interesting. She's met a lovely feller . . . and Daddy, d'you know she writes to Sunny? Isn't that the nicest t'ing, now? She's ever so kind, is our Grace.'

Deirdre, knitting socks beside the kitchen fire, smiled encouragingly across at her daughter. 'Your letters are lovely, and give a deal of pleasure,' she said. 'It's a hard life aboard ship, we know it, so Martin and Sunny are thrilled to bits when your letters arrive. But I didn't know Grace wrote to Sunny; did she tell you in that last letter?'

Polly nodded so vigorously that her short yellow curls danced on her forehead. 'Yes, she did so. She said she'd gone and given Sunny the measles, or good as, anyway, so he wrote and told her he was in hospital and she wrote and said how sorry she was. Well, she was sorry, because she'd been cuddling the little kid who was sickening for measles too, only Grace thinks she had it when she was six or seven. She said all the Carbery kids did, or at least she thought so.'

'Dear me, measles can be nasty,' Deirdre said, finishing off a row and flicking her work around to begin the next. 'Oh, me darlin' Polly, war work comes in a lot of different forms. Don't fret yourself; in the not very distant future you'll be joining the forces – the WRNs, I mean – I've no doubt of that. But until you do, keep on with those letters and little parcels, and don't forget that if you didn't have your good job you wouldn't be able to buy treats for Mart and Sunny.'

'Good job!' Polly said witheringly, but she pulled the pad of paper towards her again. 'I know I'm almost the only one left in the office wit' decent short-hand and speedy typing, the only one young enough to run messages over half Liverpool, but I'm not one whit appreciated, Mammy. Mr Slater would sack me tomorrer if he thought he could replace me with someone else.'

'Well, you've the satisfaction of knowing he can't—' Deirdre was beginning when someone knocked on the kitchen door, at first feebly and then with such a rattle that Polly fairly flew across the room to open it. It was November, and a wild night, with a high wind howling along the narrow street and when she wrenched at the door it was not only a slender, storm-battered creature who tumbled inside, but a miniature gale, as well as a good few dead leaves and a gust of rain. The girl in the dark coat began pulling off the garment even as Polly said hospitably, 'Evenin', Monica! You're quite a one for making an entrance, aren't you! I thought you were living it up in Southport, what on earth are you doing here?' She began to help her sister-in-law out of her wet coat. 'Oh, don't say Martin's coming home again!' she exclaimed, remembering the last time Monica had come rapping on their door. 'When did you hear? He and Sunny are on the same ship, you know, which means they'll both be back!'

Monica gave a moan and pulled off hat and gloves, dropping them on the floor with a complete disregard for the linoleum, which had been brushed and mopped clean directly after the family's high tea.

Then she produced a crumpled half-sheet of yellow paper and held it out to Peader, who had stood up to greet her with his customary hug and whose face, at the sight of that piece of paper, lost all its colour and looked suddenly haggard and old.

'H-he's missing,' Monica said brokenly. 'H-his ship went down . . . There was a battle . . . It was weeks ago, but the Admiralty waited . . . Oh Dad, I can't bear it!'

Chapter Eleven

MARCH 1942

Polly put the rest of her gear into her canvas issue kitbag and took a last, leisurely look around her, at the room where she and her friends had spent a good deal of their lives over the last six months. She was sorry to leave it in a way, but Scotland was a very long way from home, and though she had enjoyed herself well enough, learning her job, getting to know the other WRNs, she had often been homesick for Liverpool, for her family and friends.

She remembered her many moans in civvy life about letter-writing; how her letters to her brothers, to Sunny and Tad and Grace, had seemed so dull, with nothing very much to say. Yet she soon realised that life in the services, fascinating though it might be, did not take away her letter-writing chores, and because of the censor, her service letters might well be as dull as her civvy ones had been, for though the scenes in which they were set were more interesting to her, they concerned people that her correspondents had never met, with only occasional remarks about Liverpool, or her parents, to make them more personal.

What had really changed her life first of all, of course, had been Martin's ship going down, and Martin being lost. With the first real tragedy that she had ever suffered, the war had become personal to her. She thought of Martin with a deep and painful grief, because they had not been as close as they might have been, because she had not liked his wife, had disapproved of his marriage. So it was partly guilt that had sent her marching into the insurance office to tell Mr Slater what to do with his job – that had given her enormous satisfaction – and then she had gone along to the parachute factory in Hanover Street where her mother worked and signed on with them. Making parachutes had been fun, she had enjoyed the company, the chatter, and the feeling that she was doing her bit to kick old Hitler in the goolies – not her own expression, Bev's – but it had not quite made up for the impersonality of it. For many weeks after the news of Martin's fate she had felt angry, felt that she wanted to see some damned Jerry suffer the way her parents – and Monica – were suffering because of what they had done. Munitions might have been better, knowing that the shells and bullets would actually go to kill the hated enemy, but munitions dyed your skin the most awful yellow colour which would not, Polly had decided judicially, have gone very well with her yellow curls. So she had stuck to making parachutes, putting a great deal of care and enthusiasm into the task, until the May Blitz.

Deirdre had been working at the time in the Hanover Street parachute factory in the old Littlewoods building, and she and Polly had been on the night shift with high explosive bombs and fire bombs raining down on the city, when it was considered too dangerous to allow the workers to stay at their machines, but it had been no joke trying to make their way home, either. The streets had been chaotic. Walking to work together earlier that evening Polly and her mother had talked about the destruction caused the previous night: Lime Street Station had been hit, so trains were no longer running from there and fire bombs had landed on the Crawford Biscuit

Works, totally destroying it. 'Not that they were making biscuits,' Deirdre had said darkly. 'Oh, I wouldn't mind a nice packet of custard creams, right this minute.'

But that had been before half past ten when this raid had started with a ferocity that Liverpool had never known before. It had been bad enough when they were both working, with other girls chattering to distract them from the mayhem outside, but walking through the streets lit by fires from buildings which only hours before had looked impregnable was truly terrifying. It did not seem possible that their factory could possibly escape, but neither did it seem likely that the two of them would reach home safely.

However, they had done so, and Peader, fire watching in the city centre, had also been unhurt, though he had not returned home until lunchtime the following day.

It had been the worst eight days of Polly's life. The destruction had seemed to be total. The overhead railway had been hit two or three times as had ordinary rail lines, making travel by such means impossible. Blackler's, where Polly had worked as a schoolgirl, and Lewis's, where she and her mother had shopped, were no more. Bankhall Bridge was destroyed, effectively cutting off the city from the north, and there had been considerable loss of life. Despite the fact that St Sylvester's had been razed to the ground, that her old school had been bombed almost out of existence and that Silvester Street itself had been gutted, the O'Bradys and their neighbours had suffered no fatalities. The barrage balloon site at the end of their road had been a casualty, though; none of the cheery RAF personnel had lived when the bombs had started fires which had destroyed their accommodation, their supplies of hydrogen, and their vast, inflated charges, which had taken to the air, casting flames on everything below, until they had burned out. Polly had got to know the Bops – balloon operatives – pretty well, and hated to think that those bright-eyed young men were all dead, but she had not known them as she had known Martin.

So when the May Blitz ceased, the O'Bradys had been left with a windowless, doorless, almost roofless house and no means of making it whole again, not whilst the shortages of building materials lasted. Peader, however, said that they had got their lives, which was what mattered, and shortly after the house had been pronounced unfit for occupation had calmly moved them out to a small, draughty bungalow on Morton Shore, owned by an elderly woman whose husband had been killed on his way home from a night-shift in the city and who was nervous, she said, of living alone through such times.

'It's her house, the place she and her husband saved for and bought when they were first married, so the good God alone knows how we'll all get on together, because two women into one kitchen usually don't go,' Deirdre had said doubtfully to her daughter, when Peader had announced the plan. 'But anything's better than this.' She had gestured around her, at the church hall where they had been told to stay until they found somewhere better. 'It's bedrooms which will be most difficult, because it's a two-bedroomed bungalow, which means one for Mrs Marshall and one for the rest of us. But you can have a bed on the couch in the living room, I daresay, and when the boys and Grace come home we'll manage something. Besides, you know how practical your daddy is – he'll find some way of getting the

Titchfield Street house put right before too long, you mark my words.'

But Polly had had enough of being a dutiful daughter and doing her best to please parents who, she had long ago realised, had no intention of going off to some safe haven, either in England or Ireland, and who were perfectly capable of looking after themselves.

'I'm going to join the WRNs, Mammy, so count me out when you come to dividing up the bungalow bedrooms,' she had said airily. 'I'm old enough, so I am, and I've been wantin' to do me bit ever since . . . well, for a year or more. I wouldn't have left you and me daddy whilst you were living in Titchfield Street, in the heart of the city, but out at Morton Shore you should be safe enough – as safe as you'll let your-selves be, that is.'

So Polly had joined the WRNs, had agreed to serve anywhere she was sent, and was duly despatched to Scotland, where she and her fellow-entrants had been trained for the work they were to do. Now she had a long and complicated train journey ahead of her, which would no doubt be further complicated by the heavy snow which still lay thick on the ground here in the north, but at the end of it there would be an interesting new posting – and who knew what she might have to learn when she reached Holyhead, on the Isle of Anglesey?

Once the train was on the move and was crowded with service personnel and a few civilians, mainly mothers with small children, going about their normal business, Polly got out her writing pad, albeit with a martyred sigh. She had best write to everyone she knew, telling them about her posting, so that she might receive letters when she got to Anglesey. Life, she mused as she got out her fountain pen, had a way of giving with one hand and snatching back with the other. Letters must be written no matter what.

It was not easy to write letters on the train, but fortunately in one sense at least, there were a good few hold-ups, when Polly's pen fairly sped across the page. Tad was still in Yorkshire with his beloved Beaufighters, but Grace had moved to Norfolk, where she seemed to spend a good deal of her time trying to keep out of the wind which, she said, blew constantly across the great flat expanses of the countryside. Polly knew she would have to write to them both – and Sunny – and send them her new address but decided that, for once, she would write them just the one page. To Tad first. Tad who she hadn't seen since her childhood, but who she still missed.

Despite himself, for he was a man grown now, Tad thought a good deal about Polly, though he usually thought of her as she had been when he had last seen her, a child of ten with a mop of primrose-coloured curls and such sweet and loving ways that she had been universally adored. She had been a little imp, but everyone had loved her and when she left Dublin to go with her parents to Liverpool, in England, how horribly he had missed her! There had been no one like Polly for sticking by a feller, no one like her to share in your adventures.

He thought about Polly more because of Angela's defection, of course. Poor Angela. She had hated having to break it to him that she'd met someone else but thank the good Lord she had had the courage to do it. The world was full of pretty girls eager to make an airman's life happier and Tad did not intend to deprive them of his charms. Polly was an old mate but she was not here. And truth to tell, he had been finding it hard, for some time, to bring Angela's face into his mind's eye when he wanted to remember her. It got muddled up with his memories of Polly – so much stronger, even after their long parting – so that Angela's pale, well-tended face with its elegant little nose and light blue eyes became confused with Polly's rosy, wickedly dimpled smiles; whilst Polly's sturdy ten-year-old body got equally muddled up with Angela's slender waist and firmly jutting breasts. Tad supposed somewhat doubtfully that Polly, too, would have a proper waist, and nice, rounded breasts by now, but somehow he could not imagine it. He could only see *his* Polly, the one he had teased and tickled and bawled at and comforted all those years ago. She had asked him tearfully to help her when she needed help and had shouted rudely at him to leave her alone now and bleedin' well buzz off when she was cross. And, peculiarly enough, he missed her.

There was his work, the most absorbing, exciting, challenging work that Tad had ever embarked upon.

He serviced the engines of the Beaufighters which flew from his station. He treated every plane as though it was the most important piece of machinery on the station, and not only that, as though he felt personally responsible for the slightest failure. He knew, to the last note, how an engine should sound.

Because of this, the pilots in his squadron began to offer him short trips in the planes, whenever a test-flight was needed after he had done a repair. And because of his interest, they began to show him how they flew the planes. As a result of this, no sooner were they off the ground than Tad would take over the controls, and he grew daily more expert, even landing – and taking off – more than once.

Sometimes it was suggested by one of the young airmen that he might like to change over and become air crew but much though he enjoyed flying, Tad knew that if he once agreed to fly, that would be the end of his close and loving association with the aero engines which were his abiding passion. He also knew that though he might become a pretty good pilot, he would never become a top-flight one. And he was a top-flight mechanic.

So though Tad enjoyed the company of pretty girls, right now, he was a Beaufighter man, and was well content to work in their service. So he did not repine unduly over Angela's defection. He wrote to his brothers and sisters and to his sweet-faced, long-suffering mother, and to Polly, of course. And he coaxed and coddled and cosseted his Beaufighters and was, though he probably never thought about it, that rare thing, a happy and contented young man.

Deirdre and Peader had been sad to leave the bungalow on Moreton Shore behind them, but it was a long way out when it came to getting into work each day, and Peader, though he joined the ARP there, as he had in Liverpool, found it less exciting than being with a big city force. So when Deirdre got chatting with Mrs Ayton from Snowdrop Street who worked alongside her in Hanover Street, she was interested to hear that Mrs Ayton's neighbours had recently moved out of their house three or four dwellings further along the road, and gone to live with relatives near Mold, North Wales.

'Will it be goin' up for rent?' Deirdre asked with

seeming casualness as the two of them drew the soft parachute silk through the maw of their machines, checking every stitch though the stuff fairly flew along, for was it not a matter of life and death to see that the silk was not bunched up or had gaping seams? 'I'd like to be nearer the city, so I would, and it's a long trail home at nights, when I'm tired half to death. What's more, my Peader's frettin' out there wit' so little to keep him occupied. Oh, he likes the gardenin', and he gets on well wit' Mrs Marshall, our landlady, but he'd see a lot more of me if we could move into somewhere like Snowdrop Street.'

She did not add, which she could have done with perfect truth, that Mrs Marshall, now that the worst of the bombing seemed to have calmed down, had made it clear that she was no longer afraid to be alone. She liked having Deirdre and Peader and made no objection to the occasional bursts of having a house straining at the seams when members of their large family got leave and came to stay, but she knew that Deirdre was itching to have Brogan to visit them when he got leave. Brogan had come over as a member of the American Army and was stationed at Burtonwood and though it was fairly near Liverpool he had not, so far, managed to get away from the camp.

So when Mrs Ayton came into work a couple of days later and told Deirdre that the house was indeed to be let, the O'Bradys had been delighted. Peader had joined his wife on the train into work that morning, she having arranged to have a morning off, and they had inspected the house. It was not newly decorated and needed a good deal of work, but Peader had seen at once that with a bit of help they could make it into a nice home.

'Building materials are hard to find,' the landlord had said doubtfully when Peader pointed out some of the faults – the back kitchen roof was leaking and there was no plaster on one wall and the privy in the back yard was full of cobwebs and had a large hole in the door and no bolt on the inside, either. 'You might get hold of some old roof slates from some of the bombed buildings, but I dunno about stuff like plaster – you need permits for that kind o' thing, to say nothin' of wood. Why, I've even had to go down on me benders for a few nails!'

But he agreed to a slightly reduced rent provided that Peader saw to such things himself and did not expect the landlord to perform miracles, and so in February, after a tearful farewell with Mrs Marshall, the O'Bradys had moved into Snowdrop Street.

'We'll tell the children right away, so's our post keeps coming straight to us,' Deirdre had planned busily, putting a couple of buckets in the main bedroom where the front of the roof persisted in leaking despite Peader and a pal having put a number of uncracked slates over the gaps.

But right now, it was Saturday morning and Peader and Deirdre had enjoyed a nice lie-in, since Deirdre did not work on a Saturday, and then they had got up slowly and gone downstairs to the kitchen to have a nice leisurely breakfast before deciding what they should do that day.

'Not that there's all that much choice, alanna,' Peader said ruefully as they sat down to toast and gooseberry jam and two good, strong mugs of tea. Deirdre had made quantities of gooseberry jam from the fruit in Mrs Marshall's garden, and that good lady had insisted that the O'Bradys should take a good half of the jam back to Liverpool with them. 'If we do some shopping this morning, though, we might go to a flick this afternoon. What d'you t'ink of that, eh?'

'It depends what's on,' Deirdre said, turning the pages of last night's *Echo* as she bit into her toast. 'I wouldn't mind taking a look in at TJ's this morning, though.'

TJ's was still managing to do a good job for their poorer clientele despite wartime shortages and Deirdre, who had thought the big store a regular heaven when she had first been introduced to it, was a frequent shopper there still.

'That suits me, we can catch a tram and mebbe do all our shopping up an' down London Road—' Peader was beginning when they heard the post come rattling through the front door and Deirdre jumped to her feet and ran to fetch it. She came back with a good handful, two air letters amongst them, and sat down again, abandoning the newspaper but beginning to crunch toast once more.

'Thank the good Lord we can still buy bread, and isn't this Sample's loaf twice as good as the stuff poor Mrs Marshall got, even though it's only a national loaf, same as hers?' she said, staring at the envelopes and putting them into the middle of the table one by one. 'There's a couple from the boys, one from Grace – what a good girl she is, Peader! – and one from Polly. Ooh, which shall we open first?'

'What's rare is precious; open the letters from the boys first,' Peader said, grinning. He loved his sons but acknowledged that letter-writing was not their forte, any more than it was his.

'One of them is from Niall,' Deirdre confirmed. She hesitated, twisting the letters in her hands. 'Oh, all right, I'll start wit' the boys.'

'It won't take you long,' Peader said comfortingly,

as she began to open the airmail letters. 'A minute, no longer, and you'll be free to start readin' what's been happenin' to your ewe lamb.'

Deirdre tutted and began to read, and he was right. Neither of the missives took longer than thirty seconds or so to read. Both Niall and Bev were happy. Niall had joined the Australian Air Force and was being trained at somewhere which the censor had seen fit to clip out. Bev was in the Air Force and was training to be a navigator. He seemed to relish the active life after his years at university, but like his brother, seemed to have very little to say save that he had met a very nice girl and might bring her home with him on his next leave.

'Good, good,' Peader said approvingly. 'Now let's open Polly's.'

'It's been an age since we've had our Poll under our roof,' Deirdre said wistfully. 'I wonder if she's getting leave soon. Wouldn't it be nice if she and Grace managed to have a few days at home together?'

'I wouldn't count on Polly gettin' leave at the same time as Grace, alanna,' Peader said mildly. 'Will you read me the letter now, Dee.'

'It's a long one,' Deirdre said joyfully. 'You know our Poll, she can't stop having a crack whether it's on paper or in person. Why, even her phone calls go on rather, though she can't afford long ones. Good thing they don't charge for letters by the page, or—'

'Oh, read it, woman,' Peader said, losing patience. 'Or I'll snatch it from your hand and read it for meself, so I will.'

'Right,' Deirdre said. She began reading.

It was, as she had anticipated, a good, long letter, filled with news, with scraps of information about her work, her friends, and her social life. It also contained her new address. 'Well, would you believe it, she's going to be working in Holyhead, where the boats go to Dublin,' Deirdre broke off to remark. Her eyes filled with tears. 'Oh, Peader, isn't she the lucky one, then? To be within spittin' distance of Dublin, where she was brought up! Why, she might even go over, on a visit. Oh, Peader, there's a bit here about her angel. Listen, whiles I read it to you.'

I don't see my angel as often as I did when I was smaller. But that doesn't mean I don't see her at all, because I do. Only it's strange, Mammy and Daddy, that she's a girl-angel, or so everyone else in my billet seems to think. Not that they know about her, for never a word would I speak to anyone. Not even Grace knows. But we got to talking about angels in the billet one night, and they all said angels were fellers. Only they're not Irish, like meself, so maybe 'tis only colleens that have girl-angels. Anyway, I wanted to tell you that I never see her full-on any more, the way I did when I was a kid. I don't even see her in the corner of my bedroom, or on the half-landing, like I did before I joined up. Now I see her if I'm out on the sea in one of the small boats in the darkness, and then it's just a shape and a sort of knowing she's there, rather than actually seeing her lovely little face. I suppose she couldn't come in to the billet, with so many other girls around me, but when I pad over to the ablutions sometimes she's right at the end of the building, where it's all dark and hardly anyone goes. She'll only be there for a moment, mind, but I'd not like to lose her altogether. Maybe, when I'm really old, she won't let me see her. But I reckon I'll always know she's there, somewhere, just out of sight, watching out for me.

'Now I wonder what brought that on?' Peader said mildly. He reached for the last piece of toast and

spread margarine on it, then dabbed on some gooseberry jam. 'She's not mentioned her guardian angel
for a long while, not when I'm about, at any rate. Do
you t'ink it's because she's feelin' a bit strange over
leaving' that Scottish island?'

'Probably because she's so near Ireland,' Deirdre
suggested. 'It set her thinking about home, that's
what. Now quiet or I can't finish.'

Peader, a quiet man, raised his brows but said
nothing and presently Deirdre, having given him a
severe look, continued.

*I've just now written to Grace, to tell her where to send
letters in future. Oh, I do love Grace, Mammy, she's as
good as a sister to me – I wish she was my sister, so I do!
We're going to try to get leave at the same time, because
she's the best person to go about with, apart from you
and Daddy, and the best person to share a secret. Sara's
lovely, my favourite sister-in-law, but she's a deal older
than me so it's not the same. Besides, she's married, so
she's a woman growed, whereas me and Grace are still
getting there. Sunny writes when he can, but sometimes
I get a grosh of letters all in the one post and then I go
without any for months and months. It's always the
same with the Navy, everyone says, because they can
only post their mail when they're in port, which doesn't
happen all that often when they're on convoy duty. I
miss Sunny a lot, but I expect I'll soon make other
friends in Holyhead.*

The letter ran on in Polly's usual bright, inconse-
quential way and Peader waited until his wife had
finished reading and put the letter down beside her
plate with a satisfied smile before raising the question
which, he thought, must be in both their minds.

'Deirdre, d'you t'ink this is the best moment to tell her? Tell Grace too? After all, so far as we've been able to find out they're the only two Carberys left. They should know that they're really sisters.'

He was watching his wife's face as he spoke and saw the bright colour drain from her cheeks, saw the way her hand flew to her throat. 'Oh, Peader, I can't bring meself to say a word about all that – isn't it dangerous, still, to let anyone know, this side o' the water?'

'I'm not suggesting we should broadcast it to the whole city, alanna,' he said gently. 'Polly's a good girl, and Grace is another, despite their background. When we'd explained how we'd taken Polly for our own to keep her from a drunken and violent father and an indifferent mother, then she – they – would both understand that we meant no harm by it. We thought, then, that it was for the best and we think so now. But Polly does so long for a sister, and one of these days someone is going to ask why she's so fair when the boys are all so dark ... and there's a look, I can't explain it, but there *is* a similarity, put it no stronger, between Grace and Polly. Wouldn't it be better to tell them now, rather than to have them find out from a chance remark? Remember, the boys do know she's not our child, though they've never so much as mentioned it since we told them not to, all those years ago.'

Deirdre was silent, remembering. Her son, Brogan, coming into the kitchen and opening his coat to show them the bright-eyed baby nestling against his chest. The boys had crowded round – Bev had been the baby then – whilst Brogan told them how he had found the baby in a snowstorm, and had decided to steal her for his mammy when her older sister, who had had the care of her, had been killed by a train.

She had told her sons that they must pretend the new baby had been left behind by a cousin from the country who could no longer keep her, but within a very short space of time Polly had been accepted by everyone as an O'Brady. Deirdre had guessed the child to have been eight or nine months when Brogan had brought her to Ireland, and by the time she was two she very much doubted whether the boys ever thought about her arrival, or the secret that they all shared concerning her. She was their adored and spoiled little sister and they would have dealt harshly with anyone who had indicated otherwise.

The angel episode had shaken Deirdre, though. When Polly had told her about the girl with the raggedy shawl who had appeared in the dark stairwell, smiling at her, she had felt terrified. Did this mean that Polly was going to start remembering that other, darker life which she had lived before she came to Dublin? She had told Polly that the girl must be her guardian angel . . . Then Polly, when taunted by the little friend who had been with her at the time, had said that the angel's name was Jess . . . it could still turn Deirdre's skin to gooseflesh thinking about it, for had not Polly's sister, who had kept the little girl alive, been called Jess?

But right now, there was Peader's question to be answered. She sighed, took a deep breath, let it out slowly, shook her head. 'I can't tell them, Peader. I just dare not. We *stole* that baby, there's no two ways about it, stole her from her rightful parents. If we were still in Ireland, now . . . but we aren't, we're here, in Liverpool, in the very city where it all happened nigh on eighteen years ago. I *dare* not tell 'em, not yet, not whilst the war's on, and there's all this uncertainty.'

313

'Well, it's up to you, so it is,' Peader said equably. 'But don't say I didn't warn you, alanna. There's a likeness, I'm tellin' you.'

'I can't see it, meself,' Deirdre said obstinately. 'Why, our Polly's pretty as a picture and though I love Grace dearly . . . well, her hair's mousy, she's tall as a stalk and thin too, and she's shy, there's no – no *glow* about her. I can't see anyone thinkin' them alike, honest to God, Peader.'

'It's not the hair colour, nor the height, nor the figures of 'em that's alike,' Peader said slowly. He scratched his thick, greying hair. 'I couldn't put me finger on it no matter how hard I tried, but I – I'm *aware* of it, me love. Still, mebbe it's only because I'm close to the pair of them that I notice. Mebbe it's that.'

Deirdre opened her mouth to say, pretty sharply, that she was closer to Polly than anyone else could possibly be, and then closed it again. No, she couldn't say that, or Peader would expect her to notice this mythical likeness which she honestly could not see, though she had tried often enough. She did think that from Polly's description it was quite possible that Grace and Jess had been rather alike, but Jess had been dead a long time now, and she doubted very much whether Grace could remember the older girl at all, let alone clearly. So she would let sleeping dogs lie, for the moment, at any rate.

Finishing her breakfast and beginning on the washing-up, she said as much to Peader, who nodded resignedly. 'Oh aye, alanna, I thought that's what you'd say and mebbe you're right. Anyway, it doesn't look as if Poll's due for any leave for a while, not now she's been posted. So it can wait.'

'I know you're right, Peader, I know we've got to tell Polly one of these days,' Deirdre said, eager to agree with her husband now that the immediate danger seemed to be over. 'Only I've – I've got to prepare meself before I can work out how to do it.'

'Sure, I'm after knowin' you'd tell Poll, all in good time,' Peader said with all his usual good humour. 'And now let's wash up the delft and clear it all away so's we can go shopping!'

Chapter Twelve

It was a warm June day with the sky blue as a blackbird's egg and the breeze coming off the land for once, and smelling of the country, instead of the sea. Polly had soon settled into her new life, though it was very different from the life she had lived on her Scottish island. She had always loved the sea and the beach, and she found Anglesey an enchanting place. Unlike her Scottish island, where it had seemed to be dark nine-tenths of the time and cold and rainy ten-tenths, here she had come straight into spring, into peace almost, you could say.

Not that peace was all that obvious, since the island swarmed with uniformed members of the armed forces. So far, she had just acted as a messenger here, taking documents from the naval headquarters at Llys-y-Gwynt down Llanfawr Road and on to Turkey Shore, from whence it was flat pretty well all the way to the quay where the ships were moored. She and a dozen other WRNs were billeted on London Road, in a tall, elderly house overlooking the railway line so that washing hung out in the narrow garden was apt to come indoors a good deal dirtier than it had gone out. However, a great many items of uniform could be laundered, and stockings and collars, issue brassieres and the respectable knickers which they were supposed to wear were taken into the kitchen of the rambling old house where they could be hung on a drying rack which was hauled up to the ceiling so that wet clothing was out of the way. An elderly woman called, predictably, Mrs Jones, acted as part-housekeeper part-chaperon to the twelve girls, but she was only on duty from eight in the morning until two in the afternoon, which left the WRNs pretty free to look after themselves.

Not that they minded. In fact, they much preferred it that way, for Mrs Jones was a tight-mouthed strait-laced little woman who thought that a girl in uniform was heading fast for hell anyway. Today Polly walked slowly along Lands End, looking alternately at the tall houses which lined it on her left and the blue water in the harbour on her right. It was her afternoon off and since she and Diane, her best friend in the WRNs, were going to a dance in the old lifeboathouse on the promenade that evening, they had planned to go up and down Market Street to see if anyone was selling lipsticks. Both girls had long ago used up the small amount of make-up which they had managed to acquire before the shortages reached epic proportions, but everyone knew that it was the early bird which caught the worm, and most WRNs went into town at least once a week to see if the shops had got supplies in whilst they were not looking, so to speak.

'Not that I care much about lipstick, if I'm honest,' Polly had told Diane the previous evening as they ate mashed potatoes and a rather grey-looking stew in the canteen. 'But I could do with some face-powder. It 'ud cover my freckles; no sooner does the sun come out than freckles pop up all over me.'

Diane had looked at her friend critically. She was older than Polly by a couple of years and a good deal more sophisticated; in fact, Polly thought, they were an ill-assorted pair. Diane came from a rich county family, the male members of which were all something very high up in the Navy. She had a beautifully tailored uniform and never lacked silk stockings or pretty underwear and was on nodding and smiling terms with every officer in the place. She was very pretty, with shoulder-length black hair, china-blue eyes and the very white skin which frequently goes with such colouring. She was also easily the most disruptive element in the wrennery, always getting herself – and others – into trouble and falling into absurd scrapes from which she somehow managed to extricate herself just before news of it got through to the hierarchy under which they lived. She and Polly had formed what the other girls called an unholy alliance from the first day they had met and stood by one another through thick and thin. They followed each other's lead and enjoyed a deep and satisfying friendship which not even their many boyfriends could spoil.

'I don't want a permanent relationship until the war's over,' Diane said, and Polly agreed with her – though this did not stop either of them from going to every dance which they could get to and giggling over the lovesickness of their many swains.

The trouble was, the other WRNs told them severely, that they were both spoilt. One by having everything she wanted from the day she was born because she was the only girl in a family of boys, the other because her parents had all the money and position anyone could desire and doted on their youngest child.

'You're two of a kind,' the other girls said gloomily. 'You get away with murder just now, but it won't last. You'll get your comeuppance, the pair of you.'

So far, however, Polly concluded, they had not got

into any trouble from which they could not extricate themselves, or each other. And tonight they would go to the weekly dance held in the old lifeboathouse and have a marvellous time. If they were a little late getting home, they would climb up on to the roof of the scullery and from thence to the landing window, which was always left a little open for just such an emergency. Then before anyone had realised they were out after hours they would be padding quietly up the long flight of stairs to the attic room which they shared as the two newest members of HMS *Bee*.

In the end, Polly and Diane couldn't find a single lipstick in their whole afternoon of shopping, but the dance to which the girls had so looked forward was as good as they had anticipated and led, in fact, to a new friendship for Diane. Polly noticed that her friend was spending a good deal of time dancing with one of the local lads, and rather wondered at it; uniforms were what most of the girls went for and usually Diane was no exception. What was more, there were some American Air Force men and everyone in the room knew that they came over with their pockets full of nylon stockings and chewing gum and bars of chocolate which they insisted on calling candy. But Diane was sticking mostly with a tall, dark-haired Welshman called Meirion, and turning down what appeared, on the surface, to be more attractive offers.

When the dance ended, Polly waited for Diane and got quite annoyed with her friend when she was still hanging about at past midnight. The doors of the wrennery would have been locked a good while, and a wind had got up, coming straight off the Irish Sea and making Polly clutch her jacket round her and rather wish she had brought her lovely warm overcoat. What was more, a strong wind made climbing the slate roof of the scullery extension rather fraught, especially when the slates were wet, and there had been a shower just before the wind got into its stride.

In fact, it was a quarter past twelve and the streets were deserted as the two girls made their way back towards London Road. All the available buses had gone long since and taxis, though they might meet the ferries and the London trains, did not hang about in order to give WRNs a ride back from the harbour to their nest. So it was foot it or sleep on the beach and accordingly, the girls set out at a brisk pace.

'What was so fascinating about Meirion?' Polly shouted rather resentfully as the two of them bent their heads against the force of the wind and began to slog up Victoria Street. 'And why didn't you come straight out after the dance was over? It's not like you, Di.'

'He's nice, but it wasn't just that,' Diane said breathlessly. 'Oh Lord, if you want the full story we'd best stop in a doorway; this wind is trying to get back down my throat and blow my lungs up until I burst!'

'Better not, we're late already,' Polly shouted. 'Tell me once we're indoors.'

So they used all their energy to battle against the wind and were delighted to find themselves turning the corner into the backs of the houses on London Road.

'We should have come back at the same time as the others, Di,' Polly said breathlessly as they gained the shelter of the high wall which separated their houses from the railway sidings. 'It'll be pretty horrid on that roof in this wind . . . and the rain makes the slates slippery too. Shall I go up first?'

'Perhaps you'd better,' Diane said, then gave a squeak of dismay. 'Oh, dear heaven, where's the box?'

In order to gain the roof of the scullery the girls stepped first on a solid wooden box and then scrambled on top of the rainwater butt and from thence to the roof. Now, one glance was enough to tell them that the box had been blown away by the wind, and the most careful look around the back yard did not reveal its whereabouts.

'Unless it's that pile of broken slats in the corner it must have blown out over the railway sidings,' Polly said. 'Oh, isn't that just our bleedin' luck! But you can make me a back, I suppose?'

For answer, Diane crouched beside the water butt and Polly, giggling, climbed nimbly on to her friend's back and then sprang to the top of the barrel with such suddenness that Diane was knocked clean over, landing on the cobbles on all fours whilst giving vent to the sort of language which nice little WRNs, Polly told her, should not even understand, let alone use.

'I'm wounded, you horrible little bogtrotter,' Diane moaned, tottering to her feet whilst Polly clung to the edge of the gutter and braced herself against the wind. 'First you kick a great hole in my back, then you knock me on to the cobbles – my lovely stockings are in shreds, you toad – and it's just occurred to me that I've given you a bunk up but who's going to do the same for me?'

'I'll sneak down and unlock the kitchen door,' Polly said. 'See you in a minute,' and with that she began to scramble up the roof, not daring to stand up but clinging grimly on to the roof ridge. And presently she looked up and saw, to her horror, that the landing window, always left a little ajar, was closed. Someone must have thought the wind would slam it shut and shatter the glass, she supposed bitterly, sitting astride the scullery roof ridge now and reaching up to give a half-hearted tug to the clearly closed window. Oh dear God above, now what should they do? They could not possibly hope to wake anyone, not with the wind shrieking and moaning the way it was, and besides if they woke some of the more hidebound girls they would be in as much trouble as if they had handed themselves over to an officer.

But . . . Lilly Sumner slept in the bedroom nearest to the landing and she was a sport all right. If Polly knocked on the glass, was it possible that Lilly would hear, and come to her rescue? Polly got so close to the glass that her face was almost resting on it and raised a hand to knock. The blackout curtains were drawn across, of course, but if only Lilly woke, and realised that someone was still out . . .

Polly's hand was about to descend on the window when there was a sudden commotion and a hand, startlingly white against the blackness, came out from between the curtains and, seizing the window catch, pushed the window out with considerable force. Polly felt the wood of the window hit her squarely on the nose and then she lost her rather precarious balance and found herself bouncing down the tiles and across the gutter, to land heavily on the cobbles below.

In fact, she landed on Diane and not the cobbles, or the story, she reflected later, might have had a very different ending. As it was, Diane's startled *woof* as all the air was suddenly expelled from her lungs was so funny – or so Polly thought – that it completely took Polly's mind off her sudden descent and made the bruises from the encounter seem of little account.

'Sorry, Di, but the window was shut, and just as I was about to knock on it someone shot it open and it banged me on the nose and I fell,' Polly explained as soon as she and the older girl had untangled themselves. 'Will I climb back now, and get in? Oh jay, I'd better, it must be one in the morning, and we'll be in awful trouble if we're caught now, so we will.'

'Well, you aren't climbing on my back,' Diane said, breathing heavily and still clasping her skinned knees as she sat on the cobbles, leaning against the water butt. 'I'm very sorry but this time *I'll* climb the bloody roof and you can make me a back. Tell me when you're ready.'

'You're heavier than me,' Polly said doubtfully, getting to her feet. 'I didn't knock you over on purpose, Di, honest to God I didn't.'

'Well, I shall knock you down deliberately if I possibly can,' Diane said grimly. 'I'm a mass of cuts and bruises thanks to you, O'Brady.'

'I suppose it is my turn,' Polly said peaceably, bending down and gripping the water butt as tightly as she could. 'Go on then, up with you!'

Diane reached the top of the water butt and set off across the tiles whilst Polly sat on the cobbles and laughed as silently as she could at the sight of her tall, slender friend climbing like a huge daddy-long-legs across the slippery roof. Presently, Diane reached the now wide-open window, slung a leg over the sill, paused a moment, and then disappeared inside. And after only a very short time, during which Polly wondered apprehensively whether whoever had opened the window had lain in wait for Diane in the darkness and was now marching her off to bed in disgrace, the back door creaked open and Diane beckoned her friend inside.

'What a bloody awful night,' Diane said as the two of them threw their clothes off in their attic room and hurled themselves into their little iron beds. 'Oh, the dance was all right, I know you're going to say that, Polly, but the rest! Well, it beggars description.'

'So describe it,' Polly said from her cosy bed. 'Oh damn, I forgot to pull back the blackout curtains and open the window. It was my turn, wasn't it?'

'It was,' Diane said, but leaned over and jerked back the curtains so that the windy night could peer in at them and they could see the ragged clouds scooting across the star-drenched heavens. 'But I don't think we ought to open the window, the gale will probably set every door in the house slamming. Now are you ready to hear just why it was that I wasted – I mean spent – my entire evening in the company of Meirion Williams?'

'Won't it keep?' Polly said drowsily. Her nose hurt and all the various bumps and bruises collected on her descent from the roof were beginning to make themselves felt. 'I'm ever so tired, Di, and you can't be feeling all that good. I mean, I landed on you when I fell, so you got a double lot of bruises. Can't we talk in the morning?'

'We could, but I want to get it sorted out tonight,' Diane said stubbornly. 'Poll, has it ever occurred to you to wonder where the fellow in that little shop gets his supplies from? And why there are girls on this island with silk stockings and others who haven't anything better than lisle?'

'Ours are silk,' Polly mumbled. 'But what does it matter where the feller gets his stuff from? Black market, I suppose.'

'He gets all sorts from Ireland,' Diane said in a

thrilling whisper. '*Your* Eire, Poll, not this island. And the ferries go over there every other day!'

'So what? And as for the ferries, don't we all know it? We must watch them sail several times a week. I think they're very brave, the men who take the ferries across, because everyone knows that there are wolf packs of U-boats in the Irish Sea, just waiting to torpedo anything they can reach. Only of course our chaps go out at night and try to bag U-boats themselves, I've heard the sailors saying so. I say, Di, I wonder why the ferries don't sail at night, when our chaps are out U-boat-spotting, instead of during the day when there's no one to defend them?'

'Polly, will you stop rambling and *listen* for once?' Diane said, exasperated. 'Meirion told me that some girls go over on the ferry and buy stuff in Dublin, stuff that we can't get over here. And others take stuff the Irish need – tea is very popular, he said, and we have loads of tea in the stores – and swap for . . . well, for stockings, and lipsticks, and cheese . . . It seems a long while since I've had my way with a great, crisp pile of toasted cheese.'

'They go over to Dublin, *my* Dublin?' Polly asked, suddenly forgetting to be sleepy and sitting up on one elbow. 'But I thought you'd need special papers and all sorts to go over there.'

'Nope,' Diane said, shaking her head. 'All you need is a ticket. But of course it must help if you know the city, because you'd know where to go to find the sort of things you were after. Stockings and lipstick and so on, I mean.'

'Ye-es, but it can't be as simple as that,' Polly said. 'How d'you buy a ticket?'

'Meirion said that if I gave him the money he'd get you a ticket, and then—'

'Me? Oh no, you aren't getting me into that sort of a scrape, Diane Burlington,' Polly said roundly. 'Go yourself!'

'I can't, can I? I wouldn't know where to go for things, and I'd stand out like a sore thumb over there, as English as anything. But you, Poll, you could go over and be safe as houses!'

'I don't know,' Polly said gloomily, but in her heart she was beginning to get excited at the thought of seeing Dublin again. 'What about my uniform, though? I'm not a rich member of the Burlington family. All I've got is me uniform. You know very well that if I tried to go over in me uniform I'd be thrown in the Tower or something.'

'I'll lend you some civvies,' Diane said. 'And I'll give you the money, of course. Oh, and pay for the ticket and so on. Don't you want to go home? You're always talking about Dublin and how wonderful it was when you lived there.'

'Yes, and so it is,' Polly said stoutly. 'But I was only ten when I left . . . not that I've forgotten so much as a paving stone, for I've not, indeed. Kids always run the messages in Dublin, same as they do in Liverpool, so I know all the best shops for this and that. There's a dairy on Thomas Street where they sell the most wonderful Irish cheese . . . oh, it makes me mouth water just to think of it! But that doesn't mean I'm prepared to get into the worst trouble of me life, and get thrown out of the WRNs in disgrace, just so you can have a new lipstick.'

'Oh, it won't come to that,' Diane promised. 'If the worst comes to the worst I'd say it was all my fault. Besides, you'll never be found out; why should you? No one's interested in a girl going over for a few pairs of silk stockings. Come on, Poll, be a sport.'

'It's too risky,' Polly said obstinately. 'I'd love to see Dublin again, I don't deny it but—'

'Oh, come on, Poll, I know you can do it,' Diane said eagerly. 'You'll have to put in for some leave, of course, but they're pretty good about that sort of thing, and it isn't as if you'll need a week or anything like that. A forty-eight will be plenty.'

'A forty-eight? Why would I need that long? If I catch the— What time does the *Hibernia* leave tomorrer? She's on this week, isn't she?'

'Yes. She leaves at two o'clock, so you won't even have to get up terribly early. Not that you'd want to go tomorrow, because you'll need to get some supplies packed up carefully, so folk won't notice them. We said tea, didn't we? And I believe parachute silk's awfully popular over there. I can lay my hands on a nice big piece if you give me a few days.'

'Well—' Polly began, then frowned. 'Hey, the *Hibernia* leaves here at two o'clock in the afternoon, but what time does she get back?'

'Ah! Well, that's another good reason for yourself going over, Polly,' Diane said in a honeyed tone. 'She comes back in at noon the following day, so—'

'Oh! So I'd have to stay overnight,' Polly said. 'Why, all I'd have time for would be to have a night's sleep and then it would be time to get back to Dun Laoghaire for the ferry home! You're an idiot, you are—'

'That's another good reason why I can't go myself, Poll,' Diane said, keeping her voice low. 'No matter how willing, because I'd have nowhere to spend the night, and I wouldn't want to be cashiered or whatever they do to WRNs found sleeping rough in a foreign city. But you, Poll, you must have a thousand pals in Ireland, all panting to put you up for the night, especially if you took them some tea and some of those nice little sugar lumps they use in the officers' mess. Well? What do you say?'

'I say no way, not if I have to be there two whole days,' Polly said firmly. She lay down again. 'It 'ud all go wrong, I just know it would, plans you make always do. Come to that, plans made by me don't always go too smooth,' she added honestly. 'So something we've cooked up between the pair of us is doomed, positively doomed! As for me wearing your civvies, can you imagine what a figure I'd cut? You're a foot taller than me and about twice as broad – I'd get taken up for a vagrant, or a spy. Because me pal Tad's mammy told me that the city's stiff with bleedin' Jerries, you can't hardly step a pace in the big shops without treading on one of them. No, Di, I'm afraid your plan isn't going to include me!'

'It'll take some arranging, I grant you that,' Diane said as though her friend had not spoken. 'But I'm a good organiser; you won't be left without a plan of action, trust me for that. As for clothes, I said I'd lend you some but I didn't say they would be mine, did I? Flicky Andover is about your size and she got a lovely white pullover from her boyfriend and an old grey duffle coat . . . We'll fix you up so that your own mother wouldn't recognise you, Poll. I know you won't want to take a kitbag over, either, so I've arranged to borrow one of those knapsack things that you sling on your back when you go camping. Some of the fellers go over to the mainland to climb in Snowdonia whenever they've got a forty-eight, and Jimmy says we can borrow his whenever we want it.'

'It strikes me,' Polly said slowly, lying down in her bed again but fixing her friend with a round, reproachful eye, 'it strikes me that you've done a divil

328

of a lot of planning without so much as consulting meself. How long have you been hatching this?'

'Only tonight, guide's honour,' Diane said promptly, lying down herself and pulling the blankets up over her exposed shoulder. 'All the loans – the knapsack and the clothes, I mean – were promised ages ago, when I talked about going climbing too. Lots of people owe me favours, I'm just calling in a few of them, that's all.'

'Well, the answer's still no. If you want someone to go over to Dublin, go yourself,' Polly said firmly. 'Goodnight, Diane; sweet dreams.'

A week later Polly found herself getting off the train at Tara Street Station in Dublin and walking briskly along Luke Street. Home! This was home to her in a way which Liverpool had never really become, because her happy childhood had been spent here. It was here that she had first gone along to the small convent school where her mammy and daddy had decided she should get her education, but it was also here where what she felt was her *real* education had begun, what you might call her street education. Here she had kept nix for her brothers when they were up to some mischief or other, had run messages for the mammy and had gone in and out of the shops, both big and small, as of right. She turned into Townsend Street and immediately left into College Street, remembering now the many times she had trodden this way when the family had gone off on the train for a day's cockling down at Booterstown beach, or had been meeting someone off the train at Tara Street Station.

Every twist and turn of the narrowing streets which led her into the heart of the Liberties held a memory for her, almost all nice ones. Street games, marbles, tops, Piggy beds, she had played them all, mainly in company with Tad, who had been such a good friend to her. Yes, she could scarcely look around her now without getting a mental picture of Tad, small, square, sturdy despite the fact that he was always hungry, helping her, protecting her, codding her about ghosts and boggarts, taking her boxing the fox in the orchards on the outskirts of the city, teaching her to swim in the canal, half-drowning her in the Liffey . . . The memories swarmed into her head, bringing tears to her eyes and a lump to her throat. Oh janey, but she'd been a lucky kid to live here, to have had such a pal!

Still, all that had been a long time ago, and she had not heard from Tad now for . . . well, it must be getting on for a year. She had continued to write to him at first, doggedly determined to keep their friendship alive, but finally his lack of response had got to her. If he cared so little for her then he might whistle for her letters! She had continued to write to Mrs Donoghue, though, because she guessed that Tad was a poor correspondent to his mammy as well as his best friends, and Mrs Donoghue wrote back from time to time, though they weren't an awful lot better, if Polly was forced to be honest, than the letters – grubby notes – Tad had sent on the rare occasions when he had bothered to write at all.

That was now, and the Tad she was remembering was a boy of twelve or thirteen, a boy who mitched off school more often than he attended, who worked like a slave to keep his mammy in pennies and his numerous brothers and sisters at least fed and moderately clothed in the cold weather. He had had, in those days, to battle against a drunken father who beat his wife and knocked his kids about when he could get hold of them. Tad had been good at avoiding the older Donoghue, but every now and then he would do his best to defend his mammy and would be seen on the streets the next day with a black eye, a split lip or an arm held awkwardly.

Polly sighed at the memory. Perhaps she had been wrong to stop writing to Tad but a good deal he must have cared, she reflected bitterly now, since he had not even written to reproach her for her silence.

Right now she was too excited at the thought of what was to come to worry about her old friend's behaviour. She had heard from his mammy or one of her other friends, that Angela had given Tad the go-by. Anyway, she would soon get all the gossip because she meant to spend the night with Tad's mammy, knowing that her old friend would welcome her.

Glancing around her as she walked, she realised she had reached the Cornmarket and now turned left into Francis Street, a place redolent of her childhood. As always, the street was busy, with chisellers playing games and small girls running messages. Threading her way between them, seeing the bare feet and ragged clothing, Polly realised sharply how different her life had been since crossing the water. There was poverty in Liverpool, she knew that, but because of rationing, perhaps, things were more fairly distributed now. The rich bought luxuries on the black market, everyone knew that, but at least the poor got the food to which they were entitled, and though some did sell their clothing coupons, they managed to clothe their children better than they had done when things were more easily available. Also, wages were very much better now, with men being

331

provided with clothing and food in the forces, and having an allotment taken out of their wages and sent home to their wives and children whether they wished it or no. And then there was the money paid to women working in factories and shops; it had got better and better as labour became scarcer. Yes, things were definitely looking up in England, but here in Ireland, where there was no war, nothing seemed to have changed. Barefoot children queued for the family's bread, women in long black skirts with shawls wrapped around their heads stood and gossiped, shrieking to their children to 'Get away outta that,' and men lounged on street corners playing toss ha'penny and melting into the shadows whenever anyone in authority – a guarda or a priest – appeared.

But they've not got to fear the thrum of an aero-engine overhead and the whistle of descending bombs, nor the whizz and clatter of machine-gun fire, Polly told herself stoutly, pausing alongside a group of small boys who were obviously about to try their luck at one of the street stalls. The stalls, she noticed, were not so well-provided as they had been when she had lived here. Oranges and bananas were no longer available, though there was locally grown fruit and vegetables in plenty. She saw a whole stall covered in round, shining brown onions and determined to take some back with her and send them to Liverpool. Deirdre was always bemoaning the lack of onions, and Peader had said that when he tried to grow them on his allotment he had to keep a nightly vigil over them or they would be stolen by some wide-boy who would promptly sell them for ten times their worth.

As she watched, amused, it occurred to Polly that it might be a nice thought to take her unwitting hostess a gift of something other than the tea, sugar and bottled coffee which bulged through her knapsack. She glanced around her, and then dived into a fish and chip shop which seemed to be doing a roaring trade. Kids, she knew, would always eat fish and chips. It was a pity that she would have to queue, but the men behind the counter, sweating freely, were working like demons to get their customers served so she should not have long to wait.

She was halfway up the queue when she noticed that one of the lads behind the counter – he could not be more than fourteen or fifteen – was wearing a curious badge made out of some shiny silvery metal pinned or stuck to the breast of his grease-stained overall. She stared . . . and saw, with a frightened bump of the heart, that it was a swastika, with the German eagle above it. Horrified, she glanced about her, and realised that several of the boys in the queue wore badges, some of them the hated swastika and others cheaply made imitations of Air Force wings and roundels.

It was odd how it affected her, she thought now, trying not to stare too obviously at the badges. She had known, because Tad's mammy had told her, that some of the boys were making a game of the war, taking sides, swearing that they wanted the Germans to win because 'that would teach ould England a lesson, so it would!' But Polly now realised that it was one thing being told a fact, and quite another seeing it with one's own eyes. She felt hurt and rage combining; thoughts of Martin, dying at sea and leaving his wife a widow, thoughts of all the other young men . . . But it was no use blaming these boys for their ignorance and prejudice, they were just kids, chisellers who knew no better, who considered that if one were a true republican then it was Germany who one should back. And anyway, wasn't it just a game, hadn't Mrs Donoghue said as much?

Polly was at the head of the queue now and ordering her fish and chips. The youth behind the counter with the swastika badge on his shirt had a bright, cheery face and a pleasant manner. 'Will you be wantin' some vinegar?' he asked, holding the parcel open whilst glancing enquiringly at her. 'Will I put some on for yez?'

'It's all right,' Polly muttered, taking the parcel and folding the newspaper tightly round the delicious contents. 'I'm taking 'em to me friend's house, so I am – there'll be vinegar and salt there.'

She turned and walked out of the chipper, unable to throw off completely her feeling of distaste over the swastikas, but reminding herself that some of the boys had worn Air Force wings and RAF roundels. It didn't mean anything, really, not to them. Safe out here, watching a war going on as they'd watch the pictures and newsreels on a Saturday morning in the cinema, scarcely differentiating between what Tom Mix did in the big feature and what was happening on the other side of the Irish Sea.

Regaining Francis Street, she began to hurry on her way, anxious to get to Gardiner's Lane before the food got cold when someone drew level with her, turned to give her a casual glance and then grabbed hold of her by both shoulders, swinging her round to face him.

'Well, by all that's wonderful, if it isn't me own little Polly O'Brady! Poll, what in the divil's name are you doin' here? Last I heard . . .'

Polly's heart sank into her boots for a moment. She was wearing civvies and had pulled a truly hideous felt hat down over her curls. She had also borrowed a pair of 'props' – spectacles from one of the local amateur dramatic groups because they had plain glass in their lenses, but would help, she thought, to disguise her. And now here was this tall, broad-shouldered young man, his face difficult to see against the late sun which shone directly into her eyes, greeting her as though he had no shadow of a doubt who she was! Accordingly she pulled away from him, scowling.

'Sure an' it must be mad you are,' she said frostily, clutching her packet of chips to her bosom and wishing she could see her companion's face more clearly. The voice sounded familiar, but that was probably simply because he was using the brogue which, after so long in England, had begun to die out of her own voice. 'Who *are* you, anyway?'

'Don't tell me you don't recognise me, Poll!'

'I can't perishin' well *see* you,' Polly said irritably. 'The light's in me eyes, and you're in shadow.'

The man moved so that the light fell on his face. Polly gasped, then very nearly let go of her parcel of fish and chips as she moved involuntarily closer. 'Tad! Oh, Tad, you're just the same only a bit taller, and it's great to see you, so it is, but how can you ask me what *I'm* doin' in Dublin when you're in the Roy—'

'Ssh, Poll, do you want to get the pair of us hung up from the nearest lamp post?' Tad said in an urgent whisper. He took her hand in a large, warm palm and his touch sent a thrill through Polly, though she told herself severely that it was no way to feel, especially when, for all she knew, Tad might have become a deserter. 'Look, where are you rushin' off to, anyway? I'll walk along wit' you until we get off the main street.'

335

'I'm going to Gardiner's Lane,' Polly said, her voice reflecting more than a trifle of foreboding. 'I knew you were in England – well, you were a year ago, when you last deigned to write me a horrible little scrap of a note in answer to one – more likely a dozen – of me lovely letters. So I thought there'd be room for me to kip down on the floor somewhere.'

'Oh, there's bound to be,' Tad said. He then walked along, still holding her hand but saying nothing until they were in a comparatively deserted street, when he turned to her once more. 'Polleen, me darlin' girl, whatever brought you back to Dublin? All your family's in England, aren't they? And last I heard, you were in Scotland.'

'Oh, so you did get my letter?' Polly said sarcastically. 'No, I shan't tell you a word until you tell me what *you're* doing here, Tad Donoghue! Why, for all I know you might be a deserter, and if you're after bein' one of them, I'm none too sure I want to walk along beside you.'

Tad laughed. 'No, I've not left me pals in the lurch,' he said serenely, 'any more than you would, Polleen! I've come over wi't some stuff for me mammy and the little 'uns, and to make sure they're all right. Oh, I know everyone says that Dublin's got it easy, but apart from the money I send, Mammy doesn't do that well, not bein' able to afford the black market. So I pop over now and then wit' whatever I've managed to get hold of which will help her. Besides, I like comin' home, it's the big bonus of workin' in Valley instead of Yorkshire. Now what about you?'

'Valley? You mean Valley on Anglesey?' Polly gasped, quite overcome at this coincidence. 'Well, would you believe, Tad, I'm on HMS *Bee* in Holyhead! We're neighbours, as good as. How long have you been there? What are you doing? Do you come into town much? I've only been there a couple of months, but you'd have thought we'd have bumped into one another, wouldn't you?'

'Oh, I dunno. I don't go into town that often, except when I'm on me way over here,' Tad said. 'What really *is* odd is that we didn't spot one another on the ferry. I take it you've just come over on the *Hibernia*?'

'That's right,' Polly said. 'But it was very crowded and I got meself a spot up near the bows and sat down on me knapsack and just looked out over the sea and dreamed of home. Oh, and I'm here on a buyin' spree. I've brought tea and sugar and parachute silk and I'm hopin' to get butter and cheese, lipsticks and silk stockings. The girls paid me fare over and then gave me a list.'

'Trust you, Poll,' Tad said. He looked at her newspaper parcel. 'Though that looks more like fish and chips than tea or sugar or silk. Still, don't you know the trouble you could get into for coming over here when the country's at war? Mind, I'm not one to talk, I do it as well and I've not been caught out yet.'

Polly turned and looked at him. He was wearing grimy overalls over a dark grey shirt and wellington boots. He could have been a farm hand or a garage mechanic, she supposed. Certainly one would not have connected him with the Royal Air Force. 'No, you don't look much like an airman,' she admitted. 'And I don't look anything like a WRN, we're always smart, you know. So mebbe the pair of us will get away with it. I certainly hope so. But you've not got a knapsack, Tad. Where's your stuff hid?'

'I'm only bringing stuff for the family, don't forget,' Tad said as they turned into Gardiner's Lane and headed across the filthy paving stones for the

337

tenement block in which the Donoghues lived. 'I
bring a bit of sugar and some tea, they're in me
pockets, and I've got three or four jumble-sale jerseys
tied round me waist, but I'm not tradin', like you are.'

'I'm not,' Polly said rebelliously. 'Not much,
anyway. Don't you take butter and cheese back, then,
Tad? Only if you did you could finance your next trip,
couldn't you?'

'I could. I do take stuff back,' Tad admitted. He
squeezed her hand. 'Well, I can't get over it – me little
pal, growed up, and growed up pretty, an' all.'

'Don't be so rude,' Polly scolded, but she did not
pull her hand out of his. She eyed him covertly as they
began to mount the stairs, side by side. He was tall,
probably as tall as Sunny, and broad shouldered, and
his taffy-brown hair had been cut neatly, so that you
could see the nice shape of his head, but he was really
very little altered from the boy she had once known so
well. He still had a blunt nose, square chin, and the
sort of grin which made him look as though there was
not much he wouldn't do, given the chance. He
wasn't handsome, she knew that all right, but he had
a look of self-reliance and a sort of pride in himself
which she had noticed before amongst members of
the forces. Before, Tad had been scruffy, a bit spotty,
but now, though he was wearing greasy old clothes,
you could tell, somehow, that the dirt was not even
skin deep. It was something which you could tell
instinctively would be washed off every night . . .
Other than that, he's just the same, Polly told herself.
He's my friend and I'm fond of him, though he has let
me down rather, over the writing business.

Up the stairs the two of them went to the familiar
landing, only it, too, had changed. It was clean, the
floorboards actually polished, and the door to the

338

Donoghue flat had been painted a bright, dark blue. A small brass lion's head hung in the middle of the door and Tad lifted it and let it bang down before pushing the door open and bellowing at the top of his voice: 'I'm home, Mammy, and guess who I've got wit' me – only you never will!'

Polly stood in the doorway, her eyes rounding with astonishment even as her lips curled with pleasure. The room that she remembered as dirty and drab was shining clean and bright, the furniture polished, the big table in the centre of the room spread with a decent checked tablecloth, the fire burning brightly in the hearth and a large pot suspended over it, sending out delicious smells. There were three or four young people in the room, all neatly dressed, and Mrs Donoghue was dishing up potatoes from a pan which had been stood on the side, and turned a beaming face towards her son and his friend.

'Polly O'Brady, by all the saints! Well, no colleen could be more welcome, alanna! Come in, come in – where did you find her, Tad me boy? What's that you've got? Don't say you've been to the chipper, spendin' your money like water when I've a pot full of taties on the stove and a fine stew on cookin'. But I know someone who'd rather have fish an' chips than the best stew in the world, so I do! Meg, go an' fetch up the little 'uns and tell them we've a visitor, and she's been to the chipper on her way back!' She turned, still smiling, to Polly. 'Eh, we've missed you something sore, alanna, but you're here now, so take off that jacket an' hat, it's crushin' your curls, and come and sit down. The kettle's on the hob, I'll have a cup o' tay in your hands in one minute flat, then you can tell us why you're here! Tad, it's grand to see you, so it is, you sit beside our Polly and you'll be suppin'' tay before you're a minute older. Then you can both tell us how you came to arrive together this day!'

Lying on her improvised couch later that night, when the fire had died down and the others had all gone either to their beds or off on errands of their own, Polly thought over her day. From the moment of meeting Tad, she reflected, all the fears and uncertainties which she had been suffering from had fled. She had felt at once, as she had felt as a child, that Tad was to be trusted; he would take care of her. And when, after they had eaten their evening meal, he had taken her off for a stroll around the familiar streets, they had talked over her errand. Tad had promptly solved all her problems regarding the things the girls craved.

'Sure an' haven't I been doin' these deals for the past six months, meself?' he said cheerfully, tucking her hand into the crook of his elbow and grinning down at her. 'What's more, alanna, there's no need for you to hang about in Dublin all day and then to spend another night wit' the mammy, glad though she would be to have you. We'll get up early – the mammy does so anyway, she's still cleaning in Switzers – and get all your shoppin' done and be back in Dun Laoghaire in good time for the ferry, never you fear.'

It had sounded impossible, but Polly had thought of the many times that Tad had managed to get her out of scrapes, and did not doubt that he could solve her problems now. If he said she would be on the ferry tomorrow morning, with all her wheeling and dealing done, then he was right. All she needed to do was to put her trust in Tad; he would not let her down.

But though she might tell herself that he was simply her old friend Tad, grown a little taller and a great deal stronger, she knew that this was not really the case. They were almost like strangers, and in the eight years or so which had passed between their last meeting and this one, they had lived different lives. If we're to go on being pals we've got to get to know one another all over again, Polly told herself just before she fell asleep. Tad's a grand feller, so he is, but when it comes down to it, I only know the chiseller he was, not the grown man he has become. Why, I know Sunny a good deal better now than I know Tad. Only Sunny's so far away, and letters aren't the same . . . Still an' all, Tad's me best friend, and it'll be grand being near one another on the island, and grand getting to know each other all over again too.

And on this happy thought she fell asleep at last.

'Here we go, then! Give a wave to me little sisters, Poll. It were grand of them to come to see us off . . . Bye, Meg, bye, Biddy!'

Tad and Polly stood at the rail of the ferry, with their loaded knapsacks at their feet, waving lustily as the ferry drew away from the quay and the tiny figures of Meg and Biddy grew smaller and smaller. When they had melted into the distance, however, Tad took Polly's hand and lifted up both their knapsacks, slinging them over one broad shoulder. 'Come on, there's coffee below decks. Might as well wet our whistles since we missed breakfast. Are you hungry, alanna?'

'I am that,' Polly admitted, following him down the companionway to where a good smell of cooking came wafting up to greet them. 'Tad, you've been a real pal to me, so you have! By the time I was halfway

341

across, yesterday, I was beginning to realise I'd bit off more'n I could chew, and then along you came an' rescued me! I thought I'd find someone standing on the dockside waiting for me to offer him tea and sugar, I think, or I thought your mammy would tell me where to go and how to set about swapping one thing for another. Tell me, when did you do it all?'

'Last night, after you were in bed,' Tad said, grinning. 'Sit yourself down whiles I fetch us some food . . . Will you be havin' coffee, or is tay more your tipple this early?'

'Coffee, please,' Polly said, and watched him shoulder his way to the counter, give his order and presently return to her, bearing two mugs of steaming coffee and two hefty-looking bacon sandwiches. 'Oh, that smells so good!'

'Yeah, no rationing aboard the *Hibernia*,' Tad said, taking a large bite out of his sandwich and sitting down opposite her. 'Now, as to last night – have you never heard of the pubs, alanna?'

'Ye-es, that's where they do a lot of black-market trading and so on,' Polly said. 'But I've never seen anyone doing anything other than drink and sing and lark about. Not that I go into pubs all that often,' she added. 'Because we've got the NAAFI, and the mess, and our wrennery, of course.'

'That's right. Well, if you go into a certain Dublin pub and put it about that you've trading goods, sooner or later the person wantin' those particular goods will turn up and you do a deal. That's about all,' Tad said. 'They know most of us who come across the water come over one day and go back the next, with no time to do much in the way of shopping. So they come to us, see?'

'And they bought me silk, and sugar and tea, and

sold you butter and stockings and lipstick?' Polly said incredulously. 'It can't be that simple – I bet you've never wanted lipsticks before, have you? Let alone silk stockings!'

'Well, I'm not in the habit of buyin' lipsticks,' Tad said, looking a little self-conscious. Polly realised that he might well have bought stockings for the WAAFs on his station and felt a stab of something remarkably like jealousy, which was a bit thick considering she had been telling herself ever since last night that the two of them were more or less strangers. 'But I moved about a bit, and managed to get everything on your list. All right?'

'Oh, sure an' I am grateful,' Polly said hastily. It was not fair to ask him questions, she thought guiltily, when he had done her such a favour. 'That girl Angela – I suppose she doesn't want silk stockings or lipsticks, seeing as how she's still living in Dublin?' she heard her voice say as though it had decided to ignore the advice its owner had been handing out so prodigally. She clapped a hand to her mouth but Tad, heavily engaged in his bacon sandwich, seemed to notice nothing amiss.

'Angela? I dunno. She's got another feller,' he said thickly. 'How about the bloke wit' the peculiar name? Sammy, was it?'

It was tempting to ask what was peculiar about the name Sammy, but Polly reminded herself severely that she should never have mentioned Angela and bit her tongue. 'Sunny,' she said in as offhand a voice as she could manage. 'He's on the Russian conveys, so I've not seen him for months and months, they sail from Scapa Flow, you see. But he writes regularly, like I do, so I know he's doing pretty well. He's a leading signaller now, and hoping to become a

343

yeoman of signals before too long, and he's only young . . . about your age,' she finished.

'Oh aye? So you're still . . .?'

He didn't finish the sentence but Polly said quickly: 'Friends, d'you mean? Yes of course we are. He's a grand feller, Sunny. You'd like him.'

She half-hoped that Tad would look glum and say roundly that he would not like Sunny at all, but instead, Tad said cheerfully: 'Sure I'll like him if he's a pal of yours, Poll. And I daresay you'll like Maisie when you meet her.'

'Who's she?' Polly said bluntly. She, too, continued to eat her sandwich as though it was the most important thing in her life at this minute. 'Is there any mustard?'

Tad pushed the mustard pot across and took a long drink of coffee. Then he said: 'Maisie? Oh, she's a little WAAF working on the station. She's in the control tower, talking the kites down safely. We've been seein' quite a bit of each other lately. You'll like her.'

'So I will,' Polly said, inwardly deciding that she would heartily dislike anyone called Maisie, and wondering, just why the term 'a little WAAF' should sound so exceedingly friendly. 'If I meet her, that is. I don't get away from the old Bee all that much.'

'I'll see you get asked to our next dance,' Tad said. 'Want another coffee?'

Polly said that she would love another one, and watched his backview disappear into the scrum round the counter with an unaccountable feeling of annoyance. Why could he not have said *I'll ask you to the next dance*, instead of *I'll see you get asked to our next dance*, with its tacit inference that, since he would be taking the wretched Maisie he could not ask her, too. Not that it matters, she told herself fiercely, swinging round in her seat to examine the other people in the dining area. I've got Sunny so why shouldn't he have his horrible little WAAF? She's probably got sticking out teeth, frizzy hair and a bad case of dandruff. *And* she'll be flat chested. And have spots. And not all the stockings in the world will be able to make those matchstick legs look good!

Tad, returning with two more cups of coffee, changed the subject and for the rest of the voyage they talked about the changes – all for the better – which had taken place at the flat in Gardiner's Lane and the delights of visiting Dublin, albeit briefly.

'Next time I come over I'll get in touch wit' you and we can go together again,' Tad said as they were queuing to leave the ship. 'We might have a bit of a get-together wit' some of our old pals from school. We could go round to Swift's Alley too – you had a grosh of pals there when you were a kid.'

But Polly, agreeing, thought that this was unlikely. She had done what Diane had asked of her and saw no reason for a return trip to Dublin, particularly in the company of someone who was clearly in love with a skinny, spotty WAAF named Maisie!

Chapter Thirteen

It was a brilliant summer day and for once the wind, which seemed to Tad to blow continuously from the sea which was only just out of sight from where he was working, had dropped from a gusty force six to a gentle breeze. Tad was working on a Beaufighter Mark II belonging to number 456 Squadron fitted with Merlin XX engines, but he had just about finished and now he replaced the cowling, rubbed oil marks off with the piece of soft rag which hung at his belt, and jumped down on to the grass.

Finished now, he glanced at his watch, saw that it was time for his canteen meal, and turned back towards the huts. He would clean up, go and get himself some food, and then perhaps he would get out the old motorbike and go into Holyhead; you never knew, Polly might be at a loose end and glad of his company.

Accordingly, he turned his footsteps towards the hutments clustered at the end of the runway, beginning to think about Polly and how her being so near had complicated his life. The truth was that he had not really thought of her as a girl, let alone a breathtakingly pretty one, until that trip to Ireland. She had been his little friend, the kid he had bullied, protected and teased, he had never really thought of her as a young woman. Seeing her on Francis Street had been quite a shock, but then meeting her in the full splendour of her WRNS uniform had been an even greater one. The dazzling blue of her eyes, the soft primrose curls, the rosy mouth nearly always curling into a smile, had made her very much sought after, and it riled Tad to have to take his place in the queue, so to speak.

Not that he ever let Polly know that he was one of the many admirers who would have given a great deal to be able to call her his girl. No fear! He knew his Polly too well to let her see that he was just like the others. He took advantage of their old friendship, laughed at her, carefully asked other girls to dance at the weekly hops – and kept a jealous eye on her all the time, in case she began to show real favour to anyone other than himself. But it seemed that she was 'just pals' as she put it, with half the armed forces upon the island, and that she was saving herself for that Sunny Andersen who had been such a bad influence on her as a child.

As he crossed the concrete apron in front of the mess hut he sniffed the air. 'Bangers and mash and cabbage,' he decided, not ill-pleased, for he thought the RAF food very good indeed and was always ready for his meals. And then there was a homely sort of smell of boiling cloth, which probably meant a jam duff. It might be blackberry jam, or even rhubarb and ginger, but it didn't matter much to him. When you had spent your childhood and early teenage years fighting for a bit of bread and maggie ryan to keep off the hunger pangs then jam of any description was a treat.

Tad went into the canteen and took his place in the queue at the counter behind another fitter, Phil Dunlop. Phil turned and grinned at him. 'Finished? I bet that kite's fair shinin' with every little nut and bolt looking like burnished silver! Coming into town

347

later? I know you've got some little gal tucked away there, you dirty old Irishman! Who is she? Do you get your oats there? Is that why you aren't seein' so much of Maisie?'

Tad gave his companion a good-humoured swipe then picked up a plate from the pile and checked that his irons were in his pocket; they were. 'There's a girl I grew up wit', she's with HMS *Bee*,' he said carefully. 'I'm – I'm keepin' an eye on her, like, to see she don't get into mischief. I know her parents, and they – they expect me to see she stays on the right side of the law.'

It did not sound too convincing, even to Tad himself, but no one, not even a pal like Phil, could be told about his feelings for Polly – indeed, when she was at her most aggravating, he was none too sure of those feelings himself. All he knew, in fact, was that he could not bear the thought of any other feller with his arms round her, even if she was not precisely his girl – especially not that Sunny bloke.

'You? A guardian of decent girls? God awmighty, them parents can't know you very well, Tad! If I were a dad I'd take precious good care you din't get too close to no gal of mine, I'm tellin' you straight! Why, I'd as soon give a nice little lamb chop to old Bowser to keep safe!'

Tad grinned. Old Bowser was an enormous alsatian, one of a pair who paraded the perimeter track by night, making sure that no unauthorised person got too near the aircraft. Both dogs were friendly enough with the personnel on the station, old Bowser would probably have helped a spy to climb up into the nearest kite provided that same spy gave him a chunk of meat first.

'You shouldn't say such t'ings about the ould feller,' Tad said now, reprovingly. 'That dog had a bad puppyhood, his handler told me so. Why, he was half-starved until he was six months old, so naturally he'll do – well, anything – for a snack.'

'And you'd do anything to have your way wit' some pretty little WRN,' Phil said. 'Wouldn't we all?'

Tad said nothing but held out his plate for sausages, then moved along to the WAAF cook who was hurling spoonfuls of mashed potato on to the plates as though she had a personal grudge against it. How did Phil know I had a girl in Holyhead, Tad wondered. Then, sighing, told himself that Anglesey was a small island and Holyhead a small port. Everyone knew everyone else's business sooner or later, plainly someone had seen him with Polly. And anyway, he was glad enough to have been seen with her, because she looked so very pretty in her uniform, with her cheeky little sailor hat tipped over her eyes and her bell bottoms hugging her neat and rounded bottom. Of course she only wore her bell bottoms when she was working, but that was how he liked to think of her, tearing down the Turkey Shore Road with her hat seemingly stuck on to her curls and her slim legs going like pistons, whilst the bundles of documents she held under one arm flapped in the breeze of her going.

But anyway, even if she was working he would quite likely see her this afternoon. The girls were allowed far more latitude in the WRNS than in the WAAF, and Polly would deliver her messages, whatever they might be, and then come down to the shore. If he could find her they could have a cup of tea and a bun with him without anyone being any the wiser. She was his friend still, he knew that, but he sometimes worried a bit that it was really his motor-bike that she was interested in rather than himself.

349

She was desperate to become a WRN despatch rider and not just a messenger, and as soon as she had discovered that he owned a motorbike she had begun to pester him to teach her how to ride it. She was pretty good already, and liked nothing more than to persuade him to take her to some quiet country road, or to a hard, deserted beach, so that she might practise on the bike. Tad wondered sometimes just how Polly would explain her sudden ability to ride a motorbike to the Powers that Be, for she intended to apply for a despatch rider's job just as soon as she felt she was proficient. Knowing Polly, however, he thought ruefully, she would work something out in time – something which was both convincing yet not too far from the truth. In the meantime, if teaching her to ride his bike was his best way to keep close to her, then teach her he would.

'It's treacle duff for afters,' Phil said as he received a spoonful of overcooked cabbage and turned away from the counter. 'Grab the Flag, old feller, I can't face sawdust sausages without a good covering of sauce.'

'Right,' Tad said, obediently picking up the nearest sauce bottle and heading for the long table where most of the flight mechs seemed to have gathered. 'Treacle duff, eh? I thought I could smell something good!'

Polly and Diane had the afternoon off, so since it was a brilliant day, they had agreed to cycle over to Treaddur Bay for a swim. They met at Llys-y-Gwynt soon after two o'clock and set off together, Diane on a hired bicycle, down the long hill which would lead them on to London Road. They saw Tad from afar as they were skimming down the hill, with their hats on the extreme backs of their heads, though only Polly recognised him. 'It's me pal Tad,' she shouted to Diane above the breeze. 'He'll be coming over to give me a lesson on the motorbike, I daresay. Oh, damn, and I was looking forward to a swim, so I was. What'll I do, Di?'

Diane managed to shrug, not easy on a speeding bicycle. 'Tell him you can't play this afternoon,' she advised. 'After all, Poll my little parrot, you and I have planned this swim ever since the beginning of the week. You wouldn't let me down, would you?'

"Course not,' Polly said rather indignantly, the more so, perhaps, because she had definitely considered, just for a moment, begging Diane to let her off their planned expedition. She did so love the excitement of riding the motorbike and knew that Tad did not find it as easy to get time off as they did. 'Only he doesn't get as much time off as we do . . . so could he come along with us this afternoon, d'you t'ink?'

'He'll spoil it,' Diane said grimly, slowing to a halt as they reached the corner since Tad was now fast approaching along London Road. 'Besides, I don't like swimming in front of an audience. Tell him to come back another day.'

Polly giggled. Diane was a superb swimmer, very much better than her but Diane was going to be wearing her old school swimsuit which was decidedly skimpy in the bust region and, since it was made of black wool, rather baggy around the bottom. Diane had applied to her important relatives several times for a newer, roomier costume – well, roomier in certain areas, and tighter in others, Polly reminded herself – but so far they had been unable to come up with the goods. I expect all the swimwear factories are making diving suits or something, Polly told herself vaguely as Tad drew to a halt beside them and pulled off his forage cap. Still, no use being silly about it. Oh dear, thought Polly. If I tell Tad where we're going he'll come along, invited or not, and he'll see Diane's suit and won't give a thought to it, knowing Tad. Indeed, she privately thought, in some dismay, that Tad might very much enjoy the view, for the sight of Diane overflowing from her swimsuit was the sort of spectacle that most red-blooded young men would appreciate, she felt sure.

'Afternoon, girls,' Tad said politely as the girls drew their steeds to a halt beside him. 'Not going anywhere special, are you? Only I thought as it was a nice day, like, that Polly might be able to have a lesson on me old bike.'

'Oh, did you?' Diane said with more than a touch of sarcasm. 'Well, as it happens Polly and myself have a – a previous engagement. But no doubt she'd enjoy a lesson on your motorbike if you gave her some warning, and didn't just turn up as though she'd never got anything better to do.'

'Nasty, nasty,' Tad said with what seemed to be unimpaired cheerfulness, though Polly saw a slight flush steal across his cheekbones. 'I would have rung up, only she's hardly ever available during the day and I didn't know I was going to be free today until quite late on. I've been servicing kites all morning, but I got through sooner than I expected, and it's a lovely day . . .'

'I'll be free this evening,' Polly said quickly. 'In fact, by teatime, probably. Only I did promise Di . . .'

'Oh, it's just the two of you, then?' Tad said. 'Just going for a bike ride, are you? If so, why can't I tag along?'

'Because you go a good deal faster than us, and we

were planning a quiet afternoon, just the two of us,' Diane said in her crispest, most authoritarian voice. 'Honestly, airman—'

'If you tell me where you're going, I could be there ahead of you,' Tad said. He looked hard at the carriers of their bikes and clearly realised that the bundles so neatly strapped into place were towels. 'Oh, going swimming, eh? Now there's nothing I like better than seeing two beautiful girls takin' to the water . . . but I'm prepared to put up wit' watching the two of you, since it seems that's all that's on offer.'

Even Polly felt this was a bit cheeky, but rather to her surprise Diane giggled and surrendered, though not with very good grace. 'All right, all right,' she said, hitching herself on to the saddle of her borrowed bike and scooting forward a few paces.

'We're going to Treaddur Bay for a swim and I suppose I can't stop you coming along. But if you do, airman, you can bloody well swim too, then we shan't feel silly.'

Tad grinned and roared off but Polly, mounting her own bicycle, said: 'But he's not got bathing drawers wit' him, Di. He'll probably want to swim in the altogether, and I don't fancy that at all, at all.'

It was Diane's turn to grin. 'He might swim in the altogether if it was just you and himself, my dear girl, but he won't attempt to do so with me present,' she assured her friend. 'He'll probably come in in his horrible Air Force undies, whatever they may be. Why, it might be an even more interesting experience for you and I than it will be for him. Cheeky sod, making it just about impossible for us to freeze him off!'

'Oh well,' Polly said peaceably, pedalling away. 'I've always wanted the two of you to get better acquainted, so I have, and it looks as though me wish is about to be granted.'

When the two girls reached the beach it was to find Tad's motorcycle propped up against the sea wall whilst Tad himself was already in the sea and swimming strongly.

'Showing off,' Diane said icily, changing amongst the rocks on the right-hand side of the bay. 'Well, let's hope he stays well out there whilst we go in.'

Presently, respectably, if scantily clad, the two of them ran down to the waves and splashed in, shouting as the cold salt sea gradually rose to chest level. Further out, Tad did a graceful duck-dive, which caused Polly to squeak.

'Oh janey, Di, it's nekkid he is,' she gasped, turning her back on Tad in considerable confusion. 'How does he dare? Ooh, I do think he's awful!'

'I expect he's wearing his underpants,' Diane said, though without total conviction. 'Where is he now?'

'Over by the island . . . don't *look*, Diane, he'll think we're awful strange if we look.'

'Well, at least it'll stop him looking at us,' Diane owned. 'If he really is bare, that is. Oh come on, forget him and enjoy your swim.'

'Ye-es, but he hasn't got a towel,' Polly moaned presently, after doing some fancy strokes in the cool, salty water. 'If he shakes like a dog I'm goin' to die of embarrassment, so I am. I know he's me pal, but I'll never look him in the face again, I swear it.'

'It isn't his face you'll be looking at,' Diane said, giggling. 'He's a marvellous swimmer, though, isn't he? When he does the crawl he looks like a steam tug he moves so fast.'

'And splashily,' Polly said with a shiver. 'I'm going out now, Di. If he comes near us—'

'He's coming over,' Diane said. 'Not that I care.' But she began to retreat towards the beach nevertheless, whilst Tad came on faster, until he was near enough to speak to them.

'Why don't you come out a bit further?' he shouted. 'It's marvellous out here, and it's always easier to swim wit' a bit of depth under you. Well, Polly O'Brady, I never knew you were a water-funk until now!'

'I am nothin' of the sort,' Polly shouted back, stung by the remark. 'It's just . . . What are you wearin', Tad Donoghue? Because we aren't goin' to get ourselves court-martialled through bathin' wit' a bare airman!'

'Come and see,' Tad said provocatively. 'Come on, the pair of yiz, unless you're both yeller as – as flag irises!'

Diane turned her shoulder on him but Polly, enraged by such remarks, splashed back into the sea again, launched herself forward, and began to forge her way towards Tad in a rapid sidestroke. When she got near enough she trod water, staring at her old pal, whereupon he did a porpoise leap out of the water and back in again, revealing that he was clad in a pair of skimpy but respectable underpants.

'Well, I didn't think you'd be out here swimmin' in your birthday suit,' she said untruthfully. 'Only I didn't see what else you could have found to bathe in. Glory be to God, Tad, you'll be horribly wet and soggy when you have to get yourself dressed.'

'Shan't. I'm gettin' out now, and I'll lie on the rocks until I dry off,' Tad said complacently. He gave a short bark of laughter. 'Hey, didn't I have the pair of you in a state, then? Frightened to see something you

355

weren't supposed to see, and thinkin' me a shameless sort of feller!'

'So y'are,' Polly said stoutly, turning for the shore once more. 'I doubt that Diane will ever forgive you for making her feel a fool though, Tad, and I did want you to be pals.'

'Oh, pals,' Tad said, with a shrug in his voice, Polly thought crossly. 'That's what you and me are – pals. But we go back a long way, so we do. I don't make friends wit' people that easy.'

'Unless they're WAAFs,' Polly said under her breath. 'Unless they're pretty little WAAFs who t'row themselves at your head, Tad Donoghue! Why, everyone knows that WAAFs are easy, and sleep around wit' anyone. It's only the WRNS who have a bit of discretion.'

'What was that?' Tad called. There was laughter in his voice but Polly knew she could not possibly have been overheard and ignored him, continuing to swim for the shore. Presently she hauled herself out on the sand and went over to where Diane was already draped across a smooth, flat rock, her face blissfully held up to the sun and the salt water drying on her body. She opened her eyes a slit and smiled at Polly.

'If it wasn't for your precious pal we could have sunbathed naked,' she murmured, then laughed at Polly's shocked exclamation. 'Now, now, Polly, less of that middle-class morality! I know you want to learn to ride his motorbike, but don't you think it's a bit unfair to lead him on? I mean, you always say that the naval signaller is your real feller.'

'Sunny,' Polly said. She lay down on her own towel and relaxed, letting the heat begin to soak into her sea-wet limbs. 'Oh aye, he's me feller . . . but Tad and I have known each other for ever. I like him in the

356

same sort of way I like you, Di. What's wrong wit' being friends with a feller?'

'Nothing's wrong with that, so long as he understands that you're only going to be friends and nothing more,' Diane said lazily. 'This chap seems to me to be rather more involved than you, though, Poll. Still, I daresay you know your own business best.'

'I do,' Polly said a trifle huffily, and closed her eyes firmly. As the sun began to dry her wet hair and costume, she thought about Sunny. She knew she wanted to be Sunny's girl though she hadn't seen him for ages. She only had to think of his hand caressing her neck and moving round along her jawbone to find that her stomach had begun to churn in an exciting way, whilst her knees turned to water. Resolution seemed to disappear; it no longer mattered that she was a good girl, a decent girl, intent on saving herself for marriage. Sunny's touch made her feel wicked, daring . . . and it made her want to do something more, to . . .

With dear Tad, however, it was quite different. She and Tad had been exchanging blows, wrestling each other to the ground, kissing better, for more years than she could remember. His hand on her arm, or round her waist when they danced, brought warmth and a strong feeling of safety and security. It did not thrill her one little bit. It was a shame, she supposed idly, but there it was. Sunny was wickedly exciting, poor Tad was more like a brother, and you didn't go around wanting to marry your brother. So however much she might like Tad, he was not going to be the one for her.

Satisfied with her musings – and slowly beginning to roast in the hot sunshine – Polly rolled on to her face and gave the back of her a chance to swelter. And

357

presently, without at all meaning to do so, she fell asleep.

When she woke it was because Tad was standing over her, flicking seawater on to her extremely hot flesh and telling her that if she didn't get a move on there would be no time for a motorbike lesson before he had to return to Valley. Polly, feeling stiff and sandy and rather cross, got stumblingly to her feet and saw that Diane, looking smug, was already fully dressed, as was Tad.

'You're mean, Di,' she said accusingly, picking up her clothes and retreating to a sheltering rock. 'You could have woke me. Come to that, you could have as well, Tad,' she added in an aggrieved tone. 'Oh, I'm all burned, me legs is like lobsters and – and when I brush the sand off it hurts like hell, so it does.'

'I did try to wake you, but you swore at me and went on snoring,' Tad said unkindly. 'Look, Di, if you want to start cycling back we'll follow as soon as Polly's dressed.'

'Don't you dare go, Di,' Polly squeaked, tearing her swimming costume off with scant regard for the proprieties, though since the beach was deserted apart from themselves and she was in a private tumble of rock from whence she could see nothing but the curve of the bay she was safe enough from prying eyes. 'I won't cycle back wit' Tad on his motorbike very likely trying to hustle me to go faster than I can. Oh, and me shoulders feel like a couple o' burned steaks, so they do! You're a cruel pair, and I thought you were both me friends.'

'Sunburn is a self-inflicted wound and you could be court-martialled for it,' Tad said smugly just as Polly, fully dressed but still sandy and cross, emerged from her hiding place. 'Do you want to abandon your bicycle and come home on me pillion, though? I'll come back for the bike later, if you really can't use it.'

But this Polly refused to do, though she cycled along slowly, because the friction of her shirt against her skin was very painful. Since she was in uniform she had not dared to leave off her underwear and stockings, though even the thought of the long cycle ride, clad in full uniform, dismayed her. But still, hot and uncomfortable though she was, at least she would arrive back in Holyhead properly dressed. And once they got going it was a bit cooler, with the sun sinking now towards the west and the worst of the heat gone from the day.

'I've never envied Sunny his Arctic seas before, but I do now,' she grumbled to Diane as they cycled slowly along the country roads. 'Oh, I could murder an ice cream, so I could! Come to that, I'd give a small fortune for a nice cold bath. But when we get back to the wrennery I suppose I'll have to let Tad give me a lesson, after mucking up his afternoon.'

But by the time they got back to London Road, however, Tad told them that he would have to return to Valley. 'Sure an' you're looking mortal hot, Poll,' he said, not unkindly. 'The best place for you is bed, once you've had a bath to wash off the salt and the sand. I'll see you in a day or so.'

By this time Diane had disappeared into the house and Tad and Polly were alone in the small back yard. Polly tried to banish her bad temper and smiled gratefully at her companion. 'Oh, Tad, I'm sorry to be such a grouch,' she said. 'But I hurt all over, so I do; I don't think I could concentrate on riding your motor-bike even if you didn't have to go back to the station. I'm really sorry . . . but next time, do ring up first.'

'Sure I will,' Tad said. He glanced round quickly,

then propped his motorbike against the back wall and came over, trying to take Polly gently in his arms. 'Sleep well, alanna, and I'm sorry I codded you about being sunburnt. It's horribly painful, I know, and—'

'Don't touch me!' Polly shrieked. 'Honest to God, I'm as raw as a peeled shrimp and you go touchin' me! Gerroff, Tad Donoghue!'

Tad apologised and left and Polly stomped off indoors and presently she lay in a cool bath watching the sand float down to the bottom and feeling a good deal better and even a little ashamed of her abrupt dismissal of her old friend.

But it just went to prove, she thought drowsily, flapping her hands up and down in the water to make little waves, that she was right to wait for Sunny. And presently she got out of the water, patted herself dry and went and got into bed, where even the touch of the sheets was uncomfortable. I'll be all right once I'm asleep, she told herself, cuddling the pillow. And tomorrow I'll be right as rain, and I'll begin to have a lovely tan, just like Tad's got on him, the lucky feller. And when I see Sunny . . . Her mind drifted off into a pleasant dream in which she was back in Liverpool in peacetime, with the sun shining and Sunny holding her hand and telling her she was the only girl for him . . .

Polly slept.

It was decidedly odd getting off the number 24 tram on Stanley Road and heading for the O'Bradys' new home. Weird, really, Grace thought, that the area which she had once known so well should seem so strange to her because she herself had very likely been born on Snowdrop Street – certainly it was amongst her earliest memories. The Carberys had been at least the semblance of a family then, with a mother, a father and eight or nine children, Grace being the youngest-but-one, but by the time Grace was four or so, the family had moved away from Snowdrop Street and begun to disintegrate. Her mother was a mean, cowardly woman who would – and did – blame her children when anything went wrong so that the force of their father's wrath fell upon them rather than on herself. Stan Carbery had been a drunken brute of a docker who had become more violent and unpredictable as the years went by and the drink ate into him. They had been kicked out of the house in Snowdrop Street because they didn't pay the rent, Grace could still remember that much . . . as she could remember her father knocking her mother downstairs in a drunken fight one evening, and breaking her neck. The scuffers had come and decided to treat it as an accident, but the kids, all of them, even little Grace, had known better. They also knew that their father would keep his threat to strangle anyone who told the truth, so they had kept their mouths shut. Indeed, by the time Grace had been eight or nine she had rarely, if ever, returned to the filthy slum in a back-court where her father screamed and beat anyone who got in his way and drank not only all his own money but any that his kids might be lucky enough to make.

I wonder what would have happened to me if the Salvation Army had not taken me in and given me some pride in myself and a home at Strawberry Field? Grace wondered now as she walked, kitbag slung over one shoulder, and her greatcoat over the other, along Stanley Road. I'd never have amounted to much even if I'd lived – how could I? I was filthy, half-starved, in mortal fear of any sort of authority and constantly sleeping rough. I would certainly never

361

have joined the WAAF, worn a smart uniform and helped to fight for my country. Indeed, she would never have gone off to America to help bring up Jamie. Yes, if it had not been for the Army and the love and schooling they had given her, her life would have been very different.

Grace reached Snowdrop Street with Thompson the tailor on one corner and the Manchester Laundry on the other and turned down it, squinting along the damp pavement, trying to remember which house the Carberys had once inhabited. Number 24? Or was it 26? She did not recall ever referring to the house by its number, she had just headed for the place which she knew was her home, though usually, in those very early days, she had been either carried or led along by Jess, her big sister, the one who had been like a mother to her until the baby, Mollie, had been born and had taken her, Grace's, place. She walked slowly along the pavement, trying to conjure up memories which were pleasant, but found herself almost totally unable to do so. It had been so long ago, and after Jess had died and Mollie had been lost, their stay here had been brief. As an older child she had once or twice been drawn back to this street, wooed by vague memories of a time when she had been Jess's little favourite and of her baby sister, but even then she had been unable to recapture those happy times, so why should she expect to remember them now?

She looked hard and curiously at the houses that she passed, though they were all very much neater and cleaner than she remembered. Their front door had had a great hole in it which someone, probably their mother, had patched rather badly with a wobbly piece of cardboard. She remembered one of her brothers coming in through that cardboard one night when someone, again almost certainly either their mother or father, had locked the door and sworn that any child not indoors by a certain time would sleep on the street. She even remembered that it had been a bitterly cold night, that there had been snow, and that the missing child had left the cardboard dangling on one side so that the draught had come sidling meanly up the filthy, bare boards of the stairwell, to rouse even the soundest sleeper with its damp and chilly breath.

But right now it was summer, though the rain was falling steadily, and Grace pushed aside her memories of this street and hurried, turning towards the house now occupied by the O'Bradys and tapped on the green-painted front door.

There was a short delay, then the door shot open and Peader stood there in carpet slippers, old grey flannels and a woollen jumper which had seen better days. But his smile could not have been more welcoming had it been his own daughter standing on the doorstep and the way in which he shouted 'It's our Grace, alanna; come and help me to get her unravelled from her luggage!' was enough to warm the cockles of a heart far less susceptible to kindness than Grace's.

'Oh, Uncle Peader, it's so good to be back,' she half-gasped, as he and Deirdre took her kitbag and somehow managed to detach her from her greatcoat and began to pull her across the narrow hallway and into the back kitchen. 'Isn't it a rotten night, though? You'd never think it was summer, it's so damp and chilly.'

'Never mind, love, I've got the kettle on and there'll be a mug of cocoa ready before you've so much as settled in your chair,' Deirdre said, pushing Grace gently into the shabby old armchair which she had last seen in the house in Titchfield Street. 'We didn't know what time you'd arrive so I've got a liver casserole cooking in the oven which must be done to a turn by now. Are you very hungry?'

'Starving, Auntie Dee,' Grace said, holding out her hands to the fire. 'Liver casserole, my favourite.' She looked about her at the solid, comfortable kitchen furnishings she had known for so long. 'Have you heard from Brogan or Sara and Jamie?'

'Brogan's been posted to a base in Suffolk, Laken-heath,' Deirdre said, bustling over to the oven.

'It feels really strange to be in Snowdrop Street again,' Grace said. 'As I walked along I tried to recognise our house . . . but it was so long ago . . . You knew I was born in Snowdrop Street? I think we lived here for four or five years.'

She glanced across at Deirdre. The older woman was sitting as though turned to stone, staring at her, and when Grace looked interrogatively at Peader he, too, was staring, round-eyed.

'What's the matter?' Grace said, smiling. 'Didn't you know I were born in Snowdrop Street? Not that it matters, particularly as we weren't able to pay the rent so we had to leave. I was trying to remember the neighbours, wondering whether there were any left from when we were here, but I daresay they've all either moved on or forgotten all about us. It was ages ago, after all – I was about four when Mollie was lost and Jess was killed. That was nearly twenty years ago which is a long time for memories to go back.'

'You're right there,' Deirdre said after a rather long pause, Grace thought. 'Yes, memories are short.' She got to her feet and moved over to the oven. 'I'd best dish up before we're all as hungry as Grace.'

Grace frowned across at the fire. All of a sudden the small room seemed less cheerful, less secure, as though a chilly little wind had blown under the door.

Peader cleared his throat, glanced at Grace and then at his wife, and said rather lamely, Grace thought: 'There's nothing like a liver casserole to warm you through on a chilly night.' Grace felt that the atmosphere, which had been so warm and comfortable when she first entered the house, had become strained in some way. What could she have said? So far as she could recall she had said nothing to remind them of the war. Then suddenly she remembered a topic of conversation which would please them. 'Oh, you said in your last letter that Monica had got herself a job in a factory making uniforms because she felt that she was doing nothing towards the war effort. Has she settled in well?'

'She has indeed,' Peader said heartily. 'I don't deny there's been times when we thought her rather . . . But all that's past. I don't believe she's ever looked at another feller since Martin's – Martin's ship went down, and now she's working in a factory on a big commercial sewing machine. It's not glamorous work, but useful. She's always been a keen needle-woman and seems to have taken to the work. At any rate she's a supervisor and does special jobs for them. And whilst Sara was here she used to go over to the Eventide homes to help out, and to the Strawb, as well. Oh aye, she's turned out all right has our Monica.'

Grace smiled at the 'our', because she still remembered when Monica had been very much an outsider. But how sad that a tragedy had had to happen before Monica had truly become an O'Brady. Still, that was life, she supposed.

'Come up to the table the two of you,' Deirdre said presently, carrying a steaming casserole across the kitchen and putting it down with a plonk on the scrubbed wooden table. 'Peader wouldn't eat his share earlier, so I made do wit' a sandwich. Now we're all ready for our food!'

And the three of them settled themselves round the table whilst Deirdre dished up and Grace, mouth watering, picked up her knife and fork. Home cooking, she thought ecstatically. Bliss after months of canteen food.

'It was the ideal opportunity, alanna, so why didn't you take it?' Peader whispered to Deirdre very much later that night as the two of them lay in their bed. 'You could have just said straight out that our Polly was adopted when she was a few months old, and that she was really Mollie Carbery. I meant to speak meself, but such a look you gived me – it scared the livin' daylights out o' me, I tell you straight!'

'I think Polly should be the first to know,' Deirdre insisted. 'She's our girl, we should tell her first. Grace is a dear, but we didn't bring her up, love her from the time we first laid eyes on her as we did wit' our Poll. Oh, and I'm scared that if we tell anyone we'll be in mortal trouble. I know the mammy and daddy died, but there may be relatives . . . I can't face it, so I can't.'

'Well, you're going to have to tell the pair of 'em, some time,' Peader pointed out. 'And Grace so longs for a sister! Why not tell her now, make it easy on yourself? The good Lord above knows when Polly will be on leave next, and you'll not put such news in a letter, that I *do* know, so why not grit your teeth and tell? If Sara had been here she'd have blowed the gaffe, I'm sure of it.'

'Why? Why should Sara say anything?' Deirdre asked in an aggrieved tone. 'She's me daughter-in-law, not me conscience!'

'Because didn't you hear what Grace said after supper, about Sara's gran living on Snowdrop Street too? Sara knew the Carbs, I know she did, and naturally she and Brogan both know all about Polly's being brought over to Ireland to keep her safe. Oh, Deirdre, no good ever came of deliberate deceit!'

'We've been deliberately deceiving ourselves for all of Polly's life, just about,' Deirdre pointed out. She felt tears come to her eyes and turned, burying her face in Peader's pyjama-clad shoulder. 'I don't think it's right to tell one girl and not the other, anyway. Next time they're both home on leave I swear on the Holy Book, Peader, that we'll have it all out. Will *that* satisfy you?'

'It will,' Peader said. 'Let's hope it will be sooner rather than later, then. I know Polly was only a tiny baby when she left this area, but if I'd realised we'd have been bringing her back to the very street on which she was born . . . well, I don't know but I'd have turned the house down.'

'I would have,' Deirdre said fervently. 'Still, next time they're both home on leave . . .'

She left the sentence unfinished and was soon asleep but Peader lay awake for some time, staring into the darkness. It was all very well to insist that they tell the two girls the truth and let them enjoy their relationship, but what would it do to Polly's relationship with her adoptive parents and brothers?

'Me pal Grace is home!' Polly squeaked, putting the

367

first page of her letter down on the table and turning shining eyes on Diane, sitting beside her and eating slightly burned porridge with as good a grace as she could manage. Polly was not a good cook and it had been her turn to make the breakfast. 'Well, she will be by now, at any rate, since Mammy wrote this . . .' she flicked the letter before her with one finger, '. . . a couple of days ago. I wonder now, could I get a forty-eight?'

''Course you could,' Diane said crisply. 'Why, if Tad was able to do the same he could take you back home on the motorbike! Go on, if she's your best friend it 'ud be nice to meet up again and you've not been home since you joined HMS *Bee*. Go and ask as soon as you get into the offices,' Diane suggested, finishing her porridge and reaching out a hand towards the teapot. 'Any more tea? Though I do think the mess should provide coffee for brekker. My mama would faint if she knew her ewe lamb was reduced to drinking tea before work in the morning.'

'Your mama must have got used to bad news about her ewe lamb by now,' Annabel Ridge remarked from her place further down the table. The three girls were having an early breakfast and none of the other WRNs had yet appeared. 'What about diving into the harbour and having to be dredged up by a whole platoon of soldiers, then? What did mama think of that?'

Diane giggled. 'Not a lot. But I didn't dive into the harbour, you utter idiot, I was coming ashore from one of the MTBs and a wave sort of jiggled it and I fell in the drink. And only two soldiers came in for me, not a platoon.'

'She's accident prone,' Polly said, finishing her toast and pushing her empty cup towards Diane, who was waving the teapot about rather uncertainly. 'Pour us another cup, me darlin', then we'd best get a move on. I want to tackle the Leading WRN before she gets all snarled up in other business.'

Chapter Fourteen

On her first day, Peader took Grace on a ramble along the Scotland Road, where Grace was duly dismayed at the empty shelves and windows filled with pictures of goods often no longer even available. They had quite a good lunch though, in a tiny workingmen's cafe filled with large and noisy dockers, and after that Peader went home and Grace went to Strawberry Field.

She caught a bus, walked up the drive, and was immediately filled with nostalgia for days past. She had been so happy here! Matron came out as she entered the familiar hall and gave her a hug, then bore her off to the staffroom where a number of Salvationists were having tea and introduced her to those few that she did not already know. Then they sat and talked and Grace told them all about being a driver, and quite a lot about Graham, who was a Salvationist as well and had introduced her to a whole host of his friends.

'You won't go far wrong with another Salvationist, chuck,' an elderly member of the staff said comfortably. She was a Mrs Farrow, a retired teacher who was 'helping out during the emergency', which seemed to mean that she was doing a very good job and would continue to do it so long as the war lasted. Which, Grace thought soberly, looks like being quite a time – it's a good job Mrs Farrow enjoys the work and loves the kids.

She refused, with real regret, an invitation to stay and share the evening meal but went through into the playroom and talked to the children for a bit. They loved meeting 'old girls' they told her and wanted to know all about the services so that they could join the right one when they were old enough.

'With luck, the only force you'll join will be the Salvation Army,' Grace told them, smiling. 'I pray the war will be over long before you're old enough to join up. But Matron tells me you've done a great deal of work in raising money for our chaps. She says you must have bought a whole Spitfire with all the old iron you collected, to say nothing of newspapers, rags and the like.'

She was back on Snowdrop Street by the time Deirdre was beginning to scrub the potatoes and prick the sausages, for it was to be bangers and mash tonight. 'Tomorrow we'll have fish and chips from the shop down the road, if they've got any, that is,' she said as Grace crossed the room towards her. 'We thought we'd have an early tea tomorrow, just a cuppa and some bread and jam, and then go to the flicks. After that we'll have the fish and chips. Would you like to do that? Only we don't want you to waste a minute of your leave, alanna.'

Grace agreed with all the plans Deirdre had made and began to lay the table for supper.

'Fish and chips and a visit to the flicks will be lovely,' she said contentedly, putting round the knives and forks. 'But the best thing of all, Auntie Dee, is being with you – being back here, in Liverpool amongst me pals. They were prime to me at the Strawb, and Uncle Peader and I had a good laugh, looking at what the shops aren't selling. But I never asked – how did your day go?'

'Grand, thanks, chuck. Oh, and I met Monica, and she's coming with us to the flicks tomorrow and having supper after that. She's looking so pale and ill, I thought it would do her good to meet someone who wasn't a hundred years old and stuck on a sewing machine.'

Peader, sitting by the fire reading the *Echo*, laughed. 'There's other girls in that factory, I'll be bound,' he said. 'Still, I know what you mean, me darlin'. Monica said right from the start that she didn't believe Martin was dead any more than our Polly did, but I sometimes wonder if it isn't a good deal worse waitin' for a feller to write, or make himself known to you, than if you accept he's dead and you won't see him again. On the other hand, whilst there's hope, there may be life as well.'

'She's right to hope, I think,' Grace said. 'With the Navy, it's awful hard to say for certain what's happened, I know that. You know Sunny and I write to each other? Well, he's on convoy duty still in his destroyer, he's on the Russian convoys now though, and in one of his letters he was telling me how his ship was dodging round the convey, keeping it safe, a bit like a sheepdog circles a flock, he says, when they suddenly realised that they were a ship short – a big merchantman had disappeared. He says it was broad daylight, with no enemy aircraft overhead for once and nothing under the surface either, so far as they could judge. Yet the ship just simply disappeared and no one saw it go. But very much later, he found that one of the men had been picked up by another member of the convoy, and was safe. Only the one – but even he couldn't say just what had happened, save that he was woken by water sloshing round his hammock and a lot of noise. He said he managed to wriggle through a hole and shot up to the surface, despite not wearing a lifebelt, and found a half-submerged life raft and clung to it.'

'Well, there you are, then,' Peader said placidly. 'There's hope for Mart yet – if he was picked up by a German ship . . .'

'That's right. Or I suppose he might have swum ashore . . . oh, I don't know, but I do believe that Monica is quite right to hope,' Grace said. 'I'll be glad to see her tomorrow, in any event. I never really got to know her before, but now, perhaps, we'll have a bit more time.'

Tad was unable to get a forty-eight, or even to find time to take Polly home on the back of his motorbike.

'The truth is, Poll, that you'll be safer on the bus and train,' he told her bluntly when she rang him that evening at the station. 'My bike's not a new machine, you know. She's totally trustworthy on a run of twenty miles or so, but it's a good deal more than that to reach Liverpool, and I'd be afraid that if she broke down and I'd not got the right spare parts with me, I might make you miss your pal Grace. If you'd given me some advance warning, it would have been different, but as things stand, you're better off by public transport.'

Polly sighed and said that she would take his advice and rang off, but she had not the slightest intention of doing anything so tame. Instead, she set off on a round of all the drivers she knew, and the next morning managed to get a lift with a driver returning to Chester after delivering supplies to the naval base.

Immensely pleased with herself, Polly proceeded to hitchhike the rest of the way and as a result arrived within a few hundred yards of her new home no later than eleven in the morning with her money still intact and feeling fresh and perky. The man who had taken her on the last stage of her journey was heading for the docks and he dropped her on Commercial Road, very near the end of Snowdrop Street, and drove off, beeping his horn cheerfully in farewell.

Polly turned into the short street, reminding herself that she had now got extra time to enjoy her forty-eight and rat-tatted cheerfully on the door. She wondered who would come in answer to her knock and hoped it would be Peader, though of course if it was Grace that would be wonderful too. It could not be her mother, who was working in the parachute factory and she was still wondering who would answer the knock when the door opened and Peader stood before her, his eyebrows gradually rising into his hair whilst a big smile spread right across his face and delight beamed out of his dark eyes. Polly bounced across the short distance that separated them and straight into his arms.

'Oh, Daddy, isn't it just great to be here? Oh, I do love you, so I do!'

'Polly! Be all that's wonderful, how've you come here? Why, me darlin' girl, you couldn't have arrived at a better moment – d'you know your pal Grace is here? She got up late this mornin', because we've planned an outing tonight, and she and meself was about to go off on the tram to the posh shops on Bold Street and round there . . . But come in, alanna, and sit yourself down. Oh, just wait till I tell young Grace who's here!'

Together, father and daughter entered the house, closing the front door firmly behind them.

*

374

Polly had a wonderful day. She and Grace went off by themselves in the end, Peader having admitted that he could do with a couple of hours on his allotment, and they talked non-stop, scarcely noticing the lack of goods for sale, even in the poshest of posh shops. Grace told Polly all about her work and Polly was very impressed, feeling that Grace was doing more for the war effort by rushing around in ambulances and ferrying the aircrews to and from their kites and the messes and admin buildings than she herself was doing in taking documents and messages from ship to shore and from one centre of administration to another.

'But we're all doing our bit,' Grace said comfortingly, when Polly voiced her thoughts. 'Why, without you, Poll, enemies of the state might listen in on the wireless waves or whatever they are, and hear the secrets that you carry. Anyway, didn't you say you were learning to ride a motorbike? Despatch riders are important, and they have a very interesting sort of life as well. I think I'd rather be a despatch rider than a bus and gharry and ambulance driver any day of the week! Here's Lewis's, though and they're still serving quite a decent meal, cheaply too. Shall we indulge ourselves for once?'

'But won't Daddy expect us home?' Polly asked rather anxiously. 'I know he said he'd rather dig his allotment, but I felt mean taking his morning off away from him, so I did.'

Grace, however, was reassuring. 'He was just being polite to a guest,' she assured her friend. 'Auntie Dee tried to get a day off to take me around, but the factory weren't keen, so your dad said he'd take me instead. The trouble is, most of me old pals are working so I was at a bit of a loose end. You're a sight for sore eyes, queen, and your dad's glad he can get out of a lot of window-shopping, I promise you. As for going home for a meal, he and I had planned to eat out, so I'm sure he'll expect you and I to do the same.'

So the two girls went and had lunch at Lewis's and after that they 'did' the cheaper shops in Byrom Street and the Scottie, before getting themselves a cup of tea and a bun at the nearest cafe.

They caught a tram home and told Peader all about their day and when Deirdre got back, tired after a long day at her machine but thrilled to see Polly, they had another cup of tea whilst they waited for Monica to join them. She, good girl that she was, came in just as the tea was brewing, so the five of them hurried off to the Gaiety Cinema, where the girls had a most enjoyable snuffle in the sad bits and laughed heartily over the cartoon. They walked home after the cinema and ate the fish and chips which Peader had bought from Podesta's, opposite the cinema, and then Grace and Polly walked Monica back to her tram stop before returning home and making their way, tired but happy, up to bed.

That night the two girls talked exhaustively, despite the fact, as Grace remarked, that they had been doing so all day, and did not get to sleep until the early hours, with the result that they woke late, got up leisurely and decided to spend the day calling on old friends, or at least on the homes of old friends.

Grace took Polly to the citadel, where they were clucked over and made much of by the mainly elderly people still working there, then they had the rather dispiriting business of going along familiar streets and finding that a good many of their friends had moved away after their homes had been either badly damaged or completely destroyed in the May Blitz.

Polly was sad that St Sylvester's church was still in ruins, as was the school where she and Sunny had first met, but she had seen enough of the bombing before she left to realise it was impossible to rebuild at present. There had been too much damage and building supplies of all descriptions were in short supply. Indeed, at the house in Snowdrop Street they had odd slates on the roof and the plaster on the end kitchen wall was kept in place mainly, Peader had assured them, by the thick layers of paper which he had stuck over it.

'Anyway, they're better off in Snowdrop Street,' Polly said as she and Grace made their way back towards it later that morning, for Polly's forty-eight officially came to an end at midnight and she meant to leave and start back to the island as soon as they had eaten their dinner. 'It's much nicer than Titchfield Street, don't you think, Grace? There's more room, and more neighbours too. They're nice as well. Mammy said some of them have been there years, and can remember Sara's gran – she used to live here, now isn't that a strange coincidence? Think of our Brogan coming courting all those years ago!'

'Yes, I rather like Snowdrop Street,' Grace agreed, glancing into shop windows as they made their way along Stanley Road, though the displays could not be described as tempting. 'Did your mammy not tell you that I used to live here as well, once? Oh, it was long time ago, before my older sister died, but we did live here for a few years. I was only a kid when we left though, so I couldn't tell you which house.'

'*Did* you?' Polly said. She heard the surprise in her voice and felt guilty, but she knew that the Carberys had been a poor, feckless sort of family, knew that Grace had had a hard childhood, and this did not seem to fit in with living on Snowdrop Street. 'No, Mammy never told me that – perhaps she didn't know.'

'Probably not,' Grace agreed. 'Now I can tell you're wondering what a – a family with eight or nine kids, and all of them neglected, were doing in a nice street like this. No, don't shake your head, Polly O'Brady, I don't blame you for thinking it because I thought it meself. The truth is, my father was usually in work when I was very small and though he drank like a fish and beat up anyone smaller than he was, he must have been able to manage the rent at first. Then, when it all got too much, we were chucked out, and went off to live in one of the courts off the Scottie. Still, it's true that we were here for a bit. I daresay Sara's gran knew the Carbs quite well.'

'Well, isn't life strange now?' Polly wondered as they reached the corner of Snowdrop Street. 'We'll go round the back jigger because they always hide the key under one of the slates and I know which one. Daddy may be home, of course, but once he gets gardening, you know, he forgets the time.'

They were about to turn down the jigger when a voice hailed them and, turning, Polly was astonished to see her mother hurrying along the pavement towards them and brandishing a key. 'We'll go in the front door,' she called as soon as they were near enough. 'I've got some time off work, so I have, since it's me daughter's last day. The boss said as I do so much overtime it would be all right. I'll go back to work after you're on your way,' she added a trifle apologetically. 'But there *is* a war on, as everyone keeps saying. Come along in, girls. Peader won't be long.'

The three of them hurried into the house and

Deirdre began to cut bread for sandwiches, since the main meal of the day was always eaten at night. 'It's only spam and tomato,' she said apologetically, as she worked. 'And you won't get a decent meal, Polly me darlin', until you're back in Anglesey. But I've not the time to do much cooking before you'll want to go off, and I want a word wit' you before then.'

'Oh? What've I done wrong, Mammy?' Polly enquired, immediately aware of a certain tenseness in her mother's voice, even in the way she was slicing bread and spreading margarine. 'I've only been home two minutes, for goodness' sake!'

'Oh, alanna, you've done nothing wrong,' Deirdre said. 'It's just . . . It's something we've been meaning to tell you . . . Oh, here's Peader! Let's get this dinner down us – there's cold apple pie for afters.'

Deirdre did not enjoy her meal. She and Peader chatted to the girls, joked, laughed, ate their food. Or at least, Peader ate; Deirdre crumbled her solitary sandwich and pushed a piece of apple pie round and round her plate. Not even the addition of custard, made, admittedly, with water and dried milk, could make it palatable to one who was rehearsing over and over, inside her head, what she would presently say to the two girls. She and Peader had talked it over the previous night, and had decided that it would be best, perhaps, to speak to both the girls at once.

'After all, we're goin' to tell them that they're sisters,' Peader had said reasonably. 'Why should we not tell them together, the darlin's? I know it will be good news for our Polly, but even better for Grace, situated as she is.'

But now that it had come to the point, Deirdre wondered whether they were doing the right thing.

Or rather whether she was doing the right thing, since it had been agreed between them that the news would come better from her.

So presently, with the meal finished and Polly not due to leave the house for an hour, she and both girls stayed in the kitchen to wash up and clear away and to talk whilst Peader took himself off to the front parlour with the newspaper.

Deirdre cleared her throat a couple of times, then decided she would start the washing-up and sort of – sort of throw the information over her shoulder as she worked. Accordingly, she began, though with far less ease than she had intended – or imagined – herself doing.

'I want to – to tell you a story, girls. A long time ago, when you were only three or four, Grace, and Polly here was a little baby . . .'

Peader, sitting uneasily in the parlour trying to concentrate on the paper, could only hear their voices as a sort of murmur through the wall. But he heard the shriek, closely followed by the thunder of feet on the stairs. He got slowly and awkwardly out of his chair and went into the kitchen to find Deirdre standing with her back to the sink, her hands to her face. Tears fairly spouted out between her fingers and Grace was standing beside her, patting her shoulder awkwardly and saying: 'Now come on, Auntie Dee, it were a surprise for me – well, surprise is putting it mildly, truth to tell – so what must it have been like for Polly? For me, it's really wonderful to know I've got a sister of me own, a proper blood sister. But for her . . . well, what you didn't seem to realise you were telling her was that she may have gained a sister but she's lost the parents and the brothers that

380

she's always thought were her own. Oh, don't you *see*?'

'Where is she?' Peader said bluntly, realising that this had not gone at all as they had expected when he and Deirdre had talked over the telling of their long-held secret.

Deirdre opened her mouth to speak but was spared the necessity of answering by the thunder of feet descending the stairs and the hurling open of the kitchen door. Polly stood framed in it for a moment, looking . . . well, looking as Peader had never seen her. Her face was deathly white, her eyes scarlet-rimmed and swollen with crying. But her mouth, that gentle, generous mouth, was held so tightly that it looked lipless and the eyes, when she turned them on him, were so cold that it was like a knife through his heart.

'Polly?' he said uncertainly. 'Me darlin' child, why are you lookin' at me like that? As for poor Mammy, we t'ought you'd be pleased to know you'd a sister as well as a grosh o' brothers, we never t'ought—'

'I'm not Polly,' Polly said, her voice still tearful. 'I'm not Polly O'Brady at all, at all, Mr O'Brady, and you aren't my – my daddy, nor is *she* . . .' she pointed at Deirdre, '. . . my mammy. I'm Mollie Carbery, the little kid no one wanted once her sister was dead. And – and I'll never forgive you for lettin' me think I was one of you, wit' a proper home and a proper family of me own, when all the time I were just – just a bit of a stray kid Brogan had picked up on the railway, to oblige a dead girl.'

Peader felt tears in his own eyes and crossed the kitchen unsteadily, holding out his arms, beginning to try to explain how they had not dared to tell her at first in case the news got around and someone tried to take her from them, how they had loved her as much – more – than they would have done had Deirdre actually given birth to her. But Polly swerved round him and shot across the kitchen, hurled the back door open and ran out into the yard. Her kitbag, untidily packed, swung from one shoulder but even thus burdened, she was out of the yard, along the jigger and off up the Scotland Road, Peader guessed, before he, with his halting steps, had even reached the back door.

'Stop her, Grace! Peader, for the love of the good God, bring my little girl back to me,' Deirdre shrieked. She cast down the apron she had been wearing and ran past Peader who, following as fast as he could, was still hobbling along the jigger when his wife returned, defeat in the slump of her shoulders, the misery in her face.

'Oh, Peader, what'll she do?' she asked breathlessly, clutching his upper arms and staring earnestly into his face. 'She's in a terrible state, so she is – she'll be on a tram and halfway to Lime Street by now – I never dreamed she'd take it so badly.'

'We should have thought it out more carefully,' Peader said heavily as they returned to the kitchen, where Grace was stacking plates, cups and dishes on the dresser and looking worried half to death. 'It never occurred to me that she'd stop seeing herself as an O'Brady. I just thought she'd be mortal glad we'd stole her away, and even gladder to find she'd a sister as well as her brothers. As for what she'll do, alanna, God alone knows.'

'She'll go back to her wrennery and come to terms with it,' Grace said, heaving the big black kettle over the fire and warming the teapot. 'Give her a few days to get her sense of proportion back and she'll come round. You know our Polly, she doesn't have a nasty bone in her body; she'll see that you meant everything for the best, and get in touch to tell you not to worry. But . . . well, it must be a terrible shock, to be told that you aren't who you've always thought you were.'

'We've little choice but to wait,' Deirdre said ruefully. 'I wish there was something . . . If we could go to her . . . but she'd not see us, either of us, for all our love.'

'Perhaps not. But she'll see me,' Grace said, finishing her task and turning towards the kitchen door. 'I'm going after her, Auntie Dee; I'll catch the next tram down to Lime Street, then I'll start the journey to Holyhead. And as soon as I've talked to her I'll drop you a line, or telephone your factory, Auntie. We'll get this sorted out, never fear.'

'Oh, would you? But dear Grace, this is your week's leave, it really isn't fair—'

'It's my choice,' Grace said firmly. 'What sort of enjoyment could I have, knowing Polly – my sister – is in trouble and deeply unhappy? I think I can help her; it's the least I can do.'

She left the room, closing the door quietly behind her. Deirdre walked into Peader's arms and they stood for a moment, hugging, both with tears running down their cheeks.

'It'll come right, alanna,' Peader said at length, smoothing a big, calloused hand down her face. 'You see, it'll come right. What we did for our girl we did with the best of intentions and she'll realise it, when she's calmer. And she's right, you know, we should have told her long since that she wasn't an O'Brady by birth but only by love.'

'You wanted to tell her,' Deirdre sighed. 'And I

wouldn't – I was afraid. Oh, Peader, I pray to God we get our girl back!'

Tad was in the mess, playing cards with a group of friends, when Toby Carruthers, who had gone across to answer the almost constantly ringing phone, turned towards him.

'Tad! Tad Donoghue, there's a call for you.'

'Oh?' Tad said, getting up from his chair with a sigh and laying his cards carefully down on the green baize table. He glared menacingly round at his three companions. 'Don't you go lookin' at me hand nor changin' me cards, because I've a photographic memory, so I have and I'll kill anyone who stops me winnin' this round.' Crossing the room, he thought bitterly that it was just his luck; the first time he'd had a decent hand all week and the bleedin' phone had to ring. However, he grinned at Toby and held out a hand for the receiver. 'Who is it? Not me mammy?'

'It's a female,' Toby said, putting a hand over the mouthpiece so that his words would not be heard on the other end of the line. 'I think she's crying, old feller, so you'd best go gentle. Been getting some nice little WAAF into trouble, have you?'

'Not that I can remember,' Tad said, but though he smiled he took the receiver rather hastily, almost dropping it as it changed hands. He held it to his ear. 'Hello? Tad Donoghue speaking.'

There was a pause, and then a dry sob, a gustily indrawn breath, and a voice said: 'Oh Tad, Tad! Thank the good Lord . . . Oh Tad, it's so awful, I can't be after tellin' you how awful it is . . .'

He would have known that voice anywhere, even coming distorted over the line, and ending in sobs. He said sharply: 'Polly! What in heaven's name has happened to you? Where are you? I t'ought you'd be back in Holyhead by now . . . Are you back? If so, I'll come right away.'

'I'm – I'm not back,' Polly said, her voice sounding small and snuffly. She began to cry again. 'Oh, Tad, I'm in terrible trouble, so I am – can you come?'

'Where? Where are you, in God's name?' Tad shouted, terribly frightened by the fear in Polly's tone. 'Get a holt of yourself, Poll, and tell me where I can find you.'

'I d-don't know exactly,' Polly said, her voice perilously close to a wail. 'It's lost I am, Tad, and it's dark and it's pouring with rain and I just bolted into the first telephone box I saw, so I did. It's not Chester, it's further on than that . . . Oh Tad, will you come?'

'Of course I will – but, Polly me darlin', you must pull yourself together now. Have you some more pennies?'

There was a short scuffle and then Polly said in a slightly more composed tone: 'Yes, I've some more pennies.'

'Good,' Tad said. 'Now, alanna, are you in a town or in the countryside?'

'I – I'm in a sort of village, I think,' Polly said, after a moment during which she must have peered out through the glass windows of the telephone box, breathing heavily. 'But you know what it's like, Tad, they don't put big signs out no more tellin' you where you're at, in case of an invasion.'

'Right. Is there a pub near? Is it safe for you to go to the nearest pub and then ring me again? Don't worry, I won't move from the phone.'

'Ye-es, but – but suppose he's out there some-where, hidin' round a corner waitin' for me?' Polly quavered, with the fear so strong in her voice that Tad felt his own hair begin to rise on his scalp. 'Oh, Tad, I feel safe wit' you on the other end of the line . . . Can't you just come? I must be on the way back to the island, because the feller said he was goin' to catch the Irish ferry . . . Please Tad, don't make me leave the box. It's nearly dark out there and the rain is drivin' somethin' awful.'

She was desperately scared of someone . . . What on earth did she mean, *the feller said he was goin' to catch the Irish ferry*? She was supposed to have caught the bus and then the train . . . but suppose she had missed one or the other? Besides, she was on her way back now . . . If she had been coming back towards the island it might be possible to pinpoint her whereabouts if only he asked the right questions. He took a deep, steadying breath.

'Look, alanna, what time did you leave Liverpool? I take it you've been given a lift by someone? Well, how long d'you reckon you've been on the road?'

'Hours, I think,' Polly said after a rather long pause. 'Oh . . . don't go, don't go!'

The telephonist's voice cut across Polly's plea. 'Your time is up, caller. Do you wish to pay for another three minutes?'

'Yes. Yes,' Polly gabbled and Tad could hear the money rattling through the coin slot. They were not disconnected though they might easily have been; this was wartime and telephonists did not encourage long calls because there was always someone else waiting for a line. 'I'll stay right here, but Poll, you must take your courage in both hands and make your way to the nearest pub,' Tad said, putting all the command and sternness he could into his voice. 'I could spend the whole night and all day tomorrow hunting for you, else. Now, be my brave girl . . . peep

386

out of the box, and see if you can see something which might look like a pub.'

He could imagine Polly, stuck in that little, blue-lit cube in the middle of an unknown town or village, pushing open the door, peering round it . . .

'There's buildings,' Polly said presently, her voice a little stronger. 'A shop – well, it's got a shop window, anyway, then what looks like more houses . . . Oh, I can see something with a sign, swinging in the wind. All right, Tad, I'm goin' to put the receiver down and run like hell towards the house wit' the sign. Don't go, will you?'

'Good girl,' Tad said encouragingly. 'Watch your footing, though, don't go tripping over the kerb and breaking your leg or something. And ring me back the moment you know where you are – the landlord will lend you his telephone, if you can't pay him I will, when I get there.'

'Or I could leave the phone off the hook here, run up to the pub and find out where I am, and run back,' Polly said with longing in her voice. But Tad decided that he had better veto this. After all, any half-decent man, seeing Polly's distress, would take care of her until help came.

'No,' he said authoritatively. 'Now, Poll, off you go – put the receiver down *now*!'

He heard the receiver click on to its rest and put his own instrument down, then turned and faced the mess. To his astonishment no one was taking the slightest notice of him; men went on playing cards, talking, throwing dice, writing letters. No one, he realised, could have known that he was talking to a desperately frightened girl to whom something awful but so far unexplained had happened. At the card table he had left one of the fellers called out to him, reminding him, reproachfully, that they were in the middle of a game and he had better come quickly and play his hand or he would ruin the session.

'Oh . . . one of you can play my hand,' Tad said. What cared he for cards or poker or the two bob he had hoped to gain when Polly was in trouble? 'I'm waiting for an incoming call, I don't know how long I'll be.'

In fact, he was beginning to wonder whether the call would ever come, whether he had put poor little Polly in even more jeopardy by insisting that she should find out where she was, when the telephone rang again. He had it off its rest almost before the ring had properly begun and was speaking into it.

'Polly? Is that you, alanna? Oh, thank God, I was beginnin' to think . . . but never mind that. Tell me where you are and I'll be with you just as soon as I can.'

'I'm in a pub, like you said. It's called the Bear's Paw and it's in a place called Frodsham. Oh Tad, I don't t'ink that feller was tellin' the truth when he said he was on his way to catch the ferry . . . Oh Tad, can you come?'

'Of course,' Tad said, outwardly cool but inwardly in a ferment of doubt. Frodsham? He had never heard of the place, for all he knew she could be somewhere in the wilds of Scotland! Then he remembered that she had only been travelling from Liverpool, surely she could not be that far away? Still in his calm, steadying voice he said: 'Stay where you are, alanna, and I'll be wit' you as soon as may be. But you'd best ask the landlord if you can stay with him until I arrive . . . It's nigh on eight o'clock now, it could be midnight before I reach you. But don't you worry now, I'm as good as on me way. D'you want me to have a word wit' the landlord now? Explain t'ings a bit?'

But this, Polly assured him, was not necessary. She would stay where she was, quietly in a corner, until he arrived. Closing time was ten o'clock, Tad reminded her, but Polly said, with another muffled sob, that if closing time arrived before he did, then she would be sure to find somewhere near at hand where she might wait. 'You'll be as quick as you can possibly be, I know it,' Polly assured him, sounding a little braver now, though still obviously shaken. 'Don't worry about me, Tad – just come and find me. People are awful nice, I'm sure the landlord won't turn me out into the rain – it's pourin' cats and dogs out there, so it is.'

'That's grand then, alanna,' Tad said, greatly relieved. Polly had clearly got herself in deep trouble, but she had managed to extricate herself and would surely be all right now until he arrived to bring her back to Holyhead. 'Don't you worry about anything either, alanna. Just stay put until I come.'

A couple of hours later, Tad was driving a car which did not belong to him along a road he did not know, with only the haziest idea of how to reach his destination. But he had an elderly road map spread out on the passenger seat and the words of his pal Micky echoed in his ears: 'You can't miss Frodsham – lovely little village. Head for Manchester and you'll see this damned great hill looking as though someone's took a bite out of it. The village sort of nestles under the hill, with woods above it. And the Bear's Paw is sandstone buildings on your left as you go through the village. How far? Well, I suppose it 'ud be a three-hour run normally. But in this rain . . .

Still, there shouldn't be much else on the road . . . you'll mebbe make it by midnight.'

Micky had not known, of course, that he intended to steal a car and had been imagining that Tad would be on his motorbike. Come to that, Tad had not known he intended to steal a car. Not that he had stolen it, exactly. It was more or less like borrowing it, only the owner did not know. Well, he had not been around to ask. Had he known, Squadron Leader Alan Pierce would surely have told Tad to go ahead, but Squadron Leader Pierce was not around, having gone off on a course, leaving his elderly but reliable Sunbeam Talbot to be serviced and generally fussed over by the mechanic he most trusted – Tad Donoghue. By a great piece of good fortune Tad had worked on the Sunbeam the previous day until it was in as near perfect condition as he could make it. He had even filled it with petrol so that when its owner came back he could drive it straight off. Then Tad had put it carefully away in one of the work sheds and forgotten all about it – until Polly's phone call, that was.

He had scarcely considered the motorbike as a means of rescuing Polly, however. He had known he would have to beg, borrow or steal a car or a gharry or, dammit, a perishing blood waggon, sooner than leave his Poll alone and afraid, miles from home. But no sooner had he stepped out of the mess than he had remembered the Sunbeam; remembered, too, that its owner was off in Suffolk or Norfolk somewhere . . . and had gone confidently off to the work shed.

He had not done much to prepare for the journey either, so worried was he by the state Polly had got herself into. He simply told Micky an old pal, a little WRN from his home town, was in trouble, explained her whereabouts, took Micky's advice and his map and got into the car and drove off. Now, after two hours of solitary driving through this wild night, he wished he had thought to fill a bottle with cold tea since he was parched with thirst, but it was too late for such might-have-beens. He was stuck in the car, driving steadily along black and winding roads, occasionally catching up with a military convoy.

He wished the rain would stop, though. The low grey clouds overhead and the driving rain, to say nothing of the howling wind, probably meant that there would be no activity in the air above him on such a night, but he could see very little through the slits in the car's headlights and was in constant fear of missing a turning – or finding a ditch – and so lengthening his journey still further. Once he had spotted a stream and had climbed out of the car and slaked his thirst, but that had been ages ago. Now he was thirsty again, his mouth dry as much with fear as with the long drive, and his eyes were beginning to feel tired, as though someone had thrown sand into them.

He glanced at his watch. Eleven o'clock! It could not be much further, surely? He had seen, against the cloud, the hill with the bite taken out of it, coming and going as the road wound and snaked and seemed to curve back on itself, but always there. It was appreciably closer now – surely he would arrive soon? He glanced apprehensively at the petrol gauge, but it was going to be all right. He had fine-tuned the engine and it was being gracious, sipping rather than devouring his precious juice. Of course, the slow speed at which he had been forced to drive for a good deal of his journey would have eased the petrol consumption. He grinned to himself in the dark, for it was now pitch black except for the tiny patches of light from his heads reflecting on the gleaming wet tarmac. Soon be there, he comforted himself, peering ahead. Soon be taking his Polly in his arms and hearing what had happened to her. At the thought of the fellow who had given her a lift, lied to her, deserted her, he ground his teeth with impotent fury. He hoped Polly had got his name, the number of his vehicle, anything, so that he, Tad, could find him and use his bleedin' guts for bleedin' garters just as soon as he'd settled his Polly safely back in her wrennery.

Tad slowed to negotiate a curve, glanced up at his hill and found it appreciably nearer. Grimly, he continued to drive steadily onward. At his present rate, he should be in Frodsham well before midnight.

It was not long after midnight that Tad found himself back in the car once more, but this time with Polly beside him. She sat quietly, very small and pale and huddled in one of the two rugs which Squadron Leader Pierce kept in the boot of his beloved car – a relic from pre-war outings, Tad imagined. He had found her slipping out of the pub and walking across the pavement towards him almost as he drew up. She stood in the rain for a second, glancing doubtfully at the car, and then, as he stepped out and went to meet her, she gave a strangled sob and hurled herself into his arms.

For a moment he had held her, but then she had disengaged herself briskly and returned to the pub door. She pulled it wide, called something softly – he thought it was to the effect that her pal had come – and then she closed the front door cautiously and returned to the car. Tad helped her in, noticing as he did so that she was shivering and went round to the driver's door, climbing in behind the wheel and starting the engine. After nearly four hours of difficult and tiring driving he felt strongly inclined just to sit where he was for a moment, to ask her just what had happened to her, to pull himself together, but instead, he engaged first gear, released the handbrake and turned the car in the wide road so that they were facing towards the mountains of Wales once more. It was not until they were several miles from the village that he chose a quiet stretch of grass verge and drew up on it. Then he turned to her.

'Hadn't you better drive on?' she said. 'Whose car is this, Tad?'

'I borrowed it from a – a pal,' Tad said evasively. 'Look, what wit' the rain and the wind and bein' so worried over you, Poll, I don't reckon I can drive and listen to what you're going to tell me, so why not tell me now? For a start, why didn't you catch the train?'

'Because – because it seemed silly when I could hitch,' Polly said, her voice muffled. 'And – and – I left in rather a hurry. It was all right, at first. I got a lift from the city right through the tunnel and beyond Birkenhead, but then the rain started. I walked for miles – well, it felt like miles – and then a man in a big lorry . . . Oh Tad, I don't want to talk about it! I don't want to remember!'

'Did he hurt you?' Tad said bluntly after the silence began to stretch. 'Did he get fresh wit' you, alanna?' He felt his teeth snap shut and all the muscles in his body tense at the thought of anyone offering any sort of unwanted attention to his Polly. 'Just tell me what happened, as brief as you like.'

'He *tried* to get fresh,' Polly said. 'He was hateful, Tad. Only I remembered what the Chief WRN said to us when we were doing drill, and self-defence and

393

stuff like that. She said if a feller got fresh to kick him where he joins, so I did and he shrieked like – like the bleedin' banshee, Tad, and then he flung me out of his horrible old lorry – not that I cared, I wanted to get out – and just drove off!'

'Oh,' Tad said rather inadequately. 'But he didn't hurt you, alanna?'

'No,' Polly said firmly. 'He tried to kiss me and put his hand up my skirt so I—'

'Yes, I know, you kicked him,' Tad said hastily. 'Where were you? Still in the lorry cab? How on earth did you—'

'Yes, we were still in the lorry; he'd pulled over on to the verge, though,' Polly said. 'When he tried to kiss me I thought maybe that was all right since he'd given me a lift and promised to take me right back to the wrennery, but when his hands started moving about – *you* know how they go on, Tad – I bit him as hard as I could on his horrible chin and then I tore a great lump out of his hair and then I kicked him in the—'

'Well, you did right,' Tad said. He was beginning to feel almost sorry for Polly's assailant. Still, it would teach the feller not to give lifts to young girls in order to try his luck with them. And besides, he had abandoned Polly miles from anywhere on a filthy night in a rainstorm . . . no, he deserved all that Polly had handed out and more, Tad decided. 'But another time, alanna, don't go hitching lifts unless you're wit' a pal because . . . Oh Polly, love, what've I said?'

For Polly was crying again, the tears chasing down her pale cheeks. 'It – it's just that everything's so awful,' she said, fishing out her hanky and blowing her nose hard. 'The feller in the lorry was a bastard, all right, but it – it weren't him that got me so upset, not

394

really. Tad, did you ever think . . . well, that I wasn't meself?'

'Sometimes, when we were kids,' Tad said rather cautiously. Sometimes, he remembered, Polly's temper had flared up at him and he had thought her a termagant and not the loving little Polly he knew so well. And he knew that Ivan had often grumbled at his sister's making him do more than his fair share of the housework. Was that what she meant, though?

'You did?' Polly brightened for a moment, but then began to cry more dolorously than ever. 'Well, I never even t'ought of it, but Tad, I'm not Polly O'Brady at all! Mammy and Daddy aren't me mammy and daddy, and the fellers aren't me brothers. And they've known all along, but never a word did they say until this afternoon . . . Oh, and they seemed to think I'd be quite *glad* to be told they just took me in out of pity, glad that I was really a child of one of the meanest, nastiest, rottenest families in the whole of Liverpool . . .'

'Liverpool?' Tad said, thoroughly startled now. He wondered if the man's attack had knocked Polly clean off her trolley, because he could still remember the baby Polly sitting on her mother's hip, patting the head of any chiseller who came within reach, always smiling, always sunny. 'But Polly me love, you were born and bred in Dublin, same as me!'

'No, I wasn't,' Polly said drearily. 'I was born in Liverpool . . . Well, I'll tell you how they telled me and then you'll know why I didn't much care, at first, if that feller upped and killed me, I was so unhappy. Why, if I'd not been crying half the time, d'you think that feller would have dared to put a hand on my – my chest, let alone up me skirt? If I'd been like I

395

usually am he wouldn't have tried anything, I'm telling ye!'

'Yes, I can see that,' Tad said slowly. He was beginning to think back, to remember. There was Polly's story, oft-repeated, that she could remember being born, being brought out of the doctor's bag and into a firelit circle of admiring male faces. Tad, with his superior knowledge of the facts of life – he was not eldest in a family of eight for nothing – had always found this scenario difficult to credit, but now he wondered whether Polly had, in fact, been remembering her arrival in the O'Brady home in Dublin, but as a child of twelve months or so instead of a new-born babe. He also remembered neighbours whispering, a rumour in the early days that Polly had come in from the country . . . but they were such vague rumours, and of so little interest to him, that he had never really taken them seriously. Polly was an O'Brady, her entire family worshipped her, and he, Tad, had quite agreed with them that she was a darling, and worthy of the love which folk gave her so readily. But she was still sobbing, so he put a gentle arm about her shoulders and gave her a bit of a squeeze. 'All right, Polleen, suppose it's true, that you were adopted. Well, what's so wrong wit' that, then? You said *out of pity* but people don't take on an extra child in a big family out of pity. They do it out of love, alanna.'

'Th-they wanted a girl,' Polly said, her voice still heavy with tears. 'If I'd been a boy baby . . .'

'Nonsense,' Tad said confidently. 'Why, were you ever given love which belonged to Ivan, or Bev? Tell me truthfully, Poll, don't go making things up.'

There was a long pause before Polly said grudgingly: 'No-oo, Mammy always loved us all and so did

396

the daddy. And – and they were fair as well. Even when it made me mad as fire, I knew they were being fair.'

'Well, there you are, then. Being adopted is – is a sort of compliment, I'm after thinking. Can't you see it like that?'

'They should have told me,' Polly said, after another silence had stretched until Tad had begun to wonder whether she intended to reply at all. 'Me brothers *knew*, Tad – the older ones, anyway – and they never said a word. Why, it was Brogan who brought me home, in the front of his donkey jacket, but never a word out of him to explain to me that I wasn't his little sister at all, that I wasn't even Polly!'

'But, alanna, you are Polly O'Brady by adoption,' Tad insisted, giving her another squeeze. 'So was that the reason you left home in a hurry, and hitched a lift? Because you'd flown into a temper and run out on your mammy and daddy? Alanna, they'll be worried to death, wondering where you've gone, what you've done. We can't telephone now, of course, but you must do so first thing in the morning. I suppose you didn't phone from the pub? It never occurred to me that you might have left them not knowing . . . Oh, dammit, Poll, how could you?'

'Grace is still there,' Polly said defensively after a moment. 'And don't you go tellin' me off, Tad Donoghue! And what'll I tell the WRNS? Because they've got me down as Polly O'Brady, so they have, and I'm really Mollie Carbery.'

Tad heaved a sigh. He was very tired indeed, and beginning to feel more than a little impatient with his Polly. But he tried to explain again. 'You may have been born one thing, but when the O'Bradys took you on you became something different. It – it's a bit like

397

marriage, alanna. You knew you wouldn't always be an O'Brady, didn't you, because you knew you'd marry some day, and go and live wit' your husband? Well, you'll be married as Polly O'Brady, not as Mollie . . . what did you say the name was? And what's this Grace girl got to do with it?'

Polly took a deep breath and launched into the story, this time starting at the very beginning, with the girl Jess – her sister – carrying the baby out of their strife-torn household and down on to the railway, to keep warm and safe in one of the gang huts until morning. At first the recital was punctuated by sniffs and gulps, sometimes even by sobs, but by the time she reached the climax Polly seemed to have got a hold of herself, and the story, a rivetting one, Tad considered, was told with considerable relish. She painted the Carberys so black, indeed, that Tad felt the hair on the back of his neck stand up with horror; from what she told him, she would have been unlikely to live had she been left with the likes of them. And Polly, having got Tad up to date, turned a soulful face towards him, clearly expecting sympathy.

'Well, now I know what it's all about I can't help thinking that Brog did you just about the best service one person can do for another,' he told her. 'With your big sister gone, what sort of a chance would you have stood of being brought up properly, alanna? Indeed, from what you've said, it's Grace who has a right to feel sorry for herself. She was really left out in the cold, wasn't she? You say you're ashamed of being a Carbery, incidentally, but Grace did well for herself, didn't she? And your big sister, Jess, sounds just lovely, alanna – very like yourself, in fact. So don't condemn all the Carberys because the parents were bad, wicked people. And probably, you know, your real mammy, Mrs Carbery I mean, was a good person until her husband began beating her up and draining all the goodness out of her. Are you beginning to feel a bit better, now? Shall I get moving again?'

'I'm never going to get married,' Polly said, shrinking down in her rug once more. 'Nor I shan't have kids . . . and I do t'ink you might feel a bit sorrier for *me*, Tad, with everything I believed turned upside down.'

'It's been a dreadful shock for you, so it has,' Tad agreed diplomatically – and truthfully, now he came to think of it – pressing the starter and putting the car in gear. 'You'll come to terms with it, Poll, given time. And you must ring your mammy at work first thing tomorrow and let her know you're all right. Promise?'

'Oh, all right,' Polly said. 'And now I'm goin' to sleep so you mustn't talk to me any more, Tad Donoghue. I'm very grateful that you came for me, but I don't like you very much right now. You won't try to understand, and you say you're sorry for Grace when at least she really is who she thought she was. Goodnight.'

And with that she huddled herself right into the rug and turned away from him.

Tad could have done with the companionship of an occasional word or a look, but he drove on, realising that to Polly what had happened had been a major tragedy. She would come to her senses in the end, he knew that – his Polly had never been one to bear a grudge. And he acknowledged that finding your family were not your family, your parents not your parents, must have taken some swallowing, especially for the spoiled and adored Polly. He felt it a little unfair that he was being punished for it, for driving alone with Polly beside him and pretending to be asleep – now and then he saw her eyes glint as she glanced stealthily sideways at him – but he had enough imagination to guess pretty accurately at how she must be feeling and continued to drive in silence.

However, once they reached the island he pulled over again and turned towards her, giving her a gentle shake when she hastily closed her eyes and once more pretended slumber. 'Polly, I think you'd best wake up now. Your wrennery will be locked up for the night, and it can't be more than four o'clock now so there won't be anyone stirring for a bit. I'm out without leave too . . . but I've worked out how to get round that. What about you, alanna?'

'There's always someone up around six o'clock,' Polly said. She yawned. 'Don't worry, I'll get in wit'out any fuss. Diane will have signed in for me, I expect.'

'Right. Then I'll put the other rug round me and we can both snooze until around five.' He leaned over to the back seat and pulled the second rug across, then glanced sideways at Polly. 'Shall we both snuggle up under the two rugs, alanna? Then we can share each other's warmth and have the warmth of both rugs instead of one each.'

'I don't think we should,' Polly said, with an edge of frost in her voice. 'What would people say?'

'Not a lot,' Tad said, grinning. 'I'm not suggesting we get into the back seat, alanna! 'Tis just for warmth, you know.'

'Well, I suppose it might be all right,' Polly said, clearly not wanting to come down off her high horse but probably needing the warmth as much as he did, for Tad, by this time, was very cold indeed. His hands felt as though they might have frozen to the wheel and his feet were very little better. 'After all, you're more like a brother to me than—' Her voice wobbled and Tad heaved the rug off her and took her in his arms.

'All right, all right, darlin',' he said, his voice rough with love and compassion. 'You've had a shocking time, so you have, and here's me been trying to make you see that it wasn't so bad when it's been cruel hard on you. Now give your Tad a nice cuddle and we'll go off to sleep like a couple of babes in the wood and it'll soon be morning. Indeed, the sky's trying to lighten in the east even now.'

'Pull the rugs over us, then,' Polly said, snuggling against him. 'Oh, Tad, isn't this nice and comfy? You are kind – I wish you really *were* my brother. You'd have told me I was adopted if you'd known, wouldn't you?'

'I don't know,' Tad said, innate honesty compelling him not to give the easy lie. 'But it's not your brother I want to be, alanna. When this lot's over I want you to change your name again, only this time to Donoghue.'

He said it with a dry mouth and thumping heart, for though he had known he loved Polly and wanted to marry her ever since they had met as two adults, he still did not really know how Polly viewed him.

Polly stirred in his arms and laughed sleepily. 'Silly! I'm going to marry Sunny Andersen, I'm sure I told you that ages and ages ago. I love you ever so much, Tad, just like I love me brothers . . . well, I mean just like I love the O'Brady boys. But it's a different sort of love, isn't it! Now let's try to go to sleep or we'll be wrecks.'

Polly· slept quite quickly after that but Tad stayed awake, his heart sick and sore within him. She loved him like a brother! She was going to marry that Sunny Andersen – ridiculous name – because for him she had a 'different' kind of love! He had been a fool not to have courted her more openly, letting her believe that it was just friendship which brought him into Holyhead whenever he had a few hours free, just friendship which made him give her lessons on his motorbike, teach her how to service it, take him so for granted that she could phone him up and ask him to get her out of trouble without a second thought. She knew Tad – good old Tad – would not let her down because he was like a brother to her!

It was a long while before he slept.

Next morning, Tad was closeted with his squadron commander for a long time, rather to the surprise of his friends, for they knew that Tad had got away with his unexpected absence and also with his 'borrowing' of the car. When he came out, however, he was pale but composed, grinning cheerfully at his friends and telling them that he would surprise them all yet.

A couple of days after that, he rang Polly at her wrennery.

'Hello, Poll. Did you ring your mammy and daddy?' he enquired, for all the world as though they had parted best of friends instead of with a chill between them. 'You did? It's glad I am. Well, next time you speak to them, tell them I've been posted, will you? I'm off to foreign parts to train as a pilot, so you won't be troubled with me for a while.' And when she would have asked questions, he just said, still with unimpaired cheerfulness: 'Take care of yourself, Poll, and no more hitchhiking. Bye, love. See you – oh, some time, I guess.'

He rang off. No point in hanging around where you were not wanted, he told himself grimly. Besides, the powers-that-be had offered to train him as a pilot. It would . . . take his mind off things.

Whistling, Tad set off for his hut to get his gear packed.

Chapter Fifteen

1944

Sunny came up from the warm depths of the ship on to the icy deck and instinctively ducked his head deeper into the thick scarf wound round his neck and the lower half of his face. By God, but it was freezing out here, though that was nothing new. In the Arctic waters at the top of the world, where they took their convoy of merchantmen to the Russian ports of Murmansk and Archangel, it was always cold. Indeed, cold scarcely described it, Sunny thought morosely now. The air was so icy that it was dangerous to draw it sharply into one's lungs and even through the muffler he knew from experience that all too soon the damp of his expelled breath would form icicles on the soft white wool.

He glanced towards the rail and saw the white-tipped waves, though he had known the sea would be rough. When was it ever anything else, up here? He had been on the Russian convoys for two years – more – and had grown accustomed to the constant bucketing of the ship, the constant straining to see through the thick dark and the wicked, unrelenting cold which attacked every man as soon as he left the warmth of the mess deck below. But no one, Sunny thought now, could get used to the almost perpetual darkness up here. How did they bear it, the inhabitants of these arctic coasts, where they only saw daylight between eleven in the morning and two in the afternoon and that a pretty grey and overcast daylight at this time of the year? He and the rest of the crew, after their first few trips, had speculated on why in heaven's name did the Jerries want this God-forsaken land? Why should they fight to possess the great, sprawling mass of Russia, a land made up of empty, ice-ridden wastes and surly, ignorant peasantry? But it was all part of the war effort, to keep Russia alive and armed, so they continued to bring the convoys across some of the worst seas in the world, to suffer the perpetual dark and the endless cold, to say nothing of the dangers inherent in such seas.

However, staring out at the sea would scarcely bring them in to port any faster so Sunny made for the bridge, where the man waiting to be relieved grinned at him and then made his way as quickly as he dared across the iced-up deck and down the companionway, where he would seek his hammock and would get himself as warm as he could during his time off watch.

On the bridge, the officer of the watch acknowledged Sunny's arrival and he took his place beside him and raised the night glasses to his eyes scanning the convoy keenly for the first blue flash of a signal from another vessel. The ships showed no lights, but he could see the dim shapes of the merchantmen and could guess that the deeper darkness on the port bow was another corvette, circling their flock, as the *Snowdrop* was doing. He wondered where they were; they had rounded the North Cape a day or so earlier; going on past voyages they must be in the approaches to the harbour by now. He thought rather wistfully of his earlier days at sea, when he had sailed through warm, tropical waters and, when the ship docked at a foreign port, had taken pleasure in their surroundings, strolled around the streets, smiled at the people, admired shop windows.

Russia was different. Very different. There could be no talking to the locals because the Russian police saw to that. They were a constant presence, patrolling the dirty, wooden quaysides as though some great treasure was hidden there.

There was a slight scuffle on the bridge and moving closer to the rail he saw the ice-breaker looming up in the darkness. So the port was near! Out here, where the sea was so constantly rough, so constantly in motion, the ice did not form but as soon as the ships got into the shelter of the land – such shelter as it offered – then the sea began to freeze over. Russian ice-breakers were essential to force a way into harbour for the convoys and their escorts and now, on the port bow, Sunny saw, through his binoculars, the quick flicker of a blue light – a signal from the Russian ship. Sunny scribbled the message on his pad and read it out to the officer of the watch who told him to acknowledge it, so that the crew of that rusty, elderly vessel would know that this was the convoy for which they waited.

Very soon, Sunny was signalling the other ships to follow the icebreaker into harbour. The *Snowdrop* and her fellow guardians would not be the first into port; the merchantmen, which went right up to the quay-side, were always first with the war ships following them in like sheepdogs shepherding their flock. Once the merchantmen were tied up, Sunny knew from experience that the Russian dockers would come swarming out of the collection of wooden huts which, it seemed, constituted a Russian port, and begin to unload the convoy. Meanwhile, the warships which had protected them on their long and arduous journey would not be allowed to tie up against the quays but would anchor in mid-pool. The intention,

Sunny was sure, had been to see that no British sailors went ashore, since the police must have had their hands full just watching the dockers, both men and women, working on the ships. But since the ice formed hard enough to walk on with complete safety after no more than half an hour it was possible for anyone to walk ashore.

Someone came and stood close by Sunny's elbow at the rail. It was Freddy Sales, a fellow Liverpudlian. The two men had become good friends, particularly since Sunny's mother's death the previous year when she had been killed by a stray bullet during a daylight raid on the shipping in Portsmouth harbour and though Sunny had been at sea at the time he had been given compassionate leave when the ship had docked. He had made his way to his mother's cramped little house, only to find it already occupied, since because of the bomb damage housing was at a premium in the area. Since Sunny had never spent more than a few days in the house it had never seemed like home and though he visited her grave he had left Pompey with few regrets. He and his mother had drifted apart once he had joined the Navy, and though her morals had never worried him as a youngster, he had found it more difficult to accept her way of life once he was in the Navy himself. On the couple of occasions when he had taken himself off down to Hampshire she had been 'entertaining' a friend and though she was not embarrassed to find her son on the doorstep, both Sunny and her new playmate were. He had heard nothing of his father since the start of the war, and reverted to Liverpool on his leaves, glad to return to the city where he had been born and bred. It had seemed very much easier to go back to the city where he still had many friends, including the O'Brady family, who were always warm and welcoming. They were happy to let him sleep in their spare room if he had nowhere else to go, though he usually managed to find a shipmate who was glad enough to have him to stay for the brief period of his leave. Besides, he was ruefully aware that it was far easier to make his way to Liverpool than it had been to Hampshire. At least it enabled him to get there and back in the time allotted to him.

And of course, there was the lure of seeing Polly, because she had been back in Liverpool now for eighteen months, and sometimes, when he was on leave, he managed to see a fair bit of her.

Although he acknowledged sadly to himself that his Polly had changed. She was a despatch rider now, and took her job very seriously. She whizzed all over the place on what seemed to him a very large motor-bike, taking messages, instructions, secret papers quite often, she told him proudly. She was still a darling, of course, he told himself loyally now, but . . . well, different. Harder. Less – less interested in his war, being far too occupied with her own. And, he had to admit it even to himself, less interested in him. It was not as though she had another feller, not that he could discover anyway, and Polly was not the sort of girl to try to deceive anyone. No, she was honest and straightforward. It was almost – well, almost as though her interest in young men in general and him-self in particular had flagged. Been beaten down by the war, perhaps, and all the various things which had happened to her. So, though he always tried to see her when he was on leave, he was uneasily aware that there was something missing; the old Polly, the light-hearted, carefree one, was gone, and that he did not really know the more serious young woman who had taken her place.

On one of his leaves about a year ago he had had a stroke of luck. Grace Carbery had also been on leave, and they had managed to meet several times. Polly, wrapped up in her work, had been happy for her friends to get to know one another better, but Sunny had been rather guiltily aware that by the end of his three days at home, the relationship between himself and the young leading airwoman was possibly a trifle warmer than the old Polly, at any rate, might have liked.

For Sunny had found that it was easy to become fond of Grace. Of course she was not like Polly had once been, not by any means so bubbly and loving, but she had, he discovered, her own charm. She was far more serious, you might even say she was a bit solemn, but she was still a very feminine young woman. Polly, he thought now, had put away her femininity for the duration. She almost always wore trousers, bell bottoms, in fact, as he did himself, and now that he thought about it, he did not think she wore lipstick, or went to dances, or if she did, she had not done so when he was in the city.

Another thing about Grace was that he and she had had their fill of the horrors of war. Grace, working on an airfield in Norfolk, was used to the tragedy of the young aircrews who were laughing and fooling around in the mess one day and missing the next. And it had changed her, made her more serious, less light-minded. Polly, though she worked hard and did a job which could be dangerous, did not have the same proximity to death which had become a way of life to himself and Grace.

Even as he thought this, Sunny felt vaguely

ashamed. He had been crazy about Polly for so long now that he took it for granted that other girls, whilst a welcome diversion, were just that. When the war was over, he was sure that Polly's conviction that she was as good as any man would change, that she would become his own his lovely, loving Polly once more. And heaven knew, by that time he would *need* the old Polly. He knew that a good deal of his own light-hearted approach to life had gone for ever. Gone with the companions who would not make it to the peace, the artificer who had been swept overboard as they passed along the Norwegian coast in a gale, with those poor devils, Martin amongst them, who had disappeared along with their ship whilst Sunny had been in hospital, suffering from the indignities of measles. He knew, now, that he had been a light-weight, someone who never thought about the morrow, who seldom worried about anything, never spared a thought for others.

It was different now. He was aware of a sombre streak in his nature, the realisation that every day might be his last. Someone had once said that the sea was a cruel mistress – well, she was that all right, but it was not simply the sea which had taken the feckless enjoyment out of his life. It was, he supposed, man's inhumanity to man, which struck home doubly hard when you considered the conditions. The icy cold which could kill you before ever you hit the sea; the sea itself, its very turbulence guaranteed to sink almost instantly any small life-raft which was cast upon its stormy bosom. Then there was the possibility of being iced to the deck, literally between one step and the next, and consequently drowned by the coming aboard of a great, heavy sea. And as well as all this, there were the U-boats, lurking beneath the surface, waiting to strike. Enemy war ships, prowling round the convoy, trying to stop the cargoes getting to their destination. And the aircraft, which came out of the blue and followed the convoy until other planes came up and the convoy could be efficiently attacked, dive-bombed, fired on, utterly destroyed.

So when he went home for his leave, it was nice to have someone who understood his sudden silence in the middle of a group of noisy drinking companions. Why he sometimes wanted to be quiet, to appreciate something other than war, violence, something other, even, than the ceaseless round of gaiety which seemed to satisfy some of the other combatants in what he was beginning to see as an increasingly terrible war.

Because of the conditions on the Russian convoys, most of the men had grown beards, and Sunny had a magnificent one. Long, blond and curly, he had grown it for a bet and now rather liked it, though it had an odd effect on girls. Some liked it, others seemed to hate it. Polly, for instance, had been instantly antagonistic, had said it was ugly, made him look old, got in the way of a kiss. Sunny had tried explaining about the cold, but Polly said flatly that she thought he had grown it more to impress than to keep warm. Grace, on the other hand, ignored it, simply, he thought now, because to her it was not important, any more than he suspected his looks were. Polly, bless her, thought that his beard detracted from his good looks, whereas he knew, or thought he knew that Grace liked him as a person and would have continued to like him had he gone bald as a coot and begun to squint. What was more they had soon discovered that they enjoyed the same sort of things – visits to the cinema, long walks on the shore, talks about what they would do when the peace came. And singing.

Sunny had not really thought very much about singing until he joined the Navy and had begun to sing with an amateur choir got up by the ratings on his first convoy to Russia. To his surprise, he had a good strong tenor voice and found it easy to keep a tune in his head. Singing relaxed him, gave him something to think about other than war. When he had gone to the Seamen's Mission for one of his leaves and had met up with Grace, staying with the O'Bradys, he had discovered that she, too, loved singing.

'I'm a member of the Salvation Army, and I sing in the choir. I was a songster – that's what they call the younger members – from the time I went to the Strawb, pretty well. Why don't you come along to a service? I'm not trying to convert you or anything like that, but you'd be welcome, and I think you'd enjoy it. Our hymns are much . . . well, much *jollier* than the hymns sung in more established churches, and somehow we seem to sing them with much more joy, and – and verve. We've a great choral tradition, us Salvationists – I often think that the roof of the citadel must be fixed down extra strongly, or we'd sing it clean off!'

He had gone along, mainly, if he were honest, to be polite because Grace was Polly's pal and was staying with the O'Bradys. But after that first visit he had known that Grace was right; the enthusiasm with which both choir and congregation sang and the simple, unassuming friendliness, was a balm to his tired, overstrained mind and body. He found that he was returning to his duty not exactly uplifted by the Army, but somehow soothed by it, by the very ordinariness of singing along with people who sang quite simply for the love of God, without giving themselves airs, or having to create an atmosphere in which, Sunny now believed, pomp and ceremony played a more important part than simple belief.

So though he had no illusions about his relationship with Grace – they were friends, nothing more – he still found sharing his leaves with her was infinitely better than being in Liverpool alone, and did his best to arrange that, when they were home, it was at around the same times. Grace, working on her airfield in Norfolk, was able, to an extent, to choose when she would take her leave, so Sunny formed the habit, as soon as he got ashore in Scapa, of ringing her and telling her when he would be having sufficient time off to get back to Liverpool. If she was able to make it at the same time that was marvellous . . . not that he ever pretended to Grace herself that they were anything other than good friends, of course. Good friends who shared an interest in music, particularly singing, though Sunny had recently bought, from a fellow rating, a somewhat battered trumpet which he was learning to play. He was being tutored by the rating, who had bought a superior instrument but was happy to show Sunny how to get the best out of his old one.

But of course, Sunny reminded himself now as the ship began to nose into the clear-water path across the harbour, Polly was still his girl. She was wrapped up in her work as a WRN despatch rider, that was why she seemed not to have the time for him that she had once had, but when the war was over . . .

There was activity now on the bridge as the first officer gave the order to let go and the chocks were knocked out, allowing the anchor chain to run out.

413

Above them, the sky was a cold grey and before them, the merchantmen were lining up alongside the quay. Sunny looked at the cleared path of water around them as the icebreaker, with a valedictory grunt like an old pig in a wallow, turned and made slowly for the open sea once more. He would go below now and get some rest, then when the ice had reformed and was hard enough to take a regiment of sailors, perhaps he and a pal would go ashore; there was not much to do when you got there apart from strolling along beside the ships they had accompanied to this place, and since they were, when on shore, representing His Majesty's Royal Navy they would have to wear their number ones, but it was better than spending the time below decks, or wandering round and round the corvette's tiny deckspace. Sunny wanted a long, brisk walk in this sort of weather and though they would be speedily turned back by the police if they attempted to go far from the quayside, you never knew. All Russians, his reason told him, could not be peasants bundled up in rags, too terrified of their own police guards even to exchange a smile with a visiting sailor. Somewhere, he imagined, there must be civilised men and women, some of whom might even have a few words of English. Whenever he went ashore he always took a couple of bars of the dark and bitter chocolate or even a screw of tea and sugar; one of these days he would find someone with sufficient courage to accept such gifts when offered – but so far there had been no takers. And he was sure that the people were hungry; he longed to make contact with someone, anyone, who would give him a smile, acknowledge that they were fighting the same war, facing the same enemy, damn it, *needed* each other. Why otherwise would he and his companions have come halfway across the world to this bitterly cold, dark land, bringing food, clothing, implements of war or agriculture? He didn't really know what they carried save that it was desperately needed; why could the Russians not behave as allies and friends, instead of looking at English sailors as though they might eat them?

But then Russia wasn't like other countries and Uncle Joe wasn't like other leaders, either. Sighing, Sunny went across the bridge to report to the first officer that he was going below. He would check the signal log and then get some sleep and by that time the ice would have formed again and someone else, with luck, would be awake and ready for a tramp outside.

Polly was sitting astride her motorbike at the top of Everton Brow, admiring the city and the burnished gold of the Mersey as it lay in the setting sun before her, when the engine gave an apologetic cough, a couple of hiccups, and stopped.

Polly, who had been feeling fairly peaceful, immediately felt annoyance start to tighten her muscles. It was not fair! For a start, she should not have been up here at all, feeling mistress of all she surveyed, when she had been sent from HQ to Birkenhead with important messages; she should, by now, have been back at the Liver buildings, informing her superior officers that her task had been successfully accomplished. But it was such a beautiful, golden late afternoon, and suddenly the temptation to go a bit out of her way for once had come over her. What was more, there was a sweet shop on Salisbury Street which sometimes had a few off-ration goodies which the proprietor, fat little Mrs Mobbs, handed out in tiny amounts to service personnel.

Then there was the fact that her engine had done quite a bit of sly coughing when she was actually doing her duty, on a part of the road which she should have been on, and she had done nothing about it. Now that she lived at home, she had reasoned, she could wait until the weekend and then strip the machine down in the back yard. Ivan would be delighted to give a hand and she was familiar enough with her engine to be able to pick out what was wrong pretty quickly. What was more, the engine had never actually died on her before, just spluttered a bit and then recovered. Dirt in the carburettor, Polly had told herself – and had ignored it, when she could easily have taken it into the transport section and got one of the mechanics to see to it for her.

Still, she had been well taught by Tad before he had gone off to train as a pilot, and usually did all her own maintenance. And at least it had happened at the top of one of the best hills in Liverpool, she told herself, reaching into her pocket for one of the homemade toffees which Mrs Mobbs had sold her and tucking it comfortably into one cheek. She would coast down the hill, get the engine going again, and make her way back to the Liver buildings, then on to the depot where she would hand her machine over for once, and take a tram home to Snowdrop Street.

For Polly had opted to live at home over a year ago, when she had returned to Liverpool as a despatch rider. After the awful business – she admitted, now, that it had been an awful business, and all her own fault – of the row when she had discovered that she was adopted, she felt that it was the least she could do for Mammy and Daddy. She had been forced to admit, soon enough, that they had treated her as well if not better than their own natural children; that they

416

loved her dearly, with the sort of love that can't be put on or pretended. And though she had run away from them on that first fatal night, she had gone back a few weeks later, driven there, she had told herself rather sullenly, by Saint Grace Carbery, who had come to her in Holyhead and read her lectures and told her off just as though she had been a thoughtless and selfish school child.

For Grace had indeed travelled down to Holyhead the day after Polly's horrid adventure, if you could call it that, and had tackled her head-on about her attitude to finding that she had been adopted, and further, that Grace was her sister.

'Peader and Deirdre have been kinder to me than almost anyone else, apart from Brogan and Sara, in my entire life,' Grace had said gently. 'And just think, Poll, if you'd not been adopted! Why, the sort of life I led . . . I don't think I've ever told you about it before, but . . .'

And she had proceeded to tell Polly things that had made Polly's hair stand up on her head with horror – a father who had in all probability killed his wife, a mother who was too worn down and weary to try to protect her numerous children from a violent husband, and after they had both died, her own struggle for survival. For the first time, Polly heard of Grace sleeping rough in parks and jiggers and other people's sheds. Of being attacked by a rat – Grace took Polly's hand and made her trace the faint marks of the rat's teeth, still there on one otherwise smooth young cheek – and of being constantly hungry, constantly in fear.

At the time, shocked though she had been, Polly had not intended to show it. She had turned a sulky shoulder on her new-found sister and had said: 'Sure

417

and I'm – I'm not after sayin' that I'd have enjoyed meself in Liverpool the way I did in Dublin, am I? It's the deceit, Grace, that's what I can't take in me stride. Why in God's name didn't they *tell* me I was adopted, instead of letting me believe I was their own little daughter?'

'You know the reason, Poll; because Brogan stole you, that's why,' Grace had said with a sort of weary patience which, at the time, Polly had thought was an insult in itself. 'You were only a little kid; you might have said something to anyone, anyone at all, and they couldn't risk that, couldn't risk Brogan being took up for kidnapping. Now could they?'

And in the end, of course, Polly had had to come round, to understand why Deirdre and Peader had said nothing to her, why Grace herself had been kept in ignorance. Indeed, she was forced to admit to herself that 'Saint Grace' was a better person than she, because Grace absolutely longed to acknowledge her as her little sister, to tell people that she did have a proper relative, after all. But because of the various difficulties of the situation she had to be content with being Polly's pal, which wasn't quite the same thing at all, as Polly, in her more generous moments, acknowledged.

A few weeks after Grace's visit to Holyhead, however, Polly had felt obliged to return to Snowdrop Street and to tell her mammy and daddy that she was sorry for all she had said, that she *did* understand why everyone had behaved as they had, and to promise them that she would never think one whit the worse of them for not telling her earlier that she was adopted.

And then, when Polly had applied for the job of despatch rider attached to the Liverpool HQ of the

Navy, Deirdre had had her brainwave. 'Your daddy and meself have been thinking,' she told Polly as the two of them sat in the kitchen, knitting industriously for various members of the family who were in the Navy and needed warm clothing. 'What would you say, alanna, if we adopted Grace? Officially, I mean.'

Polly had been so astonished that for several moments she could only stare, and Deirdre, interpreting this as dislike of the idea, hastily said that it was only . . . that it seemed a sort of solution . . . that poor Grace had had a rotten deal one way and another . . .

'But she's a woman grown,' Polly had said at last, on a gasp. 'Can you do such a t'ing, Mammy? Adopt a woman grown?'

'You can; and then she can change her name by deed poll to O'Brady and the two of you will be sisters,' Deirdre said. 'Or wouldn't you like that, alanna?'

For a moment Polly had very meanly thought that indeed she would not like it. She was the only girl in the O'Brady family, the boys wouldn't want another sister thrust upon them and Polly was not too sure, in her heart of hearts, whether she truly wanted 'Saint Grace' to share her name, her brothers, her whole family. But then the more generous side of her nature came to the fore and she said: 'Well, if that's what Grace would like, it would suit me just fine, so it would. It's rare kind of you and Daddy, Mammy, when you've so many kids already.'

But as it turned out Grace, though grateful for the suggestion, had turned it down with unexpected firmness. 'It's awful kind of Auntie Dee and Uncle Peader,' she had said almost apologetically. 'But I really think it would only complicate matters.

Besides, Poll, you're going to be changing your name from O'Brady pretty soon – as soon as the war ends, in fact. Then we can be sisters without people wondering.'

'I'm not going to change me name—' Polly had begun, quite offended, before light suddenly dawned and she giggled. 'Oh! You mean *marriage*, I suppose. But you'll be changing your name as well, Grace – sooner than me, probably.'

'I might,' Grace had agreed cautiously. 'But I don't have fellers hanging on me every move like you do, Poll. Besides, isn't Sunny . . .'

'Oh yes, I reckon I'll marry him one day,' Polly had said offhandedly. 'But I dunno when – it might not be for years yet.'

But that had been some while ago, and right now, sitting astride her bike and looking down on the city as the light of the setting sun slowly deepened from gold to rose, from rose to crimson, she reminded herself that the way she was going on, she should be glad to marry Sunny just as soon as peace was declared, since she seemed to have cast off all her other boyfriends – and mostly, with no tears shed, on her side at any rate.

As for Tad . . . well, she was still cross with him, even after almost two years' absence. For as soon as he had 'phoned her at her wrennery, telling her that he was going abroad to train as a pilot, she had regretted her cruel words. Not that there was anything cruel in telling someone she thought of him as a brother, exactly – she had a high opinion of all her brothers, hadn't she? – but she had known she was hurting Tad even as the words passed her lips. And it wasn't true, not really, it was just that she had known him for so long that it was difficult to take him seriously as – well, as a boyfriend. So of course she hadn't tried, not really. And though he was her pal, and a better feller never breathed, he wasn't anywhere near as handsome as Sunny. Well, he wasn't handsome at all, he was downright plain was Tad. It was just that he was familiar, and very much her friend.

Which was why, she reminded herself now, that she was so bleedin' cross with him. Called himself a pal and yet had he answered her letters, which she had sent at least once a week for the first half year of his time abroad? No, he hadn't. Oh, he'd sent a couple of those miserable standard letters which meant that he had ticked boxes – I am well, the weather is fine, we have been swimming – and a couple of scruffy notes too, but they hadn't been letters. In fact, they had been downright unfriendly, as though he were telling her that if she wasn't prepared to swoon before him then he meant to forget her and the sooner the better.

This, Polly reflected now, sucking on her sweet, had been totally unacceptable. She wanted her friend Tad as a pal, not a lover. She had Sunny to take her about and impress her friends with his good looks. She wanted Tad for . . . well, for the sturdy independence and friendship which he had always shown her. The plain truth was that she missed him, infuriating though he was, but Tad's behaviour had proved that this was futile – it was all or nothing for him. So she had gradually stopped writing to him, had allowed her letters to get briefer – and colder – and had tried not to mind when still he did not bother to reply to them. And then, out of the blue, she had discovered the worst thing of all; ten months ago – ten *months* – he had returned to Britain, to fly some plane or other – she did not know whether he was still with his beloved Beaufighters – from an airfield in Lincoln-shire and despite being back in Blighty he had not once so much as dropped her a line or telephoned her or – or anything. If she had not happened to meet up with an old friend of his who had told her that he was back in England, she would not even have known that much.

She had considered getting in touch, naturally, but had finally decided against it mostly because she felt that he should have been the one to get in touch with her. After all, she had written and written and he had not replied. If he was so indifferent to her then she would take the hint and leave him alone.

Nevertheless it was on her mind, and a bit like an aching tooth; she could not stop thinking about it, examining her conscience, wondering whether, since it was she who had told Tad so unequivocally that she did not intend to take him seriously as a boyfriend, it should also be she who should break the barrier of silence and contact him. But she had done so, had she not? The first three letters she had sent had been mainly apologies for her behaviour, she remembered that clearly enough. And though she had not rescinded her words – how could she, without telling downright lies, since she did not have the slightest interest in Tad as a proper boyfriend? – she had definitely said she was sorry if she had been unkind. Further than that, she told herself severely now, no girl should be expected to go. And if Tad was not interested in her then she was not interested in him either. Though she did miss him most awfully, and sometimes wished ... wished ...

She had mentioned the rift to Grace a month or two back and Grace had reminded her that Tad would not know that she was now working as a despatch rider in Liverpool and living at home once more in Snowdrop Street. 'How can he contact you when he's only got the Holyhead address?' she had asked in her sensible, practical way. But though Polly's heart had given a little leap at the thought that maybe Tad had been bombarding Holyhead with letters for months and months, common sense made her reluctantly discard the lovely thought. The Navy were very good at seeing you got your post – why, she had once sent Sunny a seven-page epic in a box of Mammy's homemade fudge with some ginger snaps which she had laboriously made herself, and Sunny had got both eventually, though by then the fudge had mould all over it and the biscuits were so hard that no human teeth could break them. He had described how he had battered them into fragments with a sledge hammer and then sucked the bits – she had laughed like anything over that, she remembered.

So no hope that Tad had not been able to discover her new address. If he had wanted to reach her he could have done so. The plain old truth was that he was now as indifferent to her as she was to him, and she should forget him, push him to the very back of her mind. All that was now due to him was an invitation to her wedding, when she and Sunny got spliced, she told herself vengefully. And he wouldn't come to the wedding anyway, she knew that, since he hadn't even bothered to answer her letters.

Still. Sitting there in the late sunshine, Polly told herself that however she might feel about Tad, her feelings about Sunny were at least, very definite. I'm crazy about him, she told herself now. He's the best looking, nicest, cleverest feller I've ever met, and I'm madly in love with him. Why, when he touches my hand my bones turn to jelly and my heart thumps like a drum, and when he kisses me . . . !

But this would not get the baby a new bonnet, Polly told herself, yet still she lingered. Somehow, up here on the hill with the city spread out before her, she seemed to be able to think more clearly. Being billeted at home, she acknowledged to herself, was a mistake. She missed the companionship of the other girls, the feeling that they were all in the same boat, the easy-going sharing which went on so that when kit inspections were called, each girl would help the others over some missing bit of equipment. Stockings would be passed from bed to bed, small items such as a hat or a decent pair of shoe-laces would be shot along the row of beds when the officer wasn't looking . . . All of that was impossible, of course, when you lived at home. If you lost equipment you applied for a replacement which was supplied and they could stop the cost of it from your pay if they thought you had been careless. But somehow, the fun had gone out of it. And though Mammy's meals were a good deal tastier than the food frequently served up in either the canteen or the WRNnery itself, it wasn't quite the same. Sitting down with your parents round the kitchen table at the end of an exciting day was an anti-climax for it was impossible to say much because a good deal of what she did was confidential.

But of course her rotten behaviour over her being adopted had meant that she had little choice. She could not very well live in billets in the city when she had treated her dear Mammy and Daddy so shame-fully, she had felt obliged to go home to live.

However. Polly took a deep breath and expelled it in a long sigh. She should be getting back to the transport section just as soon as she could so that her bike might be put right in time for work in the morning.

Deirdre was darning a pair of Ivan's socks which were more darn, she thought ruefully, than sock and keeping half an eye on the bake oven, where a peculiar dish of her own invention was slowly cooking on a low heat. It was a vegetable pie, made more interesting by the addition of finely minced bacon rinds with the pastry the richer for some beef dripping which the butcher on Stanley Road had slipped into her basket the last time she had been in his shop. Deirdre knew that the beef dripping was a thank you for a couple of large onions which Mr Hartley had been delighted to receive the week previously. Peader's allotment provided the family with many small treats. So now she waited for the moment when she could produce the pie from the oven, cooked to a lovely golden brown, and receive the congratulations of her family and also of Monica, who was coming to tea this evening.

Monica, Deirdre thought, finishing off a black sock with navy blue wool and telling herself that she was lucky to have found any darning wool at all, despite their initial doubts, had turned out to be a good little daughter-in-law; one of the best.

When Martin's ship had gone down she had gone into a factory which made uniforms and when this no longer satisfied her, had joined the WRNs as a writer, which was what they called the office staff. Peader and Deirdre had wanted her to live with them in the house in Snowdrop Street where there was plenty of room and where she would have been very welcome, particularly to Polly, but Monica said she would rather go the whole hog and live with her fellow

WRNs. So she had moved into the wrennery at which had once been the Royal Hotel on the Marine Terrace at Waterloo, and was a good deal happier there, Deirdre thought, than she would have been sharing a house with them and reminded of Martin at every turn.

So now, sitting in front of the fire with her darning more or less finished, Deirdre was able to contemplate the evening ahead with some satisfaction. Polly would be home very soon and then she, Deirdre, would pop into the oven the eggless, fatless sort-of sponge pudding which she had prepared, and then Polly could read her post. The back door opening brought a smile to her face.

'That's a grand smell so it is,' Peader said, taking off his earth-caked boots and knocking them on the cobbles and, stepping into the kitchen, he pulled the door to behind him. 'I hope the girls won't be long. I'm hungry enough to eat me own boots, so I am. Diggin's such hard work . . .'

The abrupt re-opening of the back door again put an end of Peader's words.

'Mammy! We're not late, are we?' It was Polly, looking flushed and pretty in her uniform, with Monica close behind her. 'Only me bleedin' bike broke down and I took it in to the MT yard, and one of the fellers said he'd fix it so that I could use it first thing tomorrow. And Monica came out of the Liver buildings as I was passing and so we came on together. What's for tea?'

'A lovely vegetable pie with beef dripping,' Deirdre said. 'And I'm just about to mash the spuds wit' a smidgin of milk; then we can eat. Oh, and there's letters for you on the mantel behind the clock.'

Afterwards, she was to wonder what had made her

say such a thing in front of Monica, for usually she tried not to remind Monica that there were no letters for her; not any more. But today, for some reason, she simply told Polly about the letters, though she added hastily: 'You may not want to read them now; wait until later when you're alone, will you?'

Polly was sensitive about letters, too, but she reached up and took the envelopes off the mantel-piece, weighed them thoughtfully in her hand and then went and sat opposite Peader by the fire, whilst Monica, having removed her jacket, put a wrap-around overall over the rest of her uniform and began to mash the potatoes for Deirdre, whilst her mother-in-law made gravy with the vegetable water and some cornflour. 'I'll have a quick glance, just to make sure everything's all right,' Polly said, and slit one of the envelopes, then pulled out a number of sheets. 'Well, would you look at that! Sunny writes a grand letter so he does, but not usually a – a *book*.' She grinned at Peader, then began to read.

Later she glanced up at Monica, then away again, before shoving the letter back into its envelope as her mother told her that the meal was ready. And presently, when the first edge of their hunger was taken off, she said thoughtfully: 'Isn't it odd, now, that this letter should have arrived wit' Monica here? Because there's a bit of it which Sunny thought I ought to pass on to you, Monica. I'll read it presently, but first of all I'll tell you that Sunny wrote it on his return voyage, after he'd been in one of those Russian ports, all darkness and ice, which is where the convoys go. He said that he'd decided to go ashore – they're allowed, but they don't think the Russians like it much – and take a look around. A pal of his had meant to go with him but for some reason he wasn't

427

able to, so Sunny went alone. He set off across the ice . . .'

Sunny, in his number ones but with his biggest muffler wound twice round his face and once round his neck and his greatcoat collar turned up, with his thickest socks – two pairs – on his booted feet and his cap pulled right down to his eyebrows, set off across the ice. He was alone, but had already decided that he would not go ashore alone. However, someone from one of the merchantmen or even from another member of the convoy guardships would surely want to get a breath of fresh air. Going ashore alone, they had been told, might well be dangerous. The Russians, or the dock police, at any rate, were a queer bunch. They would not set on a group of sailors, and indeed if they did so it would mean the end of the life-giving convoys, but no one was absolutely sure that they would not pounce on a solitary sailor, using the excuse that he was spying, and obstinately deny that they had even seen the fellow. Might, Sunny morbidly imagine, even claim that the sailor had fallen through the ice and been drowned. They could probably produce a body without too much difficulty, Sunny thought now, eyeing the straggle of dark figures unloading the nearest merchantman. He could not be sure, of course, but he certainly suspected that the men and women who acted as dockers and unloaded the stores were prisoners of some description. Certainly the way the dock police treated them meant that they were, at any rate, not held in much esteem. Life is cheap here, Sunny thought, and was grateful when he saw three muffled figures coming towards him across the quay. He hailed them.

'Hi, there. You from the SS *Rangoon Princess*? Been ashore here before?'

They had not, but wanted to see as much as they could. 'Which won't be much,' Sunny told them gloomily. 'I've been ashore several times, but there's really nothing to see. Flat, snow-covered ground, a huddle of wooden huts, and sometimes you see lorries, lining up to take the stuff away from here. As for the locals, if they *are* locals, I've never succeeded in getting so much as a word out of any of them.'

Nevertheless, the four of them walked briskly along the snow-covered quay towards the long line of muffled figures hefting the bags and boxes which were already piling up on the quay. But as he predicted, in a lowered voice, to the sailor nearest him, as soon as they got within ten feet of the working party a couple of dark-clad policemen detached themselves from the group and came towards them, making signals that they were to come no closer, whilst they spoke harshly in their own tongue.

'Right you are, mate,' Sunny said, and the four of them swung around and walked away from the working party, towards the huddle of huts.

They skirted the buildings and went on past them, into the snow-covered wilderness beyond, but after only a short way it was clear that Sunny's new companions had no urge to explore further.

'There's nothing but snow and dark,' the man nearest Sunny said disgustedly. He turned to one of the other men. 'It's a far cry from your neck of the woods, Eggy, but even if you want to see more of it, I don't reckon the rest of us do. We'll be gettin' back, see whether there's any grub going.'

'Just because my parents originally came from Italy and my brother's been troop carrying in the Med, that doesn't mean to say I want to hang about in this God-awful place,' the man called Eggy said cheerfully. He turned to Sunny. 'My brother has been taking troops across to Italy for the invasion, and bringing back wounded and so on. Lucky devil! At least he's been warm and not perpetually frozen, like our lot.'

'Italy?' Sunny said, surprised. 'Don't tell me we've taken Italy!'

The other man laughed. 'Well, not yet I don't imagine, though you must know our troops have been fighting their way up from Sicily for months and months now. And my brother . . . but look, why not come aboard the old *Princess* for a noggin and I'll tell you about it. Cooky might find us up something hot, seeing as you're one of our brave escorts.'

Sunny, agreeing, went on board the *Rangoon Princess* and was soon comfortably settled in a corner of the mess deck with a large mug of cocoa and a bacon sandwich and as soon as he could do so he asked Eggy, who proved to be a short, stocky young man with very dark hair and eyes and a swarthy skin, to tell him what had been happening to his brother.

'My brother is younger than me and so when war came he joined the Navy, whereas I was already in the merchant service,' he explained. 'Because Ben – that's my brother – speaks pretty good Italian he was given the job of talking to ex-POWs and some prisoners who were brought aboard his ship for transportation back to the UK, and he had some strange stories to tell. The partisan movement isn't highly regarded in Italy and the peasants fear them almost as much as they fear the Nazis but even so they readily give shelter to anyone they consider as oppressed as themselves. You can tell by the marvellous way they treated fellows who managed to escape from the Germans, and aircrew who weren't picked up by the jerries but managed to find friendly locals to shelter them. Of course, when they spoke Italian, as some did, it was even easier for them to stay out of jug, I imagine.'

'Yeah, speaking the language must have helped.' Sunny said, taking a large bite out of his bacon sandwich. 'And if the allies have only recently been pushing ahead, I suppose you might have been better off in a prisoner of war camp – at least they'd feed you. Or would they head for a neutral country? Switzerland, perhaps?'

'I wouldn't have tried to cross into Switzerland,' Eggy said, pulling a face. 'I wouldn't trust a Swiss further than I could throw him and that's a fact. No, if it were me I'd stay shtum in various villages and waited my chance.'

'That would be all right for you, knowing the language,' Sunny said sagely. 'It might have been a very different story if you'd been like meself, for instance. I don't speak a word of any language but English – unless you count scouse, of course.'

'Well, I dunno about that,' Eggy said. 'Ben talked about other fellers who'd been taken prisoner but escaped, or who had been sheltered by fishermen and so on, and none of them had a word of Italian to their names. Not when they first got there, though I think most of 'em picked some up. Why, he picked up one feller who had some Italian, and he told him he'd been in a remote little village in the Calabria area of the country, being hidden by a peasant family and fed on whatever they could spare – mostly goat's cheese, unleavened bread and grapes – when a cousin from another village came visiting. She was a pretty thing, and was getting married. The old woman I was staying with was a noted dressmaker, apparently, and this girl had brought her some material to make up into a wedding dress. It was pretty stuff, real

431

quality, not the sort of thing you would ever find in a remote hill village, so this young feller asked her where she got it. She beamed at him and said it had been given to her by a young sailor that her father had fished out of the water quite early on in the war. She said he was English, couldn't speak a word of Italian, and was carrying the material wrapped round his body under his clothing. It wasn't spoiled by the sea-water for it was wrapped in some sort of oiled paper, and when he moved on somewhere else, after weeks and weeks of staying with the young bride-to-be, he gave it to her. The feller told Ben it was really pretty, a sort of cream-coloured silk covered with bronze poppies.'

Sunny stared, his sandwich halfway to his mouth. 'Are – are you sure? What was the feller's name, did the girl say?'

'I dunno, I can't remember. Ben may not ever have told me his name . . .'

'No, I don't mean the story teller's name, I mean the – the chap who they fished out of the 'oggin with the silk wrapped round him,' Sunny said quickly. 'What was his name, d'you know?'

Eggy wiped his hand across his mouth and after a few moments' thought, shook his head. 'No, I doubt that Ben would have remembered it, even if the girl had mentioned it to the other feller. No, she wouldn't have used a name, them being foreign to her. And it might not have been too safe anyway, what with the jerries and everything.'

'The thing is,' Sunny said, his mouth suddenly dry. 'I've a pal called Martin O'Brady who was lost at sea when his ship went down. His wife is a dressy little thing and he got me to buy him a dress length of silk whilst I was in Gibraltar. I did as he asked and bought him a length of cream-coloured silk covered with bronze poppies. It was very unusual stuff, and . . . well, it seems strange . . . Martin's my girlfriend's brother and if it was him they fished out of the 'oggin, and he's still alive . . .'

Eggy, finishing up his own sandwich, shrugged. 'Bit of a coincidence, but things like that's always happening in wartime,' he observed. 'I can't think two sailors would have a dress length of material like that. I bet it was your pal, Sunny!'

And Sunny, grinning broadly, said that he suspicioned it was, too. But though the pair of them talked for some while after that, they could come to no firm conclusion. 'I wonder if I ought to write to Mart's wife, tell her the story?' Sunny said at last as the two of them stood once more on the windy quay, with loose snow blowing into their faces. 'I don't want to raise false hopes, but . . . well, what would you do, Eggy?'

'I'd just tell her the story and let her make what she could of it,' Eggy decided, after some thought. 'No, tell your girl, let her decide. But if it were me, I'd rather have hope than none at all, wouldn't you?'

'I think I would,' Sunny agreed after a moment. 'If only someone had mentioned a name . . .'

Eggy, shrugging, watched him climb down the rope ladder, and, as Sunny's feet met the quay, he thought of something else. 'Hang on a mo, old feller,' he shouted, cupping both hands round his mouth so that his voice carried clearly across the ice. 'One thing me brother did say – the girl said he called her "alanna", or something like that. If that's any help, of course.'

Sunny turned and grinned up at him. 'Oh, the

433

times I've heard Martin use that word, me ole shipmate! That decides it; I'll write to my Polly this very night.'

Polly and Monica danced around the table and hugged each other when the letter was read, and even Peader and Deirdre allowed that 'It looked as though Monica had been right all along, and Martin was still alive.' No one said that he had been alive in 1942 but might well have died in the interim, but it was probably at the back of every mind. Monica, however, pointed out that had Martin been taken prisoner they would have been informed, but that, living on the country as it appeared he was, he could scarcely have let anyone know his whereabouts.

'The allies are pushing up Italy as fast as they can go,' she said contentedly, as the family sat round the fire that evening, for although it was October it was pleasant to sit in the warm once darkness fell. 'We'll get confirmation soon enough, I'm sure. Oh, and I'm so grateful to your Sunny, Poll! Now that I know he reached land, I'm content to wait.'

Chapter Sixteen

SPRING 1945

Polly lay on a smooth, sheep-nibbled stretch of turf, with the sun hot on her closed eyelids and the sound of the sea gently lapping at the shore below the cliffs, and basked. She was on her holidays, or at least she felt as if she were, for when one is in the WRNS, and suddenly gets a whole week off, and lives at home, what is to stop one spending that week somewhere else? Peader had his allotment and his coupon-checking and points-additions and Deirdre still worked in her parachute factory on Hanover Street so if Polly had stayed at home it would have been a lonely sort of leave.

If Grace or one of Polly's pals had been able to get some leave as well it would have been a different story. But despite the fact that everyone knew the war was going to end any day now, Grace was needed on her station, and Sunny was probably still with his ship, halfway, Polly thought gloomily, between Scotland and Russia, either coming or going. At any rate, she hadn't had a letter for ages, so she had decided to spend her leave visiting old friends, visiting a place, she thought now, where she had been happier than one usually was in wartime.

Anglesey. Holyhead. In fact, in the very house where she had been billeted when she had first joined the WRNS, for Diane was still there, and most of her other friends were still in Holyhead. So Polly had rung up and asked permission to spend her leave in the tall house in London Road, and Diane had told her that she was as welcome as the day was long, and added that they would not mention her presence to anyone in authority.

'We've a spare bed or two, with people on leave, and others having left for different jobs,' she had said breezily. 'Oh, Poll, I have missed you! It'll be grand to see you again – are you coming down here to see that fellow, the one you made so unhappy? Only I've not seen him around since you left.'

'No, of course I'm not coming to see Tad,' Polly had said, annoyed. 'Why on earth should I do such a t'ing, Di? Besides, he's up north somewhere – I don't know where, we've lost touch.'

'Oh,' Diane said. She sounded a little doubtful. 'Well, you know your own business best, of course, but I always thought—'

'I don't know what you thought,' Polly had said rather reproachfully. 'But you shouldn't leap to conclusions, Di. I've told you over and over that I've got a feller, a serious one. Sunny, the chap whose on the Russian convoys. He's a signaller, and—'

'Oh, yes, I know all about your Sunny,' Diane had assured her, sounding not in the least cast down by Polly's words. 'Still, no point in talking about it now, when we're going to see each other so soon. I'll get some time off . . . Oh, Poll, I can't wait!'

So Polly had caught a train and arrived at Holyhead on the first day of her leave. She had settled into the old house as though she had never left it, and in the bright April sunshine had begun to enjoy her holiday. For the first couple of days she had revisited old haunts around the docks and the town, had gone into the clubs and messes to meet old friends and generally caught up with the local news. But even in the bustle of the naval headquarters she had the feeling that everyone was waiting. Waiting for the inevitable end of it all which could not be far off, not now.

And all the time, in the back of her mind, was a feeling of vague dissatisfaction. She had been so happy here – why could she not recapture that happiness, feel the warm glow of it in her veins? She supposed it was because she was no longer truly a part of it, as she had once been. She had no real place here, no actual purpose. And a good many of the men she had worked with had moved on, perhaps manning the invasion fleet which had left from the channel ports the previous year, perhaps taking the place of other men on the convoys or in the dock-yards, putting right the damage which had been done to such vessels. So earlier that day Polly had decided to get some food from the girls' kitchen and make herself some sandwiches. Then she could take a picnic somewhere quiet, and enjoy the wonderful sunshine.

She had borrowed a bicycle and pedalled slowly around the coast, ending up here, on the quiet, sunny cliff, sunbathing, occasionally taking a drink from the bottle of cold tea she had brought with her, and thinking.

What had gone wrong with her life of late? she wondered. She had not seen her angel for ages now, since joining the service, in fact, and had told herself rather miserably that seeing angels was presumably something which you left behind with girlhood, because now she was a woman who no longer needed an angel. But she missed that sweet-faced presence which had always made her feel safe, and loved. And now, she fell to wondering why she had ever had that guardian angel, because she had had Mammy, and

Daddy and her brothers, to say nothing of Tad . . . Her thoughts broke down in confusion, until she reminded herself that she had meant she had had Tad when she had been just a kid, in Dublin, that his presence – or absence – would most certainly not have affected her need of an angel.

But Grace, who had needed an angel so desperately, her thoughts continued, had never had one. That was strange, wasn't it? She had asked Grace several times, very carefully, mind, whether Grace had ever been aware of a presence, of something glimpsed, not straightforwardly, but out of the corner of one's eye, so to speak. More an inward conviction of another's presence than a proper sighting. She had made it plain that she did not mean recently, of course, because now Grace, like herself, was a woman grown, but long ago, when Grace had wandered the streets alone, always in need, usually in fear. Grace had looked mildly surprised by the question but had said, a little regretfully, that never, during that sad time, had she ever felt any sort of strange, other-worldly presence, or not one which was well-disposed towards her at any rate. So Polly had dropped the subject, and had told herself fiercely that she should be eternally grateful for her own immense good fortune in being able to see her guardian angel now and then – as a child, of course – and not feel so deprived and cheated now that she could no longer do so.

Having settled that matter to her satisfaction, or almost so, she turned her thoughts back to her stay on the island. She had been to a dance held out at Valley, and had not enjoyed herself as much as she had hoped. She and Diane had had a lovely day out with two young naval bods. They had gone out in a dinghy and bathed from the boat, swimming in water a great deal deeper than they could have reached from the beach. It had been fun, but somehow, the faint disappointment which had seemed to come over her even as she smiled her delighted greeting to the island where she had been so happy would not be dispelled. There was something wrong, something missing . . .

Restlessly, Polly rolled from her back on to her front and studied the tiny, gold-centred daisy almost beneath her nose, with its oriole of pink tipped petals. She was being quite absurd, wholly ridiculous, and it was time she snapped out of it. She turned her thoughts to a favourite theme: her wedding. There she was, poised and lovely in a long white dress with a full skirt and narrow sleeves. She wore a white veil which billowed out beneath a wreath of lilies of the valley and her feet were clad in white, satin, high-heeled shoes. She had her hand – with the sapphire engagement and the gold wedding rings on the third finger – tucked into Sunny's uniform sleeve, and she was smiling up at him as he was smiling down at her, their eyes meeting with a look of perfect understanding and love . . . and nearby, her parents beamed, both with their eyes full of tears of love and pride as they saw their only daughter wed. And there was Diane (who often doubled in the dream as her bridesmaid, along with Grace and Monica, of course) in her uniform getting eight girls in neat WRNS navy-blue to form a triumphal arch so that she and Sunny could run the gauntlet of all the rice – no, confetti, because she would not be marrying in wartime, not now, when the whole thing was more or less over – which would be thrown between the porch of the church and the lychgate.

It was a nice dream and Polly, smiling, rolled over

on to her back again and then sat up and reached for her picnic. She bit into a corned-beef sandwich, liberally doused with brown sauce, and gazed blissfully up at the brilliant blue of the noonday sky. She had found a bag of dried apple rings and a few sultanas as well as the sandwich ingredients when she had poked about in the pantry and had decided the girls would not miss these odds and ends, deciding that she had done very well considering that no one, as yet, had asked her for her ration book. Indeed, apart from the vague feeling that she no longer belonged here, no holiday, she told herself, could have been nicer or more satisfying.

Sitting there, with the wind lifting her fair hair off her shoulders and the subdued sound of the waves on the rocks far below in her ears, Polly thought that the only unsatisfactory thing about her wedding dream was that she could never force herself to go any further with it. She could not imagine the going-away suit which she would wear, or the hotel, or guest-house more likely, where she and Sunny would spend their honeymoon. She could not imagine them enjoying their wedding reception, far less climbing into their marriage bed. And as for the ordinary things, her making his breakfast, him going off to work, this seemed totally beyond her. In fact, she thought now, folding her sandwich paper into a neat square and shoving it into the pocket of her uniform jacket, she could not imagine herself spending a few weeks with Sunny, let alone the rest of her life.

The thought, coming spontaneously, jolted her. She frowned down at her black lace-up shoes and then did something she had not done for years and years. She pressed the heels of both hands into her eye sockets and pushed and pushed until she could see scarlet and gold with black squiggles and strange patterns shooting across her inner vision, until she felt as though her head were a huge balloon which must burst at any minute. When she could bear it no longer she took her hands away from her face and opened her eyes. And for one startling, extraordinary minute she saw, vaguely, the faint outline of a face, and seemed to hear, equally faintly, the echo of a voice. Then both faded and she was just Polly O'Brady, sitting in the sunshine feeling remarkably foolish, and knowing, with startling clarity, the answer to the questions which had been plaguing her of late. The wonderful wedding of which she had dreamed was just that – a dream. It had no hint of reality, no possibility that it might, one day, actually happen. You've been a complete and total fool, Polly O'Brady, she told herself furiously, beginning to cram the remains of her picnic into her pockets and standing up to brush the crumbs off the front of her skirt and the creases off the back. But just because you've been a fool until now, doesn't mean you have to go on being a fool for ever. You came back here to find the happiness you thought you had lost – well, you didn't find it because it isn't here, not any more. It's – it's up in Lincolnshire somewhere, and if you don't go up and see Tad and tell him you've made the biggest mistake of your life and ask him to forgive you, take you back, then whatever happens next, it won't be marriage to Sunny because he isn't the feller for you and you aren't the girl for him.

Why, when Sunny comes back on leave are you so thrilled at the thought of just seeing him again that you can't think of anything else? When you're with him, do you hang on his every word, want to please him, put yourself out for him? No, Polly O'Brady, you do not do any of those things. You are pleased to see him all right, but you don't want to make any special arrangements and very soon after his arrival you begin to wish he wasn't quite so sure of himself, quite so handsome and self-opinionated. You find fault with him – oh, not aloud, but in your head. He doesn't come up to your imaginary expectations, so you find yourself pretending. Pretending that the two of you are perfectly matched, that you'll marry, have a family, be happy together. When all the time – all the time, Polly O'Brady – you're really trying to fit him into quite another shape. To make tall, handsome, blond-haired Sunny into . . . into . . .

She picked up her bicycle from where she had rested it against a handy gorsebush and began to coast down towards the road. It crossed her mind to wonder what Sunny would think when she told him that it had all been a mistake, that she really wasn't the girl for him. She could write to him, a sort of 'Dear John' letter, except that it wouldn't be a letter like that at all because now that she was looking honestly at her relationship with Sunny, she realised that in all probability Sunny had been aware of the problem for some time.

She reached the main road, if you could call a winding country lane a main road, and turned left along it. She would go back now and tell Diane that she wouldn't be spending any more time on the island. She could say anything, she could even tell her the truth, because she and Diane had never had any secrets from one another, and she saw no reason why she should be secretive with her friend now.

Polly gritted her teeth as she slogged up the first of the hills which lay ahead. Diane thought I'd come back to see Tad, she remembered, and though of course I hadn't, perhaps, in a way, she was right. Perhaps it was really Tad who had made Holyhead so special.

But as she rode into the outskirts of Holyhead, it did cross Polly's mind to wonder what exactly she should do next. She had three whole days of her leave left, enough to get up to Lincolnshire – and back again, she supposed vaguely – but she did not have very much money, and she realised that knowing which airfield Tad was stationed at did not mean she would be able to run him to earth easily. The chances were, she knew, that the airfield would be some considerable way from the railway station, and Tad, being a pilot now, wouldn't be available all day as he had been as a flight mech. She could go up there and find he was flying the first night she arrived, in bed all the next day, and flying the following night. I could hang around there for a week and not see him and be court-martialled from the Navy for being AWOL, she told herself, pedalling desperately. Though if Tad knew I was there, surely he would get out of bed and see me, if only for a few minutes? She would have to borrow some money from Di for the rail fare and the taxi fare out to the airfield. Now she actually began to think about it, what was more, she would need to stay somewhere overnight . . .

But she had reached the lane which led to the backs of the houses in London Road and turned down it, reminding herself rather grimly that obstacles such as she had been outlining to herself were there to be conquered. Besides, she could scarcely rush off now, without a word to her hostess; Diane would be home from work in an hour; she would have a chat with her then and between them they could work out what best to do.

'Ring him,' Diane said, when Polly had blurted out her sudden and surprising change of heart. The two of them were sitting in the kitchen, preparing high tea, for Polly had agreed to defer rushing off anywhere until the following morning at least. 'No use tearing off to Lincolnshire only to find that your chap's gone off on leave, or is having a day's sleep before a big bombing raid or something. Ring first; be sensible for once.'

'I don't know his number,' Polly wailed. 'That's to say I don't know the number of the airfield, let alone what mess he's in. They're huge places, these airfields, Grace talks about them sometimes. What I t'ink is, Di, that they wouldn't wake him up for a telephone call from someone they'd never heared of, but if I was actually there, on the spot . . .'

'Ye-es, I know what you mean. But – oh, hang it, Poll, you're old enough to realise that fellers aren't made of stone! You've not been in touch, not so much as seen each other, for nearly two years – what on earth makes you think he's not got himself another bit of skirt in that time?'

'Another . . . oh, no, Di, you don't know Tad, he's not like that, he's—'

'You got yourself a feller, and what's more, you more or less boasted about Sunny to Tad from what you told me. He might have got himself a girl in a fit of pique, almost, and then found . . . well, he might have discovered he really did like her. Didn't you tell me about some girl in Dublin . . . I can't remember her name . . .'

'It was Angela,' Polly said, giving a derisive sniff. 'Little miss Angela, all sweetness and light. Huh! She didn't wait for him for long either, did she? First it were undying love, then it got a bit cooler, and then she t'rew him over for someone who was on the spot and probably better off, too.'

Diane giggled. 'I'm sorry, Poll, but whenever you get ratty your brogue comes back hot and strong,' she said, when Polly gave her an enquiring look. 'Anyway, I'm just warning you for your own good. You've treated Tad badly, you said as much earlier, so you couldn't be too surprised, surely, if he – well, if he'd decided there was no hope and had – had moved on, could you?'

'Yes, I could,' Polly said indignantly. She could feel the warmth rising to her cheeks at the mere suggestion that Tad might have looked at another girl. After all, they had been sweethearts for *years*. If she had been foolish enough to turn away from him for a matter of months, surely that would not change Tad? 'I'm only a kid; Tad's a man grown and he made up his mind he wanted me so why should he have changed?'

'You aren't only a kid or you wouldn't have been considering marriage to Sunny,' Diane reminded her shrewdly. 'Honestly, Polly, when you want to twist things to your best advantage there's no one who does it better! Well, if you're determined to go rushing up to Lincolnshire don't blame me if you get given the cold shoulder and end up with a broken heart. In a way,' she added, frowning at her friend, 'you almost deserve it, after the way you treated poor Tad.'

'Oh, pooh,' Polly said rudely.

Polly spent the evening sorting herself out, as Diane put it. First she buttonholed a naval rating who came from up north and got him to explain to her the exact

445

location of Tad's airfield and the railway station to which she must go in order to visit it. Then she got train times from the booking clerk at the station, and when asked, he proved enthusiastic over helping her to plan her rather complicated cross-country journey. That done, she sat down and wrote to Sunny.

'What do you want to do that for?' Diane asked curiously as Polly settled herself at the kitchen table with a piece of borrowed writing paper and her fountain pen. 'You haven't even spoken to Tad yet, you've no idea what you're going to find when you do see him. Why, he might be married with a kid for all you know.'

Polly looked up at her, puzzled. 'So? What difference would that make? I'm writing to Sunny, not Tad.'

'Oh, for heaven's sake,' Diane said, really exasperated. 'What can you tell Sunny when you don't know a bloody thing yourself, woman? Use your loaf for once, O'Brady!'

Polly laid down her pen and looked up at Diane, then took a deep breath. 'Di, don't you *see*? You pretend I'm thick, but I can't compare wit' you! I've made up me mind that Sunny and meself really aren't suited, and that it's Tad I want – Tad I always wanted, I suppose. So the right thing to do is to let Sunny know as soon as possible. And don't think I'll be breaking his heart – Sunny's I mean – because it's my belief he probably hasn't really thought much past the end of the war and getting back to – to – well, whatever he wants to do in Civvy Street. Fellers don't think about marrying and such the way women do, I don't believe, so if he's thought of marriage at all it won't be with me. Just with some girl, I suppose. So you see, regardless of what happens when I see Tad,

I've got to tell Sunny that there's nothing between us.'

'Burning your boats, you mean, I suppose,' Diane said slowly. 'It's all very grand and honourable, but what if . . . what if . . .'

'If Tad turns me down I know, now, that if I love anyone it's him and I couldn't possibly turn to Sunny,' Polly said sturdily. 'Surely you see that, Di?'

'Ye-es, only . . . look Poll, a couple of days ago – no, a *day* ago, you were saying that you and Tad were just pals and the feller you really loved was Sunny! Don't you think it's just possible that when you see Tad again – and it's been two years, love, don't forget – you might easily discover that no matter how *he* feels, you – well, you don't really want to marry him, after all?'

'Mebbe,' Polly said. She picked up her pen again and began to write. 'But even so, I know it won't be Sunny. He's awful nice, but . . . Oh, I can't explain because you aren't in love with anyone, you don't know how different someone feels when . . . well, I can't explain.'

'Then if it all goes wrong I suppose you'll end up a spinster,' Diane said. 'What a waste that would be, you conceited little baggage! Oh, go on, burn your boats, chuck out the baby with the bathwater, cut off your nose to spite your face and all the rest. Only don't come crying to me when it all goes wrong.'

'Yes, I shall, and you'll sympathise wit' me and tell me all men are bastards,' Polly said, and Diane, despite herself, gave a chortle of amusement. 'Di, you're the best friend a girl ever had, but do buzz off and let me write me letter!'

It was a long and tiring journey across country to Lincoln, the nearest railway station to Tad's airfield, and then, Polly knew, a good taxi drive. As the train

447

neared her destination, however, she became more and more worried by what she meant to do. Simply to turn up at the airfield, she was beginning to realise, would not get her very far – would get her nowhere, in fact. It was not as if she were in the WAAF; she was in another service and could scarcely expect to be allowed simply to walk across to the mess and demand to see Sergeant Pilot Thaddeus Donoghue – if that was still his rank, of course. By now he might be a warrant officer, or a flight lieutenant . . . Oh, anything might have happened to him, including, she supposed, demotion instead of promotion. No, she could not just walk in as she had planned, she would have to telephone first.

So when she reached Lincoln she went down the road, booked herself into a guesthouse where a wiry little woman in a stained wraparound apron was charging four bob for bed and breakfast, and set off for the nearest telephone kiosk. She found one only a few streets away and went rather timidly into its noisome interior, standing and dithering for several moments, undecided what to do. Indeed, it was only when a rat-faced RAF corporal rapped on the glass with a penny and mouthed at her that she snatched up the receiver, asked for the number and pushed her pennies into the slot.

She waited, moving restlessly, shifting her weight from one foot to the other. Suddenly, she was not at all sure that she was doing the right thing. Her mouth felt dry and her heart was bumping so loudly that she felt sure she would not be able to hear the voice which spoke when someone lifted the other receiver.

The bell rang, then stopped abruptly and a voice gave the name of the station in a clear, businesslike manner. Polly's heart, which had seemed determined, two seconds earlier, to crash its way out of her chest, was suddenly suspended, along with her voice and her breathing. For vital seconds she could not say a word, then began to speak whilst, on the other end of the line, the voice repeated, with some sharpness, the information it had already given.

Oh God, it must be one-way transmission, she could hear him but he couldn't hear her! What should she do? In another moment . . .

'Press Button A, caller,' a small, impersonal voice said. 'Have you pressed Button A?'

Polly's heartbeat returned to more or less normal and her ability to breathe came back. She pushed Button A, heard her pennies rattle irrevocably into the greedy maw of the telephone box, and spoke.

'H-hello? Oh, I w-wonder if you could help me . . . I'd like to speak to Sergeant Donoghue, please.'

'You've come through to the officers' mess,' the voice said a little impatiently. 'Hold on, though . . . you don't mean Tad Donoghue, I suppose? He's Pilot Officer Donoghue.'

'Oh! Y-yes, that's him,' Polly stammered, all her normal self-confidence gone. 'Umm . . . is he there?'

'Nope. Sleeping,' the voice said laconically. 'Try tomorrow around lunchtime.'

'Oh! But I only want a word wit' him,' Polly said pleadingly. 'Won't he be around before then? Or is he flying tonight?'

It was the wrong thing to say. Walls have ears and telephones, Polly knew, were at the mercy of every interested girl on every little local exchange. So she was not unduly surprised when the voice said, suddenly suspicious: 'Who *is* that? Because if it's you, Jenny, you ought to know better than I do what's going on up here. And if it isn't—'

'I'll try tomorrer, around noon,' Polly gabbled. 'Sorry to have troubled you,' and she slammed the receiver back on its rest and almost ran out of the kiosk, completely forgetting her gas-mask case and her purse until the rat-faced corporal shouted her back.

She almost ran back to her lodgings, tired after her long journey, hungry as a wolf now that the packed lunch the girls had provided was no more than a memory, and humiliated by the embarrassing telephone call. Who was Jenny, anyway? And what was she doing ringing Tad Donoghue, who was . . . Oh dammit, he *wasn't* her feller, that was the truth, and she was behaving every bit as stupidly as Diane had said, trying to run him to earth, never considering, not really, whether he wanted to see her again.

She went in through the front door and headed for the stairs to her attic bedroom, then paused in the small, square hallway. She was terribly hungry – she wondered if Mrs Rabbit or Tebbit or whatever she called herself might be willing to provide her with a cup of tea and a sandwich? She hadn't seemed a particularly welcoming woman but surely she would not see a WRN starve before her very eyes?

Polly was standing there, considering the question, when a door in the back of the hallway opened and her landlady appeared. She stared at Polly in a manner which seemed somehow accusatory, Polly thought.

'Yes? Forgot your room key?'

'No, but I've – I've rung me pal and – and he's workin' tonight and I'm starvin', so I am,' Polly said desperately, clutching her matelot's hat in both hands and feeling like a street beggar under the woman's sharp and condemnatory eyes. 'I wondered if – if—'

450

'Chip shop two streets away, but be sure you eat 'em outside and don't trek the smell of fish in here or I'll likely be havin' complaints,' the woman said so sharply that Polly jumped. 'I lock the front door at eleven o'clock, but if you want a key . . .'

'Oh! No, it's all right, I won't be long,' Polly said, and shot out of the front door before the older woman could say another word. Horrible old hag, she was thinking. Here's me, wit' me belly flappin' against me backbone and her not willin' to give me so much as an apple to keep me alive till morning. Still, I wouldn't mind some fish and chips. What's more, it'll give me something to think about until bedtime.

She found the chip shop, which had a couple of gingham-clothed tables in the window and bought a pot of tea and a plate of fish and chips which she ate on the premises, not grudging the extra sixpence since it meant she could have as much vinegar and salt as her food required. Then she made her way back to her lodgings and went straight up to bed. And though she had expected to lie awake half the night worrying, she was so tired, and so unhappy, that she slept as soon as her head touched the pillow.

Polly spent a miserable, rainy morning waiting for the time when she could ring the airfield once again and feeling frightened, apprehensive and generally far from her usual cheerful self. But the time passed and at last, at noon, she returned to the telephone box, lifted the receiver and asked the operator for the number and this time asked for Pilot Officer Donoghue.

'I'll fetch him,' the telephone answerer said laconically, and Polly thought, a trifle dismally, that she should have left her name the day before, and asked that Tad be by the telephone at noon. It would have saved time . . . but she had a little tower of pennies standing on the side waiting to be put into the slot and anyway, it was no more than a couple of minutes later that Tad said: 'Hello? Tad Donoghue speaking.'

'Tad!' Polly said, her voice coming out high, and squeakier than usual. 'Oh, Tad, it's me, Polly.'

'Who?'

'Polly O'Brady,' Polly said, dismayed to hear a slightly apologetic note creeping into her voice. 'It's ages since we met . . . and though I wrote to you over and over, you didn't reply apart from a couple of notes. So – so I thought it might be nice to meet up again.'

'You did?' He sounded so surprised that a hot colour rose in Polly's cheeks. 'Well, it's always nice to meet old pals, but I don't get off the airfield much. Where are you, anyway?'

'Lincoln. Staying at a guesthouse in town,' Polly said. 'I – I had some leave and I thought it would be nice to – to see each other again.'

'So you said.' There was a long pause. 'But don't you think it might be better, perhaps, to let sleeping dogs lie? I don't want to upset you, but . . . Oh, how's Sunny, by the way?'

Polly felt like blurting out that she didn't know, hadn't seen Sunny for months, that it was Tad she cared about, Tad she wanted to see, but innate caution made her say airily: 'Sure and he's fine, though he's at sea a good deal. How's Jenny?'

'Jenny?'

'When I phoned last night they asked me if I was Jenny,' Polly muttered. 'So I know she's a friend of yours. How is she? Who is she, for that matter?'

'Oh, Jenny. She's fine. She's one of the WAAFs on

452

the station,' Tad said. 'So you're in Lincoln. How long for?'

'I'm going back to Liverpool tomorrow,' Polly said stiffly. 'It doesn't matter, it was just a thought since I happened to be in the neighbourhood . . . It's been – been nice hearing your voice again, Tad, but—'

'What are you doin' in the neighbourhood, any-how?' Tad cut in. 'We don't see many WRNs in this neck of the woods!'

'Oh! I – I came . . .' Polly thought about inventing a friend, then abruptly changed her mind. She had come to see Tad, she was desperate to see him, if he was going to tell her he had met someone else, wasn't interested in her any longer, then that was sad, but she would at least know it was no good hoping. So she took a deep breath, squared her shoulders and almost shouted into the receiver. 'I came to see you, Tad, because you'd not writ, and we're old pals and I missed you. But if you're too busy to come down and meet me, that's all there is to it and I'll go back home.'

'Well, I daresay I could spare half an hour,' Tad said cautiously. 'Do you know the Albion Hotel? It's in St Mary's Street – not far from the railway station.'

'Yes, I know it,' Polly said rather gloomily. She felt she could have answered a stiff examination paper on this wretched town since her landlady had turned her out at nine o'clock and she had spent the entire morning roaming the rain-soaked streets. 'What time, Tad?'

'Well, it's noon, or just after, now. Say, one o'clock? The landlord does quite decent sandwiches – I'll buy you lunch.'

'Thanks,' Polly said. 'Oh . . . the pips! See you at one, then. In the lounge bar?'

'One o'clock,' echoed Tad and put his receiver

down just as the operator asked Polly to cut her connection since others were waiting.

Polly came out of the box almost at a run, hot-faced and humiliated. He had not wanted to see her again, and she had more or less forced his hand, made him do the decent thing and see her. Well, when they met she would come out with it, baldly, tell him that she realised she had made a mistake, that she did not love Sunny, and ask him to give her another chance.

Outside in the rain, she turned up her coat collar, pulled her cap down further over her eyes, and sloshed through the puddles towards the Albion. This was easily the worst thing that had ever happened to her in her entire life – she had thrown herself at Tad and he had, verbally, pushed her away. He had not wanted to meet her and she had insisted even when it was plain that Tad felt it was a mistake. I've cheapened meself, Polly thought as she slogged on. Oh, well. At least we'll get it over and then I can start trying to rebuild my life with someone else, not Tad, clearly, nor Sunny, but someone as yet unmet.

A trifle cheered by this thought, which sounded exciting, and even more cheered by the recollection that her shame and humiliation were hers alone, that no one else would know that she had chased all the way up here only to be turned down, Polly continued to slog onwards, with the rain now beginning to channel down her neck and find its chilly way to her uniform underwear. At least, she comforted herself, she was going to see Tad presently, and surely, once they set eyes on each other, they would speedily recapture their old friendship? But in her heart she was beginning to doubt it.

Tad came off the phone and stood in the mess for a

moment, gazing in front of him and trying to conquer the big grin which was beginning to spread across his countenance. Polly had rung him, admitted she had come all the way to Lincolnshire especially to see him. Surely that must mean something, indicate that her old fondness for him was still there? He crossed the room and went out of the door to get his mackintosh, for there was no point in leaving the airfield it in this downpour. He was halfway back to his hut when someone caught up with him. Jim Stratton grabbed his arm.

'Where you goin', Tad old feller? I thought you and me were going to have some grub in the mess and then going to see a flick? Who was it on the telephone, by the way? Jenny? Only I thought she was away on a course or something.'

Tad descended abruptly from the clouds. 'No, it wasn't Jenny, it was a girl I was friendly with in Dublin,' he said slowly. 'She thought she'd look me up – we were good pals once, so we were.'

'Oh? But I thought you and Jenny had a thing going.'

'I've told you often enough that me and Jenny are just friends,' Tad pointed out. 'Anyway, meeting a girl doesn't mean you're going to marry her, does it? I'm only *meeting* Polly since she's in the neighbourhood.'

'Oh aye? Isn't she the one who gave you the brush-off just before we all left for Rhodesia? Didn't she write for a bit, only you wouldn't reply, said it was best left.'

'Oh damn you, Jim,' Tad said, grinning despite himself. He and Jim had been together now for more than two years and he must have told Jim a hundred times about his Polly and how she was going to marry

455

another feller. 'Yes, that's Polly. I don't know why she's come to see me, but . . . . well, I can't help hoping that she's realised that Sunny feller isn't the one for her.'

'And you are, I suppose,' Jim said, breaking into a run as Tad did so that they crashed into the hut together. 'Remember the last time she got you to go chasing off after her? Someone had got fresh with her and who did she turn to? It'll be the same this time, you mark my words. She wants something, that one, and you'll go chasing after her all over again and get asked for . . . well, whatever it is she wants. Likely she's in the club and wants advice.'

'In the . . .? Good God, Jimmy, whatever makes you think that? She said Sunny's mostly at sea, she didn't say she was in any sort of trouble, didn't even suggest that she was after help or advice. You're a bleedin' cynic, that's your trouble. Probably she simply wants to say she's sorry for the way she treated me that time. Anyway, I'm meeting her in the Albion in an hour. There's a bus which stops at the main gate in fifteen minutes, if I'm quick.'

'Shall I come in as well, then? Oh, I won't come to the Albion, I do have *some* tact, but we could meet up afterwards to see that flick,' Jim suggested as Tad dived into his room and began to sort through his possessions. 'Or are you going to spend the afternoon with her?'

'I don't know,' Tad said. He sorted out some money and shoved it into the pocket of his tunic, then grabbed his mackintosh. 'Look, I'm sorry about the flick, but I don't think it's on. I'll see you when I get back, though.' He grinned at his friend. 'Come in on the bus by all means, but you'll miss whatever delicacy the mess has to offer, and the Albion only does sandwiches.'

456

'I won't bother,' Jim said. He turned away. 'Have fun, Tad, and don't forget, if she's after something just you think twice before knuckling down and handing it to her on a plate. Especially if she's looking for someone to take on responsibility for a bun in the oven.'

In too much of a hurry to answer him back, Tad merely cuffed his friend across the ear as he tore past, and by a dint of running, managed to get aboard the bus, which was early. He settled himself on the back seat, shook as much rain off his coat as he could, and then concentrated on getting his fare out of an inner pocket and asking the conductor what time he expected to arrive in the city.

Having satisfied himself that he would be on time at the rendezvous, Tad then sat there and began to wonder whether Jim could possibly be right; could Polly have come to see him because she was in trouble of some kind? The more he thought about it the likelier it seemed. After all, when he had been at Valley Polly had been friendly with him because she wanted to learn how to ride his motorbike, and to service it too. And the only time she had been in trouble, the night she had been more or less kidnapped by the lecherous lorry driver, she had rung him up, with just that little catch in her voice that he so loved, begging him to rescue her.

But . . . a baby? It just was not possible that Polly could be having a baby by some bloke, or that she would dream, for one moment, of turning to him for help if the father had not wanted to marry her. But there was, he supposed wretchedly, a fair chance that she was in some other sort of scrape, that she had felt he was the only person to whom she could turn. In a way, it was nice that she still trusted him, still felt he

457

would help her, but dammit, that wasn't the way he wanted Polly to think of him, as a mug to get her out of trouble! He wanted . . . The truth was, he did not know what he wanted. I'll just have to wait and see what happens when we meet, he told himself, hunched down in his seat staring through the smeared window at the lashing rain outside. After all, this time he was in a much stronger position than she. She had come running to him and he could either accept her or send her home with her tail between her legs, depending how he felt. And as the journey continued he found that his intentions were crystallising into a firm resolve not to be hurried or pushed into anything again, not even mere friendship. She's let you down with a big thump in the past, Donoghue, he reminded himself. This time, play it a bit more cautiously. Besides, she'll have changed, as I have. We're almost like two strangers meeting after all this time, and strangers shouldn't leap into each other's arms. I'll play it cool, and remember what Jim said. If she's in trouble then she should ask her good friend Sunny to get her out of it!

In the train going home, Polly sat back in her seat and thought of the last couple of days and, most of all, of the meeting which had taken place between Tad and herself the previous lunchtime. It had been sticky, she reminded herself, especially at first. She had been sitting in a corner of the lounge bar when he had entered the room and had sprung to her feet and gone towards him, eager for his usual beaming smile, his hug.

Instead, he had taken her hands, gazed seriously down at her for a moment, and then said: 'Well? What's gone wrong, Polly? Because I don't imagine you've come all this way just to tell me you're well and happy!'

Whether it was his words or the way he stared at her Polly could not have said, but suddenly it was just plain impossible to say: 'I came because it's you I've wanted, all along. The whole business with Sunny was a dreadful mistake, and I've never thought of you as a brother, honest to God, Tad. Will you make up, so's we can go back to being friends? Well, I hope we'll be more than friends.' Instead, she stammered that of course there was nothing wrong, that she was in her usual good health and she had come to see him because . . . because they were old pals, weren't they, and she had some leave owing, and it had seemed like a good idea at the time . . .

Here she ran out of steam and Tad, guiding her to a corner table and going over to the bar, seemed not to notice the garbled half-sentences which she had uttered. He did not ask her what she wanted to drink but came back with two halves of bitter and the good news that sandwiches were on their way. Polly, who detested bitter, sipped cautiously and tried not to pull a face, and whilst they waited for the food, Tad first of all stared into space and then, apparently deciding that this was a waste of what little time they might have together, addressed her seriously.

'Polly, it was good of you to come, I appreciate it, don't get me wrong. But you know, you've changed a great deal in the last couple of years and I guess I have too.'

Polly nodded, trying not to eye him too obviously. He was broader, more substantial altogether than the Tad she remembered, and his skin was so brown, so healthily tanned! In Dublin the pair of them might have given the outward appearance of a tan but it was usually dirt, particularly in Tad's case. This tan, however, was a real one, made by the sun which had lightened his hair from mid-brown to fudge-colour streaked with gold, and it gave him an additional confidence. So she had to admit that he had changed and supposed, with real uncertainty, that she, too, must have altered.

She had said as much in a rather small voice just as the sandwiches put in an appearance. Tad handed the plate to her, then took one himself and spoke somewhat thickly through his first mouthful. 'Look, alanna, are you in – in some sort of trouble? Because if so, I've got to know about it before I can do much to help. If I can do anything, that is.'

Polly, with a sandwich halfway to her mouth, frowned across at him. Until that moment he had seemed calm, sure of himself. Now for some reason the colour in his cheeks had darkened and he looked ill at ease, as though he thought that she must have a guilty secret which he did not much wish her to reveal. So it was rather sharply that she said: 'In trouble? Me? No, indeed, Tad, I'm fine, so I am. What about you?'

He grinned, but did not answer her last question. 'Well, all right, you're fine and just came up here to – to renew old acquaintance. Is that right?'

'Yes,' Polly said baldly. She would have left it at that, gone on to talk of other things, but suddenly a sort of wild defiance took hold of her. Why should she be ashamed to tell Tad that she was no longer going out with Sunny? Why could she not tell him that far from thinking of him as a brother . . . Hastily, before she could change her mind, she spoke. 'Tad, you once said you wanted us to be more than pals. Do – do you still feel the same?'

He looked at her then, round brown eyes rounding still further, looking first astonished and then, to her chagrin, slightly amused. 'Well, next t'ing I know you'll be proposin' marriage, Poll, and it's not Leap Year for a while yet!'

Polly felt so annoyed with him that for two pins, she told herself, she would have leaned across the table and rammed his sandwich down his self-satisfied throat. But she remembered Diane's cautions and spoke calmly, or as calmly as she could. 'I'm pro-posin' nothing, Tad Donoghue, I'm just asking you. Do you or do you not want to – to be a bit more than just pals?'

This time Tad neither laughed nor turned away. He gazed thoughtfully at her, clearly considering his reply, and when at last he spoke it was seriously, with no lurking smile. 'Look, Poll, you might have been right when you said – well, that I'd been like a brother to you. The truth is, I loved you when you were a little girl, a kid of three or four, but now you're a woman, and as you said earlier, we've both changed. I – I think I'd like to get to know this new Polly better, that's what I think. So how about it? I know we're a long way apart but the war's going to end soon, everyone knows it, and in the meantime we can ring each other up, write letters – well, no, all right, I'm a lousy correspondent, you've told me so – and meet up now and then. I have leaves and so do you; we could meet halfway, or if I've got a week I could come over to the 'Pool and if you've got one you could come up to Lincoln. What do you say?'

Polly stared at him, two entirely different emotions warring within her. In one way she was glad of his suggestion, because he was right, they had both changed and she felt that she needed time to get to

461

know this sturdier, more self-confident Tad. But her other emotion was that of pique that he had almost thrown her attempt to get close to him once again back in her face. Polly had had a great many boy-friends, a great many young men had vied for her attentions. Never before, she realised, had any of them suggested that they ought to get to know one another better before going on dates and canoodling at dances. Still, she could see Tad's point. If, as seemed possible, he had only loved her with what they called puppy love, then clearly he was going to have to get to know her all over again before embarking on a more serious relationship. So finally, having thought it over for at least five minutes, she heaved a sigh and nodded. 'Right you are, Tad. But how will I know when to ring? I mean, you're flying at night and sleeping during the day . . . and I can't say ring me, because we aren't on the telephone at home – did you know I was living at home now? – and I'm hardly ever at the depot, not now I'm despatch riding.'

'You just have to phone the mess, and if I'm not there I'll leave a message that Polly O'Brady's to be told when I'm available,' Tad said, so blandly that once more, Polly's fingers itched to give him a ding round the ear. 'I could drop you a postcard when I've got leave, if I've not been able to speak to you on the telephone. Would that do?'

'I suppose so,' Polly said grudgingly, and began to concentrate on her sandwiches and beer. The beer wasn't too bad, she discovered, if you stopped breathing through your nose, swallowed hard and quickly jammed a hunk of sandwich into your mouth. She felt let down, with a sort of inner ache in the pit of her stomach, because she had had such romantic ideas of this meeting. She had been going to run into Tad's arms and their lips would have met and they would have – have melded into one person, love enveloping them in a warm glow, every eye softening with tears, mouths trembling into gentle smiles . . .

Still, there you were. It was not going to be so easy, but that didn't mean she intended to give up. She had made up her mind years and years ago that one day she would marry Tad, and though she had gone astray a bit in between, the resolve was strong in her again now. Tad was doomed, whether he knew it or not, and she, Polly, would simply have to make the best of every opportunity to see him so that he fell under her spell once more and wanted to marry her as badly as she wanted to marry him.

So the two of them drank their beer and ate their sandwiches and in between bites Tad told her a little of his life in the Air Force. His work was often highly secret, and always interesting, because his Beaufighter was what they called a pathfinder, which meant that he went ahead of the heavy bombers and their fighter escorts and saw the attackers safely to their targets. Sometimes he dropped leaflets over enemy territory, sometimes he carried a photographer, sometimes he simply went on reconnaissance flights. He talked so interestingly that Polly almost forgot to eat, but it occurred to her, uneasily, that what he did was very dangerous. Even now, with peace looming, he was in danger, she thought, whenever he flew. Of course she had known that flying was dangerous, as she had known that Sunny's voyaging through the Arctic waters on his way to and from Russia was dangerous, but she had never really thought of it quite like this. Tad's sturdy, self-reliant body could as easily spiral down to earth in a blazing plane as anyone's . . . I'm going to worry now every time I think of him night-flying, Polly thought with deep foreboding. Oh, if something were to happen to Tad I just couldn't bear it, whether he'll be my proper boyfriend or not. I wish I hadn't come, then I wouldn't have known . . . but then I wouldn't have seen him, wouldn't even have had a chance of getting close to him again, and that would have been worse, much worse. Everyone worries in wartime, she concluded, drinking the last of her horrible bitter, so why should I be any different?

When the sandwiches were eaten and Polly had told Tad a bit about her own life and work they went and saw a flick, and Tad had not even held her hand in the sad bits. He had bought her an ice cream in the interval and passed her his handkerchief when she began to snivel a bit, but that was the closest he had come to touching her. And then, when they came out of the cinema and walked back to her lodgings, she had meant to invite him in and see if he would try to kiss her, either in the privacy of her bedroom, if her landlady was not around, or on the hard little sofa in the ugly, overfurnished front room if she was. But before she could even open the front door with the key the landlady had lent her, Tad had taken her hand, squeezed it between both of his, and told her, in an infuriatingly avuncular manner, to run along in now, since he would have to belt across the city to get the bus back to camp or he would be late for his briefing and that would never do.

Polly had stood and stared after him as he had hurried away, almost unable to believe what was happening to her. This was Tad, who adored her, who had always tried to please her, who had vowed undying love at least twice when they were both stationed on Anglesey. But then the front door had

464

opened behind her and her landlady had said: 'Are you coming in now, Miss O'Brady? I'm making meself a cup of tea, you're welcome to share the pot if you're not on your way out again,' and pride had stiffened her backbone, driven the tears out of her eyes, and got her into the kitchen to drink the proferred cup.

And now, sitting in the train chugging back to Liverpool, she wondered rather dismally where it would all end. Not, she thought glumly, with her having to fight Tad off, that at least was plain. She was going to have to woo him, by the looks of it, and she was not at all sure that she wanted to do any such thing. It was his job to woo her, not vice versa!

But oh, it had been good to see him! The way his hair fell, the deep, wicked dimple which came and went in one cheek when something truly amused him, even his habit of cracking his knuckles when he was embarrassed . . . Yes, it was worth fighting for Tad, she decided, suddenly remembering the voice on the phone asking her if she were Jenny. She had not managed to cross-question Tad about Jenny . . . but she could drop an artful little question or two into their very next telephone conversation, at least she could find out whether Jenny was competition, or merely an acquaintance.

And then there was the worry; worrying over his safety, she could see, was going to become a part of her life until this wretched, horrible war ended. She felt strongly that no one should be expected to worry over the safety and well-being of a fellow who was not even prepared to make a play for you, but there it was. When you loved someone, you worried about them whether you wanted to or not. It was even possible, she supposed, feeling a little glow of satisfaction at the thought, that Tad would worry about her now. After all, she was dashing around on a motorbike, living in a port, a prey to all sorts of dangers – oh yes, Tad ought to worry about her, all right.

Satisfied on that score, Polly leaned back in her seat and prepared to work for Tad, as well as worry over him.

Tad returned to the airfield feeling extremely pleased with himself. Dear little Polly, how cast down she had been at his apparent lack of interest, and how her eyes had sparkled as, he guessed, she decided that he *should* fall in love with her whether he wanted to or not! The truth was, he knew, that he had never stopped loving her, but he had realised long ago that Polly, little darling though she might be, did not value what came easily in the way she would value something she had had to fight for. So he had not told her he loved her and wanted her desperately, had not told her that Jenny, nice little WAAF that she was, was only a friend. In fact, he had told her he was flying tonight though he would not be doing so for another forty-eight hours. It had gone to his heart to deceive her, but if she believed she had competition for his affection, it would make her value him more.

So he felt like dancing as he made his way to the mess; he felt that his life was on course once more.

Sunny got the letter when he next came ashore, and was far less troubled by it than Polly had anticipated, in fact it relieved his mind considerably. For a start, she had said she intended to make friends with Tad again, and this, he thought approvingly, was a good thing. He had been aware for some time that Polly missed Tad and wanted to get back on good terms with him, and he had been equally aware that he was no longer the boy who had once talked of sharing his future with Polly. The war had changed them both. Indeed even the peace, when it came, was uncertain because he was going to have to make up his mind what he wanted to do after the war, and he was not at all sure that he could face up to Civvy Street. Nor, when he came to think about it, did he altogether want to do so. His skipper had suggested that Sunny might carry on with his job, for a while at any rate, and Sunny thought that it might be the best thing to do. Once peace was declared, he assumed that the need for the Russian convoys would cease, but that did not mean that ships would not be wanted.

So Sunny wrote back, saying despite her letter he hoped they could still be friends and promising to come and see her the next time he was in Liverpool.

Chapter Seventeen

From the moment that Mr Churchill announced that Tuesday, 8th May was to be 'Victory in Europe Day', and that everyone would have a day off in order to celebrate, Snowdrop Street became a place of wild excitement, with everyone planning what they should do.

Folk had known that the moment would come, of course, they just had not known exactly when, and they had been saving up goodies for weeks. Months, in some cases, Deirdre said proudly, fishing her little hoard out from the tin box under the lowest shelf in the pantry. There was to be a street party, and a bonfire, despite the fact that the government had said bonfires were forbidden. 'Who'll be on the watch if everyone's to have a holiday?' Deirdre had said when Peader had been doubtful about the bonfire. 'Besides, how else can we get rid of the beastly blackout if there's no bonfire to burn the blinds on?'

Church bells, which had been silent for the whole war, only to be sounded in case of an invasion, would ring out once more. Lights would blaze, flags would fly, folk would sing and dance and there would be a spread the like of which none of the kids in the street had ever seen.

Polly had been as wildly excited as everyone else, and had done all she could to help, both because she was looking forward to the celebrations and because of a private reason of her own. She intended, a day or so before the great event, to ring Tad at his Lincoln-shire station and invite him to spend his leave – he would surely have leave? – at the house in Snowdrop Street. They would be together at last. She was in a mood of wild exhilaration, making plans for what they would do now that the end of the war had at last arrived. And in that atmosphere of gaiety and victory, surely it would be no particularly hard matter to persuade Tad to forget the bad times and remember only the good? There was the wretched Jenny, of course, but Polly always tried to put Jenny out of her mind. Tad had assured her Jenny was 'just a friend', and by and large she believed him. There was no doubt that Tad liked Jenny. He said she was great fun to be with, even-tempered and easy to please. Naturally, in view of this, Polly had sometimes suppressed a desire to say something sharp to Tad and had been as mild and biddable as possible, and she was sure it must be paying off, and that Tad would, very soon indeed, succumb to her charms and tell her that he loved the new Polly as much as the old and ask her to be his wife. Dreamily, she contem-plated a future shared with Tad and looked in jewellers' windows at engagement rings.

So, as she worked, she was quietly content, quietly planning her own celebrations which would, of course, take place just as soon as Tad was hers once more. She intended to marry him in due course but occasionally common sense came to her aid and reminded her that no one, not even she and Tad, could live on fresh air. They would both have to get jobs in Civvy Street before they could possibly start planning their future together.

The bonfire which the street had planned might have been difficult some years earlier, for Snowdrop

Street was right in the city with few open spaces, but now, thanks to Jerry, there were plenty of large bomb-sites, already thickly overgrown with the tall pink spears of rosebay willowherb. These open spaces were just the sort of area where a nice big bonfire could blaze without danger of hurting anyone's property and all over the country, Polly imagined, they were being put to the same use. So she helped the kids from the surrounding streets, the flower streets, to collect everything burnable and piled it high, and then she went and helped Deirdre to bake a number of cakes and pies, and she and Peader borrowed every trestle table they could lay their hands on from church halls and schools, and then they sat back and waited hopefully for a fine day on which to celebrate.

At the weekend Polly put in her usual call to Tad, determined to persuade him to get leave and come to the Snowdrop Street party.

She got through easily and in her new, gentle tone, greeted Tad enthusiastically and asked him what he meant to do the following Tuesday.

'Tuesday?' Tad said, apparently less aware than Polly of the importance of the occasion. 'I dunno – why?'

'Oh, Tad,' Polly cried, softly reproachful. 'You can't have forgot – Mr Churchill's given everyone the day off to celebrate – it's VE Day!'

'Oh aye,' Tad said. 'Well now, what had I meant to do? Stay in bed late, I reckon, and—'

'Stay in bed later, wit' all the country celebrating?' Polly asked incredulously. 'You can't do that, Tad – think what you'll be missing! Why, we're having a street party, we've all give food and Mammy's made *vats* of lemonade and ginger beer, and there's to be fireworks, and flags, and games . . . We – we t'ought, all of us, that you'd come across to see us, and stay for the day and mebbe the night too. There's no one in the spare room, and I know you're bound to have leave owing, because you've not had any time off since that day in Lincoln an' even then you had to go off early, flying.'

She had tried not to sound injured, but knew that she sounded at least disappointed at his failure to leap at her idea like a trout at a fly, but she kept her tone wheedling rather than reproachful, bearing in mind that wretched, goody-goody Jenny.

'Oh, I couldn't do that,' Tad said immediately, however. He sounded quite shocked. 'I couldn't let me pals down, Poll. There's all sorts of goings-on planned in Lincoln and the NAAFI are running a big dance and a special dinner . . . No, I couldn't let me pals down.'

'But just now you couldn't even remember what Tuesday was,' Polly wailed. 'And won't your pals have just as good a time if you aren't there, then? Because you can't have done much, or you wouldn't have forgot. Oh, Tad, I've done no end, honest I have. I've beetled about getting fuel for the bonfire, and I've helped Mammy wit' the cooking and Daddy wit' fetching chairs and tables and I've even done sewin', and you know how I do hate me needle.'

Tad sighed. 'Sorry, love, it can't be done,' he said, his tone complacent. 'Well, you have fun now, and t'ink about me stuck up here doing me best to have fun as well.'

It was at this point that Polly's careful plans deserted her. 'Who with?' she demanded, her voice strident with suspicion. 'Are you goin' to watch fire-works and eat your dinner wit' that Jenny you telled me about?'

'She's bound to be there,' Tad admitted. 'After all, as I've told you a thousand times, Poll, she's me good friend so there's no reason—'

Polly cut across this thoroughly infuriating sentence. 'Tad Donoghue, if you don't want to come to our street party then I can't make you,' she shouted wildly into the receiver. 'But I'm tellin' you, when you *do* deign to come back to Liverpool, don't you bother calling in Snowdrop Street, because I shan't be after wantin' to see you! I'm going to send a telegram to Sunny this moment, asking him to come and stay and be me – me partner. Well? What do you say to that?'

'I'm sorry, Poll,' Tad said, but he didn't sound sorry, he sounded amused, which only added fuel to Polly's anger. 'But I suppose, if you feel that strongly—'

'I do,' Polly shrieked, discretion cast to the four winds and temper and disappointment bringing tears to her eyes. 'Why, if you had any feelings for me, Tad Donoghue . . .'

'You're my good pal,' Tad said soothingly. 'Calm down, Poll, and remember—'

He got no further. Well, he might have done had Polly not slammed the receiver back on its rest and stalked, trembling with rage, out of the telephone box. And presently, when she was calmer and could think straight, she realised that the careful work she had been putting into her relationship with Tad ever since the visit to Lincoln had just gone up in smoke. He would be telling himself this very minute that Polly had not changed at all, she was still the bad-tempered, spoilt child he had known in Dublin. And he would he turning to Jenny and asking her . . . asking her . . .

Tears blinding her, Polly turned round and rushed back to the telephone box. She asked the operator, in trembling tones, for the number and had a considerable wait – 'Line's busy,' said the operator impersonally – before at last she got through to the mess.

But not to Tad. 'He's not here,' the officer who answered the telephone said. 'Is that Polly? No, he's had to go out – wasn't he on the telephone to you just now? I thought he said you'd just spoken to him.'

'I – I had,' Polly said, tears running down her cheeks and tasting salt in her mouth as she opened it to speak. 'But – but I've j-just remembered something I – I forgot. I'll ring later.'

She had rung later, but somehow, Tad was never available, and it seemed pointless to write a letter. She could say she was sorry, hadn't meant a word of it, would accept him on any terms, but what was the use? If he wouldn't speak to her then he was unlikely to take much notice of a letter. So, on the eve of the day for which she had longed so passionately, Polly went to bed in a very subdued frame of mind, quite seeing that her horrid temper had ruined her whole life for her and quite at a loss, for the moment, as to how she was to mend the breach she had caused between Tad and herself.

Besides, she thought drearily, as she turned out the light and rolled up the blackout blind for the last time, by now he's probably asked that horrible Jenny to marry him, and I hope she makes him very unhappy, so I do!

Then she got into bed and after indulging in the luxury of a good cry into her pillow she settled down and, despite her conviction that she would never sleep, was soon dreaming.

On the morning of 8th May, Polly woke early to find

pale sunshine pouring in through her bedroom window. It was early, but she slid cautiously out of bed and padded over to the window, telling herself that she might as well check that it had not rained in the night because if it had, some work might be needed on the bonfire, and there might be work to do on the street itself, which must be dry and decent before they could set out the tables and chairs.

But all was well. The night, clearly, had been as fine as the day which now beamed down upon Liverpool. The sky was a deep blue, there was not a cloud in sight and the sunshine was growing brighter as the sun rose in the heavens. It's going to be a marvellous day, Polly told herself, going over to her washstand and struggling out of her nightdress. Well, it would be a marvellous day if . . . but there's no use repining. I lost my temper and now I've lost Tad, and I've just got to make the best of it. Anyway, it wasn't kind of him to refuse to speak to me when I phoned, and heaven knows I phoned often enough to show anyone I was sorry, so I was. But that's Tad for you: unforgiving. And who wants a feller like that, a feller who can't forgive a person for making one little mistake and having a bit of a shout because they were disappointed?

Unfortunately, however, Polly knew very well that the answer to this rhetorical question, which should be a firm 'No one sensible wants a feller like that,' was in fact, very different. One person wanted a feller like Tad – no, not a feller like him, she wanted Tad himself – and that of course was Polly O'Brady.

However, she could not stand around in her room feeling miserable, not with such an important day about to start. She chucked her nightdress on to her unmade bed, poured water from her jug into the pottery basin and seized the small piece of soap which was all she had left until Mammy found some more, somewhere. She washed all over, rinsed herself, dried on the small scrap of towel hanging beside the washstand and began to dress, her uniform all cleaned and pressed for this special day.

Once she was ready she headed for the stairs. Deirdre was already in the kitchen, with the kettle boiling on the hob and a panful of cold potatoes frying over the flame. Some rather suspicious-looking sausages were sharing the pan and Polly gave a sigh at the sight of them. Now bacon would have been nice but was rarely available, so it would have to be sausages and some of those delicious fried potatoes.

'Morning, Mammy,' Polly said, going over to the Welsh dresser and beginning to lay the table. 'Is Daddy about yet?'

'He's walked down to the tram to meet Monica,' Deirdre said, turning the potatoes and sucking in her breath as the fat spat. 'They'll be back in a few minutes, so we can all have breakfast together. Be a love, alanna, and slice me some bread and put it on the plates.' She glanced round the kitchen as though walls truly did have ears. 'I managed to get a few shell-eggs, so I thought we'd begin our celebration early wit' them and the sausages and spuds. After all, heaven knows when we'll have our dinner, and the party won't start until four o'clock so's everyone can be there.'

'I heard from Grace; she's coming back to the 'Pool if she can manage it, and Sunny says he might come too, because his ship's in dock for some sort of a refit,' Polly said, getting the loaf out of the crock and beginning to slice. 'Oh, it'll be a grand day, so it will, but it'll be best of all to see me pals, if we manage to meet up. Only I guess there'll be crowds everywhere, and neither Grace nor Sunny could say for certain where they'd be, or at what time.'

'Never mind; if they're home they'll make their way to Snowdrop Street sooner or later. But it's a pity Tad can't get away,' Deirdre said with a shrewd look at her daughter. Polly, noticing it, sighed inwardly. She had not said much about Tad since the fateful phone call the previous weekend, but she realised that her mammy, who knew her so well, probably guessed what had happened. 'Still, everyone will be wanting leave for today, I reckon,' Deirdre continued, moving the pan off the heat. 'Mebbe next week or the week after our Tad will turn up here, eh?'

Polly finished slicing the bread and turned to her mother with a deep sigh. She might as well spill the beans, she was no use at telling fibs, never had been. And besides, Mammy and Daddy wouldn't blame her; they would be comforting and loving. It would ease her conscience to tell Mammy the truth. 'Tad won't be coming, not today nor in a few days,' she said bluntly. 'I shouted at him when I rang to invite him here and he said he couldn't let his pals down. I – well, I lost me temper, Mammy, and telled him that if he didn't come today he needn't bother to come at all. I – I said I'd write to Sunny and get him to come instead. I was horrid, so I was.'

'Lovers' tiff,' Deirdre said comfortably just as the back door opened and Peader ushered Monica inside. 'Don't you worry, alanna, these things happen no matter how we try to avoid 'em. Monica, me dear, sit you down, I'm just going to dish up.'

Sunny and Grace had met that day entirely by chance since neither could possibly have known the

476

whereabouts of the other. Sunny's ship had come in for a refit but though he had hoped to be in Liverpool for the celebrations he knew that everything depended on the trains, on the hour that his ship's captain saw fit to dismiss him, and on luck.

In the event, luck and his skipper were definitely on his side, with the result that he was told good-humouredly the previous evening that he could make himself scarce so long as he was back at his post before the ship sailed on the Wednesday, and managed to catch the milk train next morning, arriving in Liverpool after various changes and connections, to his own delight and astonishment, before noon.

He had come into Lime Street, of course, along with a great many other men and women in uniform, and the first person he saw as he got down from his train was a neatly uniformed WAAF with light brown, shiny hair and a pale, heart-shaped face, walking along the opposite platform. As she turned towards him her face lit up in a smile of such sweetness and genuine pleasure that he felt his heart give a little leap. 'Grace! By all that's wonderful, if this isn't the strangest thing! So you *did* get leave, after all, and the first person I see when I reach Liverpool is you!'

'Hello, Sunny,' Grace said. Her smile did not falter but he saw a certain wariness come into her blue-grey eyes. 'I daresay you're off to Snowdrop Street as well?'

Sunny had been about to agree that he was indeed off to Snowdrop Street when he changed his mind. He held out a hand and took hers and watched pink roses bloom on her cheeks. 'No, why should I go to Snowdrop Street when you're here, and we can have a good time, just the two of us?' he said. 'Oh, we'll mebbe go round there later, queen, but not yet, eh? There's a lot to do and see in the city and two's easier than half-a-dozen, wouldn't you say? Besides, they've gorra street party and all sorts this afternoon. We'll spend the morning together, just catching up on what's going on, shall us?'

Grace had nodded eagerly, squeezed his hand – then sighed doubtfully. 'Well, I'd love that, Sunny, but . . . don't you think Polly will be expecting you?'

'No,' Sunny said light-heartedly. 'You know our Poll, she'll enjoy herself no matter what, and there's plenty of fellers around today. She wrote a while back, said something about someone called Tad . . . I got the feeling that he was special to her. So come on, where'll we go first? I haven't eaten since last night, how about a meal? We might find some fish and chips!'

And the two of them had set off, heading for Byrom Street where Sunny remembered a place which, in peacetime, had been famous for its excellent food.

As Sunny had said, there was plenty for two young people to do and see in a city celebrating the end of a long, hard-fought war. They ate their meal, talking eagerly about their jobs, their friends, fleshing out the letters that they had been exchanging regularly, now, for a twelve-month. And then they went out into the excited crowds to begin to celebrate.

By nightfall, Sunny and Grace had watched the firework displays, danced in the street, eaten food which had been offered to anyone in uniform at various street parties and caught up with each other's news. With some reluctance they had returned to Lime Street since both were due back in their service positions by next day, and sat on a wooden seat under

478

the clock waiting for their trains and discussing their future. Sunny waxed eloquent on his captain's suggestion that he should stay with the service, and told Grace impressively that he could have a fine career in the Navy even in peacetime. He didn't want to be a sailor for the rest of his life, he told her, but just for a few years, until things were more settled. As he talked, Sunny caught hold of Grace's hand and thought that this was the first time he had noticed a likeness between Grace and Polly, though he knew that they were sisters. Of course Polly was a little raver for looks and Grace no more than passable, but somehow, today, he thought that had he had to choose he would have put Grace as the more striking of the two. Polly had golden curls and blue eyes and a dear little face, but Grace . . . Grace had style, he decided, and a sort of elegance which the bubbly Polly most certainly did not possess. I'm proud to be seen with her, Sunny thought, and was astonished at himself. He was a catch and he knew it, girls flocked round him, always had, and here he was with a girl he had never thought so much as pretty, admiring her style and elegance, two attributes which he had never even thought about before. But he dragged his mind away from his companion's looks and listened to her conversation, noticing also for the first time what a pretty voice she had, with almost no trace of the scouse accent which he himself had retained.

Grace, knowing nothing of his thoughts, continued to talk naturally and earnestly. She had told him several times of her life in New York with Sara, and of how she missed Jamie and her other friends, so now it seemed quite natural to tell him of her plans for the peace. 'I've had a lovely letter from Sara, telling me that I'm welcome to live in the flat again just as soon as I can get a passage,' she said. 'Poor Sara, it's been a horrid time for her, though she's known nothing of the shortages and the bombing and so on. But she doesn't think Brogan will get back as quickly as they would both like, so I suppose she'd be even more pleased to see me.'

Sunny stared at her. He could feel his mouth dropping open and, what was more, suddenly heard his own voice, with a note of almost desperate incredulity in it, say, 'Get a passage? You don't mean . . . you can't mean you're thinkin' of goin' back to the States when the war ends?'

Grace, in her turn, stared. 'Well, I think so,' she said slowly. 'I don't suppose there will be much for me here, Sunny – in the way of work, I mean. What's more, though I could live at the Strawb for a bit, I suppose, I couldn't expect the O'Bradys to take me in again. They'll be having all their family home, not just Polly. No, it's better that I go back to Sara. She says the delicatessen where I used to work were delighted to hear I'd be returning there and said my job was waiting for me. So you see—'

Sunny interrupted her without apology. 'But Grace, you – you don't want to go off, half a world away from – from your pals,' he said. 'Oh, I know I said I'd stick with the Navy for a bit and so I shall, but – but sailors marry, you know, make a home ashore, raise a family. And you and me's always got on great, wouldn't you say? So why go all the way to America, when I'm on your doorstep, queen.'

There was an astounded silence. Sunny, watching Grace's face closely, saw her cheeks flush very becomingly and her eyelids droop over her eyes. Was she angry? Had she not guessed that he was fond of her? Oh, he might not have declared himself so soon, in fact he had made up his mind to tell her that they must meet more often now that peace had been declared, but at the thought of her going right away a lump of ice seemed to have frozen his stomach and a sense of panic assailed him. She was the nicest girl he knew, they had a great deal in common, he couldn't let her go without a struggle! But she was still looking down at her hands and not answering and Sunny realised that he hadn't actually said – well, what he wanted to say. So he took a deep breath and then spoke with more earnestness than he knew he possessed.

'Gracie, I want – I want you to be me girl, not just me bezzie, like you have been.'

'Oh, Sunny,' Grace said, lifting shining eyes to his face. 'It sounds – it sounds . . . But I thought you and Polly . . .'

'Polly's me pal, but only a pal,' Sunny said at once. 'A grand girl, I agree. But she's not the one for me, Grace, and she knows it. I've got me eye on quite a different sort of girl. One who won't fly up into the boughs if I say I'm staying in the Navy for a while, for instance. One who doesn't think an awful lot of herself, but who suits me just fine.'

There was a longish pause before Grace said quietly: 'Oh. I'm sorry, Sunny, I didn't realise you – you had a girl, I just hope I've not spoiled your day, taking it for granted that we'd go about together.'

'That was my idea, not yours,' Sunny said. He leaned across her and took her other hand, pulling her round until they were facing each other. 'Grace, you must know that I like you, enjoy being with you.'

'I hoped you did,' Grace said shyly, the pink colour slowly blooming in her cheeks once more. 'Only there was Polly . . . and there have been heaps and heaps of other girls, you've told me so yourself.'

'Oh aye, but none of them meant anything, really, not even Poll when it came down to brass tacks,' Sunny told her. 'So if you don't mind me staying in the Navy, how about us going steady? We've done a lot of getting to know each other today and we'll need time and a lot of meetings before – well, before we think about getting engaged, but . . . well, how about it?'

'Oh, Sunny, I'd like that,' Grace said breathlessly. 'If you're sure, that is? It 'ud be better than going to the States – better than anything!'

'I'm sure,' Sunny said, and was leaning across to kiss her when, with a shriek of brakes, a train drew into the platform. Above them, the echoing voice of a railway official informed them of the train's various destinations and Sunny stood up. 'No time for anything even when there's a peace on,' he grumbled. 'I'm for this one . . . come and see me off, then I can kiss you without anyone thinking twice about it!'

The day had begun well and went on better, Polly decided as she and Monica, with Deirdre on one side of them and Peader the other, fought their way first on to a tram and then off it again, to surge amongst the cheering, stamping, flag-waving crowds and to cry a little because everyone was so happy. The crowd cheered wildly – Mr Churchill first, of course, then the King and the Queen, then the royal children. In the midst of such excitement it would have been hard to remember one's own personal troubles. Polly, determined not to think about Tad, found that for the moment at any rate she was simply responding to the happiness around her, and when someone started to play the National Anthem on an accordion she joined in with the rest, bawling out the words raucously.

'Do you realise, Mon, that some of these kids haven't ever heard the church bells ring before?' Polly shouted at one point as the bells of the nearest church began their long, loud-mouthed clamour. 'Well, I suppose they might have, but not that they can remember, I mean.'

'I know what you mean,' Monica shouted back. 'Look, fireworks!'

It was a waste, but who could resist letting off fireworks when they were so glad? Polly squeaked as the rockets whizzed past her and up into the blue, bursting in a shower of almost invisible sparks, so strong was the sunshine. And presently she began to pick out the faces of people she knew – old friends from school, mostly in uniform, neighbours, shop-keepers, even. It's an odd thing, so it is, Polly found herself ruminating, but to Liverpool people the city's like a honeypot to bees – they have to come back. They can go to the ends of the earth, I do believe, but at the end of the day they'll come back to Liverpool. Why, neither Sunny nor Grace had any thought about spending VE Day where they were stationed; they both wanted to come home, to come back here, and so they have, no doubt. If they aren't here yet, they soon will be, I'm sure of that. Oh, I do hope they come round to Snowdrop Street, otherwise . . . well, it will be a quiet sort of day for me.

It was a day to remember, the sort of day, Polly reflected, which would still be in people's memories in fifty or so years' time. People who scarcely knew one another hugged and danced together, boys climbed on to the statues in St George's Plain and hung flags from the ears of a great bronze horse, girls put wreaths of spring flowers on the statue of Queen Victoria and decorated the huge stone lions crouched on their plinths in the same way. And as darkness fell everyone watched the uprush of rockets, the whirl of Catherine wheels, the flaring brilliance of Roman candles.

The street party in the late afternoon had been a great success, with the children so excited at first that they could scarcely eat, and then so drunk with the wonder of it that they could scarcely stop and crammed their mouths with sausage rolls, sandwiches and little cakes until their parents declared they were quite ashamed – though they, too, had been busy reducing the feast to a memory.

Yet two things stood out in Polly's mind as the family made their way slowly homewards. One had occurred halfway through the afternoon, when she and Monica had gone off for half an hour to join in the dancing taking place in a nearby gardens, and she had seen, through the crowd, a young man she was almost certain was Sunny. Well, she told herself reasonably, how could she mistake that bright blond hair and the height of him?

She had caught Monica's arm, shouting that she had seen Sunny, that he was probably searching for her . . . and then, even as she fought her way towards him, she had seen him sling an arm around the shoulders of his companion and lean down, to lightly kiss the side of her face. The girl had looked up and in that instant, Polly had recognised her and stopped pushing her way through the good-humoured crowd.

It was Grace! Grace Carbery who was Polly's sister and whom Polly had always considered to be good but plain. But now, in that fleeting moment, Polly saw that Grace was not plain at all, she was very pretty, with silky brown hair and a straight little nose. And when Grace looked up at Sunny – for it was definitely he – Polly also saw, with a cold little shock, that Grace's eyes were brimming with affection for the young man whom she, Polly, had once thought of as her own property. Oh, she did not want him, not if she could have her dear old Tad, but nevertheless . . .

It had shaken her considerably, however. She stood where she was for a moment and saw the couple swallowed up in the crowd, and then turned and made her way back to Monica. 'Did you find Sunny?' Monica asked, pushing her hair behind her ears and smiling at Polly. 'Only the crowd's so thick—'

'No,' Polly said shortly. 'Never mind. Come on, let's go back to Snowdrop Street.' And they had done so, with Polly trying very hard not to keep searching the surrounding faces for Tad, because though she knew he was not coming, she could not help hoping that he might still turn up.

The second thing that she would remember, she thought now, plodding tiredly along beside Monica through the dark and emptying streets, was Monica herself. At one point, when the fireworks were at their most dazzling, Polly had looked at her sister-in-law and she had seen that Monica's face was streaked with tears.

It had brought it home to her, then, that on this wonderful day which she was enjoying so much, there were people shut up in their homes with hearts which must be breaking when they thought of their own young people, their husbands, children, lovers, who would not be coming home now that the peace had come. There were girls like Monica who were brave

485

and loving, who told themselves every morning, every night, that they were waiting for news, that their husbands, lovers, brothers were safe. But in their hearts there had to be a little seed of doubt, a suspicion that what they were rejoicing in was premature, that for them there might be no cause to rejoice.

As the glare from the rockets died down Monica turned away for a moment, and when she turned back Polly saw that she had rubbed her face dry, that her eyes seemed to be no brighter than other eyes in that great throng. 'What a day!' Monica said, taking Polly's arm. 'We shan't forget today in a hurry, our Poll!'

And Polly, giving her a hug, talking brightly, though with a little catch in her voice, thought that Monica was braver and more loving than anyone she knew. She wouldn't want to spoil anyone's fun by showing a long face on this day so she was putting all her courage and strength into an enormous pretence – Oh God, let Martin be safe, Polly prayed. I'll buy the biggest candle in the city and light it for Martin tomorrow so I will. And I'll have a word with God about Monica, too, while I'm about it. Because it had been two years since the last sighting of Martin, if it had been Martin, and in that time the allied forces had over-run Italy, releasing prisoners and searching out the men who had gone on the run. Even to Polly's desperately optimistic hopes it seemed strange indeed that Martin had not got in touch with them. If he was alive that was. Peader, with his eyes full of sympathy, had tried to tell her not to expect miracles.

'Hope is good, but I can't help thinkin' if our Mart had been alive that someone would've been in touch,' he had said. 'Just you pray, alanna, same as your mammy and I do.'

But right now Polly turned to Monica with her brightest smile. 'I'll walk up to the Pier Head with you because you'll be wanting a number 17 and then I'll have to come back here to catch my own tram,' she said. 'It's been such a grand evening that making it last a little longer suits me just fine.'

When the two girls reached the Pier Head, however, there were still a great many people about and the queue stretched a considerable distance. 'But it doesn't really matter,' Polly said as they joined the end of the queue, 'because we'll be able to lie in for a bit tomorrow morning. Oh, but you've got to walk from Seaforth to Waterloo if you catch this tram . . . Is there anything that would take you all the way, alanna?'

Monica, however, assured Polly that she did not mind the walk and since there were several WRNs in the queue ahead of them she would have company all the way home. The wrennery, which had once been the Royal Hotel on the corner of Marine Terrace, was an enormous building and housed a great number of girls, so some at least of the WRNs in the queue would be making their way back to it. Indeed, Monica spotted several friends ahead of them and assured Polly that the walk, in such company, would be more enjoyable than a taxi ride – and far less expensive.

'Not that we'd gerra taxi at this time of night,' she added comfortably. 'Don't you worry, Polly, your mam said I could stay over if I wanted, but I decided to go back. Me and me mates will have a good jangle before settling down to sleep, and – and it takes me mind off things.'

And presently, two trams, both 17s, drew up at the stop and Monica crammed on to the second one, Polly stepping back but waiting to wave as the tram drew away.

'It's been a grand day,' Monica shouted over her shoulder as she was pushed and shoved further down the tram. 'Tell Mam and Dad I'll come over later in the week. Night, Poll!'

'It was much more fun 'cos we were together, Monica,' Polly called back, and then turned away and with one last wave started to make her way towards Lime Street and her tram home. Polly was luckier than Monica, boarding a 24 no more than two minutes after arriving there and when they reached her stop she got thankfully down off the step into the comfortable warmth and brightness of Stanley Road. What a good thing the blackout's done with at last, she told herself, for with most of the shop windows brightly lit she could see her way perfectly. Only fancy, she said to herself as she turned away from the tram stop, this time last month the sight of one of those lights would have brought a warden's wrath down on the head of whoever had neglected to draw curtains or blinds. Oh, isn't peace a wonderful thing now?

Smiling to herself, Polly turned her steps towards Snowdrop Street and her own bed. She was very tired indeed, and now that she and Monica had parted and the excitement was over she could no longer deny a sort of inner flatness, as though the day had sucked all the life and enthusiasm out of her, leaving her little more than an empty husk.

It's that old Tad, I did think he might have turned up despite what he said, Polly told herself as she plodded along the pavement, but though she was no longer buoyed up by the mad excitement of the day she soon began to enjoy the walk. Lights streaming out of so many windows despite the lateness of the hour were still a novelty, a bonfire on a bomb-site glowed red and the trams, bicycles and occasional cars making their way along the street were comforting to one used to the pitch darkness of a blacked-out city.

And presently, Polly reached Snowdrop Street and turned down it, realising that her legs were extremely tired, that she would not be at all sorry to climb the stairs and get into her bed, even though her day had not been quite what she had planned. Her house was in darkness, however, which meant that if she went by the front door she would have to wake someone up, so she retraced her steps and went down the jigger, finding her way easily despite the fact that it was a good deal darker here than in the main street. She opened the gate into their own yard, headed for the back door and the key always kept hung up on a nail behind the bird-box fixed to the wall – and gave a startled squeak. A man detached himself from the shadows where he had apparently been waiting and came towards her.

'Polly?'

Polly's hand flew to her heart. It was Tad, after all – Tad, who had said he couldn't get here, wouldn't get here! He was right here in front of her, a grin on his brown face, teeth gleaming white, hands going out to her . . .

She had meant to say that he had frightened her, she had even meant to reproach him a little before admitting that she was glad to see him, but somehow nothing happened quite as she had intended. Instead, she heard herself give a muffled sob as she crossed the distance between them in one jump and threw herself into his arms. Those arms closed round her, infinitely

489

warm and comforting, and Tad's voice said in her ear: 'You're not cryin', are you, Poll? And I t'ought you'd be pleased to see me, so I did!'

'Oh, I – I am pleased, I am, I am,' Polly snuffled against his tunic. 'Oh, Tad, I was horrid to you, wasn't I? And I do love you most awfully much, so I do, and I t'ought you didn't like me one bit and I couldn't blame you because I'd been horrid, not a bit nice, and I was jealous of that Jenny girl, and I wanted to punish you . . . Only Tad, I love you more than anyone else in the world, and I want to be with you even if you know I'm not a nice girl at all. So there!'

'That's good to hear,' Tad said, a hand smoothing the curls away from Polly's hot forehead and then caressing her cheek, wiping away the wet of her tears. 'But we need to talk, Poll. Where can we go?'

'Indoors,' Polly said at once. She reached up and plucked the key from its hidden hook. 'In the kitchen; there's no one still up, Mammy and Daddy will have been in bed hours since.'

As she spoke she was unlocking the back door and ushering Tad into the kitchen, still warm from the day of sunshine as well as from the fire smouldering away in the stove. Now, she took off her coat and hung it on the back of the door, motioning Tad to do likewise. Beaming with a pleasure which she was quite unable to conceal she lit the lamp with a taper from the fire and then turned to her companion. 'We can talk very well in here,' she said, pulling one of the chairs nearer to the fire. 'I'll put the kettle on – how long were you standing in our back yard waiting for me to get home, dearest Tad? And when did you leave Lincoln? Oh, and why did you come, when you said you wouldn't? Couldn't, I mean,' she amended hastily as Tad opened his mouth to speak. 'I know it wasn't your fault really, I know you were only being fair to your pals, but . . . well, here you are, so . . .'

'Here I am,' Tad agreed. He had taken off his own coat and hung it next to Polly's and now, as she bustled about getting out tea, milk and cups, he sat himself down in the chair she had indicated. 'Well, the truth is, Poll, that I didn't altogether trust your sudden desire for me companionship. After all, alanna, you'd spent months keeping me at arm's length, you'd told me over and over how fond you were of Sunny What's-his-name, you'd assured me that you thought of me as a brother . . .'

'I didn't mean it,' Polly muttered, turning back towards him. 'I – I was all mixed up that night, you know, Tad. I know I was thinking backwards – all wrong, I mean – but it's a strange t'ing to discover that you're not your own mammy's and daddy's girl, after all. I reckon I didn't know what I was saying, not really. Oh, and I know I probably said the same thing again in me letters, but I was still all muddled up in me mind, you see,' she added hastily. 'For ages and ages I just told meself that I wanted you as a friend. Then I realised that I couldn't bear a – a future which didn't have you in it.'

'That's grand to hear, so it is,' Tad said, but Polly thought he still didn't sound as though he completely believed what she was saying. 'The trouble is, Poll, it took me a long while to get you out of me system, like, and I don't fancy having to do it again if your mind does one of its quick-change tricks. You see, I don't know *why* you've suddenly decided that – well, that I'm the feller for you and not Sunny What's-his-name.'

Polly began to pour the tea. The trouble was, she reminded herself, that her own realisation that Tad was the only person she could ever love had come, not as a result of any one thing, but more as a gentle flow of gradually increasing conviction. In fact, now that she thought about it seriously, it had been her awareness that Sunny was not the man of her dreams which had made her realise it was Tad who mattered to her. But how to explain to him so that he would understand, see that this time there would be no changing of her mind, no going back. She was the old, loving Polly who had known from the time she had been just a child that Tad was her other half, her mate. This, she realised, was an important moment in her life and this time there must be no mistakes, no wrong words or misunderstandings. This time she must make Tad see that she was in deadly earnest.

So she carried the tea over to the fire and sat down in the chair opposite him. 'It happened because I wanted to go back to Holyhead, where I'd been so happy, and have a leave there,' she said, speaking slowly, her eyes on his face. 'I needed some time alone, I think, Tad. Time to consider just what I did want in my life. So anyway, I went back, and some-how, Holyhead wasn't as special as I'd expected it to be. It was almost as if there was something missing. Anyway, I went off by meself to the clifftops above the sea with sandwiches and that, and I lay on the turf and thought. I thought about Sunny, and being married, and then I *knew* that marrying Sunny would be the greatest mistake of me life. He's a grand feller, he's handsome and tall and girls like him, but . . . I realised when I had a chance to think properly, on that quiet clifftop, that I didn't love him. Not even a tiny bit and – and the feller I wanted to be beside me for ever wasn't tall or golden-haired or any of that rubbish, it was – well, it was you, Tad.'

'Right. And this was how long ago?' Tad asked rather dryly. 'A year? Nine months?'

'Well, no, it wasn't as long as that—' Polly began, to be swiftly interrupted.

'You mean it was just weeks ago? Oh, Poll, who's to say you won't change your mind again in another few weeks? After all, you've not seen Sunny once since your trip to Anglesey, have you? You might set eyes on him—'

'I have seen him, so,' Polly said vehemently, standing her mug down on the floor beside her and getting to her feet. 'I saw him this very afternoon, and did I get one single feeling that he was me feller? No, I did not! He was with Grace, what's more, but if he and she were to get together – which I know very well they won't – Oh, Tad, I want you!' The last words came out almost as a wail and with them, Polly cast herself at Tad's knees, clasping them tightly and then burying her head in his lap. 'Don't – don't you want me even a little bit?' she said on a snuffle.

There was a moment's silence and then Tad leaned down and heaved her on to his lap. With both arms tightly round her and his mouth against her hair he said: 'Polly me darlin' girl, you don't know how much I want you! You're all I've ever wanted, that's God's truth, and when you decided you didn't want me – well, I was cut to the heart, so I was, and for a bit life just didn't seem worth living. Only I made meself think sensibly and I got over it, more or less. That's why I don't want to go through all that pain again.'

'Oh, Tad,' Polly muttered. 'Oh, Tad, it wasn't the real me, it was just plain stupidity, and – and being a bit bedazzled by Sunny's looks. But all that's over and done, I swear it on a stack of Bibles, I'll never look at

493

another feller so long as we both live.' She looked up at him, seeing him through a dazzle of tears. 'Won't you give me a chance to prove I mean it, though, darlin' Tad? Because if you won't – or can't, even – then I don't know what I'll do.'

'Well, we'll give it a go, then,' Tad said, suddenly cheerful. 'Ooh, you're a cuddly armful, so you are! But we can't sit here like this all night. I've only got a forty-eight, so I'll have to be off back to Lincoln at the crack of dawn, which means trying to grab some sleep tonight. I'd best see if I can find a lodging house still open.'

'You'll do no such thing,' Polly said softly but with determination. 'Mammy and Daddy would be shocked at me if I let you go off when we've an inch of space to spare. And – and tomorrer, I'm coming wit' you back to Lincoln so's we can talk some more, because there's things we need to say, Tad.'

'But not tomorrer,' Tad said with emphasis. 'I don't want to see you court-martialled, alanna. We'll do everything the proper way, for once. I'll go back to Lincoln and get meself some leave and you'll go back to being a despatch rider until you're demobbed. Agreed?'

And Polly, opening her mouth to say hotly that she would do no such thing, that she did not care if she were court-martialled so long as she was with Tad, heard her own voice saying meekly: 'Sure an' if that's what you think is best, darlin' Tad,' and knew that she had grown up at last.

It was comfortable in the O'Bradys front parlour, with a couple of blankets and a pillow and the comfortable couch all to himself, but even so Tad found it hard to go to sleep. For one thing, he was uneasily conscious that it was past midnight which meant that

494

he could only sleep for about five hours at the most. His squadron leader had given him a forty-eight as a special favour, it really would be a shabby thing if he was late back, so he must be at the station early because he had no idea what time the first train heading for Lincoln left, but no matter how unearthly an hour it should prove he really meant to be aboard.

For another thing, though, he was as pleased and excited as he had ever been, and pleasurable excitement is no aid in getting to sleep. He knew, now, that he had been right to call Polly's bluff when she had simply turned up unannounced in Lincolnshire to tell him she was fond of him and wanted to resume their old relationship. He had not told her so this evening, but in fact he had decided not even to try to get back to Liverpool for the celebrations, only once the great day dawned he had found it quite impossible not to try to get to Polly just as soon as he could. Having told his squadron leader that he would be staying on the station he had had to explain that things had altered and leapt aboard the first transport heading into the city. He had gone at once to the station and from then on had cursed every slow train, every missed connection, as he worked his way steadily cross-country towards his girl. But he had made it at last, only to realise that the house in Snowdrop Street was deserted. He had imagined Polly in Sunny's arms, being comforted because he, Tad, had been so cruel to her, and had ground his teeth with rage at his own foolishness. Why hadn't he admitted that he loved her, wanted only her? Why had he played out the charade that he was too hurt to risk being hurt again? But now he was glad, because his little darling really was his little darling now. He had no more doubts, only a wonderful, warm glow of certainty. Polly was his and he was Polly's, and now they could stop wasting time and start to plan their lives together.

So after he and Polly had kissed goodnight she had gone upstairs to fetch blankets from the spare room, and had come down again with a pile of bedding and the information that Mammy had still been awake, and had said to say sorry she wasn't coming down herself to welcome him but it was awful late, and would he make himself at home, please, and not to leave in the morning before Polly had got up and made him breakfast and a packed lunch for the train.

Tad had felt good after that. He was no longer an interloper in the O'Brady house but an invited guest, and since Polly had promised to set her alarm for five o'clock so that she might come down and wake him and see to his breakfast he should have had no qualms about going to sleep and fitting himself for another day of travel on the morrow.

The trouble was, he could not sleep, and it soon occurred to him that Polly, too, would be wide awake and this re-activated his worry about her finally dozing off and sleeping through the alarm clock's bell, and very soon he was sitting up on the couch, with the pillow across his shoulders, determined not to risk so much as half an hour of slumber.

When, after about an hour of this, the parlour door creaked open and a small figure wrapped in a pink eiderdown and with an alarm clock in one hand and a very guilty expression crept into the room, he was so pleased that he nearly cried out. In fact, he remembered in time that there were two O'Brady parents upstairs and merely whispered: 'Poll! I can't sleep, I was scared of not waking in time for the early train, but I see you guessed how it would be and brought me the clock – thanks, alanna. But you need your rest, you've had a long day, same as I have, so you go up again now, and go to sleep and don't bother about waking up for me. I can get meself a bit of bread and scrape and a cuppa and then be on my way. Off wit' you, Polly me darlin'.'

Polly, however, came over to the couch and sat down beside him, standing the alarm clock on the small occasional table in front of it. She smiled at him but shook her head in a very determined fashion. 'No, Tad, I'll not be going back upstairs to lie awake and worry that you'll miss the bleedin' train,' she told him in a very composed tone. 'Besides, there's a lot we've not had time to talk about, I want to ask you . . . oh, about lots of things. And since we can neither of us sleep – I'm still all lit up and excited inside about us, and about not being at war, and remembering the fireworks and the bonfires – we might as well be awake together, don't you think?'

'So I do,' Tad said, giving in happily and putting an arm around her slender shoulders. 'Lean on me, Poll, and let's talk!'

'Where will we start, though?' Polly said, settling herself comfortably in the hollow of Tad's shoulder. 'I feel as if I've lived *years* that you don't know about, Tad. Are you goin' to tell me what you did after I'd said – the things that I said? Only I don't think I want to know.'

Tad laughed. 'No, I don't suppose you do, and it wouldn't make very interestin' listening,' he agreed. 'So let's start with you, Poll. You don't mind about being adopted now, do you, Poll? And you don't mind that Grace is your sister?'

'No, I don't mind, exactly,' Polly said in rather a subdued voice. 'Because I know that Mammy and Daddy love me ever so much and did everything they

497

could to make me happy. But I do wonder about my angel, Tad. Do you remember her? I told you about her when I was only a kid, and you thought I was going soft in the head I daresay, but – but I really did see her, Tad, often and often. In fact, it's only this past year or so that I've not seen her.'

'I believe you saw your angel,' Tad said. 'I'm not saying I understand it, Poll, but I do think you saw . . . well, something, at any rate.'

'Someone, not something,' Polly put in. 'But what I don't understand, Tad, is why the angel came to me? Why didn't she go to Grace, who needed an angel so very badly? She was the one who was left alone, not me.'

'Oh, Poll, you will keep looking at things from your own point of view and never from anyone else's,' Tad said, sighing and kissing the top of Polly's curly golden head. 'Can't you see, even now? Your mammy told you that she thought your angel was really your big sister Jess, didn't she?'

'Sure she did, and I suppose she might have been right,' Polly said rather grudgingly. Tad, grinning, thought that if you'd imagined a guardian angel with great white wings and a good deal of influence with the Lord it was rather a comedown to admit that the angel was just a skinny, dirty little slum child who had been killed by a train whilst searching for shelter in the shunting yards. Still, Polly was clearly coming round to the idea. 'But if it's true that my angel was really Jess, then why didn't she take care of Grace? Grace was her sister too, remember.'

'That's what I'm trying to tell you, alanna,' Tad said gently. 'Sure an' you will look at things from your own point of view all the time – amn't I telling you so, time and again? Look at it from Jess's angle, won't you! She

498

was in charge of a young baby, the baby she had looked after almost from birth. And because she was cold and worried and in a hurry she went and got herself killed by a train, leaving that little baby to fend for itself. Don't you see now, alanna?'

'But I was all right; Brogan took care of me, carried me over the sea to Mammy and Daddy, and after that I didn't really need anyone – except for you, Tad,' Polly said quickly. 'So that dog won't run, me fine friend!'

'But Jess wasn't appearing to you because you needed her, Poll. She was doing it because she needed *you*,' Tad explained as patiently as he could. He had found it hard to understand himself, at first, but now that he had come to terms with Polly and her angel it seemed impossible that Polly should still not see. 'I guess that she loved you with a deep, possessive love – and why should she not? She'd made a pretty good job of bringing you up from what Brogan told your mammy, and she *needed* to see you, to watch over you, to make sure you were all right.'

There was a long pause whilst Polly clearly gave this new idea all her attention. Then she heaved a great, deep sigh. 'I do see, now,' she said at last. 'Then – then I won't ever see my angel again, will I? Because I'm really grown up now – and I've got you, Tad. For ever and ever.'

'That's right, Poll,' Tad said gently. 'You've got me now, for ever and ever.' And he put both arms around her and drew her close. 'Do you know, I've never kissed you, Poll? And if we're giving it a go, then I think . . .'

Polly put her face up to his and their lips met and clung.

*

At five o'clock the alarm went off and by six Tad was kissing her goodbye and setting off for the station. Polly would have liked to have gone with him, but Tad said she should go up to her room and get a bit of sleep before her work started later. Polly agreed, therefore, to telephone his airfield that evening to make sure he had got back safely, waved him off and then went meekly back into the house. Light was beginning to filter through the curtains as she climbed the stairs to her room, filled with a happiness yet with a thread of sadness running through it because she was going to have to say goodbye to her angel, and, she knew, to her carefree girlhood.

I've grown up at last, so I have, she thought to herself, sleepily climbing the stairs. I thought I was a woman ages ago, but now I know it took almost losing Tad and then finding him again and sharing a real, proper love to grow me up. And as she reached the head of the stairs she looked back . . . and thought she saw, standing on the half-landing, a barefoot girl in a long, draggly shawl who looked up at her fleetingly for a moment and gave her the most beautiful smile before she was gone, and only the shadow of the bannisters remained, and dust motes swirling in a pale sunshine's ray.

Polly stopped still for a moment. 'Goodbye, Jess,' she said in a voice no louder than a whisper. 'I'm proud to have known you, and in a way I'll miss you . . . but I'll have Tad now, so long as we both shall live, and that's enough for anyone.'

For a moment she waited. For a sign? For one more glimpse of that sweet, fragile presence? But she knew suddenly, with a deep inner certainty, that she would never see her angel again. Not, at any rate, in this world.

As she let herself into her bedroom she realised that there would be no more blackout, no more dark, dangerous streets, and very soon no more despatch riding, no more exciting uniform. No more war.

Polly crossed the room and threw the blanket she had wrapped herself in back on to the bed, then climbed between the sheets. What a day – well, what a night, come to that! She and Tad had talked and talked, and worked out how their life would go on for the next few months and she hadn't thought once about a white wedding or a wonderful honeymoon somewhere exciting, she had simply thought how marvellous it would be not to have to say goodnight to Tad and go their separate ways. I'm lucky, so I am, she thought, snuggling down. Peace is beginning and Tad and I will tackle whatever it may bring together. Come to that, everyone is having to tackle it now. Sunny will leave the Navy and Grace the WAAF and the boys will come home and . . . For a moment she thought about that odd sighting across the crowd, of Grace and Sunny in each other's arms. Had she really seen them? If so, what did it mean? But her own happiness was so enormous that she could not speculate for too long on anyone's else's future. Tomorrow, she thought drowsily. Tomorrow I'll get down to wondering what Sunny and Grace were doing together, tomorrow I'll think about Martin and the others and pray they all get home safe, tomorrow . . .

And Polly was asleep.

A Long and Lonely Road

For Dorothy Nelson, of Appley Bridge, whose story of the bombing of Liverpool on the worst night of the Blitz I have shamelessly borrowed. Thank you Dorothy!

Acknowledgements

Grateful thanks go, as they have gone so many times, to Alan Hague, a stalwart supporter of the Flixton Aviation Museum, whose knowledge of Norfolk and Suffolk airfields, and the planes that flew from them, is truly unparalleled.

Thanks go also to Graham Jones of Rhosddu, Wrexham, who shared his knowledge of life – and death – in submarines and to Flt Lt John Taylor of Rhuddlan, who lent me a rare book on Liverpool during the war which had not previously come my way.

And then there is Gwyn Thomas of the Suffolk Records Office, who set us on the track of a hurricane which caused extensive damage in 1943. And thank you Gwilym Williams of Wrexham, for straightening me out on the Welsh language and correcting my spelling.

And last but not least, grateful thanks to Joy Thomas of The Heritage Museum in Wrexham, who worked extremely hard to track down the evacuation of Liverpool children to the small town of Ruthin during the war.

Chapter One
1938

'Petal! What the devil are you doing? Oh, if our mam saw you now, she'd give you such a wallop! Come on out of it this minute, d'you hear me?'

Four-year-old Petal twisted round to look up into her elder sister's face. She tried to move and when this proved impossible, she gave Daisy a sweet smile but remained where she was, crouched on the dirty paving stones with one arm thrust as far as she could get it between the iron bars of the drainage grating. 'I'm stuck,' she said. 'Me cherry wob bounced out of the downpipe and went straight into the drain. I could see it so I put me hand in to gerrit back, only – only it were further off than I thought an' now I can't pull me arm out, though I've tried ever so hard, honest to God I have.'

Daisy gazed despairingly down at her small sister. Petal had soft fair curls, big blue eyes and an enchanting smile, yet she was always in trouble. Often she got away with it because grown-ups could not believe that such an angelic-looking child could be as naughty as Petal was. They thought it far likelier that Daisy, who had straight brown hair and a thin, intelligent face, would be the one who thought up all the mischief. But now Petal's enormous blue eyes were beginning to brim with tears; it was clear that in her imagination she was never going to escape and would be in the most awful trouble.

Daisy sighed, and had crouched on the paving stones

to examine her sister's plight more closely when a shadow loomed over her and a voice spoke in her ear.

'What's the little tyke done this time, then? Gawd, Daisy, when I thinks how your mam sends you out each mornin', clean as a whistle an' fine as fivepence, then how your kid ends up the way she does . . . well, it's downright strange, that's wharrit is.'

Daisy turned round and eyed the speaker indignantly. It was Nicky Bostock, who lived two doors away at No. 11, Bernard Terrace, and how he dared criticise anyone else for being dirty she could not imagine, for Nicky was filthy, from the top of his dusty head to the soles of his bare and blackened feet. Daisy knew he was not altogether to blame for this because he was what her mother called 'a passed-down child'. This apparently meant that his own parents had disappeared long ago and he had lived, for as long as he could remember, with a foster mother and father, neither of whom was related to him by blood. In fact, Mam said she thought Nicky coped very well, maintaining as much independence as possible and steering clear of the Ryans whenever Mr Ryan was drunk, or Mrs Ryan wanted a scapegoat.

Right now, however, Nicky was grinning down at her and Daisy felt she should support her small sister. 'It isn't her fault this time,' she said defensively. 'She must have fallen over and her arm's got jammed down the bleedin' drain. Anyway, what business is it of yours, Nicky nosy Bostock?'

Nicky grinned, clearly not at all insulted. 'Fell over!' he said derisively. 'Who d'you think you're kiddin', Daisy McAllister? I seen her playin' cherry wobs wi' young Jacky; she were fishin' out one what went down the drain, that's what she were doin', dirty little bugger.'

Daisy's eyes widened. She sometimes swore herself when in company with her peers, but the word 'bugger' was strictly forbidden to her and Petal, though they heard it often enough on their father's lips. She was about to reply indignantly that he should mind what he said and stop cussing, when Petal piped up.

'I isn't a dirty little bugger,' she said tearfully, if untruthfully. 'Oh, Daisy, do stop arguing and help me! I'm stuck, I tell you!'

'Let me have a look,' Nicky said gruffly, kneeling down next to Daisy. The child had rolled up the sleeve of her ragged cardigan to well above the elbow and had jammed her arm in so hard that two purplish marks showed where the bars had caught it. But surely, if her hand had gone in, then it should have come out, Daisy thought confusedly. She was still trying to work out what best to do when Nicky spoke. 'Aw, Gawd, trust a bleedin' girl,' he said, leaning over and seizing Petal's arm, none too gently. 'She put her hand in to fetch out the cherry wob flat like, but now she's gorrit in her fist. So, a' course, she can't gerrit out again.' He shook Petal's arm impatiently. 'Lerrit go, you little thickhead, or you're there for life, I'm tellin' you.'

Petal gave a wail of protest, so Daisy said reassuringly: 'Nicky's right, Petal. If you flatten your hand out, it'll come out easy peasy. After all, it's only a cherry wob, when all's said and done.'

'It ain't, it's three,' Petal wailed, her fist still obstinately closed. 'I found two others in the mud when I were diggin' for mine, an' if I flatten me hand out I'll lose 'em all. It took me ages to reach them an' I got ever so mucky. I *can't* leggo of them now.'

'Then you're there for life, kiddo,' Daisy said grimly. She knew better than to try to reason with Petal;

3

threats might work, diplomacy never would. 'Well, I'm off home, it's dinner time. Are you coming, Nick?'

Petal's face grew pink and she tugged fruitlessly, then turned to her sister once more, a smile curving those angelic lips. 'Oh, Daisy, I've had an idea, a real good 'un! We can do it if you'll help me and it won't take more'n a few seconds. If I open me hand, you can put two fingers through the bars – they'll fit easy – an' take the cherry wobs off of me. I can't do it meself 'cos me other hand's proppin' me up. Oh come on, Daisy, be me pal.'

Daisy could not help smiling to herself. When it came to getting what she wanted, Petal could outsmart most. She was about to agree to have a go when Nick intervened. 'You're that sticky wi' mud, I reckon that the cherry wobs will come up with you if you goes through the bars slow an' careful, like,' he said. 'As soon as your palm's clear of the grating, I'll pick 'em off.'

The manoeuvre was completed successfully and Petal stood up, rubbing her cramped knees and grinning happily as Nick handed over the precious cherry wobs. Her face was dirt- and tear-streaked but her smile was so sunny that both the older children found themselves smiling in return. 'Thanks, Nicky,' Petal said gratefully. She turned to her sister. 'Is it really dinner time, Daisy, only I'm starving.'

'Me, too,' Nicky said. 'I'd best go in an' see if I can talk old Ma Ryan into givin' me some bread an' a cut o' cheese.' As the girls headed for their door, he strolled alongside them, suddenly remarking: 'You doin' anythin' after dinner, Daisy? Fancy a stroll down to the river? Or we could go to the gardens?'

Daisy looked doubtful. She had suspected for some time that Nicky rather liked her; he tended to hang about in her vicinity, and often walked home from school with her, though he seldom attended himself. The trouble was, he was generally known to be what her mam called 'a bit on the sharp side'. Daisy knew he stole, nicking fruit off the stalls, rooting through the bins at the back of Taylor's bakery shop in Stitt Street for stale buns, or broken sausage rolls. She knew he had to do this – food was always short in the Ryan household – but knew, also, that adults did not condone such behaviour and would blame her equally if he stole whilst in her company. So she said that she and Petal were going out with their mam and gave Petal a glare when the younger girl opened her mouth to argue. She looked a trifle apprehensively at Nicky because she did not want to hurt his feelings – he had rescued her little sister after all – but he appeared to have taken the remark at its face value.

'Okay,' he said cheerfully. 'I'll mebbe walk you home from school on Monday, then,' and with a casual wave of one hand, he was gone.

Daisy turned to Petal as they went down the jigger, heading for their back door. 'Honest to God, Petal, the scrapes you get in!' she said. 'And where was your pal Jacky, anyway? If he were a real pal, he'd have helped you to get out, not just run off.'

'He were losin' . . . well, until my cherry stone went down the drain, he were,' Petal said sunnily. 'He ran off with all the cherry wobs except the one down the grating, so I'm going to kill him after I've had me dinner.'

Daisy laughed. 'If Mam hasn't killed you first,' she observed. 'She sent you out clean, if not tidy, and Nicky was right, now you look a real little scruff bag.' She bent over her sister to straighten her stained and spattered cardigan, then reeled back, a hand flying to

5

her nose. 'Petal, you stink! You smell worse'n the privy on a summer's day. It's a good job our dad ain't due back in port till tomorrow or he'd have had your hide – and mine, and Mam's as well – if he got one whiff.'

'I can't help it, Daisy. Drains is smelly things an' I were stuck in that one for hours and hours,' Petal said. 'Anyway, it weren't *my* idea to try to get the cherry wob back, it were horrible Jacky's. He tried with a stick but that weren't no good, so he said since I had the skinniest arms and it were my stone, I'd better have a go meself. It were him rolled up me cardy sleeve,' she added, with a touch of resentment, 'and when I first put my hand through the grid and the pong came up, he said I were a ninny and bet me two liquorice sticks that I'd never reach it. He dared me, Daisy, and no one can refuse a dare, can they?'

'No, I suppose you had to have a try, though I wouldn't have,' Daisy said. 'It's too bad of Jacky to put a dare on a kid of four – why, he's seven, isn't he?'

'Six or seven,' Petal admitted. 'But it's no use saying I'm only four, because if I do that he won't let me play with his gang, an' I like boys' games better'n girls', so I do.'

'Oh, come on, Petal,' Daisy said reproachfully. 'You and Fanny play at shop and tea parties and all sorts when she's around. I bet you were only playing with Jacky because Mrs Hanson had taken Fanny to do the messages.'

'Ye-es, Fanny weren't there. But I *do* like playing with Jacky's gang,' Petal said obstinately. 'And he owes me two liquorice sticks because I got the cherry wob back, didn't I, Daisy? So it's ya boo and sucks to him, isn't it?'

Daisy laughed; she couldn't help it. Jacky was a

6

right little bruiser but Petal wasn't afraid of him, not she. 'All right, have it your own way,' she said, as she opened the back door. 'But I wouldn't be too keen to tackle Jacky meself.'

'Yes, but Jacky says his teacher told them that boys were never to hit girls, so that's all right.' She turned large blue eyes up to her sister's face. 'Only if boys shouldn't hit girls, then why is it all right for dads to hit mams?' she enquired, as they entered the kitchen. Daisy felt her face warm as the blood rushed to her cheeks and she looked guiltily across to her mother frying potatoes in a large blackened pan on the stove, but Rose McAllister did not appear to have heard. She turned as the two children entered, and Daisy thought how pretty her mother was with her dark hair tied back from her face with a piece of twine, her cheeks flushed from the heat of cooking and her big, dark eyes with their curling lashes seeming to smile at them both. My mam's always smart, though her clothes are old, Daisy thought with pride. Why, even with the big calico apron wrapped round her, you can see how small her waist is and how clean and neat she is.

'Oh, Mam, Petal's got herself mucky. I'll give her hands and face a bit of a wipe at the sink, but her cardy's covered in mud; can I take her upstairs to find a clean one?'

Daisy did not want to tell her mother that her little sister stank like a midden but soon realised it would not be necessary. Rose glanced down at Petal and gasped as the smell hit her. 'Cripes, Petal, whatever have you been doing? If that pong is coming from your woolly, you'd best dump it in the sink and I'll deal with it later,' she said, as Daisy picked up the dishcloth and began vigorously rubbing at her sister's face and hands. 'I'd ask what you've been up to only I bet I'd rather not know.' She watched as the filthy cardigan was dropped into the sink and said, as her children trotted past her, heading for the stairs, 'Don't be long now, these spuds are almost ready; I give you two minutes at the outside.'

'Awright, Mam, we'll be back before the cat can lick her ear,' Daisy said cheerfully, shepherding her little sister out of the room. 'We love fried spuds, don't us, Petal?'

Rose turned the fried potatoes gently in the pan, smiling to herself at her daughter's ingenuous remark. Not that it was ingenuous really; it was a fair enough question. Why was it that boys were taught not to hit girls, yet when they became adults a great many men thought nothing of battering their wives or giving their kids a good hiding for the most trivial offence?

Steve McAllister was a case in point. He was a stoker aboard the SS *Millie May*, a coaster plying between the small ports of South America, so his times at home in Liverpool were blessedly infrequent. When he came ashore drunk, Rose could understand his truculence, even his violence, but the truth was, like his father before him, he was a man of vicious and capricious temper. After nine years of marriage, she knew how suddenly he could change from a relatively good mood to a foul one, and until a couple of years previously she had feared and dreaded his homecomings.

Not any more, though. On that winter's day, two years ago, she had been frying liver and onions on the stove when the back door crashed open. Steve had lurched into the room, eyes bloodshot, and had stood swaying in the doorway for a moment. 'Wharra you cookin'?' he had demanded, his voice slurred from the drink. 'Whassin that bleedin' fry pan?'

'It's liver and onions,' Rose had replied levelly, though with a wild and thumping heart. 'It's your favourite dinner, Steve.'

He had scowled and taken a couple of shambling steps towards her. 'Not today, it ain't,' he had said thickly. 'Today, I fancy fish 'n' chips an' a bottle o' porter. Put that bleedin' pan down an' go an' buy some, quick.'

'I've no money,' Rose had said truthfully. 'An' I'm not going anywhere. You'll have to make do with liver and onions.'

He had taken two more steps towards her and Rose had known what was coming. Once, she would have let go the pan and tried to run round the table, slipping out of the door before he had turned back towards it, but now, suddenly, she was filled with defiance. She took the big iron pan in both hands and swung it in a wide arc. Liver, onions and hot fat flew across the short distance which separated them, splattering Steve's face and hands. For a moment he stopped short, then, with a howl of rage, he grabbed for the frying pan, clearly meaning to turn her weapon upon herself. But the pan was almost red hot from the heat of the fire, and for a sickening moment Steve was unable to let go of it, though his roars of pain and rage reverberated around the small room, which was filled with the smell of sizzling Steve.

Rose had given a short, harsh laugh. 'I warned you,' she had said, in the most threatening tone she could produce. 'I've had enough of it, Steve. The kids are in bed, thank God, but I'll not let you touch me again in one of your moods, so be warned.'

But he hadn't been listening. The moment he had

torn himself free of the pan, he had rushed across the kitchen to bend over the pail of water under the sink and plunge both hands in it, whilst uttering a stream of abuse and sobbing with the pain of his burns.

Rose had eyed his rear thoughtfully, still swinging the frying pan. One good whack on that tempting, trouser-clad target, and Steve would end up with his head in the pail of water as well as his hands. But she had felt that such a move might be carrying the war one step too far and, still holding the frying pan, had begun to clear up the liver and onions.

Presently, Steve had stood up. She had glanced across at him. His face had been red and blubbered and tears were running down his cheeks. He had glared at her but to her secret astonishment – and great delight – she had read something very like respect in his glance. Oh, there had been hatred there and a desire for revenge, but it had been clear that her action had surprised him. She had thought he would think twice before attacking her again.

And so it had proved. She had made a point of letting him see that she would no longer allow herself to be a victim, that she would hit back with any weapon to hand if he threatened her again. Of course, there had been other times when he had hit out at her and she had had no chance to defend herself, but she always made sure that afterwards he suffered in some way, and gradually he had learned to keep his distance.

Sometimes, she thought back down the long years to their courtship and wondered how on earth she had been so blind. She told herself that a girl of seventeen, kept too close by strict and elderly parents, had had no idea what marriage and a family involved. But the truth was partly that she had been swept off her feet by the handsome, swaggering young seaman, who had brought her presents from faraway places and taken her dancing and to the theatre and the cinema – three things of which her parents disapproved – and partly that to go out with Steve had shown her parents that she was no longer a child who could be told what she might and might not do.

So they had married in the teeth of deep parental opposition, though her parents had not withheld their consent, and moved into the little house in Bernard Terrace. Her parents had kept a small shop on Stanley Road, but after her marriage they had sold up and moved out to Great Sutton, on the Wirral, where a newspaper and tobacconist's shop, with a flat above it, had provided them with a decent living. As her own marriage degenerated, Rose had been less and less anxious to take Steve to visit her parents because her pride could not let her admit how right they had been. However, she had taken the girls to see their grand-parents as often as she could, and both her mother and her father had adored the little girls, softening towards them in a way they had never done towards Rose. Sadly, when Petal had been two and Daisy six, first her father, then her mother, had succumbed to influenza, which they had neglected in order to keep the shop open. They had sent for Rose, asking her to take over the shop for a few days, but it had been too late.

Rose had always had to save hard and plan well ahead for her visits to Great Sutton, but when they came to an end she found she missed both the trips away from the city and her parents. Mrs Darlington had been well past forty when Rose was born, and now that she was a mother herself Rose realised how difficult it must have been for the couple to find them-selves parents at such an advanced age. Both only

11

children, they had not understood Rose's need for the companionship of young people like herself, or her yearnings for independence from the narrow and rigid lives they led. And truth to tell, having grandchildren had mellowed them beyond belief.

Now, Rose turned the potatoes in the pan and glanced, anxiously, towards the kitchen door. The *Millie May* came into port tomorrow so she and the children would make do with fried potatoes for their dinner today. She would save the liver and onions for the following day, as she always did. Petal had asked her, when Steve was last in port, why they always had liver and onions on her daddy's first day home and Rose had smiled grimly at Steve, over the child's blonde head, and said sweetly that it was Daddy's favourite dish. Steve had glanced quickly away, refusing to meet her eyes, but Petal had been quite satisfied with the answer, especially as she was fond of liver and onions herself.

Rose fished out the tin plates and began to serve the potatoes, just as the kitchen door burst open and the children ran into the room. Petal was wearing a fawn-coloured cardigan which had once been Daisy's, and looked considerably better than when she had entered the kitchen earlier. When Petal was born, Rose had breathed a sigh of relief because she would not have to buy much in the way of clothing, though Steve had been bitterly disappointed, or so he had claimed. Now, Rose thought that Daisy was a motherly little soul and took as much pride in Petal's appearance as she would have done had she been the child's mother. She had brushed out Petal's soft curls and straightened the child's long grey stockings. She had even rubbed most of the mud off Petal's worn black plimsolls, and done her best to brush the child's short grey skirt. Rose wished she could have afforded decent boots for the children to play out in at this time of year, but it took her all her ingenuity to have them properly shod for school. Petal had started in the infants' class the previous September so now, Rose thought ruefully, she had two decent sets of clothes to keep clean. It was not that Steve was ungenerous; because of his long absences, the shipping company who owned the *Millie May* paid her an allotment every month, but it was not really sufficient for all the expenses of home and family. Rose had to work, but since the majority of women living in the terrace were in the same position, she thought nothing of it. The only real problem was that work was so hard to find and so poorly paid. 'Haven't you heard about the Depression?' employers would say, grimly, when offering one a tiny wage for work that would mean many hours of slavery each week. 'You're lucky I'm offering you work at all, so if you ain't content with the money I pay, you'd best go elsewhere.'

Only there wasn't an elsewhere, Rose thought now. She put the crockery on the table and went to the cupboard to fetch the sauce bottle. Doling a meagre amount on to each plate, she smiled approvingly as Petal ran to fetch the cutlery and Daisy filled a jug of water at the sink. Then she took her own place, poured water into their enamel mugs, and picked up her knife and fork.

'I do love fried potatoes,' Petal said earnestly, carefully dipping a piece into the puddle of sauce. 'But it ain't as good as liver and onions . . . I wonder what Daddy will have brung us back?'

Rose sighed. Steve was so unreliable, that was the trouble. Christmas was not far off, but even so, you could never tell. He might come home laden with

13

presents for his small daughters – he never brought Rose anything – or he might come in empty-handed, then hand the girls half a crown apiece. Or, of course, he might come in roaring drunk, having spent his wages at some dockside pub or other, and try to persuade her to fork out her hard-earned money so that he could start another pub crawl as soon as possible.

Sometimes, when he was drunk, he would tell the girls in a self-pitying voice that he had brought them a grosh of presents – beautifully dressed dolls, a parrot in a cage, even a puppy – but that these objects had been stolen from him as he left the ship. With tears in his eyes, he would explain that, because of his loss, he had taken 'a l'il drink or two' to cheer him up, which was why he now felt so ill that he would have to go straight upstairs and lie down.

Rose could never tell whether there was any truth in these stories because there were occasions when Steve did bring the girls presents. Of course, she knew they had not been stolen, thinking it likelier that he had simply put them down somewhere, or even shed them on his passage home. What she did know, for sure, was that the gifts would not reappear and that Steve would spend the rest of his time ashore drinking with his mates, only returning to Bernard Terrace for food or a night's sleep.

Still, there were worse fates than Steve, Rose told herself, eating her fried potatoes and wishing she had been able to afford a bit of meat or fish to go with them. Charlie Briggs, young Jacky's father, was a docker and usually out of work. When he was in work he drank and when he wasn't he stole, either from his wife or from his old mother, who lived three streets away. Poor Nellie Briggs had to put up with his constant presence, often sporting black eyes or a limp, for her husband was even more violent than Steve. The kids avoided him whenever they could, but it wasn't always possible and they, too, were often marked.

'Mammy? It isn't long to Christmas, is it? *Will* Daddy bring us presents, d'you think?'

'I don't know, queen; if he can, he will, I suppose,' Rose said, coming abruptly back to earth. 'But isn't it Santa Claus who brings presents at Christmastime? Remember the poem Daisy's been telling you?'

Petal nodded eagerly. 'Oh yes, I 'member.' She closed her eyes and rocked herself gently backwards and forwards. '*'Twas the night before Christmas and all through the house, Not a creature was stirring, not even a mouse . . .*'

'That's right, so you hang up your stocking on the end of your bed, and you never know . . .'

Regardless of whether Steve remembered Christmas or not, Rose was determined that this year the children should have something in their stockings. Last year had been a really bad one. She had been employed as a waitress, earning reasonable money and determined that they should have a good Christmas. She had meant to order a piece of pork from Mr Pollard on the corner of William Henry and Salisbury streets and had planned various little treats to be bought on Christmas Eve, when shopkeepers, fearing to leave goods unsold over the holiday, would drastically reduce their prices. Then Daisy had come out in spots. It was chickenpox, and seven days later Petal had followed suit. Rose had begged her employer for a few days off – just a few days – whilst the infection was at its height, but Mr Grundy had told her, sadly, that this was his busiest time of year and unless she could find a babysitter, he would have to replace her. She had found a woman willing to brave the chickenpox, but she had only lasted a day. Rose had come home at seven that evening, exhausted after a ten-hour shift on her feet, to find the fire out, Petal burning up with fever and crying dolorously, and Daisy trying to fill a stone hot water bottle from the kettle, because she was so cold. The old woman was fast asleep and snoring on Rosie's own bed and had been most indignant to be turned off without pay, swearing that she would have the scuffers round next morning and take Rose to court, if need be, to get her money.

Of course it had been an empty threat, but it had meant that Rose had had to give up her job. Steve had not come home – which was a blessing – but nor had he sent any money to ease matters, though Rose had written to him explaining that she was out of work through his daughters' illnesses, and could do with some financial help. So they had had an absolutely awful Christmas. Stockings had not even been hung up because Rose needed all the money she had left to pay the doctor; indeed, Christmas Day had passed like any other day, with the children still in bed, though their temperatures were beginning to ease. None of them had referred to the holiday until long afterwards, when it occurred to Petal that she had been cheated.

'Didn't Santa even *try* to come down our chimney?' she had asked plaintively. 'Didn't he leave even an orange? Or a few sweeties?'

Rose had answered, diplomatically, that of course he had visited them. 'Only I used the orange to make you a nice hot drink and you sucked the sweeties when your throat was so sore,' she had said.

Now, Petal's knife and fork clattered on to her plate and she glanced hopefully up at Rose. 'Them spuds was lovely but I've still got a little chink in me belly what needs filling,' she said plaintively. 'Is there any pudding, Mammy?'

'You should say tummy, not belly,' Daisy interposed. 'Or I suppose you could say stomach; that's what the teacher says in school. And I don't see how you can still be hungry. You're littler than me, but you ate just as many spuds.'

'Smaller than me, not littler,' Rose said absently. She liked the children to speak nicely. 'Daisy, fetch the loaf from the bread crock, and Petal, you can see if there's any jam left in the big jar on the bottom shelf of the pantry. I'll have to get some more tomorrow, with your dad coming home, because he likes a jam butty to round off a meal.'

Petal slipped off her stool and went over to the pantry, closely followed by Daisy, and presently the children returned with their spoils. Rose cut a thick slice, halved it, and eyed the jam in the jar. She doubted if there was sufficient even to cover the one slice, then remembered a trick her mother had often used and, fetching the blackened kettle from its place on the hob, poured half a teaspoon of boiling water into the jar and began to swill it around. Then she tipped the jar on to the bread, spread the thin jam carefully, cut the slice of bread in half, and handed a piece to each child. 'There you are, something to fill the chink,' she said cheerfully. 'And when you've eaten that and I've washed up and cleared away, we'll go up to the shops and buy something nice for tomorrow's dinner.'

'Liver and onions,' Petal said gleefully, through a mouthful of bread and jam. 'Will Daddy be at home for Christmas, Mammy, or will he have gone back to the *Millie May* by then?'

'It's only three days to Christmas, so I suppose

they'll probably remain in port over the holiday,' Rose said, trying to keep gloom and foreboding out of her voice, though feeling both. Steve was bound to get drunk over Christmas and it troubled her that he might spoil things for the kids if he ran out of money and could not go out on a pub crawl every night. So far, Steve had never laid a finger on the children, though since hearing Petal's remark as she had entered the kitchen earlier Rose had been aware that her girls must know full well that Steve could be violent. However, there was no point in meeting trouble halfway; she would simply have to hope that the spirit of Christmas would triumph over the spirit of Guinness and that he would leave the three females to enjoy their holiday whilst he went off to the pub to drink with his cronies.

Presently, the meal washed up and cleared away and the fire banked down, the three of them donned their coats and hats, picked up Rose's marketing bags and headed for the shops. Once, Rose would have pushed the big old pram, but a year ago it had mysteriously disappeared. Since it was during one of Steve's periods at home, and since he had been unusually short of money, she imagined that he had sold it. It was annoying, of course, and she felt that if anyone had had the money it should have been she, since it was her parents who had presented her with the pram when Daisy was born. Naturally, she had said nothing to Steve about it; she had merely served up a dinner of blind scouse and dumplings, and when Steve had poked, disparagingly, at the vegetables, demanding to know where the meat had gone, she had said simply: 'To the same place as the pram, I dare say,' and had noticed with satisfaction that he had avoided her eyes, though he had eaten the rest of his stew without complaint.

'Mam, where's we goin' first?' Daisy asked, as they descended from the terrace into Salisbury Street. 'If we've got ever so many messages, we ought to gerron a tram and go up to St John's market. Stuff's cheaper there, everyone says so.'

'That's just what we're going to do,' Rose said, taking Petal's small hand in her own and setting off along Salisbury Street in the direction of Islington. 'Petal's little legs aren't up to walking all that way and coming back, and when we're laden with heavy bags, our little arms aren't up to it either.'

That made Daisy laugh, though she said wistfully: 'If we still had the pram, Petal could have had a lift among the messages, coming home, which would have saved a penny or two. I wonder what happened to that pram?'

'Oh, Daisy, me darlin', you sound like a little old woman sometimes,' Rose said. Daisy's old-fashioned ways amused her but they also made her sad. Because of their circumstances, Daisy had had to grow up and take responsibility for her little sister in a way which Rose thought unfair. However, she knew that most of the children of Daisy's age who lived in the poorer districts of the city were in the same boat and, like Daisy, none of them seemed to resent it.

They emerged on to Islington, crossed the busy road and joined the queue at the tram stop. Rose had never told Daisy what she thought had happened to the pram and did not intend to do so now but said, instead: 'Never mind the pram, queen. You like a tram ride, don't you? And if we'd had the pram, we couldn't possibly have got it aboard! Ah, here comes one now!'

Steve came home, announcing that he would be with them until after the New Year, but his mood was far more sober – in every sense of the word – than usual. Rose had bought some chestnuts from a street vendor and Steve had made a punch, using liquor which he had brought back with him, and some of the fruit which Rose had purchased earlier in the evening from the stalls on Scotland Road. She had been astonished when Steve had suggested that they all go and do the messages together, and downright flabbergasted when he had said he wanted a quiet evening at home. She had asked him, solicitously, if he were feeling well, and he had given her a strange look. For the first time, he had actually seemed interested in the children's activities, had carried Petal in his arms when she got tired, and had persuaded Daisy to sing the carol which she had sung as a solo in the school concert.

So now the two of them settled down in front of the fire and Steve arranged the chestnuts on a shovel which he pushed beneath the hot coals. Then he poured a small quantity of hot punch into two mugs, and handed one to Rose. 'There you are,' he said gruffly. 'I've put the stuff I brought back in the cupboard under the stairs. It ain't a lot, but it'll be more'n they got last Christmas.' He lowered his head, then looked up at her, his expression still one that she had never seen on his face before and found difficult to read. 'I got you something an' all,' he added. He sounded almost ashamed, Rose thought with amusement, and once more she wondered what had happened, why he was not off drinking with his pals, or trying to pick a fight with her.

'I've not got you anything because we don't exchange presents, do we?' she said, after the pause had begun to lengthen. 'I told you I'd had some pre-Christmas work in the bakery, but I spent all the money I earned on grub and a few bits for the kids. I – I'm sorry, but you know how it is.'

'Aye, I know how it is,' Steve mumbled. 'But me and the fellers was talkin' after old Chamberlain came back from Munich, waving his bit of paper an' sayin' "Peace for our time" and that. I ain't much interested in politics, nor what they call world affairs neither. But there's a feller what slings his hammock next to mine, called Alby Cohen. He's from Liverpool, like what I am, an' he's a Jew. He told us about that there Crystal Night, where them Nazis dragged women an' children out of their beds, an' killed 'em, just for bein' Jewish. He said Chamberlain were a fool if he thought he could stop that there madman . . . what's 'is name, oh aye, Adolf Hitler . . . from swallering up as much of Europe as he could gerr'is hands on. He said he reckoned this 'ud be our last Christmas before old Hitler sent his Nazis across the Channel, our last Christmas without – without wonderin' if there'd be a knock on the door, if some storm trooper were goin' to come in an' drag our kids out on to the street.' He swallowed. 'It made me think, like; seamen don't get to see their kids at Christmas all that often, and . . .' His voice petered out. Then he cleared his throat and started again. 'Alby's clever, not like the rest of us. He knows a thing or two, does Alby. I reckon if he says there's goin' to be a war, then he's right an' Chamberlain's wrong. So Alby's signed off from the old *Millie May*, so's he can join the Royal Navy, and – and I'm goin' to do the same. I reckon they'll be needin' men when war comes an' Alby says if we gerrin first we'll likely get the better jobs, bein' more experienced, like.'

Rose stared at him. She had always thought him a man of few words and had never before heard him talk for so long. This Alby, she reflected, must be a pretty strong character to have made such an impression upon her usually unimaginative husband. But he was looking at her, clearly expecting a reaction. 'But suppose Alby's wrong, Steve?' she said slowly. 'You've never said much, but I've always thought you were happy enough aboard the *Millie*. If there isn't a war . . .'

He interrupted her at once, shaking his head almost reprovingly at her. 'No, no, you don't *understand*. Alby's been there, he knows all about it. He's got relatives living in Germany; some of 'em's already in these here camp things, what the Nazis have set up, but others are trying to go on with their lives, an' they've talked to him, told him things. There *will* be a war, Rosie, you've gorra believe me.'

'I – I think I do believe you,' Rose said hesitantly. He had not called her Rosie since Daisy was born, and though she could never forget how badly he had treated her in recent years, it was wonderful to think that his attitude might change, that he might become a softer, pleasanter person. 'I've not thought much about Hitler, or what's going to happen – I've been too busy seeing the kids get fed and the rent gets paid – but I know the newspapers think there's trouble coming, and if it does, we're all going to have to pull together.'

'That's it,' Steve said eagerly. 'And there's somethin' else, Rosie, something I've not told anyone, 'cept for Alby. A couple o' times, when I've been on the booze, I've – I've seen things.' He shuddered. 'Horrible things – hands chopped off at the wrist an' oozing blood, creepin' across me blanket, headin' for me throat. Giant crabs and great, slimy crocodile things, slitherin' down the bulkhead . . . Once, I got fightin' mad wi' the things an' started attacking them; I thought a great old snake was curlin' round me, tryin' to squash me ribs, but it were Alby, tryin' to stop me goin' mad. He said it were the drink; well, I knew it were. He said if I didn't ease off, I'd end up mad or dead.' He grinned, suddenly, and for a moment Rose saw the swaggering young seaman for whom she had abandoned her home, broken her parents' hearts and almost ruined her own life.

'So I'm off the drink, 'cept for the odd glass now and then,' Steve said. 'Hey, them nuts is done to a turn; I'll peel you a couple. They reckon stokers have asbestos fingers. Now we'll see if they're right.'

For the rest of the evening, the two of them examined the presents they had bought for the girls. There were two real dolls, proper ones with eyes that opened and shut, curly hair and soft, huggable bodies. Rose knew the girls would be absolutely delighted, though in her heart she doubted that these grand babies would ever replace the home-made rag dolls which Daisy and Petal cherished. Then Steve had bought each girl a rubber ball – one red, one blue – and pretty little jackets made of what he told her proudly was angora wool. 'They'll love everything,' Rose told him warmly. She had bought them the new plimsolls they so desperately needed, and a skipping rope each, as well as some hard-boiled sweets and two small bars of Nestlé chocolate. 'They're going to have a wonderful Christmas, Steve,' Rose said, as the two of them made their way up to bed. 'A lot better than last year, I can tell you.'

And sure enough, Christmas Day was celebrated to the full. Steve's gift to Rose was a necklace of crystal beads, and though she had had no present for him, she had made sure that his day was a happy one. Towards evening, though, he grew restless, and when the children were in bed he slipped on his coat and announced that he needed some fresh air.

Telling herself, grimly, that he would doubtless return in a drunken rage, Rose went early to bed and fell asleep almost at once. She did not wake until eight o'clock next morning and realised, when she did so, that he could not have been on the drink, since he had managed to slip into bed beside her so quietly.

This happy state of affairs lasted until New Year's Eve. Steve left the house as soon as the girls were in bed, and had not returned by closing time. Rose went to bed, armed with the coal shovel, and heard her husband crashing into the house in the small hours. He was swearing and shouting at her to come down and pull his bleedin' boots off, and twice she heard him come stumbling up half a dozen stairs and then fall heavily down them. The last time he did this, he shrieked to her to come down at once. 'Gi' me a hand up, you snooty bitch, 'cos I'm thinking I've broke both me bleedin' legs, an' it's a wife's duty to gerra feller into his own bed,' he bawled. 'Aw, c'mon, Rosie, or it ain't only my bleedin' legs that'll be broke come mornin'.'

Rose sat up in bed. It had been so nice having him home sober that she felt almost tempted to go downstairs, but past sad experience told her that this would be a mistake. He would hit out at her, or grab her; might injure her so that she could not return to work, and the money she earned was a necessity. Besides, even if she had wanted to, she was not strong enough to propel him up the stairs, and anyway by morning he would have forgotten everything, have a horrible hangover and probably want to spend the rest of the day either on the sofa or in bed.

Slowly, Rose slid under the covers again, pulling the blankets up over her shoulders. Steve's voice had sunk to a mumble; probably he was more asleep than awake. She was beginning to drowse herself when a small voice spoke, almost in her ear, causing her to give a convulsive leap. 'Didn't you hear Daddy call you, Mammy? He were hollerin' pretty loud. He woke me up. Daisy woke up and started to cry, but she's gone back to sleep now. I took a peep down the stairs, but I can't see him. Are you going down, or shall I?'

Rose sat up in bed once more and put her arms round her little daughter; Petal was shivering. 'Yes, I heard him, queen, but I didn't go down because I don't think Daddy is quite himself.'

'Oh, you mean he's drunk,' Petal said matter-of-factly. 'And when daddies is drunk, they sometimes hit mammies, don't they? If I go, will Daddy try to hit me? I know Mr Briggs hits Jacky, but Daddy's never hit me, has he?'

'No, darling,' Rose said, trying not to remember the number of times she had had to get between Daisy and Steve. He had threatened the child in the past but, she was bound to admit, had never actually struck either of his daughters. Only his wife. 'Look, Petal, you slip into Mammy's nice warm bed and I'll go very quietly down the stairs and make sure he's all right.' She slid out of bed on the words and tried to pick Petal up and pop her between the covers, but Petal resisted.

'No Mammy; if you're going down, then I'm coming with you,' she said, and set off for the stairs at a brisk trot. It was a cold night. Rose whipped a blanket off her bed and wrapped it round her shoulders, then followed her daughter's small, determined figure. Petal pattered ahead of her, and presently the two of them stood in the empty hall. Steve was nowhere to be seen, but through the open kitchen door Rose could hear rich, vibrating snores. She and Petal tiptoed into the room and there was Steve. Since he had managed to heave himself on to the sofa he was obviously not suffering from broken legs, and although his snores were not musical, at least they seemed to indicate that he was well enough. Mother and daughter exchanged relieved looks and then Rose removed the blanket from her shoulders and placed it, tenderly, across Steve's slumbering body, tucking it in so firmly that he would have a job to escape from it. She wondered whether to place a large jug of water conveniently to hand since she knew he would wake with a raging thirst, but decided against it. On a previous occasion she had done so, and Steve had drunk the water and then piddled all over the sofa. If, on the other hand, he had to get up to reach the water, he would use one of the buckets, might even stagger to the outside lavatory if he was sober enough.

'Poor Daddy,' Petal whispered as they retraced their steps. 'He'll have a rotten headache in the morning, won't he, Mammy?'

Agreeing, Rose accompanied Petal back to her bed and tucked her in, glancing across at Daisy as she did so. Poor little soul! She must have been woken by her father's shouts, but her memories of him were clearer – and more unpleasant – than Petal's. His bubbly, blonde little daughter had always been his favourite, though Rose had to admit that he treated them fairly so far as presents and so on were concerned. But he could be harsh and sometimes quite spiteful towards Daisy, whilst treating Petal with obvious affection. Of course, Petal found it easy to show her own affection, having no bad history with her father. She would climb on to his knee, throw her arms round his neck, even play that she was a dog, pretending to bite his outstretched fingers and crowing with amusement when he acted as if he had been hurt. He would suck in his breath and roll his eyes, exclaiming that she was a real little devil, so she was.

He never played like that with Daisy, never had, probably never would. So of course the child was afraid

26

of him. Rose had seen her elder daughter looking wistfully on when Steve and Petal played together, or when Steve read to Petal from a book, but Rose knew there was nothing she could do about it. If Steve really kept off the drink, if he could show some sort of warmth towards Daisy, then there might be hope of closeness in the future. But Steve would have to earn Daisy's trust, and for the moment at least he seemed pretty well indifferent towards his elder daughter.

Rose tucked Petal in, turned to leave the room, then turned back. 'Where's Millie? Come to that, where's Maudie?' she asked, a sudden suspicion entering her head. 'When I put you to bed the night before last you were both cuddling your new dollies, but now I can't see either of 'em.'

'No. That's why poor Daisy were crying,' Petal said. 'When we come up to bed tonight, they was gone, and Daisy said Dad had took 'em. I don't mind much – I loves Josie Ragget best – but poor Daisy were real upset.' Petal sat up on one elbow, gazing across at her mother in the flickering candlelight. 'I say, Mam, if he's took 'em to Uncle's, then you could gerr'em back when it's safe, couldn't you?'

Despite herself, Rose gave a little choke of laughter. Petal was that knowing! Once or twice, when times were hard and extra expenses cropped up, Rose had had to go to the pawnbroker's on the corner of Islington with some article or other. Mr Parr or Mr Mordaunt would hold the object until she could redeem it, but she did not think she had ever explained any of this to Petal. However, the child clearly understood the intricacies of pawnbroking, so she might as well use the knowledge to comfort her girls.

'Yes, if your dad has taken them to the pawnshop we'll redeem them as soon as his ship sails,' she said

27

comfortingly. 'Petal, who told you about – about Parr and Mordaunt's?'

'Jacky, of course. His mam pops his Sunday kecks on a Monday morning and gets 'em out again the followin' Saturday,' Petal said sleepily. 'I do like Mrs Briggs, Mam, she's ever so kind. If you can't get our new dollies back, I could ask—'

'No!' Rose said with rather more force than she had intended. 'Don't say a word to anyone else about your dollies, please, queen. I'll get them back as – as soon as I possibly can. Will you promise me you won't say a word to Mrs Briggs?'

'Awright,' Petal mumbled. 'Night night, Mammy.'

'Night night, chuck. And don't forget: not a word to anyone about your dollies.'

'I promise,' Petal said, yawning. 'I do love you, Mammy!'

Daisy lay curled up, with her old rag doll clasped firmly against her chest, and listened to Mam and Petal talking. She did not wish to admit that she was awake because she knew it should have been she who had accompanied her mother downstairs; she who understood very well how dangerous it could be for Mam to venture anywhere near Dad when he was drunk.

The trouble was, she had been so upset at the loss of her brand new doll that she had sobbed herself into quite a state and it had simply not occurred to her that she should go and wake her mother when her father had fallen down the stairs. Indeed, she had felt downright relieved at the crash because it meant that he was unlikely to come up and start trouble when he reached his bedroom.

But Petal had not hesitated. Daisy had heard her get up and trot through to Mam's room, had even heard the slight creaks as they descended the stairs. She had sat up in bed, thinking guiltily that she should really go down and lend her support, but before she had even poked a toe out from beneath her blankets she had heard her sister and mother returning. Quick as a flash, she had cuddled down again and was glad she had done so. She gathered that her father had been asleep and had given them no trouble, and when Petal had explained about their loss of the dolls she had been delighted to hear Mam say that she would get them back as soon as Dad had left for sea once more. Until Petal had talked of Uncle, it had not occurred to her that the dolls might have been pawned. She had imagined that Dad would have taken them to the pub and sold them to someone there, but if they'd really been pawned, and Mam seemed to think it likely, then they could be redeemed as Mam had suggested.

Now, Daisy turned over and put her warm arms round her sister's solid little back. Petal was so brave, but then she had never known what it was like to be in Dad's bad books, to be growled at and cursed, and, if Mam was in the other room, to receive a stinging slap round the legs, merely for the crime of walking past his chair and getting between him and the warmth of the fire for half a second.

Still, I'm brave in some ways, Daisy told herself defiantly. I never let anyone bully Petal and I help Mam all I can. And tomorrow morning, I'll go down early and help her with the breakfast, even if Dad's awake and shouting. And as soon as he's gone, we'll get our beautiful dolls back from Mr Parr's shop.

On that happy thought, Daisy slept.

Chapter Two
1939

It was a beautiful, sunny Whit Monday, and since the children had a day off school Rose had decided to take them to New Brighton. They had caught the tram down to the Pier Head, crossed the floating bridge, in company with a great many other people also intent on a day out, and were now aboard the ferry. The two little girls were hanging over the rail and chattering excitedly to one another, but Rose had read the headlines on the fly sheets that morning, and her pleasure in the day out was tinged with apprehension. The news was so bad! Ever since Steve had joined the Royal Navy, she had been conscious that, despite Mr Chamberlain's 'peace for our time', the rumbling of war in Europe had not gone away. In fact, it had got worse. It was impossible not to worry when you had small children in your care and a husband at sea, though Steve's desire to stay on the wagon had not proved very long lasting. He had been home twice since Christmas and on each occasion had come back full of good resolutions, only to fall by the wayside the first time he walked through the door of the nearest pub. Rose had remonstrated with him, reminded him of Alby Cohen's words, and when he was sober he always assured her that his drinking bouts were at an end, but this had not, again, proved to be the case.

However, he no longer attempted to use physical violence against either her or the children, because Rose had made it plain that such behaviour would be met with all the force she could muster. Fortunately, drink made him noisy as well as abusive, and she usually heard him coming as he tumbled across the threshold, cursing as he mounted the steps and blaming everyone else if he slipped and fell.

Rose sighed to herself. What was she doing, ruining a beautiful day by thinking about Steve? She had acknowledged to herself long ago that she had been a fool to marry him, but at least now she was in a much better position, financially, than she had ever been in her life before, and she had rumours of war to thank for that. Conscription had come in in April, though so far only for men aged twenty, and she had managed to get a job making uniforms, in a large factory on Long Lane. The pay was excellent, the other girls were friendly and the work itself was well within her capabilities. Rose paid Mrs Briggs to give an eye to the children when they came out of school, and a slightly larger sum to take care of them during the holidays. She had worried at first, knowing that Mr Briggs was a violent man, but she soon realised that Mrs Briggs was quite capable of controlling her husband when money was involved. After all, the girls played out with the other children when the weather allowed, only going into the Briggses' house when a meal was forthcoming, and during the Easter holidays Mrs Briggs's eldest, a strapping fourteen-year-old called Dulcie, had kept the girls happy and amused, even on wet days.

'Mammy.' Petal's shrill voice cut across Rose's thoughts. 'We're moving! We're at sea, like Dad is. There's lots of ships in the docks – one of 'em might be his!'

Rose shook her head, smiling at her little daughter. Because she was now earning regular wages, she had not brought a carry-out with them, but had promised them that they should have their dinner in a real café.

Because of this, both girls had insisted upon wearing the pink gingham dresses which Rose had been fortunate enough to spot on a stall in Paddy's market, and had immediately snapped up. She had had to let the hem right down on Daisy's dress, and had taken out the darts on Petal's, but thought that her daughters looked both sweet and smart, and was proud of them.

'Mammy, might one of the ships be Daddy's?'

'No, queen, I don't think so. If Daddy was in port, he would have either let us know or come home himself. But his ship has gone up to Scotland for manoeuvres, whatever that may mean. In his last letter, he said it might be two or three months before he was back in Liverpool, so we don't have to worry – I mean . . . oh, well, his ship can't possibly be one of the ones you can see,' she finished lamely.

'Good,' Daisy said roundly. She caught her sister's reproachful eye and gave Petal a little push. 'Oh, I know you're Daddy's favourite, but even you can't have forgotten what happened last time he was at home.'

'I try to forget,' Petal said, rather wistfully. 'After all, it were my best coat as well as yours that he took.'

'It weren't the coats I were thinking about,' Daisy said, with dignity. 'I were thinking about the row when Mam found out they'd gone and told him off. And don't pretend you weren't scared, Petal, because you were shaking like a leaf. I had my arms round you and I felt you trembling like anything.'

'Well, it was all right; when your dad saw I was really angry – and I'd picked up the poker – he simply walked out of the room,' Rose said, smiling to herself. If Steve had had a tail, it would have been clamped between his legs, she thought now, remembering how his self-righteous fury had oozed away into mumbles when she had raised the poker. She wondered how he could believe that she would ever dare to actually hit him, but supposed that a violent man expected violence from others. Whatever the reason, he must have acquired some money from somewhere – she did not like to imagine where or how – because he had turned up several hours later, no longer drunk, and with the missing coats over his arm. Now she assumed that he must have pawned the coats, but had been saving the money for a binge, which, if she had not intervened, would have started as soon as his favourite pub opened its doors.

'Well, I were a bit afraid,' Petal admitted. 'But it was all right, wasn't it? Dad takes things because I suppose he needs some money, but we get 'em back. We got our dollies back as well as our coats, didn't we?'

Daisy heaved an exaggerated sigh. 'Mam got the dolls back, not Dad,' she said severely. 'An' tell the truth now, isn't it nicer at home when Dad's at sea? No rows, no fights, no swears . . .'

But Petal had tired of the whole conversation, it seemed. She swung round and headed for the bows of the ship. 'C'mon, Daisy. If we're right in the front, we might see a mermaid or – or a penguin, or even a whale,' she shouted excitedly. 'First one to see a mermaid gets to choose which café we has our dinners in.'

Rose, following her daughters more slowly, thought what an odd mixture Petal was. Did she truly believe she might see a penguin or a whale? Petal was nearer babyhood than her sister, could still half believe in such things as mermaids and fairies. Rose had noticed that if they had cake for tea, Petal invariably thrust a few crumbs of it into her pocket, and could be seen, later, spreading such crumbs out on a nearby wall. When questioned, she had said that it was for the fairies, though Jacky Briggs had scoffed at the idea.

'It were mice, more'n likely, or mebbe bleedin' rats,'

he had said scornfully. 'You'd believe anything, you!'

'It weren't mice, it were sparrows, 'cos I've watched 'em come down and peck away. But it might be fairies, don't you see?'

Jacky had not seen, but Rose, overhearing the conversation, thought she had. Petal knew, with the practical side of her mind, that sparrows ate the cake crumbs, but according to the dreamy, imaginative side, it could have been fairies.

'She'll go far, that 'un,' April, the girl at the next machine, had said comfortably, when Rose had told her of the conversation. 'She'll be a perishin' lawyer, or the Prime Minister one of these days, tek my word for it!'

So now Rose watched indulgently as her daughters scanned the foaming bow wave, hoping for goodness knows what weird or magical creatures in the water below. And presently, when the ferry was alongside the dock and beginning to disgorge her passengers, she took Petal's hand in hers and bade Daisy catch hold of her small sister. Rose's other hand was encumbered by what the children called the outings bag, for though she had not brought food with them, she carried some bottles of lemonade, a couple of towels and the brief bathing suits she had made for them out of remnants bought on Paddy's market.

As the three of them began to walk up New Brighton Promenade, Petal burst into song. '*Here we go gathering nuts in May, nuts in May, nuts in May,*' she carolled, breaking off to remark, 'Oh, that's the wrong song 'cos it's not a cold and frost morning, is it, Mammy?'

Daisy laughed and swung her sister's hand vigorously. '*Oh I do like to be beside the seaside,*' she sang. '*Oh I do like to be beside the sea, Oh I do like to stroll along the prom, prom, prom, Where the bands all play tiddly om pom pom . . .*'

Singing lustily, the McAllisters continued to head for the beach.

Steve and Alby came off watch together and went down to the seamen's mess. Despite the fact that it was almost June there was a heavy swell running and it was too cold to spend more time than you had to out on the deck. Steve looked at Alby as the two of them settled on one of the long benches. He was a small man, a good six inches shorter than Steve himself, with curly black hair, sallow skin and very dark eyes, fringed with thick stubby lashes. He was also very much more intelligent than Steve knew himself to be, though Alby never shoved it down your throat that you weren't brainy, as some of the others did. Sometimes, Steve wondered why they were friends, because they were so different. Alby's locker was packed with books, some of which were novels, though many were impressive tomes on politics, international affairs and history. He had offered to lend them to Steve, who had given him a pitying glance. 'I ain't goin' to waste my time readin' a lot of stuff I wouldn't even begin to understand,' he had said honestly. 'Readin' is hard work for me, not enjoyment. Why, even when I'm listenin' to the wireless and the news comes on, me mind goes wanderin' off an' I come back to reality to find the bloody news bulletin's over. Why don't you play cards or do crosswords, or have a go at shove ha'penny, like the rest of us?'

Alby had laughed; one of the things Steve liked about him was that although he was clever, he never tried to influence other people, never made you feel small. 'I don't mind the odd game of cards from time to time because I reckon you're right: everyone needs to relax now and then. But you need other people to play cards with – unless it's patience – and when we come off

35

watch, it's sometimes hard to get a card school going.'

Now, the cook leaned through the hatch and grinned at them as other men came trooping down the companionway and into the mess. 'Come and gerrit,' he bawled. 'It's bacon chops, boiled spuds an' cabbage wi' a currant duff for afters.'

There was an immediate jostling rush to grab tin plates from the pile and to get into a queue, and very soon both Alby and Steve were digging into their food. 'I know the cabbage is only dried, same as the mashed spuds is, but it's good grub, ain't it?' Steve said, through his mouthful. 'Is your old woman a good cook, Alby? Mine has her faults, but she turns out a grand meal when the dibs is in tune.'

'Aye, Rachel's a grand cook an' all,' Alby said dreamily, pausing with a fork full of meat halfway to his mouth. 'Her suet dumplings are the nicest I've ever tasted. Her mam's a good cook, too, only she's more for foreign food, having been brought up in Lithuania. She didn't come to England till she were in her twenties and of course she brought her cookin' with her, so to speak.'

'Aye, like the Chinese,' Steve said knowledgeably. 'They're good cooks, though when I were a kid me brothers an' meself used to believe they ate dogs an' rats an' that.' He grinned at his friend. 'I dare say your Rachel can turn a couple o' rats into a tasty dinner, if she's a mind.'

'You cheeky bugger,' Alby said. He punched Steve's shoulder, then stood up to carry his empty plate back to the hatch and fetch his currant duff. 'Mind you, if she were pressed, I reckon Rachel could make something tasty out of three old cabbage leaves and a sole of a boot.'

Laughing, the two men joined the queue at the hatch for their duff.

* * *

As soon as the meal was over, Alby went and fetched one of his books from his locker and settled down into a corner to read. He had said nothing to Steve, as yet, but the first officer had told him he had put Alby's name down to take the examination next time they went ashore which, if he passed, would set him on the road to promotion in the Royal Navy. So now, though he seldom mentioned books to Steve, Alby studied in every spare moment. He was not aiming to run the Navy exactly, but he was very attracted by signals and thought that that would be a career which would satisfy him, particularly once the war he was expecting started. The Yeoman of Signals would be either on deck or on the bridge with the captain, and he would be using both manual skills and the knowledge which he was even now acquiring. Oh yes, if he could start on the ladder which would lead to his becoming a signaller, he would, he thought, get a good deal of satisfaction from the job. Of course, the extra pay would be very welcome too, now that he and Rachel meant to set up home together, for though they had married the previous year, they were still living with Rachel's parents and saving up for a place of their own.

He was immersed in his book when someone tapped him on the shoulder. Glancing up, he saw Steve looming above him, looking excited. For a moment, Alby felt annoyed at the interruption, then grinned up at his friend. Steve did not realise he was studying, he remembered. 'Yes, old feller, what's biting you?' he enquired, closing his book but keeping his finger inside to mark his place. 'I thought you'd joined the card school; don't say the game's over already?'

'No, no, nothing like that. But, Alby, the fellers were talking and Dan Williams has brought down a notice off of the board. It says the Navy is looking for submariners

– fellers to man submarines – and the pay is grand, better'n we're ever likely to get aboard HMS *Jericho*.'

Alby took the notice and read it, frowning slightly as he did so. He had never actually been aboard a submarine but could guess from the pay alone that it must be pretty grim. 'How are you in confined spaces, Steve?' he asked shrewdly. 'Ever been shut in a broom cupboard by your dad, or an angry teacher? I reckon a submarine's a bit like that, only one hell of a lot worse. Money ain't everything, old feller.'

Steve scowled down at the notice, clearly thinking it over, and Alby felt guilty because, though money was *most* certainly not everything, he was studying in order to get better pay himself. Poor old Steve never even thought of promotion and would not, Alby knew, be happy in a higher position. He was definitely not born to command, and though he could be both arrogant and overbearing towards those younger and less important than he conceived himself to be, he had never shown the slightest desire to rise from his present lowly rank.

On the other hand, Steve had a wife and two kids. He had told Alby that Rose was now earning good money, making uniforms for the forces, and Alby guessed that a man like Steve, who considered all males superior to all females, would secretly resent being out-earned by a woman.

But Steve was still thinking and it was several moments before he answered. 'Well, I dare say you're right and a sub would be a bit cramped like. But, Alby, you've always said we've gorra fight this 'ere war with everything we've got, else the bloody Huns will overrun us, murder our kids and tek our wives off to Germany for slave labour. And the money's good, ain't it?'

This was the moment, Alby realised, to tell Steve

of his own plans. It would not be fair to discourage Steve from applying to join a submarine by allowing him to believe that he and Alby would remain ship-mates. Alby knew it was not naval policy to put a man who had gained promotion on the same ship in which he had served as a rating; discipline was easier to main-tain when you were amongst strangers. Accordingly, he cleared his throat and began. 'Steve, old feller, you'll have to make up your own mind on this one, because – because I've been meaning to tell you I've decided to try for a job in signalling. Mr Jenkins told me what exams I'd have to take and how to prepare myself for them, so I've been doing a lot of studying and next time we're in port I'm going to sit the prelims . . . they're the first exams you have to pass to get a foot on the ladder. So you see, there's no point in my signing up for submarines because I doubt they'll need signallers and anyway, I don't like enclosed spaces.'

Steve frowned. 'You're real clever, Alby. You'll pass them exams all right, never you fret. But I don't see why it should matter that you want to go for a signaller. You'll still be me bezzie, won't you?'

Alby was touched by Steve's remark and tempted to let it go at that. After all, Steve would find out, in the fullness of time, that he, Alby, would almost certainly be moved to another ship upon his promotion. But one look at Steve's anxious face decided him that it would be wrong to take the coward's way out. He must explain to Steve that his promotion would prob-ably mean his departure to another ship.

He did so, making sure that Steve understood, seeing the disappointment dawning in the other man's eyes as he took it in. It was obvious that Steve had never consid-ered that they might be parted and was taking it hard, but even as Alby tried to think of some words of comfort, Steve's face cleared. 'Suppose you do get shifted, like you think, what's to stop me requestin' a move as well?' he asked eagerly. 'Oh, I know fellers mostly stay with the same ship, but when the war starts things will be different, won't they? Come to that, I might go for a submarine and then say I didn't like it an' get meself moved back to whichever ship you're on.'

Alby grinned; he couldn't help it. He and Steve had only been in the Royal Navy for a few months, but they had both noticed the difference between naval and merchant shipping. Discipline in the Navy – which was the Senior Service after all – was far more rigid than in the merchant fleet. With the best will in the world, Alby could not imagine the Service letting Steve flit from ship to ship as the fancy took him. But he knew his friend too well to try to make the point now. The best way of getting unpleasant facts into Steve's mind was to imitate the Chinese water torture: drip, drip, drip. You had to keep plopping the same idea over and over into Steve's apparently indifferent ear, and, eventually, he would assimilate what you were saying. But Steve was talking; he had better listen in case a reply was needed.

'. . . so you see, if our Rose finds out that she's earning more'n me, she'll put on even more airs,' Steve was saying earnestly. 'She were an only child, so her mam and dad spoiled her rotten, and I know she's cleverer than me, though only in a bookish sort of way, of course. She weren't so bad a few years back; she minded what I said, did what I told her, but now, because she's gorra good job . . . well, life ain't that easy when I go home, to tell the truth.'

'Oh, I'm sure you're wrong and she still respects you as much as ever,' Alby said tactfully. 'Tell you what, Steve, next time we dock in Liverpool, I'll take you home to meet my Rachel, and then I'll come round to your place an' meet your Rose. How about that?'

Steve brightened. 'You might tell her she's wrong, once or twice, put her in her place,' he said eagerly. 'She'd tek it from a clever feller like you.'

Alby laughed. 'I shouldn't think that would make me exactly popular with your wife,' he pointed out. 'Specially if she came in and said, "Dinner's ready!" and I said, "No, it ain't!" I should think she'd give me a thick ear, and it 'ud be well deserved.'

Steve laughed too. 'Right then. And next time we're in Liverpool, I'll enquire about submarines.'

Alby was worried by the thought of Steve, who was six foot two, getting inside a submarine and then discovering that he, too, suffered from claustrophobia, but he very soon stopped worrying on that score, at any rate. When they went ashore in Kirkwall, in early June, the first thing they heard, when folk realised they were from Liverpool, was the word *Thetis*. Eyes rounding with horror, Steve listened to the dreadful details of how the *Thetis* had sunk in Liverpool Bay when undergoing sea trials. He heard how, for three terrible days, the men inside had tapped out Morse messages of despair on the hull, which had reared for a quarter of its length out of the sea. The Admiralty had eventually winched the submarine from its watery grave by looping chains around its body, but by then only four men had escaped and over seventy had either drowned or died from carbon dioxide poisoning.

'Well, the *Thetis* has made me mind up for me,' Steve said to Alby, as they climbed into the liberty boat to return to their ship. 'Why, only a madman would volunteer after that, and though I'm none too bright, I don't mean to lose me life for a few extra bob in me pay packet.'

'I think you're very sensible,' Alby said gravely. 'No

41

point in putting yourself in more danger than you need, old feller.'

'No, and you might not pass the exams after all,' Steve said brightly, and looked puzzled when Alby laughed.

'Mammy, if there isn't going to be a war, why do we have to have gas masks? I hate mine, I does. It smells of poo an' I won't wear it.' Petal looked with distaste at the small black-snouted gas mask with which she had been issued. 'I shall throw it away when I get home.'

Rose and the two children were walking back to Bernard Terrace. It was a fine summer afternoon and Rose sighed despairingly as she looked down into her small daughter's defiant face. 'No, Petal, you can't throw it away because if there is a gas attack, it could save your life,' she explained patiently. 'I know it smells funny – that's because it's made of rubber – but it's better to be alive than dead, wouldn't you say?'

Daisy, viewing her own gas mask with equal distaste, reached round her mother to rumple her little sister's fair curls. 'Don't be daft, Petal,' she said briskly. 'Mine smells horrible, too, but I bet gas would smell worse. Anyway, it's just a pre— pre— oh well, it's just in case there's a war. An' those Nazis are so horrible they might easily cheat an' send gas over without lettin' on a war had started, so just you keep your gas mask ready, like it says on the posters.'

Petal stuck out her lower lip. 'But it makes a roarin' sound when I breathe,' she objected. 'And it pinches me round my face an' that horrible rubber thing pulls my hair.'

Daisy sighed dramatically. 'Yes, it pulls my hair, too,' she agreed. 'But when we get home, Mam'll fix it so it's comfortable. And anyway, if there isn't going

42

to be a war, they'll expect you to hand it back in, I suppose, for the next war, you know,' she ended, with the practicality of childhood.

'You're probably right, Daisy,' Rose said with a chuckle, 'but actually, everyone seems to think it's only a matter of time before the war starts. Still, no need to spoil a nice summer day by talking about it.'

Daisy agreed and when they reached home, Rose took their gas masks in their small cardboard cases and hung them, with the coats, on the back door. She devoutly hoped that all the talk of war would come to nothing, but she did not believe that the government would be placing huge orders for uniforms if they did not consider war was imminent.

Life, however, had to go on. She and her friend Maisie, who lived next door, often talked over what they would do if – when – war started. Both young women were aware of the air power which Germany had used in support of the rebels in the Spanish civil war, and everyone assumed that they would start air raids over Britain the moment war was declared. Liverpool, with its busy docks, was bound to be a target and Maisie had talked about evacuation of children, half fascinated, half repelled by the idea. Like Rose, she only had two children, a girl of fourteen and a boy of six. 'They're sayin' some mams can go along wi' their kids but, for one thing, I'd die o' boredom, stuck in the bleedin' country,' she had said frankly. 'And for another, I'm in the best paid job I've ever had an' I don't mean to give it up wi'out a struggle.'

'I can't afford to give mine up,' Rose had replied. 'But perhaps the kids won't have to go, perhaps it won't come to that. It's all right for you, Maisie, you've got Dick workin' on the docks, so that'll be a reserved occupation, and your Trixie's selling china in Bunney's, so she won't be evacuated, 'cos it's just school kids. I know your Freddie would have to go, but you'll still have some company. But I'd be all on me lonesome, and I don't fancy that, I'm telling you.'

But that conversation had taken place several weeks before. Now it was the last day of August, the school holidays were drawing to a close, and somehow war no longer seemed something which might or might not happen, something which could be pushed to the back of one's mind as a problem for tomorrow. The last time he had been home, Steve had bought her a wireless set and commanded her, brusquely, to listen to the news bulletins. 'If there's anything important in 'em, mind you tell me in your letters,' he had said. 'Alby's Rachel is goin' to do the same, but of course letters foller us for weeks sometimes, afore they gets delivered.' He had looked at her keenly. 'What did you think of my pal Alby, then?'

Alby had come round to Bernard Terrace on Steve's last leave and Rose had taken to him at once. He was short and swarthy, with a large Roman nose, and he was one of those men who even grew hair on the back of their hands, something Rose usually abhorred. But somehow, within a few minutes of meeting Alby, one forgot his looks and was only aware of a strong and delightful personality. However, Rose had looked at Steve cautiously, because she never knew how her husband would take even the most ordinary remark. 'Alby? Well, he's no oil painting, is he? But he seemed really nice,' she had said, trying not to sound either insincere or too impressed. Before they were married, a friend of Steve's had asked her to dance. Naturally, she had done so and had been astonished at the depth of Steve's fury. She knew now that, had they been married then, he would probably have become violent

44

as soon as they were alone, but at the time, though she had felt a little uneasy, she had not read the signs aright.

Now, however, caution was second nature in her dealings with Steve. Besides, much though she had liked Alby, she knew Steve would never have cause to be jealous in that direction. Alby adored his Rachel, was proud of her, brought her name into every conversation and generally made it clear that he was a man deeply in love.

'Can we play out now, Mam?' Daisy's voice brought Rose's thoughts abruptly back to the present. 'After all, we'll be in school again in a few days' time.'

'Yes, all right, only your tea will be on the table in half an hour, so don't go too far,' Rose warned. 'Petal, stay with Daisy, there's a good girl.'

She wondered whether she ought to make them take their gas masks then prudently decided against it. She could just imagine Petal carefully placing hers in the path of one of the big shire horses who pulled the brewery carts, or balancing it on a tram line, or getting rid of it in some other fashion.

'Right you are, Mammy,' Petal said briskly, heading for the back door. 'If me pals are playin' out, then—'

The back door opened so abruptly that Petal gave a squeal of alarm and jumped back, then leaped forward and cast herself at the intruder. 'Daddy, Daddy, Daddy!'

Steve swung her into his arms and gave her a hug, then put his arm round Daisy's small shoulders; an action unusual enough to make Rose stare.

She smiled at her husband, though a trifle cautiously. What on earth was he doing here? He usually tried to let her know when he would be in port but, of course, letters went astray or were posted too late to arrive before ships docked, and this must be a case in point. 'Hello, Steve. Fancy seeing you,' she said, reaching for the big iron ladle which hung on a hook beside the stove.

Steve saw the movement and gave an exasperated sigh before standing Petal carefully down on the kitchen floor. 'I aren't drunk, if that's why you're grabbing for the ladle,' he said gruffly. 'We're mobilising down south, but we needed some new parts in the engine room, so we're here till tomorrow noon. Looks like we won't back down over Poland, so war's a certainty.'

Rose had been doing her best to follow the complicated manoeuvres which were going on in Europe, but had more or less given up. She knew that there was a pact between Britain and Poland – each one promising to defend the other – and knew that Germany was threatening to attack that country in order to gain access to the Baltic Sea. But of the diplomatic moves which were being made, she knew nothing. Mr Chamberlain's 'peace for our time' had become meaningless and she realised that Steve, as a member of the armed forces, was far more likely to know what was going on than a mere machine worker in a uniforms factory. Quietly, she turned away from the ladle and went across to the pantry. 'I didn't know you were coming but if bacon and egg and a pile of fried potatoes will do you, I can have it ready in five or ten minutes,' she said. 'If there's going to be a war, I s'pose I'd best spend me savings on any food which is likely to be rationed. What do you think?'

'Good idea,' Steve said. He turned to the children who were standing, staring open-mouthed. 'Go on, you two, gerroff an' play wi' your pals while you've got the chance.'

As soon as the girls had banged the door shut behind them, Rose began to pile bacon, eggs and cold potatoes up on a plate and heat a knob of lard in the big black frying pan. As she had said, it was no more than ten minutes before she was able to place a plate of cooked food before Steve and hurry over to the pantry to fetch a bottle of his favourite HP Sauce. Only when he was tucking in did she venture another question. 'When do you think it'll start then, Steve? Only they're saying in the factory that this war will be an air war and Liverpool will be a prime target. I know you said, ages ago, that if war came you wanted the kids out of it, away from here, but I can't go with them. My war work isn't as important as yours, but as they conscript more and more fellers – and girls – for the armed forces, they'll all need uniforms. And anyway, the money really is a help. Only – only I feel it's a bit hard on the kids, sending them off alone.'

'You send them,' Steve said, shovelling in the food. 'They'll be a deal safer away from the city. But they ain't goin' to send 'em far, just into North Wales, I dare say, or the Wirral. You'll be able to visit 'em. As for when it'll start, weren't there some sort of ulti— ultimatum? I reckon it'll start when that runs out.'

All through the evening, Steve was good with the children and behaved reasonably towards Rose. Next day, she went with him to see him off, a thing she hadn't done since the early days of her marriage. Her feelings towards him were still ambivalent, but he was going into danger, there could be no doubt of that, and the least she could do was wave him off and wish him well.

On the dockside, she saw Alby and his wife. They were clinging unashamedly, and tears were running down the woman's pale cheeks. Rachel was small and plump, with very large dark eyes, thickly curling black hair, and skin as pale as milk. When Steve called out to Alby, she hastily wiped away her tears and turned towards them, revealing a smile of great sweetness. 'I'm

47

being awful silly, because I know they'll come home safe,' she said in a small voice, addressing Rose. 'Only it's so hateful seeing them go off after only a few hours ashore.' She turned back to her husband. 'Now mind you take care of yourself and write me lots of letters,' she said, in a voice that she strove to make practical. 'And if you're right, and the war really does start quite soon, then I'm going to leave me Auntie Leila's shop and take up some war work, like what Rose here has done.' She turned back to Rose. 'I'm real good wi' me needle,' she confided. 'D'you think they'd take me on?'

'I'm sure they would, because most of us are just machinists and they always need workers in the finishing department,' Rose said encouragingly. She was guiltily aware that her own lack of emotion over Steve's departure must be putting her in a bad light with the younger woman, but she could not help it. For many years, Steve had beaten and bullied her and she had dreaded his homecomings; the fact that he now seemed to treat her better could not make up for the bad times. She knew that, for some time at least, the mere sight of his tall figure would be enough to start the cold trickle of fear down her back and the churning of apprehension in her stomach. But now Alby was wrapping his arms round Rachel, stroking her hair and kissing her with a degree of tenderness which made Rose's stomach lurch, this time with envy. How wonderful it must be to be loved like that! All around them, other men were saying goodbye to their womenfolk, mostly showing little emotion, though several of the women had tears on their cheeks. Alby released Rachel and turned towards the gangway and Steve grabbed Rose's shoulders – she could not help a quick wince – and kissed her briefly on the forehead. 'Mind you take care o' them girls o' mine and see they're sent off somewhere safe,' he said. And before she could reply, he was mounting the gangway, leaving her without so much as a backward glance.

Rose and Rachel stood and waved until their men had disappeared into the bowels of the ship, then Rachel wiped away the tears, blew her nose and smiled up at the other woman. 'You're so sensible, Rose,' she said in a small voice. 'But you an' Steve have had years together; Alby an' me's only been wed a twelvemonth. I expect I'll get used to sayin' goodbye to him, given time.'

The two women turned away from the quayside, heading back towards the city. Rose did not want to tell Rachel how she felt about Steve, yet it seemed like cheating to pretend that she was hiding deep emotion, able to conquer her sadness by strength of character. Hesitantly, she remarked that her married life had not been all plain sailing. 'Steve wouldn't think much of it if I wept all over him. And besides, I've been seeing him off for the best part of ten years now,' she confided. 'To tell you the truth, Rachel, there have been times when I were downright glad to see him go. He – he's not so good when he's downed a few pints, if you see what I mean.'

Rachel looked up at her, her big dark eyes full of understanding. 'I did wonder, from something Alby let fall once . . . but he said all that was a thing of the past. He said Steve's been off the drink . . . oh, for ages.'

'He's been much better,' Rose acknowledged, as they crossed Islington. She paused on the far pavement. 'Want to come back wi' me for a cuppa and a scone? You could meet Daisy and Petal; they're good kids but if Steve's right, and war really does break out, I'm goin' to send them to the country, so you may not meet them again till the war's over.'

'I'd like that,' Rachel said gratefully, falling into

step beside her. 'When d'you think I could call round to your factory, ask them if there's any jobs goin'?'

'Come on Monday morning, around nine o'clock; Mr Mellors's assistant will be in then and she'll tell you when to come for an interview,' Rose said.

The two young women chatted amicably as they made their way back to Bernard Terrace. Rose had left Daisy and Petal in the charge of Dulcie Briggs, knowing she could be relied upon to keep the children out of mischief and to organise them into games which would not lead to fights or damage to property. As they entered the terrace, Rose saw that today it was skipping. Two big girls turned a rope while at least a dozen smaller ones dashed in and out, chanting the strange, sometimes meaningless catches and songs which accompanied jumping rope. Daisy, her pony tail bobbing as she jumped and her face pink with exertion, saw her mother and ran out and Petal, who had seemed absorbed in a game with a number of other small girls, came flying over as well.

'Why didn't they come to see their daddy off?' Rachel enquired. 'Surely they would have enjoyed that?'

'I'm afraid it's rather old hat for them,' Rose said. 'They're back to school on Monday so they want to play with their friends whilst the holiday lasts.' She shot a quick sideways glance at Rachel. 'To tell you the truth . . .'

'Mam doesn't usually go down to the docks to see Dad off,' Daisy interrupted. 'Usually, Dad goes down earlier to have a jar or two with the fellers. Only today, he asked Mam to go since she weren't working. We could have gone, me and Petal, only the dock's always so crowded when a ship's leaving and we get shoved and pushed around, you know, being small.'

Rachel laughed. 'I'm small meself, so I know what you mean,' she said cheerfully. 'D'you know who I am?' She pointed a finger at Daisy. 'I know you must be Daisy . . .' she transferred the pointing finger at the younger girl, 'and you must be Petal; but do you know who *I* am?'

Petal said nothing. She put her index finger in her mouth and regarded Rachel solemnly before suddenly remarking: 'It's rude to point, missus; my mammy says so and so does our teacher.'

Rachel laughed again. 'You're right,' she acknowledged. 'But aren't you even going to have a guess?'

Petal did not reply, but Daisy said thoughtfully: 'You might be a pal of me mam's, someone what works in her factory, but I don't think you are. I think you must be the lady what's married to Dad's friend Alby. I think you're Mrs Cohen.'

'Clever girl,' Rachel said approvingly. She fished a small purse out of her handbag, flipped it open, and handed each child a round, brown penny. 'There you are, a prize for being so clever. Now don't go spending it all in one shop.'

'Thank you *very* much,' Daisy said fervently. 'Can we go and spend it now, Mam?'

Rose agreed that they could go to the corner shop, but Petal hung back, gazing from the penny in her fist to Rachel's face. 'Only – only I didn't guess, so I shouldn't have the penny,' she pointed out. 'It isn't fair that I should have a penny when I couldn't think who you were.'

'Ah, but you reminded me that it's rude to point,' Rachel said, virtuously, but with a twinkle. 'So you see, you are just as entitled to your penny as Daisy is.'

Petal thought this over for a moment, then nodded vigorously. 'Okay,' she said, joyously. 'Come on, Daisy, I'll race you to the corner shop.'

Chapter Three

The first Sunday in September was warm and sunny, and when Rose looked out of her bedroom window her first thought was how nice it would be to take the children to the beach. Next day they would be back in school and who knew what the weather might do in the days ahead. But then she remembered that they were to spend today with Aunt Selina and Uncle Frank, which was an even nicer prospect than a day on the beach would have been. No sand in the sandwiches, no long journey, and no fretfulness towards the end of the afternoon because Aunt Selina and Uncle Frank would make sure that the day was as perfect as possible.

Selina was not, in fact, Rose's aunt but first cousin to her mother, though Rose had always called her Auntie since Selina was a good twenty-five years her senior, and it had seemed more natural, somehow. Selina and Frank lived in a neat house in Penny Lane. Frank ran the corner shop, helped out by his wife, whilst his elderly sister Ethel, who lived with them, saw to the house when her sister-in-law was working.

The children always enjoyed their visits to Penny Lane for they were much indulged, since Aunt Selina and Uncle Frank, childless themselves, adored children. There was always a delicious roast dinner with a special pudding for dessert, a high tea containing all the children's favourite food and, in between the two meals, a walk in nearby Prince's Park, with a bag of bread to feed to the ducks. If the weather was too wet to make outdoor pursuits possible there were various board games – old-fashioned, but none the worse for that – and usually some small gift to take home: a couple of brilliantly coloured gobstoppers, one of Ethel's home-made finger puppets, or a large and juicy orange. In short, the children always looked forward to a day spent in Penny Lane and Rose shared their feelings. Telling Aunt Selina and Ethel all about factory life, repeating the funny things the children had said or done, and hearing, in return, stories of life in the corner shop, was soothing, relaxing. The fact that the McAllisters were given delicious food which appeared on the table as if by magic helped to make each visit a memorable one, though Rose knew that they would have enjoyed their visits to Penny Lane even if they had only been given bread and margarine to eat and water to drink.

Having checked on the weather, Rose washed and dressed quickly, then popped her head round the girls' door, not at all surprised to find them already prepared for the day ahead. As the door opened Daisy, engaged in buttoning her small sister's cardigan, beamed across at her mother. 'We are almost ready,' she said proudly, 'because Aunt Selina said, last time we saw her, that if today was sunny, we could have an early dinner and take a picnic in the park. Oh, Mam, Aunt Selina's picnics are the best in the world and there'll be bread for the ducks, and perhaps some cake crumbs for the little birds. And Uncle Frank said he'd take us out in a boat on the lake if we were really good. I do *love* Uncle Frank!'

'Then we'd better have jam butties for breakfast so we can eat them as we walk down to the tram stop,' Rose said practically. 'I'll nip down and put the kettle on so we can have a cup of tea before we leave, though.'

'I'd rather have milk,' Petal observed. 'Or lemonade . . . could me and Daisy have lemonade, Mam?'

Luckily, Rose had made lemonade the day before, and presently the three of them set out for the tram stop. It was early, not yet nine o'clock, and the streets were quiet, the heat of the day already bringing with it a certain lassitude, though the children ran along in front of their mother, calling to one another and carefully avoiding the cracks in the paving stones.

They reached the house in Penny Lane and were warmly welcomed by Selina, Frank and Ethel, Selina telling them that despite the warmth she had prepared a roast dinner. 'Frank wants to listen to the Prime Minister's speech on the wireless, otherwise we might have had a cold dinner in the park,' she told them. 'But we'll eat early – I reckon we can leave the house soon after noon – and take a picnic tea out with us. I dare say there'll be a stop-me-and-buy-one in the park, so if you get too hot on the boating lake we can have a round of ice creams to cool us down.'

The children were delighted at the prospect of an early dinner and a long afternoon spent in the park, and very soon they were gathered round the dining table, watching eagerly as Uncle Frank began to carve the joint, which was beef today. It was flanked by a great many golden brown potatoes, whilst a dish piled with teacup-sized Yorkshire puddings stood in front of Aunt Selina and a tureen containing cabbage and cauliflower awaited Ethel's attention. Rose was in charge of the gravy jug, golden-bubbled and smelling delicious, and Uncle Frank had just dug his carving fork into the joint when he glanced at the clock on the mantelpiece and seemed to remember something.

'Best switch on the wireless set for a moment, Selina,' he said, pointing to the brown, box-like structure which stood right in the middle of the sideboard. 'Unless I'm much mistaken, Neville Chamberlain is going to tell us what's happened with that German feller. I can't believe they'll march into Poland, but we'd best listen to what the Prime Minister's got to say.'

Aunt Selina stood up and went over to the sideboard. For some moments, strange sounds issued from the large brown box. Then there was music, faint but recognisable. Aunt Selina twiddled the knobs and a voice, speaking harshly in some foreign language, boomed out.

Uncle Frank gave an exclamation of impatience and laid the carving knife down on the dish. 'Sit down, Selina,' he commanded, though not unkindly. 'You never will leave well alone. It were tuned into the Home Service earlier; all you had to do was turn the bloody thing on.'

Rose stared. Frank was seventy years old and had never previously used strong language in her presence, but before she could comment, another voice came from the radio. '. . . no such undertaking has been received and that consequently this country is at war with Germany.'

For a moment there was a stricken silence, then Frank began to carve the beef. 'Well, it were only what we must have expected,' he said heavily. 'We gave 'em chance after chance, but in the end the chances run out and it's war.'

Rose looked round the table. Her daughters seemed both solemn and puzzled, and Aunt Selina and Ethel had tears in their eyes, though neither let them fall. Rose herself felt a great many emotions, but realised that the chief one was relief. Whatever lay ahead, at least they now knew where they stood; they were at war and because they were an island, they could start pulling up the drawbridge, so to speak. It had been different for Poland; there had been no declaration of war, no warning of intent. Germany had simply invaded, aware of her immense military superiority, heedless of the rights and wrongs of the case. Rose's worst nightmare – that they might wake up one morning to find storm troopers at their door – no longer seemed a possibility. Forewarned was forearmed, and Mr Chamberlain's words – 'we are ready' – must mean something, after all.

Uncle Frank, at the head of the table, continued to carve, laying the big slices of beef tenderly on a plate which he then passed to his wife, who added roast potatoes and Yorkshire puddings before handing the plate to Ethel for vegetables. Rose, last in the line, poured gravy and passed the plate to Daisy, who regarded it with satisfaction, though the manners dinned into her by her mother prevented her from so much as touching her knife and fork. Uncle Frank was cutting Petal's meat into smaller pieces, and as he did so he glanced across at Rose. 'I saw in the *Echo* that plans for the evacuation of schoolchildren are already made,' he observed. 'You'll send these two? Only we all saw pictures of what happened in Poland. I know they can't march across the Channel – France is in the way for a start – but them Heinkels and Dorniers don't take no heed of such things. The only safe place will be deep in the country where there's nothing worth bombing.'

'Steve and I talked it over and agreed they'd have to go,' Rose said uneasily. She had tried to prepare the children, making evacuation to the country sound like a huge adventure, but it was one thing to talk about the possibility of parting and quite another to realise that it was actually upon them. When they turned up at school next day, Daisy and Petal would be labelled and led off to Lime Street station. Parents would not know their ultimate destination until they received the postcards which the children had been given to send, and Rose dreaded the moment when she would see them off on the first journey they would ever have taken without her.

Everyone now had a laden plate before them and Uncle Frank took the remains of the joint over to the sideboard, then returned to the table and sat down again. He picked up his knife and fork, the signal the children had been waiting for, and they all began to eat, though Rose felt that the food on her plate could have been sawdust, for all the attention she gave it.

Selina, however, was made of sterner stuff. 'I've made a steamed apple pudding with custard for dessert, but no one won't get any if they don't finish up every mouthful of their first course,' she announced. 'This here war is bound to mean shortages, rationing and that. So we'd best make the most of this grand dinner. I want to see clean plates and big smiles from everyone, because war or no war we're taking that picnic to the park and having a grand old day of it.'

'I'm sure we'll all eat up,' Rose said gaily. 'And tomorrow, you two girls will be starting the biggest adventure of your lives. I expect you'll be living on a farm, with animals all around you, and they'll let you help with feeding the little lambs and milking the cows . . . oh, you'll be doing all sorts! Don't I wish I could go with you, but now we're at war uniforms will be needed even more urgently, so I can't just abandon my job.'

'We'll all be doing something towards the war,' Aunt Selina said approvingly. 'Well done, Petal, well done,

Daisy, those plates are so clean I'll scarcely need to wash 'em up. Now come along, Frank, you're going to be last again.'

'When I were young, my gran told me to chew each mouthful a hundred times,' Frank observed, grinning at the children. 'I doubt if this pair so much as tasted their grub, let alone chewed it a hundred times. Still, they look pretty well on it.' He finished his last potato and heaved a satisfied sigh. 'Now who's going to help Aunt Selina to clear these plates and bring on the pudding?'

'Mammy, I know I'm not in Daisy's class at school, but – but I can stay with her on the train, can't I? And what about when we get to – to wherever we're going? Only I'd rather be with Daisy, even than with the other kids in my year, and – and who'll help me dress in the mornings and tell me to change my socks if I aren't with Daisy?'

Petal's small face, looking anxiously up at her, wrung Rosie's heart. Petal had put into words what had been worrying Rose herself, for though the teachers had assured parents at a meeting some time earlier that every effort would be made to keep families together, they had admitted that this might not always be possible. But Rose smiled reassuringly down at her little daughter, determined not to let her own fears show. 'I've told Miss Adams, and Miss French, that you must be kept together so I'm sure they will see that you aren't parted.'

As she spoke, the untidy group of children and mothers entered Lime Street station and Rose, glancing up at the clock, realised that she must begin to make her way to the factory, for lateness would not be tolerated. The teachers were rounding the children up, trying to get them back into line, and Rose bent over Daisy and gave her a hug. 'Take care of your little sister, queen,' she said quietly. 'You've got your post-card? You won't forget to write it as soon as you arrive, letting me know your new address? I'll do my very best to come and see you at the weekend, but if I can't make it I'll write back to let you know your postcard has arrived safely. Have you got your carry-out? Your gas mask? Your toothbrush and your little suitcase? Yes, I see you've got everything; you're a good girl.'

Tears trembled on Daisy's long lashes but she caught hold of Petal's hand and smiled bravely up at her mother. 'Yes, we've got everything, Mam; you've checked us at least six times this morning already, and we've not had a chance to put anything down,' she said. 'I'll do everything you told me and I won't let them separate me and Petal, no matter what.' She glanced round her rather wildly. 'But – but I haven't seen Nicky, Mam. He'll be coming with us, won't he? I know he's not often in school, but he won't stay in Bernard Terrace when all the other children have gone, will he?'

'No, no, he'll be here somewhere, along with the Ryan kids,' Rose said, rather absently. She felt tempted to add that they might not recognise Nicky with his layers of dirt washed off and his best clothes on, for everyone had been warned that the children must look respectable. At that moment, however, she caught sight of him. His hair had been cut cruelly short and he wore a shirt and trousers, both far too large for him. Rather to her surprise, his gas mask case was slung over one shoulder and one pocket of his shabby jacket bulged with what was, presumably, his carry-out. He saw her watching him and came over to them, grinning cheerfully.

'Mornin', missus; wotcher, girls,' he said. 'You awright, Daisy? I'm lookin' forward to it, me. Be a change from Ma Ryan's awful cookin', any road.' He turned to Rose. 'And don't you go worryin', missus, I'll keep an eye on these two for you.'

'You won't be able to; you're eleven an' Daisy an' me's younger,' Petal pointed out dolefully. 'Oh, here comes Miss French; she's shouting at you, Nicky.'

Miss French bustled up to them, telling Nicky crossly to get back to his own age group, waiting until he did so before patting Rose's arm and assuring her that she would take care of Daisy and Petal. 'And I don't mean to have my girls mixing with toughs like that young fellow,' she said decisively. She turned to the children. 'Say goodbye to your mother, my dears, our train has arrived.'

Rose turned to the girls and kissed them, lifting Petal up in her arms first and then doing the same to Daisy. 'My darlings, take care of yourselves and each other,' she said urgently. 'And – and have fun and be good.'

'We will be good, Mam,' Daisy said. 'Now you go off 'cos you mustn't be late for work. We'll be all right, see if we ain't!'

It had been a long and tiring day and the children's carry-out was nothing more than a memory before they arrived at their destination, the small town of Ruthin, set deep in the Welsh countryside. The children were ushered off the train and lined up in a long crocodile on the platform. The teachers were reinforced here by half a dozen friendly and efficient-looking country women who were to show them the way to the Town Hall, the temporary reception centre where they would meet the people who would take them in.

As they left the station, Daisy looked around her. Ahead of her, rearing above the slate roofs of the little town, she saw a church steeple and the face of a gold-figured clock; saw too that though the town itself was in a hollow with hills all around, it was also built on a hill so that the road up which the ladies were leading them was a steep one. Daisy looked round her with pleasure; in the warm September sunshine she thought it a fairytale town, a far cry from the huge imposing buildings and crowded streets of Liverpool but none the worse for that. She took Petal's hand, for her little sister had begun to lag. 'Not far now,' she said encouragingly. 'And when we get there the lady said we'd get give a nice tea. You'll like that, won't you?'

'Yes, I'd like to have me tea,' Petal admitted. 'I shouldn't have ate me carry-out so quickly – you did say I shouldn't – but I was so excited that I couldn't wait.' She heaved a deep sigh, dragging on Daisy's hand. 'Is it much further? Only me little legs is achin' like billy-o.'

Daisy was about to reply when she saw the children at the head of the crocodile turning into a large stone-built building. It had narrow windows, above which were pointed, almost churchlike, arches and over the double oak doors there was a carving of an ancient castle. Daisy and Petal, still holding hands tightly, went through the doors into a milling crowd of children and adults, feeling somewhat at a loss. Their teachers could not be immediately identified in the throng, but before Daisy could begin to panic someone grabbed her elbow and she turned to see Nicky Bostock grinning down at her. He had a plate in one hand piled with sandwiches, biscuits and buns, and a mug of tea in the other. 'Ain't this just prime?' he said, pushing the plate into Daisy's hands. 'Go on, gerroutside o' that lot, the pair of you. Us fellers were sent ahead and I'm already full to burstin'. Here, Petal, hang on to me mug o' tea and I'll fetch you an' Daisy one – or would you rather have milk? There is milk – I see'd a big jug of it.'

Both girls opted for milk and Nicky disappeared into the crowd once more, so Daisy steered her little sister to a vacant chair and they sat down with the plate of food in Daisy's lap and began to eat. A big, commanding-looking woman with cropped grey hair and a weather-beaten face saw them and came over. 'You've not lost much time,' she observed. 'Well, I just hope you can eat all that food since you've helped yourselves to such a quantity. You should never forget there's others just as hungry as yourselves, you know.'

Daisy was so humiliated at this suggestion of greed that she only stared, open-mouthed, but Petal was made of sterner stuff. 'We was give it, we didn't ask for it,' she said, her voice shrill with indignation. 'We's too little and weak to push through that great crowd round the food tables, so don't you say we took more'n our share, 'cos we never did. Our mam's brung us up not to grab, missus!'

The woman's face grew so red that Daisy thought she was about to burst but, apparently, she was not angry, only amused, for she gave a great bark of laughter and ruffled Petal's long fair locks. 'I apologise unreservedly . . . that means I'm sorry I misjudged you,' she said, still smiling. 'And anyway, the ladies' committee have been truly generous and provided enough food for double the number of children who have arrived here today, so you tuck in and enjoy it. Want a drink?'

Once more, Daisy opened her mouth to reply but was forestalled by the arrival of Nicky carrying two

62

Bakelite mugs of milk. He handed them over and took his own mug of tea back from Petal, then dragged over another vacant chair and sat down on it, grinning up at the large lady. 'The bossy woman in the blue check dress told me to give her a hand and take some drinks round,' he informed her. 'Them what's supposed to be servin' is stuck behind the trestle tables and the crowd's so thick that little kids can't get through; or the mugs get knocked out of their hands, which is worse. I'll just down me own tea and then I'll gerrin the scrum again, see if they need any more help.'

Daisy watched with awe as Nicky drank his tea in one long swallow and then disappeared into the crowd once more. She glanced across to where the elderly woman had stood, but she had disappeared so Daisy sipped her milk and ate the food, and told herself that she was lucky to have a friend like Nicky who would look out for her and Petal, in this land which was as strange to him as it was to herself.

They had just finished their food, and Daisy had placed the plate and the empty mugs neatly beneath the wooden chair she and Petal were sharing, when a large man in a tweed suit got up on a chair, clapped his hands loudly and asked for silence. 'Now you've had your teas, children, we're going to start moving you out of here,' he said briskly. 'The folk who will take you in will come to *you*, so if you could all sit down quietly, on the floor, you'll either hear your names called or someone will come over and introduce themselves. In the meantime, stay where you are unless you hear your name. Is that clear?'

All round the hall heads were nodded, and now that everyone was seated Daisy saw, for the first time, that there were a great many grown-ups in the doorway, some of them pushing and jostling and all of them scanning the children's faces eagerly, and giving little smiles and nods of encouragement whenever they met a child's eye. On either side of the doorway there were middle-aged men holding lists and talking to the waiting women and then some of the women were handed sheets of paper and waved into the room. The first women called out names, children raised their hands and at long last Daisy could see that things were beginning to move. She and Petal sat cross-legged, gazing with interest at the faces of the women as they advanced into the room. Most looked kind and interesting, but there were one or two, Daisy thought apprehensively, who had mean, pinched faces or tight little mouths, which she thought augured ill for the children they were given.

Presently, however, the hall began to empty, though the press of women in the doorway did not seem to have decreased by very much. Nicky, sitting beside her, leaned over. 'I heared someone say that a good few of the kids what was expected haven't arrived,' he whispered hoarsely. 'I wish we could choose the women, 'stead of them choosin' us, specially now there's so few kids left.'

'So do I,' Daisy murmured in heartfelt tones. She looked at Petal, whose fair curls were rumpled and whose eyelids were beginning to droop, then down at her own neat person. She had seen Fanny Hanson and her sister Esme go off with a fat and comfortable-looking woman, and wondered why two girls renowned for being both untidy and dirty had been chosen in preference to Petal and herself. She voiced the thought to Nicky, who said reassuringly that this was not the case. 'Them women gets give name by the fellers – someone said they're council officials –

standin' each side of the doorway,' he explained. 'You'll get took by someone nice, don't you worrit. And so will I, of course,' he finished, his tone of bright optimism contrasting oddly with the worried look in his eyes.

And presently, there were only six children left, and Daisy saw Petal's eyes filling with tears and felt angry enough to jump to her feet, even though she was immediately told to sit herself down again by one of the ladies' committee. 'I shan't,' Daisy said, defiant for the first time in her life. 'We – we don't care if no one wants us, my sister and me, 'cos we've got a good mammy back in Liverpool and if none of these ladies wants us we'll go back to her right now, even if we have to bleedin' well walk every inch of the way.'

There was an indignant murmur from the waiting women and one of them surged forward and took both Daisy's hands in a warm and comforting clasp. 'It's a scandal the way they've arranged things, my little love,' she said warmly. 'There's a dozen women here what 'ud be happy as larks to have you live with them, but we aren't allowed to choose else a nice little couple like you and your sister would have been took among the first.' She reached out to pat Petal's cheek. 'What's your names, loves?'

'We're Daisy and Petal McAllister,' Daisy said, rubbing her eyes with the backs of both hands, 'and – and the boy what's with us is Nicky Bostock. He lives near us only he's got no mam and dad, so he lives with the Ryans, and – and they went ages ago.'

'McAllister and Bostock, McAllister and Bostock,' the woman murmured. 'I guess there's someone at the back of this lot . . .' she indicated the women in the doorway, 'who can't get through to you, but I'll soon put that right. You wait on a moment.'

She turned and pushed her way through the crowd and presently reappeared with a broad beam almost splitting her face in two. 'They are for Mrs Blodwen Williams of Ty Siriol,' she said breathlessly to the nearest council official. 'She came in the pony and trap and meant to leave the pony in front of the station where there's tethering posts and that. But someone has left a couple of wild sheepdogs tied up there, and Myfanwy – that's the pony – wouldn't settle, so Mrs Williams had to wait until the dogs' owner turned up. She's down there now, doesn't like to leave the pony, so if you'll tick them off I'll take them out to the trap.'

The man to whom she had been speaking consulted his list, marked it, and then nodded, and the woman took Daisy and Petal by the hand and would have led them out, but Daisy hung back. 'Wharrabout Nicky?' she asked wildly. 'He's the only one left now and I told you, the Ryans went ages ago!'

The men consulted their lists with worried frowns, shaking their heads, but the woman who held the girls' hands was of a more practical turn of mind. 'Count up the Ryans,' she said suddenly. 'If this lad lives with the Ryan family, I guess someone simply didn't realise he wasn't a Ryan too. Go on, count the Ryans.'

There was an anxious moment whilst the men scanned their lists, then one of them said, slowly: 'There's more'n one family of Ryans, you know, but I've got a group here, eldest Nicky, then four others, the youngest Tommy.'

Daisy gave a crow of triumph. 'Nicky's a Bostock . . . I *telled* you so,' she said. 'Is he to go with 'em, after all? Can someone show him the way?' She looked back. Nicky was standing in the hall with both hands shoved deep into the pockets of his trousers. His lips were pursed as though he was whistling, but no sound emerged, and though he had ducked his chin and was staring down at his feet, Daisy thought there were tears on his stubby black lashes. She did not wonder at it, for the tiny taste she had had of being unwanted still hurt her with an almost physical pain.

'He can't go to Mrs Hepzibah Evans; she was grumbling she hadn't got room for the children she did take, so she won't thank you for an extra one . . .' one of the men was beginning, when the woman who was holding Petal and Daisy let them go and surged back towards Nick. 'Get your stuff, young man, you're coming with me,' she said briskly, ignoring the murmurs from the women in the doorway and the council officials. 'I'm Mrs Foley and my husband and me have got a flat over our butcher's shop in Clwyd Street. You look a likely lad to me and the child I was expecting hasn't turned up yet . . . besides, I can always squeeze in an extra one.'

Nicky looked up at her. 'Thanks, missus,' he said gruffly. 'I – I won't be no trouble.' As the woman and the three children pushed through the crowd in the doorway, he gave Daisy's shoulder a poke. 'Thanks, Daisy, but I knew it would be all right, really,' he muttered. 'See you in school tomorrer, I reckon.'

They emerged into a cool dusk with a sliver of moon already showing as the daylight faded. Mrs Foley handed the girls over to another woman before bustling Nicky away in what Daisy guessed to be the direction of Clwyd Street, and the girls were led back down the hill to the station where they saw a pony and trap from which a large woman was descending. She had bright red cheeks, thick grey hair plaited into a coronet around her head, small twinkling brown eyes, and an expression of great friendliness; Daisy liked her on sight and knew, from one glance at Petal's face,

that her sister felt the same. Their companion led the
girls up to the trap, saying as she did so: 'Here's Daisy
and Petal McAllister, Mrs Williams, come all the way
from Liverpool to stay with you until it's safe for them
to return to their own home.'

Mrs Williams held out two arms like bolsters, and
gathered the girls into a warm embrace. 'Sorry I am
that I couldn't come into the hall after you, fynwy
fechan i, but Myfanwy has a mind of her own and
there was nowhere to tether her where she wouldn't
be in the way,' she said. She produced, from her pocket,
a couple of lumps of sugar and handed one to each
child. 'Want to get on her good side? Know how to
feed a horse?'

'You must keep your hands flat or they'll nibble
your fingers,' the girls replied in a chorus, for Mammy
often gave them a piece of carrot or perhaps even a
bit of bread to give to the milkman's old dappled
mare. We may not be country children but we do know
something about horses, Daisy thought proudly, as
she felt the pony's soft lips twitching across her palm.

With the pony satisfied, Mrs Williams helped the
two children into the trap. Before climbing up herself
she checked that nothing obscured the white painted
bands across the back of the trap, though there
seemed to be very little traffic around at this time in
the evening.

As soon as she had taken her seat, she clicked to
the pony and the equipage moved forward. Daisy
looked around her as the pony began to trot along a
curved road and across a bridge over what Mrs Williams
told her was the river Clwyd. Then they turned right
into the road which led, their companion said, to Ty
Siriol, which was the name of her farm. On the left
hand side Daisy saw a stone-built school with gabled

68

windows and a sizeable playground, and when she remarked on it Mrs Williams told her that it was Borthyn School, where she and Petal and their schoolfellows would be attending classes.

She began to ask Mrs Williams about the farm but had scarcely got out more than a few words when Petal spoke in an urgent undertone. 'Daisy, is we going far? Only I need the lavvy ever so bad.'

Despite the fact that she had almost whispered, it was Mrs Williams who replied. 'You poor little thing. I'll draw up just as soon as we're clear of the houses and I dare say you can use the ditch, for we've had nigh on two weeks of dry weather and the farm's still some way from here. Dilys – she's my daughter – will have supper on the table for when we get home.' As she spoke, she drew the trap into a gateway and indicated that the girls should get down. Petal leaped out with such alacrity that she almost fell and Daisy, following more slowly, realised that she, too, needed to spend a penny, and the sooner the better. She steered Petal towards the gate, unlatched it and swung it partly open, then looked into the meadow beyond and changed her mind, shutting the gate before Petal could venture through it. 'There's huge cows in there; we'll do what Mrs Williams says and go in the ditch,' she announced. 'No one will see us 'cos of all that tall grass and wild flowers . . . oh, Petal, I said in the ditch, not on the bank! You can be seen for miles, I should think.'

'I don't care,' Petal panted. 'I'm in a *hurry*, Daisy, and that means I can't wait. But you can go in the ditch if you like. Can I get back in the trap when I've finished?'

'No you can't, you can jolly well wait for me,' Daisy said crossly, bobbing down. 'I shan't be a minute . . .

oh, Petal, your skirt's got tucked into your knickers. Wait a minute and I'll straighten you out.'

'I want to get back in the cart,' Petal whined. 'I stung me bum on a stinging nettle and I want to sit on it and squash the sting out of it else I shan't be able to sleep tonight. Come *on*, Daisy!'

Presently, the children got back in the trap and the pony set off once more, trotting briskly along the road, though Mrs Williams kept well to the side.

During the drive, Daisy suddenly knew that she would remember this journey all her life. As they had left the town behind she had seen the great humped shoulders of a mountain range on her right, and she could even make out the dim shapes of sheep and cows in the meadows. In places, the road was tree-lined, in others, pasture. The breeze which blew into her face smelt of sweet country things, without a hint of smoke from factory chimneys or Mersey mud. Above her, stars swam in the dark blue of the sky, and the silver eye of the moon lit up the road ahead so clearly that it could almost have been day. The quiet was only broken by the creaking of the pony's harness and the tappety-tap of its hooves on the tarmacked road, and Daisy thought these sounds were far more beautiful than the sounds of home: the clank and clatter of trams, the hooting of ships on the Mersey, and the constant hum of traffic and shouts of noisy, exuberant people going about their daily business.

Mrs Williams began to talk, telling the children that her name was Blodwen and that they should call her 'Auntie Blod'. 'You'll meet my daughter, Dilys, and Mr Williams – you must call him Uncle Gwil – when we reach Ty Siriol,' she told them. 'I have a son as well as a daughter; his name is Gareth, but he's in the Rifle Brigade and abroad at present, so you aren't likely to meet him. We've farmhands who work for us, of course, and neighbours who come and go, but a farm in the Welsh countryside is probably very different from your own home.' The children were seated one each side of her and now she looked a trifle anxiously first at Daisy, then at Petal. 'I guess you'll be homesick at first, but we'll do our best to see that you're happy and I'm sure you'll soon settle in,' she told them. 'Someone will drive you into Ruthin to school each day – it'll probably be Dilys or myself – so you won't lack for friends, and your mam can come and stay whenever she's able, though I believe she has a job?'

'Yes, she does; she makes uniforms for soldiers and sailors and airmen,' Daisy said eagerly. 'It's very important work; she's helping with the war effort. But she'll come and visit us just as soon as she has some time off, she promised.'

'Well, isn't that grand?' Mrs Williams said heartily. 'I understand from your teachers that none of you will be expected in school tomorrow, and maybe not the day after either, so you'll have time to get to know the farm before your mam arrives. Dilys will take you round tomorrow, and show you where everything is – hens, pigs, sheep, barns and stables, cowshed and byres – and you'll find you soon grow accustomed.'

'Will we be able to help on the farm?' Petal squeaked. 'Our mammy said there were all sorts of jobs what needed doin' on a farm. Feedin' animals and c'llectin' eggs and cuttin' corn . . .'

Mrs Williams laughed. 'We'll teach you to do all of it in time,' she said reassuringly. 'And we've a quiet old pony which Dilys used when she was a girl; you can learn to ride on Feathers if you like.'

'We'd love that, wouldn't we, Petal?' Daisy said

71

eagerly. 'Do you have dogs and cats? Petal and me's always wanted a dog or a cat, but Mam said it were just another mouth to feed, and besides – besides, our dad doesn't like cats or dogs. I see him kick a cat right across Bernard Terrace once, when he thought no one were lookin'. The poor thing were only walkin' along, mindin' its own business, when it found itself flyin' through the air on the toe of Dad's sea boot.'

Mrs Williams said something under her breath, in a language which Daisy guessed must be Welsh, then smiled apologetically. 'Sorry, I was forgetting. As you say, a good reason for not keeping a cat, but to answer your question, we've three sheepdogs and probably half a dozen cats. So your dad's a seaman, is he? Then I dare say he won't be home all that often.'

Daisy agreed, thinking that Mrs Williams sounded as though she had no wish to be visited by a man who kicked cats. She wondered, rather doubtfully, if she should not have told this lovely, comfortable woman about that particular incident, but then the trap turned right, into a wonderful leafy lane which wound between high banks. Trees grew on either side, sometimes leaning over the lane so that their mingling branches turned it into a mysterious tunnel, and Daisy sat forward on her seat, gazing ahead with all her might, spellbound by the beauty and strangeness of it.

'Not far now, chicks,' Mrs Williams said, as though guessing how tired they both were. 'Now don't forget, you may call me Auntie Blod and Mr Williams will be Uncle Gwil, because there's no sense in formality when you're all sharing a house. Here we are then, home at last!' As she spoke, she turned the pony into a large, paved yard, surrounded on three sides by what Daisy imagined must be farm buildings. Ahead of them was the farmhouse. It was a low, whitewashed building, slate-roofed and somehow reliable-looking, as though it had been there for many hundreds of years and would still be there in the hundreds of years to come. There were no lights showing, but as Mrs Williams drew the trap to a halt someone opened the door and a great rush of golden light spilled out. The room thus exposed by the open door was warm and homely, with a big table covered by a red and white gingham cloth, upon which stood a large pot of something which steamed.

But before she could begin to wonder what was in the pot, a figure emerged and came towards the cart. Mrs Williams began to speak in Welsh, then stopped abruptly, heaving herself out of the trap and holding her arms out to Daisy. 'Got to remember to speak English, I have,' she said, in self-reproof. 'Dilys fach, this is Daisy and the littl'un's Petal.' She stood Daisy down on the cobbles, lifted up the drowsy Petal, and handed her to the girl called Dilys. 'You take the children inside while I deal with the trap and Myfanwy here.'

Daisy saw, as soon as they entered the lamplit kitchen, that Dilys and her mother resembled each other closely. Dilys was a tall, sturdily built girl, with rich golden hair and rosy red cheeks, very like her mother's. But Daisy found herself concentrating on the contents of that steaming pot and was grateful when Dilys, following the direction of her gaze, said with a laugh: 'We cooked a mutton stew because Mam thought there might be some delay on the road – and how right she was!' She had carried Petal into the kitchen with as little effort as her mother had shown, and now she put the child down in a comfortable ladder-backed chair, well supplied with cushions, and indicated that Daisy should sit on the one next to it.

'In the normal way we'd wait for my mam, we would, but I reckon the sooner you get fed and into bed the better.' She began to ladle a generous portion of stew and potatoes on to two dishes which she put down in front of the children. 'Eat up, my little ones, and tomorrow I'll take you round the farm and show you what sort of place it is.'

Next day, Daisy woke to find sunshine streaming through a crack in the window curtains. For a moment, she lay there, wondering where on earth she was and why she appeared to be sunk in some delicious warm softness which cradled her like a mother's arms. She remembered being told that this was a beautiful goose feather bed. Petal, no doubt, was still sound asleep beside her, and this was Ty Siriol . . . and today, the beautiful, golden-haired Dilys was to show them round the farm.

She sat up and immediately realised why the shaft of sunlight had only now struck her face. Petal was not in bed, but at the window, spread-elbowed on the broad sill with her nose pressed to the glass. The window, a sash one, was open at top and bottom, and now that she was properly awake Daisy could hear a number of fascinating sounds: buckets clanking, boots clumping across the yard, a cockerel crowing some-where in the distance, and a cow – perhaps several cows – making the low contented sound which Daisy had always been told was mooing.

'I say, Petal, what's out there?' she said eagerly, jumping out of bed and hopping across to the window.

Petal turned and beamed at her. 'It's cows, and two black and white dogs, and heaps and heaps of chickens,' she said excitedly. 'Let's go downstairs, Daisy. I wants me breakfast but I wants to go out into all that lovely sunshine more than anything else. Oh, Daisy, ain't we lucky? The lady with the golden hair what helped me undress last night just came out of that shed with two buckets full of milk. I bet I can have some for breakfast if I ask nicely.'

She headed for her clothes but Daisy grabbed her shoulder and jerked her to a halt. 'Washing first,' she said firmly. 'A nice strip-down wash first thing, Mam said, *and* we're to clean our teeth. Is there water in that tall jug or do we have to go down and fetch it?'

'There's water,' Petal said. 'It were too heavy for me to lift but I dabbled me hands in it, honest to God I did, Daisy. Won't that do, just for today?'

'No, it will not,' Daisy said firmly. She found that Petal was not the only one who could not lift the jug but she managed to tilt it so that water ran into the round basin. She helped Petal to wash first, then washed herself, shivering as the cold water touched her warm skin, but determined to have what her mother would have called 'a proper wash'. Once they were both clean, she helped Petal to put on her underwear, cotton dress, socks and sandals, then dressed herself and brushed her hair. Petal's long wavy hair had already had the brush dragged through it. Daisy would have liked to plait her own hair or make a pony tail, but could not manage it, so left it loose. Then she and Petal plumped up the pillows and pulled the blanket across the feather bed. As they left the room, Daisy glanced round it. Whitewashed walls, a wooden floor, black with age and as uneven as the surface of the sea; a wide window with a broad sill overlooking the farmyard and framed with yellow curtains, and a roller blind which Petal must have let up in order to watch the activity below; the wash stand with its jug and basin and an enamel bucket beneath . . . aha, that would be for the slops. It was too late to call Petal back – she was already halfway down the stairs – but Daisy retraced her steps, emptied their washing water into the bucket, and peered under the bed. She remembered Dilys telling them there was a chamber pot stowed away there, for their use, but doubted whether Petal had woken for long enough to take advantage of it. However, she heaved it out and examined it critically, glad to find it empty but awed by its proportions. It was a giant pot, fit only for a giant bottom; Daisy knew she would never dare perch on it in case she fell backwards and got wedged. She wondered if they could ask for a smaller one, then dismissed the matter and, hefting the slop bucket in both hands, made for the stairs.

Their first day on the farm was a wonderful one for both children. They met Mr Williams, a small, wiry man whose checked cap seemed to be a permanent fixture, since he did not even take it off when he sat down to dinner. Because his wife and daughter talked all the time, Daisy thought he seemed a very quiet man. He ate enormously, answered any question put to him in monosyllables, had a mug so huge to hold his tea that Daisy thought a mouse could have enjoyed a good swim in it, and smoked a pipe which Auntie Blod told them smelled so terrible that he was never allowed to use it in the house. The only time he volunteered any information was when Petal asked the identity of the young man in the photograph on the parlour mantelpiece. It happened that Dilys and her mother were engaged in noisy conversation at the time, so Mr Williams was the only person to whom Petal could address her question. He grinned at her, revealing surprisingly white and perfect teeth. 'That's Gareth, our eldest,' he said briefly. 'Joined up. Rifle Brigade.

Won prizes for his shooting . . . competitions and that . . . has our Gareth.'

At this point, Auntie Blod and Dilys began to dish up and the conversation turned to what task the farmhands would undertake that afternoon.

As soon as the children had got up, Auntie Blod had taken them round the farmhouse. It was a large, rambling building, built on several different levels, so that there were steps up and down all over the place. Daisy was intrigued by what Auntie Blod called her stillroom, a sort of walk-in pantry or larder, lined with shelves upon which stood rows and rows of jams, bottled fruit and pickles of every description. The children gazed with awe at such a quantity of food, for though their mother fed them as well as she could, she did not store food in the house and had never made jam, or preserved fruit, in her life. 'Why aren't there apples or pears? Don't you grow them?' Petal had asked, having scanned the shelves. 'There must be everything else in here, except for apples and pears.'

Auntie Blod had given her an indulgent look. 'These here are all soft fruits . . . soft vegetables too,' she had explained. 'You don't see no 'taties, nor turnips or swedes either, because, although we keep 'em, we keep 'em raw, not cooked. Presently, we'll go outside and take a look at the dairy, and then I'll show you the apple loft and the potato clamp.' She chuckled richly. 'Farmers don't waste nothing; we grow too much to eat it all while it's in season, so we store the surplus.'

True to her word, when breakfast was over, she escorted them round the farm buildings. Daisy was very impressed with the dairy which had recently been built, where Auntie Blod spent several hours a day. There was a butter churn, huge marble slabs upon which containers of milk stood to cool, and a great many gleaming pans, ladles and other instruments for the making of butter, cheese and cream. Tentatively, she had asked if she might help next time Auntie Blod made butter or cheese, and was delighted to be told that, when they were not in school, they might help in all sorts of ways.

Auntie Blod had then returned to the house to prepare the dinner and Dilys had taken them all round the farm. They had seen enormous pigs – which Dilys called sows – surrounded by little pink babies. They had seen the great lumbering cows and their wet-nosed, long-legged calves. They had been introduced to the great Clydesdales who worked as hard as any man on the farm, Dilys had told them, and she had given the children carrots to feed to Myfanwy and Feathers, the ponies who pulled the trap and had once been ridden by Dilys and her brother, Gareth, when they had been younger – and a good deal lighter – and needed to get about without constantly begging lifts from their parents.

When dinner was finished, they were told they might feed the hens and were given a small scoop of corn each. Normally the hens were fed morning and evening, and not in the middle of the day, but Dilys said they must grow used to the way the poultry mobbed anyone leaving the farmhouse – she had clearly noticed that both Petal and Daisy had clung very close to her when the hens had appeared to be about to attack.

Daisy and Petal set off across the yard feeling a considerable degree of trepidation when the hens rushed towards them, flat-footed and splay-legged, making the most unholy din. Some of them actually took to the air in order to see what was in the metal scoops the children held, but as soon as Daisy, gritting her teeth, hurled a handful of grain on to the cobbles, they abandoned their attempts and began eagerly pecking, shouldering each other aside, stamping on each other's feet, and generally behaving like the undisciplined, greedy louts Daisy had thought them.

'I shan't mind the hens any more,' Petal confided, when the last of the grain had gone. 'You know that big shed on wheels, in the next field? Auntie Blod said she shuts the hens in there at night, because of foxes. She said they lay their eggs in there as well – did you peep inside when Dilys took us past it? I'd like to collect the eggs but I don't want to have to fight a great heap of chickens – hens, I mean – if they'd rather keep them.'

'The way you said it, it sounded as though foxes laid their eggs in the hen house,' Daisy said, with a giggle. 'I know the hens are all right, really – Auntie Blod said so – but I'm not going into that old shed when they are in there, not for a fortune. I did peep inside and the smell made me eyes water. There are lots of smells on a farm, aren't there? I thought the pigs would pong most of all, though I like their smell, but hens really stink.'

By this time, the hens, having eaten all the grain, had wandered off, so the children turned their steps back towards the farmhouse. They had reached the kitchen and were about to ask Auntie Blod what they should do next when Daisy clapped a hand to her mouth, giving a muffled scream. 'Oh, Petal, the post-card! We promised Mam we'd send a postcard just as soon as we knew our address! Oh lummy, she'll be so worried . . . she thought we'd arrive yesterday after-noon, not late at night, and I don't suppose there's a post box for miles!'

Overhearing, Auntie Blod turned towards them.

'It's my fault, so it is,' she said guiltily. 'Promised, I did, that you'd write as soon as you were settled, but it doesn't matter; fetch that postcard, cariad, and you can take it to the box at the end of the lane.'

Daisy ran up to her bedroom and fished the card – already stamped – out of the string bag which Rose had given her to carry their small, personal possessions in. Then she thundered down the stairs again and shot into the kitchen. Petal was eating a hot buttered scone and drinking a mug of milk, and Daisy settled herself at the table beside her with her postcard and a pencil. Starting was easy . . . 'Dear Mum . . .' but with so much to say and so little space, Daisy wondered what first to choose. Thinking it over, she realised that a lyrical description of the farm might make her mother feel that her daughters were not missing her at all, yet if she started off by saying they were homesick, her mother would be very distressed. In the end, she asked Auntie Blod what she should best do.

Auntie Blod considered. 'Just say you've arrived safely, that Ty Siriol is a farm and that Mrs Williams will be pleased to see her – and put her up for the night – just as soon as she can spare time to come,' she instructed. 'I'll write the address for you, so there's no mistake, and tell her what bus to catch.'

Petal lifted her face from her mug and stared at Auntie Blod. 'Does a bus come past here?' she asked incredulously. 'We haven't seen one all day, have we, Daisy?'

Auntie Blod laughed. 'They doesn't come all the way up here, cariad, but they stops at the end of the lane, like. Only two buses a day, there are. They leave Ruthin at eleven in the mornin' and five in the evenin', so if she drops us a line and tells us which one she'll

80

be on, you girls can go over and meet her – give her a hand with her bag.'

'That will be lovely; but our mam works shifts at her factory and she doesn't seem to get much time off,' Daisy observed. 'But I'm sure she'll come just as soon as ever she can.' She held up the postcard. 'Have I left you enough room for what you want to write, Auntie Blod?'

Auntie Blod sighed. 'Better drop her a line myself, this evening, when I have a bit more time,' she decided. 'I can't cram all I want to say on no postcard, and I need to think before setting things down in writing.'

The farmer's wife picked up the card and scrutinised it, then took it from Daisy's hand and sat heavily down at the table. Painstakingly, she wrote the address, the tip of her tongue emerging between her lips, very much as Petal's did when she was trying to write neatly, and Daisy saw that Auntie Blod's writing was large and round; very similar to her own, in fact.

'There you are!' Auntie Blod said presently. 'I'll give Shanna a shout – she's the oldest sheepdog. She'll go down the lane with you and make sure you get there safely.' Chuckling, she added, 'Dilys would tell you Shanna's so clever she could post the card herself, and she's not far wrong at that. Now eat up your scones and drink your milk and when you come back, we'll walk down to the birch pasture and you can watch Bess and Becky – they're Gwil's two younger dogs – workin' with the sheep. You'll like that.'

Returning from her shift at the factory, Rose pounced on the postcard, realising at once that it had come from Daisy. Although the children had only been gone a couple of days, she was already missing them dreadfully. The house seemed to echo with the ghosts of their childish voices, and because she was now alone, she did not bother with cooking or a fire. She was buying a gas cooker, paying for it in weekly instalments, so she always made herself tea and toast, but it wasn't like a proper meal, and oddly enough she went to bed early because there seemed nothing worth staying up for.

She carried the card over to the kitchen table, lit the gas under the kettle, and then sat down to read the very first communication she had ever received from her elder daughter, for they had never been parted before. Daisy had not written much, merely said they had arrived safely and were living on a farm and liked it very much, but there was something reassuring in the fact that the children's foster mother – if you could call her that – had added a line of her own. *Your girls is grand*, she had written. *You are lucky! Letter follows. Yours faithfully, Blodwen Williams.*

The kettle boiled and Rose made herself a cup of tea, then went over to the bread crock for a loaf. She cut a thick slice, then hesitated. To be sure, there was a good canteen at the factory and she had had sausage-meat pie and chips there, earlier in the day, but now she realised she was hungry, no doubt because she was no longer anxious about the children. Deciding to have something more substantial than tea and toast, she went to the cupboard and scanned the shelves, pulling a face as she did so. She had been too busy to go shopping on the two previous days, although Rachel had warned her that she really ought to get in some groceries since folk were buying up everything they considered might be rationed – or unavailable – as the weeks went on. Her pantry shelves contained a tin of baked beans, a bag of rice, two tins of condensed milk and a tin of carrots. The meat safe was empty and there was, she knew, only half a loaf of bread in the bread crock. I'll have to pull myself together, Rose thought, because I don't intend to sit here and starve! Goodness, there's no more than a pinch of tea in the caddy – I really must get to the shops before they close, or I'll see nothing but empty shelves.

Having decided to eat a proper meal, she realised that beans on toast would not be sufficient, but there was always Wilson's fish and chip shop on the corner of Mary Terrace; it was only five minutes' walk away. I'll nip down there and buy myself some . . . and perhaps I'll pop in on Rachel and find out how she got on at the factory because she'll have had her interview by now . . . she's lucky really to be living at home, because I'm sure her mum cooks her a hot meal every night of the week.

Rose glanced at the clock above the mantel. Yes, the chip shop would be open; probably there was already a queue, but that didn't matter. With the children gone, one thing she did have was time.

Rose bought her fish and chips and carried the newspaper parcel round to Mrs Edelmann's house. If her friend was successful, Rose remembered, she and Rachel had planned to walk to and from work together when they were on the same shift, for since Rachel had applied for a job in the finishing department, and Rose was a machinist, they would be in different parts of the building, so though they might meet each other in the canteen from time to time they would have little contact during their actual working day.

Reaching Rachel's home on Langsdale Street, Rose tapped on the door and then stood back, suddenly realising that she could scarcely march into someone else's house carrying fish and chips which would undoubtedly make their presence felt, for she had sprinkled them with salt and vinegar in the shop, and the smell of hot vinegar was already making her eyes water.

She was just considering whether it might be better to walk swiftly away, hoping that her gentle knock had not been heard, when the door swung inward and a small woman in a pink wraparound apron, stood looking enquiringly up at her. She had black hair, parted in the middle and pulled back into a bun on the nape of her neck, and large, doe-like dark eyes. She was not pretty, being strong-featured with rather sallow skin, but there was still a degree of similarity between herself and the much prettier Rachel. Rose thought that she would have known this was Rachel's mother even if they had not met on the Edelmanns' doorstep.

'Yes?' Mrs Edelmann said.

'Is Rachel in?' Rose asked hesitantly. 'I'm – I'm a sort of friend . . . we don't know each other very well, but our husbands are aboard the same ship, and . . .'

Mrs Edelmann's face cleared, her big, dark eyes becoming soft and friendly. Then she smiled and stood back, gesturing for Rose to pass her. 'You must be Mrs McAllister,' she said, and Rose noticed that she had a slight foreign accent. 'Go through, Rachel is in the kitchen.'

Rose began to protest, to explain that she did not wish to fill their house with the smell of fish and chips, but this only made Mrs Edelmann laugh. 'My house is full of the smells of cooking; your fish and chips are nothing,' she said. 'Go through, go through. Rachel will be delighted that you have come calling. She has been lonely since Alby sailed.'

She shepherded Rose through an open doorway into a large kitchen. It was growing dusk outside and the room was lamplit, whilst a bright fire burned in the open-fronted stove. Rachel was standing by a pan of fast-bubbling water, dropping shaped pieces of what looked like pastry into it, but she looked round and beamed a welcome as Rose entered.

'Mrs McAllister, how nice of you to call! I expect you've come to ask how I got on with Mr Mellors this afternoon. But I'm forgetting my manners – would you like a cup of tea? Some cake, perhaps?'

'I'd love a cup of tea,' Rose said, suddenly aware that she was thirsty. 'But I've just bought fish and chips for supper because, to tell the truth, I've no food in; it doesn't seem important to get the messages now I've only myself to feed.'

Rachel smiled, swung open an oven door set in the wall beside the fire, and, taking the parcel from Rose, tucked it into the oven and slammed the door. 'It'll stay hot whilst you drink a cup of tea,' she said comfortably. 'Now sit down, do. Have you heard from the children yet?' she added, turning back to Rose.

'Yes, there was a postcard when I got back from work,' Rose said. 'They're on a farm and seem really happy, though it's early days yet, of course. But their foster mother is writing me a letter, so obviously she's a nice person.'

Rose settled herself in the chair and presently the two young women, both with a cup of tea before them, were seated on opposite sides of the table whilst Mrs Edelmann took Rachel's place at the stove.

Rose sipped her tea, then glanced questioningly across at Rachel. The younger girl smiled. 'I'm to start tomorrow morning, in the finishing department,' she said, jubilantly. 'I'm to have a month's trial but Mr Mellors gave me some work to do and left me for half an hour; when he came back I'd finished and he seemed really pleased with the result, so it looks as though you and I will be working together, Mrs McAllister.'

'I'm Rose and you're Rachel,' Rose said, smiling. 'Our husbands call each other by their first names so it would seem very odd if you and I did not follow suit. I've only been in the finishing department once, when I was sent to take a pile of uniforms through, and to tell you the truth, I can't remember a thing about it. Will you be working with a lot of other girls? Did you know any of them? Did they seem a friendly crowd?'

Rachel gave a trill of laughter. 'What a lot of questions! I think there are four other girls and one man doing the finishing,' she said. 'Mr Mellors took me through and introduced me but didn't leave me with them. One girl – she told me to call her Liz – will show me the ropes when I start and check that I'm doing as I ought. I don't know whether you know her – she's a tall girl with gingery hair and freckles and a mole on her cheek, just below her left eye. She seemed friendly enough so I hope we'll get on.'

'Oh, Rachel, I *am* glad,' Rose said warmly, reaching across the table to give the other girl's hand a congratulatory pat. 'What shift are you on tomorrow? I'm on days this week, which is eight in the morning till four in the afternoon.'

'I'm on days for the first month, I think,' Rachel said. 'And it would be lovely to go together, but there's no need for you to come out of your way. I'll walk up to the main road and wait on the corner. What time would be best?'

'We'd better say half past seven, since the buses are pretty crowded with folk going to work in the early mornings,' Rose said. 'We can go to the canteen together as well, as we're both on days, and I can introduce

86

you to my friend April. She's really nice, you'll like her.'

As she spoke, Rose began to get to her feet. She realised that she wanted to get home so that she could eat her fish and chips and have a read of the new Denise Robins romance before going to bed. For the first time since the children had left, she believed she would be able to concentrate on the book, and not find her mind wandering. 'Thank you very much for the tea, Rachel, Mrs Edelmann,' she said politely, going across to the oven and taking out her parcel of fish and chips with some care, since the newspaper was now very hot. 'I'll see you tomorrow, Rachel, at half past seven prompt.'

Mrs Edelmann nodded but Rachel accompanied Rose to the front door and let her out. She said wistfully: 'I do not ask if you've heard from Steve because I'm sure you have not, but I expect, like me, you watch for the postman every day in the hope that a letter will arrive. And now you'll be waiting for the children's letters as well. If – if you hear before me – for letters can go astray – you will tell me, won't you?'

'Of course I will,' Rose said warmly, then gave a little wave and set off along the pavement. For the first time it occurred to her that being in love with your husband had some very real disadvantages. Rachel worried about Alby, wondered how he was getting on, longed for a letter from him as much as she herself had longed for her children's postcard. I wish Steve no harm, she told herself as she hurried along in the deepening dusk, but with the best will in the world, I can't put the clock back and feel about him the way I did in the early days of our marriage. Come to that, the early days of our marriage weren't all that rosy either. His bullying had begun the first time he had

87

returned from sea and, until the incident of the frying pan, had continued relentlessly ever since. Things were better now – the frying pan and Alby had seen to that – but with Steve, you simply never knew.

Rose turned into Bernard Terrace and headed for her own front door, feeling a glow of contentment at the prospect ahead of her. A fish and chip supper, a big pot of tea and then an early night, curled up alone in her double bed with a good book: a far better and less dangerous companion than Steve would have been.

Rose fished the key out from round her neck – no need to leave it dangling through the letter box now that she was the only occupant of the house – and let herself in. She went through to the kitchen and lit the gas under the kettle, but did not take off her coat for the empty house felt chilly. She bustled about, getting a plate from the dresser and a bottle of tomato sauce from the pantry, and, when the kettle boiled, made herself a cup of tea and tipped the fish and chips on to her plate. By now she was extremely hungry and she ate quickly, drinking the scalding tea as soon as it was safe to do so. Then she washed up her plate and mug and headed for the stairs. If the children had still been living at home, she would have prepared breakfast and laid the table, but for herself, bread and jam and a cup of tea would be quite sufficient.

Presently, she climbed into bed and opened her book, telling herself that now she knew the children were safe and well, she could enjoy her solitariness without feeling guilty. Even so, she was conscious of the quiet of the house around her. If Petal lay on her back, she snored, just a gentle little rumble, and Daisy sometimes talked in her sleep, and Rose found herself missing such small sounds. At the end of the first chapter, she put the book down and blew out her candle, nipped out of bed to let up the blackout blind and open the casement, then got back into bed and gazed, a little resentfully, at the bland face of her alarm clock, set to go off at half past six. It should have comforted her to remember that, had the children been at home, the alarm would have sounded at six, for she would have needed the extra half-hour to get them ready for school, but somehow it did not. What was an extra half an hour when compared with the pleasure of her children's company?

Telling herself brusquely not to be such a fool, Rose pulled the blankets up round her ears and settled herself for sleep. No doubt the morning would bring a letter from Mrs Williams, and anyway, she meant to visit this Ty Siriol just as soon as she had a day off. Despite the war, trains and buses were still running, though the government had cancelled all public assemblies such as cinema and theatre shows. Yes, she would visit the children just as soon as she could. On that thought, Rose fell asleep.

Chapter Four

By December, Daisy felt as though she had lived on the farm all her life. Naturally, she and Petal attended the local school but only on a part-time basis. One week they had lessons from half past eight to half past twelve, the next from one o'clock to four. Their classes were somewhat disorganised by the fact that whereas at home boys and girls had followed a different curriculum, here boys and girls shared the lessons as well as the classrooms. It was soon seen that in some subjects the girls were well ahead of the boys whilst in others the boys did best, but no one seemed particularly bothered by this. Daisy noticed that even the teachers were more relaxed, seldom punishing anyone for lateness or inattention and being particularly careful to see that no child felt left out or ill done by.

The school was a low, old-fashioned one-storey building, with a slate roof and tortoise stoves in every classroom, though these had only recently been lit for the weather had continued mild right up to early December. Now, however, when Daisy and Petal left the farm, sitting behind Myfanwy in the trap, they passed through a veritable fairyland, for the trees were rimed with frost as was every twig in the hedge, every blade of grass on the verges. Daisy had never seen anything so beautiful, and loved to walk across the frosted grass when she crossed the pasture, hearing it softly crackle beneath her stout wellingtons.

On this particular morning, they left the farmhouse

just as the sun came up over the eastern hills. It was round and red and so brilliant that it took Daisy's breath away. She clutched Petal's hand and pointed and saw that Petal, too, was dazzled by it. Even Auntie Blod, who must have see the sun rise a thousand times, stood for a moment, staring, before leading them over to the stable where Dilys was just finishing tacking Myfanwy up and strapping her into the shafts of the trap.

'Mornin', girls; *bore da*,' she said cheerfully. She led the pony out into the yard as she spoke. 'I'll be meeting you myself when school's finished, to give Mam a chance to do her dairy work.' The two children scrambled into the trap and settled themselves on the leather seat, pulling up the horse blanket, which was always kept on the bottom boards, to cover their legs, for their socks ended at the knee and their skirts began six inches higher, leaving an area much prone to chilblains. Dilys glanced reproachfully up at Daisy. 'I thought you were going to get up early so that you could come with me when I took the churns down to the main road for the milk lorry to pick up.'

'I did mean to,' Daisy said remorsefully. 'But we don't have an alarm clock and Auntie Blod didn't wake me early . . . well, I forgot to ask her to,' she added honestly. 'Couldn't you wake me yourself, Dilys? Only I would love to come with you.'

'Maybe I'll wake you tomorrow,' Dilys conceded. Auntie Blod picked up the reins and Dilys stepped away from the pony's head, giving Myfanwy an encouraging slap on the rump as the pony began to move. 'See you at half past twelve, girls, and don't you be late,' she added, raising her voice. 'You must love your school, 'cos you're always last out!'

Daisy and Petal waved and shouted until Dilys was

out of sight, then they settled back to enjoy the journey. Daisy, who felt the cold, was careful to keep her hands under the horse blanket, though she was wearing the thick mittens which her mother had knitted for her and brought to the farm last time she visited. Both girls had a pair and pronounced them lovely and warm, but once the trap was moving the wind nipped at their noses and pinched their cheeks to scarlet, and a hand left outside the horse blanket, even when warmly mittened, would soon have frozen fingers. And frozen fingers mean chilblains, Daisy reminded herself. She had suffered from chilblains ever since she could remember and dreaded the itching which was worse even than the flea bites that had tormented them when they first came to the farm, though now the cold weather seemed to have sent the fleas into temporary hibernation. Auntie Blod had explained that you could not wash feather beds, but she hung them across the washing line from time to time, beating them vigorously with an instrument shaped like a three-leafed clover on a long handle, and this seemed to do the trick.

'I wonder what your mam will do for Christmas?' Auntie Blod said idly now, turning the pony and trap into the main road. 'Likely she'll come to us, do you think? We'll have one of them gobblecocks for our dinner and I've already made a big ol' puddin' and a Christmas cake what'll scarce fit into my largest tin, so there'll be food to spare.'

'It'd be lovely if she could come,' Daisy said wistfully, 'but it all depends on the factory, you know.'

'Well, hope for the best, we must,' Auntie Blod said philosophically. 'I 'spect you're doin' all sorts of Christmas things at school, aren't you? I remember, years ago, Dilys were the Angel Gabriel in one of them nativity plays which Miss Bronwen Jones organised; comes of having a yaller head, she said. An' the next year, she were the Virgin Mary. Are you doin' a nativity play this year?'

Despite the difference in their ages, Daisy and Petal were now in the same class, though the teachers gave them different work. Because numbers were falling there was a mix of country children and evacuees in each class, and the girls were learning to get on well with the local children. One of the teachers, Miss Dodd, had returned to Liverpool, but the remaining staff managed well with their dwindling classes. After Christmas, the rumour went, everyone would be having full-time school again; not something to be relished, exactly. But Auntie Blod had asked a question; Daisy shook her head. 'No, not this year; this year we're giving a concert,' she said. 'Some of us are going to sing carols and do dances; the boys are going to recite a poem, verse and verse about, you know, and the really tiny ones – that means you, Petal – are going to do a nativity *scene*; there's a cardboard donkey and a cardboard ox and we're all to bring a shoe bag full of straw or hay for the stable and Miss Bronwen Jones is going to get costumes from the dressing-up cupboard. Petal's the Virgin Mary and Sandra is lending her new doll for the baby Jesus. Its eyes open and close and when you tip it back it goes waa-aa, waa-aa, like a real baby,' she ended, rather wistfully, though when she thought about it, what was a doll compared with the charms of a kitten or a puppy, or a little new, milky lamb?

'And how do you like being the Virgin Mary?' Auntie Blod asked, turning to smile at Petal. 'An important part, it is, cariad.'

'Ye-es, but I'm not allowed to say anything,' Petal

said aggrievedly. 'I wanted to say "No room at the inn" and I wanted to look at the baby and say "It's a boy!" but Miss wouldn't let me. She was really mean. She said I was rude and I'm not rude, am I, Daisy?'

Daisy considered this as the pony clip-clopped along, its ears pricking forward and the breath rising from its nostrils in a cloud of steam. 'We-ell, I think you were a bit rude,' she observed. 'You shouldn't have pulled up the dolly's skirt before you said, "It's a boy!" That's what Miss Bronwen Jones thought was rude.'

'Yes, but how could I tell if it was a boy or a girl when it has almost no hair and only a long nightie thing?' Petal asked. 'I didn't know about boys having that little tassel until I saw Danny Spellman in the school toilets, but I knew that cows are different from bulls and boy dogs from lady dogs, so what's wrong with looking at a dolly?'

Daisy would have answered her sister sharply, but Auntie Blodwen tactfully changed the subject. 'Well, well, never mind,' she said. 'Are you making Christmas cards and paper chains and that? Out here in the country, there's holly and ivy for the asking – mistletoe too – and I dare say you'll be decorating your class-rooms. Is it very different at this school from your old one?'

Daisy considered. She had been happy enough at St Ambrose Council School in Prince Edwin Street, but nowhere near as happy as she was now. For a start, her school day was very much shorter, but it was not only that. In this school, everything was geared to the countryside which surrounded them. There was a big nature table in each classroom and the pictures on the walls were all of country things. The children were expected to know the names of the trees even when they could not be identified by their burden of leaves, and pictures of field mice, shrews, stoats and weasels, rabbits and hares were pinned up all over the place.

Having considered the matter, Daisy said: 'I like this school ever so much better than the old one. It's – it's slower, somehow. Quieter. The teachers don't get as cross as they did at home, and they teach nicer things, stuff that's easier to understand. Things about animals, and plants. And Mel – he's a boy in our class – told us that in summer we'll go for nature walks, and be allowed to help on the farm during school time, if there's haymaking, or harvesting.'

Auntie Blod nodded, then drew the trap into the side of the road, for they had reached the school and could see children streaming across the asphalt playground, calling out to one another and greeting Daisy and Petal.

'Right you are. Dilys will be fetching you at dinnertime, so don't dawdle coming out. See you later.'

Blodwen sat in the trap and watched the children joining up in small groups in the playground, waiting until the bell rang and the pupils began to line up. She saw the young lad, Nicky Bostock, who lived with the Foleys on Clwyd Street engage Daisy in earnest conversation and smiled to herself. Nicky had been to the farm twice for tea and she had liked him; guessed she would see a good deal of him over the coming weeks. Only when the children had disappeared into the building did she click to the pony and set off on her journey back to Ty Siriol. Although she had said nothing to either Daisy or Petal, she had been anxious for some time about the number of children who were returning to the city. She supposed it was natural enough for parents to miss their offspring, and many

of them found the long journey to visit both expensive and time-consuming. Others, of course, did not
bother to visit, but wanted any child who could be
useful back with them once the first fear of an immediate air attack had worn off.

For it was clear that such fears were needless. The
war had been a fact for more than three months, but
there had been no sign of the invasion which the
government had feared, let alone attacks from the air.
Once or twice enemy aircraft had been reported
approaching the coast, but all they had done was drop
leaflets, which had seemed to make the whole idea of
evacuation pretty pointless. For her own part, Blodwen
thought the parents should leave their kids where they
were, for the time being at least. Why take a child
back into danger? Oh, the danger might not be immediate, but it could surely not be discounted so early
in the game? At the time of the Spanish Civil War,
Blodwen had been to the cinema and seen the news-
reel pictures of what the German air force had done
to the great cities of Spain; could such scenes be
forgotten so easily? But she had realised, as soon as
the children began to get into lines, that the evacuees
were very much thinner on the ground than they had
been. She thought that of the hundred or so evacuees
who had become pupils at this particular school only
fifty-odd still remained. The children had told her that
one of the teachers had gone back to Liverpool, and
she had heard from another farmer's wife that at least
one more would not be coming back to the school
when term started again in the New Year, but surely
Mrs McAllister, a sensible woman, would not try to
take her children home? She had a full-time job, was
sufficiently well paid not to grudge the cost of the
journey to Ty Siriol, and was obviously very attached

to Daisy and Petal. Surely she would leave them where they were so happy, at least until they were certain that there would be no bombing, no invasion?

So far, Mrs McAllister had shown no signs of wanting to take the children home, but the truth is, Blodwen Williams, that you've grown so fond of them that parting would be a real blow, the farmer's wife told herself severely. She had liked them from the first, and the more she got to know them the fonder she grew. At fifty-five, she was hoping for grandchildren, she supposed, but there was little chance of that. With Gareth in the forces and Dilys stuck out here on the farm, she might have to wait as much as five or ten years, she thought, and in the meantime Daisy and Petal were with her, making her laugh, curling up beside her on the couch of an evening to learn a poem or practise writing or even just listen to a story on Children's Hour. Losing them would be unbelievably painful. She had always liked children, especially small girls, but these two, she had long decided, were thoroughly delightful. Bright, intelligent and loving, they were a credit to Mrs McAllister's upbringing, which could not have been easy since Blodwen did not think that the girls' father had been much help.

Reading between the lines, she had gathered that Mr McAllister was not a good father, though because he was at sea a great deal she supposed that his relationship with his children would naturally be a good deal less close than that which existed between Gwil, Gareth and Dilys. But Daisy was afraid of Mr McAllister, and that was all wrong; children should love their parents, even if they regarded them with some awe. Blodwen had not sensed that either Daisy or Petal was in awe of their father, and she knew very well that both Dilys and Gareth thought of Gwil as a friend, someone to be admired and imitated, but never, in any circumstances, to be feared. No. There was no escaping the fact that Daisy feared Mr McAllister, and even Petal thought of him as unpredictable, though it was clear she was her daddy's favourite. As for Mrs McAllister, she never referred to him if she could help it, except in the vaguest and most general of terms.

The trap rattled along, and as Blodwen turned the pony into the rutted lane she made a mental note of a huge holly tree, heavily laden with scarlet berries. She would get Elias to come down later with a pair of shears and a basket, to cut holly for the house. Perhaps the children would like to accompany him and, if so, he could take them along to the orchard too, for there was an ancient apple tree there upon which mistletoe grew in round, circular clumps. It was too high for Elias to reach but if he lifted Daisy into the lower branches she would be able to climb up and break off some mistletoe twigs. Yes, the children would enjoy that, and Blodwen thought it was good for Daisy to climb trees and behave like a tomboy occasionally. Petal was the bolder of the two in a good many ways, but lately Blodwen had been encouraging Daisy to enjoy pursuits such as tree climbing and swinging from the knotted rope which, long ago, Gareth had attached to one of the lower branches of the great beech tree at the back of the stables, and Daisy had proved to be just as athletic as her sister.

And when I finish my dairy work, I'll write to Mrs McAllister and suggest that she comes for Christmas and spends a day or two with us, Blodwen decided, as the trap emerged from the lane into the farmyard. We're awful lucky that she's such a nice woman and so easy to get along with. Some of the mothers . . .

dear heaven, that woman whose boys stayed with Mrs Evan Williams, she were really rough. The language! And the dirt! They never washed properly, if at all, and their clothes were mostly rags. And Mrs Evan Williams said the mother's table manners – and the boys' – simply didn't exist. They all crammed their mouths with food, talked while they ate, jumped up from the table in the middle of a meal without so much as a by your leave, and didn't know the meaning of please and thank you. Oh aye, Gwil and I were real lucky we were given the McAllisters.

Blodwen climbed down from the trap, led the pony into the stable and left old Ben to deal with Myfanwy. Yes, there was no doubt about it, she was lucky with her evacuees and would write and invite Mrs McAllister to stay for the Christmas holiday this very day.

Rose saw Rachel waiting for her at the bus stop as she hurried along Shaw Street, and quickened her pace. The letter from Mrs Williams had arrived just as she was leaving the house and reading it, as she walked along, had obviously slowed her down, since a glance over her shoulder revealed that the bus she wanted to catch was only yards behind her. Panicking, she broke into a trot and reached Rachel, halfway down the queue, breathless but triumphant. Fortunately, the bus drew up almost as she arrived and those people behind Rachel were too eager to get aboard themselves to point out that she had jumped the queue. It was, of course, perfectly legitimate for a friend to save you a place but there were people who simply barged in and they were becoming increasingly unpopular as queues grew longer.

Petrol had been rationed since mid-September but it was food shortages which were hitting city dwellers hardest. In the last year of the previous war there had been rationing of foodstuffs, and Rose was beginning to think that even rationing would be better than traipsing from shop to shop in a vain effort to buy something perfectly ordinary, like a bag of sugar or sultanas, in order to make some sort of cake for the festive season.

She said as much to Rachel as they boarded the bus but her friend only laughed at her, shaking her head. 'You should see my mam's larder; the shelves are so laden I'm surprised they don't collapse,' she said. 'The older folk remember the last war, when you couldn't buy so much as a loaf of bread without queuing for half an hour, and things like sugar, bacon and butter were all rationed. I told her she was a wicked old hoarder, reminded her that the government had said hoarding was unfair, but she just stuck her nose in the air and said I'd be glad enough of her larder when Alby comes home wanting a decent meal. I'd offer to let you have some sultanas and that, but why don't you come round to us for Christmas? You can be sure of a good feed and a warm welcome – Mam and Dad thoroughly approve of you, Rosie!'

The two young women were sitting side by side, having been lucky enough to get aboard just as a couple of elderly men were alighting. Rose gave Rachel's hand a squeeze. 'You and your mam are so kind, I don't know what I'd do without you. But I had a letter this morning from the girls' foster mum; she's invited me to join them for the holiday and to stay overnight, if I can, and I really would love to be with the children, see their faces on Christmas morning. But I'll have to ask Miss Marriott if I can be off for four days in a row and then work straight through for eight days, say. She's norra bad old stick; I'm sure she'll let me have the time off if it's possible.'

Rachel smiled at her. 'Well, you certainly won't be short of food if you're going to that farm. Why, she sent you home with eggs and butter and home-made bread last time you visited, and the time before, you had so many apples and pears in your bag that you could hardly walk. Mam was most impressed; she just wished I were young enough to be an evacuee so she could stock up her larder all over again.'

'I gave you half of everything,' Rose reminded her. 'Since the stuff was perishable, it was the sensible thing to do. Why, I had omelettes for four days in a row; I felt quite egg-bound.'

'Don't think I'm not grateful,' Rachel said hastily. 'Mam were made up with all that fresh country food.'

'And I took Mrs Williams's advice and laid the apples and pears out on newspaper in the children's room,' Rose continued. 'I have a look at them every now and then – and eat one or two – and they're keeping really well, just like she said they would.'

'Tell you what, Rose, if Miss Marriott can't spare you, you come to us. No need to let us know until nearer the time because, as I said, Mam's catering for a dozen, by the looks of it.'

The bus came to a juddering halt and both young women got to their feet and headed for the exit. 'Thanks, Rachel,' Rose said, as they jumped down on to the pavement and began to make their way towards their workplace. 'It'll be a real treat to have four whole days off at once.'

'Ye-es, I know what you mean,' Rachel said. 'But suppose something happens and the fellers come back? You'd – you'd want to be at home then, surely?'

'Yes, of course, only we've not heard that there's any chance of them being back in the 'Pool for some time,' Rose pointed out. 'And anyway, Ty Siriol isn't that far away, and Steve knows how to get there. The girls write regularly – and so do I, of course – so he'd just have to hop on to a train and then get the bus . . . or I suppose he could hitch-hike.' She looked almost appealingly at her friend. 'I can't let the children down on the off chance that Steve's ship might come in, can I? I think Christmas is more important for children than for the rest of us and I'm sure Steve would agree. He – he's quite fond of the children in a way, especially Petal.'

If Rachel noticed anything strange about Rose's last remark, she did not comment, and the girls joined the short queue to clock on. They always tried to arrive early, so the fact that they had to queue to clock on did not bother them. Rose took her card from the rack on the left, pushed it down into the machine and pulled the lever, then checked that the time had registered before sticking it into the rack on the right, and Rachel followed suit. Then the two girls went their separate ways, Rose calling out as she did so: 'See you in the canteen at half twelve; save me a place in the queue if you're first and I'll do the same if I am.'

When Rose had left Liverpool on that Saturday morning it had been cold but clear, with no sign of snow, but by the time the train chugged into the small Ruthin station snow was falling gently from a lowering sky and the wind seemed to have dropped completely. Rose got down from the train and thanked a burly young farm worker for lifting down her case, then looked hopefully around her. Schools had broken up two days before and Mrs Williams had written that someone would meet her, since the arrival of the train did not coincide with one of the twice daily bus departures. The platform looked bare, and though the flakes fell softly, they were sufficiently frequent to make it difficult to see more than a few yards. Sighing, Rose bent to pick up her suitcase and even as she did so heard rushing footsteps and was nearly knocked backwards by her daughters' enthusiastic welcome.

'Mammy, Mammy, Mammy! Oh, it's so lovely to see you! Auntie Blod's waiting in the road because Myfanwy doesn't like being tied up and left when the snow covers all the grass and she's got nothing to chew on.' That was Petal, her eyes bright, her cheeks rosy as apples.

Daisy, hanging on to her mother's arm and jigging with excitement, said importantly: 'Poor Mammy, I bet you're cold and tired from the long journey. Was it cold in the train? Auntie Blod's brought a stone hot water bottle for you to put your feet on and she says the kettle's on the hob so there'll be a nice hot *panod*.'

'Yes, it was freezing on the train,' Rose said with a reminiscent shudder. 'A hot water bottle sounds lovely, darling; but what's a *panod* when it's at home?' she asked, imagining a small pancake of some description. 'No, don't try to carry my case, it's far too heavy for you. Daisy, you can take my handbag and Petal can carry my umbrella. There's not much point in putting it up because umbrellas are only good for rain, not for snow.'

'A *panod* is a cup of tea, I think,' Daisy said, as they reached the pony and trap. Mrs Williams climbed ponderously down, seized Rose's heavy case and tossed it into the bottom of the trap as though it weighed no more than a feather. Then she kissed Rose on the cheek, told her she was as welcome as flowers in spring, and boosted her into the trap with such force that Rose was quite surprised not to clear it all together and find herself standing on the further side. However, she sat down, with a child on either side, thanked Mrs Williams fervently for meeting her in such dreadful weather, and settled down as her hostess clicked to the pony and the small party headed for the hills.

'Was it snowing in Liverpool, Mammy, when you left?' Petal asked eagerly, once they were on the move. 'Auntie Blod says it nearly always snows at Ty Siriol but they never get thick yellow fog like we do at home. And usually the snow comes after Christmas, not before, so Auntie Blod says it won't lay. That is what you said, isn't it, Auntie Blod?' she added anxiously.

'That's right, cariad,' Mrs Williams said cheerfully, but she did not take her eyes off the road ahead and kept the pony to a walking pace. Even so, Myfanwy stumbled a couple of times and when they reached the lane Mrs Williams climbed down, announcing that she would lead the pony because the surface of the lane was so rutted and uneven Myfanwy could easily take a wrong step and end up with a broken leg.

Eager to seize what they clearly saw as a great advantage, the children scrambled out of the trap and ran ahead, Daisy leaping up to grab at branches and tip their light powdering of snow down into the lane. For her part, Petal walked just ahead of the pony, turning back to warn the sturdy, rough-coated creature of potholes and other hazards as she went.

Rose, too, had climbed down from the trap, though she regretted her decent leather shoes. Wellington boots would have been practical but she had not even considered the possibility of snow when she had set out, and although her case contained a great many things, it held no boots. However, if Mrs Williams was right and the snow did not continue for long, she supposed that boots would not be necessary. She said as much to her hostess, who laughed, but shook her head. 'The snow won't last but it'll leave a deal of mud behind it,' she observed. 'Farmyards is mucky places and knowing your daughters as I do, I guess they'll want you to go with them to feed the poultry, take fodder out to the ponies, watch the milking and so on. You'll need boots all right, but we've plenty to spare. You can use a pair of Dilys's; better that than ruining good leather.'

'I feel ashamed,' Rose said ruefully, as they entered the yard. 'But on both my previous visits the weather was dry and I wore sensible brogues.' She wrinkled her nose at the black court shoes, now mud-spattered, which had been her Christmas present to herself. Still, they would clean up and could be worn whenever there was no possibility of having to leave the farmhouse.

'Come on in, Mam. You can pull the kettle over the fire and make the tea while Auntie Blod sees to the pony and trap,' Petal said, running to open the kitchen door.

'Indeed she cannot,' Mrs Williams said roundly, smiling at her guest. 'You go up to your room and make yourself at home, unpack and so on, and by the time you come down I'll have a nice cup of tea and a piece of Victoria sponge all ready for you.'

Christmas Day dawned clear and bright, though with a sharp frost. The hours at the factory were long and the work quite hard, needing a good deal of concentration, so Rose was happy to agree not to try to get up when the children did, but to have a bit of a lie-in. She suspected that she would wake at six anyway, but slept deeply and was awoken by the children giggling as they opened her door.

Rose shot up in bed just as Mrs Williams entered

flanked by Daisy and Petal, with a tray in her hands. Rose began to apologise for her tardiness, but was assured that her daughters had hoped she would not wake early, since the surprise they had arranged for her depended upon her remaining in bed a little later than usual. 'We made your breakfast ourselves, tea, toast, and bacon and egg,' Daisy said proudly. 'Only the tray is so heavy we couldn't carry it, norreven between us. Put your knees down, Mam, then Auntie Blod can stand it down.'

Mrs Williams, smiling broadly, settled the tray comfortably in front of Rose. 'The girls is saving opening their presents until you come down,' she said. 'And I'd be much obliged if you'd use me given name – Blodwen – because having you call me Mrs Williams all the time seems a bit formal, like.' She pointed to the tray. 'There's marmalade in the jar with bluebells on and a nice pat of our own farm butter in the little glass dish. Now we'll leave you to have your breakfast in peace, or at least I will. I expect Daisy and Petal will watch every mouthful; they've had their own, by the way.'

'Oh, Mrs Will— I mean Blodwen, you really are too good,' Rose said, looking hungrily at the bacon, eggs and mushrooms which filled the plate. 'I hadn't realised how hungry I was.' She began to eat as the older woman left the room and beamed at the children as they climbed on to the bed. 'What a wonderful Christmas present! You couldn't have given me anything nicer than a proper cooked breakfast, on a tray.'

'We thought you'd like it,' Petal said, clearly gratified by this enthusiastic response. 'Daisy and I made the toast and filled the milk jug, and Daisy curled the butter with Auntie Blod's little butter-curler. But of course, norreven Daisy were allowed to fry the stuff, 'cos fry pans is dangerous, Auntie Blod says so.'

Involuntarily, a picture of herself in her kitchen at

home, swinging the heavy frying pan in order to keep Steve at bay, appeared before Rose's eyes and she choked back a giggle. It wasn't really funny, she knew, but it was better to laugh than to cry, and Petal was clearly unaware that her remark about the danger inherent in a frying pan could be taken two ways. And now Daisy was chattering, full of plans which she was anxious to share with her mother, so Rose brought her mind back to the present.

'. . . and after dinner, there's to be a party – they have one every year – with Auntie Blod's sisters, and their husbands, and all their children coming here,' she said excitedly. 'Some of the kids is our age – a couple of them are in our class – and Auntie Blod says there will be all sorts of games and fun, as well as a lovely tea. But of course, the animals have to be fed and the cows have to be milked, so we'll be able to help, just as we usually do.'

Rose began to spread butter on to her toast, looking thoughtfully at her daughters as she did so. When she had left Liverpool, it had been on her mind that she might bring the children back to the city when she returned there on Wednesday. It would make her life a great deal more complicated but she had noticed that most of the children who had left on 4th September were already back in Liverpool. Schools which had been closed were reopening, teachers were returning, and despite such things as the blackout, conscription of men between 19 and 41 save for those in essential employment, and shortages of most basic foodstuffs, life was returning to normal. The panic which had caused the mass evacuation of children was subsiding and though there had been no official admission that this exercise had not been necessary, the streets of Liverpool teemed with children once more.

The trouble was, Rose could see how happy Daisy and Petal were and knew, in her heart, that they were far better off on the farm than they would have been in Bernard Terrace. The Williams family were almost self-sufficient and although Mr Williams grumbled that no doubt laws would be brought in which would interfere with his farming practices, as had happened in the last war, Rose was certain that the sturdy independence of the family would make sure that they were not unduly interfered with.

So what to do? She missed their companionship horribly but was not selfish enough to think that more important than their happiness. But perhaps the children should be consulted over such an important matter. Rose took a sip of tea, then put her cup down and cleared her throat. 'You like it here, don't you, darlings? I know you're a big help to Auntie Blodwen and Dilys, but what about school? At first, you were with your friends, but a good many of them have come home. Do you miss them?'

Petal began to say that she would quite miss Fanny, who had gone home for Christmas and did not mean to come back, but Daisy, shrewder than her sister, interrupted. 'Oh, but we've made new friends, haven't we, Petal? And when we start school full time in the new year, we'll soon get to know the rest of the children. And in the spring, your friend Maldwyn Griffiths is going to take you birdnesting and fishing for tiddlers in the brook and if Nicky is still here he and me will come along as well. And there'll be little lambs, some of 'em orphans; they're the ones Auntie Blod feeds with a real baby's bottle. And there's primroses and violets – not to buy, to pick – all over the banks . . . oh, spring is going to be wonderful this year.'

Rose smiled lovingly at her daughters, reflecting

that Petal's genius for friendship was a truly enviable attribute. Petal made friends easily and could pick and choose her companions, whereas poor little Daisy, she knew, would have missed Nicky Bostock fearfully had he gone back to the 'Pool and would have found it hard to replace her old friend with a new one.

'So you don't miss Bernard Terrace too much? Or me, or your daddy, either?' Rose asked, rather wistfully. She wanted the children to be happy, of course she did, but she wanted them to miss her, too. At these words, however, both small girls hurled themselves at her, hugging and kissing her and assuring her that they missed her very much and only wished she could be with them at the farm, and not stuck, all by herself, in Bernard Terrace.

'But you come and visit whenever you can, don't you, Mammy?' Petal said, as Rose carefully stood her tray on the bedside table. 'And Daddy might come when he's next on leave, I suppose.'

She did not sound unduly thrilled by this last suggestion, but Rose was comforted. Her daughters truly loved her, truly missed her, but living on the farm was like a wonderful holiday, the sort of holiday they would never have enjoyed but for the war. She crossed the room and began to pour water from ewer to basin, then turned to shoo the girls out of the room whilst she washed and dressed. 'Don't worry about the tray, I'll bring it down when I'm ready,' she said briskly. 'Now, off with you, and help your Auntie Blodwen.'

She would have closed the door on them, but Petal turned a beseeching face towards her. 'You will hurry, won't you, Mammy?' the child asked anxiously. 'We haven't opened a single one of our presents yet, but

Auntie Blod let us have a feel of what she's bought us, and oh, oh, I *do* want to see if I've guessed right!'

It was hard to wake up on Wednesday morning, very, very early, before the sky had even begun to lighten, for Mr Williams was going to drive Rose to the station to catch the milk train, which would get her back to Liverpool in time to catch her usual bus to work. Rose had borrowed Dilys's alarm clock and when it shrilled, she wished, passionately, that she could hurl it through the window and go back to sleep. However, she got groggily out of bed, dabbed shrinkingly at her warm flesh with a wet flannel, dressed hastily, and headed for the stairs. Duty called and though Mr Williams had assured her that he was often up at this hour, she felt it was an imposition for him to get out their old Austin to take her to the station.

Downstairs in the kitchen, she was surprised to find Dilys, very bright-eyed and cheerful, frying sausages and cold cooked potatoes in the big, black pan. Rose stopped short, staring across at the younger woman. 'Oh, Dilys, don't say you've got up specially to make breakfast! I could have managed perfectly well with a slice of bread and jam; that's all I ever have at home.'

Dilys tutted, much as her mother would have done, Rose thought. 'That's no way to start the day,' she said severely. 'Besides, I'm on early milking this morning and either Mam or meself always gets up to feed whoever is on earlies. 'Da' will be in any moment, so you and I aren't the only ones looking for a cooked breakfast.'

Secretly, Rose wondered whether she would be able to eat a cooked breakfast at such an early hour, but somehow, when the food was dished up on to the plates and Dilys, Mr Williams and herself were seated at the table, her appetite returned with a rush. She finished off her meal with toast and marmalade and two large mugs of tea, and then Dilys picked up a stout brown paper parcel which had been standing on the dresser and handed it to her. 'Mam has put you up a piece of cheese, some cold fowl and half a dozen eggs, as well as some links of our home-made sausages,' she said rather shyly. 'It's been grand having you, Mrs McAllister, and I hope it won't be too long before you're back again.'

Dilys then picked up her suitcase and carried it out to the car, while Rose, cradling the parcel, tried to express her gratitude to these two hard-working people who had found room for her children in their lives and in their hearts.

It seemed strange to be driving along the lane with glass separating her from the frosted beauty of the trees and hedges, for she had grown used to going on foot, or perhaps in the pony trap, during her stay with the Williamses, but it was a good deal warmer and also quite a lot faster than the other methods of transport, and it seemed no time at all before Mr Williams was drawing up outside the station and hopping out to carry her suitcase.

'Thank you so much, Mr Williams,' Rose said, trying to take the case from him. 'I can manage this, honestly I can, and I know you'll want to be off back to the farm to get on with the work. I keep trying to tell you how grateful I am to all of you . . .'

But she was speaking to empty air. Mr Williams had stridden ahead of her on to the platform and placed her suitcase a foot from the line, and even as he did so she saw the train approaching, the steam from its smokestack rising white against the black and frosty sky. It drew to a halt alongside the platform and immediately the station, which had seemed to be deserted, sprang into life. Milk churns rattled as they were heaved up into the guard's van, a man with a large flag came running out of the ticket office to have a word with the engine driver, and a couple of passengers appeared and climbed aboard.

In the dim blue light which was all the illumination allowed, Rose selected a corner seat and tried to thank Mr Williams again, but he was having none of it. 'A pleasure it is,' he said gruffly, and shot a surprisingly large, calloused hand. Rose put hers into it and they shook briefly. Mr Williams stepped back as the guard came along the train, slamming doors, and Rose let down the window on its leather strap and leaned out.

'Please thank Mrs Williams for the parcel of food,' she called, as the train began to chug out of the station. 'And thank you again, Mr Williams.'

He grinned; she could see the flash of those incredibly white teeth, even in the dark, then she pulled the window up and sank into her corner seat. She told herself that she was lucky to have had such a wonderful break and be going back to work with many happy memories, but all she could think about was how cold and lonely the house would seem, and how much she would miss Daisy and Petal.

By the end of January the snow, which had begun to fall in earnest on the hills of North Wales some time earlier, reached Liverpool for the first time. Rose got letters from Daisy extolling the marvels of sledging, for Maldwyn Griffiths and a group of other children had accompanied Daisy, Petal and Nicky up to the long, sloping pasture behind Ty Siriol armed with rough wooden sledges, and had instructed them in the art of choosing a smooth pathway and descending on the sledge – or indeed, on a sturdy tray – at incredible speed.

Daisy's letter had been almost incoherent as she struggled to get her feelings into words; the wind in her face, the enormous cold, the thrill as one steered one's vehicle round a bump and the astonishing way one took to the air and soared into a snow bank when one's conveyance hit an obstacle. Then there was the return to the farmhouse, cold but elated, to drink tea and eat hot Welsh cakes and boast of their prowess.

Rose envied the children but hated city snow. Pavements became treacherous in the extreme and Bernard Terrace had to be negotiated with considerable care, since the children made slides which were occasionally hidden and could cause a most unpleasant fall. Of course, all the houses were cold, but because Rose was alone and often did not bother to light the fire, her house felt like an icebox. Draughts she had scarcely noticed before seemed to stab at her through every available crack around windows and doors, and because she had no time for shopping – working girls could not join long queues – her meals became little more than hasty snacks. She told herself that she had a good hot meal in the canteen every working day and usually either cooked something or went round to Rachel's house on her day off, but even so, she dreaded another fall of snow and longed for spring.

Oddly enough, she soon realised that many of her neighbours thought her a strange parent to have left her children in their foster home when so many others had brought their families back to Liverpool.

On this particular day, as Rose hurried across to her house, Maisie, her next door neighbour, laden with marketing bags, stopped her. She was an old friend and had clearly decided to give Rose a bit of a talking to, for she began the conversation by saying, bluntly, that she thought Rose was foolish to leave the children in North Wales. 'They'll be more that Blodwen's kids than yourn, by the time this bleeding war's over,' she commented. 'I wouldn't be without my Freddie for longer than I had to; that's why I brung him back at the beginning of December. Besides, he'd started bed-wetting so he couldn't have been happy.'

'Well, Daisy and Petal are extremely happy,' Rose said, rather defensively. 'But it was different for your Freddie; he didn't like his foster mother, did he? And you said he were with a big family and felt left out. Of course it makes it easier for my Daisy and Petal, because they're together. The Williamses have taken the girls to their heart, I'm telling you.'

Maisie nodded. 'Aye, you did tell me, and that's why I say them girls won't want to come back, ever, if you don't shift 'em soon,' she said, almost aggressively. 'And if they were home, you'd have to keep the house warm and cook yourself decent meals once in a while. You're beginning to look right peaky,' she finished.

Rose sighed but did not attempt to defend herself further. 'I may bring them back in the spring,' she said reluctantly. 'I'm only trying to do what's best for them, Maisie.'

'I know that,' Maisie said, standing her marketing bag down and giving Rose's shoulder a reassuring pat. 'But there's others as don't, and of course, you leavin' the girls in a safe place gets up some folks' noses, 'cos they feel guilty about bringin' their young 'uns home. I do meself,' she added, with a burst of honesty. 'Tell you what, queen, I know you're havin' a job to get your messages, what with workin' every hour God sends, so why don't you pop an envelope through me front door with a list of what you need and a few bob to cover the cost? It'll be no skin off me nose to buy a bit extra as I go round the shops.'

Rose thanked her and promised to leave a list the very next day, and went indoors, heartened by the conversation in one way, though also a little cast down. She was trying so hard to do the best for her children! It seemed unfair that she should be criticised, particularly as she would much rather have had the girls at home. But being a parent was never easy, she concluded. She went into the kitchen and lit the gas under the kettle. Then, because of the conversation with Maisie, she got together paper kindling and some small pieces of coal, and laid and lit the fire. Maisie was right about one thing: she really must make more of an effort to eat properly, so she would start by cooking some of her bacon ration and putting it between two thick slices of bread. She got up and fetched pan and bacon, and as soon as the rashers started to sizzle the delicious smell sent her back to the pantry; she would fry a couple of rounds of bread as well, and heat up a tin of beans, and when she had eaten she would write a letter to Steve, telling him all about the fearful weather and the children's ecstasy over the snow. After that, she would write to Daisy and Petal. Then she would tune in her small wireless set to keep abreast of current affairs, and when the nine o'clock news was finished she would go up to bed, snuggle down under the great mound of blankets – for she had put the children's bedding on top of her own – and forget her troubles till morning.

Once this plan had been followed, however, and she was tucked up in bed, she found herself mulling over Maisie's words. She did not really think that the children would grow fonder of Blodwen than they were of herself, nor did she think they would resent coming back to Bernard Terrace when the time was ripe. Naturally, they would miss the country, but she supposed that, when the war was over, she, Steve and the girls could visit the Williamses from time to time, keeping the friendship green. If only Steve did not return to his pre-war drinking habits, then perhaps life could be pleasant for all of them, though she supposed, sadly, that when hostilities ended her lovely well-paid job would go too, and she would be forced to work very hard indeed, for long hours, in order to earn half her present salary.

Next door, the sound of feet thundering up the stairs came clearly through the thin wall and Rose sighed. Because she was alone in the house, she had become much more aware of the sounds from neighbouring properties. It was odd, because it had never occurred to her before that Maisie McBride and her family were noisy, but they certainly seemed so now. Dick shouted at the children, and Trixie shrieked with laughter, banged her bedroom door, and turned the wireless up so loud that Rose sometimes thought Steve need not have bothered to buy her a set.

On the other side, the Gray family were even worse. Maud Gray had six boys still living at home, the eldest sixteen and the youngest four. When they fought, which was often, they thumped into the wall with such force that Rose's pictures jumped, and Maud's strident voice could surely be heard all the way down to the Mersey as she bawled imprecations and poured curses down on the heads of her rumbustious young.

It isn't as if my children were ever particularly noisy, Rose told herself now, so why I should be so aware of my neighbours, I really don't know. But I am, and that's all there is to it. Of course, when Steve was home and started a row, I suppose the neighbours pricked up their ears and thought us as rowdy as themselves, so I really shouldn't grumble. Oh, but how I wish the girls were curled up in the next room right now!

Next door, Trixie's door slammed, and after perhaps ten minutes of comparative quiet, the Gray brothers came thundering up the stairs on the other side. Most of them were already in bed, Rose judged, so this would be the two eldest, and to give them credit, once they got into their room, they were careful not to make a noise which would wake the younger ones.

Nevertheless, Rose continued to listen to the boys as they got ready for bed until, at last, she fell asleep.

Chapter Five
April 1940

'Use your eyes, girl!' Maldwyn's voice was low but Petal could hear the touch of impatience, nevertheless. 'Look for a thickening in the hedge, move your head slowly from left to right, then up and down. The leaves on the hawthorns are so tiny still that almost anywhere where there's a thicker bit could mean a nest. Now come along, I've showed you half a dozen, so you must find the next one.'

Petal and Maldwyn were in the Three Acre Wood, or rather they were skirting it, looking for birds' nests in the hawthorn hedge which surrounded it. The wood itself was mixed, with some mature trees, some saplings and good thick undergrowth. There would be many nests within it, but Maldwyn was a practical boy and believed in covering as much ground as possible in a workmanlike fashion. When they had found all the nests in the hawthorn hedge, he explained, they would pick out the ones they wanted, taking one egg only from the nests of their choice.

Petal agreed to this because she agreed with everything Maldwyn said. Over their time at Ty Siriol, he had become her best friend; he had taken her sledging, taught her how to sail a home-made boat on the pond at the back of the farm, gone with her to the picture house in Ruthin for the Saturday morning show, even helped her to understand the Welsh which most of the local children spoke when out of school. He was the third and youngest son of the Griffiths family, who farmed half a mile up the road from Ty Siriol. A thin, dark-eyed, dark-haired boy, only a little older than Petal herself, he had taken her under his protection when the children returned to school in early January, translating remarks made in the playground until, almost without realising it, Petal began to understand well over half of whatever was being said in Welsh.

But right now, birdnesting was important because it would be her mother's birthday in another five weeks and Maldwyn was going to show her how to make a beautiful – and free – present, for which birds' eggs were an absolute essential. So she scanned the next section of hedge eagerly, spotted a nest and was rewarded by Maldwyn's quick, shy smile and by an emphatic nod of his head.

'You done well,' he whispered. 'It's a blackbird's nest and their eggs are greeny-blue; real pretty.'

Having peered into the nest to verify the truth of this statement and to count the eggs, the two children moved on, discovering another four nests – robin, blackcap, song thrush and blue tit – before Maldwyn decreed that they should now retrace their steps. 'We need, say, half a dozen blackbird eggs, three thrushes and one or two each of the smaller birds,' he said instructively. 'We'll have to blow them really carefully . . . but it's easier to show than tell, and don't forget, only one egg from each nest.'

By dinnertime, the soft collecting bag which Maldwyn carried with such care contained the right number of eggs and the children turned their steps towards Ty Siriol once more. Normally Nicky and Daisy would have accompanied them but today they had gone to a picture show in Ruthin so the two young ones had gone collecting on their own.

I must be the luckiest person in the world, and the happiest, Petal thought, as they headed for the back door. When Auntie Blod and Uncle Gwil listen to the news I know war is horrid, but I do so love the farm, it's perfectly splendid, and oh, how I wish Mam could come and live with us, too, so that we could stay here for always.

She and Maldwyn entered the kitchen. Maldwyn had been invited to have his dinner with them when he had called for Petal earlier in the day and now he went across to the sink, as of right, to wash his hands and face before the meal, greeting his hostess cheerfully as he did so. 'We've got the eggs, one from each nest, like I said, and after dinner I'm going to show Petal how to blow them without making cracks or spoiling them in any way,' he said proudly. 'What's in the pot?'

Auntie Blodwen turned from the range and smiled at them. 'It's lambs' tail stew, and I'm saving Daisy's share for suppertime.'

Petal winced and saw Maldwyn do the same. Uncle Gwil had told her that lambs' tails had to be docked because otherwise they were a prey to infection, getting caught in the undergrowth and trailing on the muddy ground in wintertime, but even so, she hated the thought of eating a tail whose owner was even now gambolling in the fields. However, Auntie Blod thought this reaction was ridiculous. 'You eat mutton, which is a dead sheep when all's said and done, and you eat eggs, which would turn into hens if we left 'em under the broody,' she said. 'Besides, there's a war on and it's wicked to waste food, Mr Churchill said so.'

But settling down at the table, Petal decided to feed Uncle Gwil's sheepdogs with the meat in her portion, whenever no one was looking.

⋆   ⋆   ⋆

Steve McAllister arrived back in Liverpool late one afternoon in May, just a couple of days before his wife's birthday. Not that he remembered that, he just thought the date vaguely familiar. He and Alby hefted their ditty bags and walked together up the sloping road from the docks, Steve at least feeling both exhausted and angry, for their ship, HMS *Jericho*, had been involved in enemy action out in the Atlantic, where she had been accompanying a convoy from the United States, and Steve had actually felt a shot pass within inches of his head, and had known sickening fear when a torpedo had struck somewhere below the water line. But they had been lucky; the torpedo had done minimal damage, and though water had been coming in and the pumps were in constant use, they had got home safely. And now the *Jericho* would be in dry dock for at least five days or possibly six, whilst the damage was properly repaired and the ship revictualled.

Part of Steve's bad temper had been caused by his friend, who had refused to nip into a dockside pub for a few bevvies before returning home.

'It's all right for you,' Steve had growled, slowing to a snail's pace and gazing longingly at the Goree Vaults. 'Your missus will give you a grand welcome and there'll be a hot meal set on the table in a trice. All I'll get will be a cold look and a bit of bread and scrape.'

'If you go home drunk, then it's all you'll deserve,' Alby pointed out. 'For the Lord's sake, why anticipate trouble? Very likely, she'll rush down to the chip shop as soon as you enter the house . . . unless she's already got something hot on the stove, that is.'

'How can she, when she don't know I'm in port?' Steve groaned. 'And I'm that hungry, me belly thinks me throat's been cut. I'd like to get hold of whoever buys supplies for the *Jericho* and ring his bloody neck.'

Alby sighed. 'Yes, something definitely went wrong,' he agreed. 'No ship with a full complement should run short of food two days before docking. But I suppose it were a longer journey than they'd anticipated, keeping out of the way of the wolf packs and so on.'

'Well they ought to have antic— anticipated it,' Steve grumbled. He heaved a sigh and straightened his shoulders. 'Still, you're right; no point in looking on the black side. Rose ain't a bad wife; she's a grand little cook, so she is. It's just that if the kids is still in North Wales, she don't bother all that much wi' makin' meals. She said so the last time she wrote.'

'Aye, I dare say we'll both notice some changes,' Alby admitted. 'My Rachel's never worked before so she won't be at home all the time. It'll seem strange when she goes off in the mornings, the way I used to do.'

'Yeah, but it's worse for me,' Steve said, unwilling to admit that anyone could suffer as he was suffering. 'You've got your ma-in-law to cook meals an' clean the house an' that; she'll darn your socks and front-to-back your collars and sew buttons back on. I bet Rose won't even offer to get me a hot meal, not when she's got a good excuse to come home and sit on her bum after work.'

Alby stopped dead and grabbed Steve's arm, swinging him round so that they were facing one another. 'You've got a right nasty chip on your shoulder, you have,' he said accusingly. 'I thought your wife were a real nice woman; I only saw your girls once, but Mrs McAllister had made sure they wore pretty clothes and were clean as a couple of little whistles. She put a good tea on the table for all of us – I reckon her home-made bread takes some beating – and now that she's not got the kids to look out for, the place will be like a new pin and there's bound to be nice food in the house. So stop expectin' the worst and start deciding to enjoy your leave, hear me? And if things does go wrong, come round to our place and we'll see you're fed and watered, old feller.'

Steve could not help laughing and reluctantly agreed to do as Alby said and give Rose a chance. Then they climbed up Everton Brow and Steve turned right into Salisbury Street, leaving Alby to continue on his way. Presently, Steve turned into Bernard Terrace and headed for his own front door.

It was locked. Steve groaned but put his hand through the letter box, fumbling around for the string. It was not there. He stood back, asking himself what the devil his wife was playing at, feeling the anger rise and a tide of heat stain his cheeks. She had no right to lock him out. The key should have been there; suppose the kids came back early from school.

He remembered then. The bloody kids were in Wales, his bloody wife was working at the uniform factory on Long Lane and he was bloody well locked out of his own home. For a moment, he was so furious that he stepped back a pace, preparing to attack the door like a human battering ram. Dammit, was he no longer master in his own house? He had been locked out like a naughty child; it would teach her a lesson if she came home to find he had broken the door down.

Luckily, however, common sense prevailed. The door was old but both sturdy and solid. There was a back door, which led straight into the kitchen, but for all he knew she might have bolted that before leaving.

She could not lock it since there was no lock, but the bolts top and bottom rendered it even more impregnable than the front one. Restlessly, he went back along the terrace and turned down the jigger and into his tiny backyard. There was a lean-to scullery or washhouse at the back, with a sloping tiled roof, and, to his joy, he saw that the back bedroom window was slightly ajar, no doubt because it was a warm day. Steve glanced around him. If he put his foot on the kitchen window sill, he should be able to scramble up on to the scullery roof and thence to the bedroom window. The trouble was, it was bloody undignified and anyone passing by might see him and realise he was locked out of his own home. Still. It was either go in by the bedroom window or stay outside, and it pleased him to think how shocked Rose would be when she returned from work to find someone in the house. He told himself that if there was no food in the place, he would hide behind the kitchen door when he heard her coming, and give her a good buffet round the ear to show her who was boss.

Despite the fact that he had long legs and strong arms, he found it extremely difficult to get from the yard to the roof. He made it in the end though, clutching so desperately at the slates that he brought two of them crashing into the yard. Unfortunately, this drew the attention of a couple of urchins passing along the jigger. The first one nudged his companion and said, in ringing tones: 'There's a bleedin' burglar climbin' on the McAllisters' roof! Ooh, he looks a real bad 'un; he's got one o' them faces burglars have in the Beano. C'mon, Charlie, let's run for the scuffers.'

Charlie, however, demurred. 'They'd never believe us, norrunless we take the feller captive ourselves,' he said. He bent and picked up a stone which he hurled, with great accuracy, at Steve's head. Steve's roar of mingled pain and wrath seemed to egg the boys on, for a positive rain of missiles followed. Bits of rotting vegetable matter, stones and even lumps of coal bounced off his head and shoulders, whilst the boys screamed at him to get bleedin' out of it and come down afore he were knocked off of his perch.

'When I get down, I'm gonna bleedin' kill you,' Steve howled and was almost glad when the noise brought Rose's friend Maisie out of her back door.

'What the devil . . .? Oh, it's you, Steve,' she said. 'Why on earth . . . oh, I reckon you're locked out, is that it?' She did not wait for an answer but turned to the two boys, who had ceased raining missiles upon the enemy now that an adult had hove into view. 'Off with you, kids,' Maisie said. 'You done right to try an' discourage a burglar, only he ain't one. He's been an' gone an' locked himself out, that's all. Go on, get home, before he comes down and clocks you one.'

'Are you sure he ain't a burglar, missus?' the younger boy said plaintively. 'He looks like a burglar, he's got a right nasty face on him. And he's broke the slates on the roof and he throwed bits o' stuff at us.'

'You threw first . . .' Steve started, then realised that it was beginning to sound like a kids' quarrel, and shut his mouth firmly. Ignoring the watchers below, he scrambled on to the ridge of the roof and began humping himself towards the window. He could hear the boys' muffled giggles and a quick glance showed him Maisie grinning like a Cheshire cat, but by now he was past caring. All he wanted was to get into the house and plan a revenge upon Rose.

Once down in the kitchen, he searched for food and found only bread and margarine and half a jar of rhubarb and ginger jam: a concoction which he hated. He was quite glad the fire was not lit since it was a warm day, but he lit the gas under the kettle and made himself a pot of tea, tipping the last of the sugar into his cup out of sheer spite. It made it far too sweet, but when Rose came home she would have to drink her tea without any sugar at all.

Having eaten two thick slices of bread and margarine, he decided to go out, using the back door and leaving it unbolted, of course. He had no idea what time she would be home but thought he would go to the pub and have a couple of bevvies; then he would take his friend Alby up on his offer.

Acting upon this resolve, he left the house and was soon ensconced in the Salisbury Arms, tipping back a pint of porter and trying to remember the way to Langsdale Street.

Rose was on a late shift, which had meant starting work at two in the afternoon and not finishing until ten. It wasn't a bad shift – in some ways she quite enjoyed it – since the bosses usually worked during the day and so things were a little more relaxed on both the two until ten and the ten until six shifts, though she had never got used to sleeping in the daytime and was glad that the late shifts only came round about once a month.

As a finisher, what was more, Rachel, like the bosses, only worked days, and Rose missed her company dreadfully. This afternoon she had set off for the bus alone and presently reached the factory, taking her place on the bench alongside April, and beginning to assemble the various parts to be fed into the maw of her commercial sewing machine.

She had been doing the work for a year now and it had become almost automatic, which was a blessing, since it allowed her to let her mind wander. With only a couple of days before her birthday, she was thinking of her two days off, which she would spend at Ty Siriol, and of seeing the children again. She was more delighted with them every time she visited, she told herself now. Daisy was sensible, nowhere near as nervous as she had been, far more self-confident; Nicky was still billeted in Ruthin, though Mrs Ryan was always threatening to get him back since he was useful and kept an eye on her younger children, and Daisy spent a good deal of time with her old friend. The two of them took excellent care of Petal and her friend Maldwyn, seeing that the younger ones were never bullied and did not get into too much trouble.

'Penny for your thoughts,' April said suddenly, when they had been working more or less in silence for a couple of hours. 'I reckon it's time for a break. That last seam I done weren't as straight as it might have been, but five minutes of movin' around and a nice cuppa would do us both a power of good.'

Rose glanced up at the round face of the clock on the wall. 'She won't blow the whistle for the best part of an hour,' she pointed out sadly, 'but there's always the lavvies . . . you go first, since it was your idea.'

April waited her moment, then hurried from the room. When the supervisor passed behind April's chair and gave Rose an enquiring look, she pretended to be surprised but said that April must have been caught short. The supervisor accepted this, though she frowned and pursed her lips, and when she was once more at the other end of the long room Rose also abandoned her work and hurried off to the toilet block.

When she returned, Rose joined in the general chatter which was going on. The girls discussed the rises in the price of a stamp, the Prime Minister, Winston Churchill, the new film at the Rialto and the chances of their going off on a firm's outing when August arrived, despite the war. Then it was time to go to the canteen for a hot meal – bangers and mash with baked beans on the side, followed by apple pie and custard – and before she knew it, a whistle shrilled and the girls began to tidy their places, leaving for the cloakroom just as the new intake hurried in to take over their machines.

It was a mild night, with a gentle wind blowing, and as she climbed off the bus in Shaw Street and headed for home, Rose's thoughts reverted to her days off once more. She loved her visits to the farm and congratulated herself that her girls were getting the sort of childhood she herself would have loved. They knew so many things that had completely passed the young Rose by! She had watched Daisy carefully measuring boiled potato peelings and other vegetable leftovers into a bucket, adding hot water, and then staggering out to the grain store where a vast bin contained large quantities of meal. Her daughter used a tin scoop to measure meal into the bucket, stirring it vigorously with a long metal spoon until it was apparently of just the right consistency, before adding a few handfuls of corn, stirring the mixture once more and hefting the bucket out to the yard.

The hens, alerted by heaven knew what sounds, flocked to her side, some making a spirited endeavour to leap into the bucket, but Daisy fended them off with the metal spoon, laughing as they flapped eagerly around her. Then she began to dole out the mixture, throwing it as far as she could so that all the poultry got a share, and when she could get no more out of the bucket she laid it on the ground for a moment, so that the greedier hens could peck out any last scraps of food still adhering to its galvanised sides.

Rose knew that Daisy had been frightened of the chickens when she first went to the farm. She had been nervous of horses, would not have dreamed of feeding the pigs in case they decided that she herself would make a tasty morsel, and went out of her way to avoid the great grey and white geese, with their big orange bills, their venomous hissing, and their huge, splayed feet. Rose herself was not fond of the geese but now Daisy – and Petal – knew just how to deal with the aggressive birds. They would kick and clout their way through the creatures, though they were careful never to turn their backs, for an angry gander, especially one who had been kicked, would think nothing of nipping at bare legs or arms, provided the owner was not actually looking at him at the time.

Blodwen has been so generous to me and so good to the children that I really ought to take her a little present, Rose was telling herself as she put her key into the front door. It was half past ten and the houses were quiet, not even the Grays creating the usual din they made when Mrs Gray began to hustle the younger boys off to their beds. Rose locked the door behind her and headed for the kitchen. She would make herself a cup of tea but she would not eat anything since she had had a meal not much more than three hours ago. She went into the kitchen and across to the stove, then something made her pause. She glanced round her, frowning slightly. Something was . . . different, though right now, she could not say exactly what. She went across to the window and pulled down the blackout blind, then reached up and lit the gas lamp. Then she turned back to the stove, carefully shielding the match she had used, hoping to be able to light the gas under the kettle with the same flame.

Afterwards, she wondered what had made her pick up the kettle, for normally she put enough water in it to make a cup of tea before she left the house, but now, to her surprise, the kettle was empty.

Frowning, Rose considered, glanced at the stove top to see if the kettle had suddenly sprung a leak and examined the floor. No dribble of water from sink to stove to indicate that the kettle had leaked on its journey earlier that day. Shrugging, she carried the kettle to the sink and half filled it, carried it back to the stove, lit the gas and perched it on the ring. Then, waiting for it to boil, she looked around her once more. What *was* different about the room? It was warm, a bit stuffy, but then the day had been warm, and the house did tend to get stuffy with all the downstairs windows shut. Another glance round convinced her that the only real difference was that the pantry door was not quite shut and investigation quickly eased her mind. Earlier that day she had asked Maisie to buy her a small loaf of bread, a packet of teacakes and some fruit, whatever was available. Strawberries were coming into the shops soon; she would have liked some strawberries.

Rose went over to the pantry and checked and sure enough there was a small loaf and a packet of teacakes. The fruit looked like apples, though – but it was still a bit early for strawberries, she supposed, and apples would be just as good.

The kettle hissed and began to whistle and Rose grabbed it off the stove before it screamed like a soul in torment, the way whistling kettles will if only half filled and left over the flame. She made herself a pot of tea, waited for it to brew for five minutes whilst she ate a teacake, then drank the tea. She always cleared up before going to bed because she hated facing a dirty kitchen and a piled-up sink next morning. She began to tidy up now, humming to herself as she worked. Next day she would be on the two until ten shift again, and the following day as well, but then there would be two wonderful days off to spend with her children, two dreamy country days.

Because she was happy she cleared the kitchen in record time, refilled the kettle, then headed for the stairs. She was halfway up them before another thought occurred to her; a thought which stopped her in her tracks, brought a cold sweat breaking out on her forehead, neck, breasts.

Maisie did not have a key to Rose's house, so how had the messages managed to get into the pantry? Rose had often toyed with the idea of having another key cut, but somehow she was always too busy, and anyway, Maisie never minded hanging on to a few groceries until Rose was able to go next door to pick them up. It was not as though Maisie had to wait for the money, because Rose always paid in advance.

Puzzled, Rose remained where she was for several moments, halfway up the stairs, staring before her, trying to work it out. Then, with another shrug, she began to climb the stairs once more. Fool that she was, she must have forgotten to lock the front door . . . no, that couldn't be the answer because she had just unlocked it, hadn't she? On the other hand she had not checked the back door . . . yes, that must be it. She had been in a hurry to leave earlier in the day, must have forgotten to bolt the back door, and Maisie had let herself in, dumped the messages and gone out again.

But that would mean the back door would still be

unbolted, and if it was, Rose should really retrace her steps and shoot the bolts before going up to bed. She half turned, then weariness attacked her again. Why should she bother with the back door if it had been unbolted all afternoon and evening? She had nothing worth stealing, so there was no need for her to go downstairs again tonight.

With a light step and a lighter heart, Rose climbed the rest of the stairs and crossed the narrow landing towards her bedroom door. She opened it and went straight across to pull down the blackout blind. She had her arm up to the cord when some small sound – the creak of a board, an intake of breath – told her that there was someone, or something, else in the room. She gave a gasp of sheer terror and half turned, even as something hit her a heavy blow between the shoulder blades and she fell forward, striking her head against something hard and cold. For one moment longer, she was conscious of a voice, a presence. Then she plunged into blackness.

Rose came to herself aware only that she was lying on something soft and in pretty complete darkness, though when she moved her head slightly she became aware of a lighter square and realised that this must be a window. But her wits were still addled by what had happened and terror still blurred her thought processes, making it difficult to concentrate. She tried to move her head again and moaned as pain stabbed at her brow, then opened her eyes to find a dark figure bending over her. Immediately, fear told her to pretend she was still unconscious and she closed her eyes quickly.

'Rose? Rose, wharrever's the matter? It were a joke, for God's sake! I come home soon after two o'clock to find meself locked out, and when I did manage to gerrin, there weren't no food, norreven a bottle of ale. I were that disappointed; I've been dreamin' about gerrin' home ever since the ship were damaged and the officers told us she'd be in dry dock for a week.' Somebody was chafing her hands; rough fingers pushed the hair back from her damp forehead. 'Rosie, for God's sake, speak to me! I didn't mean no harm, I just thought I'd surprise you. Only that bleedin' blind got wrapped round your hand somehow and it brought the whole lot down and your forehead hit the window pane. Rose? Rose?'

Rose opened her eyes. She looked up at her husband's bulk and thought, bitterly, that she should have guessed he had come home. And hiding away in order to terrify the life out of her was just the sort of thing he would do, though on this occasion his 'joke' had gone a little too far, even for him.

'Rose? Oh, thank Gawd, you ain't dead.' His voice, which had been uncertain, almost pleading, suddenly became aggressive. 'Trust you to give me the fright of me life, you perishin' little bitch. Why, I go to tap you on the shoulder and next thing I know you're flat on the floor an' out cold, an' I s'pose you'll blame me for it. Well, blame away, I can't stop you, but I'm tellin' you, that great lump on your forehead ain't nothin' to do wi' me. *And* I'm sober as a judge, wharrever you may like to think.'

He had been bending over her and Rose, groggily beginning to sit up, realised that his breath did not smell of drink, and his speech was not slurred. She put a hand to her sore and aching forehead and felt a warm wetness, saying as she did so: 'I don't understand. If you didn't go to the pub and you docked at two, where have you been?'

'Are you all right now? Here, I'll give you a hand to get down to the kitchen because I daren't show a light, not now you've dragged the blind down. But I can still see there's a nasty cut on your forehead – I can see it in the moonlight – an' I just hope you ain't goin' to blame me for that an' all!'

Rose was tempted to reply acidly that, since he and she were alone in the house, she could scarcely blame anyone else, but bit her tongue. It would not help to antagonise him further, and right now it seemed that guilt and remorse were fighting for supremacy. She would try to give him the benefit of the doubt, for the time being at least. Perhaps it had just been a joke, though she thought it likelier that he had meant to give her an awful fright to pay her back for being out when he had come home. Still, no point in giving him an excuse to be even nastier to her.

'Rose? Can you hear me? Lemme give you a hand to stand up.'

He pulled her up and Rose stood, swaying for a moment, trying to collect her thoughts. By his own admission, he had been ashore since two o'clock, and it was now getting on for eleven at night. If he had not been boozing, and she was pretty sure he hadn't, where had he been?

She did not ask the question at once, however, but waited until they were safely downstairs in the kitchen. Then she watched whilst he drew down the blinds, lit the lamp and set a match to the ring beneath the kettle. Still feeling weak and with her heart banging unevenly, she settled herself in an armchair, sipped the hot cup of tea he handed her, and decided she must sort this matter out. 'I'm sorry, Steve, but I'm still very confused. If you've been home all day . . . oh, I don't understand! There was something –

something in the pantry, something that shouldn't have been there. Oh, it was the groceries I'd asked Maisie to buy. If you were here when she delivered 'em, you could've ate the lot, I wouldn't have grudged you, and Maisie would have told you I was on the evening shift. If you knew I'd be home by half past ten, why didn't you wait up for me? You could have given me a fright just as well in the kitchen as in the bedroom.'

Steve shrugged; he had the grace to look more than a little ashamed. 'Oh, I dunno . . . it just seemed . . . the fact is, I took meself round to Alby's place. I couldn't go out of the front door, because you'd locked it, so I went out the back and left it unbolted. That inteferin' cow next door saw me comin' in an' knew I was home, so after I'd gone she nipped in with wharrever she'd bought for you an' stuck 'em in the pantry.'

'Oh, I see,' Rose said wearily. 'Well, I suppose the same applies; Rachel must have told you my shift ended at ten.'

Steve heaved an enormous sigh. 'She did. And since you're bound to find out anyway, they gave me a grand supper – that woman's a prime cook – and then we played cards until nine o'clock or so. Here, the cut on your forehead has stopped bleeding. So if you've got a bit o' plaster, I'll stick it on. And if the cross-questioning and blaming has finished, then I reckon we ought to forget about it an' go up to bed.'

Once more, Rose was filled with an overwhelming desire to be truthful, to tell him that she did not wish to share a bed with someone who had played such a mean trick on her, but again she held her peace. To be fair to Steve, though his advances in bed were rough, he had never deliberately caused her they were making love and though tenderness was unknown to him, his satisfaction afterwards usually meant that he rolled away from her and slept at once, freeing her to go to sleep herself, secure in the knowledge that he would snore until the alarm clock went off.

So she accompanied him meekly up to their bedroom and climbed into bed, though when he flung a rough arm across her body and tried to pull her against him she feigned sleep and presently, muttering beneath his breath, he turned away from her and was soon snoring.

Rose, however, lay awake for some time. The sticking plaster made her forehead prick and burn and various bruises from her fall were beginning to make themselves felt, but worst of all was the recollection of her two days off, which she had meant to spend at Ty Siriol. She supposed she could suggest that Steve accompanied her – Petal would be pleased – but because of her husband's unpredictable behaviour, her little holiday would be fraught with worry instead of the relaxing time she had anticipated.

Rose sighed, lying very stiff and quiet between the sheets. How nice it had been to be able to sleep alone in this bed, without fear. But presently, despite her anxiety, the rigours of a long and eventful day took their toll; Rose slept.

That night, curled up close in their bed, Rachel burrowed her head into the soft spot of Alby's shoulder, so that his chin rested on her hair, and said, sleepily: 'Well, I'm glad I've got to know Rose's husband at last. He's awfully nice, isn't he, Alby? And how he loves his little daughter. I wonder if he'll go down to the farm when Rose does? When I told him she meant to go for her birthday, he looked a bit cast down, said he'd been planning a surprise for her, wondered whether he might bring the kids home, just for a few days, you know. He seemed to think they'd be safe enough and I know Rose misses them dreadfully. I agree with her that the countryside is safest, but just for a few days . . .'

Alby pulled his wife's soft and yielding body even closer and turned his head to plant a kiss on her temple, feeling the flutter of the pulse which beat there against his lips and aware of a rush of tenderness, mingling with desire. He was so lucky! He and Rachel had met at a dance and from the moment he had taken her in his arms, he had known with absolute certainty that she was the girl for him.

'Alby? I was just saying . . .'

Alby chuckled. 'You always are – just saying, I mean. The thing is, sweetheart, that I'm not at all sure how Steve would enjoy a stay in the countryside. He likes pubs and dances and snooker halls and, above all, the company of other men. It's odd because, personally, I enjoy the company of men or women, but there are some fellers who literally dislike the opposite sex and I believe Steve is one of them.'

'Dislike? But how can you say that, my dearest? Steve was very sweet to me, and to Mother as well. He praised her cooking, asked her about her Wednesday Sewing Circle, complimented her on her choice of paintings for the sitting room wall . . . and when I talked about work, he seemed truly interested.'

'Yes, but I suspect he was being polite. It's difficult to explain, love, but whereas I talk about you a great deal, aboard ship, he scarcely ever mentions Rose. He seems to think that simply being a male of the species confers wit and intelligence, two things a woman cannot possibly possess. Didn't you notice that some of his remarks – even the complimentary ones – were . . . condescending, as though he were doing your mam a favour by praising her choice of pictures?'

There was a pause whilst Rachel appeared to mull over his remark, and when she did speak, it was slowly and more thoughtfully. 'Ye-es, I know what you mean,' she said at last. 'But how can he believe Rose isn't intelligent? She's ever so quick and clever and – I don't want to insult your friend, Alby, but he's really not at all quick on the uptake, is he? Not clever, either. Well, Rose showed me one or two of his letters and he doesn't write as well as Daisy does, and his sentences are all short and sort of chopped up.'

Alby laughed. 'Yes, and that's one of the reasons why he and Rose don't hit it off the way you and I do,' he explained. 'Steve bitterly resents having a wife who he secretly knows is cleverer than he is, so he spends a lot of time plotting to take her down a peg, if you know what I mean.'

'That's horrid!' Rachel said indignantly. 'Why doesn't he try to get cleverer himself, though? I mean he could read books, study, like you have. I expect he'd feel much better if he got made a Leading Seaman, or whatever it's called.'

'It's hard to explain,' Alby said. 'But I think the reason is that while he believes himself to be superior to all women – not just Rose – he still has a sneaking suspicion that he'll never really get much further, either in the Royal Navy or in the merchant fleet. And now just you stop talking for one minute, or it'll be time for breakfast and we shan't have slept a wink.'

A week later, Rose locked her front door carefully behind her and hurried along the terrace in the pearly, early morning light, turning into Salisbury Street and hoping that she was not going to spoil her first day of freedom by missing the bus. It was odd to think of it as her first day of freedom because she had been back at work for two days, but in the early hours of this morning the *Jericho* had sailed on the tide. With her husband aboard her, and not liable to return to the city for several weeks, Rose had been aware of a strong feeling of relief as soon as she awoke and now she found herself eager to get to work, knowing that the next time she came home again her stomach would not clench with dread at whatever might await her.

In actual fact, however, Steve had been perfectly reasonable, for once. Embarrassed by the cut on her forehead, the black eye which had appeared next day, and the many bruises on her arms and knees, he had been quick to explain his wife's appearance as being the result of an unfortunate accident. She had been pulling down the blackout blind when the whole thing had collapsed and she had fallen against the sash window, cutting her brow, blacking her eye and bruising herself considerably in the fall. Most neighbours had appeared to accept this explanation without question, but Maisie had lived next door for too long. She had raised sceptical eyebrows and had actually snorted when Steve had said that the trip to the farm had had to be cancelled because of his wife's injuries. 'Anyone who believes that, would believe anything,' she had said to Rose when Steve had wandered back indoors. 'If he gives you more stick, queen, you want to go to the scuffers. They'd mebbe give him a taste of his own medicine which might make him think twice before doing it again.'

But, for a variety of reasons, Rose had decided to go along with Steve's story. After all, he was hardly ever home. In future, she must be more careful. She had allowed him to take her front door key and have another one cut, but she had decided that she would never again leave the house without first smearing the hall floor with a light dusting of either flour or cocoa powder. Then she would be able to see immediately if someone had come in, and could act accordingly.

Despite her resolve, however, she had taken no precautions before leaving the house that day. He had only just sailed, and anyway she meant to go down to the farm as soon as she had finished work, even though she would have to return by the milk train the following morning. The children had made her a surprise birthday present, and their disappointment when she had written to say she would be unable to visit them had been severe. Daisy, aided and abetted by Blodwen Williams, had telephoned the factory during Rose's dinner hour and had begged her mother to come to Ty Siriol, if only for a few hours.

'It took ages and ages to make your present,' she had said plaintively, her voice very tiny and strange in Rose's ear, for this was the first time she had spoken to her daughter on the telephone. 'And it's ever so delicate, Mam, not the sort of thing you could send through the post. It – it would end up in a thousand pieces, Auntie Blod says.'

So Rose had promised and Daisy had put Auntie Blodwen on the line. 'Just tell us the time of the train you'll be arriving on, cariad,' she had said briskly. 'Someone will be there waiting. And we'll deliver you with the milk churns, first thing the following day.'

It had taken some arranging, nevertheless. Rose had changed shifts so that today she was on mornings and tomorrow she would be on afternoons, which should give her time enough to get to the farm and back. Fortunately, by now, Rose was a quick and experienced worker, so her supervisor had agreed to her swapping shifts, anxious to keep her staff happy.

Now Rose turned into Shaw Street and headed for the bus stop, then waved as she saw Rachel hurrying along the pavement towards her. This was the first time she and Rachel had met since Steve's return and Rose beamed at the younger girl, suddenly realising that Rachel's feelings over the departure of the *Jericho* would be the exact opposite of her own. She wiped the smile off her face and was about to say something sympathetic when Rachel spoke. 'Rose, whatever's happened? You look as if you've been in a road accident! Steve never said you'd been hurt when I saw them off last night.'

'Oh, that,' Rose said airily, indicating her still puffy eye and the sticking plaster across her forehead. 'It were the stupidest thing, Rachel, but it happened almost a week ago, so I'd all but forgotten about it. I was in my bedroom, pulling down the blackout blind . . .'

By now, Rose had told the story so often that she was almost word perfect, and had no difficulty in sounding as though it were no more than the truth; in fact, she almost believed it herself. Watching Rachel's face, as they joined the bus queue, she was pretty sure that Rachel had believed it too.

'I bet the children got a surprise when they saw their darling mam looking like a prize fighter,' she remarked with a chuckle, as the bus came to a halt beside them and the queue began to inch forward. 'It must have been lovely for them to see both of you, though. It'll be the first time for ages that they've had their mam and their dad together . . . and it was your birthday, too.'

'Oh, Rachel, thank you so much for the birthday card,' Rose said belatedly. The children had made her cards, but Rachel's had been the only shop bought one, since Steve did not believe in marking such occasions and always left the buying and sending of cards to her, birthdays being women's work. But she must answer Rachel's questions, or her friend would get a totally distorted view of recent events. 'But I didn't get to see the children, unfortunately. I was knocked unconscious when I hit the window pane and Steve thought I'd best not go off into the country. Besides, he wanted to arrange a little party . . . just family, I mean,' she added hastily, seeing the trap yawning before her. 'Only I wasn't quite well enough to do any catering, so we went to the Derby cinema on the Scotland Road, instead. We had a meal first. The following night, we went to relatives and had a pretty good time.'

'I see,' Rachel said slowly, as they climbed aboard the bus and moved up the central aisle. 'Steve did say something about a surprise when he came round to our place that first afternoon.' She looked, shrewdly, at her friend. 'Rose, are you sure you only banged your head on the window pane? Only, I know how keen you were to go down to the farm and see the kids and I wouldn't have thought . . .'

Rose laughed, trying to make it sound as though the suggestion were genuinely amusing. 'What else did you think I'd done? And of course I was disappointed over not seeing the children, bitterly disappointed, in fact. But in wartime, we wives have to put our husbands first, don't you think? And anyway, I'm catching the first train to Ruthin this afternoon when my shift finishes, so I shall see the kids all right. They've made me a birthday present which is too fragile to post so I couldn't let them down.'

She was watching Rachel's face as she spoke, and saw her relax, begin to smile. It was annoying that she had to lie to her best friend, but better in the long run. Steve had been much easier to live with since he had palled up with Alby, and Rose did not intend to do anything to spoil such a useful friendship.

By the time they reached the factory, Rose had told Rachel all about the film she and Steve had seen, the dance they had attended, the evening they had spent with Aunt Selina and Uncle Frank in Penny Lane, and Rachel had reciprocated with her own news, for she and Alby had gone house-hunting, or rather flat-hunting, and had seen a couple of places which they both liked and could afford.

'Only they aren't so near the docks; they're even further out than the factory,' she disclosed as they approached the time clock. 'It would be nice for me in one way . . . there are gardens and things . . . but you and I wouldn't be able to travel to work together. Still, we could meet in the canteen as usual.'

Rose tried not to look dismayed, but realised that she felt it. The journey to work was long and dull, only made bearable by Rachel's company, but she could scarcely say so. Instead, she wished Rachel luck with her house-hunting, but could not forbear reminding her friend that she would miss having someone waiting at home for her each evening, would miss her mother's cooking, too. 'And she does your messages for you as well,' she pointed out, a trifle reproachfully. 'Believe me, being all on your own is no picnic, queen.'

'Oh well, it will probably come to nothing.' Rachel said equably. 'But it was fun looking.' They punched their cards and set off for their places of work.

★   ★   ★

143

Daisy and Petal were waiting on the platform when Rose's train drew in, for though they now attended school for a full day since so many of the evacuees had returned to their own homes, the routine was less strict than it had been before the war. Children, especially the older ones, were allowed off school as a matter of course if they were needed on the farms, and for an event as important as meeting a parent who had rushed over just to be able to spend a few hours with her small daughters there had been no question of denial.

'Come in early tomorrow,' the teacher had instructed them. 'And Petal, you can show your mam how nicely you read; she'll be pleased, I'm sure.'

Now, as Rose stepped down from her carriage, Daisy and Petal flew forward, immediately asking her what she had done to her face and Rose explaining that she had fallen over when pulling down the blackout blind. Then they were hugging, kissing and chattering. Rose kissed them both, lifting them into the air to do so and noticing how much heavier they had both grown, then they set off across the station and into the road where Blodwen Williams awaited them, sitting in the pony trap and beaming all over her face.

'Hop in, Rose,' the older woman said briskly, as soon as Rose was near enough to hear her. 'Walked into a door, did you?'

Rose explained, as she climbed into the trap, closely followed by her daughters.

'Come along, girls . . . and don't go sitting on that parcel, Petal, or you might just as well have sent it through the post!'

'Oh, Mammy, do open it,' Petal cried as soon as they were all packed comfortably into the trap. 'Maldwyn helped – he's awful good – but me and

Daisy did all the threading. It took ages . . . oh, it's the prettiest thing!'

The 'prettiest thing' was revealed as a long piece of fine waxed thread, upon which were strung the most beautiful birds' eggs, each one selected for colour and size. Rose marvelled over it, touched that the children should have made her something which had cost them a great deal of effort, whilst Daisy assured her that they had taken no more than one egg from each nest, because otherwise it would not be fair on the little mother and father birds. 'And we blew them by making a teeny hole in each end of the egg and puffing air until all the egg white and yolk had come out; then we washed them ever so carefully in warm water – Petal did that – and then, when they were dry, we strung them. And Maldwyn says you can loop them across the mantelpiece in your parlour, or across a picture rail, if we've got one,' she continued. 'Do you like them, Mam? Do you really and honestly like them?'

Rose assured her daughters that it was the loveliest present she had ever received, and after that the hours seemed to fly by. She and Blodwen talked about the possibility of the children's returning to Liverpool and Rose admitted that she felt they would be safer at Ty Siriol than they could possibly be in Bernard Terrace.

'So for the time being at least we'd like to leave them here,' she said. 'Why, they're even learning Welsh – it would be a sad thing, to my mind, to drag them back to the city when they're so happy.'

Blodwen had nodded vigorously. 'Aye, you're right, and we love having them,' she assured her guest. 'They're a help already in a great many ways, and will get even more useful as they grow older. And next time your husband's home on leave perhaps the two

of you could come over for a couple of days? I'd be
– interested to meet him.'

So now Rose, making her way home on the milk
train, told herself that she was very lucky indeed. The
Williams family loved her children and would take
every care of them. If she took them home they would
have to go to a child-minder, and though there were
excellent women minding children in the neighbourhood they could not hope to compete with the
Williamses. Steve had asked, a trifle wistfully, if she
would not do better to bring the children back now
that the danger seemed fairly remote, but Rose thought
this would be downright selfish. If Steve had been
prepared to put himself out he could have gone down
to the farm with her and seen his children for himself.
But the thought of being a long way away from the
docks, his pals and even the pubs he frequented, though
he had drunk only the odd pint now and then, had
been enough to push the thought of seeing his children into the background.

She decided that, if he could give her advance
warning of his next leave, she would have Daisy and
Petal back in Bernard Terrace for a few days. And
then she leaned her head back and went gently to
sleep, only waking when the train pulled into the next
station and people began to come aboard.

Chapter Six
September 1940

'Do you know, Petal, that we've been here a whole year? Isn't that amazing? When we get home I'm going to write to Dad and tell him we can both speak Welsh pretty well, because he's going to come to Ty Siriol on his next leave, and it would be nice if he knew about us speaking Welsh.'

Petal sniffed and gave her elder sister a chilly look. Did Daisy think she was daft or something? She was doing well at school, had headed her age group in the last end of term exams, so naturally she was well aware that they had been in Wales for a whole year. The two children were no longer picked up from school in the pony trap, because the Williamses were too busy most of the time, but they had arranged a sort of rota with other local farmers who had either children of their own or evacuees, and today it had been the turn of Mary Jones, whose family lived another two miles away from Ruthin. She was a pretty, lively girl who had recently volunteered for the WRNS and had told the children that this would be her last trip into town since she had been accepted and would leave for London early the following week.

Because the lane which led from the main road to the farm was just over a mile in length, the children were always dropped off at the corner, which was wonderful in warm summer weather – like today – but not so good when it was raining cats and dogs or blowing a hurricane. Petal, who had no objection to walking when the weather was clement, idled along, thumb in mouth, admiring the first flush of autumn colour in the hips and haws beginning to brighten the hedgerows and wondering what was for tea today, whilst her sister rehearsed what she would say when she wrote to her parents later on.

'Only Auntie Blod said not to say she'd been rather poorly,' Daisy reminded her sister. 'You'll be writing as well, Petal, so you must say we're all pretty stout. That's what Dilys calls it, anyway. And that's rather annoying, because Aunty Blod's better now, but if we can't say she was poorly last week then we can't say she's better, either. Shall we write separate letters this time, or will you add a bit to the bottom of mine?'

'Separate to Daddy, the other to Mammy,' Petal said quickly. She was well aware that Daisy did not love Steve as she did, though she had no very clear idea why. It was true that Daddy spoiled her and sometimes did not seem to notice Daisy, but she thought this was because Daisy jumped and went pale when Daddy tried to pull her on to his knee or talk to her about his ship, or her school, as he had done when they had gone home to see him while he was on leave last month. The trouble is, you've got to have a good memory to remember your daddy when he's been at sea for . . . well, for a long time, and perhaps Daisy's memory isn't as good as mine, so she treats him a bit like a stranger, and daddies don't like that.

'Righty-ho,' Daisy said now, and began to skip. It wasn't far to the turn in the lane which then widened out into the farmyard. Petal began to skip as well. Soon be home! Soon be having a nice big slice of apple cake – she did love apple cake! Auntie Blod had announced her intention of having a baking day since she had missed it last week, being poorly, so there would be other good things as well as apple cake. Meat and potato turnovers, delicious little round cakes with their initials marked on each one, shortbread to take to school for elevenses, and lots more, including the big cottage loaves for eating at home and the tin-loaves for taking as carry-out.

As the farmhouse came into view, Daisy began to run; for all she was so much older, Petal guessed that her sister was just as eager to reach the kitchen and be invited to 'try one of me special jam tarts' by dear, kind Auntie Blod as Petal was herself. The two of them entered the kitchen at a gallop, only to stop short, staring. The kitchen table was laden with good things, steam was rising gently from the oven in the range, but Auntie Blod was sitting slumped in a chair, her face grey, her lovely hair tumbling out of its coronet of plaits. Her eyes had been closed, but they opened as the two girls erupted into the room and, after a shocked moment, her pale lips moved.

'Daisy? Is that you, cariad? I – I'm glad you've come home because I – I'm not feeling so good. There's such a bad feeling in my innards . . . need help I do, more than I ever dreamed I would. D'you think you could run out to the field by the wild rose copse and fetch Dilys, or Uncle Gwil?' She put out a hand to them and, to Petal's horror, it was trembling. Auntie Blodwen, the best person in the world after her mother, was frightened! Petal took the hand in her own small, warm ones, and was frightened herself; it was so cold, and wet, too, despite the warmth of the kitchen.

'Daisy will go,' she said quickly. 'But I'll stay here with you, Auntie Blod. I – I'll make you a nice *panod* and you'll better in a trice, see if you aren't!'

Daisy glanced from one to the other, showing relief when Auntie Blod shook her head. 'No, ducky, I don't fancy nothing, to tell you the truth. Sick to my stomach I am, and right strange I do feel. But if you'll stay with me, cariad . . . I own I'd feel better.' She turned her eyes to Daisy, without moving her head, and Petal saw that her skin was saggy and grey and looked as wet as her hand felt. 'You'll hurry? Tell Dilys . . . and her dad . . .'

But Daisy was already out of the kitchen. Petal watched her cross the yard at a fast run and disappear in the direction of the wild rose copse. Then she pulled up a chair so that she might continue to hold Auntie Blod's hand but could do so sitting down, for she now had to acknowledge to herself that she was very badly scared. Auntie Blod had always seemed young and strong and wonderfully capable, but now one glance at that grey face and sagging body made Petal realise that her foster mother was old . . . old as the great, hump-backed hills of the Clwydian range which formed a backdrop to Ty Siriol. Old as the ex-headmaster, Skinny Skelton, who lived in a house in the square and sometimes came tottering into school to present a prize, or take an ill teacher's place.

'Auntie Blod? Are you *sure* you wouldn't like a cup of tea? I can make you one, honest I can.'

Petal's voice sounded very small and scared in her own ears, and she was just hoping that Auntie Blod had not noticed when she felt the hand, which had been lightly gripping her own, slide out of her grasp, felt it slump back on to the older woman's lap . . . and thought, for one horrified moment, that Auntie Blod had . . . had . . .

Petal gave a small gasp, said in a tiny voice: 'Auntie Blod, you mustn't die, please don't die! Petal's here, I'll look after you!'

And even as she spoke the words the kitchen door

crashed open and Dilys entered the room, closely followed by Daisy and Uncle Gwil. 'Mam, oh, Mam!' Dilys said, falling on her knees in front of her mother, whose eyes remained closed and whose head drooped in a terrifying fashion. 'Oh, Mam, and you kept saying you were better . . . Da, fetch a blanket. She's cold as . . . as charity!'

'In a moment,' Uncle Gwil said, his voice surprisingly steady. He bent over his wife. 'Blod, my dear one, can you hear me? I'll get Elias to fetch the car round and we'll take you to see Dr Evans; just you hang on there and we'll see you right.'

Petal did not expect Auntie Blod to answer, but after a moment she said, her voice slurred and slow: 'I hear you, Gwil. Hang on I will, boyo!'

Uncle Gwil actually chuckled before straightening up and heading for the stairs. 'I'll fetch that blanket,' he said briskly, then turned back to address his daughter. 'The doctor will likely want her in hospital. I shan't be two ticks.'

Daisy crossed the room to Petal's side and took her hand. 'Auntie Blod will be all right,' she whispered comfortingly. 'Don't worry, queen. Once the doctor sees her he'll make her better in no time.'

Petal mumbled an agreement, but privately, eyeing Auntie Blodwen's crumpled face and sagging body, she was not so sure.

Rose was shopping, something she scarcely ever did now because Maisie, only working three days a week, usually did it for her. But today she was on the night shift, which meant she had time to herself, and fairness dictated that being free for once, she should do the messages for Maisie as well as for herself. She had called round at her friend's house earlier, to pick up the ration books, and now she was queuing at Annie Baker's greengrocery in William Henry Street. She had done the grocery shopping, keeping an eye on the list Maisie had given her in the pious hope of finding some of the unrationed, but also unobtainable, goods for sale, and now she was queuing for early apples which were beginning to appear in the shops, for potatoes, carrots and, hopefully, for oranges.

'Hey, Rosie! Get some for me, will you, then I won't have to join the bleedin' queue, which already goes halfway round the block!'

Rose glanced behind her and grinned at the speaker. It was one of the girls from her bench at the factory, Helen Foster. Helen had recently moved into Bernard Terrace to live with her mother. She had four small children, ranging in age from eighteen months to seven years, and had been openly critical of Rose's keeping her children on in the country when she could have had them home. Rose had pointed out that Helen's mother looked after her four while she was at work, whereas she herself had lost her mother some years earlier and would have had to find a child-minder for Daisy and Petal, but Helen had been a bit dismissive . . . until last month, that was. The bombing of London and other British towns, as well as the dog-fights which were taking place daily over the south of England, had made people realise that the cities were not safe places for either adults or kids, though so far Liverpool, which should have been a prime target with the route across the Atlantic from the United States ending there, and the docks busier than they had ever been, was comparatively unscathed.

So now Rose smiled back at Helen and said she was queuing for apples, carrots, spuds and oranges, if they had any. Helen came over, ignoring the fact that half the queue were glaring at her, and pressed some money into Rose's hand.

'Fetch us a stone o' spuds and a couple o' pounds o' them apples then,' she wheedled. 'Oh, by the way, what's up at your place, eh?'

'Up? Nothing, so far as I know,' Rose said, staring, 'an' I can't carry a stone o' spuds, even if Mrs Baker would let me have 'em, which she won't.' Was Helen trying to tell her that Steve was home? But when she asked if Helen had seen her husband around, Helen shook her head.

'No, or I'd of said. But the telegraph boy was knockin' as though he were a-goin' to have the door down as I came past. You expectin' a telegram? Anyroad, he went next door, to old Maisie's – I saw him knocking.'

Rose's hand flew to her mouth and she pushed her purse and her shopping list into Helen's hand. 'A telegram? My God, I must get home at once! Be a dear, Helen, and finish my messages for me. You can take my place in the queue – no one will mind.'

Helen agreed and Rose hurried home. As she turned into Bernard Terrace she saw a telegraph boy pedalling his bicycle along in the gutter, and waved him down. 'I'm Mrs McAllister; I live at number seven. I believe you were trying to deliver a telegram earlier, when I was out doing my messages . . .'

Even as she spoke, the boy was fumbling in his bag and held out a small, yellow envelope. 'Any reply, missus?' he asked cheerfully, as Rose spread out the small sheet of paper and began to read. 'A reply's sixpence – if it's short, that is.'

Rose's heart, which had begun to beat overtime, steadied to a more normal pace as she read the words. *Mrs Williams took ill stop Going to hospital in Wrexham stop Please come urgent stop Williams*. For a moment, she could not think straight, then she made up her mind. She had given her purse to Helen but she ferreted around in her handbag and found two threepenny bits. The boy had his notebook out and was looking at her expectantly. 'Just say, *Will be with you soonest possible, McAllister*,' she said, and watched the boy's pencil take down her words. She knew she ought to tip him and rooted round in her bag once more, finding a couple of pennies and pressing them into the boy's hopefully extended palm. 'Thanks very much. How soon will it reach the Williamses, do you suppose?'

The boy shrugged, glancing at the address. 'It'll take me ten or fifteen minutes to get back to the post office, so it should be there in the time it takes the young feller in Ruthin to cycle to . . .' he looked at the address, 'to the sender,' he finished, obviously not wanting to try to pronounce the Welsh words. 'Don't worry, missus, it'll be there before you are, even if you was to fly.'

'But Mammy, *why* did we have to leave? Auntie Blod was always telling us what a help we were and anyway, you keep saying she'll be right as rain in no time, now she's in hospital. And there's school, all our friends . . . how long will we be away for?'

Petal's small voice was beginning to hold a distinct whine and Rose sighed to herself as she answered the question which had already been asked and answered a dozen times. 'Darling, Dilys will be far too busy to look after you properly, just think about it. There will be all the farm work, all the housework, all the dairy work, to say nothing of baking, doing the washing and ironing, feeding the stock . . . oh, a hundred different things, and only poor Dilys and Uncle Gwil to tackle the lot. Because of the war, farmers have to produce as much food as they possibly can and, of course, all the younger men have been conscripted into the forces. The ones who are left, Elias, and old Dewi, aren't as strong, can't do as much in a day as the younger fellers did. That will put a heavy burden on Dilys, but as soon as Auntie Blodwen's well again, I'm sure they'll want you back.'

The three of them were sitting in the train heading for Liverpool. Daisy, who had let Petal do all the complaining, wondered whether it was time to speak up, but decided against it. Last night, she had been so worried about Auntie Blod that she had been unable to sleep, so had stolen downstairs. Reaching the kitchen, she had found Uncle Gwil and Dilys still up and had climbed, miserably, on to Dilys's large and comfortable lap. The two were talking in Welsh and after a moment, during which Dilys soothed Daisy as though she had been a baby, clucking and patting, father and daughter continued their conversation, clearly believing that Daisy could not understand a word.

'It's a big operation, Da, but Mam will come through it all right. She's ever so strong, the surgeon said. But she won't be no manner of good so far as the farm's concerned for at least six months, maybe longer. When she's recovered from the operation, they'll be sending her to Rhyl to convalesce, so it could be as long as ten weeks before she's even back with us.'

'Aye; it'll be the first time we've spent so much as a night apart since we were wed,' Uncle Gwil said glumly. 'If only our Gareth were home, we'd manage somehow. But without him, I tell you, my love, I don't know which way to turn.'

'Well I do,' Dilys said, with a briskness Daisy had never heard in her voice before. 'We must apply for a Land Girl – more than one – and tell the Ministry it's urgent. Other folk have Land Girls and reckon they're a real boon.' She lowered her voice. 'The only thing is, we shan't be able to keep the children because Mam won't be well enough to cope and the Land Girls can't be expected to do anything in the house – they're farm workers, really.'

Uncle Gwil digested this for what seemed like an age to Daisy, but when he spoke, it was decisively. 'Aye, you're right. We've been managing somehow, with the older fellers and me – and you, girl – working every hour God sends, and more, but harvest time made me realise that we'd do a good deal better if we had more pairs of hands at our disposal. Your mam's a wonderful woman; she thinks nothing of starting her work at five in the morning and not stopping till ten at night. Mebbe it's that which has brought her so low. But the truth is that when she comes back she'll need more time to herself, because no matter how she sees it, she's not a young woman any more. Yes, we'll apply for a couple of Land Girls next time we go into town. I don't suppose we'll get anyone for a while, but I'll explain to the Ministry chap and I'm sure they'll do their best.'

Daisy had listened to this conversation with only half her attention and presently Dilys had carried her up to bed and popped her in beside the still slumbering Petal. Warmed and comforted by Dilys's cuddles, and by the fact that both father and daughter had seemed certain Auntie Blod was going to get better, Daisy had not allowed the significance of their words to worry her until she awoke next morning and began to think. If the Williamses were going to have Land Girls – and many of the farmers in the area already employed such young women – and Auntie Blod would not be well enough to look after them for many weeks to come, then she and Petal would have to go back to Liverpool whether they liked it or not and a return to the farm in the near future was unlikely, to say the least. The two of them would have done everything they could to help, but in her heart Daisy knew that the reliance which they all placed on Auntie Blod could not be fulfilled by two children.

So now, sitting in the railway carriage whilst her mother tried to calm Petal's fears, she wondered whether Rose had been told about the Land Girls and the impossibility of the children's returning to the farm until Auntie Blod was completely better, or whether she believed that they would soon go back to Ty Siriol. And another point: if Auntie Blodwen was going to be in hospital for a long time, could the McAllisters visit her there? Wrexham was a bit nearer Liverpool than Ruthin was, so perhaps they could all go – armed with a bunch of chrysanthemums – and see for themselves that their dear Auntie Blodwen was actually getting better. Daisy thought she'd never forget that fearful grey and sagging face, the slurred and cracking voice. If only she could see Auntie Blod looking more like herself, then she knew the nightmare – that Auntie Blod might die – would begin to recede.

Daisy waited until her mother had stopped speaking and then put forward the suggestion that they should visit Auntie Blod in the Wrexham hospital, just as soon as they could. 'Because Dilys said they'll send her to Rhyl to con— conva something or other, and Rhyl is a long way off,' she observed. 'What do you think, Mam? We could go on your next day off and take her some flowers.'

'That's a very good idea,' Rose said approvingly,

smiling brightly at her daughter. 'You're a good girl, Daisy, thoughtful and kind. Yes, as soon as she's allowed visitors, we'll make our way to the hospital in Wrexham; that's a promise.'

In the event, it was almost the end of November before the children actually got to see Auntie Blodwen again, and then it was only because the staff agreed that, for once, they would waive their 'no children on the ward' rules since Mrs Williams was to depart in another few days to Rhyl, where she would convalesce.

They arrived at the small station at noon so Rose, who knew Wrexham quite well from previous visits to Auntie Blod, took them to Steven's Café in Hope Street, where they had a first rate meal, Petal announcing that the sausagemeat pie with mashed potato on top was almost as good as Auntie Blod's.

After that, they walked through the narrow streets to the War Memorial Hospital, an imposing modern building, built of red brick and sandstone, with elegant balconies overlooking a small side street. The children had grown accustomed, if not reconciled, to the idea that they would probably not return to live at Ty Siriol for a long, long time. *If ever*, Daisy said mournfully inside her head, but that was one idea she did not share with Petal, for her small sister had whined and wept and even wet the bed upon first returning to Bernard Terrace. Daisy knew that in her heart of hearts Petal still believed in a happy return to the farm, and she did not intend to be the person who disillusioned her little sister.

But now, standing outside the building, staring upwards, Petal seemed surprised that the balconies were not crowded with eager patients – Auntie Blod well to the fore, obviously – waiting to greet the visitors. She held a tiny bottle of lavender water in one hot hand whilst Daisy grasped a bunch of shaggy tawny chrysanthemums, and both children were eager to hand their gifts over and be extravagantly thanked, for they had saved their weekly pennies up and bought both perfume and flowers out of their own money, with only a little assistance from Rose.

'Come along, children,' Rose said briskly, taking a hand of each, for suddenly they had both hung back, overawed by the size of the place and by the strangeness of it, neither having even visited a hospital before, far less been a patient in one. Rose, who had visited Auntie Blodwen twice already, led the way in as though she owned the place, and Daisy was glad they had someone with them who knew the ropes, for the hospital's steady refusal, until today, to allow them to visit had made her imagine the whole place as a sort of prison and the nursing staff and doctors as warders, and not always well-disposed ones either.

'Up here, along here, round this next bend,' their mother was saying, and as they reached the entrance to the ward a nurse came towards them. She recognised Rose, and greeted her as Mrs McAllister.

She was an elderly woman, whose collar and cuffs were so rigidly starched that she had pink marks at neck and wrists, and she told them they must not stay too long. 'Mrs Williams has had a very serious operation and must not become too tired,' she said gravely. 'Very fond of children, she is, which is why I agreed to this visit, but it must be a short one; do you understand?'

Considerably awed by this little speech, the children nodded, round-eyed. But then Rose was ushering them through the doors on to the ward. It was a long room with tall windows, though no balcony that Daisy could see, and someone was waving to them, smiling, gesturing to them to come closer . . .

Daisy hung back for a moment, unsure. To tell the truth, she had been secretly dreading that the Auntie Blod in the hospital bed might look like that other Auntie Blod, the incredibly old, grey-faced one who had collapsed in the kitchen on that memorable, dreadful, afternoon. But to her infinite relief, the Auntie Blod in the hospital bed was the real one, the one who had taken them in, loved them, spoiled them. To be sure, her hair seemed to have rather more white in it than Daisy remembered, and her rosy apple cheeks were pink rather than red, but the blue eyes twinkled and the mouth was curved into a real, unaffected and happy smile and the arms she held out were strong-looking . . . young-looking, even.

Still Daisy held back, embarrassed by the number of nightgowned women in the beds on either side of the central aisle, not wanting to make a fool of herself – was that really Auntie Blod looking so well and fit or was she just imagining it? – but as usual, Petal had no such scruples. She dashed forward and flung herself into Auntie Blod's arms with such force that that stout person reeled for a moment. But then she laughed and heaved Petal on to the bed and held out her arms to Daisy, and Daisy gave a strangled sob which she tried to turn into a laugh, and the next moment she was being hugged too, and her chrysanthemums were being declared the most beautiful flowers ever to be brought into the hospital, just as the lavender water was the very thing for which Auntie Blod had longed, particularly since she would soon be going away to the convalescent home in Rhyl, and would want to impress all the nurses and doctors and other patients she would meet there.

'And are you settled, glad to be back with your mam again?' she asked presently when the first ecstasy of greeting was over. 'Hard it is on children to be carted from pillar to post, I always think. But if there's no danger, the place for a child is with its mother, that's what I say. And the child-minder? Mrs – Mrs Briggs, is it? She's kind to you? A good woman who is fond of the little ones?'

'She's all right,' Daisy acknowledged. She knew it would be tactless, unkind almost, to say that Mrs Briggs's idea of tea was bread and jam. Daisy understood, now that she had actually suffered from the rationing, that they had been tremendously lucky at the farm. Because they grew, or reared, so much of their own food, the shortages really hadn't affected them at all, but now . . . well, Mrs Briggs's teas were a case in point. Also, because she looked after other children as well as Daisy and Petal, they had to put up with a certain amount of competition at the tea table. Amos and Andy, eleven-year-olds, could eat twice as quickly as anyone else and had often cleared a plate of bread and margarine and eaten half the horrid seed cake Mrs Briggs provided before Daisy and Petal had done more than take a couple of tentative bites of their own portions.

However, they could scarcely tell Auntie Blod what they had not brought themselves to tell Rose, so Daisy said sedately that Mrs Briggs was very kind and her daughter, Dulcie, great fun. When questioned, she admitted that it was nice to be with all her old school friends again . . . though she missed the farm and the Williamses. Nicky had returned to Liverpool within days of their own homecoming, which was blessing for Daisy as there was no one at her present school who was half as nice and kind as he.

Petal opened her mouth to say something and Daisy shot her a warning glance. Petal shut her mouth again. They had both been reminded by Rose that they must not upset their kind foster mother by admitting how much they missed Ty Siriol, and Daisy, at least, was determined not to say how horribly unhappy they had been at first. Often, she thought of their time on the farm as a sort of lovely dream which had happened in another life, and when she had told Rose this, her mother had smiled sadly and said that they were very lucky kids to have a time like that to look back on.

'When I'm grown up I shall marry a farmer,' Daisy had said, and Petal, always keen to go one better, said scornfully: 'Oh, Daisy, don't *marry* anyone. I shan't. I shall *be* a farmer, just like Uncle Gwil.'

It had made her mother laugh, Daisy remembered, and she was just about to tell Auntie Blodwen how funny Petal had been when she happened to notice that the lovely pink colour which had come into Auntie Blodwen's cheeks as they talked seemed to have disappeared; and even as she noticed this, she saw her mother move, make a tiny gesture with one hand. *It's time we left*, the gesture said. *Auntie Blod's getting tired.*

Immediately reading the message correctly, Daisy got to her feet and kissed Auntie Blod and bade Petal follow suit since she had just noticed the time, and they really must not miss their train. Auntie Blod kissed and hugged them, kissed Rose, said goodbye, reminded them that they would always be welcome on the farm, though until she got home again things might be a trifle awkward, and though she was feeling ever so much better she didn't think she'd be much use as a worker for a while . . . the stitches caught at her when she tried to walk . . . oh, but they were not to forget her, she would never forget them, would expect them to write regularly, as indeed they had done throughout her stay in hospital . . . She was still waving as they left the ward, and as they retraced their steps along the corridor her mother gave Daisy's shoulder a squeeze. 'You are a kind little girl to make it easy for us to leave without upsetting Auntie Blod,' she said. 'Actually, we'll have an hour to kill before the next train, so we'll take a look at the shops. There's a Woolworth's here, I seem to remember; we might buy a little toy, or some sweets perhaps – I've still got some coupons left.'

'I don't see why you say Daisy's so good,' Petal said, much aggrieved. 'I'm every bit as kind as old Daisy, and a lot littler. Why don't you say *I'm* a kind little girl? And if she's the only one getting sweets, or a toy, it ain't bleedin' well fair!'

'You won't get anything at all if you swear, young lady,' Rose said severely, though Daisy noticed she was trying to hide a smile. 'And you're a good girl, too, mostly, so you shall have a toy, or some sweets, when we reach Woolworth's. Wasn't it nice to see Auntie Blod looking so much better? And wasn't she pleased to see you both? As for writing letters, you've both been very good about doing so whilst she was in hospital, so I'm sure you'll write just as much when she's in Rhyl.'

The children agreed that they would do so and it was not until they were in the main shopping street that Petal began to cry. 'I want Auntie Blod to be back at the farm so we can visit her there,' she wept. 'I love her so much, Mammy, and I like people to be in their own places; Ty Siriol is her place, not horrible hospitals, or that other place in Rhyl. Oh, Mammy, I miss Auntie Blod so much.'

'So do I, Petal, but at least we're with our own mam, and not with someone else,' Daisy said, whilst Rose tried to distract her little daughter by pointing out that Woolworth's was only a few yards up the road. 'Think of Jenny Platt, living with that horrible old grandmother because her mam has been and gone and joined the ATS. And Bernard Terrace is nice, isn't it? We've got lots of friends there, and – and Dulcie Briggs lets us play really good games . . . oh, *do* stop crying, Petal, everyone's staring!'

Petal gave a deep sigh, and allowed her mother to blow her nose and wipe the tears from her cheeks, then she smiled bravely up at her sister. 'I'm all right now,' she said huskily. 'I hope they sell little Dinky cars in Woolworth's because I don't see why boys always have to have the best things, and I'd like one of my own.'

'Only another five days before Christmas,' Rose said, as she and Rachel met on Shaw Street and turned their steps towards the nearest bus stop. 'I'm off for three whole days because I've got the children; are you working over the holiday, Rachel?'

'Yes, but I've got the twenty-eighth, twenty-ninth and thirtieth off,' Rachel said. 'It's different for us . . . we don't much mind when our holiday comes so long as we have one. And Alby may suddenly arrive home, which would make my Christmas, even if it was a bit later than yours.'

'Yes, it would be lovely if the *Jericho* came into port, though I don't suppose Steve will have had a chance to get the children presents,' Rose said. 'But still, I've managed to fill a stocking for each of them. And we'll have a Christmas dinner, though it may not be all that lavish.' She looked curiously at her friend, noticing the pink flush on Rachel's cheeks and the brightness of her eyes. 'What's up, Rachel? I do believe you've heard from Alby . . . are they coming home?'

'I wish they were, because I've got some news for Alby and I'd dearly love to see his face when I tell him,' Rachel confided. 'Oh, Rosie, I've got to tell someone or I'll burst! I'm going to have a baby in the spring . . . well, in May. I've told my parents, of course, but Alby will be absolutely delighted; if only he were coming home!'

By now, the two young women were standing at the bus stop and Rose turned to give her friend an exuberant hug and a kiss on the cheek. 'That's wonderful news, the best news I've heard in weeks,' she said joyfully. 'Just think, Rachel, this time next year we'll both be scouring the shops for toys, or games, or children's books. Can I tell the kids? Petal won't mind one way or the other, but Daisy is always nagging me to give her a baby brother or sister.' She laughed, a trifle self-consciously. 'I did try to explain, but despite knowing all about sheep and cows I don't think she understands the . . . facts of life yet.'

'At ten years old I should hope she doesn't,' Rachel said virtuously. 'And yes, you can tell them, if you make them promise not to say anything to Steve when they write. I'm going to write to Alby with the news, of course, because who knows when the *Jericho* will come back to Liverpool? Why, the last time they were in port, it was in Southampton, I think, and they weren't there for long enough to get home, even for a few hours.'

'Perhaps I won't say anything just yet then,' Rose decided, as they climbed aboard the bus. 'Did I tell you that Maisie next door has an aunt in the country, who makes her own mincemeat, the sweet sort? She's given Maisie a couple of jars of it and Maisie is giving me one of them, so this afternoon when I get home, I'll be baking mince pies. Fortunately, I've been saving my flour and marge ration for weeks and weeks, so I could do a big bake for Christmas.'

'My mam does all of that, bless her,' Rachel said smugly as they squeezed along the aisle, past passengers already standing. 'Don't forget, Mam's invited you and the kids to tea on Boxing Day. My father has been keeping a bottle of sherry to toast the baby's health when he's born, but he said we would all have a tiny glass to celebrate when you come round.'

'Lovely,' Rose said, trying to sound enthusiastic, though she disliked the taste of all alcohol and much preferred a nice cup of tea. 'And don't worry, I wouldn't miss one of your mam's high teas for all the world.'

'Mammy, when the mince pies is done, can me and Daisy share one? I know they're really for Christmas Day, but it's *nearly* that, only another five days to go and I'm hungry *now*. Me and Daisy ate up all our sausage and mash but we've still got a little gap, just about the size of a mince pie. Oh, Mammy, do say we can.'

Rose was about to reply when the sirens started to wail. She glanced towards her oven, which already contained a tray of mince pies, and at the table, where another trayful had just been completed. There had been raids, on and off, ever since the children had returned home, but none of a particularly serious nature – not if you lived some distance from the docks, at any rate. The McAllisters were used to them, took them in their stride, though Rose resented the broken nights which made work next day seem so hard. But whenever the siren sounded she popped the children into the Morrison shelter, where they slept soundly enough, whilst she herself curled up alongside them and usually managed at least some sleep. There had been several such alarms in November, culminating in a raid on the 28th during which almost two hundred people had been killed and many homes destroyed. This had almost frightened Rose into sending the children away once more, though heaven knew who would take them since the Williamses could not do so, but the attack had been followed by a quiet period when no enemy aircraft had even been seen in the skies, and this had made it seem unnecessary to split the family up once more. Now, despite a most unpleasant sensation in the pit of her stomach at the sound of the sirens' wail, she decided she could not possibly go to the public shelter immediately or the mince pies would be ruined, and it was infuriating to think of spoiling good food for what might very likely turn out to be a false alarm. And of course the sirens sounded just the same, even if the enemy aircraft were heading for Wallasey, or Birkenhead, or perhaps further up the coast, at somewhere like Barrow-in-Furness. She decided that the children must squeeze into the Morrison shelter, which took up a good deal of room under the big kitchen table, just until the mince pies were cooked. After that, if it seemed that the raid might be a bad one and provided it was safe to do so, she would take them, and all their impedimenta, along to the shelter; hopefully, they would not be there long. She glanced up at the clock above the mantel; it was half past six. In normal circumstances, the children would begin their bedtime preparations in half an hour anyway, so they might as well do so now, in case later they were in the shelter and unable to clean teeth, brush hair and get into their nightgowns.

'Mammy? Did you hear that? Does it mean they're going to start dropping bombs again? I thought they'd give up on us, honest to God I did. I hate the noise, Mammy, it frightens me ever so. Oh, I wish we were back on the farm, so I do!'

Daisy had been curled up in a chair, reading her comic paper, but now she stood up and came over to the table to put a reassuring hand on her small sister's shoulder. 'Let's peep out of the window and see if the sky's clear of aeroplanes,' she suggested.

Rose was about to remind her eldest that they must never go near windows during an air raid, and the safest place for them right now was inside the Morrison shelter, when they all heard it: the steady, menacing thrum, thrum of enemy aircraft approaching, and then the scream of descending bombs and the explosions as they hit their target.

Immediately, mince pies were forgotten. Rose seized the children and hustled them into the Morrison shelter. Petal was crying, but Daisy, though white-faced, seemed calm enough. Rose had already placed blankets and pillows beside the shelter, as well as their night clothes and Petal's almost bald teddy bear, and now she handed these to Daisy, who promptly began to make a nest. 'Don't be long, Mam,' she urged, trying to keep her voice steady, Rose thought. 'When you come into the shelter as well, you can tell us a story – or read to us if you like. I've put *Simple Susan* on the sofa and one of the *Amelia Anne* books. It'll – it'll stop us listening for the next crash.'

Rose was about to say that she would come into the shelter at once when the smell of cooking reached her. With a squeak of dismay, she rushed across the kitchen and grabbed the mince pies from the oven. They were done to a turn, and for a moment she looked regretfully at the uncooked pies before resolutely turning off the gas. If, by some awful mischance, the house was hit, then a fire in the kitchen, fuelled by the gas oven, would not be a good idea.

The thrumming was directly overhead now; she could imagine the dark and evil shapes blotting out the stars, death falling from them on to the innocent citizens below. An enormous crash almost stopped her heart, and she was still holding the tray of mince pies ten seconds later as she joined her children under the table. Daisy, looking white and frightened, had an arm round Petal and was telling her a story, but when the children saw the mince pies their faces brightened and Rose, without a word, handed them round.

'Should we go to the shelter, Mam?' Daisy asked presently, as the sound of explosions and the noise of enemy aircraft got louder. 'The house keeps shaking. I'm scared it'll come down on our heads.'

'It won't,' Rose said with a confidence she was far from feeling. 'But it will be really dangerous out in the streets, queen. Those planes are right overhead . . . we'll stay where we are this evening. But I'm afraid tomorrow night we'll just have to get to the shelter early, whether or not there's a raid. Auntie Maisie used to do that most nights when the raids were bad; says she's got used to sleeping on a concrete bunk with strangers all round her.'

'Oh. Right,' Daisy said. 'Can you read to us, Mam? Only my voice isn't loud enough, and . . . oh, look at that!'

Rose, wrapping a blanket around herself and pulling her pillow into position beneath her head, followed the direction of Daisy's pointing finger, then smiled, torn between astonishment and sheer, undiluted relief. Petal was curled up under her blanket, her thumb in her mouth and her golden eyelashes fanned out on her cheeks. She was fast asleep.

A couple of days later, Rose and Rachel met in the canteen for a chat. The raid which had caught Rose making mince pies had been followed, the very next night, by an even worse one. Bombs had rained down upon Liverpool and no one had got much sleep, though Rose and the children had gone to the shelter as she had promised. The atmosphere down there was a good deal happier than it was when you were shut up in your own house, for the older women organised sing-songs and there was a good deal of laughing, story-telling and question and answer games. Rose managed to get a bunk for herself and the children and had the satisfaction of seeing them drop asleep as the night wore on, but she herself could not so much as close her eyes. So now she was asking Rachel, in all seri-ousness, whether she was right to keep the children in the city when the danger was so real, so terrible.

'I expect you ought to send them into the country,' Rachel conceded as they ate their braised liver and onions. 'But where would they go, queen? It isn't as if you could trek – go into the countryside each evening and return in the morning, I mean – as lots of mothers with kids do, because you want to keep your job, don't you? Oh, I'm sure someone would have them, but finding that someone will take time. It's not as though there were a general evacuation, as there was directly war broke out.'

'No-o, but I feel so bloody guilty, letting them stay here when the danger is so great,' Rose said, spearing a potato and chopping it into the gravy. Canteen food was pretty good, all things considered, and it meant that she could feed the children better since she did not need to share their evening meal. 'My aunt and uncle, the ones who used to live in Penny Lane, have moved out to Formby, but they've scarcely any room to spare and though they've said they'd pack the kids in somehow, they're – well, they're awful old, Rachel. They used to spoil the kids, and I doubt very much if they could discipline them now, see that they went to school and so on. And when I suggested it, Daisy went all bolshie on me, and said she wouldn't leave me in danger because if she did I'd be bound to get hurt. Oh, she would go to the Williamses like a shot, but not to Aunt Selina and Uncle Frank. Kids are weird, but Petal backed her up so I said I'd think about it and left the subject alone.'

'I can understand in a way,' Rachel said, pushing her empty plate aside and pulling forward her pudding, a dish of suet roll and custard. 'When they went off to Ruthin they were with all their classmates; it was an adventure, with lots and lots of their friends and teachers around them. They made heaps of new friends on the farm and at the school, and got used to them, were truly fond of them. But going off to an ancient aunt and uncle – no, I know they aren't ancient really, but they must seem that to your little girls – without a soul they know, joining a new school, being away from you . . . well, it's a lot to ask.'

'Yes, I suppose you're right, especially at Christmas time,' Rose admitted. 'Goodness, only another couple of days and it will actually be Christmas! Oh, Rachel, surely the Luftwaffe will want to be in their own homes at Christmas, and not bombing us? I do hope so!'

'You aren't the only one,' Rachel admitted. 'Mam and Dad simply won't hear of going to the shelter and so I feel I can't walk out and leave them. But when the bombs are close, and you can hear the planes' engines overhead . . . well, I wouldn't mind a nice hefty shelter over my head, and people all around me in the same boat.'

'After what happened when bombs managed to get below that shelter before they exploded, and sent almost fifty people to kingdom come, I'm not all that sure that going to the shelter is the safest thing to do,' Rose observed, beginning to eat her own pudding. 'The trouble is, whatever I do may be absolutely wrong . . . still, it's the same for all of us. And for the moment, we'll stay put and take our chance along with everyone else. In the New Year, if things get worse, I'll have to think again.'

Steve met Alby as the watch was changed and saw at once from his friend's face that he had had good news. He loped over to the smaller man and raised his eyebrows. 'Well? It can't be a letter because we ain't in port.'

Alby grinned exuberantly. 'Signal,' he said. 'I've passed my final exams and will be a signaller, starting when we next go to sea, and I can stay with the old *Jericho*, for the time being at any rate.'

It was a nasty, grey day with snow gusting across the open deck from time to time and a bitter wind blowing, but Alby's face was alight and Steve saw that he must be glad for his pal, though inwardly he was dismayed. Ever since Alby had passed the preliminary examinations he had been fearing that the two of them would be parted, and though it was good news that Alby had been made up without, as was usual in peace-time, having to change his ship, he knew that this was now bound to happen sooner or later.

'Congratulations, old feller,' Steve said. 'And I've

heard a bit of good news, too; we'll be back in the Liverpool docks in four or five days, and we'll get a chance to see our folks this time, since unloading the merchant fleet takes a day or two. So it won't just be letters; we'll sleep in our own beds for a couple of nights.'

Alby's smile grew even broader, then faded a trifle. 'If the wolf pack don't find us and scupper half the merchantmen,' he said. 'They say the U-boats hang about just outside the Mersey estuary. And then there's the Luftwaffe . . .'

'Oh, don't be so bleedin' miserable,' Steve said reprovingly. 'We've had a good run this time. We've not seen so much as an enemy—'

'Shut your great big blathering mouth,' Alby said, suddenly furious. 'Do you want to bring every perishin' U-boat on our track? I tell you, if anything stops us getting a couple of days at home, I'll personally break both your bloody legs.'

Considerably startled, for Alby rarely swore and never lost his temper, Steve mumbled an apology and gestured to the younger man to go ahead of him, down the companionway. 'I dunno what made me say it,' Steve said humbly, as they entered the seamen's mess and went to line up at the hatch which separated the men from the galley. 'But won't it be grand to be back in Liverpool again? I told you the kids had come back from the farm, didn't I? It'll be good to see them after so long.'

To his relief, Alby grinned at him. 'And you'll see that pretty wife of yours,' he said reprovingly. 'I can't wait to see Rachel, meself, though we still haven't got a place of our own. Her parents are grand; they never interfere, understand how precious a couple of days can be when you've not seen each other for months.'

'Oh aye, it'll be grand to see Rose, of course,' Steve said, realising with some surprise that it wasn't altogether untrue. She was a good cook, was Rosie, and when she wasn't working the house was real homelike. He imagined the firelit kitchen, the soft easy chairs, the delicious smell of bread baking, or a meat pie simmering away in the oven. For the first time for absolutely ages, he thought about his mother and her ill-kept, disorganised house. He remembered dirty kids underfoot, his brothers' perpetual quarrelling, his father's violence and the fits of ill-temper, so bad that he and his brothers had dreaded his father's return at the end of each day. His father had been dead for five years, killed in a dockers' brawl, and Steve rarely visited his mother because her whining got on his nerves, though whenever he had a few bob to spare he would go round to the house in Regent Street and slam the cash on the table, grudging every penny, but knowing that the old girl would make better use of it than his hard-drinking father would have done.

Ahead of him, Alby turned away from the hatch, his tin plate full of stew and dumplings. Steve swallowed; the food both looked and smelled good, but the gravy was thin and the dumplings were not as satisfying as potatoes, which could be mashed into the gravy and would have filled him up nicely. Although they always took on supplies in New York, potatoes quite often ran out before they docked again, mainly because a convoy had to steer a zig-zag course so that they did not make a perfect target for the wolf pack, shadowing them beneath the waves.

Steve took his plate of food and went and sat next to Alby on the bench. Ever since his brief flirtation with the idea of working in submarines, he could never think of the U-boats without shuddering. At Alby's suggestion, he had painstakingly read everything he could lay his hands on concerning submarines. He knew about the cramped conditions, the bad air, the way they lay quiet in the very depths of the ocean, the men warned not to make a sound, not to move, whilst above them the enemy sat with their hydrophones clamped to their ears, listening for a man to cough or sneeze, giving away their position. And there was the sonar, whose blip, blip, blip, could detect objects lying on the floor of the ocean, and of course the depth charges, which could destroy a submarine so completely that sometimes only fragments came to the surface to prove to the attacking ship that she had made a killing.

But he also remembered that U-boats fired torpedoes, which could finish a ship off within moments of their first strike. In fact, from having been happily devoid of imagination, he thought resentfully, thanks to Alby he now seemed to have more than his fair share. He could quite see why Alby had been annoyed with him, too; the dangers were always there, either above or below you, and only a fool would tempt fate by announcing, in mid-ocean, that they had had an uneventful voyage. He turned to Alby to voice this thought, just as the ship reverberated to a shuddering crash and all the lights went out.

Chapter Seven
January 1941

There was no panic. Steve felt for Alby's arm and gripped it tightly, whilst all around them men produced torches and began to make for the nearest exit. Steve and Alby followed, clattered up the companionway and emerged on to the deck. Since they had last been up here dusk had fallen, though there was still sufficient light to see each other and to recognise the officer who was marshalling them into a line – not easy, since the deck was already at an angle of 45 degrees.

'What happened?' a burly seaman ahead of them in the line asked. 'I were in me bunk and when the crash came I were thrown out, on to the floor. I slipped and slid towards the companionway and looked down the corridor and, begod, there were water roaring towards me. It were up to me waist by the time I'd climbed the first half dozen steps . . . I doubt if another soul gorraway besides meself. If I'd realised what were happenin' . . . me bezzie, Lofty, were snorin' like a motorbike . . . mebbe I should ha' gone back . . .'

'No point,' someone said succinctly. 'It were a torpedo. No enemy shipping about, so it must ha' been fired by a U-boat.'

'Not just one torpedo, two, fired in quick succession,' someone else said. 'It's near blown us apart, which is why they're launching the boats. Our only chance, see. We're too far ahead of the rest of the convoy to swim back to 'em.'

'I hope they've scarpered, now they know we know

they're here,' a small red-headed rating said apprehensively. 'Last time I ended up in the oggin, the
buggers fired at us, damn near blew me 'at off.'

Alby laughed. 'Oh well, that's all right,' he remarked.
'I'm not wearin' me hat, so I'll be okay then.'

As they talked, the line had been moving steadily
forward, and now Steve reached the rail and was able
to watch what was happening. Despite the difficult
circumstances, the lifeboats were being launched efficiently and coolly, since this was the side of the ship
nearest the water. Steve noticed, with a sick churning
in his stomach, that the sea was getting closer every
moment, indicating that it would not be long before
the poor old *Jericho* slid quietly beneath the waves.

It was also clear that the boats could not possibly
hold the entire crew, but Steve realised that a great
many of the men must have suffered the same fate as
that which the burly seaman had described: in their
bunks, or at their stations below decks, they would
have been helpless to escape the terrible inrush of
water.

Ahead of him, Alby had reached the front of the
queue and was clambering aboard the lifeboat. Steve
glanced back. He had not realised that he and Alby
were quite near the end of the line, for there were
only a dozen or so blokes still to come as he took his
place in the lifeboat beside his friend. In fact, within
moments, the deck was empty, and the young officer,
having checked that no one else was waiting, launched
the lifeboat, and then jumped aboard himself, saying
breathlessly as he did so: 'Grab an oar, you men, and
let's get out of here! When she goes under, she'll take
us with her if we don't put a good distance between
us.'

Everyone did their best, and afterwards no one was

quite sure whether it was the suction of the sinking of the *Jericho* or whether the unseen enemy had fired another torpedo. But suddenly there was a huge wave, as high as a house, bearing down on them. They were at the wrong angle to ride it, even if such a thing were possible, and could do nothing when ton after ton of water, green and salt and cold as ice, crashed down upon their cockleshell craft.

Steve came ashore with nothing worse than a cut over one eye, a great many bruises and a strong desire never to return to sea again, even though he knew he was one of the lucky ones. He and the young red-haired rating had been picked up – eventually – by the SS *Coromandel Queen*, carrying grain, and he knew that Alby had been picked up, too, since there had been much frantic signalling amongst the fleet when day had dawned.

So now Steve stood on the quayside and waited, because he did not intend to make his way back to Bernard Terrace until he had seen his friend face to face.

He did not have long to wait. Alby came ashore only thirty minutes after Steve himself had landed, but his first remark proved him more alert than his friend. 'Did you see the damage as we came up the Mersey?' he said. 'The docks and Bootle seem to have taken a fair pasting. I hope to God the girls are all right.'

It was the first time that Steve had even considered that they might not be. To his mind, war was a man's business; women moaned about shortages, said there was nothing to buy in the shops, sent their children into the wilds of Wales. He acknowledged, of course, that the Luftwaffe would bomb the docks, the

178

grain warehouses, and other such places, but it had honestly not occurred to him that his neighbours, his wife, his children even, might have been killed or injured whilst he was fighting his own battles at sea.

In fact, as he and Alby walked through the shabby streets, he realised that he still could not believe anything had happened to Rose or the girls. Bernard Terrace must be at least half a mile from the docks; there was nothing in the surrounding area to attract the attention of the bombers, so he could not bring himself to waste time worrying about them. They would be all right; he knew it in his water.

And so it proved. He and Alby said cheerio on Shaw Street and went their separate ways, and presently Steve crossed Bernard Terrace and went into No. 7. The back door was closed, but he opened it and a wonderful smell of cooking came out. He had not realised it was a Saturday, but now he knew it must be, since his daughters were seated on stools drawn up to the kitchen table, busily painting in two colouring books. Rose was cooking at the stove and, to do her credit, when his head appeared round the door there was only the slightest of hesitations before she cried: 'Steve! I'm so glad you're safe.' And, leaving the pan she was stirring, she crossed the kitchen, gave him a quick peck on the cheek and then said: 'But what have you done to yourself? Don't say you've been fighting!'

She ushered him into the room whilst he explained, briefly, what had happened and the children stared at him, round-eyed. It had been five months since they had seen him last, he thought ruefully, and that must be why they were both looking at him doubtfully. He crossed the room and bent over Petal, who had always been his favourite. 'Don't you remember me, queen?' he asked, and suddenly his voice was rough with unshed tears. This kid had been fond of him, had never shown fear in his presence, had always hugged and kissed him, but of course she was older now; would she turn against him as Daisy had done?

But it seemed as though surprise alone had stopped her running to him, for she pushed her picture away and jumped up, casting herself into his arms. 'But Daddy, Daddy, your poor face . . . but the doctor will make it better,' she gabbled, as he lifted her off her feet, settling her on his hip. 'Was your ship sunk? Was you nearly drownded?'

'The old *Jericho*'s sunk to the bottom of the sea, but me and me pal bobbed up like a couple o' corks an' gorra lift home with one of the merchant ships,' he said gaily. 'But if I'd had to, queen, I'd have swum all the way home, just to see my little girl again.'

Daisy had left her seat as Petal did, and now she reached up and patted his arm. It was a timid gesture but the nearest she had ever come to showing any sort of affection for him, so Steve rubbed her cheek, feeling foolish in a way he never did when caressing Petal. He told himself she was older, more reserved, and did not examine his own feelings for his elder daughter in any depth. He loved Petal and tolerated Daisy; what was wrong with that? He knew many men who did not care for any of their children and felt no guilt over his secret dismissal of Daisy. She's her mother's daughter, he told himself; Petal's Daddy's girl.

Whilst he talked to the children, Rose had dished up. It seemed that the meal was to be some rather odd-looking rissoles, a handful of carrots and three large boiled potatoes, and all of it was being put on one plate. He was still pondering the significance of this when Rose carried it over to the table and set it down in front of him. 'I'll just make some French toast and fry up a bit of bacon for the rest of us,' she said. 'It won't take a moment; then we can all eat.'

Oh, so that was why there were three rissoles and three potatoes, Steve thought, picking up his knife and fork and reaching for the HP Sauce. It would have been their meal had he not turned up. He began to eat; the rissoles looked rather strange and home-made but they were delicious, full of flavour and cooked crispy on the outside and soft and meaty within. Just as he liked them, in fact. The children sat down again and began plying him with questions, whilst behind them Rose dipped thick slices of home-made bread into the egg and milk mixture she had concocted, then fried the soggy slices in the pan alongside a few thin rashers of bacon. Steve, eating steadily and helping himself to a couple of thick wedges of bread and margarine, rather enjoyed being the centre of so much attention. He went over his recent experience, from the crash and thunder of the striking torpedoes to the moment when he, the red-haired rating, and Alby had been fished out of an increasingly rough sea and hauled aboard two of the merchant vessels.

'Oh, Dad, it must have been awful, really terrifying,' Daisy breathed, and Steve was gratified to see that there was hero-worship in her small face instead of the usual mixture of fear and defiance. 'Weren't you and Alby and the other man lucky, though? What happened to the rest of the men in your lifeboat? Were they rescued too?'

Steve shook his head. 'No, the rest of 'em was all drowned,' he said. 'But me an' Alby, I reckon we've got charmed lives, same as Andy – he's the rating what came home on the same ship as meself – because of the whole ship's crew, only eighteen came ashore today.'

'Why do you say Andy has a charmed life?' Rose asked, putting three more plates down on the table. She pushed Petal's chair in, then handed both girls knives and forks and sat down before her own plate. Steve saw she had no bacon but only the French toast – or eggy bread as Petal called it – but thought nothing of it, though he had not realised before that she did not like bacon. He wanted to say: *You can't afford to be fussy in wartime, you should see some of the meals I've been forced to eat aboard ship*, but decided against it. Rose might see it as criticism and the atmosphere at present would not be helped by Rose's getting snooty with him.

'Steve? Why does Andy have a charmed life?'

Steve polished his plate with the last slice of bread and looked hopefully round. Where was the pudding? But then he saw the children were still eating and held his tongue. Doubtless a pudding would appear in the fullness of time. 'Andy? Oh, didn't I tell you? This was the third time his ship had been torpedoed under him. Some fellers is like that, they seem to have bad luck in that they are aboard ships which get holed or shot up or something of that nature, but they always gerroff scot-free themselves. Well, I had me cut eye and bruises but that were only done when I were being hauled aboard the merchantman. Oh aye, I reckon me an' Alby are lucky, awright.'

'I see. Well, I'm most awfully glad Alby was saved as well, because . . . well, me and Rachel are very good friends, and – and I don't suppose it will matter if I tell you now, because it's the first thing Rachel will tell Alby. They're expecting a baby, Steve; isn't that nice? Rachel is thrilled to bits and she's certain Alby will feel the same. Apparently they've always wanted a family, and though they won't move out from her mam's place until things are . . . more settled, like, they'll do so as soon as the war's over and Alby's home again for good.'

'Grand, grand,' Steve said absently. He wondered if afters would be jam roly; easily his favourite. He decided not to ask about the pudding; instead, he contented himself with remarking that he'd enjoyed the rissoles. He tried to smile at Rose, but the way she had just spoken stuck in his craw: *Well, I'm most awfully glad*, she had said, in that annoying, smug way she had. And then she couldn't say: *Rachel's gorra grin on 'er gob what stretches from one lug to t'other*, like any decent scouser would. She had to say: *Rachel is thrilled to bits* – stuck up cow! Still, there you were. He had married her knowing her mam and dad thought she were a perishin' princess and had done his best to knock the nonsense out of her, though clearly without very much success. Oh, well; he remembered Alby saying once that you can't change people, only time and experience can do that. Then, he hadn't really understood, but now he thought he did. Once a snob always a snob; and anyway she were a good mother to his kids and a cracking cook. He watched as she cleared away the plates and felt considerable relief when she went over to the cooker and opened the oven door once more. Baked apples! She had a special way with baked apples. She cored 'em, filled the middles with sultanas, brown sugar, bits of peel and the like, then wrapped them in pastry, her specially rich pudding pastry as he always thought of it. The result was . . . oh, just grand! He hoped there would be custard; he was fond of a spot of Bird's finest.

He watched hungrily as three baked apples were removed from the oven and was a little disappointed to see that they were being put on to three plates. Not all for him, then. But he doubted he could have eaten three, though two would have gone down very nicely. There wasn't much custard, either, but it would have to do. He watched jealously as Rose poured the sauce and was pleased to see that he was getting the largest apple and a good-sized pool of custard. Well, it was fair enough; he was a hero, wasn't he, and anyway girls had smaller stomachs; well-known fact.

He had almost finished his pudding when he saw that Rose was beginning to wash up. His brows rose. Really, it seemed she had gone off baked apples and custard now; what was the world coming to? Didn't everyone keep telling everyone else that there was a war on? But the kettle had boiled and she had made the tea; it was sitting to one side of the stove, brewing, and presently she came over and poured conny-onny into a cup and then added the tea. It was dark brown and sweet, the way he liked it. He grinned at her as she handed him a large mug. She wasn't so bad . . . he knew many a man who, coming home unexpectedly, would have been told to get himself down to the fried fish shop, but snooty Rose, for all her faults, had dished up a prime meal, prime!

He began to sip the scalding tea.

It would not have been true to say that Rose regarded Steve's homecoming with nothing but pleasure, because she was still extremely wary of him, and sometimes she caught him looking at her in a very odd way, almost as one would look at a tiger which was caged behind bars of astounding frailty. At other times, she could read downright dislike in his glance and knew, sadly, that this dislike was mirrored in her own answering gaze. Yet he is trying, she told herself as she and Rachel, on the same shift for once, hurried back along Shaw Street. Ever since he stopped drinking so much – ever since he met Alby, in fact – he's been a good deal easier to live with. But now she began to listen to Rachel, who was chattering away, telling her that Alby would be starting aboard his new ship in two days' time and would be acting Signaller.

Rose had only been listening with half an ear, but now it occurred to her that if Alby knew about his new berth then Steve would probably have heard also. She wondered whether they would be aboard a corvette, a destroyer, or perhaps even a battleship, and decided that as soon as he knew for sure, she and the girls would accompany him down to the dock to take a look at what would be, in effect, his new home. It would be sensible to take an interest, she decided, and nice for the girls to be able to picture the size and strength of the ship their father sailed on. A true daughter of Liverpool, she knew that a corvette was a very small fighting ship and that a battleship was huge. But that was about the extent of her knowledge. She guessed that Steve, however, would enjoy telling the girls all the details and found herself quite looking forward to arriving home.

When she did so, Steve was lounging in a chair by the fire, with a copy of the *Echo* spread out on his knees, though she did not think he was reading it. She glanced, at once, towards the sink, hoping that he might have seen fit to peel the bowl of vegetables which stood on the draining board, but was not surprised to find them still just as she had left them, untouched. The evening before, she had mentioned that she would leave them on the draining board and had asked him, humbly, to peel and prepare them if he had time, but probably he had not given the matter a thought. Better to say nothing, she decided, hanging her heavy coat on the back of the door and making for the sink. Anyway, what did it matter? In a couple of days he'd be off again and she wouldn't have to peel a great mound of spuds, carrots and swedes in order to make up for the small amount of meat she had managed to obtain.

'Hello, Steve,' she said cheerfully, as her husband stirred, yawned and stretched. 'Have you had a good day? Alby came up to the factory and told Rachel he's got a berth, so I suppose you know which ship you're sailing on by now.'

Steve grunted, then knuckled his eyes. 'Put the bleedin' kettle on, gal,' he said thickly. 'No, I've not been to the office yet. Mebbe I'd best go down to the docks before the kids come home. Then, if they want, I can show them which craft Alby an' meself will be 'onourin' with our presence.'

He said the last four words in a strange, falsetto voice, which Rose took to be an imitation of her own since he had carped over her accent ever since he had arrived home. Sighing, she wondered why men almost seemed to want to drag you down to their level rather than applaud your efforts to speak good English and bring your children up properly, then chided herself for such a narrow view. Many men, such as Alby, her own father and Mr Edelmann, were a very different kettle of fish.

While she was thinking, Rose had filled the kettle, put it on the stove and lit the gas, and Steve had hauled himself out of his chair, grumbling that he was gasping for a cuppa and could do with a bite of something as well. Rose immediately went to the pantry and got out the loaf and a jar of mixed fruit jam, but by the time she was beginning to spread the jam on the bread, Steve had unhooked his overcoat and cap from the back of the door, and was clearly about to leave.

'You could wait for the kettle to boil . . .' Rose was beginning, but once more, Steve simply grunted and left the room, slamming the back door behind him. Rose shrugged and glanced up at the clock above the mantel. The bread and jam would do for the children, who would be in soon and always arrived starving hungry, and she could do with a cup of tea herself, so would make a pot anyway. It really was a pity that Steve couldn't be a bit more civil, couldn't at least acknowledge that she was making an effort to sustain good relations.

At the sink, Rose peeled, chopped and sliced, and then carried the pans over to the fire. Then she got down the big old frying pan in which she would gently part cook the precious onion which the greengrocer had saved for her, and the cubes of stewing beef rolled in flour, which she had prepared that morning before leaving for work.

When the back door burst open, her stomach contracted and she scolded herself for being a fool; then she realised that it was only the children. They bounced into the room full of talk about their day's doings, and pounced on the bread and jam as though they had not eaten for a week, though Rose knew for a fact that they had had a cooked dinner at school that day. 'Where's Daddy, Mam?' Petal asked, as soon as her appetite had been at least partially satisfied. 'He said he'd be home when we came out of school. He said he'd try to buy us some sweeties, if he could find a shop selling any.'

'Daddy's gone down to the docks to find out which ship he'll be sailing on in a couple of days,' Rose told them, pouring out two mugs of weak tea as she spoke.

'Alby went down earlier and was given all the details but I didn't ask Rachel the name of the ship; in fact, I didn't even ask her what class of vessel he'd be on, but we'll know when Daddy gets home.'

'Oh goody,' Petal said joyfully. 'I love going down to the docks and Daddy told us he'd take us to look at his new ship as soon as he knew which one it was. Will we go tonight, Mammy, do you think?'

Rose shook her head. 'I doubt it, queen,' she said gently. 'I know we've not had a raid for three weeks or so, but that's no guarantee that the planes won't come over again, and no one wants to get caught out during a raid, do they?'

'Especially not down by the docks 'cos everyone knows it's the docks the horrid Germans are after,' Daisy said wisely. 'Never mind, Petal, I expect Dad will take us down there tomorrow and we wouldn't see much in the dark, anyway, what with the blackout and everything.' A sudden thought seemed to strike her. 'Do you know that a lighted cigarette can be seen from a plane hundreds and thousands of feet above the city? Dicky O'Neil told me so when we was walking home from school, and Dicky knows everything, just about, because his dad's a scuffer. Mam, why aren't you a firewatcher or in the ARP, or the WVS? Some of the other mothers are and Miss Hebden does something with the Red Cross, I don't know what.'

Rose laughed. 'It's because I've got two horrid little children to look after and a full time job,' she explained. 'I wish I could help more but the fact is, queen, it's all I can do to keep going sometimes, because I'm so tired. Now, do either of you have any homework?'

It transpired that Petal had to learn a poem and Daisy to write an essay on what her mam did to help the war effort. By the time these tasks were satisfactorily concluded, the meal was ready. Rose wondered whether she should dish up at once or wait for Steve to reappear, but decided, in the end, that she really had no choice. It would be a crime to spoil good food in wartime and that was just what would happen if she kept the stew simmering for too long. I'll warm Steve's up as soon as he gets in, she told herself, turning off the gas and beginning to ladle the stew on to her own and her daughters' plates. He won't be long, unless he falls in with a group of friends and stays to have a crack with them. Thank heaven it's not chops, or rissoles, or a nice piece of cod!

She and the children ate their portions and had bread and jam instead of a pudding, and still Steve had not arrived. He was still absent at bedtime, and Petal whined to be allowed to stay up until her daddy got home, but, at a glance from Rose, Daisy grabbed her sister and hauled her up the stairs. Giggling, Petal let herself be pulled into her bedroom, though she turned in the doorway and shouted back to Rose that at least her mammy should send Steve up to read them a story, or possibly come herself if her father arrived home very late indeed.

Rose finished clearing up the meal and looked doubtfully at the stew congealing in the pan. What on earth was Steve playing at? She supposed that he might have met a pal and bought fish and chips, but why, for goodness' sake? She knew he enjoyed the atmosphere in a pub but did not think he would spend a whole evening there, because he had admitted once, when in a mellow mood, that there was no enjoyment in watching other fellows drink.

The hours ticked by. When eleven o'clock came, Rose, who would have to be up at five next day, decided that she would simply have to go to bed. Steve would not want to eat at this hour, so she transferred the stew to a large bowl, covered it with a plate and popped it into the pantry. Then she made her way up to her room, undressed hurriedly and was soon asleep.

In her own room, Petal was still lying awake when she heard her mother mount the stairs. Usually, she slept as soon as her head touched the pillow, but tonight, for some reason, sleep eluded her. She had a most uneasy feeling that all was not well with her daddy. She knew, of course, that he was not to be relied upon, could say one thing and do another, but he had promised to take Daisy and herself to see his new ship and she guessed, from her mother's attitude, that Steve had not intended to stay out for the entire evening. This was worrying. Daisy sometimes mentioned that Daddy used to drink too much and had been known to thump both Mammy and Daisy herself when full of drink and in a bad mood. But she had also said that Daddy did not drink like that any more, intimating that this was a good thing. So why, why, why was he not home?

Uneasily, Petal lay and listened to the sounds of her mother changing into her nightdress. She heard the springs creak as Rose got into bed, heard her turn restlessly a couple of times before settling down. Then, some time later, she heard the clock strike twelve. Midnight! She had never been awake at midnight in all her years and did not think her daddy had ever come home so late before. She wondered if she should go through and wake Mammy, and when the clock struck the half-hour, slid out of bed, her warm toes curling indignantly away from the icy lino, and her warm body making it plain that it did not wish to wander the house and would much prefer to return to bed.

By now, however, Petal's blood was up. It would not be fair to wake her mother, whose alarm clock would go off at five in the morning and who would leave the house soon afterwards in order to reach the factory by six. But Daisy started school at the same time as Petal did, so she was the proper person to wake. Petal shook Daisy's shoulder vigorously, then leaned over and sang softly in her sister's ear: *'Wake up, wake up, wake up, you lazy devil, I feel so sorry for you!'* which was the reveille her father had taught her in one of his more expansive moments.

Daisy awoke groggily, knuckling her eyes and remarking, in far too loud a voice, that Petal was a little beast and it surely couldn't be getting up time yet.

'No, it ain't,' Petal said inelegantly. 'But our daddy hasn't come home, Daisy, an' I'm afraid something horrid has happened to him. He's got a cut face and lots of bruises, remember; if he fell, he might not be able to gerrup again.'

'Ye-es, but what could we do if we found him lyin' on the ground?' Daisy asked reasonably. 'We're not strong enough to pick him up; he's ever so heavy, our dad.' Despite her objection, however, she had got out of bed and was slowly following Petal's example, for Petal had begun to dress herself, pulling her clothes on over her nightie. 'Anyway, if he was at the Edelmanns' house and it got late, they might have asked him to stay the night, don't you think?'

Though Petal did her best not to show it, this suggestion was so sensible that she nearly gave up the whole idea, but having got Daisy out of bed and into her clothing, she decided to go ahead with her plan. It would not hurt, after all, to walk down as far as the docks and if Steve was nowhere to be found, then at least they had tried, and could come back to bed with a clear conscience.

So, presently, two small figures emerged from Bernard Terrace and began to make their way down Everton Brow.

An hour later, the same two small figures approached the house in Bernard Terrace, trying to be as quiet as possible. They had not been successful, despite searching diligently in all the likeliest places, and were now returning home feeling that they had done their best and that no more could be expected of them.

Daisy's hand was actually on the front door knob when both children heard someone turn into the terrace and head towards them. Petal squeaked: 'It's Daddy!' and Daisy, turning a moment later, saw that she was right. She swung open the heavy front door and opened her mouth to speak, but before she could say a word she found herself roughly grabbed and hustled inside the house, along the hall, and into the kitchen.

Petal, following, said plaintively: 'Where have you *been*, Dad? We waited and waited and you didn't come, and then poor Mammy had to go to bed because her alarm clock goes off at five, so Daisy and me decided . . .'

Daisy tried to wriggle out of her father's grasp, tried to explain that they had been searching for him, but one glance at his bleary, bloodshot eyes and one whiff of his spirit-laden breath told her that she was unlikely to get him to listen. 'Where have *you* been, you deceitful little bitch?' he shouted. 'Oh, you think you're so grand, Rose McAllister, so much better'n me, but you're just a little slut, really. Off after some other feller the moment me back's turned. Oh, I'm goin' to teach you a lesson you won't forget in a hurry!'

As he said the last words, he transferred his grip from Daisy's shoulders to her hair and actually heaved her off her feet by it, tearing a shrill scream from her lips. Daisy struggled and kicked and knew, vaguely, that Petal was joining in. She saw, through tear-blurred eyes, that Petal was attached to her father's leg like a small bulldog, but her own pain was so great that she was scarcely conscious of anything else. Steve was raving at her, calling her Rose, repeatedly hitting her across the face whilst still gripping her hair so tightly that she could feel the roots giving way. She was almost fainting, waves of black coming and going, a sick dizziness possessing her, when she heard a sound like someone striking a great gong, *doiiing, doiiing, doiiiiing!* Then she was falling to the floor, sobbing for breath, weak with terror and pain. She felt the quarry tiles come up to meet her, slapping her hard on the knees and the palms of her hands, then something large and heavy fell on top of her and, for a few blissful moments, she plunged into darkness.

Rose had entered the kitchen at the height of the fracas. She had not understood what was happening, or why, but she did not waste time in conjecture. She simply seized the frying pan and brought it down on Steve's head with enough force to make him let go of Daisy and fall, senseless, on top of her.

Rose grabbed at his seaman's jacket and hauled him, bodily, off her daughter, inadvertently treading on his hand as she did so and not giving a damn. She had never been so angry in her entire life and hoped, fervently, that she had done Steve some mortal damage, though she doubted it. His head was hard as a rock, and because he was clearly drunk as a skunk she doubted that she had done him nearly as much harm as he deserved. The devil takes care of his own, she thought bitterly, lifting Daisy up in her arms and carrying her over to the easy chair nearest the dying fire. Petal had been sobbing wildly but now she came over to her mother and they both looked anxiously into Daisy's small, white face, already beginning to turn scarlet and blue in stripes where Steve's hand had caught her.

'Oh, Mammy, it's all my fault. Will she die?' Petal said fearfully. 'It were my idea to go and search for Daddy, so I woke Daisy and made her come with me. We searched and searched and couldn't find him, only when we got home he – he sort of appeared. He were angry wi' Daisy, only he kept calling her Rose, and then he dragged her indoors and started hitting her. I bit him in the leg and I did my best to make him leave our Daisy alone, but . . . but . . .'

Daisy's eyes flickered open and Petal gave a huge sigh of relief, echoed by her mother. 'She's alive! Oh, Mammy, I'm so glad she's alive!' She glanced behind her as she spoke, to where her father sprawled face down on the floor. 'I wonder if he's alive, too?' she said, her tone so academic as to bring a quivering smile to Rose's lips. 'I hope he stays asleep, though, because he's mad, isn't he, Mammy? He *must* be mad because he thought poor Daisy was you, and you wouldn't have let him drag you by the hair, would you, Mammy? You'd have hit him, bang, wallop, with the frying pan.'

'He's not dead,' Rose said grimly. 'But he'll wish he was, when he wakes up! Daisy, darling, if I help you, can you get upstairs, do you think? You poor little thing, and you were only trying to help the great, bullying . . . I mean you were only trying to help Dad. But he's drunk, you see, and men . . . well, they don't always know what they're doing when they've a good deal of drink inside them. Oh, your poor little face, you're covered in bruises. I've a good mind to fetch the scuffers, then your father could enjoy a bit of peace and quiet in a police cell, *and* answer to the local magistrate for the way he's behaved.'

Daisy sat up, wincing as she did so, and looked fearfully around her, but when she saw Steve, still prone on the floor, her anxiety seemed to ease a little. 'Don't get the scuffers, Mammy,' she said in a small, cracked little voice. 'Only . . . only do we have to go on living in this house, where he can come whenever his ship docks? Can't we go away, all of us, and live somewhere – somewhere safer? I know we can't go back to Ty Siriol, and I know you need your job, but . . . oh, *do* let us go away from this house!'

'We'll do something,' Rose promised. 'Once he's at sea and out of the way we'll find somewhere better to live, somewhere nearer the factory, perhaps. But right now, pet, we'd best all get to bed, or no one will be going anywhere in the morning.'

She carried Daisy up the stairs, with Petal bobbing at her heels, but when she had tucked the girls up and would have gone downstairs to check on Steve, both children begged her to stay with them, not to sleep in her own bed. 'Dad's drunk, you said so. He – he might hit you and kill you by – by mistake,' Daisy said wildly. 'Please, Mam, sleep with us tonight! We'll squeeze up small as small to give you room, won't we, Petal?'

And in the end it seemed the most sensible thing to do. Rose went downstairs and saw Steve was conscious again and sitting on the sofa, though in no very amenable state of mind. He had vomited on the kitchen floor and shouted at her when she advised him to clear it up before morning, but the shouting was half-hearted and she could see that he was having difficulty in remembering anything that had happened in the previous two or three hours. 'Why were I on the bloody floor, instead of in me bloody bed?' he asked, the belligerence fainter, for once, than the puzzlement. 'I don' unnershtand . . . I met me pals for a quick bevvy, never have more than the one now I'm on the wagon . . . nex' thing I know me head's ringin' an' I come to meself on the bloody *floor*, for God's sweet sake!'

'Yes, you were on the floor because you attacked your little girl and I hit you with the frying pan,' Rose said grimly. 'You stink of drink, strong drink, not just a beer or two, and I'm locking my bedroom door against you, so don't expect to sleep anywhere but the sofa tonight. I've had enough, Steve. If it wasn't for the fact that it's two in the morning and I'm dead tired I'd have handed you over to the scuffers without a second thought. So just you kip down on the sofa and we'll talk in the morning.'

'But you'll be at work,' Steve said craftily. 'Shan' be – be able to talk to me, nag me. When a feller's drunk he don't know what he's doin', you can't blame me for what I didn't know . . . aw, to hell with it, you'll find a way to blame me somehow.'

Rose snorted but said nothing more and presently left him. He heaved himself on to the sofa, demanded a blanket in a voice which told her that he had small hope of receiving one, and was snoring fit to wake the dead before she was halfway up the stairs.

Three in a bed, when one of the three – Petal – kicked in her sleep, was no picnic, but Rose heard her alarm clock go off at five through the thin partition wall which separated her room from that of the children and got reluctantly out of bed. She would not dare go in to work today, leaving Steve in the same house as the children, for even if he behaved himself, Daisy was in no fit state to get herself up and to school, let alone that she would be terrified to so much as catch her father's eye for a long time to come. She padded out of the house, therefore, and round to the Fosters. Fortunately, both women were on earlies, so Helen was up, and proved quite willing to take a message in to work explaining that Rose's daughter was ill but that Rose would be in as soon as she had sorted something out.

'And though I don't believe a word of it, I shan't go splittin' on you,' she said, yawning behind her hand. 'Your old feller was a-screechin' and a-yellin' last night, bawlin' out that you were a tuppenny tart . . . oh, don't worry, queen, no one won't listen to his bad-mouthin', because I reckon they all knew he was half seas over, as the sayin' goes.' She looked inquisitively at Rose. 'He didn't knock you about? You're bloody lucky, queen. Most of 'em get nasty when they've a skinful.'

'No, he didn't hit me, he hit Daisy,' Rose said grimly. 'So you see, I've a lot to sort out, but thanks ever so, Helen, you're a pal. And now I'd best get back to the house just in case someone beside meself wakes up.'

Back home once more, Rose went quietly into the kitchen where she found Steve at the gas cooker, making a cup of tea. He looked up as she entered, then looked quickly down again and she saw, for the first time in her life, that he was blushing. Steve McAllister, actually blushing, showing embarrassment! She said nothing, however, going over to the dresser and taking down two mugs. Without a word, she poured conny-onny into each, then stood them next to the teapot which Steve had just filled. When the tea was brewed and poured, she took her own cup, still in silence, and sat down at the table. Steve followed suit and as he leaned forward and put both hands round his mug – it was bitterly cold in the kitchen for the fire had gone out and had not yet been relit – Rose met his eyes for the first time, her gaze steady yet penetrating. She saw that his own eyes wavered, his glance shooting from his mug of tea to her face, and then wandering, uneasily, round the kitchen. Had he not behaved so badly, she might have felt sorry for him, for never had she seen him look so hang-dog. Guilt was written all over his face and his first words proved it.

'How's the kid?' he said gruffly. 'I don't remember touchin' a hair of her head, though I know I hit you a couple o' times, but – but you said it were her . . . I dunno, I were that confused . . . what were I doin' down at the docks, anyroad? And why did I go to the pub after?'

'You went to the docks because Alby had gone down earlier in the day and been told which ship he was to join . . .' Rose began, but got no further. She saw a look of horrified comprehension dawn on Steve's face and then, to her astonishment, he buried his head in both hands and began to sob.

Once again, she felt a faint stirring of pity; Steve never showed any emotion other than anger and here he was, crying like a baby. Tentatively, she leaned across the table and touched his hand and felt an immediate revulsion, so strong that she snatched her hand back as though his had been red hot. Remember, you're in this fix because you were once fool enough to fall in love with this pathetic creature, she scolded herself, and don't let him get away with anything because he's got to know what he did, and you've got to know it will never happen again; you owe it to yourself and the children.

'Steve? Whatever is the matter?'

He looked across at her, shamefacedly rubbing the tears from his cheeks with his enormous, grimy hands. 'Alby's norron the *Harrier*, an' I am,' he said. 'He's gorr'is promotion, but he's on one of the flower class corvettes.'

'So?' Rose said coldly. She knew the two men were friends but this was ridiculous. He was behaving as though he and Alby were lovers, not pals, using the fact that they would no longer be shipmates as an excuse to drink himself silly and to punch up his daughter. She began to say as much, but was interrupted.

'But you don't understand. Alby kept me off the drink, stopped me thinking I had to have a skinful every time I reached port,' he said thickly. 'Before I met him, I always had bottles of the hard stuff stashed away somewhere aboard. I've used me pay to buy other fellers' rum rations . . . I'd do anything for a drink. Then I met Alby—'

Rose interrupted him without compunction. 'Steve, you sound like Pinocchio, as though you're incapable of existing without Jiminy Cricket to tell you how to go on. For God's sake, you're a grown man, not a child, and must learn to take decisions for yourself. You've cut down on the drink once and we'd actually begun to get along quite well, but one little setback and you almost kill your own daughter. What on earth were you thinking of?'

'I thought she were you,' Steve said sulkily, after a short pause. 'I dunno why, 'cos she's not very like you, but me brain was addled by all the drink I'd taken. They say when you come off the wagon, you can get drunk on two or three bevvies, and I'd had just about as much as I could hold.'

Rose heaved a deep sigh. 'It's not good enough, Steve, because once you're back on the drink, the same thing could easily happen again, and with worse results. Come to that, you'll probably attack me, and who will look after the kids if I'm in a hospital bed, or six foot under? I think it would be best if you stayed in the Sailors' Home next time you're in port, and kept well away from us. I've not told the scuffers this time, but there isn't going to be a next time, understand?'

Steve stared at her as though he could not believe his ears. 'But Rosie, this is me *home*. I pays the rent and you get my allotment from the Navy, same as the other wives. You can't simply kick me out of me own home.'

'I don't need your money; I'm a supervisor now, so I can cope with household expenses, the rent . . . the lot, in fact,' Rose said. 'Besides, if I don't have to feed you when you're home, I'll be a great deal better off.'

'But – but wharrabout me kids? I dare say Daisy's not feelin' too fond . . . you must tell 'er it were an accident – say I didn't mean it – but Petal's me little princess, she loves her daddy, she'll be that upset—'

His words were cut off by the opening of the kitchen door. Petal came into the room. She was rosy with sleep, her fair curls tangled, but her eyes bright. She looked across at her mother, her eyes seeming to look straight through Steve. 'Mammy? Are you awright? I heared you talking an' I thought – I thought . . .'

'Well, if it ain't me favourite little girl. Come an' sit on your ol' dad's knee an' tell your mam it 'ud break your heart if she didn't let me come home no more,' Steve said coaxingly. 'I weren't meself last night, I were ill, but I never meant to hurt nobody, only your mammy don't understand. She thinks . . .'

He put out a hand as though to pull Petal on to his knee but she eluded him easily, and went round the table to stand beside her mother. Rose, glancing down at her, saw hostility in every line of the child's face and body. Petal looked up at her. 'Oh yes, Mammy, it would be lovely if *that man* never came into our house again,' she said, pointing at Steve. 'I don't like him at all. In fact, I hate him. Poor Daisy is still asleep, but earlier, when she turned over, she cried. Her face is all red and purple down one side and some of her hair's come out. Can you make him go away before Daisy gets up?'

Rose glanced across at her husband and saw that he was crying again and felt nothing but contempt. How dared he expect Petal to love him when she had seen him beat up her older sister only hours before? But Steve was lurching to his feet, and for a moment Rose feared that he might actually attack her daughter. She pulled Petal to her, but the little girl pushed her off and ran round the table. 'Go on, gerrout of our house!' she shouted. 'We doesn't want you here after what you've done to our Daisy. Go on, beat it!'

'I'm goin',' Steve said unsteadily. He turned to Rose. 'As for not wantin' my money . . . well, mebbe a rating's pay ain't worth much for all I'm fightin' for me country. But I know a way to earn more and you and the kids shall have every penny, 'cos I don't mean to start seein' them crabs crawlin' up the walls an' droppin' off on to me bunk to try an' eat me alive. I'll stop drinkin', I swear it, an' then you'll be sorry you turned me out.'

Neither Petal nor Rose said a word as Steve lurched towards the back door, grabbed his jacket and crashed the door shut behind him. Then Petal turned to her mother. 'What did he mean about crabs eating him alive?' she asked fearfully. 'It – it sounded horrid, Mammy. Do crabs get inside ships?'

'No, queen, but if a fellow drinks too much, he has awful nightmares,' Rose said tactfully. 'We shan't have to worry about your father for a bit, though, because I've told him to stay at the Sailors' Home next time he's in port, and I shall have the front door lock changed so that he can't get in whilst we're out. Now let's go up and see whether Daisy fancies a nice bowl of porridge for her breakfast.'

By the time she and the girls had washed, dressed and eaten breakfast, Rose had made a decision. No matter how careful she was, she could not keep her job and protect the children against another attack from their father. She remembered how often, when they were first married, Steve had sworn to lay off the drink, and how such episodes had never lasted more than a few weeks. If only Mrs Williams had been able to take them back, she would have had no hesitation in sending them off to Ty Siriol, but as it was she would speak to the head teacher of the local school, and find out whether there was any sort of scheme at the moment to take city children into the safety of the countryside.

By teatime that evening, she knew that she could send the children to safety in the next week or so; she had decided that it would be best if she kept Daisy by her until the bruises had faded and the memory of Steve's attack had grown less vivid. But then, provided she accompanied her daughters and saw them safely settled, they should be happy enough knowing that they were safe from their father, as well as from more nights of horrendous bombing, and she would assure them that she would visit them as often as possible.

'You're going to Wrexham, my loves, the town which we visited when Mrs Williams was in hospital there,' Rose told them. 'It's a nice big house, I believe, just outside the town, owned by a gentleman who is working in London, so it is being run in the meantime by his wife. The billeting officer said she took four boys when war was declared, but could not cope with them, and this time has asked for nicely behaved little girls, so it sounds to me just the place for the two of you.'

'I'd rather stay with you, Mam,' Daisy said fearfully. 'Maybe Dad won't try to come home any more. Or you said we might all move – you as well – which would be grand if we could find somewhere Dad didn't know about.'

'Yes, but we will need my job more than ever if we aren't going to get your father's pay,' Rose explained. 'And that means I can't live out in the country because I wouldn't be able to get to the factory each day.'

Daisy looked undecided. 'But suppose Dad finds out where we're staying and comes there? The lady wouldn't know what he's like; she might let him take us out for a w-walk or a p-picnic. And – and you wouldn't be there to bonk him over the head with a frying pan.'

Rose hesitated. 'I had to explain to the billeting officer that your dad was a violent man and must not, in any circumstances, be given your address,' she said carefully. She turned to Petal. 'That means no letters, queen, neither from you to him, nor from him to you. Can you understand?'

'Yes, and I don't want to write letters to someone

so horrible,' Petal said vehemently. 'Nor I don't want letters from him; he's our worst enemy, ain't he, Daisy? We hate him like we hate the bleedin' Germans, and the Luft—Luftwhotsit.'

'Luftwaffe,' Rose said, as Daisy nodded agreement with her sister's sentiments. 'Right then; I'll take you to Mrs Wyn Roberts in a week or ten days, and stay there with you for a day or two, just to make sure everything's all right. I'm awfully sorry that it means yet another change of school, but I'm afraid things like that happen in wartime. And now I'm going to make you a nice big high tea and then we'll all have an early night, because we didn't get much sleep last night, did we?'

'Daisy an' me slept all right, once we got to sleep,' Petal said. She picked up her sister's hand and cuddled it against her cheek. 'I love Daisy next best to you, Mammy, in the whole world, so it won't be *too* bad going away from Bernard Terrace. But – but can you sleep in our bed again? I know there's no lock on the door but we can swing the bed round and jam the brass rail thing under the door handle, then we'll be safe as houses, won't we?'

Rose sighed inwardly; so it was not only Daisy who was going to remember Steve's attack with dread for the rest of her life. It had clearly affected the normally ebullient Petal as well. She did hope that neither would start bed-wetting once they got to Wrexham because constantly laundering sheets and mopping up puddles was enough to put the most perfect foster mother off her charges. However, there was no point in meeting trouble halfway. The billeting officer had told her that Mrs Wyn Roberts kept a spare room for the use of parents and, in view of the violence which had precipitated this move, had written a letter to the factory, explaining that Rose would need to be away for at least a week, though she gave no actual reason.

'I don't need to do so; your employer will take my word for it that the time off is needed,' she said, when Rose looked doubtful. 'You say your husband's ship sails in a couple of days, and once he has left the children will be safe. Then a week should be ample. Good day, Mrs McAllister.'

Rose carried out Petal's plan of action, and by eight o'clock the three of them were tucked up in bed, though Rose had chosen to wedge a chair from the kitchen under the door handle, rather than try to move the heavy old brass bedstead. Secure in the knowledge that their mother would protect them, the girls fell asleep almost at once, but Rose, not used to such early hours, merely snoozed. When the knocking came, she was instantly awake. With considerable care, she eased herself out of bed, gently moved the chair, opened the door and padded down the stairs. It could not possibly be Steve, because he had his own key and she had not yet had time to have the locks changed. It would be a neighbour, someone wanting to borrow half a cup of sugar, or a tin of conny-onny. After all, in normal circumstances, she was rarely in bed before ten o'clock.

Nevertheless, she opened the door carefully, clinging grimly to the edge of it, in case someone tried to force an entry, for her nerves still jangled from the happenings of the night before. In the thick darkness, she could only see the outline of a man, but when he whispered hoarsely: 'Can I come in, Rose, just for a few minutes,' she knew at once that it was Steve.

She was tempted to slam the door but knew that this would be unwise since he had a key, though he had not chosen to use it. Instead, she said in a low voice: 'I thought I told you to stay away from this house, but if you meant to disregard what I said, why didn't you use your key? We were in bed, the kids and me.'

'I didn't use me key because you told me not to; you said to clear off,' Steve said, his voice almost a whine. 'Let me come in for a moment, Rose, I'm freezing cold and I can't stop anyway.'

Rose hesitated, then pulled the door wide and gestured him inside. She knew he was speaking the truth, though she didn't know how she knew. She ushered him into the kitchen, saying as she shut the door softly behind him: 'I'll give you five minutes, Steve, and then you've simply got to go. We can't take much more, me and the kids, and we need to get some sleep.' He slumped into a chair and, after a moment's hesitation, Rose followed suit. 'Well? What do you want to tell me that's so important you've come knocking in the middle of the night?'

'I came to tell you . . . oh, dammit, Rose, I – I'm real sorry for what happened, honest to God I am. No, don't start, I know being sorry isn't enough, that's why . . . that's why . . .'

Rose waited, brows lifted. She did not intend to make things easy for him; let him tell her straight whatever it was that was so important, or get out. After more hesitation and some mumbling, Steve seemed to pull himself together. 'You know Alby and me were bezzies, looked out for one another, kept each other on the straight and narrer. Well, when I heared he were being sent to another ship . . . that's what drove me back to the bleedin' drink. You see, Alby's been my – my luck, in a way. While we was together it seemed to me nothing real bad was likely to happen to either of us. And then they've separated us, and I went kind o' mad, I reckon. So – so I went to the shipping office just now, and wrote on a lot of papers and talked to folk, and now I've done it; I've signed on as submarine crew and I leave for Gosport – that's the training centre, and it'll be me home port – first thing in the morning. The money's a good deal better and – and it'll go to you and the kids, and I won't be able to get back to the 'Pool, mebbe not for years. The feller warned me that a good few o' the subs are sent to places like Malta, or Greece, and will stay there until the war's over or until they're sent home for repairs or refits or whatever. So you see, I doubt I'll be coming back to Bernard Terrace for – for a goodish while.'

He stared at Rose with what seemed like a mixture of misery and defiance but Rose's answering stare was, she knew, mainly one of puzzlement. 'So?' she said at last, when the silence between them had stretched and stretched. 'I don't see why a submarine can't have Liverpool as its home port . . . or why you've signed on for it, come to that. I'm sorry, Steve, but I just don't get the significance of what you're telling me.'

Steve jumped out of his chair and took two strides towards her but Rose was out of her own seat almost simultaneously and reaching for the frying pan. She would never take a chance again, not with Steve. He was as dangerous, and unpredictable, as – as a tiger; she did not mean to be caught napping. But, apparently, he had only risen in order to stride about the room, his face tormented, so she sat down again, though on the very edge of her chair this time, and with the poker at her feet where she could grab it in a moment.

'It's a whole different ball game, being in a bloody submarine, woman! They have to sail from Gosport or Portsmouth because . . . oh, I don't know, they just do . . . and that means I'm not liable to turn up here unannounced. If I'm given proper leave I can telegraph, write, let you know somehow. Not that I'm particularly keen to come back here, if me home's barred to me. As for the submarines, God, the money's good, and I dare say I'll get used to being crammed into one of 'em, though the thought of all those tons of water above and below . . . but I've done it – done it for you and the kids, done it to show you I'm sorry, that I ain't all bad, whatever you may think. I – I want Daisy and Petal to know I won't ever hit either of 'em again . . . dammit, Rose, I were mad wi' drink. I thought it were you I were draggin' into the bleedin' house!'

And I suppose if you had killed or half killed me, that would have been all right, Rose thought to herself, but did not put it into words, because it would not exactly help matters. And now that she came to think about it, she could not imagine tall, hefty Steve cramming himself inside a submarine. He would undoubtedly go for training – he probably had little choice since he said he had signed papers – but they would soon realise their mistake; this was the man who had once refused point-blank to get into the lift at Lewis's with her and the pushchair, but had run up all those stairs instead. However, it would not do to say so. Instead, she spoke soothingly. 'I see; I understand, Steve, but to be frank, it isn't money that's needed here at present, it's the promise that you won't come near us, won't pursue us if we leave Bernard Terrace. Can't you understand that? It's going to be a long while before Daisy stops being scared of her own shadow, after what you did.'

'Yes, I know, but there's nothing I can do about

that if you won't let me see her,' Steve pointed out, with a certain amount of truthfulness, Rose was forced to admit. 'But can't you *see*, Rose? If my home port is the other end of England then I can't just turn up unexpected – that's wharr I'm tryin' to tell you. And – and I'm punishing meself by signing on aboard a sub. I'll be going through a worse hell than any I've put the kid through. Oh, for Christ's sake, try to understand!'

Slowly, Rose nodded. 'I really am trying, and I – do appreciate what you're saying,' she said at last. 'But honestly, Steve, you must go now! Suppose one of the girls woke and heard me talking and came downstairs? I've promised you'll stay away, and . . .'

'All right, all right, I'm going,' Steve growled. He stopped in the doorway and glared at Rose before making his way out of the house, and in that moment she knew, with real sorrow, that his problem was insoluble. He might make an effort to reform, to become a decent person, but such a reform would – could – only last for a few weeks. In a way it wasn't even his fault, it was how he had been brought up. He had seen his father knock his mother about, been knocked about in his turn, and when he married he already deeply despised women. When Rose had stood up to him he had simply loathed her, as he had, in the end, loathed his mother for letting his father beat him. But there was no sense in saying any of this, because tigers did not change their stripes any more than leopards changed their spots. The kids had the right idea. They would all move away from here when the war was over, go abroad if necessary, and shake the dust of Bernard Terrace, and Steve, off their feet for good.

Chapter Eight

Rose waited a full week before she packed the children's belongings into a suitcase, told them to bring their favourite doll or teddy bear, and set off for the house the billeting officer had found for them. She was glad it was situated in Wrexham because she felt at least the town would not be strange to any of them; had they not visited Mrs Williams in the War Memorial Hospital, had a meal in Steven's Café and gone round the shops? It was a market town, small but friendly, Rose thought. The district was riddled with coal mines, and though she knew there were both army barracks and an airfield, these were separated from the town by some distance. There were certainly no docks, as it was at least thirty miles from the sea, so there was little to attract the Luftwaffe. In fact, she supposed it was a bit of a backwater. But a backwater was just what one wanted for one's children in time of war.

No taxis were waiting when they arrived at Wrexham station, so Rose and the children made their way to Grove Road on foot; Rose, at least, with a pleasant feeling of anticipation. She looked at Daisy and saw that the child was examining her surroundings with every sign of interest and without any of the caution which she had shown whenever they left Bernard Terrace on a shopping expedition. She had explained over and over that Steve had gone to a place called Gosport at the other end of England and that he would not be returning to Liverpool until the war was over, but though Daisy appeared to be reassured, she could not quite rid herself of the suspicion that he might be lurking behind a telephone box, or in the dark entry which ran between the shops and the jigger at the back.

Rose halted in front of a tall stone wall, with a pair of double wrought-iron gates set into it. The gates were painted black, and above them there was a stone arch upon which were depicted the words *The Larches*. For a moment, the splendour of the gates took her aback, made her heart begin to bump uneasily. Surely she must have made a mistake? This was the home of rich people, people of influence. She assumed that the rich pleased themselves in wartime as they did in peace, and if so, the owner of the Larches would have found some excuse not to have to accept evacuees. Then she remembered what the billeting officer had said. Mr and Mrs Wyn Roberts had had four boys billeted on them, but had been unable to cope. She supposed that ordinary people would have been told, pretty brusquely, to make the best of it, but these wealthy folk had used their influence to get the boys sent elsewhere, though they had said, graciously, that they would take a couple of young, nicely behaved girls. Oh, well. She supposed she should be grateful that the boys had not been satisfactory, because – she peered through the gates – this was certainly a far grander and more beautiful house than she had ever dreamed of staying in. Not that she could see much from here, as there was a shrubbery of evergreens to the right and a great many tall and beautiful trees obscured her view, though she could see that the house was very large indeed. Rose had stood down her suitcase before looking through the gates, but now she picked it up again, lifted the latch and pushed the gate wide, aware that the children had crowded close to her, awed by the gravel drive which crunched beneath their feet, and by the extent of the shrubbery and the garden ahead of them.

Halfway along the drive, Daisy jerked at her mother's sleeve. 'Look, Mam, under the trees: millions and millions of snowdrops. I've seen them on the market stalls, and there were a few under the big beech at the farm – we wasn't allowed to pick them – but I've never ever seen a carpet of them. Why, they're so thick you couldn't walk without treading on them.' She turned to her sister. 'Have you *seen* them, Petal?'

Petal glanced sideways and nodded, but she was clearly more interested in bricks and mortar than in horticulture. 'Yes, I see 'em,' she said impatiently. 'But oh, Mam, look at the house. It's – it's like a castle, or a palace, or something. It's huge.'

They had rounded a bend in the drive and now the house stood before them. It was built of stone with mullioned windows which came to a point, rather like church windows, and there were two turrets which, Rose supposed, had reminded Petal of pictures she had seen of castles and palaces. There seemed to be a great many windows, all staring out at the newcomers, and Rose was glad she had put on her best clothes and dressed the children as neatly as possible.

Three stone steps, well scrubbed but not whitened, led up to the front door, which was huge and decorated with large brass studs. There was a round, white porcelain bell push on the right and a large knocker in the shape of a lion's head in the centre of the door. Rose was hesitating, wondering which to use, when Petal forestalled her by pressing on the bell with all her strength, and continuing to do so even when approaching footsteps could be heard above the bell's shrill notes. Daisy snatched her sister's hand away just in time; the door creaked open.

'Yes?' An elderly woman stood there, looking at them as though she suspected them of planning to steal the doorsteps, Rose thought. She wore a large white apron over a black dress, stout lace-up shoes and wrinkled black woollen stockings, as well as a most unpleasant expression. Rose had begun to stammer that she was Mrs McAllister, and that she had told Mrs Wyn Roberts that they would be arriving by train this morning, when suddenly her embarrassment changed to annoyance. The old woman had eyes in her head; she could see the suitcase and the paper carrier bags the children held. She must know very well who they were and why they were standing on her doorstep; she was just being difficult for some reason which Rose, as yet, did not understand. So she cut off her stammered explanation, looked the elderly woman straight in the eye, and said firmly: 'We are the McAllisters and we have an appointment to see your Mrs Wyn Roberts; kindly inform her that we have arrived, please.'

She had meant to step forward into the hall, presuming that the woman would expect the family to follow her. Fortunately, she hesitated, meaning to take Petal's hand, and it was a good thing she did since the woman, without a word of acknowledgement, turned away, slamming the door behind her as she did so and missing Rose's nose by inches.

Rose put down her suitcase and Daisy gave her hand a squeeze. 'She's a nasty old woman, Mam,' she whispered. 'But she's only someone who works here, not the lady who owns it, isn't she? I expect she's cross because she thinks she'll have to make our dinners and show us the way to school and that.'

'I don't care what you say, Daisy, I think she's a rude old woman; a nasty, rude old woman,' Petal said. She did not lower her voice. 'If she's rude again, Mammy, I shall knock her horrible old legs with my little suitcase; that'll make her sorry.'

Rose was about to remind her that one should always be kind to elderly ladies when the door opened again. It was the same woman, but this time she held the door wide, gesturing them inside. Rose pushed the children ahead of her, then turned to the maid. 'I'm sorry, but there are four doors to choose from; where should I go?'

For answer, the maid slammed the front door shut, stalked ahead of them to fling open another, and then headed for the very last door, which was situated at the end of the hall and was covered in green baize. She was not quite through it when Petal's voice rose plaintively. 'Is she dumb, Mammy? You know, it's like blind, only it's your voice. If she's dumb, we should be sorry for her, 'cos Mrs Williams says we must be sorry for the afflicted.'

Rose smothered a giggle but thought it a pity that Petal hadn't kept her voice down for she could tell, by the look of hatred which the maid shot at Petal, that whatever the woman's afflictions deafness was not one of them; she had heard – and resented – every word.

And as Rose was soon to learn, she was not the only one to overhear Petal's words. The three of them went through the doorway and found themselves in a pleasant, high-ceilinged room, painted white with sprigged wallpaper, floral curtains and a round, plush carpet decorated with a scattering of roses. There was a beautiful fireplace with a tiled surround, in which a number of logs burned brightly, a wide well-cushioned window seat, and several comfortable-looking easy chairs upholstered in white and gold. Two of these chairs were occupied by middle-aged women, both smiling, and as Rose advanced towards them they got to their feet. 'Good morning, Mrs McAllister,' the taller of the two said, holding out her hand. 'I'm Mrs Wyn Roberts and this is my sister Mrs Franklin.' She was plump and pretty, with a round babyish face upon which was perched a pair of tiny spectacles. She had frizzy fair hair, hazel eyes and small but rather uneven teeth, which showed when she gave Rose a wide and friendly smile. Rose, shaking hands, liked her at once. She could tell from Mrs Wyn Roberts's smile that she had heard Petal's comment and was amused rather than annoyed by it.

Her companion was very different, short, skinny and dark-haired, with a pair of snapping black eyes, a long thin nose and a gravity of expression which vanished when she, too, smiled. Like Mrs Wyn Roberts, she was obviously well disposed towards the newcomers, and the sharp black eyes twinkled as she greeted Rose, then held out her hand, first to Daisy, then to Petal. 'How do you do, young ladies?' she said seriously. 'You will be Daisy McAllister and you will be Petal McAllister. I am Mrs Wyn Roberts's sister, Mrs Franklin, and as you can see, no two people could be less alike. So I am not at all surprised to see that you, Daisy, have straight dark hair and you, Petal, have blonde curls, but as I often used to say to my sister, when we were small, I could have curls if I wished, by the simple expedient of having a permanent wave, or wrapping each lock round a pipe cleaner every night, whereas my sister is doomed to curls, and cannot straighten them no matter how she tries.'

'But you don't curl your hair, Mrs Franklin . . .'

Daisy was beginning, when Mrs Wyn Roberts floated across to the fireplace and pressed the bell. 'Tea, tea, tea,' she sang out. 'Take your coats off, my dears, and sit down. You must be tired and thirsty after your long journey, so we thought a meal halfway between lunch and supper would be appropriate. Edith – that's our maid – will bring the tea trolley through directly.'

And sure enough, only moments later, there was a great clattering outside and Daisy jumped up from the tapestry stool on which she had been sitting and politely held the door open. Edith shoved her trolley through it without acknowledging Daisy's presence by so much as a glance. Indeed, she ignored everyone but her mistress, to whom she said in a grumbling tone: 'I made breakfast tea, like you said, Mrs Wyn Roberts, and I hopes as the sangwidges is sufficient. You said "little gals".'

There was a world of reproach in her voice but Mrs Wyn Roberts only laughed. 'They *are* little girls,' she said, beaming at them both. 'Thank you, Edith, that will be all.'

Edith gave the sort of fruity sniff which, had Petal done it, would have had Rose demanding that she use her handkerchief, but no one said anything until the maid had slammed the door resoundingly behind her.

Mrs Franklin tutted. 'I know Edith's been in the family's employ for forty years, but she really should learn that you are her employer; she who pays the piper calls the tune, you know. And what's more . . .' she glanced disapprovingly at the tiny sandwiches set out on the trolley, 'there's not enough food there to feed a sparrow, let alone the five of us. But never mind. You start pouring, Clara, and I'll go and have a word with Edith.'

Whilst she was gone, Rose and Mrs Wyn Roberts

chatted amicably and Mrs Wyn Roberts dispensed cups of tea and handed round pretty china plates and then the tiny sandwiches, advising her young guests to take four or five. The children obeyed but the postage-sized sandwiches disappeared in no time and Rose was relieved when Mrs Franklin returned to the room, bearing a large plate upon which were set out what appeared to be chunky and uneven cheese and tomato butties. She stood the plate down and turned to take another dish from the disapproving Edith, who was following her closely. The second dish held a fair-sized madeira cake, and presently they were all munching. Rose noticed, with approval, that when Edith left the room for the second time, she closed the door quietly behind her.

When tea was finished, Mrs Wyn Roberts glanced hopefully at her sister. 'Anna, my dear, would you save my poor legs and show Mrs McAllister and the children over the house? Mrs McAllister is to stay in the blue room tonight, but the children will be in our old nursery, of course. And then, if they would like to explore the garden, I dare say they can do so without any help from us.'

Rose followed Mrs Franklin willingly, eager to see if the rest of the house was as beautifully furnished as the drawing room. She soon found that it was, though Mrs Franklin told her that the dining room, breakfast parlour, living room and conservatory were rarely used now. 'My sister has breakfast in bed and takes most of her meals on a tray in the drawing room because it means she only has to heat the one room, but the children will eat with Edith in the kitchen,' she explained. 'I'm afraid you will have to talk to Edith regarding what time the children eat and what sort of food they prefer, because my sister has always left such matters in the hands of others. Before the war, when Mr Wyn Roberts lived here all the time, and did not have to spend weekdays in London at the Ministry, they employed a cook, a gardener, a boot boy, a scullery maid and Edith, who was the parlour maid. The gardener does his best to keep the place tidy, and in summer grows wonderful fruit and vegetables for the house. But the others have all gone. Mrs Jones, the cook, joined the ATS, but the scullery maid and the boot boy took more remunerative posts, at the Royal Ordnance factory in Marchwiel. I believe they make munitions there but it's awfully hush hush, you know. However, Edith is too old and too set in her ways for anything but domestic work, so she has stayed on.'

'I see,' Rose murmured. 'But – will Edith be able to manage, Mrs Franklin? As you say, she is no longer young and seems very set in her ways. I realise that you must do a great deal to help her, but . . . but . . .'

'Oh no, I do nothing, because I don't live here,' Mrs Franklin said quickly. 'I thought you realised; I'm simply on a visit. I live in Chester and I work at the Ministry of Supply, so I have little opportunity to come back to Wrexham, let alone to help my sister out. But as for managing, Edith must do quite well or my sister would not continue to retain her services.'

They had been climbing the wide staircase and now Mrs Franklin threw open a white-painted door. 'Your room,' she said briefly. 'The children are on the next floor up. I think my sister felt that the old nursery, containing, as it does, a great many of the toys and books which she and I enjoyed as children, would be more suitable than a bedroom on the lower floor.'

Rose said nothing until they were once more descending the stairs. The children had stayed in the nursery, fascinated and intrigued by the rocking horse, the doll's house, and the large bookcase, packed with shabby but beautifully illustrated books. Now, greatly daring, Rose put her hand on her companion's arm and drew her to a halt. 'Mrs Franklin, my girls are good girls, but even so, they will make extra work for everyone. They can make their own beds, bath themselves, get ready for school and so on, but they can't cook their own meals or wake themselves up in time to get to school. And they have normal appetites. If you'll forgive my frankness, the tea Edith had prepared for the five of us would have left Daisy and Petal feeling very hungry, even if they'd eaten it all themselves. I'm sure Mrs Wyn Roberts will do her best to see the children are cared for, but if too much is left to Edith . . .'

'Naturally, Mrs McAllister, you are worried that your children might not find Edith very . . . sympathetic,' Mrs Franklin said tactfully, 'but I'm sure such worries are needless. The fact is, the authorities told my sister, when the other evacuees left, that they meant to requisition the Larches for the use of senior management at the Ordnance factory. The alternative was to house at least six evacuated children here, so you see, my sister will make every effort to keep your girls happy and content. Indeed, she has already applied for more evacuees, only stipulating that they should be girls, since this is an all-female household.

'I see,' Rose said slowly. 'And – and will Mrs Wyn Roberts employ more help when the other children arrive?'

'She may well do so; but surely two women can manage six small girls?' Mrs Franklin said, beginning to descend the stairs once more. 'Don't worry, Mrs McAllister. Your children will be both safe and happy here. It's a wonderful house for children and, when spring comes, a wonderful garden. There is a Wendy house, an orchard with a swing hanging from a branch of an old pear tree, a tree house built in the big copper beech . . . a sandpit . . . I assure you, it's a paradise for children, and I should know because I lived here myself from my birth until I married.'

Rose had to be content with this, though before she left the following day, she did manage to have a word with Edith. Finding the maid alone in the kitchen, she approached her, trying to smile pleasantly, though the older woman's features did not soften and her gaze was distinctly aggressive. Rose thought that Edith looked like an angry toad with her long thin mouth tightly folded and her pale eyes bulging.

'Yes?' she said baldly, as Rose approached. 'I'm very busy, Mrs – er – Mrs McAndrews, so if you've anything to say, you'd best say it at once, and no beating about the bush.'

To say that Rose was taken aback was an understatement, but she held the woman's gaze. 'I just wanted to tell you, Edith, that I am very sorry for the extra work my children will cause, but I think you will find them co-operative and helpful. However, I have written my name and address on this envelope, together with the telephone number of the factory in which I work. If there is anything I can do, or if you need to get in touch with me, you can contact me there.' She handed Edith the envelope which contained, beside the details mentioned, a ten shilling note. 'And by the way, as you will see, our name is McAllister, not McAndrews.' Rose was tempted to add 'Ethel', but did not do so. She felt sure that the older woman would take it out on Daisy and Petal if she did any such thing.

The children walked with her to the station, chattering happily as they did so. Daisy had fallen deeply in love with the Wendy house and said that she and Petal meant to carry one of the doll's tea services down from the nursery in order to have tea parties there. Petal, for her part, could not wait to climb up to the tree house, and both children anticipated the arrival of four more small girls with pleasure. 'I expect we'll all go to this Alexandra School,' Daisy said cheerfully, as Rose climbed aboard the train and turned to give her daughters a last kiss. 'Mrs Wyn Roberts's house isn't like the farm because there are no animals, not even a dog or a cat, but perhaps they'll get one if we suggest it.'

Rose opened her mouth to warn Daisy to do no such thing, but at that moment the guard came along the train, slamming doors and shouting to those not travelling to stand well clear, and almost immediately the train began to chug out of the station. Rose waved and waved at the two tiny figures until they were out of sight, then sat back in her seat, blew her nose, and told herself that Daisy and Petal were a couple of lucky kids. That beautiful house! And all the wonderful toys which children in their position would never normally see, let alone play with. And then there was the garden, the Wendy house, the tree house . . . yes, they were lucky children indeed.

Nevertheless, the eyes that she turned on to the magazine she had bought for the journey were full of tears.

On the way back to Bernard Terrace, Rose decided that she must fill her life with activities; preferably those which would help with the war effort. Loneliness was a bad thing because it gave one too much time to think; she would be better fully employed spending her spare time, such as it was, helping others.

So, as soon as she got home, she went and visited Maisie and asked her where she should go to volunteer for part-time war work which would fit in with her factory shifts. Maisie said, frankly, that she had no idea but, as usual, knew someone who would be able to help. 'Remember Muriel Jones, who were a couple of years above us in school? She works full time at the Civil Defence Control Centre; it's a real important job, so if you go round to her place one evening – she lives in Upper Beau Street – she'll soon put you right.'

Deciding that there was no time like the present, Rose went round to Muriel's house that same evening, and by the time she was eating her solitary supper she was all fixed up. She had decided she would become a firewatcher or, if the need was elsewhere, a shelter warden. Muriel was a tall, thin woman, square-shouldered and energetic, and had understood about both Rose's factory shift work and the loneliness which she felt now that the girls had been evacuated for a second time.

'I'm glad you came to me, because I do believe that you'll be a good deal happier fitting in with other people and getting to make new friends,' she said, her rather horsy face suddenly transformed by a broad smile. 'Alone, one cannot help but imagine dreadful things during the raids – I did myself – but in company with others, everything is easier to bear. I share this house with three other war workers, all women of course, and usually we are too busy to feel afraid. How is your husband, by the way? I seem to recall someone telling me he was a seaman, so I don't suppose you see much of him.'

Rose smiled. She knew enough about the local grapevine to realise that Muriel must know she had married Steve McAllister; a man who drank too much and probably ill treated his wife. Simply answering the question, she replied: 'Yes, Steve's in the Royal Navy, so naturally I don't see very much of him . . . and now, apparently, I shall see even less. He recently volunteered for submarines, so his home port will be down south. At the moment he's on a training course in Gosport.'

Muriel looked her squarely in the eye. 'Is that bad? Will you miss him?'

Before she had thought, Rose had answered with complete honesty. 'No, it isn't bad and I shan't miss him at all. He – he is not an easy man to live with. I've put up with it for years, learned to defend myself, and to keep out of the way when he was really drunk, but after Christmas he attacked one of the children and as far as I was concerned, that was the end. I've managed to evacuate them and won't give him their country address, but by the time the war is over I hope I'll have found a permanent home for us, somewhere far away. Perhaps even abroad.'

'I see. I'd heard rumours – you know what this place is like – but whenever I've seen you in the street you've always looked smart and happy, and the children content and well cared for. Some women in your position would let themselves go, take the easy way out.'

'I did that at first,' Rose said honestly. 'I was too frightened of him to think of making a stand. Then one day I was cooking at the stove . . .'

She told Muriel the whole story, half ashamed, half proud, and was delighted when the older girl smiled broadly and held out her hand. 'Shake, Rose! My father was violent, and after my mother died he thought he could start on me. He was a scuffer; I hit him so hard with his own truncheon that he had to have five stitches in a scalp wound. That was years ago but he's still alive, and though we've not shared a house since '36, he seems to respect me now and wouldn't dream of saying a word out of place, let alone raising his hand against me.'

The two women talked a little more and then Rose left, having made out a schedule of her shifts for the next four weeks or so. Muriel had agreed to put together a programme of firewatching for Rose to follow, taking her shifts into account, and promised to push it through the door of No. 7 in the next couple of days.

So when Rose met Rachel in the canteen on her first day back in work, she was full of news. Over macaroni cheese and boiled potatoes, she told Rachel all about the Larches and Mrs Wyn Roberts, and about Edith, who had seemed so grumpy but would doubtless improve upon further acquaintance. Then she talked about the voluntary war work which she would be starting as soon as her schedule arrived. It was almost as an afterthought that she mentioned Steve's transfer to submarines.

Rachel stared at her, round-eyed. 'Oh, Rose! Alby told me Steve had thought about it once before only he was put off by the *Thetis* sinking,' she said. 'Alby said Steve was all wrong for submarines; he said he's not too keen on enclosed spaces and – and he's so *tall*. Alby said he'd have been ducking his head all the time. Whatever made him do it? Volunteer, I mean?'

Rose took a deep breath. 'It's a long story; it goes right back to when we first married, which was when Steve began to hit me when he was drunk, or in a bad mood,' she said quietly. 'I've never said a word before, Rachel, because Steve and Alby were such friends that it didn't seem fair to tell you about Steve's other side, the side only his wife and kids knew.' She looked thoughtfully across at Rachel's appalled face. 'If you'd rather not know, just say, but it's why he ended up volunteering for submarines.'

After a long and very tense moment, Rachel nodded. 'I'd rather you told me,' she said. 'Once, Alby hinted at something of the sort but I suppose I didn't want to understand, because Alby is such a grand fellow that it seems strange he should choose to befriend someone – someone who wasn't just as grand.'

So Rose told her story and at the end of it Rachel nodded sadly. 'I see. Things are a lot clearer: the lump on your forehead, and your black eye . . . the way Steve sometimes talked . . . oh, Rose, I am so sorry. If I'd known, perhaps I could have done something to help. But one thing I don't understand. Why should Steve volunteer for submarines?'

'He said that it was partly the money, which is very much better, and partly he's punishing himself for what he did to Daisy,' Rose explained. 'Also, his home port will be down south, so he won't be able to simply walk into number seven whenever he's in port. And oddly enough, I think it's partly because he and Alby were to be separated and he feels fate has kicked him in the teeth by taking his pal away. So perhaps he's kicking back by volunteering to do something which Alby had warned him against.'

There was a long silence, then Rachel got to her feet and Rose followed suit. 'I'll never understand men if I live to be a hundred,' Rachel said ruefully, as they left the canteen. 'But I'm so glad you told me everything, Rosie, and I hope you and I will always be bezzies. I wouldn't mind helping with the firewatching meself. Could you put in a word for me?'

Rose laughed and shook her head chidingly. 'They'd have to buy a bigger van just to squeeze you inside,' she observed. 'No, don't hit me, I was only teasing. I'll have a word with Muriel the next time I see her. 'Bye for now, Rachel.'

Several weeks later, Rose came home from work to find two letters on the doormat. She carried them through into the kitchen but did not bother to light the fire since the March weather was quite clement at the moment. She sat down at the kitchen table, wondering which missive to open first, and decided on the children's. She loved their letters, which were always chock full of their news, each one writing a few lines. Now it seemed that they were going to have what Petal called tests, and what Daisy called examinations, before the Easter holidays, so both girls announced that they were studying hard and that Mrs Wyn Roberts had volunteered to 'hear' such things as tables and the rules of grammar. Because of her new responsibilities, Rose had only visited the Larches once since that first time and had been delighted with the children's enthusiasm for their new school and their obvious contentment with Mrs Wyn Roberts. Daisy informed their mother that they did lots of work round the house, making beds, dusting and using the carpet sweeper as well as occasionally going into town for messages. Rose smiled indulgently, thinking that a carpet swept or a room dusted by Petal would have to be done again by someone a little more meticulous, but congratulated them on their hard work.

Rather to her surprise, Edith had not been at home when she visited and when she had asked the children where the maid was, they had exchanged quick glances and said they did not know but thought she would be home around six.

'Ah, then I suppose Mrs Wyn Roberts will be making your supper,' Rose had observed. Daisy had nodded vaguely but Petal had piped up that supper was always cold when Edith was away, and then the subject had been changed and Rose thought about Edith no more. She guessed that the woman's attitude would lead to the children's avoiding her as much as possible, but since she had asked them, tentatively, whether they were happy or had complaints, and had received an emphatic yes to the first and no to the second, she decided that Edith's attitude must have softened.

She did wonder why no more evacuees had arrived at the Larches, but Daisy told her that Mrs Wyn Roberts thought the authorities had forgotten about them. 'Only I 'spect they'll remember soon,' Daisy had said hopefully. 'Not that it matters, 'cos we've both got friends in school, haven't we, Petal? Mine's called Gwennie and Petal's is called Sian. The four of us play together at weekends, and now the evenings are getting lighter we'll probably play after school as well.'

So Rose received letters from the children with pleasure, and now she eyed the second letter with considerable curiosity. It was from Steve – she knew his writing well – and it was postmarked Portsmouth which, she knew, was near Gosport. But it was also fat, and in the past Steve's communications had never run to more than a single page of his untidy – and rather illiterate – scrawl. So she slit the envelope and pulled out the contents with more interest than usual. Immediately, she saw the reason for the thick envelope; there was a letter to herself, but he had also enclosed letters to the children. Each one had the name printed on it, though no address, and both were stamped. Rose smiled a little; clearly, Steve's intention was still to win back his children's trust, and when she felt the envelopes she was pretty sure that something more than a letter was contained therein. It might be money, or a little brooch or badge. He had obviously enclosed a small present with each letter.

But right now, the most important thing was to read her own epistle and find out whether he had become a submariner or if he had already changed his mind, so she bent her head and concentrated.

Dear Rose,

    Well, here we are, nearly at the end of our training and though it's been tough, it was certainly no worse than I expected. We've done all sorts, learned how to operate the controls, stared through the periscope until we could make sense of what we could see and used the escape hatch . . . a nasty business. But we're settling down, learning to trust one another – and trust is real important aboard a sub. I can't tell you too much about the sub we'll be joining except that she's called Centurion *and has a crew of thirty-three. I say 'we' because I've got a mate, a grand feller. His name is Ted and he's from Southampton – married, like myself, with two little girls; what a coincidence, eh? There's a rumour that the* Centurion *has come into dry dock for repairs and will go back to the Med, with us aboard, when she's fit again. Not bad, eh? All of them lovely beaches and gorgeous Maltese girls . . . but you don't have to worry about them, not looking the way you do. I think about you all the time, and the girls of course. Write often, my love, and tell the girls to write as well. I know they aren't with you but I know, also, that you'll be in close touch.*

All my love, Steve.

Rose stared at the letter, her chin dropped on her fists. There was something . . . something not quite right here. Submarine training was all very well but surely it would not have altered the style in which Steve wrote? It was his writing all right, but there was something strange . . .

Carefully, she conned the letter again, examining each word, then gave a whoop as realisation dawned; when she looked closely, she could see that, originally, the writer had begun to write one name and had replaced it with *Ted*. Suspicion growing, she realised that *Southampton*, too, had originally been something else. She sat back in her chair, scarcely knowing whether to laugh or cry. Steve had copied another man's letter, word for word. She had no doubt that, in the original, the friend's name had been Steve, and the town in which he lived Liverpool. She could imagine, all too clearly, how Steve would sprawl across the table in the mess, tongue curling out of the corner of his mouth, concentrating so hard on his copying that he had almost forgotten to transpose Ted for his own name and Southampton for Liverpool. Once, she might have been really annoyed, but now she could understand why he had done it. He had no ability with a pen, insufficient imagination to pass on to someone else what he had seen and done. Yet he had clearly wanted her to know that he was not unhappy, that he was looking forward to joining the *Centurion*, and that he had found a good friend. If he had to cheat a little bit to get the news across to her, so what? People did many worse things – Steve had done worse things himself; she should be grateful that he had taken the time to write, even if he had copied his friend Ted's letter. As she went to put the letter down on the table again the last page folded itself and she saw there was something written on the back of it. She turned it over, then grinned. *PS Rose – I miss Alby, course I do, but this feller Ted's real grand. He's goin to help me keep off of the drink.*

He had only signed the postscript with his initial, which was far more typical than the *All my love, Steve* with which the main letter had ended.

Rose carried the letter over to the dresser and put it in the drawer on the right, where she kept such things. Then she returned to the table and looked long and hard at the letters Steve had sent to their daughters. It seemed awfully sneaky to open them, but the kettle was steaming on the hob and no one need ever know. Presently, she tipped the contents of both out on to the table, keeping them separate so that they would both go back into their original envelopes. Then she read the letters which, she thought, were pretty much as her own letter had been . . . probably copies of what Ted had written to his own daughters. There was no mention of the fracas which had sent Steve off to volunteer for submarines, but she was extremely annoyed, when she opened the little cotton-wool-wrapped parcels, to find that Petal's contained a shiny new shilling and Daisy's a sixpence and a threepenny joe. She did not believe that this was meanness – it must have been the only cash he had had on him at the time – but the fact that he had sent more money to the child he had not attacked, but who happened to be his favourite, hurt her so much, for Daisy's sake, that she jumped to her feet, fetched her own purse, and found a silver shilling, thinking Steve's ninepence a fair enough exchange for peace of mind. Then she carefully resealed and addressed the envelopes; she would post them in the morning, as she went to work.

She was on her way up to bed when a thought which had never entered her head before stopped her in her tracks. When he was sober, men liked Steve. Alby had considered him good company, a grand person to be with, and Ted clearly felt the same. When they had first married, Steve had been popular with the crowd who went to the football matches on a Saturday afternoon, with his workmates, with the boy cousins he had played with as a youth. When he was drunk, they avoided him, which was both natural and sensible, but when he was sober, they actually liked him.

Slowly, Rose began to mount the stairs once more. She had heard girls in the factory speak of someone as being 'a man's man', and now she thought that this description fitted Steve perfectly. He could admire and respect a man, but never a woman, so it stood to reason that he should never have married.

And his marrying, she could admit it now, had been partly, at least, her own fault. She had found his good looks, the sheer size of him, as well as his swaggering attitude, irresistible. And then there had been the heady pleasure of defying her parents, insisting that Steve McAllister was the only man she would ever love, dogging his footsteps. He had been flattered, she was pretty sure of that. The best-looking girl in the neighbourhood, a well-brought-up, intelligent girl, albeit only sixteen, crazy about him – who would not have been flattered? She had virtually thrown herself into his arms – could one entirely blame him for catching her, marrying her . . . and then reverting to type?

But now it seemed that, having come to his senses at last, if only temporarily, he was trying to behave as other, better, men did. He had tried to imitate Alby, when the drink had been getting the better of him; and then their ship had gone down and they had been assigned to different vessels and fear, superstition, call it what you will, had sent Steve staggering off to the nearest pub to drown his sorrows. And then, of course, he had become violent, had attacked Daisy . . .

And now, in a sense, he had come full circle, she thought as she undressed and slipped into bed. Though he was still trying to reform, it was too late. When he emerged from the Navy he would be a single man once more because his wife and children would be far away, and safe from him for ever.

And on this thought, Rose slept at last.

Daisy and Petal had discussed what they should write in their letters, how much to tell their mother, and had come to the conclusion that they had best tell her only the good things about their new foster home. Indeed, most of what they wrote, and what they had told her when she visited, was no more than the truth. Mrs Wyn Roberts was kind, in her way, and was always asking them if they were happy, making friends, getting enough to eat. To be sure, they did do a great deal of housework, but they were also allowed to play with their friends in the garden or in the big attic nursery at the top of the house.

What they did not mention to either Rose or anyone else was that Edith hated them, not because they were children, or a nuisance, but because they were from Liverpool, and this meant that she hated their mother, too, and everyone living in Bernard Terrace, everyone attending St Ambrose School.

From the moment that they had returned to the house after Rose's departure, the maid had made it plain how she felt. 'Two dirty little scousers,' she had said malevolently. 'Not fit to clean my shoes, you ain't, with your thievin' ways, your filthy language. Makes me sick, you does, sick just to hear that 'orrible accent, them 'orrible expressions! I tell you, if them bloody Huns did one good thing it were to drop bombs on Liverpool. I wish they'd flatten the whole stinkin' city, that I do.'

Against such outright loathing, what could they do? Tell Mam that Edith hated them, wanted them dead? Well, they could, Daisy thought, but all it would do would be worry Mam, make her strain every nerve to get them billeted with other people, and other people might be worse. Edith fed them on the leavings from Mrs Wyn Roberts's table; once she had given them each a bowl of thick vegetable soup (she called it *cawl*) and when they had eaten it, had told them she had pissed in the pan before pulling it over the fire.

Daisy had gone green and rushed for the sink, where she had vomited the soup up, but Petal had looked coldly at Edith and said: 'I don't believe you. You say scousers are liars, but you are worse. You look like a toad and you behave like one too. You're slimy and nice to Mrs Wyn Roberts because she's important, and you're horrible to us because we aren't. Don't you know the poem: *Taffy was a Welshman, Taffy was a thief, Taffy came to our house and stole a leg of beef*? Well, I thought that were just a cruel lie, but it's true about you. You steal the food that our ration books buy, and you tell lies. I can't imagine you squatting over that little pan and piddling into it – your knees would give out, so they would!'

It had made Daisy feel better, but she realised that they had to make a stand. Edith gave them bread, potatoes and leftover scraps, but never made them a proper meal, and though they had a hot dinner at school they often went to bed hungry. She wondered about telling Mrs Wyn Roberts, tried timidly to point out that their breakfast and tea were makeshift meals, but Mrs Wyn Roberts arched her fair brows and stared at Daisy, disbelief written all over her face. 'But last night we had a beautiful mutton stew. The night before it was vegetable pie with a tiny piece of liver each, and the night before that—'

'We didn't have any of that,' Daisy had said boldly. 'We had potato and a bit of cabbage one night, and bread and jam the other. And – and not very much bread and jam, either,' she added, her voice sinking almost to a whisper.

'But Edith has assured me that she's too busy to cook nursery meals so we all have the same,' Mrs Wyn Roberts said, with an air of finality. 'Of course, I know that rich food would be bad for children – it would give you nightmares – but Edith is very careful never to overload your little stomachs. And besides, so much food is rationed that eating truly well is next to impossible. Though I do believe the food Edith has provided these past few weeks has been better than it was earlier in the year. I suppose it's because, as the weather grows finer, things become easier, though I'm sure I don't know why.'

Daisy murmured that the fact that Edith now possessed her own and Petal's ration books might have something to do with it, but Mrs Wyn Roberts was not listening. 'I've put Edith's wages up because she's trying so hard to make us good, nourishing meals,' she informed Daisy. 'After all, now that there are no other servants, she has to do all the marketing, and she goes from butcher to butcher trying to find someone who has got something available which isn't rationed.'

Daisy was so indignant at that remark that she spoke up. 'Edith gets the ration stuff but we do the rest of the messages,' she informed Mrs Wyn Roberts. 'It takes us hours after school and on a Saturday, going round the shops. We even walk out to the farm on Cefn Road for some of the messages.'

Mrs Wyn Roberts looked surprised. 'Messages!' She laughed gaily, then patted Daisy's cheek. 'Now I wonder what sort of messages my dear old Edith sees fit to send around the shops with two little girls as couriers? I expect she wants to know when various foodstuffs will become available, eh?'

Daisy stared at her, completely baffled. But before she could even try to explain, the front doorbell rang and Mrs Wyn Roberts got slowly and gracefully to her feet, shooing Daisy out of the room before her. 'Off with you to the kitchen, and tell Edith not to bother to come to the door, since I am on my way there myself,' she said briskly. 'I expect it will be Mrs Prothero with a knitting pattern which she is lending me.'

Daisy was still wondering what she should do about Edith and their meals, when Mr Wyn Roberts came home for what his wife described as 'a short break from routine, an end-of-year refresher'. The children, with the memory of their own father and his recent behaviour very fresh in their minds, regarded the announcement of their unwitting host's imminent arrival with considerable concern and Edith, seeing this, did her best to portray Mr Wyn Roberts as some sort of monster before his actual arrival. Petal said stoutly that she didn't care; if Edith didn't like him he was sure to be as nice as anything, and anyway, Mrs Wyn Roberts would not have married someone as horrible as the person she depicted. Nevertheless, both children nursed a secret dread of this 'short break from routine'.

Mr Wyn Roberts was arriving on the six o'clock train from London on Friday evening, and though the children suggested that his wife might like to meet the train she said, with a heavy sigh, that because of the war train times were no longer reliable, so she had instructed her husband to catch a taxi from the station.

'Only there isn't always a taxi,' Daisy said, remembering their own arrival. 'Suppose he has to walk, carrying his luggage? You can drive, can't you, Mrs Wyn Roberts? And there is a car in the garage, isn't there?'

'Yes, I can drive, but the car hasn't been used for months and months . . . there's probably no petrol, and anyway, as I said, the times of the London trains have been so disrupted by the bombing that I might be waiting for *hours*!'

Daisy heard the petulant note creep into Mrs Wyn Roberts's voice and realised that she should not ask any more questions; there was no point. Their hostess did not want to fetch her husband from the station and Daisy was realist enough to remember that it was, in any case, a pretty short walk, even carrying a heavy suitcase, and also that the porter had told them that the taxis were always there to meet the London train, but did not bother much for more local ones.

'We'll have dinner whenever Mr Wyn Roberts arrives . . . that is, he and I will dine then,' Daisy overheard Mrs Wyn Roberts telling Edith. 'And what should we have? I think . . . something special, but something which can be kept hot in the Aga, because heaven knows what time the train will actually reach the station. And a nice pudding, I think . . . there are still some apples in the loft over the garage, but they're past their best . . . do we have marmalade? I don't know whether you remember, Edith, because before the war you were never called upon to cook, but marmalade roll with custard was quite one of Mr Wyn Roberts's favourite puddings. Could you manage that, do you think? And perhaps cheese and biscuits with a nice cup of coffee to round the meal off?'

Edith said obsequiously that she would do her best, though she went on at some length about the difficulty of getting most of the ingredients her mistress had asked for, but since this was not at all unusual Mrs Wyn Roberts merely waited until Edith stopped telling her how hard life was and then said: 'That seems satisfactory; goodnight, Edith,' and sailed gracefully out of the kitchen and back to the white drawing room, where she spent most of her time.

On the Friday, Mr Wyn Roberts duly arrived. He was about the same height as his wife, which surprised Daisy for, without really thinking seriously about it, she had concluded that men were always taller than their wives – look at her parents! Rose was at least six inches shorter than Steve, and a great deal slimmer and more – well, more fragile, Daisy supposed. But Mr Wyn Roberts, though of a height with his wife, was downright skinny. 'You wouldn't think he were a feller whose favourite grub was marmalade pudding and custard,' Daisy whispered to her sister from their spy-hole halfway down the gracious staircase. 'He must be awful old . . . he's got hardly any hair and there are lines all over his face.'

In the days that followed, however, they found Mr Wyn Roberts, though strict, to be a good deal less fierce than Edith had led them to believe. He expected certain things of them – punctuality, particularly at mealtimes, and at getting up and bed times – politeness to all grown-ups and instant obedience when asked to perform some small task. But so far as Daisy and Petal were concerned, the happiest result of his week-long stay was a change in their routine which benefited them greatly. On the second day, Mr Wyn Roberts came into the kitchen, his wife trailing behind him, and glanced frowningly round. Edith and the children were preparing vegetables, and stopped their work as the master of the house addressed them. 'I've decided we shall all benefit if, in future, everyone, including myself and my wife, eats all their meals in the kitchen. It will save Edith carrying heavy trays up the stairs, but most of all it will save fuel. I expect you know that a great many miners – the younger, fitter men – are now in the armed forces; their place has been taken by conscientious objectors – conchies, folk call them – but they don't have the experience or the strength of the men they have replaced. So, as the war goes on, coal will become a rarer and rarer commodity. To have a fire in three rooms is ridiculous, a wicked waste, so in future, Edith, the only fire you kindle must be that in the kitchen.'

Mrs Wyn Roberts gave a bleat of protest. 'Oh, but, Henry, I can't possibly get myself up early enough to share breakfast with the children. They have to eat before eight in order to get to school on time. And how can I possibly perform all my many tasks in a room without a fire? I shall simply freeze to death!'

'No you won't,' Mr Wyn Roberts said robustly. 'You will bring whatever work you may have down to the kitchen. I've arranged with the GPO to come in and re-route the telephone so that it can be placed on the kitchen dresser. That will save either yourself or Edith having to run all the way to the white drawing room whenever it rings. As for breakfast in bed, my dear, that is a luxury no one can afford in wartime. Surely you've heard that song the soldiers all sing . . . now what are the words?'

Petal's hand shot up. 'I know it!' she squeaked. '*This is the army, Mr Jones, No private rooms or telephones, You've had your breakfast in bed before, But you won't get it here any more.*'

Mr Wyn Roberts actually smiled, though his wife stared stonily before her. 'Well, well, it seems we have quite a little songstress among us,' Mr Wyn Roberts said. 'Now I hope I'll hear no more objections to what is, in truth, sheer common sense.'

His wife stared at him with scarcely veiled hostility and Daisy realised that these arrangements had come as as much of a shock to Mrs Wyn Roberts as they had to Edith and themselves. She gazed at Mr Wyn Roberts with dawning respect. He might be old and skinny, with weak eyesight which needed the help of heavy horn-rimmed glasses, but he was not afraid to take unpopular decisions.

When no one spoke, Mr Wyn Roberts continued. 'I shall write out a timetable and suggest some menus which will be a good deal easier for everyone,' he said, in his deep, unaccented voice. Daisy had noticed that Mr Wyn Roberts, though a Welshman to the core, did not speak with a local accent. He had told the children he had never learned Welsh as he had gone to a local prep school in Chester until he was eight and from there been sent to an English boarding school.

Mr Wyn Roberts turned back towards the kitchen door, but before he could leave the room his wife spoke again, her voice unnaturally high. 'And I suppose you are going to have the front door lifted off its hinges and brought round to the back so that we shan't have to go along all those passages whenever someone rings or knocks?'

239

Daisy expected an outburst of anger from Mr Wyn Roberts, but instead he beamed at his wife with what appeared to be genuine pleasure. 'Clara, my dear, you think of everything. I am a lucky man to be married to someone with such a keen brain. Oh, I know you were only joking, but you've got the right idea; we will affix a large, permanent notice to the front door, instructing all callers to take the side path round to the back of the house and knock loudly upon the kitchen door.'

Daisy thought there was a rather tense moment whilst Mrs Wyn Roberts made up her mind how to take this remark. But either discretion was the better part of valour, or their hostess had decided to accept the praise as her due. She inclined her head graciously, then addressed the maid. 'Well, Edith, it seems that we are to learn to share this beautiful kitchen in future. I shall be able to help you with meal preparation far more easily than I have done in the past.' She turned to her husband. 'Come along, my dear; you promised to accompany me to Chester to visit my sister this morning; she won't like it if we're late.'

For several moments after the Wyn Robertses left the kitchen, Daisy and Petal sat uneasily at the table, continuing to shred cabbage. Daisy half expected an outburst from Edith, for when the older woman realised the full import of Mr Wyn Roberts's changes she was sure to be cross. With all of them sharing a meal, Daisy was sure it would not be possible for Edith to give them nothing but cabbage whilst she and her mistress feasted on stew, or chops, or sausages. Edith had stomped over to the sink and started peeling potatoes, so Daisy could not see her face, but soon the old woman dropped the last peeled potato into the pot and carried the latter across to the Aga, though she stood it to one side since their main meal was always taken in the evening.

She said not a word, but presently Daisy heard a very odd sound issuing from the old woman's direction. She looked across and saw that Edith's shoulders were shaking; surely she was not crying? Mr Wyn Roberts's changes would make her life very much easier, though of course she might not relish sharing her kitchen with her mistress.

But as Edith turned away from the stove, Daisy saw that she was laughing, laughing so helplessly that tears ran down her cheeks, uttering great whoops as though the laughter had been locked inside her for so long that it could not come out in a quiet and orderly fashion, but must emerge in whoops and gasps.

When, at last, the laughs hiccuped to a halt, Daisy gave Petal a nudge in the ribs. 'You ask her,' she muttered. 'You gerraway with more'n I can, 'cos you're only a kid still.'

Petal nodded. 'Edith, why's you laughing?' she asked baldly. 'We've never heard you laugh before, me an' Daisy.'

'I never had cause before,' Edith said. 'But the thought of that idle, fat cow havin' to get up for breakfast, which she hasn't never done since I've known her, and havin' to live in the kitchen along a' me . . . well, it was enough to make a cat laugh.' She glared ferociously at Petal. 'And don't you go tellin' no tales, sayin' that I called the mistress names, because that I never would. I – I'm . . . *hee-hee-hee* . . . I'm her devoted slave, everyone knows that.'

Later that day, on their way to the shops to purchase some bones for stock, Daisy and Petal discussed the enigma that was Edith, but came to no very definite conclusion; the only thing they did realise was that, thanks to Mr Wyn Roberts, life would be a good deal easier for them from now on. They knew Mrs Wyn Roberts was lazy but she was not unkind. Once they were all eating together, she would see that they got a fair share of the food.

'But suppose Mrs Wyn Roberts goes back to breakfast in bed and so on and doesn't live in the kitchen any more when Mr Wyn Roberts leaves?' Petal asked rather apprehensively as they came out of the butcher's market and headed for Chester Street. 'She might, you know.'

But Daisy had already thought this out and shook her head. 'Mrs Wyn Roberts is really very fond of Mr Wyn Roberts and she wouldn't do anything to upset him,' she observed. 'Besides, she has lots of visitors, you know, and most of them are friends or relatives of his who might easily let slip that they'd been given tea in the white drawing room, or something like that. And then there's Edith. You bet she can tell tales with the best.'

Petal admitted that this was so and the children returned home feeling that life had definitely taken a turn for the better.

Chapter Nine
April 1941

Steve's training was finished and he and the rest of the crew of HMS/M *Centurion* had been sent to Malta by the submarine service – or 'the Trade' as it was known to the submariners – whence they scoured the Mediterranean, attacking enemy shipping, and sometimes coming back to port after a ten-day patrol with the skull and crossbones flying and two or three more definite kills to their name.

Oddly enough, the thing that he had most dreaded had not come to pass. Steve had always disliked – feared – enclosed spaces yet he had no such feelings aboard the *Centurion*, even when she was sailing at her maximum depth. He felt safe from the terrors he had known aboard HMS *Jericho*, almost began to think of the sea as a friend. Now, *they* were the lurking peril searching for prey. *They* were the wolf pack, the terror which struck from below on a calm, blue day; it was their torpedoes which streaked through the water whilst men were relaxing, asleep in their bunks, eating a meal.

He said as much to Ted as the two of them were sprawled in the mess. 'I never thought I'd say it, but I prefer subs to surface ships,' he remarked. 'We're like – like invisible to them up above. They don't even know we're there until they feel the deck moving under them and hear the explosion. Oh aye, I'd rather be a wolf than a sheep, if you see what I mean.'

Ted was writing to his wife; Steve to Alby. The

correspondence between the two men was, naturally, of a sporadic and infrequent nature but, whenever he got into port, Steve looked as anxiously for a letter from Alby as Rachel would have done. He had been parted from his friend by fate and the exigencies of war, but he did not intend to lose touch with the other man. They were both Liverpudlians and would both return to their native city when hostilities ceased. If they kept in regular touch, then they would simply pick up their friendship where it had left off. So Steve was determined to keep up the correspondence, hard labour for him though it might be.

Ted looked up from his own letter with a grin. 'So you like being the hunter, rather than the hunted, eh? Just you wait, me old china, until we're lyin' on the bottom, pretendin' to be a rock with ten battleships circling above and depth charges goin' off all round us. I know they fired at us yesterday, but that was nothing compared to what some subs go through.'

Despite the fact that he and Ted were, so to speak, in the same boat, their attitudes were totally different. Steve paid very little attention to words or warnings. It was actual personal experience which had taught him the lessons he had learned in life. His mother had told him to be gentle with women, but his father had shown him how the force of a blow could give him power over others; showing, not telling, was what counted for Steve.

Now, Steve agreed with what Ted had said, but was only paying lip service since, so far, the *Centurion*, ably captained by their young skipper, had nipped into dangerous situations, struck with deadly accuracy at fat merchantmen, or at the warships surrounding them, and had nipped out again, untouched.

Their most recent attack had been almost unsporting

since they had sneaked into a smallish Greek harbour, sunk three caiques, and left before their presence had been so much as suspected. Steve had heard some of the men muttering but the skipper knew best and he said the caiques were being used as gun boats and were probably manned by German sailors, which made them fair game.

Steve signed off with a flourish and slipped his letter into an envelope, but did not seal it down. The censor would have to see it before it could be sent, and since he had no idea in which theatre of war Alby's new ship operated, he had no idea, either, how long the letter would be on its journey. Ted, finishing his own letter at the same time, stood up and stretched. 'Do you want me to check that for you?' he said, indicating Steve's missive. 'I will if you like . . .' but at that moment the skipper sent the crew to action stations and Steve went to his position by the forward plane controls. Taking up his position, he thought, regretfully, that this would probably delay their meal by some while. On a small submarine, there was no regular cook, the men taking it in turns to prepare the meals. Today it was his turn and he had planned to make Cheese Oosh: a delectable mixture of milk, cheese, powdered egg, tomato and mustard which was much prized by the crew of the *Centurion*. But Cheese Oosh would have to wait; Steve sat down, resting his hands lightly on the wheel before him, and prepared for action.

This time, even Steve realised that they were in a sticky situation and would need phenomenal luck to get out of it. The *Centurion* had gone in low and deep, believing the ships above them to be in a half-circle, intending to do the maximum amount of damage in the shortest possible time, whilst relying on surprise to get them out of the half-circle before any ship could retaliate.

It had not been a half circle but a full one, and since it was daylight they had been spotted through the crystal clear waters of the Mediterranean, probably by their shadow on the sandy bottom, for the Mediterranean was a tricky sea. There were hills and valleys, plateaux and rifts on the sea bed, and they had not stuck to the valleys and rifts because the skipper had been too intent on the prey and had not realised that he could be seen. Everyone had been at battle stations but they had not had a chance to fire as much as one torpedo before the depth charges began.

At times, these were too close for comfort, so the skipper had decided to make a run for it; to go deeper. Fortunately, they had almost immediately found just what he was looking for: a sea valley so deep that when they reached the bottom, it was at their maximum depth of two hundred and fifty feet and they knew they could no longer be seen, although the ships above probably had a shrewd suspicion that they were still somewhere around.

'They'll go presently,' Ted murmured in Steve's ear. 'They've got a destination to reach; they can't hang around on the off chance that we're still here. In a couple of hours, Skip will bring us up to have a look around.'

The hours passed; every now and then, a depth charge exploded, giving the lie to the hope that the enemy would move on. Once it grew dark, they would have a better chance of getting away, but turning propellers was the sort of thing the hydrophones would pick up on immediately, and then the depth charges

246

would start in earnest. Steve guessed that most of the convoy would have moved on, intent on reaching their destination, but probably leaving a destroyer behind to deal with them when they tried to surface.

The air was growing fouler; Steve's chest ached with every indrawn breath. He had been on the forward plane waiting for the signal to move his controls. But, like every man aboard, or all the ones he could see at any rate, he was now lying prone, conserving energy, conserving air, praying to God that they would be able to surface before the air ran out completely.

Beside him, someone moved. Jacky was throwing up, almost silently, into the bucket of diesel. A sour stench filled the air – what air there was – but the diesel dealt with that, and presently the skipper came quietly amongst them. He wanted a volunteer to go and change the batteries, which would give them perhaps half an hour more of breathable air. The trouble was, the space through which one had to wriggle to reach the batteries was extremely shallow – a bare twelve or fourteen inches. The skipper was sturdy, even though the men always reckoned to lose at least a stone of weight in the course of a ten-day patrol.

The skipper had written on a sheet of paper, *I want a volunteer to change the batteries*, and Steve immediately raised a hand. He had always prided himself on his slim figure and knew he was perfectly capable of wriggling through the narrow space and changing the batteries; he had done it often enough before, heaven knew.

Skip gave him the thumbs up sign and Steve stood up with great care. As the atmosphere had thinned, it had grown hotter and hotter, and he was already stripped down to singlet and shorts, his feet bare. He squeezed into the narrow space and was disconnecting the batteries when he heard, behind him, a muffled thud and an unwary exclamation. Startled, he tried to turn, then scolded himself for stupidity. He had gone in forwards but must retreat backwards; he would find out who had made that God-awful din when he was back with the others. He was actually trying to wriggle out of the narrow space when there was a tremendous explosion and the sea came roaring in. For a moment, he fought to escape. He tried to hold his breath but the sea was too strong. It roared in, unstoppable, stronger even than the *Centurion*, the old, remorseless enemy. Oddly, as he realised that this was the end, a picture of Rose as she had been on their wedding day came into his mind. The wide, innocent eyes, the adoring look in them as they fell on her new husband. What had gone wrong, he thought confusedly. She had changed; hardened. It had all been her fault, the failure of their marriage, the fact that his daughters no longer loved him.

Then the water forced itself into his lungs, stomach, ears, eyes and nostrils. Darkness was merciful as the sea took him.

Rose came out of the house in Bernard Terrace, tin hat in position, gas mask on one shoulder and two cheese sandwiches in the left-hand pocket of her coat. It was a fine, clear night, the stars bright in the dark heavens above. Because she had been on early shift that day, Rose had had a good rest in the afternoon, so when the siren sounded she had not been to bed and was able to leave the house at once, fully dressed and ready, she told herself, for anything.

She headed for the tall building where she would be firewatching as long as the raids lasted. The streets

248

were full of scurrying figures, some making for the air raid shelters, others for their posts, and Rose was greeted by several people as they hurried along. Reaching her destination, she climbed the long flight of metal stairs to the roof. The moonlight was too bright, she thought apprehensively, settling herself in the shadow of a large chimney stack. By now, everyone knew all about the bomber's moon and indeed, as she looked up at the great silver disc, Rose saw the first enemy aircraft silhouetted against the stars, heard the steady thrum of its engine. Then she saw others and her heart gave an uncomfortable jump. Great black, lumbering shapes; they came on relentlessly, and soon she heard the first bombs fall, though they seemed to be some way off. Birkenhead docks? She could not say for sure, but of course they would be aiming for the docks, for the unprotected shipping lying there, for the warehouses, full of desperately needed supplies, which lined the quayside.

Usually, there were two of them firewatching from this particular position since the roofs covered an enormous area, but there was no time to check round for Violet Pierce, her opposite number. Rose saw a fire blossom, calculated its position, and made for the stairs at a run, almost colliding with a figure coming up them. It was Violet, looking shaken.

'Sorry I'm late,' she gasped. 'But I'd just got into bed when the sirens started so I had to dress and that. Anything happened?'

Rose swung past her, calling back over her shoulder as she did so. 'Big fire over towards the docks; a warehouse, I should think. I'll report it to the warden's post and come straight back because, by the sound of those engines, we're going to have a busy night of it!'

* * *

It was a bad night, but worse was to follow. Rose was kept constantly on the go, both on the Thursday night and the Friday night, and greeted Saturday with real relief. It was her day off and she would be able to rest instead of having to work, for though many shops, factories and other buildings had been hit her own place of work was pretty much untouched, and uniforms, the boss had told them severely, were always needed; production must not be allowed to fall just because the Luftwaffe had decided to give the docks a pasting.

Only it wasn't just the docks, as the people of Liverpool soon realised. Bombs were falling everywhere. Homelessness was commonplace – you would go out to the shelter at night and come home to a smoking ruin.

Rose came off firewatching duty in the early hours of Saturday morning and went home to Bernard Terrace – and straight to bed. Once, she would have found it impossible to sleep during daylight, especially on a lovely May morning, with the sun shining from a cloudless sky, but now she was far too tired to appreciate the fine weather. She crawled into bed and slept the clock round, then got up, made herself a quick meal of beans on toast, and sat down at the kitchen table to write a reassuring letter to the children. She realised that the BBC might well mention the raids on Liverpool, though she did not think the children listened to the wireless much. A set was kept in the white drawing room so that Mrs Wyn Roberts could keep abreast of the war, but the children, busy about their own concerns, were not likely to be told worrying news by their kindly hostess.

Rose wrote steadily. She told them that she had visited Aunt Selina and Uncle Frank, who were enjoying country life. They had purchased a piglet and four hens and had intended to fatten the piglet for the table, but had grown so fond of it that she doubted they would ever bring themselves to do the necessary. There was a woman called Mrs Higgins – did the girls remember her? – who lived three doors further along Penny Lane; she had offered to run the shop for a fifty per cent share of the profits. Uncle Frank thought he could trust Mrs Higgins and had taken up her offer and now only visited the shop once a week.

Rose finished off with the usual line of kisses. Last time she wrote, she had enclosed Steve's latest letter for, to her secret astonishment, he had begun to write regularly and cheerfully, and had made it clear that he was happier as a submariner than he had ever been aboard ordinary ships.

Rose had wondered whether to send the letter to the children but, in the end, had decided to do so, in fairness to Steve. Submariners were highly regarded by the rest of the Navy, and Steve had signed on to try to show his children, and his wife, that he wasn't all bad, as he had put it. So Rose thought her daughters should know that life aboard the *Centurion* was not everyone's cup of tea and that their father, in his own way, was a brave man.

In fact, having thought long and hard, Rose had concluded that Steve loved the life, partly because of its total masculinity, and also because the thirty-three men aboard the *Centurion* were like an extremely close-knit family; something Steve had never known, or appeared to want, before. If he had had sons instead of daughters, things might have been easier at home, but as it was it had taken the Navy – and most of all HMS/M *Centurion* – to show him what he wanted from life. Having been the target of German U-boats, he was obviously prepared to put up with a good deal in order to be the wolf rather than the sheep.

When the knock came on the door, she glanced at the clock on the mantel and wondered whether Violet had come to visit. The sky was still clear and the moon would be bright later, but that did not mean there would be yet another raid. She hurried to the front door and pulled it open, and there was Rachel, smiling a little apologetically. 'Rachel! It's lovely to see you; I miss you dreadfully at work. But what on earth are you doing here . . . oh, for goodness' sake, where are my manners? Do come in. I've got the kettle on, and I dare say you'd like a cup of tea.'

She ushered Rachel into the kitchen, sat her down in an easy chair and then began to pour the tea, talking as she did so. 'Have you seen the doctor lately? You're due any time now, aren't you? I know how they keep changing one's dates – at least they did with me. When I was expecting Daisy, I told my mam I thought there was a conspiracy and that my pregnancy was going to last for at least ten years.'

Rachel laughed. 'It does seem a bit like that,' she said ruefully, running a hand over her enormous stomach. 'But I'm actually due tomorrow, and that's why I've come.'

'Tomorrow!' Rose said, staring at her friend. She could not help thinking that this was not a good time to be giving birth, with the Luftwaffe trying so hard to flatten the city. But of course no one could choose when their baby was born; it was pot luck. 'Rachel, if you don't mind, I'll work while we talk, because if there's a raid I shall be going to the shelter and I usually make myself a few sandwiches and a bottle of cold tea to take with me.'

'Oh!' Rachel said. 'Well, let's hope there isn't. The

thing is, Mam and Dad have moved out to the country – they didn't want to, not with the baby due so soon, but I told them I'd be more worried about them if they stayed than they would be about me if they went, so they agreed to go. It was a relief, I can tell you, because my mam kept telling me I was eating for two and trying to pile my plate until I told her that if I ate any more I'd burst; but you know what mams are. She's so keen to have the perfect grandchild that she doesn't care how uncomfortable I am so long as the baby's fine. And that's why she made me promise not to stay at home alone at nights once the baby was due; she made me swear on the Bible – the Old Testament, of course – that I wouldn't, and I did – swear, I mean . . . well, promise, anyway,' she finished.

'But what if there is another raid tonight?' Rose said, feeling harassed. 'I think you ought to go along to the hospital, honestly I do, Rachel. I believe they've got cellars where patients can shelter during raids, and then if anything did happen – if you started to have the baby, I mean – you'd have doctors and nurses all around you; don't you think that might be best?'

'Oh, but, Rose, the hospital might not like it,' Rachel said, looking distraught. 'I – I don't want to put their backs up, if you know what I mean. After all, I'm not a patient until my pains start.'

'Ye-es, I see what you mean,' Rose said, though a trifle doubtfully. Although she'd had two children herself, she had never seen another woman in labour, let alone helped to deliver a child, and found herself hoping, devoutly, that she never would. She honestly thought that Rachel would be very foolish to risk having the baby under any but ideal conditions. However, it was clearly useless to say so now. If there was a raid – and a glance at the kitchen window confirmed that it was another fine evening – then that was the time to decide just where her friend should spend the hours of darkness.

It was around quarter past ten when the sirens went off, interrupting Rose and Rachel, who were having a lively discussion over babies' names. Rose jumped to her feet and began to struggle into her coat, for though the day had been warm and the night was mild, she knew that the wind would be cold. Rachel stood up at the same time and began to pull on her own coat.

'I'll come with you to the shelter. I'm not going to have the baby for at least twenty-four hours,' Rachel said authoritatively. 'They told me at the hospital that babies stop moving twenty-four hours before they decide to get born and my little chap has been kicking and pounding all day, so let's get going.'

'All right, if you're sure,' Rose said, rather doubtfully. She did not recall that either Daisy or Petal had stopped bounding around inside her twenty-four hours before their arrival. And indeed, halfway to the shelter, Rachel suddenly stopped and clutched her arm. 'Rose! Oh, Rose, I feel . . . I feel . . .'

They had been about to cross Everton Brow and they could hear the planes, the thrum, thrum of their engines sounding all too familiar. Rose tried to hurry Rachel on, but her friend resisted. 'I'll have to stand still for a minute . . . there was a horrid, tearing pain . . . oh, my goodness!'

'What is it, what is it?' Rose said anxiously. Then her eyes followed Rachel's gaze downwards. In the moonlight, there was a dark stain spreading across the pavements beneath her friend's feet. 'Oh, Rachel, don't say you're bleeding! You *must* get to hospital. Really you must.'

She looked wildly around her, but already the street was almost deserted, save for a tall figure – probably an air raid warden – coming towards them. But Rachel was answering, shaking her head. 'No, I'm not bleeding, or I don't think so, at any rate. I think my w-waters have broken. You were right, Rosie, I really ought to be at the hospital.'

Rose gazed at her friend in an agony of indecision. They were a long way from the hospital but quite near the air raid shelter. The trams and buses would have stopped running when the sirens sounded and she did not think she could get Rachel to the hospital by herself. Her friend would very soon be unable to walk, but if she could reach the shelter, at least there would be others there who could help her if the baby really was about to be born. She was starting to say so, to urge Rachel towards the shelter, when a voice broke across her words.

'Excuse me, ma'am, but can you direct me to the nearest warden's post? I've offered my services but I got caught out and what with the blackout and the searchlights and the noise, I'm well and truly lost.'

Rose heard the soft American drawl with real relief. If he had been willing to help at the warden's post then surely, if she explained their desperate situation, he would be equally happy to help her to get Rachel off the street. In the moonlight, she could only see that he was tall and dark and wore a uniform of some sort.

She turned towards him, speaking briskly. 'Thank you so much, but my friend and I need your help far more urgently than the wardens could possibly do. Rachel's expecting a baby and I think it's started. She's booked into a hospital, but it's a fair way off and I'm simply not strong enough to help her to cover such a distance. If I could get her to the nearest shelter, though . . .'

The young man grinned; she could see the flash of his white teeth in the moonlight. He began to speak, but the foremost planes were overhead now and the roar of their engines and the whistle and crash of descending bombs made conversation impossible. The American looked round wildly, then put an arm round Rachel, motioning Rose to do the same. Then he shouted, 'Lead the way, ma'am. This is no place for any of us to be lingering. Point me to the shelter.'

They didn't make it. A few yards further along, someone opened a door, then hastily slammed it shut as light streamed out, for a second, on to the pavement. A man stood there, a tin hat on his head, struggling into his jacket. This time it was a real air raid warden and he addressed them angrily, wanting to know what they were doing in the street during an air raid. Rose began to explain, but the American said brusquely: 'This woman's giving birth, officer, and she needs a roof over her head. Open that durned door!'

The man complied, grumbling beneath his breath, and less than a minute later they had been ushered into the warden's sizeable kitchen. The warden did not like leaving them there – he was a small, ferrety man with mean, suspicious little eyes and a whiffling pink nose – but he had little choice, he told them. The nearest public shelter was already full to overflowing. His wife and children had taken their places on the bunk beds there some three hours previously, and they had not been the first by a long chalk. 'Don't you go touchin' nothin', nor stealin' nothin' neither,' he said nastily, turning to leave. 'I've got me duty to do, but when I checks the shelters I'll see if there's a nurse or a doctor what might pop along, give you a hand, like.'

'Thank you so much,' Rose said sarcastically. 'I take it you won't object if we boil some water. After all, water doesn't cost much and you've still got a decent fire in the stove.'

'Ah, I dare say you think she'll be wantin' a cup o' tea,' the warden said knowledgeably. 'Well, if you use any of my missus's tea, you'll have to pay us back. And don't go messin' up me kitchen or the wife'll say I were a fool to let you in and clack me head off.'

Nobody answered him. Rachel sat on a small easy chair by the hearth, moaning gently. Rose filled the kettle at the sink and carried it across to the fire, and after the warden had left and she had leisure to look around, she saw that the American was wearing Royal Air Force uniform. She also saw that he had a pleasant, craggy face, short, light-brown hair, and eyes of almost exactly the same shade. As she watched, he was removing his greatcoat, which he spread over Rachel, telling her that she was not to worry; he was going to fetch help.

He straightened up and Rose clutched his arm. 'Don't leave me,' she said in an urgent undertone. 'I've never seen a baby being born. I won't know what to do . . . and where will you find help with a raid going on?' Even as she spoke, an enormous explosion drowned her next words, so that she had to repeat them. 'The warden said he'd send a nurse.'

The American smiled and patted her shoulder. 'I'll get help of some sort,' he assured her. 'I wouldn't trust that mean little feller to remember any of us once he was out of here. Now you just keep your friend company; I'll be back before you've missed me.'

Despite Rose's fears, the American was as good as

his word. The kettle had scarcely boiled before the front door opened once more and a practical, grey-haired woman came briskly across the room towards them, a small black bag in her hand. The American hovered behind her. 'This is Sister Dawson, the local midwife,' he announced. 'She was in the shelter and volunteered to come at once.'

'Oh, thank God,' Rachel muttered. She tried to sit herself up in the chair, then collapsed back once more, but she smiled with determined brightness at Sister Dawson. 'They – they told me at the hospital to time the pains, sister, and not to start bearing down until they were coming every two or three minutes. So far, it's only every five or six, but I feel – I feel . . .'

Sister Dawson smiled reassuringly at her patient but looked disapprovingly round the kitchen, then addressed Rose. 'You'll be the friend who was taking her to hospital,' she said. 'Run upstairs and fetch bedding – and don't tell me Mr Parsons won't like it because I'll deal with him – and this young man here can bring the sofa through from the front room. I seem to remember a sofa in the front room the last time I visited here.'

Rose rushed to obey her, and when she came back to the kitchen with her arms full of blankets, the sofa was pulled up near the fire and Rachel was lying on it, her head supported on cushions. There was no sign of the American, which was fortunate since Sister Dawson had helped Rachel out of most of her clothing. As soon as she saw Rose, she took the bedding, wrapped Rachel in a sheet, and then folded it back in order to examine her patient thoroughly. Then she pressed a stethoscope against the mound of Rachel's stomach. Rose started to speak, to ask where the American had gone, but Sister Dawson shushed her impatiently and after a few moments removed the stethoscope and hung it round her neck, then patted Rachel's shoulder reassuringly. 'Well, the head is engaged, but he won't be born for an hour or two yet,' she said. 'Now, I'd best take a few details before the actual birth begins.' She took a note-book out of her capacious black bag and began to ask questions: Rachel's full name, age and address, the name of her doctor and details such as the hospital she should have entered, the names and addresses of her next of kin, her blood group, and so on.

In the middle of all this there was a small tap on the door. Rose hurried across and opened it. The American stood there, looking awkward. 'She turned me out because she said she had to get her patient prepped, whatever that might mean,' he whispered. 'She seems pretty competent so I'd have left and made my way to the warden's post, only she wouldn't let me take my greatcoat, not until you'd brought the blankets down, and I guess the air force would likely court martial me if I lost my uniform before I'd even reached my airfield.'

Rose smothered a giggle and glanced cautiously behind her, then gestured to him to enter the room. Rachel had the blankets up round her chin and was perfectly respectable, and Sister Dawson was putting away her notebook and getting to her feet, saying that they'd all be the better for a nice cup of tea, telling Rose to see if she could find a tin of biscuits in the pantry, and commanding the American to bring another chair through from the parlour, since they might as well make themselves comfortable.

She had already enquired Rose's name, but now she asked the American just who he was, and such was the authority of a pencil poised above a small notebook that he gave the information immediately.

'I'm Luke Nadolski; I'm a flyer, come over from the States to join your RAF,' he said. 'I was making my way to the nearest warden's post to see if I could help any, when I came across these young ladies. So if you've done with me, I'd best be getting along . . .'

All the time they had been speaking, the whistle and roar of descending bombs had been sounding outside, and now Sister Dawson shook her head at him. 'You're not going anywhere, Mr Nadolski,' she said reprovingly. 'For a start, there's no point in sending you out to the warden's post, because you'd never find it, not with bombs dropping everywhere and the streets full of flying glass.' She lowered her voice. 'And if anything goes wrong here, which is always possible, then I may need you.'

'Oh. Right,' Luke Nadolski said at once. 'Only I've never seen a baby born, ma'am, and I don't reckon I'll be much use.'

'You'll likely not see this one born either,' Sister Dawson said. 'But whatever happens, Mrs Cohen will have to go to hospital, even if it's after the birth, and someone will have to fetch an ambulance. Personally, I think it may be many hours before Mrs Cohen is delivered, but with first babies you can never tell. So pull up a chair and sit down.' She smiled suddenly at the American's obvious unease and winked at Rose. 'Don't worry, I'll send you out when the action starts. And now let's have that cup of tea!'

The baby, a boy, had been born as the sirens wailed the All Clear, by which time Rose felt as if she had known Luke all her life. She and he had accompanied Rachel and her baby to the hospital in the ambulance but had decided to walk back, since public transport would undoubtedly be in a state of chaos as the raid had been an extremely heavy one.

Luke had told her that he was not due at his airfield for a couple of days, so she had invited him back to Bernard Terrace for breakfast and a wash and brush-up. He had insisted upon leaving a message – and a ten shilling note – for the warden whose house they had commandeered so ruthlessly, and now they strolled along in the sunrise of a fine May morning, talking companionably, though the destruction around them was incredible; it seemed a miracle that the warden's house, and those of his neighbours, had escaped even from blast. As she and Luke walked along the littered road, glass crunching beneath their feet, she clutched his arm and pointed. 'My God! See that building over there? The one you can see right through because there's nothing left except the façade and the window frames? That . . . that was my firewatching post. If I'd been on duty last night . . .' She did not bother to finish the sentence; the hollow shell of the warehouse spoke for itself.

'My God,' Luke said softly. 'But I guess war is like that. I mean, if you'd directed me to the warden's post, I could have been killed on my way there. See what I mean?'

Rose nodded dumbly. What he said was true, but somehow the narrowness of her own escape had been like a kick in the stomach. She knew she would grow accustomed to what had happened, but felt that she needed time – and some sleep – before she would be able to come to terms with it. Meanwhile, she and Luke made their way steadily across the city, appalled by the extent of the destruction and by the fires which still raged.

They were deeply, dreadfully tired, for neither had got a wink of sleep all night. Rose had worked with Sister Dawson once the birth was imminent, pulling against Rachel's hands as she strove to give birth to her child, and when he arrived, scarlet-faced and furious, she had bathed the baby in the sink whilst Sister Dawson did all the important things and saw to the new mother.

Naturally, the American had been consigned to the front room whilst all this was going on, but as soon as Rachel was respectable once more, and the child tucked into the curve of her arm, Sister Dawson had dispatched him, with Rose as his guide, to the warden's post to get an ambulance. They had got Rachel and the baby to hospital, seen her comfortably settled, and then the two of them had set out to walk to Bernard Terrace.

When they reached Salisbury Street, Rose felt a tightening of her stomach muscles as apprehension gripped her; it would be too terrible if a bomb had landed on her little house. But there was no dust, no broken glass, no obvious destruction; Salisbury Street and its environs snoozed in the May sunshine, and as she turned into the terrace Rose felt a surge of relief. The short rows of houses faced each other, calm and undamaged, as though there had been no raid, no bombs, no raging fires.

Because Luke was a visitor, Rose did not head for the jigger but went straight to the front door, unlocking it and waving Luke hospitably inside. 'There won't be a fire, I'm afraid, but I've a nice modern gas stove, so I can heat you up some water on that,' she said cheerfully. 'Oh, but I am so tired and so thirsty! I could drink the Mersey dry and sleep the clock round . . . only we'll have breakfast first. You'll want to get back to where you're staying and sleep there before you go off to . . . Lincolnshire, was it? I'd offer you a bed but you'll want your stuff – you left your kit bag in your lodgings, I take it?' She had lit the gas under the kettle as she spoke and now turned and looked up at her companion, seeing for the first time the dark circles round his eyes and the exhaustion which carved lines on his face. She was suddenly aware that she felt light-headed with tiredness herself and realised that if she sat down and relaxed, she would almost certainly fall asleep. And it must be worse for him, she told herself, bustling across to the pantry to fetch bread and margarine, porridge oats, tea and condensed milk. He had returned the previous day from America where the air force had sent him to train as a bomber pilot. He had tried to make light of his journey back to Britain but she guessed that the strain must have been considerable; no wonder he looked so weary.

Rose worked quickly and presently they sat down to porridge, tea and toast. They talked little as they ate and drank, but by the time the meal was over and Luke had pushed back his chair and stood up, Rose had made up her mind. He began, haltingly, to thank her for the food and to ask for directions, but she interrupted him. 'Luke, there are perfectly good beds upstairs and you are far too tired to go roaming the streets and so am I. We'll both go upstairs and sleep until, say, four o'clock. I'll set my alarm so you needn't worry on that score. Then we'll go to your lodgings and make sure they haven't been bombed. Don't you think that's more sensible than forcing ourselves to go on being wakeful and alert when we need sleep so desperately? I'm on the night shift tonight, and tomorrow I'll be visiting Rachel in hospital and then doing my firewatching stint. What do you say?'

She had risen when he did. Rose was tall, but even

so, she had to look up to catch Luke's eye. He was staring at her, looking undecided, but then a wide smile lightened his face for a moment, and he nodded. 'Sure, Rose, if you don't mind my borrowing a bed, I'd be downright glad to crash out for a few hours. I am pretty well jiggered, to tell you the truth.'

'Good,' Rose said, leading the way up the stairs. They had each had a brief wash at the sink, but right now all she cared about was getting some sleep. She opened her bedroom door, then paused on the threshold. She had meant to let Luke use Daisy and Petal's bed, but now she realised that this would be unfair. Like Steve, he was long-legged and would be horribly cramped in the children's small bed, so she guided him into the room, picked up her alarm clock as unobtrusively as possible and then backed out of the room again as he stood there looking almost owlishly around him. 'I'll bang on the door at four o'clock and we'll have a cup of tea and a sandwich, and then go along to your lodgings,' she said. 'Sleep well, Luke.'

Closing the door softly, she crossed the narrow landing and went into the children's room. By now, she was so tired that undressing seemed out of the question, but she pulled off her thin jersey and wriggled out of her grey skirt, noticing how dusty both garments had become and wrinkling her nose at the smell of burning which still clung to them, for several times during the walk from the hospital they had had to make their way through smoke from burning buildings. Sitting on the edge of the bed, she set the alarm for four o'clock, doing so with such exaggerated care that she might have been a drunk, striving to appear sober. Then, smiling at the thought, she tumbled into bed and pulled the blankets up round her ears. For a moment, she lay there, enjoying the crisp cleanness of the sheets and the softness of the pillows beneath her head, thinking that she was probably too tired to sleep. She thought about Daisy and Petal, safe and secure in the Larches, and wondered what Luke was thinking about. Then, abruptly, with his face still before her inward eye, she fell deeply and dreamlessly asleep.

Luke took off his outer clothing, folding tunic and trousers carefully, rolling his socks into a ball and stuffing them into the toe of his boot. Then he sat down on the bed and contemplated the room. He had guessed immediately that it must be Rose's, and not that of the small daughters. He also guessed why she had let him use it, and as he climbed between the sheets and stretched out his long legs he was grateful to her. Beds in England – or the ones that he had slept in, at any rate – were made kind of short, so that he always felt he was stubbing his toes, but this bed was grand, with plenty of space for a guy to stretch out. Carefully, he snuggled his head into the pillow and was immediately aware of a faint, sweet perfume. Even as he breathed it in, he remembered Rose's face. It was a nice face with widely set brown eyes, a small straight nose and a mouth which, when she smiled, tilted upwards and formed a deep dimple in one cheek. Her chin was small but determined, her figure neat, with curves in all the right places. She had told him she was the mother of two girls, but he thought there was no sign of it in either face or figure; she might have been no more than twenty. He wondered what the children were like; whether they favoured her or her husband. She had told him that her submariner had blond curly hair and had shown him small photographs of her husband and the two children, though he had not looked closely at either. Rose had told him that the younger child had Steve's blond curls but had not commented on the older one, and the photograph had been too small and fuzzy to tell him much. Rose's own hair was a shining, chestnut brown, not curly or even wavy, but cut in the pageboy style which some film star had made popular. When the sun fell on it, its russet hue gleamed with touches of gold, fawn and copper; yes, it was the sort of hair which could be described as a crowning glory.

Luke yawned and put one hand beneath the pillow, feeling something soft enmesh his fingers. He grinned to himself; it was her nightie, of course, pushed under the pillow to be out of the way. Doubtless there would be pyjamas – Steve's – under the other pillow. He slid his hand further along to check, but found nothing and supposed that the submariner had either taken his pyjamas away with him or stowed them in the chest of drawers beneath the window. Thinking of the chest of drawers made him remember that he had forgotten to draw the drapes before getting into bed. He opened one eye a slit; yes, sunshine was streaming in, making it quite impossible to get to sleep. He must certainly remedy this – in a moment, he would climb out of bed and pull the drapes across. In a moment . . . but right now it was so comfy . . . he felt so relaxed, so at home . . .

He slept.

Chapter Ten

It had been Edith's weekend off, so the children had enjoyed a rest from her constant nagging and nastiness. But all good things come to an end and on Sunday evening, when they came back from playing with some schoolfriends near the allotments on Chester Road, there was Edith, cooking a meal in the kitchen. She turned as they entered the room and said snappishly: 'The mistress has gone a-visitin', so you'll have an early tea and then go straight to bed. I can't be doin' wi' the pair of you under me feet all evenin'.'

'All right, Edith,' Daisy said peaceably. She had no desire to start a row with the older woman, especially when there was no Mrs Wyn Roberts to put Edith smartly in her place if she became openly aggressive towards the children. 'But is there anything we can do to help you? We could lay the table, or . . .'

Edith turned and stared at them for a moment and Daisy saw, with some surprise, that the woman's face held a strange expression she had not seen on it before. It was not a nice expression. She had a sort of half-grin on her face, and Daisy thought it was a gloating sort of grin. But perhaps, she told herself, as Edith said she needed no help, not from the likes of *them*, it was better than the look of truly evil bad temper which Edith frequently wore when her weekend off approached. Come to that, she usually came back to the Larches in a foul mood, which often lasted a couple of days, so perhaps the peculiarly pleased look was some sort of improvement.

'Well, if we can't help then we'll play in the garden for a bit,' Daisy said, turning away from the stove and heading for the back door. 'Come on, Petal.'

Petal, however, lingered. 'What's for tea, Edith?' she enquired hopefully. 'We went over to Laura's house after Sunday school and her mam was out so we didn't get anything to eat. I'm starving, so I am.'

Edith turned and gave them a particularly nasty look. 'Snot sangwidges and sick soup,' she grated. 'That's all you bleedin' well deserve, you grubbin', grabbin' little pair. Now gerrout o' me kitchen and don't come back till I calls you.'

Daisy turned to leave the room without a word but Petal stood her ground for a moment. 'You're a rude old woman,' she said calmly. 'And if Mrs Wyn Roberts were at home you wouldn't dare say such things. If you say 'em again I'll tell on you . . . to Mr Wyn Roberts, I think. He wouldn't care if you left, you know . . . he'd probably like it, so just you watch out, Edith!'

Edith turned and began to speak, but Daisy grabbed her small sister and dragged her from the room. They both dashed into the garden and right down to the bottom of it, where a sooty brick wall, at least twelve feet high, separated the Larches' garden from that of the house at the back. Daisy was pink and furious, but Petal, giggling, told her not to get in a fuss over old Edith. 'She hates us, I don't know why, but she really is scared of Mr Wyn Roberts, because she knows he doesn't like her much, and he isn't nearly as lazy as his wife and wouldn't mind if the old horror left,' she said cheerfully. 'I know that's true, because last time he was home he said he didn't know why his wife put up with her. He said that when the war's over the first thing he'll do is send old Edith back where she came from. So you see, she won't want us telling Mr Wyn Roberts about the things she says and does when there's only us kids to hear.'

Daisy smiled, but agreed that Petal was probably right. 'And she shouldn't talk to us the way she does,' she admitted. 'Only she's got us in her power in a way . . . she can make things jolly uncomfortable for us – and for Mrs Wyn Roberts – if she puts her mind to it. After all, she cooks and cleans and so on, and I can't see Mrs Wyn Roberts doing it for herself, can you?'

'No. But I say, Daisy, I *do* wonder where Edith goes on her weekends off, don't you? She doesn't seem to enjoy herself much, does she? And she nearly always comes back here in a nasty temper.'

'I used to think she lived somewhere lovely, like the farm, or perhaps even by the Welsh seaside,' Daisy said thoughtfully. 'But if so, you'd think she'd at least set off with a smile, wouldn't you? Yet she even puts off leaving on a Friday evening, quite often, and doesn't set out for the station until Saturday morning. Still, never mind her. Let's climb up into the old tree house; tea won't be ready for a bit.'

The tree house was Petal's delight, so the two of them spent a happy half-hour high in the branches of the big copper beech, but by the time Edith called them they were quite glad to descend, for their midday meal had been a sketchy one; Mrs Wyn Roberts had already left for her friend's house but had made some honey sandwiches and some paste ones, and had put them with a jug of milk on the kitchen table. She had left a note telling the children that Edith would make them a hot meal that evening, so by the time they

269

were seated once more at the kitchen table they were eager for the food which Edith was dishing up.

It's a pity she's so horrid, Daisy told herself as she dug her fork into the slice of meat pie on her plate, because she really is a good cook. And she gets round the people in the shops, too, because I'm sure we have more meat than some folk do.

Edith took her place beside them and, catching Daisy's eye, gave her a creaky smile. Daisy thought her resemblance to a toad even more marked when she smiled but did not mean to do anything to annoy the old woman. After all, neither she nor Petal wanted to be enemies with Edith; life would be so much nicer if only the maid could bring herself to regard them with less malice. But Edith was smiling now, though with glittering eyes, so Daisy decided to see what reaction a friendly overture would receive. 'Did you have a nice weekend off, Edith?' she enquired. 'The weather has been lovely, hasn't it? Mrs Wyn Roberts got out our cotton dresses and said we might wear them for school tomorrow instead of our serge skirts and woollen cardigans.'

She half expected a snub, but instead Edith positively beamed at her. 'Oh aye, I had the best weekend of me life,' she said. 'I went to bed last night but I were woke up at ten o'clock by the sound o' bombs droppin'. So what did I do? I gorra coat on and went down to the Mersey – I go back to Birken'ead, you know, on me weekend off – an' what d'you think I saw?' She cackled triumphantly, blotchy colour rising in her unhealthy-looking face. 'I saw bloody Liverpool on fire, that's wharr I saw. I saw them great black bombers a-hammerin' of that stinkin' city until it were flattened. I saw the docks on fire and the big warehouses, and the little houses of them filthy scousers.'

She cackled again. 'I stayed up all night, cheerin' the bombers on, tellin' 'em to do a good job of it, to kill every bleedin' scouser what ever opened his mouth. Oh aye, the Jerries have taught 'em a lesson they won't forget in a hurry – 'cept I doubt there's anyone left alive to benefit by it.'

'I don't believe you,' Daisy said stoutly, after an incredulous moment. 'I think it's what you'd *like* to happen, though I'm sure I don't know why.' She squeezed Petal's hand reassuringly. 'It's just Edith's lies, Petal, like the snot sandwiches; she's trying to frighten us, that's all.'

Petal's face was white but she glared with hatred at Edith and raised her own small voice. 'You're a wicked liar, Edith. Why, if Liverpool was burned down, it would be on the news.' She glanced quickly up at the kitchen clock. 'It's nearly six now . . . turn it on, Daisy.'

'It'll be on the news awright,' Edith said gloatingly. 'But they won't say the whole place were flattened because they know the Jerries listen in an' they don't want the good news to get back to old Hitler.' She laughed, a sound the children had seldom heard before. 'I'm tellin' you, I could ha' read the *Echo* by the light of the fires blazin' and reflectin' in the water. Oh, it were a grand sight, a grand sight!'

'We still don't believe you,' Daisy said bravely, but there was a quiver in her voice. Somehow, the remark about reading a newspaper by the light of the fires rang horribly true and presently, when she turned on the wireless, the announcer's voice gave credence to what Edith had been saying. Liverpool had been heavily bombed on the previous night. Daisy did not resume her seat at the table but held out a hand to Petal, who had stopped eating as soon as Edith had dropped her bombshell. Then she looked steadily across at the old woman. 'Our mam is in Liverpool,' she said in a trembling voice. 'And all our friends . . . they're all there. And what have any of them done to you, Edith?'

Edith got to her feet and ambled across to the kitchen door, preventing the children from leaving by that route. 'You just get back to that table and eat the good food I've prepared,' she hissed. 'What have they done to me, you ask? Oh, nothin', of course! They just dismiss anyone who don't live in their stinkin' city as bein' third class citizens. Why, they even call Birken'ead the one-eyed city! They hates us . . . but not nearly as much as I hates them. I tell you I danced wi' delight as them bombs rained down. I prayed the Air Force wouldn't stick their long noses in, and nor they did. I cursed the bloody balloons and the fellers on the searchlights, an' I cheered on them Jerry pilots, wharrever they call theirselves. As for your mam, I dare say she might have gorrout somehow; you never know. Rats desert a sinkin' ship, they say, and—'

But Daisy had had enough. She ran full tilt at Edith, her head striking the old woman in the stomach and sending the air out of her lungs with a whoosh. Then, as Edith wheezed and gasped and began to curse, Daisy pushed her bodily away from the door, grabbed Petal's hand, and towed her out of the kitchen. The two of them raced up to their room and slammed the door. For a moment they just stared at each other, chests heaving, and then Petal hurled herself into Daisy's arms and the two little girls wept as if their hearts would break.

After ten minutes or so, Daisy pulled herself together and began to mop Petal's tears and tidy her small sister up. 'We know Liverpool was bombed 'cos the wireless said so,' she said. 'But it was bombed at

Christmas . . . it's been bombed quite a lot . . . and the old Germans didn't flatten it then, so I don't suppose they have now. It was just Edith being horrible and spiteful and trying to upset us.'

'Ye-es, only suppose she *were* telling the truth,' Petal said dismally. 'Suppose our mammy is hurt and wanting her little girls? Suppose she's in hospital? Oh, Daisy, suppose she's dead an' we're orfings!'

'Orphans,' Daisy said automatically. 'But I'm sure she's wrong. I'm sure our mam's all right, and all our friends as well. Only . . . only we've got to make sure. I'm going to go back right now. I'll leave a note for Mrs Wyn Roberts, telling her what's happened. I'm afraid I'll have to steal some money but you know what Mrs Wyn Roberts is like. She might not be home for hours and hours. And I want to go *now*!'

'I'm coming with you,' Petal said stoutly, rubbing the tears off her face with her dirty hands. 'Besides, if we wait for Mrs Wyn Roberts, you know what she'll say: she'll say we can't possibly go back to the city. She'll say she's sure our mammy's fine. She'll say we're in her charge and she'll promise to send a message and it'll be days before we find out what's really been happening.'

Daisy stared at Petal; for a kid of seven she was remarkably cool-headed. And presently she proved even more cool-headed, producing from her pocket two pieces of rather squashed pie, and handing one to Daisy. 'I took it off our plates while Edith were ranting,' she said cheerfully. 'I knew we'd be hungry later and wouldn't want to go back to the kitchen. Only why do we want money, Daisy?'

'Train tickets,' Daisy said briefly. 'Get me a bit of paper – tear a sheet out of your homework book – and I'll write the note. Then we'll go.'

Without a word, her small sister complied, and Daisy wrote a note in her neatest handwriting to Mrs Wyn Roberts, telling their foster mother what Edith had said and explaining that they had to go home to Bernard Terrace, but would return when they knew their mother was safe.

'In books they always pin notes to the pillow, but I don't know where the pins are kept and we can't waste time looking,' Daisy said, placing Petal's old teddy bear on top of the note. 'He'll hold it down, though, so it doesn't blow away.'

Petal gave an indignant squawk, snatched the teddy bear off the pillow and replaced it with a copy of *Five Children and It* which Daisy had been reading to her, a chapter at a time. 'Teddy's coming too,' she said firmly. 'Why, if I left him behind, Edith might cut his dear ears off, or throw him on the kitchen fire.'

Daisy realised that Petal might well be right and picked up her rag doll, pushing it into the satchel which she had just emptied out on to the floor. 'Put Teddy in your satchel, along with a cardigan and anything else we might need,' she said authoritatively. 'I expect Edith will be shovelling meat pie into her gob and thinking up more horrible lies for later, so we'll get going before she begins to wonder what we're up to.'

As quietly as they could, the children stole down the attic stairs and went into Mrs Wyn Roberts's bedroom. They knew she kept a small supply of cash in her bedside cabinet, though both children felt guilty as they opened the drawer. However, they need not have done so, for it was empty. 'Oh well, at least it's saved us from being thieves,' Daisy whispered, as they crept down the main staircase, carefully avoiding the creaky step three from the bottom. 'We'll nip out of the side door because our coats – the winter ones – hang there. If we have to sleep out of doors, then we can cover ourselves with those.'

Outside, it was still broad daylight, and the children felt almost happy as they hurried along towards Chester Road. 'If we were on the train, we'd go through Chester, or, at any rate, in that direction,' Daisy said as they walked. 'Are you hungry, Petal? If so, we'll nip into the allotments and get ourselves some peas and some new carrots. People wouldn't mind if they knew what's happened to us today.'

However, they were not destined to become vegetable thieves either, since several of the allotments were being worked by their owners, and anyway, as Petal said, the chunks of meat pie which they had messily devoured in their bedroom had filled them up quite nicely.

'I expect we'll get a lift soon,' Daisy said cheerfully, as they left the town behind. 'We'll tell people we came to visit our auntie for the weekend, but lost our return train tickets. Someone's bound to take us most of the way to Liverpool, even if not all the way. Best foot forward, Petal!'

They reached Liverpool in the early hours of Monday morning. They had been given several lifts, including one by an ATS officer and her driver on their way to Blackpool, and ended up being driven in a baker's van through the outskirts of the city. It was then that they discovered that Edith had not exaggerated, for fires still burned, lighting up the darkness, and the roads were covered in debris. Their driver, an elderly man with a thin humorous face, enormous porcelain teeth, and no more hair than a day-old baby, knew the city, he told them, like the palm of his hand and actually delivered them to Salisbury Street. The girls got out of the van, thanking him profusely, and waving until he was out of sight. Only then did they begin to look apprehensively around them. But though the sky was clear, they could see very little damage in the bright moonlight, and made their way to Bernard Terrace considerably relieved. They were approaching their own dear, familiar front door when a figure stepped out from between two houses, checked, then came towards them, wagging a disapproving head. It was a neighbour, Mr Bright, who lived further down the terrace, though at first the girls did not recognise him for his tin hat was pulled well down over his eyes, and his ARP uniform was covered in dust. He greeted the girls cheerfully, however, saying: 'What have we got here, young ladies? Oh, it's Daisy and Petal McAllister, isn't it? Why aren't you down a shelter somewhere? Don't you know there's a raid on? The All Clear hasn't gone yet.'

'Yes, it's us, Mr Bright,' Daisy admitted. 'We heard about the raids from someone who had been visiting over the weekend and we've come home because we had to know if our mam was all right.'

Mr Bright tutted indulgently. 'Oh well, I can under-stand that,' he said. 'Your mam's norrin, but I saw her yesterday evening and she were all right then; I reckon she were on her way to work. She stopped for a word – very cheerful she was – and I'm perishin' certain she had no idea you were headin' home. If you ask me, the worst of the raid's over, so mebbe you'd best go home an' have a few hours' sleep afore your mam gets back. I dare say she'll be awful mad wi' you, but no doubt you did it for the best. Come along, I'll see you inside. D'you have a Morrison shelter?'

'Yes,' Daisy said. 'I'll just fish the key up through the letter box . . .' By this time, they had reached the front door and Daisy realised, with some dismay, that there was no key dangling on a piece of string, to be fished up and used by any member of the McAllister family who needed to get inside. She turned wide, dismayed eyes up into Mr Bright's face. 'It's not there,' she quavered unhappily. 'How's we to get in, Mr Bright?'

It seemed like a knotty problem, but Mr Bright accompanied them down the jigger and across the small backyard where, to the children's great relief, he found that their mother had left the pantry window slightly ajar. It was the work of a moment for Mr Bright to hoist Petal through the window, and seconds later both children stood in the familiar kitchen, whilst Mr Bright, shouting a cheery goodnight, left them at last to their own devices.

'We'll have some bread and jam and a drink of milk, and then get to bed,' Daisy said, ushering her sister towards the kitchen table. 'And we'll have to go back to Wrexham in the morning because . . . well, because we'll have to.' She did not add that one of the many buildings missing from the familiar skyline had been the school she and Petal had attended. Petal had been very brave but there was no point in letting her see how near disaster had come. The school was only a few streets away; Bernard Terrace had been lucky.

Daisy cut thick slices of bread and spread them thinly with jam, filled a couple of mugs with a mixture of milk and water, and watched her sister drink and eat hungrily, following suit herself. The Morrison shelter had the same blankets in it which had been there at Christmas and Daisy smelt the familiar odour of brick dust, soot and damp – reminding her sharply of the Christmas bombing, when she and Petal had spent so many nights in the shelter, their mother beside them.

However, both children, utterly exhausted, slept for a couple of hours before waking abruptly to find that morning had arrived. Daisy sat up. The atmosphere of the house, which had once been so pleasant and friendly, seemed to have changed, to have become full of brooding menace. She sighed and crawled out of the shelter, not surprised that Petal followed her so swiftly that she could feel the little girl's nose bumping against the back of her legs. 'It's time we found out what's happened to Mam,' she said, straightening up. 'We can't stay here not knowing, so why don't we try to make our way to the factory on Long Lane? We can meet Mam out of work and explain what's been happening as we walk home.' She looked hopefully at the younger girl. 'Of course, if you'd rather stay in the house—'

'I wouldn't,' Petal said quickly. 'It 'ud be different if Mam were home, but – but it doesn't seem like our house, does it, Daisy? And were that the All Clear? If so, folk'll be comin' out of the shelter and someone might know if Mam's all right.'

'Right, I'm going to take the stuff out of my satchel and fill it with food for our breakfast,' Daisy said, suiting action to words, and presently the two children emerged on to Bernard Terrace once more. Daisy took a deep breath of the early morning air which, despite smells of burning, brick rubble and dust, seemed downright pleasant. No one was about yet but she still felt as though they had both escaped from some peril and smiled joyfully as they entered Salisbury Street. 'It's a lovely day; why don't we go to the gardens and eat our breakfast there? Why, we might meet

Nicky on his way to school . . . oh no, perhaps . . . or he might be coming up from the shelter any minute. I've really missed Nicky.'

Happy to be out of the house, which had suddenly seemed such a dangerous place to be, the children set off in the direction of Long Lane.

Rose woke early and looked around the small room in which she lay, totally confused for a moment. She had not gone to work after accompanying Luke to his lodging house, which was mercifully intact, because there was no work to go to. The factory had been bombed in the early hours of Sunday morning and damaged far too extensively for there to be any question of the workers returning there. Instead, she had visited Rachel in hospital to explain that some other premises would have to be found before the staff could make uniforms once more, and Rachel had begged her to spend the night in the little house which she had abandoned the night before.

'Mam and Dad won't be coming home for weeks; not until it's a lot safer than it is now,' Rachel had said. 'I'm so afraid that I may have left windows open or doors unlocked, and you know how dreadful people can be. If someone gets in and steals all our nice stuff, or wrecks the place, I'd never forgive myself, so would you be a dear and check up for me? It'll only be for a day or two; once they release me from here, I'll go straight to the house myself, though with the factory gone, it's tempting to take little Luke out into the country to stay with Mam and Dad.'

Rose had not been able to conceal her surprise, though she was pleased, too. 'You're going to call him Luke? What will Alby have to say to that?'

'Well, after big Luke was such a trump last night,

it seems the least I can do; if the baby had been a girl I'd have asked if I could call her after you. And I know Alby won't mind at all; he'll be just as grateful to big Luke as I am when he hears what happened, I'm sure. But, Rose, you will go and check on the house for me, won't you? I'll be really anxious until I hear that everything's all right.'

Rose had agreed, and when she left the hospital she had gone straight to the Edelmanns' house. She had checked all the windows and doors and then had gone round to the neighbours for a chat, explaining that she would be staying in the house to keep an eye on things for her friends until Rachel and the new baby returned from hospital. The neighbours had been really nice, friendly and helpful, but since they were in the habit of 'trekking' out of the city each night, they were not able to promise to look after anyone else's property. 'In fact, to be honest, my dear, we've been relying on Mrs Cohen to stop anyone breaking into our house,' Mrs Carruthers had said. 'She was adamant that she could not leave the area until after her baby was born, so she was quite willing to keep an eye on our place.' She was a small, wrinkled walnut of a woman, trying to do her best for her daughter and her four grandchildren, who had been bombed out of their own home and had come to live with her. She looked hopefully at Rose.

'Whilst I'm staying here, I'll do my best to keep your house safe as well as the Edelmanns',' Rose had said gently. 'But after the very heavy raid last night, I imagine the authorities may simply take over houses which are not occupied. Folk have got to live somewhere, after all.'

Mrs Carruthers had nodded sadly, her bright little brown eyes filling with tears. 'Me and my family have got to live somewhere too,' she had pointed out. 'Oh, Mrs McAllister, this is a wicked, wicked war.'

Rose had agreed and gone back into the Edelmanns' neat home, reflecting that her own house in Bernard Terrace would also be unprotected whilst she remained at the Edelmanns'. But I'll go back for a time each day, and the neighbours will make sure that no one takes it over, she had told herself. Yes, now that there's no factory, I'll be able to look after two homes until Rachel is on her feet again.

But right now, waking in Rachel's nightdress to see the May sunshine pouring between the Edelmanns' curtains, life did not seem too terrible. She felt all the better for a good night's sleep, able to cope once more with whatever lay ahead. Stretching luxuriously, she rolled out of bed and made her way downstairs to get some breakfast.

The sun was climbing as the children crossed Shaw Street and headed for Netherfield Road, and it was at this point that Daisy remembered that they could not catch a bus, even if one was running, because they had no money. Furious with her own stupidity, for the teapot on the mantelpiece always had cash in it, Daisy pulled Petal to a halt. 'We'd best go back to the house and find some pennies so's we can catch a tram or a bus when our legs is tired,' she said. 'Oh, *do* come along, Petal, don't drag!'

But Petal was tired and not at all keen on retracing her steps. However, a bus ride certainly had advantages when you were tired, so she followed her sister obediently. After all, being without any money whatsoever was not a good idea. Sighing, she tagged along behind Daisy.

★   ★   ★

Overhead, a lone Dornier bomber crippled by ack-ack fire sustained while attacking the shipbuilding yards at Barrow-in-Furness passed over the city of Liverpool, the crew no doubt rejoicing as they looked down on the fires still burning brightly below. Now, returning home, the pilot knew that the condition of the plane was so desperate that he must jettison the one remaining bomb he carried to lighten it. He pressed the bomb release and watched it plummet to earth, saw the enormous explosion in a part of the city which, from this height, looked relatively undamaged. Then he turned back to resume his interrupted conversation with the navigator.

Rose had her breakfast, checked the house once more, and then set off for her own home. There were a great many people about, some on their way to work, others hopefully carrying shopping bags, children going to school and air raid wardens and council workers roping off unsafe buildings and trying to answer a thousand questions as to the state of their homes from those returning to the city.

Rose greeted a good many people she knew, but continued on her way. She wanted to get back to the terrace as soon as she could, make sure that all was well there.

She crossed Netherfield Road, which was littered with debris, picking her way carefully around great shards of shattered glass. Men with brushes and shovels were clearing it as fast as they could, but there was nothing they could do about the tram lines which reared out of the road like angry snakes; there would be no trams running on this route today. When she reached Salisbury Street she could see no new damage and entered Bernard Terrace with a light step. She told herself that she would have to begin to look about her for another job, for though Steve's money arrived pretty regularly, she needed her own contribution and besides, she wanted to do her share towards ending this dreadful war so that life could return to normal again. She had always fancied the women's services, but because of the children – and her job in the uniform factory – she had never seriously thought of joining up. The children seemed happily settled with Mrs Wyn Roberts, however, and she certainly would not bring them back to this war-torn city.

In fact, as soon as Rachel gets out of hospital, she would . . . Rose's thoughts stopped dead, and she stopped too, unable to believe her eyes. The terrace was crowded with people, many of them friends and neighbours, but there were officials there, too, roping off . . .

No. 7, Bernard Terrace, was no longer there. Instead, there was a deep pit out of which reared a shaky-looking brick wall with the tattered remains of a double bed hanging from a beam which thrust out into empty air at what once must have been first floor height.

Rose took two tottering steps forward, then stopped again, her hand flying to her throat. It was incredible, impossible! Other houses in the Terrace showed gaping windows and someone's front door . . . it was her own . . . lay forlornly in the roadway, but otherwise, it was as though No. 7 had been scooped up by a giant hand – a hand which had taken care not to brush against Numbers 5 or 9, and had left them relatively unharmed – and crushed into dust. 'Mrs McAllister! Oh, my dear, what a relief! We thought . . . well, you can guess what we thought. Oh, thank God you're safe, but wharra terrible shock for you, to come home to this.'

It was Mrs Gray, looking white and strained. Rose

smiled tremulously. 'I couldn't believe my eyes when I came round the corner,' she said shakily. 'But why the crowd? And – and why does the rope stretch along your frontage and that of number nine? Your homes are all right, aren't they?'

Mrs Gray uttered a sound between a snort and a moan. 'You want to see the back, chuck,' she said. 'It were a lucky thing we were down the shelter 'cos the kitchen's only got three walls and no ceiling, and the back bedroom's gone. The warden just telled me your place received a direct hit, but number nine and our place got the blast. They say it ain't safe to go back in and that we've gorra find somewhere else to live for a while.'

Suddenly, her face was lit up by a wicked grin and she nudged Rose in the ribs. 'Mind you, we come up from the shelter afore the wardens an' them realised yours had been hit and me sons went into ours an' took out as much as they could. A' course we couldn't budge the beds but we got most of the small stuff out – food, pots an' pans, bedding, clothes and that – afore they roped it off.'

'I'm glad for you,' Rose said rather feebly. She wondered what the Grays would do now, how they would manage, but was aware, suddenly, that she already felt detached from Bernard Terrace. This catastrophe had made up her mind for her. Homeless now – and jobless too – she would be a liability not an asset if she remained in Liverpool. But if she joined up, then she could be truly useful, truly valuable.

One of the men who had been gingerly roping off the one tottering wall of No. 7 came over to Rose. 'Mrs McAllister? A neighbour pointed you out. I'm real sorry, queen, but I reckon you're a very lucky woman. Oh, I know the house is gone, along with all your goods and chattels, an' I know you've got nothin' left in the world but the clothes you stand up in, but Mrs Gray told me your children were evacuated to Wales a few months ago and your husband is in the Navy, so at least you've got your lives . . .'

Rose felt someone tugging her arm and looked round. Old Mr Bright stood there, his face grey with fatigue, his tin hat and uniform grey with cement dust. He said urgently: 'Missus, I'm that sorry and it were all my fault . . . honest to God, missus, I thought I were doin' it for the best. Oh, I'll never forgive myself if . . . if . . .'

For the first time since she had returned to the terrace, Rose smiled. 'I don't see how you can blame yourself for what the Jerries did, Mr Bright,' she said gently. 'It's a dreadful thing to have your home destroyed, but at least there wasn't any loss of life, so far as we know.'

'But – but there were; that's wharr I'm tryin' to tell you,' Mr Bright said, and to Rose's horror she saw tears brim up in the old man's eyes and trickle down his dust-covered cheeks. 'Them little girls o' yourn, missus, they come back last night. They wanted to make sure you hadn't been hurt, so I told them I'd seen you, and the planes had all gone, so . . . so . . .'

Rose stared at him, trying to take in what he was saying. 'The – the girls?' she quavered. 'But they're miles away, miles and miles. It couldn't have been Daisy and Petal. They're in Wrexham, in Wales. And – and they couldn't have got in. I always lock up pretty carefully before I leave the house and I did so last night. Honest to God, Mr Bright, you're mistaken, you have to be.'

Mr Bright shook his head dolefully. 'They were in there. You'd left a window open round the back and

I lifted the littl'un up so's she could squeeze through. She unbolted the back door and I told the pair of 'em to get inside the Morrison, just in case. Oh, missus, you'd best tell the fellers to start diggin'.'

Rose felt waves of faintness threaten to overcome her, but pushed them resolutely back. The Morrison shelter! People in Morrison shelters had been known to survive after their whole house had fallen on them . . . but a direct hit? She pushed her way through the thinning crowd until she could look down into the pit that had once been her home. If she could just see a corner of the Morrison shelter . . . but surely Mr Bright must be mistaken? He was old and did not know the children well. Some other child must have persuaded him that it was her home . . .

Rose looked down. There was something . . . something covered in dust, filthy and torn, but with bright brown glass eyes staring up at her. Her mind gave an unbearable jerk as she recognised Petal's teddy, and then waves of merciful darkness overcame her as she slid to the ground.

Rose came round and looked up, dizzily, at the circle of faces about her. She started to struggle, to try to get up, and found herself being lifted from the ground in a pair of strong arms. She had no idea what had happened or why she had fainted, but even as the man who held her began to speak, everything came rushing back and she burst into a storm of weeping.

'Rose! Now, Rosie, don't take on so. I know it was your home and you loved it, but . . .'

She recognised the soft American drawl at once, remembered the young airman who had been so kind, had helped her with Rachel. She wondered why he had come back, but it hardly seemed to matter. Nothing mattered but the terrible fear that her children were dead, buried beneath the ruins of their home.

She began to struggle and he set her down gently, putting both arms round her, trying to comfort her without knowing the reason for her distress. She tried to fight free of him, breaking into panicky speech. 'The children! My children! Oh, Luke, they were here. I thought Mr Bright was confused, but Petal's teddy . . . it stared up at me. Oh, Luke, they might be down there this minute, choking to death under all that rubble! I must get in there, I must!'

She would have ignored the rope barrier, scrambled down into the pit, but Luke held her firmly, but when she would have screamed and attacked him, another voice broke in, and a small and extremely grimy hand grabbed at her arm. Rose looked down and saw Nicky Bostock. He was filthy, as always, but his eyes were shining and he was shaking his head vehemently. 'They ain't dead, missus. Daisy and Petal ain't dead,' he said with emphasis. 'They gorrout of the house 'cos they were scared of bein' there without you, Daisy said. I met 'em earlier on. They'd been on their way to Long Lane when one of 'em thought to come back to the terrace to fetch a few pennies so's they could catch a bus. It's the divil of a long way out to Long Lane on foot, so they turned back, which was when I fell in with 'em. We were walkin' back to the terrace when we saw a plane kinda low; we actually saw something fall from it. We stopped where we was, starin' up – we were on Salisbury Street – and there was this huge explosion. It blew us off our feet – I cracked me elbow on the kerb an' young Petal grazed both knees and the palms of her hands. But that were all, honest to God it were.'

Rose stared at him, wanting desperately to believe

what he was saying, yet unable to forget the teddy bear, Petal's most dearly loved possession. 'But – but the teddy bear's lying there, amongst the rubble,' she said uncertainly. 'Are – are you sure they didn't go back to the house after the explosion, Nicky?'

'Course I'm sure,' Nicky said scornfully. 'Not that it would have mattered if we had gone back, because that explosion was the bomb that landed on the terrace, it must have been. But the bomb made Daisy decide not to bother about a few pennies, so we all turned back again and headed for Long Lane. I went with the kids as far as the recreation ground off Rice Lane. We had a great breakfast there, 'cos Daisy had stuffed her satchel, and Petal's, with grub. But then I remembered there might be trouble if Ma Ryan found out I'd not gone to the shelter, so I come back.'

'Oh, Nicky,' Rose breathed, almost fainting, but from relief this time. 'You don't know . . . I can't explain . . . oh, Nicky, thank you, thank you!'

She would have hugged him but Nicky, seeing the intention in her eye, stepped back smartly, holding up a grimy paw like a policeman halting traffic. 'No you don't,' he said reprovingly. 'I give you the good news but I don't expect to have you a-huggin' of me. What do you want me to do, missus? I reckon them kids will have found out you ain't at work by now.'

Rose began to answer him, to say that no doubt the children would soon return, when another thought occurred to her. She clapped a hand to her mouth, then lowered it again. 'Oh my God,' she said brokenly. 'The factory was bombed on Saturday night; they're going to think – they're going to think . . .'

Luke had released her but he still had a comforting arm round her shoulders and now he gave her a squeeze. 'I know what you were going to say, but I'm sure you're wrong; they won't conclude that you're dead or badly hurt,' he said bracingly. 'I don't know this Long Lane, nor your factory, but they've only got to ask anyone in that neighbourhood when the factory was bombed and they'll be told that it was Saturday night. And remember, they know you were alive and kicking on Sunday because they met Mr Bright and he told them so.' He turned to the old man who was still sniffing dolefully and mopping his eyes with a large checked handkerchief. 'Isn't that so, Mr Bright?'

The old man nodded. 'Aye, I told 'em you were all right when I met you on Sunday evening, when we'd had a word,' he admitted. 'And I thank God that I didn't send them to their death, oh, I thank God.'

Edith was still in a good mood when she came downstairs on Monday morning to make breakfast. She got out the porridge oats and began to measure them into a large saucepan, adding water, a little milk and then a good dollop of black market butter; she had obtained it herself, though Mrs Wyn Roberts had paid for it, so she knew it was black market. Then she added a hefty spoonful of brown sugar and carried the pan over to the stove. Mrs Wyn Roberts loved Edith's porridge, frequently remarking that no one else, not the best hotel in the country, could make better porridge than her Edith. Folk had asked Edith for the recipe but she would never give it since she was well aware that the soft life she led could only be maintained so long as Mrs Wyn Roberts could not find a better cook anywhere in the area. She lit the gas under the pan, fetched a wooden spoon and began to stir. She reflected that, in peacetime, the porridge would have been just the beginning of an excellent breakfast which would have gone on to eggs, bacon and kidneys, perhaps a nice pair of kippers or a flavoursome piece of smoked haddock, and would have finished up with freshly baked bread, lashings of butter, and as much Seville marmalade as you could pile on each round of toast. Now, of course, breakfast began and ended with porridge, so she made a great deal.

Presently, Edith began to wonder what the children were up to. Usually, at this hour of the morning, there was a considerable racket from upstairs as the girls got out their school clothes and put their weekend things into the laundry basket. Edith reflected, grimly, that she did not mind how much washing the girls made since it was done by Mrs Llew. Mrs Llew took the washing home on a Monday and brought it back cleaned and ironed on a Tuesday. Then she stayed for the whole of the rest of the day, doing what Edith called 'the rough work', scrubbing floors, brushing acres of carpet, polishing furniture and washing down paintwork, tiles, and anything else which needed cleaning.

The porridge began to simmer gently and Edith put the lid on the pan and began to pour a cup of tea, just as she heard Mrs Wyn Roberts's step on the stair. Her mistress came into the kitchen, smiling brightly. 'Good morning, Edith,' she said. 'Aren't I kind to you today? It's so beautifully bright and sunny that I woke early and thought I'd save you having to climb the stairs by taking my morning cuppa in the white drawing room. Has the post been yet? Oh, and I thought the children would already be up, but since they obviously aren't I fear you'll have to climb the stairs anyway, to rouse them. We can't have them late for school, can we?'

'No, m'm; I'll go up at once, m'm,' Edith said agreeably, but with murder in her heart. Bloody kids!

As if she didn't have enough to do without waitin' hand and foot on a pair of slummies. Still, Mrs Wyn Roberts seemed quite attached to the dirty little tykes, so she'd best go up and wake them. She would quite enjoy giving them a good shake and a slap round the face, and then saying her hand had slipped.

Edith carried Mrs Wyn Roberts's cup of tea through to the white drawing room, thinking resentfully that it would not have hurt her mistress to carry her own cup. But of course she did not voice her thoughts aloud. She never intended to let the younger woman know the depth of her dislike and resentment. She was as near happy as she could be at the Larches, and did not mean to jeopardise her position by an unguarded word.

Presently, she stomped up two flights of stairs and threw open the door to the girls' room. She was astonished to find the bed neatly made and no sign of either child, and though she had not investigated she was pretty sure they had not been in the bathroom on the first floor of the house. She supposed, angrily, that they must have gone off to meet friends before school, but then she remembered that neither child had had breakfast and thought it unlikely that they would have left the house, because it would have given her an excuse to deprive them of the meal.

She was just about to stomp off downstairs again, brimming over with righteous wrath at such ingratitude, when she saw the note. Even without reading it, she felt sweat start on her forehead, felt her hands grow clammy. She crossed the room and grabbed the note, then read it.

Dear Auntie Clara,
  Edith went back to Birkenhed for her weekend

off and told us about the bombing. She told us all
of Liverpool had been flattened and she thinks heaps
and heaps of people have been killed. She is glad of
this as she does not like scowsers but we are afraid
for our mam and our friends who are scowsers too.
We could not wait for you to come home as Edith
said you were always late when you went to call on
that silly old woman, so we have gone now (six
o'clock). We will come back when we know our mam
is safe. Please do not worry, we shall be all right.
With love from Daisy and Petal xx

Edith read the letter a second time, rage mounting
in her so fast that her breathing grew short and her
cheeks hot. Then she scrumpled the letter up and
pushed it, viciously, into her skirt pocket. Mrs Wyn
Roberts was certainly not going to read that! If she
had done so, Edith might have been blamed for the
children's disappearance, and what was more, Mrs
Wyn Roberts would have discovered that Edith thought
her mistress's sister a silly old woman. She might even
have guessed that Edith had deliberately frightened
the children, though she had never dreamed that they
would run away, silly little fools. She would just have
to brazen it out, remember that she had heard something on the wireless about the bombing of Liverpool,
pretend it had been that which had sent the children
off on what was sure to be a wild goose chase.

She was halfway down the stairs when a cheering
thought occurred to her. If the children had reached
Liverpool and there had been another raid the previous
night, then they might easily have been killed or badly
injured, which would mean that she would be shot of
them at last.

Edith descended the rest of the stairs with a spring

in her step, arranging her expression to read alarm and puzzlement. She entered the white drawing room, dramatically flinging the door wide and saying in a hollow voice: 'Oh, Mrs Wyn Roberts, their bed ain't been slept in. They've gorn orff, God knows where.'

Mrs Wyn Roberts was deeply distressed by the sudden disappearance of her young guests but did not know what to do for the best. Fortunately, she went first to the school and spoke to Daisy's teacher, who immediately gave it as her opinion that the girls must have heard about the bombing of Liverpool and wanted to see for themselves whether friends and relatives were safe.

'But how could they do such a thing?' Mrs Wyn Roberts wailed. 'They said nothing to Edith and didn't leave me a note, which is most unlike Daisy, who is a very thoughtful child. They had no money, they took nothing with them – well, apart from Petal's teddy and Daisy's rag doll – and it's an awfully long way to Liverpool. And then there's the Mersey. How could two little girls cope with that?'

The teacher, Miss Rhoda Jones, admitted that it seemed almost impossible that two penniless children could cross such a wide tract of country. 'But both girls are bright and resourceful, and in these difficult times folk are not slow to give lifts,' she reminded the other woman. 'I know the bombing was bad because a friend of mine visited her parents in Wallasey over the weekend, and said the fires from bombed buildings and shipping could be seen for miles. If someone told the children, I'm sure their one desire would have been to get back to their mother. Do you happen to know where Mrs McAllister works?'

'No, not really; I believe she makes uniforms for

the forces,' Mrs Wyn Roberts said vaguely. 'And it isn't as if they're on the telephone, otherwise I could ring.'

'Send a telegram, Mrs Wyn Roberts,' the teacher advised. 'I take it you know Mrs McAllister's Liverpool address? And you can send a prepaid reply, you know, which would mean you'll know what has been happening by the end of the day.'

'Oh, but suppose they haven't gone home? Mrs McAllister will think me careless and unfeeling to lose her children,' Mrs Wyn Roberts pointed out. 'I'm really very fond of them both – they are dear little girls, polite and helpful – but I can't be everywhere at once. I spent yesterday with my sister, but the children weren't alone. Edith – my housekeeper – was with them. She assures me she put them to bed and saw that they had everything they wanted before going to bed herself.'

'I'm sure no blame will attach to anyone,' the teacher said reassuringly. 'If the children have not yet reached home, though, the police must be alerted to keep a lookout and find the girls before harm comes to them. In fact, I think you should inform the local police in any event.'

'I'll do so at once,' Mrs Wyn Roberts said. 'Thank you so much for your help and advice, Miss Jones. I shall, of course, let you know what is happening as soon as I know myself.'

The teacher smiled. 'I shall be most grateful,' she said. 'Daisy is one of my favourite pupils – though teachers are not allowed to have favourites – and Petal is both lively and affectionate. You are lucky in your evacuees, Mrs Wyn Roberts, and I'm sure they are lucky, too.'

Chapter Eleven

There was a glorious reunion, of course. Luke had insisted on hailing a taxi to take himself and Rose out to Long Lane, and it was a good thing he had done so, since they arrived at their destination to find two terrified, ashen-faced children staring at the shell of the factory with tears running down their cheeks. Clearly, they had not had time to make enquiries about the raid which had done such damage and assumed it must have taken place the previous night. The taxi drew up with a squeal of brakes and Rose hurtled out of it, screaming: 'Daisy, Petal! Oh, my darlings, you're safe! Thank God you didn't stay in Bernard Terrace this morning.' She hugged the children convulsively, kneeling down on the pavement amidst all the rubble and glass, to get to the children's level. 'But whatever made you come back to Liverpool? Did someone tell you about the bombing? My loves, the bombing was the reason you were sent away in the first place; I wanted to keep you safe.'

'Mammy, oh, Mammy,' Petal sobbed, burying her face against her mother's shoulder. 'We did hear about the bombing – horrible Edith told us – and we had to make sure you were all right.'

'Oh, Mammy, if you'd been in the factory, you might have been killed,' Daisy sobbed. 'Can't we stay with you? Can't we all go away from the bombing? There must be somewhere safe and you can't say you've got to be near your factory, 'cos it's all in bits.'

Rose was suddenly aware that she was kneeling on something horribly sharp and got hastily to her feet, as an agonising pain shot through her knee. Glancing down she saw, to her horror, that a jagged sliver of glass was sticking out of it and that blood was pouring forth. Petal and Daisy squeaked with fright, but Luke was more practical. He crouched on the pavement and gently removed the glass, then squeezed at the wound, causing it to bleed even more freely. 'The blood will wash out any fragments of glass left in,' Luke said. 'I've got a clean handkerchief, but it's a long cut and quite a deep one; I think we should make for the nearest first aid post. I told the taxi to wait, so he can take us.'

As he spoke, he was knotting a large white handkerchief round the injury, tying it so tightly that Rose doubted if she would be able to walk, but in seconds the handkerchief was scarlet with blood and though she said, faintly, that she was sure she would be all right, did not need hospital treatment, she made no objection when Luke half carried her to the taxi and thrust her and the girls inside, then climbed in after them. 'The lady's knelt on some glass; take us to the nearest first aid post, please,' he said.

Luke did not say so to Rose, but the depth and position of her wound, and the fact that the jagged piece of glass which he had removed from it might have left splinters behind, worried him. The pavement and the glass were both filthy, and from the amount of blood pumping forth he feared that Rose might be in real trouble if she was not dealt with quickly. However, it would not do to let the children see he was worried. So he smiled reassuringly at them and introduced himself. 'I'm a friend of your mom's. My name's Luke

Nadolski. We'll get your mom some treatment, where they can put a couple of stitches in her knee, and then we'll decide what to do next.'

'When the doctors have made Mammy all right, we could go home and have some dinner,' Petal said longingly. 'We did have breakfast, didn't we, Daisy? But it were an awful long time ago.'

Luke glanced at Rose. He felt it should be she who told the children that their home no longer existed, but the poor girl was leaning back against the cracked leather upholstery, eyes closed and face ashen. He did not think she was listening to the conversation; she was probably half fainting. Sighing inwardly, he squared his shoulders and spoke as gently as he could. 'Your home was bombed this morning, honey. But we'll get you a meal somehow, as soon as your mom is better. Then, of course, we'll have to find you all beds for the night, though you'll be going back to Wales tomorrow, I expect.'

Daisy's small face set in lines of sheer obstinacy. 'We're never going back to that place again,' she said. 'Mrs Wyn Roberts – Auntie Clara, I mean – is quite a nice woman, but Edith is really, really horrible. I think Mrs Wyn Roberts is afraid of her; at any rate, she never stops her being beastly to us. Why, the reason we came home was because Edith told us that Liverpool had been flattened and that almost everyone was dead. She said the docks were on fire and she said she danced with joy as the bombs fell. We told her she was a wicked woman, but she didn't mind at all. She hates us, just because we're scousers, and we'd far rather risk being bombed than go near her ever again.'

'I see,' Luke said slowly. 'But what in God's name are scousers? Is it another word for little girls, honey?'

'It's what folk call Liverpudlians,' Rose said, in a thin, faint voice, and Luke saw that she was actually smiling. 'Has Edith been nasty to you before, pets? You've never said.'

'She's always been absolutely *awful*,' Daisy assured her mother. 'But we didn't want to upset you so we never said anything. Only this time, when she said she danced with joy to see the flames . . . oh, Mam, we just couldn't bear it.'

'The evil old witch,' Luke said feelingly. 'Doesn't that Mrs what's her name, Auntie Clara, have any control over her?'

Daisy sighed patiently. 'Mrs Wyn Roberts is kind but very lazy; Edith does all the cooking and most of the housework, so I suppose Auntie Clara closes her ears to Edith's nastiness for the sake of her treacle tart,' she said ingenuously. 'Edith is friendly with all the black market spivs – I heard someone say that – so she gets all sorts of extras. Auntie Clara has to pay for them, but she doesn't have to . . . to . . .'

'Doesn't have to dirty her hands or admit to herself that she's cheating,' Luke supplied. 'I think the sooner you're away from that place, the better; don't you agree, Rose?'

But, to his alarm, he saw that Rose was in no state to answer. Her head had fallen sideways and even as they drew up, she fell heavily against his shoulder.

Luke felt cold with fear for a moment, but then common sense came to his aid. She was breathing gently but quite normally, so far as he could judge, and one way and another she had been through quite an ordeal. So he scooped her up in his arms and ducked out of the cab, then spoke to the taxi driver. 'Wait for me,' he said briefly. 'And you kids stay in the cab until I come back. I shan't be long.'

He glanced at the girls' frightened faces and hesitated, then turned back towards them, giving them his most reassuring grin. 'It's all right, babes, your mom's fainted, that's all, and no wonder! She thought the pair of you were in the house when it was bombed, and then there's her poor leg, which must have hurt like— like nobody's business. So just you stay there and I'll be back in two minutes, see if I'm not, and your mom with me, right as rain once more.'

Because Rose insisted, they went to Bernard Terrace. She hustled the children past the remains of No.7, telling them not to look, but of course she guessed that they had done so when she saw them staring at each other wide-eyed, perhaps realising for the first time what a narrow escape they had had.

Rose meant to call on Miss Ada Finch, who was living on her own at No. 14. Rose was hopeful that Miss Finch might be able to let them have a room for a few nights, just whilst they made alternative arrangements, but this proved impossible. 'My dear, if I could help, I would, you know that,' she said warmly, clasping Rose's hand. 'But my sister Freda, her two daughters and the baby were bombed out on Sat'day night, and my brother Tom's house was hit on Sunday, so I don't have an inch of space to spare. But there must be someone else who could take you in . . .' Turning away from No.14, Rose felt her shoulders droop. It seemed she had no alternative; the children would have to return to Wrexham and she would have to find herself some sort of place to go, even if it were only an air raid shelter.

She said as much to Luke and he offered to go with her to take the children back to Mrs Wyn Roberts, though they were declaring, stoutly, that they would not leave their mother. 'If you make us go back, we'll run away again,' Daisy said tearfully. 'That Edith is the wickedest woman in the world; she spits in the soup and tells us there's snot sarnies for tea. Last week, she told Petal the sausage rolls had dog turds in and I couldn't eat my tea even though I knew it was lies. Petal told Auntie Clara that Edith had said there were turtles in the sausage rolls – she got the word wrong – but Auntie Clara just said that Edith was teasing.'

'Then Auntie Clara gobbled up the sausage rolls herself, so they weren't wasted,' Petal said dolefully. 'Mrs Wyn Roberts is greedy, Mammy, that's why she buys black market stuff and won't ever tell Edith off, or get rid of her. Oh, I won't, I won't go back!'

Rose looked, speakingly, across at Luke, as they walked back towards the ruin of No. 7. 'I don't see how I can possibly keep the children with me, since I simply have to work and we've got nowhere to live,' she murmured, drawing closer to Luke and keeping her voice low. 'I had hoped to join up – after all, I could still visit them regularly whenever I got leave – but if they won't go back to Mrs Wyn Roberts, I just don't know what I should do.'

'I guess the kids have a point, though,' Luke said. 'You wouldn't want to send them back knowing what that Edith is like, would you?'

Rose looked up into his troubled face and realised that he was absolutely right. Her children had always been truthful and it was pretty plain that no matter how kind Mrs Wyn Roberts might be, it was really Edith who had the most to do with Daisy and Petal. I must be going mad, she thought remorsefully, to consider for one moment letting them return to the Larches. But dear God, what can I do?

'No, I wouldn't – want to send them back, I mean – now that I know the situation, and I'm ashamed that it took you, a virtual stranger, to make me see sense,' she said humbly. 'My children mean more to me than anything else and I am so keen to ensure their safety that I can't have been thinking straight. Thank you, Luke, for making me see clearly.' She turned to the children as they approached No. 7, looking down at Petal and smiling encouragingly. 'If there's a warden or a worker handy, sweetheart, I'm going to ask if they can fetch out your teddy bear and Daisy's rag doll, because they were both visible when I came over earlier. Otherwise, the chances are they – and everything else – will be looted as soon as the author-ities leave the terrace.'

'Oh, good,' Petal said, beaming. 'I love my teddy next to you, Mammy – no, next to you and Daisy. I wonder if we might go back to Auntie Blod's? D'you think we could, Mammy?'

'That would be an ideal solution, of course . . .' Rose was beginning, when Luke pointed. There were men working on the tumbled ruin of the house, and already a number of artefacts were neatly lined up on the pavement: several saucepans, a pile of dust-covered blankets, some extremely chipped and dirty orna-ments, a handful of cutlery, several Bakelite mugs and plates, and next to them – oh joy! – Petal's patched and faded teddy bear and Daisy's beloved rag doll.

The children pounced on their possessions with cries of joy and Rose was just about to approach the workers to thank them for their efforts when a telegram boy skidded into the terrace and came to a halt outside No. 7. He stared hard at the ruined house, then looked across at Rose. 'You Mrs McAllister? Telegram for you.'

Rose gave a little gasp. All her life, she had been afraid of telegrams, but she took the small yellow envelope, saying brightly: 'I am silly. Of course, it will be from Mrs Wyn Roberts. I know you left a note, darling, but you could only tell her you were coming back to Liverpool; she must have been half out of her mind with worry, imagining you lost, or in bad company.' As she spoke, she slit open the envelope and pulled out the sheet within and began to read.

The Admiralty regrets to announce that HMS/M Centurion *is ten days overdue and must be presumed lost with all hands stop.*

Rose stared blindly down at the ground whilst pictures formed in her mind. Steve, on their wedding day, proud and sure of himself, giving her a hug as they emerged from the church. Steve holding Daisy in his arms when she was about a week old, looking down at her tiny face with affection; he had wanted a boy but had seemed fond of Daisy at first. Steve playing football with a crowd of kids and young men, kicking the ball so hard that it had sailed right over the rooftops and disappeared into Mary Terrace. Steve bursting into the house after his first long voyage, with a fluffy toy for the baby and a necklace of polished stones for herself. But there were other pictures, of course, pictures which she would have to try hard not to remember. Steve, red-faced and angry, punching her in the mouth, kicking her as she lay on the floor, dragging her up by the hair and screaming at her because she had annoyed him in some trivial fashion. Steve swearing at the neighbours if they knocked on the wall because of the drunken din he was making. Worst of all, Steve holding Daisy up by her hair with one hand while he hit her across the face with the other, and Petal tried in vain to drag him away. She saw them all, the incidents, petty and horrendous which had ruined their marriage, turning Steve into a monster and herself into a victim.

She realised she was folding the telegram into a tiny square, unfolding it, pleating it into an accordion, then folding it up again. Anything rather than having to take in the implications of the words on the buff-coloured paper between her hands. Oddly, Steve had been happier aboard the submarine than he had ever been in his life before, or so she had grown to believe. The cramped and dangerous life lived by the thirty-three men aboard HMS/M *Centurion* seemed to suit him completely. Shared danger, shared excitement, the new skills he was learning, combined to make him truly proud. It was sad and terrible that Steve, the submariner, was dead and maybe, in the fullness of time, she would be able to weep for him, but Steve McAllister, husband and father . . . her mind shied away from the truth, then faced it steadily. She, and her daughters, would be infinitely better off without him.

'Mammy?' It was Daisy, eyes anxious in her small, pale face. 'Mammy, is it from Mrs Wyn Roberts?'

Rose shook her head dumbly and felt Luke take the small piece of paper from her fingers and spread it out. 'No, it's not from Mrs Wyn Roberts,' he said gently. 'It's – it's bad news, kids. HMS/M *Centurion* is ten days overdue and that almost certainly means . . .'

'Our dad's on that boat,' Petal said at once. 'Does that mean he's overdue, too?'

'It does,' Luke said diffidently. Rose saw him glance hopefully at her, but shock seemed to have deprived her of speech and she listened as he went on: 'It – it may mean that your dad won't be coming home any more.'

'Well, he isn't coming home any more,' Daisy said at once. 'After he hit me and dragged me indoors by my hair, Mam promised he wouldn't come home ever again. So why is someone sending us a telegram, telling us what we know already? And why is Mammy upset?'

Rose pulled herself together with a big effort. It was not fair to leave Luke, who was almost a stranger, to try to explain to Steve's daughters that their father was dead. So she said: 'The Admiralty have sent a telegram to tell us that your dad was almost certainly lost at sea . . .' and was amazed at the firmness of her own voice. 'Can you understand that?'

Daisy nodded solemnly but said nothing, though she put out a hand and took Petal's small paw in her own. Petal's face crumpled and she turned her head away but Rose saw the tears on the child's cheeks and thought how sad it was that only Petal could cry for her father's death. She bent and lifted the child up, trying to give what comfort she could, but after a moment Petal gave an enormous sniff, knuckled her eyes and wriggled out of her mother's arms. 'I wish Daddy had just gone away like you said he would, but perhaps he'll be happier in heaven than he would have been in Portsmouth,' she said philosophically. 'Mammy, couldn't we just get on a train and go and see Auntie Blod? We did so love it there, me an' Daisy, and – and we hated the noise and the fires and that, last night.'

Rose had recently acquired a wristwatch and now she glanced down at it. It was still early and what was to keep them here, after all? It was quite possible that someone else in the Ruthin area might be able to take the children, even if the Williams family could not. A personal visit would be quicker and much simpler than trying to get in touch by letter. 'I think you're right, Petal,' she said slowly. 'Even if Auntie Blod can't have you, someone else might have a spare bedroom. There are pubs which do rooms so we could stay there for a couple of nights at least, whilst I sort myself out.'

The children beamed with satisfaction and ran ahead, beginning to chatter excitedly, and Rose turned to Luke, pulling a wry face. 'I'm so sorry to have involved you in our troubles,' she said formally, holding out her hand. 'Thank you so much for all your help; we'll never forget you, the girls and I. Goodbye; perhaps we'll meet again some day.'

Luke laughed. 'You aren't getting rid of me that easily, ma'am,' he told her. 'Any chance of me getting to this Ruthin and back in a day? If so, I'll come with you; why not? After all, I've got nothing else to do until I catch the 10.35 to Lincoln tomorrow morning. If the trains are still running by then, that is,' he ended.

Rose was guiltily aware that her heart gave a decided leap. Adult company, in her present state, would be very welcome and she both liked and trusted this young American serviceman who had come to her aid at one of the worst moments in her life so far. So she smiled up at him, assuring him that the train journey was unlikely to take more than a couple of hours, and thanked him again for his kindness.

Luke, however, would have none of it. 'I'm not being kind, I happen to enjoy your company and, as I said, I've nothing much else to do,' he told her. 'Besides, I really don't think you're in any state to cope with whatever else life might throw at you. You've lost your home, your husband and your job and whether you know it or not, you must still be in a state of shock. It'll hit you later, believe me, and when it does,

I'd be happier if you were with friends, or at least with people who are well disposed towards you and the children.'

Rose could only thank him again. At his prompting, she sent a telegram to Mrs Wyn Roberts, explaining what had happened and asking her to send the children's possessions to Ty Siriol. She knew kindly Mrs Williams would pass their stuff on as soon as they had a permanent address.

Lime Street station was closed because of un-exploded bombs so they caught the boat over to Rock Ferry where they got on a train to Chester. There, the four of them got aboard the train which would take them to Ruthin. Luke had bought sandwiches from the buffet at Chester station and a rather stale-looking pork pie, and the children regarded this unexciting fare as a picnic and began clamouring to eat it almost as soon as the train drew out of the station. He had also provided himself with a notebook and some stubs of pencil, and soon the four of them were playing word games, and I Spy, and gazing out at the sunny countryside speeding past. The journey seemed to pass in a flash and they reached Ty Siriol before noon, to be greeted with rapture by Auntie Blod, who wept with happiness as she hugged the children and Rose. Before anyone could explain, she also hugged Luke, exclaiming that it was grand to meet Mr McAllister at last and telling him that he had the best wife and the nicest children in the world.

Petal laughed wildly, but said sunnily that this was Mammy's kind friend and that Daddy had gone to Jesus that very day.

Poor Auntie Blodwen looked very confused, as well she might, Rose thought. But when the children raced into the yard to find Dilys, she was able to explain the whole situation to the older woman. Luke, ever tactful, had left the kitchen in the children's wake, so Rose and Auntie Blod settled themselves at the kitchen table with cups of tea and home-made scones, and Rose told her everything that had happened, including the unsuitability of the evacuation home which had been found for the children in Wrexham. 'It was a lovely house and the Wyn Robertses are lovely people, but they employ a housekeeper called Edith . . .'

Blodwen Williams was shocked by the story but assured Rose that she had done right to bring the children back to Ty Siriol. 'We had three Land Girls, but now I'm back on my feet and able to cope we've only got the one, so the children's room is empty again,' she said cheerfully. 'I'm afraid I can't offer to put you and your gentleman friend up – that's to say, you could share the children's room, as you used to, but—'

'It's all right, Luke is going back to the city tonight, since he is due on his airfield in Lincolnshire some-time tomorrow,' Rose said. 'But Blodwen, I wouldn't expect you to accommodate a man I hardly know myself! I did tell you we only met on Saturday night . . .'

'Of course, of course, cariad,' Blodwen said, looking embarrassed. 'I'm an old fool, but when the four of you came into the kitchen . . . well, you looked such a happy little family . . .'

'Yes, I know what you mean,' Rose said, nodding. 'Now there's something else we must discuss, because you must realise that the children have nothing, no clothes, no ration books, not so much as a penny piece between them. I didn't think when we simply headed for the train, but I suppose we should have gone to a centre somewhere, to get emergency ration cards and some sort of clothing. I have telegraphed Mrs Wyn Roberts asking her to forward the children's stuff to this address, but I don't know how long it will be before it arrives. I had planned to ask you if I could stay for a night or two, but will the authorities in Ruthin be prepared to do anything for us, or shall I have to return to Liverpool?'

'You leave it to me, my dear,' Blodwen said, getting to her feet. 'There's a centre in Ruthin, manned by the WVS . . . you stay here and give an eye to the children and get some dinner on the table. I'll take the pony trap into Ruthin and sort things out . . .'

Next day, Rose stood on the platform at Edge Hill station, seeing Luke off. The children had been so happy to be back at Ty Siriol once more that she had decided to return to the city when the American did. She knew she should have contacted the authorities and was actually able to do so before the offices closed for the day, and then she and Luke had visited Rachel, and Rose had brought her friend up to date with everything that had happened. Rachel had been deeply sympathetic, both about Steve's death and the bombing of the house in Bernard Terrace, and offered the use of her parents' house for as long as Rose needed a roof over her head. Rose had thanked her, saying that it would be lovely if she could stay there one more night, but that after that she was taking over Luke's room in his lodging house until she could make more permanent arrangements.

Luke had seen her settled into his lodging house, assuring her that she could pay him back as soon as she had sorted out her affairs. 'I'll give you my address, the telephone number of the base and the name of the nearest train station; then you can write with your own address, as soon as you've got one, and that will mean we don't lose touch,' he had told her, scribbling on a piece of white card and handing it to her. 'Put that away safely and don't you dare lose it. I've enjoyed being with you and the kids more than I can say – yesterday was just like a holiday, if a rather eventful one – so I refuse to let you chuck me out of your life, or disappear into the wide blue yonder.'

Now, they were standing on the platform, being jostled by people, mainly service men and women, hurrying to get aboard the waiting train. Luke took hold of her upper arms and swayed her gently from side to side, smiling down into her face as he did so. 'You're a grand person, Rose McAllister, and you've taken the sort of punishment which would have had a lesser woman on her knees, but you're still in there, fighting. I know there was maybe friction between you and your husband, that there wasn't much love lost, but even so, I guess there were good times and you'll want a bit of space before you let anyone else get close to you. But when you do feel you need a – friend, I want it to be me. Is that asking too much?'

Rose stared at him, then gave him a push towards the train. 'Get in, Luke, or you won't find a seat, and it's no fun standing in a crowded corridor for miles and miles,' she said urgently. 'I – I know what you're trying to say, or I think I do, and you're right. My marriage turned sour years ago and it's made me . . . well, not scared of men exactly, but – but wary of them. But if friendship is all— Oh my God, they're shutting the doors! Get in, or you'll be left behind.'

Luke grinned, grabbed her and planted a resounding kiss on her astonished mouth, then leaped into the train just as it began to move. The guard shouted at him, but he slammed the door and leaned out of the window, at what seemed to Rose a perilous angle. 'Write as soon as you're settled,' he shouted. 'And join the WAAF, if that's what you really want. Remember, Rosie, your new life starts here . . .'

But whatever words might have followed, Rose heard none of them above the clatter of the departing train and the long blast of the guard's whistle. She waved until the train was out of sight and then made her way, thoughtfully, out of the station. All she had in the world were the clothes she stood up in, her gas mask in its case, and a few shillings which Luke had insisted upon lending her. If she joined one of the services, they would provide her with everything she needed, including accommodation, and, of course, a uniform. They would pay her a wage, feed her, give her leave when it was due so that she might see her children, and transport her, free, from one place to another. What felt more important than anything else at present, however, was that, when she put on a uniform, the responsibility for her future would be hers no longer. The army, the air force or even the Navy would take that responsibility from shoulders which, she felt right now, were no longer capable of bearing the weight. Resolute at last, she began to walk towards the recruiting office.

Within three days of bidding Luke farewell, Rose also said goodbye – for the time at least – to Liverpool, and her civilian life there. She had joined the WAAF and set out for the nearest training centre with a light heart, feeling Luke had been right: her new life was beginning.

Chapter Twelve

By the time America entered the war on 8 December, 1941, Rose was a fully fledged WAAF, about to take a week's leave before going to her first permanent posting, which was to an airfield in Norfolk. She went first to Liverpool to visit Rachel, who was once more established in the little house in Langsdale Street. It had suffered some blast damage while Rachel was still in hospital, and although the roof had been roughly patched up and some of the glass in the blown-out windows replaced, it was no longer the cosy, well-furnished home it had once been, for there had been not only destruction, but also looting, and the Edelmanns – who had moved back in – and Rachel had had to refurnish the place with anything they could find. Utility furniture was available, but it was poor stuff so in the main, the family bought second hand and managed well enough.

Rose only meant to stay one night in the city and then go on to Ty Siriol, but in fact, Rachel begged her to stay a little longer so that she might see Alby, whose ship was due in any day. Rose was pleased enough to do so for the baby, now seven months old, was a delightful little chap, and since she had been made his godmother, though by proxy, she felt she ought to spare him some time. Also, Rachel wanted to know all about life in the WAAF. She told Rose that had it not been for little Luke, she, too, would have joined up. But circumstances had made it impossible and anyway, the uniform factory was flourishing once more, though it was no longer in its original building but in a huge hangar which had been converted so that the girls might continue their work. Rachel complained that it had been rather stuffy in summer and was draughty in winter, but she was good at her work and the money came in useful.

Rose was willing enough to tell Rachel all about the WAAF because she felt she had found her niche at last. The WAAF had taught her to drive a car, a bus or a large lorry, had sent her on courses to learn how engines worked and had trained her in the art of telling others what to do without appearing either bossy or self-opinionated. She had only been at the training centre for three months, then had spent three months as a sort of roving driver, being sent around to any airfield which needed her. But this posting was to be a proper one; she might remain there for the rest of her service, or of course she might be moved on. Everything depended on the needs of the air force.

'So far, I've been billeted in all sorts of places,' she told Rachel. 'Mostly, we're in what they call huts, which are pretty basic affairs. They usually hold around twenty WAAFs, and each one of us has a small iron bedstead, a very small locker for personal possessions, and a bit of wall where we can pin up photographs or posters . . . stuff like that. Most huts have ablutions either attached or a short way away, but one of our billets provided us with a tin basin each, and two of the girls would be told off each morning to go and fill great big enamel jugs with water and each girl got about a pint to wash in. Then, once a week, they marched us to the public baths, where we could have a good soak and get properly clean.'

'Lord, I wouldn't like that,' Rachel said disapprovingly. 'Don't they give you curtains or anything so you can have a good wash in privacy?'

Rose laughed. The two girls were sitting in the Edelmanns' kitchen, with baby Luke asleep in his wickerwork cradle and a vegetable stew simmering on the stove. Mr and Mrs Edelmann had gone to the cinema, knowing that their daughter and her friend would have a lot to talk about, so Rose had no hesitation in assuring Rachel that modesty was simply impossible when twenty or thirty girls were crammed into a hut like sardines into a tin. 'But believe me, queen, it's a good deal better than civvy street, when you've been bombed out,' she added. 'I'll never forget the three days I spent in Liverpool after Bernard Terrace was bombed; I knew what it was then to be a Displaced Person. The authorities sent me to a church hall where I was allocated an emergency ration card, free passes for the British Restaurant and the Public Baths, and a pillow and a couple of rather thin blankets. The WVS were marvellous, and the folk in the British Restaurants, but you couldn't help feeling you were accepting charity. If I hadn't known I would be leaving it behind me, I think my self-esteem would have disappeared without trace.'

Rachel smiled affectionately at her friend. 'I think the war has changed everyone, though not always for the better,' she said. 'But it's changed you most of all. You always seemed a little bit unsure of yourself, a bit apologetic. You always dressed nicely but you didn't have the pride in your appearance which you've obviously got now.' She hesitated. 'I – I know your marriage wasn't always a very happy one, but I think it isn't just being widowed that has changed you. I really do think it must be the WAAF.'

'It is the WAAF,' Rose acknowledged at once.

'Steve had almost convinced me that I was useless, just another silly female, good for nothing but scrubbing floors and making meals. Then the war came along and I got a proper job, and earned proper money, and I began to think that there was more to me than Steve thought. His death didn't really change anything, but joining the WAAF . . . oh, Rachel, it's been the making of me. I never thought I'd learn to drive, be taught how engines work, be a truly useful member of a big community, but I've done all those things and I don't believe I've come to the end of what I can do yet.'

'And what about Luke what's his name?' Rachel asked curiously. 'I know you exchange letters, but have you met up? He seemed to like you a lot, I thought.'

'No, we've not met since May, but he's just a friend,' Rose said at once. She stood up and went over to the cradle where the baby was beginning to stir and pucker his lips in a suggestive sort of way. 'I think the young master is hungry; can I pick him up and have a play with him whilst you get his bottle?'

In March 1942, Rose was posted to Coltishall, in Norfolk.

Now, she took the big camouflaged lorries up to HQ when supplies were needed and spent quite a lot of time in denims. She had told Rachel that she and Luke had only exchanged letters, but as she entered the mess one dank October afternoon someone called out to her that she was wanted on the telephone. Rose hurried across to the instrument and recognised Luke's transatlantic drawl immediately. 'Well hello, honey! I've been posted, along with my whole crew. We've moved from Lincolnshire to East Wretham in Norfolk, so I reckon we could meet up, if you're willing? D'you realise, it's almost eighteen months since we first met, so I thought it was high time I made contact. I'd like to take you out for a meal if you can get away this evening. Your liberty trucks will take you to Castle Meadow in Norwich I guess, same as ours?'

'That's right,' Rose said, half reluctantly. She was not sure that meeting Luke again was a good idea at all.

'I thought so. Then how about it?'

Rose hesitated. Writing to Luke was fine, but actually seeing him might be going a bit too far. Since joining the WAAF, she had discovered the joys of independence and found she had no wish to change them. She had been asked out by a great number of men and had turned them all down without compunction. She had seen other girls get involved, seen how their normal cheery dispositions changed as anxiety for the safety of the young men who flew off almost nightly on their dangerous missions began to affect them. Because she had had no strong feelings for Steve, she had not allowed herself to worry overmuch when he went into danger, but she knew, instinctively, that it would be very different if she allowed herself to love someone. Loving anyone brings anxiety in its train; she had seen how fear for Alby had made even the placid Rachel jumpy and nervous, watching the dock gates as though staring in that direction would bring Alby safely through them. But she could scarcely say this to Luke, who had been such a support to her during the May Blitz. So, since she was not on duty that evening, she arranged to meet him on Castle Meadow at around seven o'clock.

As she made her way to her hut to get ready, she told herself that sharing a meal was not like going to the cinema or to a dance hall. They would sit on opposite

315

sides of a small table, eat good food and tell each other about their lives. She supposed that he might give her a friendly kiss on parting, but perhaps, if she were quick enough, they might shake hands instead. At any rate, he had said he wanted her friendship and that was something which she might rather enjoy. She had a good many friends amongst the girls in her flight, but young men did not seem content with friendship and wanted something more. If Luke was really different . . .

Rose went to the rendezvous and did not immediately recognise Luke among all the other RAF personnel, but as soon as Luke grinned at her she knew him and was surprised at the warmth of her own pleasure upon seeing his tall figure approaching. She thought he looked somehow older since their last meeting, but she knew from her own experience that bomber pilots, with the responsibility for getting their crews, as well as themselves, to and from their targets in safety, were apt to develop worry lines ahead of their time. Luke flew Wellington bombers, she knew, though because of the censor his letters had usually dealt more with his life on the ground than with his time in the air.

But he was coming to meet her, a broad grin on his craggy, attractive face, both hands held out. 'Rosie!' he said warmly. 'I hardly recognised you. You look tremendously smart. How have you been keeping? How are the kids? Gee, we've got so much catching up to do . . . I've booked a table at the Castle Hotel for seven fifteen, so if we hurry we'll be able to get ourselves a drink before we eat. How well d'you know Norwich?'

He took her hand as he spoke; it would have seemed churlish to snatch it away, so Rose left her fingers in his as they crossed the width of Castle Meadow, avoiding a couple of buses and a swarm of cyclists as they did so. As soon as she reached the further pavement, however, she gently disengaged herself, pretending to fuss with her gas mask case. 'I know the city quite well, but I've never risen to the heights of the Castle Hotel, not even been inside its doors,' she admitted. 'I've been round the cathedral and visited several churches – there's supposed to be one for every day of the year, did you know that? – and of course, I've been to most of the cinemas and pubs. How about you?'

'I scarcely know it at all; this is only my second visit,' Luke explained. 'But there's heaps to do here, not counting cinemas, dance halls and pubs.' He hesitated. 'Things a couple of pals could do together. In the summer, there are the Broads – we could hire a boat and take ourselves off for a whole day – and the fellers tell me there are still places on the coast where the beach isn't mined, so one can swim. It's a great place for birds – waders, sea birds and the like – so we could take my binoculars and spend a day down on the salt marshes, watching for summer visitors. Still, for now, it's just a meal and a chat; is that right?'

Rose smiled at him. His words seemed to imply that he really did want friendship – only friendship. He really was most awfully nice and was not put off because she was not looking for a boyfriend, and that was good enough for her.

'There are a great many stately homes as well,' she said eagerly as they entered the Castle Hotel. 'Did you know Anne Boleyn was born and brought up just down the road from here, in Blickling Hall? I don't suppose it's possible to go inside the house in wartime, but there's nothing to stop us looking at the outside, only I don't know about buses and how often they run, and I expect it's too far to walk.'

'That's no problem,' Luke said at once, leading her to a softly lit bar, already full of men and women in service uniform. 'I've a seventh share in an old car – what the fellers in my crew call a jalopy – so we can get about in that, provided you can give me a day or so's notice of your off-duty time. The whole crew chipped in and we take it in turns to use it, but Toby – he's my tail gunner – and myself have it most often; the rest of the fellers seem to want the city more than the country, so they use the liberty truck mostly. Now, what would you like to drink?'

It had been a grand evening, Rose thought, as she climbed into the liberty truck and took her place on the little tin ledge which served for a seat. The meal had been good – as wartime meals went – and the company, she thought, had been even better. Luke had talked a great deal, filling her in on all the details of his life before the war, when he had been 'Stateside' as he called it. He had explained that he came from what he dubbed Middle America, a small introspective town where his father ran a gas station and garage, and his mother had managed the grocery store attached. Just before the war in Europe started, his father had taken his elder brother Max into the business, bought the empty lot next door, and started selling new cars. Max was good at it, using all his considerable charm to persuade folk to buy from them rather than going forty miles further on to the only other dealer in the area.

'Did you work for your father?' Rose had asked, but Luke had shaken his head so vigorously that his dark brown hair had flopped across his brow. 'No way, sister! I've always wanted to fly, ever since my Uncle Bob took me for a flip in an old string bag which was part of an air circus. I would have joined the American Army Air Force as soon as I left school, but I was too young; they wouldn't take me. So I went into what you might call civil aviation, only they wouldn't let me fly – too young again – so I learned all about aero engines. By the time the war broke out over here, I was a pretty useful aero engine mechanic. I'd done some flying on the side, mind you, pretending I had to test the engines which I'd just repaired, but then your war came along, and I volunteered for the RAF.'

'And walked straight into the Blitz,' Rose had said, smiling at him. 'Poor old Luke, what a ghastly beginning!'

Luke had smiled too, showing the amazingly white teeth which seemed typical of all American servicemen. 'No, you've got that wrong,' he had assured her. 'I came over by sea and joined up in '40 and what d'you think they did? They looked at the forms I'd filled in and listened to how I'd been involved with aviation ever since leaving school, and sent me straight back to Texas to get myself trained as a flyer. I don't believe I said, but my mom came over from the old country – England, I mean – when she was only four, and she's still passionate about the place.'

In return, Rose had told Luke something about her own childhood and adolescence, though she had steered clear of her marriage, save to talk about the children. She had told him that she had received a somewhat stiff letter from Mrs Wyn Roberts but had not let it worry her since she felt that both she and her daughters had done the right thing. Mrs Wyn Roberts had claimed that the girls had left her no note, had not even told Edith of their plans, but though Rose was certain that Daisy and Petal had told her the truth, that they had left a note, she did not think it worthwhile telling Mrs Wyn Roberts so. Neither had she pointed out that Edith had lied when she had claimed to have checked on the children last thing at night since, had it been true, Daisy and Petal would not have had time to reach Bernard Terrace in the early hours of the morning, before their house had been bombed.

'And I'm sure the Wyn Robertses and that horrible Edith soon forgot all about my girls and would probably have been happier having no evacuees at all,' she had commented. 'And the children are happy at Ty Siriol, so happy that their letters are far shorter than they were when they were living at the Larches. In fact, I believe Auntie Blod has to sit them down at the kitchen table once a week and make them write a page each, so that I know what they're up to.' She had smiled across the table at Luke. 'Not being a parent, you can't imagine how it eases my mind to know that the girls are both safe and happy.'

Luke had clicked his tongue at her. 'Just because I'm not a parent, it doesn't mean I've no imagination,' he had said gently. 'I thought Mrs Williams a very great lady, but of course I wouldn't know Mrs Wyn Roberts if we met face to face on the sidewalk.' He had cocked an intelligent eyebrow at Rose. 'I wonder what sort of evacuees she got next,' he had said musingly. 'Whoever they are, I bet she isn't finding them as easy as Daisy and Petal.'

'No, I bet she isn't,' Rose had said with a chuckle. 'I never replied to her letter because I felt she was criticising the children when she said they had not left her a note, but she was pretty nice to us, really. She always put me up when I went visiting and I believe she was fond of the girls. I wonder if it's too late to drop her a postcard, just telling her that I'm in the WAAF now and that the children have gone back to their first foster home.'

'Good idea,' Luke had said, approvingly, just as the waiter approached the table and handed them both the dessert menu. 'Gee, they've got ice cream . . . and apple pie; I wonder if I could have both?'

When the postcard arrived, it took Mrs Wyn Roberts several moments to realise who Rosemary McAllister was, for it was nearly eighteen months since Daisy and Petal had left. When she remembered, she could not help thinking that the great changes which had happened in her life would never have occurred but for those two little girls. Then she scolded herself for the thought, which she knew to be unfair. It had not been their fault that Edith had been caught out in a lie – several lies – and even though Mrs Wyn Roberts had been forced to tell the authorities that the girls had left it was not exactly their fault, either, that she now had two boisterous and unmanageable teenage boys and a mother and young baby, both of whom whined and wept more often than they smiled, living under her roof. So Mrs Wyn Roberts sat down at the table and read Rose's card and let her mind go back to what had really started it all.

She had been sitting at the kitchen table, placidly shelling peas whilst Edith peeled potatoes at the sink. It was only a couple of weeks after the girls had left and Mr Wyn Roberts was coming home, so they were preparing a special dinner for that night. She remembered she had been singing a little song under her breath, whilst Edith had been chuntering on about the rudeness of the butcher when she had suggested he might produce some kidneys for the master's breakfast. A brief knock on the back door had interrupted her thoughts and Mrs Llew had entered the room carrying two linen pillow cases full of clean washing.

'Mornin', Mrs Wyn Roberts. There you are, all nicely ironed, with the master's collars starched as good as any laundry,' she had said breathlessly. 'I put the clothes in one pillow case and the bed linen, along o' towels an' that, in the other.'

'Thank you, Mrs Llew; you're a treasure. How much do I owe you?' Mrs Wyn Roberts had asked, although the sum was invariably the same.

'Three and sixpence, if you please, ma'am,' Mrs Llew had said. 'Unless you want to wait and pay it all together at the end of the week.'

Mrs Wyn Roberts smiled but shook her head. Mrs Llew always made the same offer, but she was dependent on the money she earned and would have been dismayed had her employer not paid up at once. 'Right you are, three and six it is,' she had said, reaching across the table and abstracting her purse from her handbag. She produced two half-crowns. 'Have you any change, or would you put the extra one and six towards what I pay you at the end of the week?'

It was polite to ask the question, but again she had known what the response would be. 'I've got change,' Mrs Llew had said at once, dipping into the pocket of her wraparound overall. She fished out a handful of loose cash, then gave an exclamation. 'Bless me, I meant to give you this as soon as I walked through the door. I found it among the washing when I were sortin' it into whites and coloureds. A bit crumpled it were, so you may ha' read it and throwed it away, but even so . . .'

She had handed over a creased piece of paper, clearly torn from an exercise book. Mrs Wyn Roberts had glanced at it incuriously, then flattened it out on to the table and read every word. Only when she had done so did she turn to Mrs Llew, saying in a cold, emotionless voice: 'Where did you find this, Mrs Llew?' As she spoke, she had glanced across to the sink where Edith was still peeling potatoes, but the older woman had not so much as turned her head.

'Oh, it were in the pocket of that old grey skirt, the one with soup stains all down the front,' Mrs Llew had said blithely. 'And a rare job it was, getting those stains out, but I done it, as you see.' And on the words, she had produced a droopy grey skirt from the nearest pillow case and spread it out so that Mrs Wyn Roberts could see that it was clean.

The movement must have attracted Edith's attention for she had swung round, stared at the skirt and then at the piece of paper spread flat on the table, and even as Mrs Wyn Roberts watched, her neck and face had become blotched with scarlet and her hands had begun to writhe together.

Mrs Wyn Roberts had been so angry that she felt the heat rise in her own cheeks. 'There *was* a letter from Daisy and Petal,' she had said, her voice shaking. 'And you denied it, Edith. You went up to the children's room, read the note they had left for me, realised that it implicated you and hid it away in your pocket. Well, you weren't as clever as you meant to be because you never destroyed it and now I know what sort of person you really are.'

'I – I kept it from you because – because it weren't none o' your business . . . I mean, none of what they said about me were true. All that rubbish about spittin' in your soup puttin' dog turds in the sausage

323

rolls . . . it were just kids' lies to get me into trouble. So why should I hand it to you, eh?'

Considerably bewildered, Mrs Wyn Roberts had stared from Edith to the note and back again. 'You were glad that Liverpool was bombed and told the children so, even though you knew their mother lived and worked in the city,' she had said slowly, choosing her words with care. She realised that, in her panic, Edith had actually forgotten what had been written in the note. 'So it is none of my business if you spit in the soup, Edith? None of my business if you put dog do in the sausage rolls? What a very odd idea you must have of me! But the reason that I'm telling you to leave my house at once, and never to darken my door again, is because you deliberately tried to terrify two little children by telling them their home had been flattened and their mother was probably dead, and you were glad of it, to say nothing of the lies you've told me. Go on, pack your things.'

Edith had stared at her as though she could not believe her ears, her eyes bulging and her tongue flicking in and out to moisten her big, flat lips. For several moments, she had not spoken, then words came out of her in a torrent. Horrible words. All the spite which she must have been harbouring for years against her mistress came out in a flood of foul language and fouler sentiments, until suddenly Mrs Llew had surged forward, caught Edith by the shoulders, shoved her physically out of the kitchen and slammed the door on her. Then she turned to her employer. 'What a wicked woman; how dared she use such filthy language in front of you, ma'am,' she had said, patting her employer's shoulder with one huge, work-roughened hand. 'I hope as you won't blame me for giving you the piece of paper, but it were addressed to you and

I thought it only right. Truth to tell, I never even read it, so I'm not too sure what the children said.'

Silently, Mrs Wyn Roberts had handed her the paper and Mrs Llew had read it to herself, her lips forming each word as she did so, for Welsh was her first language and clearly reading English was a chore. When she had finished it, she turned her puzzled red face towards Mrs Wyn Roberts. 'But – but there's nothing about spittin' in the soup,' she had said wonderingly. 'Nor nothin' about dog do in the sausage rolls; why ever did Edith say . . . ?'

'She'd forgotten what was in the note, but she remembered some of the nasty things she'd said to the children,' Mrs Wyn Roberts had explained. 'Well, my husband never liked the woman, so at least someone will be pleased.'

'You'll be wantin' another housekeeper, though,' Mrs Llew had said brightly. 'I know a nice, respectable woman who'd be willing to come in daily, though I doubt she'd want to live in. Want me to have a word?'

Mrs Wyn Roberts had employed Mrs Llew's friend within a couple of days of Edith's outraged departure, for the woman had not left quietly. She had threatened to take revenge on the Larches, to burn it down, to tell the police that there were illegal goings-on, to do her mistress some mischief in the fullness of time. Then she had stormed out and it was only much later that Mrs Wyn Roberts had discovered that her housekeeper's suitcase had contained, besides Edith's own possessions, the Meissen figurines from the white drawing room, the silver cutlery used for best, all the loose change from Mrs Wyn Roberts's bedside drawer and the garnet necklace and earrings which Mr Wyn Roberts had given his wife on their wedding day.

Now, sitting at the kitchen table with Rose's card

before her, and the din of the evacuees preparing for school and thundering up and down the stairs making her wince, Mrs Wyn Roberts decided that in fairness she must write to Rose McAllister and tell her about the discovery of the note and Edith's subsequent departure. Smiling to herself, she got up and went to the white drawing room to fetch pen, ink and paper, just as Joshua and Simon came charging down the stairs, skidded across the hall leaving boot marks on the black and white tiles, and disappeared into the kitchen. For a moment, she wondered whether she should go back and dole out the porridge which was simmering on the stove, for the new housekeeper arrived at nine o'clock, after the boys had gone to school. But as she was turning back, Evelyn Brown, with her squawking baby under one arm, came down the stairs and also headed for the kitchen. Let her do it for once, Mrs Wyn Roberts thought rebelliously, closing the door of the white drawing room behind her. She's idle and discontented and it's about time she learned to pull her weight. Oh, how I long for Mrs McAllister, Daisy and Petal. Those were the days! But no matter how difficult life was for her now, she never longed for Edith.

Chapter Thirteen

January 1943

'Come along, Petal, stop mooning or we'll be late. Miss Hastings is ever so nice but she does hate it when someone comes in in the middle of prayers.'

'Oh, but the hedgerows look so beautiful with frost on everything and the sun making each twig glitter,' Petal said reverently. 'Now that Mam is away from the city and out on that airfield, do you suppose she sees beautiful frosts like these?'

Daisy was a cold little creature; no matter how warmly she was wrapped, her nose, toes and finger-tips always went numb when it was frosty, and when she got to school, and into the comparative warmth, they would throb and ache with the returning blood, and if she were unlucky she might get a crop of chilblains. Even so, she could not help admiring the beauty of the delicate frost tracery on every branch and twig and decided, on the spur of the moment, that if it was still cold at the weekend, they would go into the hills. There was a stream up there which sometimes froze in severe weather and a cavern where icicles formed, some of them as long as a foot.

She put the thought into words, adding that they would ask Nicky to accompany them. She still remembered her delight when Nicky had turned up once more in Ruthin.

It had been three days after their own return, and at first Daisy had scarcely believed her eyes. She had only caught a glimpse of him as he crossed the playground after classes had started, and since she had only seen his back view she told herself, sternly, that it could have been anyone. But when playtime had arrived, and the whole school had erupted into the yard, she saw at once that she had not been mistaken. Nicky was surrounded by a group of friends, all of whom clearly remembered him from his first brief stay amongst them, but as soon as he saw Daisy he had come across to her, his face splitting into a wide grin.

'Bet you never expected to see me, queen,' he had greeted her. 'In fact no one expected to see me, norrin this neck o' the woods, but we was bombed out on Monday night – poor old Bernard Terrace is beginnin' to look like a gob full of teeth with half of 'em missin'. I'm thirteen now, old enough to be useful, which is why the Ryans took me back to Bernard Terrace in the first place. They'd ha' kept me there, too, if the house hadn't bought it, so they had to go an' live wi' Mr Bob Ryan and his wife, and there weren't room for me, an' when I saw the WVS ladies about a billet, I said I'd come back to Mrs Foley, if she could have me. They telephoned to the Town Hall and someone went round to the butcher's shop in Clwyd Street and Mrs Foley said if I'd give a hand in the shop an' help with her vegetable garden, she'd fit me in. So a' course I agreed, an' they give me a spare pair of kecks, a jacket an' shirt and an emergency ration card, and one of 'em put me on the train, and here I am.'

He had grinned down at Daisy and she realised, suddenly, how much he had grown since the two of them had last played Relievio in the school yard. She had said as much, but Nicky had only laughed. 'You see'd me when your house were hit and we had our picnic in the rec, and that were only a few days ago,' he had reminded her. 'I don't reckon I've growed much since then.'

Daisy had laughed. 'I know what you mean but I'm not talking about *then*, I'm talking about the last time we were in this playground. I've got taller as well, so has Petal, but you've really shot up, Nicky.'

But that had been over eighteen months ago and as she and Petal had settled happily into the farm, Nicky had done the same with the Foleys. He slept in a little attic at the top of the tall, tottery house, and worked pretty hard for his foster parents. However, they were very fair with him, allowing him time off so that he could go around with his friends, and treating him more like a son than the Ryans ever had. 'It's because their sons is both growed up,' Nicky had explained to Daisy. 'The Ryans have got a heap o' kids which are *really* their own, so they didn't need me at all, except to look after the younger ones and now Bert can do that – he's next to me in age. I were just another mouth to feed, a nuisance really. But the Foleys have only got me, so they can take time to get to know me. And they notice that I work hard and want to get on; I reckon I'm in clover!'

So now, Daisy and Petal hurried into school, and when playtime arrived Daisy suggested that Nicky might like to go up into the hills with them at the weekend. He agreed enthusiastically, as she had known he would, and reminded her that the tops of the hills, at any rate, were covered by a blanket of snow. 'We can nab a couple o' trays from somewhere and go down the hills on 'em, like on a sledge,' he said eagerly. 'It'll be grand, better'n Havelock Street, 'cos once when I went down there on me tray, I couldn't stop an' I shot straight into Netherfield Road and nearly got flattened by a coal lorry.'

Daisy nodded wisely, though she and Petal had never been allowed to sledge anywhere in the city, let alone down Havelock Street, which was known to be both steep and dangerous. 'We'll get the trays . . . we might even get a proper sledge,' Daisy said, with a vague memory of Dilys telling her how she and her brother had taken their sledge up into the hills every winter. 'Have you ever made a snow house, Nicky? They're called igloos. When Dilys was a little girl, she and her brother used to make them when the snow was deep enough. I'd like to do that.'

'Me too,' Petal chimed in at once. 'We could take a sort of winter picnic; Auntie Blod always has a cake, or some sausage rolls or something, tucked away in her larder.'

'That 'ud be grand,' Nicky said. 'Tell you what, I'll get Uncle Bill to look out some bits and pieces of meat and that, to give to Mrs Williams.' He grinned at them, tapping the side of his nose and winking as he did so. 'There's always some farmer, somewhere, what's hid away a pig or a sheep for slaughter, which won't go through the Ministry books. Oh aye, Uncle Bill will gi' me a parcel o' bits when I explain Mrs Williams will be feedin' me.'

The bell rang at this point and the children had to return to their classes, but before she left to go to her own room, Petal gave Daisy's hand a squeeze. 'Couldn't we ask Maldwyn if he could come to the hills with us as well?' she whispered. 'It'll be much more fun if there are four of us.'

Daisy and Petal had made all the arrangements for a day in the hills by Thursday evening. They would not be able to set out until around noon, because Nicky was needed in the shop on a Saturday morning, but since Maldwyn also worked on the farm at weekends, and the two girls did their share of any tasks of which

Auntie Blod thought them capable, this was no bad thing. Petal pointed out that if they had waited until Sunday they could have started earlier, immediately after church, but having made their plans they decided to stick to them.

On Friday, coming back from school in the pony trap, Dilys, who was driving, remarked that Petal looked flushed. 'I've got a perishin' cold,' Petal said, energetically blowing her nose into a rather inadequate handkerchief. 'But a day in the open air will do me lots of good because it's that stuffy classroom which has made me sneeze; the chalk dust and that, you know.'

Dilys laughed, but said that she would make Petal a hot cup of tea with a spoonful of whisky in it, as soon as they reached home. 'And if I were you, I'd go straight to bed after supper,' she advised the child. 'Then you'll be fighting fit for your expedition tomorrow. It don't do to ignore a cold, cariad.'

For once, Petal did as she was told and went snuffling off to bed, clasping her rubber hot water bag, as soon as supper was over. But next morning, when Daisy hopped out of bed and swished back the curtains and pulled up the blackout blind, she turned a disappointed face towards her small sister, still cuddled down in bed. 'Oh, Petal, can you see? It must have been snowing for hours; the yard's inches deep and there's still quite a few flakes falling. I bet Auntie Blod won't let us out of the house on a day like this.'

Petal shot up in bed, indignation written all over her small face. 'But we *must* go,' she wailed. 'I went to bed early and drank that beastly drink so's we could go to the hills today. And Nicky and Maldwyn will be coming over as soon as they've done their jobs. Oh, Daisy, we must, we must go!'

'Well, we might as well get up and dress,' Daisy said tactfully. There was no point in letting Petal get in a state for no real reason, for though the snow in the yard looked deep, it was probably only three or four inches and might be no impediment to their plans. The girls got up, washed and dressed with an anxious eye on the weather, and by the time they had made their beds and descended into the kitchen, things looked a good deal more hopeful. The snow had stopped, the dark grey clouds had blown away, and the sun was shining out of a clear blue sky, although it was still extremely cold.

As soon as breakfast was finished, Daisy and Petal did their chores. Petal dusted and swept the carpet in the living room with the Ewbank whilst Daisy, muffled in her thick winter coat, went and helped Dilys to clean down the dairy and sterilise the big milk pans and the butter-making equipment. Then she went into the cowshed and collected the stainless steel milk pails, taking them back into the kitchen where Auntie Blod cleaned them out with boiling water and a good deal of elbow grease. After that, the two girls helped Auntie Blod in the kitchen until noon, making themselves and the boys a mound of sandwiches and cutting up a whole fruit cake into large wedges, as well as popping a couple of bottles of lemonade into the haversack which Daisy sincerely hoped that Nicky, as the eldest, would carry. A rap on the door heralded his arrival, complete with an old and battered tin tray under one arm and a brown paper parcel under the other. He marched into the kitchen, handed the parcel to Auntie Blod, telling her that it came from Mr Foley, and accepted her thanks graciously before turning to beam at the girls. 'Ready for the off, then?' he said cheerfully. 'It's a grand day – the air is being warmed by the sun till you could think it were summertime if it weren't for the snow. And the snow's gettin' a grand crust on it, so it'll be as slippery as hell – I mean slippery as anything – when we get into the hills.'

Auntie Blod looked surprised. 'Oh, but I thought you'd be staying here for your dinners,' she said. 'I know Daisy and Petal have made a picnic, but you can eat that for your tea. Why not eat your dinners here? I've got a casserole in the Aga.'

The smell of the casserole was enticing and for a moment Daisy wavered, but Nicky was firm. 'No, it gets dark too early in January to purroff leavin' right now,' he explained. 'Ah, here's Maldwyn; he'll tell you the same, Mrs Williams.'

Auntie Blod sighed, but when Maldwyn assured her earnestly that it would take them almost an hour to reach the best slopes, she gave in. 'I'll save some of that there casserole and you can have it when you get back,' she promised them. 'And don't you forget, you're to be home here afore dark, or you'll be in trouble. And if the weather turns bad on you, or looks like doing so, come straight home. Is that understood, fynwy fechan i?'

Daisy smiled to herself as she agreed that they would come home at once if the weather changed, because she had suddenly remembered that when Auntie Blod had first used that Welsh expression she had thought it sounded like swearing, or some sort of insult. Now, of course, she knew that it merely meant 'my little ones', because she and Petal – and Nicky, too – understood the Welsh language well and could speak some Welsh without having to think about it.

Having promised to be sensible, the children presently found themselves trudging up the lane in the sunshine, Maldwyn towing a small, home-made sledge, whilst Daisy and Nick carried battered tin trays and Petal, wellington-booted and rosy, kept trying to take the sledge's strings from Maldwyn, or darted ahead to pelt them with soft snowballs from the shelter of snow-laden gorse bushes.

By the time they reached the cavern where Daisy had thought they would eat their picnic, they were all pretty hot and only too willing to accede to her suggestion that they eat their food here, though Maldwyn pointed out that they still had a good twenty-minute walk before reaching the best sledging place. Snow had driven into the cavern, and icicles as long as Daisy's arm hung round the entrance like jagged teeth. But they pushed their way inside, Nicky loudly lamenting that they had not thought to bring a supply of kindling up with them. 'We could have made a fire and toasted the sandwiches on sticks,' he said wistfully. 'We could have hotted up the lemonade an' all, and warmed our hands and feet.'

'Well, we didn't,' Daisy said, rather crossly. It would have been fun to light a fire all right, but she thought it was almost as nice to squat inside the cavern, eating sandwiches and drinking lemonade, and watching the sun strike a million diamonds of brilliant colour from every icicle. Besides, simply being out of the snow whilst still in the sunshine was warming her up. 'Anyway, a fire would have melted the icicles and that would probably have put it out, which wouldn't have been much fun.'

Maldwyn laughed. 'And the breeze is blowing towards us, so the fire would have smoked us out like rats out of a barn,' he pointed out, in his soft Welsh voice. 'Tell you what, though, Petal was telling me about the snow houses that Dilys and Gareth used to build when they were kids. I know how to build a snow house with a sort of chimney, so next time we come up here I'll bring some dry wood and we can light a fire in that, once it's made.'

Nicky gave a crow of derisive laughter. 'Oh aye?' he said mockingly. 'If a fire will melt icicles, then I should think your old snow house would be a puddle ten minutes after you lit the first match. I'd ha' thought a farmer's lad would know better than to fill a gal's head full o' nonsense.'

'It's not nonsense . . .' Maldwyn was beginning quietly when Petal sprang to his defence.

'You don't know nothin', Nicky Bostock, you're just a stupid city scouser,' she said angrily. 'Maldwyn knows everything about the countryside. He can tell a blackbird's nest from a thrush's by the way it's built; he knows every bird's egg, every single one. He can put his hand in a stream and bring out a trout. I've seen him – it's called ticklin'. So, if he says you can build a fire in a snow house, then you bleedin' well can.'

'Yes, I reckon Maldwyn knows all sorts,' Daisy said pacifically, 'though it does sound unlikely, Petal, you must admit. I mean everyone knows heat melts snow, so why shouldn't a fire melt a snow house? But there won't be time for building such things today, not if we're to get some sledging done, so don't let's argue.' She glanced around her, then began packing the remains of the food and drink back into the haversack. 'Everyone ready to move on?'

They agreed to do so, though Daisy intercepted the baleful look which Nicky shot at Maldwyn, and was sorry for it. Maldwyn was a nice boy and never tried to show off, particularly to Nicky, a good three or four years older than he, but Daisy appreciated that Nicky was doing his best to learn country ways and probably could not help resenting the younger boy's knowledge.

However, nothing more was said as they toiled up

the steep incline, and presently they reached the field which both she and Maldwyn had had in mind. Nicky glanced approvingly at the long gentle slope, though he could not resist pointing out that the field ended in some low, scrubby bushes with a stream beyond them. 'If we go crashin' through those bushes, we'll likely end up in the stream,' he said. 'Ain't there a place where we can slide wi'out catchin' our death of cold at the finish?'

Maldwyn, however, assured him that the bushes were thicker than they looked and in fact were growing out of a deepish hollow. 'You'll never hit the stream unless your tray takes off and soars over the bushes like a pheasant on the wing,' he said, with a chuckle. 'Before my brother Eifion joined the air force, he and meself came up here every winter, and neither of us ever got so much as an inch past them bushes.'

Nicky accepted this wisdom, though grudgingly, and soon the four of them, Maldwyn and Petal on the sledge, and the other two on their trays, were swooping and shrieking their way down the field, and tumbling off into the bushes. Despite the sunshine, the snow in the shadowed hollow was dry and powdery, so all that was necessary to rid oneself of it was a good shake, before climbing the hill again and repeating the experience. After a while Maldwyn offered the sledge to Nicky and Daisy, and he and Petal took a turn on the trays, though after watching Petal, who was small and light, descending the hill at a frightening pace, he told Daisy that her sister was far safer on the sledge since he could use his feet to brake and his hands to steer, thus making certain that Petal did not descend the hill like a rocket. 'I thought she was going to do what I told Nicky me and Eifion never did; that is go so fast that the tray took off, flew over the bushes like a bird, and crashed into the stream,' he said, chuckling again. 'But she's safe enough with me, and you and Nicky manage grand on the trays.'

'Don't we though?' Daisy said, trudging up the hill with her tray in her arms. 'This is the best thing I've ever done, Maldwyn, easily the best. Well, the best of the winter things,' she amended, remembering picking primroses and violets from banks sweet with the scent of spring; long, warm days in the hayfield, learning when to turn over the piles of drying grass with her small pitchfork; and riding the rough little pony round and round a grassy meadow whilst Dilys told her to grip with her knees, to keep her hands down, and to rise to the trot. 'You are so lucky, Maldwyn, to live here all the time; I wish we did.' She glanced around her. Nicky and Petal, talking earnestly, were following them but out of earshot. Daisy lowered her voice. 'Nicky wishes he did as well, you know. That's why he's – he's sometimes a bit sharp with you; it's because you're a lot younger than he is, but you already know all the things he's trying to learn before he gets sent back to Liverpool,' she ended.

Maldwyn's thin brown face broke into a smile. 'Oh aye, and I don't blame him, but if you ask me, he won't go back, him, not ever. Why should he, after all? Petal told me he's got no family of his own – them Ryans aren't even related to him – and so far as I can make out, he's rare good at all the jobs the Foleys need doing. Oh, I'm not saying he'll work in the shop or deliver meat for the rest of his life, 'cos he'll want to better himself, I dare say, but I think he'll stay in Ruthin. Can't see no reason why not, meself.'

Daisy gazed at him, round-eyed. 'I reckon you're right,' she said slowly. 'Why, I'll be able to get a job in a couple of years and I'd like to live here, just like

Nicky. Mind, if the war ends soon, Mam will take us back to Liverpool in a trice.'

'Why?' Maldwyn said baldly. 'Your home's been bombed, your dad's been killed – Petal told me that – so why shouldn't your mam settle here as well? You like it here, you said you did, and young Petal likes it too, she often says so. She says she's going to be a farmer and keep pigs and hens, and have her own pony and trap,' he added, grinning at Daisy.

Daisy opened her mouth to reply, but at that point they reached the top of the slope and Petal came panting up beside her. 'If you and Nicky get on the big tray, and me and Maldwyn use the sledge, we could have a race,' she said breathlessly. 'Bet we could beat you, even though we're younger.'

The first swoop down the hill was won easily by Maldwyn and Petal because, of course, they were lighter and their sledge was more manoeuvrable than Nicky's tin tray, so the second race was a handicap one, with the tin tray getting a six-yard start. This time it was a dead heat, and it was only as they reached the top of the slope once more that Daisy noticed that it was getting difficult to make out the shapes of the bushes in the hollow below them. Even as she opened her mouth to say that they must get home before dark, a snowflake landed on her nose. She began to point out to the others that the daylight was fading, but before she could say more than a few words, snowflakes began descending thick and fast, and she saw that the wind was getting up. The boys realised it at the same moment and stopped discussing the handicap which should be applied on the next race, suggesting instead that they should make all speed towards the farmhouse. They set off at once, but very soon Daisy noticed that Petal was lagging behind, even though Maldwyn was doing his best to help her along. 'I'm tired and most awfully hot,' she whimpered, when Daisy dropped back to ask her how she felt. 'I'm aching all over and I feel sick. It's all your fault, Daisy McAllister. You shouldn't have brought me out when you knew I had a nasty cold.'

Daisy felt outraged at the unfairness of this remark, but saw that Petal was not quite herself and gave her sister's shoulders an encouraging squeeze. 'That's right, queen, it's all my fault,' she said. 'Let me put my arm round your waist and Maldwyn and I will help you along.'

She had to shout the words above the worsening gale and presently, when Petal pushed her away, saying that she was dragging on her and not helping at all, Daisy went ahead once more to where she could just make out the shape of Nicky, with the hump of the haversack on his back. She caught his arm, saying urgently as she did so: 'Nicky, Petal's worn out and not at all well. D'you think we should make for the cavern and shelter there until the storm passes? She's only a kid, after all, and probably she's right; I shouldn't have brought her out when I knew perfectly well she had a nasty head cold. Oh, do let's make for the cavern; it's ever so much nearer than Ty Siriol.'

Nicky was against the plan at first because he said what they all wanted was a decent fire to dry out their clothing and a hot meal in their bellies, but presently he agreed that perhaps the cavern might be a better option and the two of them turned back to tell Maldwyn and Petal the change of plan.

There was no one behind them; only the whirling flakes and the rapidly falling dark. Nicky turned back to Daisy. 'That's bleedin' well torn it,' he said, and there was panic in his voice. 'I can barely see me hand in front o' me face and I've not gorra clue in which direction that cavern lies. Have you, queen?'

Dumbly, Daisy shook her head. With the snow underfoot, she could not tell whether they were on the stony little track which would lead, eventually, to the Ty Siriol lane, or whether they had strayed far from it. She raised her voice in a loud shout. 'Petaaaaaaa! Maldwyyyyyyyyn!' But even as she called, she heard her voice being whipped away by the wind and muffled by the falling snow, and knew there was little chance of being heard. Desperately, she turned back to Nicky. 'We'd best go back, Nick,' she said urgently. 'We've simply got to find them. I wonder if they've made for the cavern? If so, and we come across it, at least we can huddle together for warmth and wait there until the storm passes.'

This time Nicky did not even hesitate. He shook his head firmly and grabbed Daisy's arm, pulling her after him. 'Don't talk daft,' he adjured her. 'Our only hope of finding any sort of shelter is to keep on going downhill. We'll never find the cavern, norrin this snow and not without Maldwyn to guide us. If they make it, they'll be okay until the storm passes, and if we make it – to Mrs Williams's place I mean – then we can send out a search party to fetch the others in.' Daisy still hung back and Nicky gave her a shove. 'Don't be a fool, Daisy; once we turn back, we'll use up all our energy searching whilst the kids will be getting colder and colder. Can't you see we've got to have help? I reckon the Williamses will know that cavern and be able to go straight to it, even through the snow, and if the kids aren't in it, there'll be torches and more folk to shout their names, and a better chance of finding them before . . . well, before something awful happens. So best foot forward, as Mr Foley would say, and no more hankerin' after turning back, understand?'

When she heard it put so succinctly, Daisy realised

at once that Nicky was right and fell into step beside him once more. After a few moments, he took her arm, saying gruffly that they must not get separated. Once or twice he encouraged their onward progress by remarking that he was pretty sure they were still going downhill and, hopefully, were still on the track. It was impossible to say for certain whether he was right, but Daisy hoped that he was. She thought they might easily have left the track but knew, as they neared level ground, that there would be trees and bushes on either side of them and presently, despite the swirling snow and the fact that it had frozen on to her eyelashes and had to be impatiently dislodged every few minutes, she thought she saw a shape looming up before her and realised that it was a great old oak tree, the one which grew closest to the track. She must have spotted it at the same time as Nicky did for he gave a hoarse shout, then looped an arm about her waist and began to hurry her along. 'Only another fifty or sixty yards to go and we'll be in the farmyard,' he said exultantly. 'We've near on made it, queen. I say, suppose Maldwyn and Petal are already in the kitchen, toasting their toes by the fire? Wouldn't that be grand, eh?'

'They couldn't possibly have passed us without us noticing,' Daisy said, a trifle peevishly. She felt as though her legs were made of lead and wanted nothing more than to rest for a bit before tackling the remainder of the journey. 'Can't we rest just for a little while, Nicky?' she asked plaintively. 'I'm so tired, I'm sure I could curl up and sleep under that oak tree, if only for a few minutes.'

'No you could not,' Nicky said, his voice outraged. 'That's how people die in the Arctic, you stupid girl. Just you keep a-moving, or you'll feel my boot behind you.'

Daisy gave a stifled sob but in her heart she knew Nicky was right. She had heard the stories of gallant Captain Oates leaving the Scott expedition and saying that he 'might be some time', knew that he had frozen to death in the snowy wastes of Antarctica, and had no desire to follow his example. Presently, she was rewarded by the sound of voices and the sight of torches, and next moment she was in Dilys's arms, sobbing out that Petal and Maldwyn were missing, that she had lost them in the snow and would never forgive herself if harm came to her little sister. Dilys picked her up and hugged her tightly and Daisy saw that there were tears on the older girl's cheeks. 'It's all right, cariad,' Dilys said comfortingly. 'Mam's in the kitchen warming blankets before the fire and soup on the stove. She'll have you and Nicky here warm as toast and well fed in five minutes, and don't you worry yourself about Petal and Maldwyn. Shanna's got a wonderful nose on her so I brought out your pixie hoods so she can have a sniff of them and know she's looking for a person and not a lost sheep. Can you cross the yard yourself, love, or do I have to carry you all the way? Only the sooner we fetches the other two back to the farm, the better it'll be for us all.'

'I can walk,' Daisy said, struggling out of Dilys's arms with some reluctance, for the older girl felt as warm and comfortable as a feather bed. 'Come on, Nick.'

Nicky, however, hesitated. 'I oughter go back wi' the others, show 'em the way to the cavern,' he mumbled. 'I just wanted to see you safe indoors, queen . . .'

But Dilys was having none of it. 'You'd be more hindrance than help, boy,' she said brusquely. 'We've got three strong men and meself, as well as Shanna, and we're none of us soaking wet, nor yet wore out, so just you get into that kitchen and no more argufying and we'll be back with Petal and Maldwyn afore you know it.'

Daisy waited for Nicky to object, to say that he was good for many hours yet, but to her relief he just heaved a sigh, nodded and grinned at Dilys, and followed Daisy kitchenwards. Daisy had scarcely raised her hand to the doorknob before the door was flung open and she found herself clutched to Auntie Blod's warm bosom and carried across the kitchen to be set down before the fire, blinking in the strong light of the oil lamp.

'Oh, my dearest Daisy, what a fright you've give us, but you're home an' safe, and that's the main thing.' Auntie Blod was stripping Daisy of her soaking clothing as she spoke, and as soon as she had done so she turned and began to do the same for Nicky, for it was clear to Daisy that what with the cold and the wet, neither of them could move their numbed hands to any practical purpose. 'Where's Petal and Maldwyn?' Auntie Blod went on, seizing blankets, hot from the fire, and wrapping one round Daisy and another round Nicky. 'I'll warrant they ain't far behind you – I dare say Dilys is giving them a bit of extra coddling, them being nobbut babies – so the pair of you can sit on the sofa while I pour you a nice mug of hot soup.'

'P-P-Petal's lost; sh-sh-she wouldn't let me help her; she s-s-said I was dragging on her,' Daisy explained, through chattering teeth. Oh, Auntie B-B-Blod, if anything's happened to P-P-Petal . . . I should've made her l-l-let me help her . . .'

Auntie Blod patted Daisy reassuringly but the look of worry deepened on her rosy face. 'That young 'un! Obstinate as a whole herd of mules, she is; if she were in one of her independent moods, you'd not have had a chance, cariad, so don't go blaming yourself. Besides, with all the men out looking, as well as our Shanna,

343

she'll be sharing the fire with you in no time, as well as this lovely thick soup.'

She was pouring soup into two mugs as she spoke and would have handed one to each of them, save that Nicky spoke before she had time to do so. 'Don't, Mrs Williams,' he said urgently. 'I can't even keep hold o' the blanket; our hands is so cold, they couldn't go round the mug handle, lerralone take the weight of it to our lips. But if we could sit up to the table and have a bit o' bread to dip, like . . .'

'It's an old fool I am,' Auntie Blod said remorsefully, standing the steaming mugs on the scrubbed wooden table. 'What's more, it's a deal too hot to drink, so while it cools I'll nip upstairs and fetch you down some dry clothing. Daisy can have her own, of course, but I reckon an old pair of Gareth's winter trousers and one of the thick old jerseys I knitted for him to wear on the farm will do you a treat, Nick. Shan't be more'n a moment.'

She disappeared and could be heard ponderously ascending the stairs, and Nicky turned and grinned at Daisy. 'I'll be rare glad o' them kecks,' he whispered. 'I'm bare as a babe beneath this blanket; she even took off me underpants, an' socks, an' everything. I hope you weren't watching, young Daisy.' He was grinning and Daisy grinned back.

'I'm bare, too; I were too busy shiverin' and aching when the fire started to warm me up to bother about what were happening to you,' she pointed out righteously. 'Besides, I seen you with no clothes on more'n once, swimming in the Scaldy.'

'Oh aye, but I've – I've growed a bit since then,' Nicky said, a trifle awkwardly. 'Mrs Foley were shocked when I told her we swam naked at home. She said I were too old for such things and gave me a pair of her Ernest's old bathing drawers.' He chuckled. 'She knitted them for him and they've stretched a bit, I reckon, over the years, but the other fellers usually wear something similar, so I don't complain.'

'I've never learned to swim,' Daisy said regretfully. She got up, still blanket-wrapped, and approached the table, gazing longingly at the mugs of soup. 'I can't wait to get some of this down me . . . what's that?'

Even as she spoke, Auntie Blod re-entered the kitchen, dumped some clothes on Nicky's lap and handed a thick jumper, a brown woollen skirt and a pair of stockings to Daisy. 'It's back they are; I heard Shanna barking and that's a sure sign she found what she were looking for,' Auntie Blod said briskly. 'Get into them clothes before the kitchen's full of folk needin' a warm. I'll just cut some bread, then you can be sitting down and eating your soup by the others come in.'

Nicky and Daisy scrambled into their clothes and Daisy rushed to the back door and pulled it open. Looking across the yard she saw that Auntie Blod had been right; Dilys was carrying Petal, the child's face pressed against her neck, and Uncle Gwil had an arm round Maldwyn, whilst Shanna danced around the small group, grinning and barking as if she knew she was the cleverest dog in the world. Behind them, the farmhands shouted farewells in Welsh and turned to go back to their own cottages, clearly anxious to be home before the weather worsened again, for the storm had eased and only a few large curled-feather snowflakes continued to float down. But the cold was still very much with them; it nipped at Daisy's face and at her stockinged feet and she was glad to close the door on the night as the last person entered. She looked on as Auntie Blod took Petal's small form in her arms and began to strip off the child's soaking clothing, whilst Dilys performed

the same service for Maldwyn. Daisy went over to
Auntie Blod, looking anxiously into her sister's small
face. Petal was very flushed, her eyelids heavy and her
mouth drooping, and Daisy heard her hoarse breathing.
She realised, all in a moment, that Petal's eyes were not
focusing on her, did not seem to see her.

'Auntie Blod? Is – is she all right? She looks so
strange and she's making a sort of wheezing sound.
Is she asleep?'

She could easily have been asleep for she made no
move, either to help or hinder, as Auntie Blod stripped
her to the skin and wrapped her in a blanket, but at
Daisy's anxious words Auntie Blod tried to smile reassuringly before turning back to the task of chafing
Petal's cold body. 'She's like ice,' she said quietly. 'But
at least she's alive . . . *this my son was dead, and is alive
again; he was lost, and is found.*'

Daisy stared at her, bewildered. 'But Petal isn't
your son, nor even your daughter,' she said in a puzzled
voice. 'Though of course, she was lost and now we've
found her. Dear, dearest little Petal, I'll never be cross
with her again.'

Auntie Blod smiled and smoothed back the tumbled
hair from Petal's forehead. 'That were a quotation from
the Bible; remember the Prodigal Son?' she asked. 'But
the child's head is like a furnace, though the rest of her
is still cold as ice.' She turned to her daughter. 'Dilys,
cariad, I'm afraid someone will have to go for the doctor;
the child's got a fever, and a high one if I am any judge.'

Dilys came over and looked down at Petal, a worried
frown on her face. 'But will I get into Ruthin with all
this snow on the road, and will Dr Clitheroe come back
with me?' she asked doubtfully. 'It's awful dark, Mam,
and I don't reckon he'd get his car out of the garage
because it's at the bottom of a slope. By tomorrow,

there'll be mebbe more chance of him visiting.'

Auntie Blod looked undecided but Uncle Gwil cut in in his usual quiet way. 'I'll go. I'll take Sweep, 'cos he's the larger of the two shires, and he's amenable to being rid bareback. Dr Clitheroe's a good man; when I tell him he's needed urgently, he'll come, even if he has to ride Sweep pillion behind me.'

Auntie Blod's face cleared. 'You're a good man yourself, Gwil,' she said quietly. 'Tell him she's hot as fire and unconscious; tell him I'm truly worried. And I'll pack you a flask of tea with whisky in so's you can have a nip whenever you feel inclined. Get that wet coat off and them wet boots; I'll fetch dry.'

She bustled out and Daisy's heart gave a startled leap as she saw that all the colour had drained from Maldwyn's face. Whilst Auntie Blod loaded Uncle Gwil with dry clothing, the promised flask and a huge muffler, as well as a great deal of advice, Maldwyn sidled over to Daisy. 'All my fault, it was,' he muttered wretchedly. 'We lost sight of you in the blizzard and Petal said she couldn't go no further, so I lifted her up and took her to the cavern, knowing it were nearby. I couldn't have reached the farmyard carrying her,' he added sadly. 'The snow was too thick, and by then I was too weak myself to take her weight.'

'Oh, Maldwyn, you did wonderfully well to get her into shelter,' Daisy said, clasping his cold hand between her two warm ones. 'Nicky and I meant to make for the cavern ourselves but we were lost and dared not turn aside from the track. I'm sure you saved Petal's life by reaching it. If you'd collapsed in the snow trying to carry her to the farm, you'd both have been dead by now.'

Maldwyn returned the clasp of her hand just as Uncle Gwil pulled open the back door. Daisy caught a glimpse of madly swirling flakes, heard the howl of

347

the wind and realised that the blizzard had started once more. She hoped Uncle Gwil and the doctor would soon return and knew she would feel much happier about Petal when they did so, for she thought the doctor both kind and clever – had he not cured her sore throat and mended Elias's broken ankle? But now, inside the kitchen, all was bustle. It was clearly impossible for either Maldwyn or Nicky to return to their own homes, so Auntie Blod and Dilys were creating makeshift beds from the sofa and two of the armchairs. At present, Petal was lying on the sofa, but Auntie Blod meant to kindle a fire in her own room and have Petal share her big feather bed. 'Then I can keep an eye on her, my love,' she explained to Daisy. 'I wouldn't be easy, knowing she were liable to cry out and me not hear her. Uncle Gwil can sleep in the Land Girl's room, since young Heather's away for the weekend and won't be back till late tomorrow or early Monday.' She glanced at the window, almost obscured now by snowfall. 'If she gets back at all,' she added ruefully. 'We've been snowed up here for weeks at a time in the past; I reckon it's going to happen again.'

By the time Dilys had carried Petal upstairs to the now warmed bedroom, the kitchen had been converted for the boys' use and a meal – casseroled beef and Auntie Blod's delicious floury dumplings – had been set out on the table. Daisy joined the others at the meal, though she felt almost guilty doing so, since Dilys and Auntie Blod took it in turns to sit upstairs with Petal. Dilys assured Daisy that though horribly hot and feverish still, her sister was awake and as cheerful as one could be in the circumstances. 'But there's no denying Mam and meself will be a lot happier once the doctor's seen her,' she admitted. 'All finished? Who's for a nice piece of apple pie with custard, eh?'

The boys responded eagerly but Daisy felt she could not eat another morsel and begged Dilys to let her go up and sit with Petal whilst Auntie Blod came down and enjoyed a share of the apple pie. Dilys hesitated, but clearly seeing Daisy's anxiety told her that she might run upstairs and have a few words with Petal. 'Only you can't look after her the way meself and Mam can,' she said bluntly. 'She can't shift herself in bed – she aches all over – and we're bathing her forehead with the lavender water you gave Mam when she were in hospital and wiping her hands with a wet cloth. You tell her as you and Nicky are safe, and Maldwyn's fine, 'cos that does seem to worry her that she can't remember seeing you in the kitchen.'

Daisy nodded and made for the stairs, glancing hopefully towards the window as she went; you never knew, Uncle Gwil and the doctor might be crossing the yard at this very moment. But she could see nothing through the blackout blind, though she could still hear the howl of the wind.

She entered Auntie Blod's room softly, then walked quietly towards the bed. Almost as though she were aware of her sister's presence, Petal's eyes flew open, but they went straight to Auntie Blod's face. She moaned softly, turning her head restlessly on the pillow as though searching for a cool spot, and Auntie Blod gently reached out and stroked a large wet handkerchief, redolent of lavender water, around the sufferer's strangely flushed face. Daisy went and stood close to Auntie Blod. She was frightened because she had never seen Petal looking like this before. Her sister's eyes were bright with fever, the blonde curls damp with sweat; and whenever she moved, she groaned. Petal had closed her eyes while Auntie Blod applied the lavender water, but now she opened them again. Her wide blue gaze fixed, vacantly, on Daisy's face, but even as Daisy clutched at Auntie Blod's arm, beginning to say 'She doesn't know me', Petal's gaze sharpened and focused and her lips curved into a tiny smile.

'It's you, Daisy,' Petal murmured, in a thread of a voice. 'Oh, I'm so glad you aren't dead. Is Maldwyn . . .?'

Daisy saw that Petal's lips were cracked and dry and that speaking was difficult for her. Auntie Blod picked up a spoon, dipped it into a mug of something which stood on the bedside table, and would have trickled it between her patient's lips except that Petal moved her head in a gesture of negation and then cried out shrilly, as the movement hurt her.

Daisy spoke quickly. 'Maldwyn's fine; and Nicky's fine, too, and so am I,' she said reassuringly. 'You mustn't worry about any of us, darling Petal. Nicky and I got back to the farmhouse quite quickly, and you and Maldwyn were so sensible! Maldwyn says you went straight to the cavern, which was what Nicky and I meant to do only we didn't know the way, so Nicky said just to keep going downhill . . .'

She stopped; a frown was creasing Petal's brow and her eyes had closed, almost involuntarily it seemed. 'Cavern? We didn't go to no cavern,' she said in a puzzled voice. 'Oh, Auntie Blod, I hurts all over, so I does. Even my perishin' toes hurt. I think someone's pulling my head off my shoulders so's my neck will be as long as a g'raffe. Can't you give me something to make me better?'

'I dussent do much until the doctor arrives, but he won't be long,' Auntie Blod said reassuringly. 'Now how about a little sip of the nice beef tea in this here cup? Or there's lemon and glycerine; it's grand for sore throats.'

Petal did not answer; she seemed to have sunk into an uneasy dose, muttering senselessly, and to her dismay Daisy saw tears squeeze out from between her sister's closed eyelids and soak into the feather pillow.

Auntie Blod turned to her, her voice sinking to a whisper. 'Go you off downstairs, cariad,' she said. 'No sense in staying up here when sleep is what she needs. I've melted an aspirin in the lemon and glycerine and another in the beef tea, 'cos an aspirin will do nothing but good. It'll ease the pain and mebbe even send her to sleep. But the quieter she's kept, the better. Run along now, me love.'

Daisy was only too glad to obey; the sight of Petal, so obviously ill, frightened her and she could not help remembering how they had all promised to return to the farm immediately if the weather worsened or before darkness fell. The trouble was, she told herself, rejoining the others in the kitchen, that everything had happened so quickly. None of them had had a watch, but if they had only remembered to glance at the sky, they would have seen that the sun had gone and the snow clouds were rolling over. Unfortunately, the excitement of racing the tin tray against the sledge had completely absorbed them, making them indifferent both to weather conditions and to the lateness of the hour. As a result, Petal, who had had a nasty cold anyway, was now extremely ill and causing a great deal of worry to everyone, for Daisy knew Auntie Blod would not willingly have sent her husband out in such dreadful conditions, had she not feared for Petal.

As she entered the kitchen, every eye turned to her, but she took her place at the table, still trying to command her voice and blink back tears. After a moment, she told them that Petal was 'sort of awake' and had known her, though she had seemed to be sleeping once more when Daisy left the room.

'Sleep's the best thing for her,' Dilys said bracingly. 'Besides, it won't be long before . . . what's up, Shanna?'

Daisy looked down at the dog, who had risen quietly from her place before the fire and was standing in front of the back door, the plume of her black, white-tipped tail beginning to wag gently from side to side. 'They're back,' Nick said joyfully, jumping to his feet. He swished the blackout curtain back and opened the door a crack, making sure that the curtain fell in place behind him. 'Dammit, I can't see a bleedin' thing.' He turned to Dilys. 'Can I nip out and tek Sweep from him, Miss Williams? Then he and the doctor can gerrin and start thawin' out whilst I rub the old feller down and dry off his saddle and bridle.'

Dilys looked a bit doubtful, but Nicky was already pulling the door open wider and letting in a quantity of the snow which had piled up against it. 'Hang on, Nick; you aren't dressed for the weather and you've got no more dry clothes,' Dilys said firmly. 'I'll show the doctor up to Mam's room and then I'll go and give Dad a hand. I've got dry clothes a-plenty, but I'll wear my rain cape and wellies, so's I won't get soaked.'

Nicky went to shut the door once more, but it was abruptly pushed wide, almost knocking him over, and Uncle Gwil appeared in the doorway, slamming the door behind him. He was so coated with snow as to be almost unrecognisable, but he spoke with his usual calm authority. 'I couldn't get through; the wind's piled the snow in the lane into drifts higher than my head, and up on the main road it's the same. We tried to take to the fields, me and Sweep, but no chance. The drifts there are worse if anything, and treacherous. Like the North Pole, it is, with not a landmark to warn of hedge or hollow, till you blunder into it. I

352

can't risk Sweep breaking a leg, so we turned back. I've put him in his stall but he needs rubbing down. I just came in to let you know we're back.' He shook snow off himself. 'How's the littl'un?'

'Not so brave, but she'll do,' Dilys said briefly. 'I'll bring old Sweep a bucket of hot mash; reckon he deserves it.'

'Aye, that he does; he's a heart like a lion, has Sweep,' Uncle Gwil said. He turned back to grin at his daughter. 'I wouldn't mind a bucket of hot mash meself,' he said, ducking his head and pulling the heavy oak door shut behind him.

In moments, the kitchen was all in a bustle. Maldwyn made the hot mash and Dilys tipped soup into a pan and pulled it over the fire, then checked that the casserole which she had saved for her father had not dried out. 'Have that when he gets indoors, he can,' she remarked, taking her shiny cape off the back door and pushing her feet into her wellingtons. 'Can you pour some of that soup into a mug, Daisy, without burning yourself? Only I know my dad. He should come indoors, of course, and get some food inside him, put on dry clothes, but he won't leave me to fettle Sweep. No, he'll stay out there till the horse is as warm and dry as he should be, and as well fed. Then he'll come indoors and see to himself; we don't want two invalids about the place.'

Daisy, carefully pouring soup from the pan into Uncle Gwil's large tin mug, had been stricken with dismay upon realising that the doctor had not been fetched, but she told herself, resolutely, that Auntie Blod had nursed her own children through any number of ailments and would doubtless be able to cope with Petal. It was only because Petal was not her own little girl that Auntie Blod had felt obliged to send for the doctor. Having poured out the soup, she handed the mug to

Dilys and then hurried up the stairs, knowing that Auntie Blod would have heard her husband's voice and would be eagerly awaiting Dr Clitheroe's appearance.

She entered the room to find Auntie Blod sitting Petal up against her pillows and trying to administer a spoonful of the lemon and glycerine, though Petal was saying, fretfully, that she would not swallow the horrid stuff and that she wanted her mam, so she did. Auntie Blod looked round eagerly as the door opened. 'I heard Gwil's voice; is Dr Clitheroe coming up?' she asked. And then, as though she had guessed what the answer was to be, her face fell. 'Oh no! He didn't get through, did he? Well, now the fat's in the fire, and no mistake. Still, if you'll send Dilys up to me, love, the pair of us should be able to get the young madam here to swallow some of this concoction, then she'll feel more the thing.'

Dreadfully worried, Daisy scampered down the stairs, pulled Auntie Blod's rain cape off the back door and wrapped herself in it. The boys were at the sink, Nicky washing the dishes and Maldwyn wiping them, and took no notice until she began to drag the door open, when they both turned to stare at her in astonishment. 'Wharron earth are y' doing, kiddo?' Nicky asked incredulously. 'Mr Williams and Dilys – I mean Miss Williams – will be managing fine without any help from you. You don't want to go out in all that—'

The slamming of the door cut the sentence off short and Daisy was out in the yard, feeling the force of the blizzard for herself, terrified by the strength of it, by the depth of the snow and by the shriek of the wind, yet still determined to slog her way across the snowy waste of the yard and take Dilys's place in the stable. She ducked her head as far into the huge cape as it would go and was pleasantly surprised to find herself entering the stable, having been neither blown off course nor defeated by the blizzard. Both Dilys and her father swung round as the stable door creaked open and Dilys began to berate her, but stopped when Daisy gasped out her errand.

'I telled Auntie Blod that the doctor wouldn't be coming – well, I didn't have to tell her; she guessed – and she asked for you to go up and give her a hand with Petal, Dilys. She's trying to give Petal medicine, but it needs two.'

Dilys had been rubbing the big horse down with a wisp of hay and Uncle Gwil, the soup finished and the mug empty, had been teasing the tangles out of Sweep's thick, black mane, but now he took the hay from his daughter and began energetically plying it over the patient animal's damp coat, saying briskly as he did so: 'Aye, I reckon it 'ud take two to get that young madam to do anything she didn't want! You go off, Dilys, my love; the young 'un and meself will be finished here in ten minutes.' He turned to Daisy. 'Brush out his fetlocks, there's a good gal, and give his legs a good rub, 'cos you ain't tall enough to reach his mane.'

'Right you are, Uncle Gwil,' Daisy said cheerfully. Dilys had shed her rain cape in order to attend to the big horse but now she donned it again, then cast an amused look at Daisy. 'You *were* in a hurry,' she remarked, heading for the stable door. 'You've got your boots on the wrong feet, so you have!' And with a chuckle, she left the stable, shutting the door firmly behind her before more snow could swirl in.

By the time Gwil and Daisy returned to the house, both boys were in their makeshift beds, though not actually asleep, and there was no sign of Dilys. Uncle Gwil dished himself up a huge plate of casseroled meat and dumplings and then told Daisy to make her way to bed. 'I'll fill you a hot water bag and you can pop your nose into your Auntie Blod's room and make sure your sister's all right, else you'll never sleep,' he said kindly, pouring hot water into Daisy's blue rubber hottie. 'I know we wanted the doctor to come, no doubt we'll fetch him tomorrow, but in the meantime your sister couldn't be in better hands. My Blod's nursed kids through whooping cough, quinsy, septic throats and croup,' he added bracingly. 'She only asked the doctor to come out because Petal's not her own kin, but she'll see her right, so don't go worrying yourself.'

His smile was so kind, so understanding, that Daisy felt tears prick behind her eyelids, but she did not mean to cry before Nicky and Maldwyn, and contented herself with replying that she was sure Petal would be fine, before hurrying up the stairs. She hovered outside Auntie Blod's room for a moment, not quite liking to enter without knocking, yet fearing that a knock might rouse Petal if she slept. She had turned the handle and pushed the door perhaps an inch ajar when she heard words which made her blood run cold. 'Neither you nor Gareth ever had rheumatic fever, but I remember Maldwyn's brother Billy bein' mortal ill with it,' Auntie Blod was saying in a low voice. 'The thing is, to keep 'em cool and quiet, and to give plenty of fluid, so we'll do that for tonight. But tomorrow someone will have to get through to Ruthin, 'cos there's modern medicines we'll need.'

'Oh, Mam, not rheumatic fever!' Dilys said, her voice breaking on the words. 'Why, it killed young Emily Pritchard from Llanbedr.'

'Aye, but that were years back . . .'

The door creaked as Daisy entered the room and both women swung round, giving Daisy what they no doubt meant to be reassuring smiles. 'Quietly, my love; your sister's asleep. She took the medicine, and by tomorrow morning . . .'

'Rheumatic fever. You – you said it were rheumatic fever,' Daisy faltered. 'Oh, Auntie Blod, a girl in my year had that and now she can't run, or play games, and her lips is blue and – and folks say she ain't long for this world. And Petal's so – so lively, she'd never quiet down and go slow, not if you were to tell her a hundred times.'

'No, no, you've got the wrong end of the stick, cariad,' Auntie Blod said, but her eyes slid away from Daisy's entreating gaze. 'Feverish she is, from the head cold and the snow, but nothing worse. Dilys and meself were just talking about other cases where – where a fever's been neglected. We'll take good care of your sister; she'll be right as a trivet in no time, just you wait and see.'

Daisy took one hasty glance at Petal's flushed face, mumbled that she was sure she hoped Auntie Blod was right, and hurried to her own room where she found temporary respite in a hearty bout of tears. She told herself over and over that she was doing no good by worrying, but it was a long while before she slept.

By the time day dawned next morning, Auntie Blod and Dilys were longing for the light to strengthen so that someone might go for the doctor. Petal had slept, but fitfully, and every time she awoke she had complained of aches and pains and had demanded her mother's presence, had not seemed to understand when Blodwen or Dilys had reminded her that she was at Ty Siriol, many miles from Liverpool.

Dilys was bathing the child's face with lavender water when her mother drew back the curtains, letting in the wintry reflective whiteness of a countryside several feet deep in snow. As the curtains swished back, Petal gave a sharp cry and pushed Dilys's hand, and the lavender-soaked handkerchief, away. 'Don't!' she said crossly. 'I hate that stuff when it goes on my neck; it stings like anything.' She turned her head, apparently without pain, to glare at Auntie Blod. 'And I don't want the curtains back, I want them closed tight as tight. The light hurts my eyes turble bad.'

Auntie Blod gave a squawk and crossed the room so fast that Dilys found herself being pushed away before she could move for herself. She saw her mother bend over the bed and snatch back the neck of Petal's winceyette nightdress. For a moment Auntie Blod peered at Petal's skin, then she sat heavily down on the bed and turned to beam at her daughter. 'It's the measles!' she said joyfully. 'Why didn't I think of that?' She gave Petal a triumphant hug. 'Oh, my little love, it's only the measles, so today you can have a nice bowl of porridge to your breakfast – and a boiled egg, if you fancy that – and tomorrow you can have a proper dinner and in a few days you'll be up and playing downstairs with your sister, though you'll not leave the house until the snow clears, 'cos even the measles mustn't be neglected.'

'Well I'm blessed,' Dilys said, examining the rash which pretty well covered Petal's body and was beginning to show on her cheeks and forehead. 'Fancy us not thinking of that, Mam, for I'm sure Merion who drives the milk lorry told me both his girls had got 'em a week ago, and they're all at the same school. Oh lor', I wonder how soon Daisy will get them?'

'I don't know and I'm blessed if I care,' Auntie Blod said joyfully. 'Measles I can cope with; I wouldn't call the doctor out for measles. I'd best go and tell Daisy, because the poor child will have been worritin' herself to flinders. She'll be mightily relieved to learn it isn't rheumatic fever, even if it does mean that she herself will be the next patient.'

But Daisy, when Auntie Blodwen hurried into her room with the good news, was able to assure her that she had had the measles a year before Petal was born. 'I'm so glad it's only that, Auntie Blod,' she said, sitting up and clutching her bedding round her, for it was a bitterly cold morning. 'I don't think I've slept for more than a few minutes all night because – because Mam expects me to look after Petal and I didn't do very well at it yesterday, did I?'

'Yes you did, you looked after her as well as anyone could,' Auntie Blod said firmly. 'If anyone is to blame, it's meself. No one knows better how suddenly the weather can change up here in the hills. Yet I let the four of you go off as if you knew the conditions as well as I did. And anyway, you weren't to know that Petal was about to come out in a rash of measles, were you?'

'No, and nor were you,' Daisy reminded her. She gave an enormous yawn then snuggled under the covers again. 'Is it all right if I go back to sleep for a bit, Auntie Blod? It's Sunday, so there's no school and the church service doesn't start until ten.'

'You can sleep all day, if you've a mind, cariad, since we're snowed in good and proper,' Auntie Blod informed her. 'Maldwyn might get home if Gwil can get the tractor started, or he might saddle up the shire and take him back, but Nicky's here till the snow clears and that could be days . . . weeks, even.'

'Gosh, weeks!' Daisy said sleepily. 'That means no school for weeks, either. I wonder if Nicky's had measles? I wonder . . . I wonder . . .'

She slept.

Chapter Fourteen
March 1943

Because Mrs Williams had been unable to contact Rose for a couple of weeks after Petal's measles had started, Rose had not asked for leave to visit her daughters at the time. It had seemed downright foolish to trek across the country just to see the girls for a few hours, particularly in bad weather, so she had decided to put off visiting them until the spring, when she would be able to ask for a week's leave. Instead, Rose had written a cheery letter, explaining that she would visit when the weather was better. She had enclosed a postal order for three and sixpence, instructing Daisy to buy Petal a colouring book and pencils, or something else which would help her to pass the time spent in bed.

Daisy, bless her, had replied promptly. She said that Petal was up and about again, and would be back in school in another week, and that at Petal's request she had spent some of the money on a pack of Happy Families cards; a game that everyone could play whilst sitting round the table in the evening. The rest of the money had gone on knitting wool since Auntie Blod had beguiled the long hours when Petal had been listless and weary, not well enough to play games, by teaching her to knit. Daisy told Rose that all the older girls were knitting for the forces and Petal had decided to do the same. She had managed to knit squares without dropping too many stitches and proudly handed them in at school, for the teachers to crochet into blankets. The teachers had told the children that folk who had been bombed out were very grateful for the lovely warm woollen blankets, which had made Petal look a little pensive. Daisy said that Petal thought that since their house in Bernard Terrace had been bombed, they ought to be allowed to keep at least one of the blankets themselves, but her sister had reminded her that they now lived with Auntie Blod and did not need such things.

Daisy, herself, was growing up amazingly, Rose considered. She was knitting socks – great big thick ones for air crew who needed all the warmth they could get – doing well at her lessons and learning a certain amount of cooking, so that she might help Auntie Blod and Dilys. Rose loved getting her letters, now so full of her doings, but sometimes she could not help having a little weep because she was missing so much of the girls' growing up.

However, Rose realised that the WAAF was changing her as much as the passing months were changing her daughters. She had recently successfully completed examinations which had earned her the rank of corporal and this had meant a small increase in pay, a slightly larger increase in responsibility and a really big increase in her self-esteem.

Now, Rose sat in the cookhouse with Kate, Jen and Mo, her particular friends, discussing their forthcoming leave. The four girls had arrived at Coltishall more or less simultaneously over a year ago and spent most of their off-duty time together. Mo was married to a tail gunner at present flying from an airfield in North Africa, Jen was the wife of a naval rating and Kate, like Rose herself, was a widow and still unattached, though as she somewhat reproachfully told Rose, at least she had a decent social life and every intention of marrying again. 'When the right feller asks me, of course,' she always added, grinning wickedly at her friends. 'The wrong 'uns are always far too keen and the nice fellers are usually married, but one day the perfect feller will go down on his knees and you won't see me for dust.'

But right now, the vexed question of what to do with a whole week's leave was the subject of conversation. Rose had announced her intention of going to see the girls, though she admitted it was a shame that she could not wait till Easter, when they would be on holiday and, of course, the weather would be better.

'Only it's such ages since I've seen them and when Petal was ill with the measles, the farm was cut off so I couldn't go down and do my share of the nursing,' she explained. 'What's more, the Wing Officer doesn't much like it if you hang on to your leave until it's convenient for you; she would rather we took it when it suits her and I don't want her putting a black mark against my name.' She smiled round at her friends, her eyes twinkling. 'And I'm simply longing to see my kids again and to make sure that Petal's eyesight hasn't been affected by the infection, because it does sometimes happen, you know,' she finished.

Kate smiled at her. 'You go; you'll have a lovely time, even if they are in school. But why don't you get on the blower; you might be able to persuade your Luke to see if he could get the same week off. You were moaning about the long train journey, saying you'd be wasting at least two days travelling back and forth, changing trains and hanging about on draughty platforms,' she observed. 'But your feller's got a car, hasn't he? If he could wangle the petrol, I bet he could get you to Wales in half a day or less, and you could spend time with him as well as with your daughters. What about it?'

'He's not my feller and I don't want to ask him for favours,' Rose said slowly. 'If he's got a week's leave due – and I'm pretty sure he has, I remember him mentioning it – then I dare say he's got plans of his own.'

Mo, who was a small, sturdy girl with dark hair and narrow, snapping black eyes, wagged a reproachful finger. 'Talk sense, woman,' she admonished. 'That Luke of yours is a stranger in a strange land. He won't be going home to his mum and dad, or visiting his sister and her family, or going to stay with old friends, and well you know it. I reckon he'd jump at the chance of visiting your Welsh farmhouse and spending some time with you and the kids.'

Jen, who had been rapidly eating baked beans on toast, nodded approval before scraping the last piece of toast round the plate and popping it into her mouth. She was a skinny, fair-haired girl with a narrow, rather serious face. She was packed with energy and never still for long and when she spoke, it was with decision. 'Mo's right, Rosie, and as for Luke not being your feller . . .' She snorted derisively. 'Pull the other one, it's got bells on! If he's not your feller, then why is he always on the phone, asking you to see a flick or go to a dance, or take a drive somewhere?'

'He may ask, but that doesn't mean I go, not every time,' Rose said defensively. 'He's a nice chap, not pushy or grabby, if you know what I mean, but taking him on leave . . . well, that would be giving him the wrong idea.' She glanced across at Kate, smiling apologetically. 'You see, Kate and meself are very different. Kate was only married to Bobby for three months, but they were a happy three months, weren't they, Katie, old dear? I were married to Steve for – oh, years – and I can't say we made a go of it. In fact, I married in haste to repent at leisure, as the saying goes, which is why I don't want to repeat the dose, get involved again with any man.'

'Not even a nice chap like Luke?' Kate said curiously.

She was easily the prettiest of them, Rose thought, with her smooth, ash blonde hair and pink and white complexion. Most of the men on the airfield – the unattached ones – wanted to date her, but Kate was extremely choosy. She kept a photograph of her husband pinned to the inside of her small locker and though he had been killed almost two years ago and Kate seldom mentioned him, Rose thought that the love between them had been a very strong emotion and one which Kate could neither forget nor push to the back of her mind. She measures every man she meets against her Bobby and they all fail to come up to scratch, Rose thought sadly. I never thought I was lucky to have married a man I couldn't love until I got to know Kate.

'I've only met your Luke a couple of times but he seemed . . . oh, reliable, and sensible, and it's easy to see he's really fond of you, Rosie,' Kate continued.

'That's because I'm almost the only person he really knows in England,' Rose said wryly, but this remark was greeted with jeers.

'The only girl he knows in England? He's air crew, he's got a car and there must be fifty or sixty WAAFs on his station, all panting for a look from him,' Jen said. 'You may be kidding yourself, Rosie, but you can't kid us. He likes you and you jolly well like him. Why are you afraid to admit it?'

Rose pondered the question seriously. Her friends were at least partly right; she did like Luke and knew he liked her, but she also suspected that he was growing weary of being kept at arm's length. If he was to decide to stop seeing her, she also knew that she would miss him, but then if Kate or Mo or Jen were moved to another station, she would miss them too. And there was no doubt about it, a week spent on the farm with her daughters at this time of year would be restful but scarcely exciting. If Luke came along as well, she knew they would all have a much better time. It wasn't just the car, though that would be extremely handy, it was Luke himself. He was good fun, humorous and always full of ideas. The girls did not know him very well but would soon do so and Rose knew that the Williamses would welcome him to their home and find a corner for him, even if he could only sleep on a makeshift bed in their front room.

The trouble was, inviting him to spend a week's leave at the farm with her was tantamount to admitting that there was more between them than simple friendship and Rose was still very reluctant to make such a move. It was ridiculous and she knew it, but the moment she saw Luke's face soften, saw him reach out a hand to touch her, she would move away, blow her nose, do anything to prevent any sort of intimacy. But you can't go through life being afraid of a handshake, she scolded herself now, sitting with her friends in the crowded cookhouse. You've got to remember that the children will come back to you when the war's over, and what are they going to think if there's no man – not even a man friend – in your life? They'll grow up influenced against men by my feelings, and that isn't fair on either of them. What's more, a family should be a partnership because the girls need a father, even if I think I don't need a husband. It isn't as if they ever see their uncles, or male cousins. No, I simply must stop believing men are my enemies. And then there's the practical side of it. I don't know what sort of work will be available for women after the war. I might have to consider marriage from sheer necessity, you never know.

Abruptly, Rose made up her mind and got to her feet. 'Right; you've talked me into it,' she said briskly. 'Luke's a good bloke and I know he's got nowhere to spend his leave and I'm pretty sure he's due for some. He was probably flying last night, but I'll give him a ring around four o'clock.'

Luke had returned from his night raid and landed just as dawn was greying the eastern sky. He got stiffly out of his seat, then glanced across at the woods on the perimeter of the airfield, seeing the first and most beautiful signs of spring: catkins and pussy willows in the hedge which surrounded the wood and the new grass beginning to cover bank and pasture. He checked that his crew were preparing to leave the aircraft. They were good guys and had been together now for longer than most. They had been lucky and had not lost a crew member; a fact of which few skippers could boast.

'Ready, fellers?' Luke said, heading for the outside world. He looked up at the sky. It was clear and cloudless; a pale milky blue which would deepen when the sun came up. It was going to be a lovely day.

Phil, the wireless operator, stretched and yawned hugely as the men made their way towards the gharry which would take them to the admin office for debriefing. 'After a spot of breakfast, I'm going to sleep the clock round,' he said, in his soft Lancashire voice. 'We're due for some leave now, you know that, don't you, Luke? We've reached twenty-five sorties, so we're entitled.'

'Yeah, I guess so, but I don't fancy going off alone

366

somewhere,' Luke said softly. 'Oh, I know everyone says *you can come home with me*, but being a guest . . . I reckon it 'ud be more of a strain. I suppose I could go up to London, see the sights . . . anyway, it's something I'll have to think about.'

Brendan, the navigator, blew a raspberry. 'Why not give the go-ahead to that flighty little WAAF who's been making eyes at you for the past six weeks?' he suggested. 'Go on, make her the happiest woman on earth.'

'Shut up, you,' Phil said. 'I've got my eye on her! I've always fancied blondes, even if it does come out of a bottle. She'd be wasted on Luke.'

Luke grinned but no more was said until the debriefing was over and the crew had gone into the cookhouse for a hasty breakfast before seeking their beds. Then Phil asked Luke why he didn't take his week's leave with the young woman he occasionally took to the flicks.

'Because she hasn't suggested it,' Luke said lightly. 'I told you before, Phil, she's got a couple of kids. They were evacuated to a farm in Wales so I guess when she gets leave, that's where she'll go.'

'You could go as well,' Phil said, though he didn't sound particularly convinced. 'Aw hell, Luke, we all need a break now and then, even an iron man like yourself.'

They all laughed, but when Luke climbed into his bed, having first drawn the blackout curtains and closed the window tight against the clatter of a working airfield, he thought seriously about the situation between himself and Rose. He thought her a beautiful and desirable woman but was uneasily aware that their relationship was not progressing as he would have liked. She may have thought he did not notice, but he dreaded the way she drew back from him if he tried to make even the simplest gesture of affection, and winced if he made a sudden movement. Once, aboard a country bus, he had raised his hand to lift their gas masks down from the overhead rack and Rose had positively cringed, as though expecting a blow. He knew she had not had a happy marriage and guessed that Steve might have hit out at his wife when he'd had a few drinks, but told himself that she could not put him in the same category as her dead husband. He had never raised his voice to her, let alone his hand, and found himself resenting the implication that he might do so. Dammit, Rose would not even let him hold her hand in the flicks and though she had danced with him, it had been like dancing with a wax model, so stiff and unbending had she seemed. And yet . . . and yet there was a warmth and a gaiety in Rose and a sweetness of character which he longed to share. He reminded himself that he had only really got to know her since she had joined the WAAF; in a civilian situation, things might be different. If he suggested that they went on leave together, she might unbend a little.

That's not a bad idea, Luke told himself drowsily, shrugging the covers up round his ears. I'll give her a ring this evening and arrange to meet; then I'll tell her about my leave, explain that I have no family or friends to go to, though she knows that well enough, and ask if we could spend the time together. After all, she can only say no.

Almost before the thought was formulated, Luke slept.

Luke saw her waiting on Castle Meadow as his gharry drew to a halt behind hers and waved cheerfully. They had not said an awful lot when they had spoken on the phone earlier that day, but he had told her he wanted to take his leave now that spring had arrived, and without prompting she had suggested he should go with her to the farm.

It had been tempting to reply that he would be delighted to go with her but he had held back. Instead, he had said he thought they ought to talk and had been honestly astonished when she had agreed.

Now, however, jumping down from the back of the truck and seeing her welcoming smile, the colour rising in her cheeks, he thought that perhaps everything would be all right. She was so pretty and had recently become so much more self-confident that surely she would begin to be less cautious in her dealings with him. At any rate, he intended to put his feelings into words and see how she responded. He had tried the friendly approach and it really hadn't worked; now he would see what plain speaking would do. So, for a start, he took her hand as they crossed Castle Meadow and went down Davey Place, telling her as he did so that he meant to take her to Lyons where they could have a good meal and a good talk. 'And don't try wrenching your hand away,' he added, feeling her instinctive withdrawal but not letting go, as he had on previous occasions, 'because I don't like being treated like a leper, darling Rose.'

He was watching her face as he spoke and saw her bright colour rise up, but he also saw the little smile which touched her lips and felt her fingers relax in his.

'Sorry,' she said, and sounded as though she meant it. 'I don't mean to be rude, or to hurt your feelings. It's just . . .' She sighed. 'Oh, it's so difficult to explain without being . . . well, disloyal, I suppose you could say.'

He squeezed her fingers lightly as they turned on to Gentlemen's Walk, almost immediately entering Lyons Restaurant. It was still early evening and the place was not crowded, so they found a quiet table for two and talked inconsequentially until the nippy, in her neat black and white uniform, had delivered their food. Only then did Luke raise the subject which he was beginning to believe was uppermost in both their minds.

'I know you mentioned you were going to spend a week at Ty Siriol and you suggested that I might like to join you. It was very generous of you, honey, but the reason I didn't jump at it was because I wasn't sure why you had asked me,' he said carefully. 'You see, you've never given me much encouragement to believe that I'm anything more than a chance-met acquaintance.'

Rose began to murmur a protest, flushing even more deeply, but Luke cut her short. 'I know it's not easy to talk about such things, Rose, but I'm – I'm real fond of you. You're a beautiful, desirable young woman, yet I'm not allowed to take your hand without feeling . . . well, that I'm being fresh. If I spent a whole week with you, I'd like to think it was because you were growing fond of me and wanted to further our relationship. But quite frankly, I'd be half afraid to try to give you a kiss in case you repulsed me.'

'I thought you understood,' Rose muttered. She took a mouthful of food, chewed and swallowed it before speaking again. 'I've been happy in the WAAF and I was pretty happy in Bernard Terrace whilst Steve was away. I – I thought you knew Steve was violent when he'd had a few drinks. I thought you understood.'

'I do know,' Luke said gently. 'But I'm not Steve,

as you very well know. Have I ever raised my voice to you? Why, I've never even told you how it hurts me when you cringe at any sudden movement I make. You can't believe I'm the sort of guy who would hit *any* woman, let alone the one I love.'

Rose looked up quickly, and for a moment Luke thought he saw in her eyes a reflection of the love which he knew must be in his own, but then she glanced down at the food on her plate. 'I know you aren't like Steve – but it isn't just that,' she muttered. 'If Steve had always been violent, I wouldn't have married him, would I? He was grand when we were courting; it was only after we got married and Daisy was born that he began hitting me. At first, I couldn't believe it; I kept telling myself that it was my fault, that I was doing something wrong. It was ages before I realised that Steve had always been a bully but had kept it hidden from me for as long as he could.' She had kept her eyes down while she spoke, but now she raised them to his. 'I don't *want* to spend the rest of my life alone, because of what Steve did to me,' she said, her eyes bright with unshed tears. 'I want to be able to love someone properly, the way my friend Kate loved her Bobby – but I'm so afraid of making another mistake.'

Luke looked at her with real compassion. What an awful fix she was in, and through no fault of her own. He said quietly: 'But don't you see, honey? You've got to learn to trust again, because there's no other way. You can't have a trial marriage with half a dozen different guys to see which of them isn't likely to turn into a wife beater. And anyway, since you seem to regard an arm slipped round your waist as being dangerous, I don't think you'd take kindly to a trial marriage!'

He spoke lightly, trying to make a joke of it, and Rose gave him a tremulous smile. 'I know you're right, and I really will try,' she said. 'For one thing, I want the girls to have normal, happy lives, and that means boyfriends in a few years and husbands after that. So if you will come to the farm with us, I'll truly do my best to behave normally, the way you would expect a girl to behave.' To his astonishment, she reached across the table and took his hand, holding it firmly in her own. 'And I'm sorry for the way I've treated you, Luke, because I like you better than any man I've ever met.'

'That's wonderful,' Luke said. 'And will you do something for me, honey? Will you just tell me exactly how Steve was when he was courting you? I never met him, of course, but from what you've told me, he wasn't a lot like me. Now think; did he make you laugh? If you were carrying a bag, did he take it from you? Was he as nice to your mam and dad when they weren't there as he was to their faces? And last, but not least, did he think he was one hell of a guy who could have any woman he wanted, so you were real lucky to get him?'

Rose looked at him for a long moment and then she began to laugh. When she could command herself once more, she mopped her streaming eyes with a handkerchief and gave him her answer, ticking her replies off on a finger as she did so. 'You ask if he made me laugh and the answer to that is pretty straightforward. He was the sort of man who took himself seriously and was always slightly suspicious of laughter. To be fair to him, I think he thought you were laughing at him and not with him . . . a kink in his self-confidence, I suppose. As for carrying heavy bags, an awful lot of Liverpool fellers would say that was women's work . . . Steve was certainly one of them. What was the next question?'

'Was he as nice to your mom and pop—?' Luke began, but Rose cut him off short.

'Oh, yes, I remember: was he as nice to my parents when they weren't there as he was when they were present.' She giggled again, clearly finding the question amusing. 'That's a difficult one, Luke, because thinking back, he was pretty horrible to them every time he came to our house. He sneered at Mam's cooking, argued with Dad over any subject that came up, and was generally difficult. I'm ashamed to admit I let him get away with it because, little fool that I was, I took him at his own valuation. He swaggered into our house as though he owned it and I was so afraid of losing him that I never told him off or criticised him in any way. Even then, I knew how deeply he would have resented it,' she ended.

'And the last question? Did he think he was one hell of a guy who could—'

Once more, Rose interrupted, her eyes sparkling. 'Oh yes, he thought he was God's gift to the universe, but not particularly to women. It sounds awfully odd, Luke, but I don't think Steve really liked women, not any of them. I remember my father once saying that Steve was a man's man and that fellers like that didn't make good husbands and by golly, wasn't he right? If I'd been as meek as Steve thought me – never giving an opinion, never arguing, never saying no when he wanted yes, it's just possible that the marriage might have worked, though I doubt it.'

'Ah, but you had the girls to protect and guys like that end up beating their kids as well as their wives,' Luke said shrewdly. 'From what you've told me, I think your marriage was doomed from the start. But now, honey, why not ask yourself the same questions, only put the name Luke instead of Steve. Go on, don't think you'll embarrass me if I fall short.'

But Rose was smiling at him with sparkling eyes and shaking her head so that her long dark hair swung violently from side to side. 'No, no, I don't need to; you're always making me laugh and it's the same with all the rest. You're as different from Steve as chalk from cheese, and it's about time I realised it and valued you for what I know you are. Dear Luke, come to the farm with us and I promise you the length of my arm will be so short, you'll scarcely notice it's there.'

Luke gave a whoop and, forgetting his surroundings, leaned across the table and took Rose in his arms, kissing her resoundingly. 'That's my girl,' he said exultantly. 'Oh, Rosie, we're going to have the best week's leave in the whole world! And now let's get out of here and go somewhere where I can kiss you properly without an audience.'

Going back to Coltishall that night Rose was astonished at how warm and happy she felt. I've been an absolute fool turning Luke's love away because I was too scared to take a risk, she told herself as the truck began to bounce along the narrow country roads. They had discussed their forthcoming leave at some length and had both agreed that it was a wonderful opportunity to put right the things that had been wrong – or rather lacking – in their relationship.

'When we get to know one another better, we may decide it's all a mistake and prefer to remain simply friendly acquaintances,' Luke had said but not, Rose thought, as though he had meant it. 'That means we'll enjoy ourselves but be prepared to go our separate ways at the end of the week with no hard feelings.'

Rose thought it generous of him but, as she now

acknowledged, Luke was a generous person. He had given her friendship and affection without any sort of return; in future, Rose told herself, things would be very different.

The journey to the farm in Luke's old car was a revelation. Crossing the whole countryside, it was as though spring was always one step ahead of them as they neared the west of the country. In Norfolk and the Midlands, buds were still tightly furled and the glorious hedgerows which lined the roads barely showed a touch of green, but as they entered Wales and headed for the hills, there was a riot of blossom as well as the brilliant green of hawthorn, and Rose knew that soon the steep banks would be starred with primroses and sweet, purple violets.

She was as excited as any child. She told Luke how Daisy and Petal had gone out with their friends in February, dipping for frog and toad spawn. Uncle Gwil had given them an old battery case which they had speedily converted into an aquarium, and now it contained a number of fat tadpoles, most of which were turning into tiny, jewel-bright frogs. 'I never had any country fun like that when I was a kid,' Rose said wistfully, as the car turned into Ty Siriol lane. 'When I was Petal's age, I didn't know a hazel catkin from a pussy willow, nor a frog from a toad, because of course I was an only child and Mam and Dad kept me pretty close. Why, I thought Princes Park was real country. I used to tell other kids that Uncle Frank and Aunt Selina lived in a country cottage, though of course it was really a terraced house in Penny Lane.' She turned to look curiously into Luke's face. 'What about you, Luke? I know you come from a small town in the middle of America, and you've got a brother, and your dad runs a garage and your mum a grocery store, but is that country? I suppose it can't be because you wouldn't sell much petrol or mend many motor cars out in the country, would you?'

Luke gave her an indulgent glance. 'It is country, though it's on the outskirts of a small town,' he told her. 'When we were kids, my brother and I, and a whole gang of us from the local school, used to ride off on our bikes and get into all sorts of mischief. In the fall, we stole apples and pears from the orchards and feasted like kings. We made ourselves catapults and either drew a target on a tree, or hid behind a hedge and tickled up grazing cattle with an acorn or a little smooth pebble. There were prairie dogs on the plains and, of course, fields and fields of maize, which grew a good deal higher than a boy's head. We had some fun in that maize, playing hide and seek, catch, anything you'd like to name. I don't suppose you've ever sat down, on a hot afternoon, and bitten into a corn cob and felt sweet white liquid running down your chin, but it's something us kids took for granted then, yet now it seems like the taste of Paradise.'

Whilst he spoke, he swung the car off the lane and into the farmyard, and as he drew up the back door flew open and two small figures emerged to hurl themselves joyfully upon Rose.

'Mammy, Mammy, Mammy!' Petal shrieked, whilst Daisy clung on to her mother's arm and nestled her head into the hollow of Rose's shoulder. 'Oh, Mammy, Felix the cat has got kittens. I'm going to have the black and white one, and Daisy wants the ginger. We're going to call them Nib and Nob.'

'I always thought Felix was a boy's name,' Luke said mildly, getting out of the car and receiving a hug from Petal, though Daisy hung back a bit, looking awkward. 'But I suppose names are different over here.'

Daisy laughed. 'No, it's more because it's difficult to tell a boy cat from a girl cat when they're kittens,' she explained. 'When Auntie Blod saw Felix getting a round tummy, she said we'd made a mistake and wanted to call her Phyllis, only the name Felix sort of stuck.' She glanced, shyly, up at Luke. 'Do you want to see them? The kittens, I mean, and Felix of course. They're in the end stall of the stable, up one corner of the manger.'

Luke said that he would be delighted to see the kittens but felt he ought to greet his hostess first, and presently the small party repaired to the kitchen where Auntie Blod poured out cups of tea, cut wedges from a fruit loaf, which she told Luke was called bara brith, and settled down for a good gossip.

'You've chosen a lovely time of year for your visit,' she told them. 'We've had a bit of a turn round upstairs so's I can put everyone up. I've put Daisy and Petal into the apple store because there isn't much fruit in it at this time of year and there's plenty of space for a couple of makeshift beds.' She turned to Rose. 'You are sharing Dilys's room, if that's all right; I haven't moved Heather, because she's in our Gareth's room anyway, and that leaves the children's room for Mr Nadolski – or should I call you Flying Officer Nadolski?'

'No indeed; please call me Luke, Mrs Williams,' Luke said quickly, which made the older woman laugh.

'If I'm going to call you Luke then you must follow Rose's example and call me Auntie Blod,' she said easily. 'Now, what plans have you got for this coming week?'

*   *   *

They had five glorious days on the farm. Auntie Blod spoiled them dreadfully, Rose told Luke, as each meal seemed better than the last, though the children assured them that they seldom had a meal which did not include meat, or eggs, or fish.

'I think things are easier out here,' Daisy said wisely. 'Nicky Bostock works for the local butcher in town and seems to be able to get hold of all sorts of things which you wouldn't even see in Liverpool. He says it used to be called bartering, only we call it swapping these days. If someone in the town who sells – oh, hardware, or knitting wool or something – needs eggs for a cake, then they'll go to one of the farmers in the hills with knitting wool, or a pound of nails, and exchange it for the number of eggs they want. See?'

Rose did see, and when she explained to Luke, adding that the Ministry did their best to stop such transactions but were mostly outwitted by the canny farmers, he said he thought it was fair enough. 'Townsfolk don't realise how hard a farmer works to rear his lambs and pigs and calves, to till his fields, lift his potatoes and cut his wheat,' he said. 'Why shouldn't he get some of the benefit as well?'

So, for five days, they lived on the fat of the land, and since their visit included a weekend Rose was able to enjoy the girls' company and to assure herself that Petal's eyesight was unaffected by the measles. 'And all the spots have gone as though they had never been,' Daisy assured her mother. 'It were a good job you couldn't see her when she were first took bad though, Mam. She looked terrible. Her eyes were all swolled up and she had so many spots, you could scarce fit a pin head between them. She was pretty good about not reading and not pulling back the curtains to look out, because the snow was so dazzling. It were a good thing I couldn't go to school, though – no one could get through, not even the milk lorry – because I sat by the bed for hours at a time, reading her all her favourite stories. And for the first few days, you know, Nicky was snowed up here with us. He were ever so good, helping out on the farm, carrying trays up so we could have our dinners with Petal, and playing games when she were well enough. I really do like Nicky; if we go back to Liverpool when the war's over, I'm going to miss him like anything.'

'But surely, Nicky will go back too?' Rose asked. 'Surely he'll want to return to the Ryans when the war's over?'

Daisy gave a derisive snort. 'Oh, Mam, why on earth should he? He's got a good job with the Foleys and they really like him, treat him like a son, he says. The Ryans never wanted him; he weren't no kin of theirs, they just kept him out of charity . . . well, if you can call it charity to treat someone the way they treated poor Nicky. No, he'll never go back.' She shot her mother a quick glance then looked rather intently down at her hands. 'Anyone who has lived in the country would think twice about going back to the city,' she muttered. 'I do meself.'

Rose had been astonished and slightly affronted by her daughter's words, but it had made her look at Daisy more closely. When she did so, she saw how her daughter was changing and maturing. When the war started, the child's figure had been almost sticklike, with no shape to it at all; now she had a proper waist, slim but gently curving hips and the beginnings of a bust, and it's not only her figure that's changing, Rose told herself ruefully. Daisy was becoming a real help around the farm. She understood about broody hens, knew how to control the great grey and white geese, whose noisy approach still scared Rose half to death, and could knit and sew, cook and clean almost as well as a woman grown. Seeing her with new eyes, Rose was also forced to see that Daisy had a will of her own. If she decided to get a job in Ruthin when she was old enough, Rose very much doubted whether she would be able to override the child's wishes and force her to move back to the city.

Petal, of course, was a different matter. At nine years old, she had little thought for the morrow and would, Rose was sure, do as she was told, though possibly not without grumbles.

Rose began to worry over these things but Luke, when she confided in him, told her not to meet trouble halfway. 'Both Daisy and Petal are your children and they love you very much. It's all very well for Daisy to talk about staying in Ruthin when the war's over, but who can tell when that will be. And for that matter, who knows where *you* will be. Your house has been destroyed and most of your neighbourhood. Oh, I'm not saying it will never be rebuilt, but judging from what I saw of Liverpool after the May Blitz, it's going to take quite a time to put things right there. Why, you yourself might prefer to live and work in Ruthin, when you leave the WAAF, which would solve everyone's problems.'

Rose realised that this was true and stopped worrying, bending her mind instead to relishing the company of the young woman Daisy had become, as well as enjoying Petal's artless conversation and refreshing outlook on life.

When Luke suggested, however, that they should leave the farm and make their way back to Norfolk a couple of days early, she was astonished and rather hurt. 'But, Luke, we've both got seven days' leave; it won't be much fun mooching round the station when we could be here, with the Williamses and the kids,' she said reproachfully. 'I thought we'd leave at about eleven o'clock on Wednesday, so that we were back in time to settle down and hear all the gossip before going to bed. Neither of us has to be back before midnight but I wouldn't want to leave it as late as that.'

The two of them had gone for a stroll up towards the hills after the children had gone to bed. They had formed the habit of doing this because it was the only time they had to themselves and Luke usually put his arm round Rose, saying that it was safer in the dark in case one of them should trip over an unseen obstacle.

At her words, Luke gave her a quick squeeze. 'I'm not suggesting we go back to the station, honey. I thought we might stop off in a pub, or a small hotel somewhere, take a look around. You see, though it's been a wonderful few days, we're not much nearer getting to know one another properly, are we?'

Rose stopped short, pulling him to a halt as well, and turned to face him. It was a clear night for once and they had got their night eyes, so Rose could see his face looming above her, catch the glint of his teeth as his lips parted in a slow smile. 'Luke Nadolski, just what are you suggesting? If it's what I think it is, then you can jolly well forget it! I don't want to be drummed out of the WAAF because I'm in trouble.'

'But I see no reason why you should be drummed out of the WAAF just because we've taken a bit of time for ourselves,' Luke said. 'Look, if you hate the idea of a couple of days alone with me, just say so, but oh, Rosie, I guess you must know by now how I

381

feel about you, and I was beginning to believe . . . to hope . . .'

As he spoke, he cupped her face tenderly in both hands, and very, very slowly, giving her every opportunity to pull back, he bent his head until their mouths met.

It was a gentle kiss, almost passionless, yet Rose felt her heart begin to beat faster and her stomach to perform unusual gyrations. She returned the kiss, then broke away from him, saying rather breathlessly: 'Oh, Luke, you're right. We'll leave early and – and have some time to ourselves. Oh, Luke, oh, Luke, I'm almost sure . . . it's just that . . .'

Luke laughed and put a finger against her lips. 'Hush, honey,' he said in a low voice. 'Make haste slowly. Now let's get back to the farm and tell Auntie Blod we'll be leaving Tuesday morning, early. That will give you another full day and no one will be surprised at our leaving, since I've told everyone that old Henrietta needs nursing along and that doing the whole cross-country journey in one day was hard on her elderly constitution.' Luke had christened the car Henrietta after an aunt of his who, at ninety-six, was still working her small farm without assistance, save at harvest time.

Rose laughed and put a hand up to stroke his cheek as they turned back towards the farm. 'Has anyone ever told you you're a devious devil, Luke Nadolski?' she asked him. 'I *wondered* why you kept on shaking your head and saying we mustn't expect too much of Henrietta, when we both know full well that she sailed across the country without so much as a hiccup.'

Luke captured her fingers and kissed them; an action which sent more thrills tingling up Rose's spine. She snatched her hand back, however, saying breathlessly:

'Just you behave yourself, Luke! You're getting me all hot and bothered when I want to be cool, calm and collected. Race you to the kitchen door!'

On Tuesday morning, Luke insisted on running the children to school in Henrietta, so that they might have a few moments more with their mother. Since Rose had assured the girls that she would be arranging for them to come across to Norfolk sometime during their summer holidays, they were reconciled to her leaving them a day sooner than they had expected, but even so, when it came to the moment of parting, they clung to Rose and then, to their mother's pleasure, they both insisted upon hugging Luke and kissing his cheek. 'We think you're the nicest man our mammy has ever had,' Petal said, squeezing Luke's hand tightly in both of hers. 'Auntie Blod says the same; I heard her telling Uncle Gwil the other night that you'd make a grand daddy.'

Daisy felt the heat rise up in her cheeks, but gave her small sister a shake. 'I don't know why you say that because, apart from our dad, Luke's the only feller Mam's ever brought home,' she said. 'You name me one other, Petal McAllister!'

'Oh! Well, if Mam had had other fellers, Luke would be the nicest and *I* think he'd make a lovely daddy,' Petal said. She turned back to Luke. 'Do you have children of your own, Luke? Are you a daddy?'

Luke was beginning to say that since he had never been married he had no children of his own either, when Daisy once more took a hand. 'For the Lord's sake, stop prattling, Petal, and gerrinto your class,' she said crossly, giving her small sister a shove. She turned to follow her, then turned back. 'I'm awful sorry, Luke; if I've told her once, I've told her a hundred times not to repeat what she only half hears as though it were gospel. Only – she didn't mean no harm, she just wanted you to know she likes you very much. And I do, too,' she added hastily. 'I think you're almost as nice as Uncle Gwil.'

Luke thanked her, gravely, for the compliment, assured her that his feelings were undamaged and his withers unwrung, and then watched with a smile as she scampered into the school, waving as she went.

'Two nicer kids you couldn't find if you searched the length and breadth of this island,' Luke said, as he put the car into gear and drove out of the small, grey town, cupped between the soft green hills. He turned his head to smile down at Rose. 'Now where do you fancy stopping for lunch?'

Rose blew her nose vigorously and dabbed at her eyes before replying. She loved the girls so much and had realised, this time more than ever, how she was missing them. Daisy's adult awareness had come far earlier than Rose's own had done and she thought that this was because Daisy had had to take responsibility for her little sister whilst she was still only a child herself. But what could I have done, she asked herself miserably. I had to earn money and I had to do my bit towards the war effort. Oh, but now Petal will start to change, and I shall miss that, too.

'Rose?' Luke asked gently. 'You're upset because you're leaving your children behind, but you mustn't be. No one could be kinder or more generous than the Williamses, and you said yourself that you could never have given them the sort of country childhood they're experiencing now.'

Rose sniffed dolefully. 'I know you're right and I suppose I'm really crying for myself,' she admitted. 'I've missed so much, Luke – so much of their growing

384

up, I mean. And they never come again, those special years which turn a little girl into a young woman.' She took a deep breath, put away her handkerchief and smiled across at Luke. 'I don't mind where we stop,' she said. 'Any nice little pub where they make sandwiches will be fine.'

Luke spotted a pleasant-looking pub just outside Melton Mowbray and they stopped there for their lunch. The fat and motherly landlady provided them with cheese and pickle sandwiches and a large piece of apple tart. The day was fine and sunny, though there was a real nip in the air, but they sat in the bow window of the pub, which overlooked an attractive garden dotted with wooden tables and chairs where, had the weather been warmer, they could have eaten their food. Both pickles and apple pie were home-made and they did not hurry over the meal, finishing up with a cup of coffee each and then enjoying a chat with the landlady, whose son was also in the air force.

'We'll be lucky if we find anywhere half as good as this to spend the night,' Luke said casually, handing Rose into the front passenger seat and then taking his place beside her. 'I thought we'd break the back of the journey today, if we can, by pressing on for a bit. Then we can have our evening meal wherever we stop and go up to bed at our leisure. There'll be no rush in the morning, so we can lie in for a bit – if that's what you'd like, I mean.'

'That sounds lovely,' Rose said vaguely. Not for the first time, it occurred to her that Luke might mean them to share a room and she looked across at him speculatively. How would she feel if he suggested it and what should she say? She was no shrinking violet and knew that in one way it would be natural for Luke to want to sleep with her. After all, he did a highly dangerous job and one never knew . . .

Horrified, she pushed the thought out of her mind. She was not going to agree that she and Luke should become lovers just because he piloted a Wellington bomber and was in danger every time he flew. There were girls in her hut who must have slept with a dozen different men, using the excuse that they were giving the fellers a taste of life – and love – because it might be the feller's only chance. Rose had never subscribed to this, thinking it an excuse for behaviour of which they would otherwise be ashamed. But now, when she suspected it was about to become an option for her, she realised she felt differently. She also realised she was close to falling in love with Luke, and if one loved, then surely one wanted to give? The greatest gift, she thought confusedly, was the gift of oneself, but she had given herself to Steve and look where that had led.

'Rosie? A penny for your thoughts.' Luke's voice cut across her musings and Rose felt the hot colour flood into her cheeks. Was this the moment to ask him . . . well, what exactly? She could scarcely say bluntly, *Do you want me to share your bed tonight?* He had told her that the folk amongst whom he had grown up were good church-going people, with a great regard for moral values. He might be shocked and horrified at the mere suggestion that they should sleep together – or rather, not sleep – before marriage.

Rose glanced quickly across at him, hoping he had not noticed her flush. Anyone would think I was an eighteen-year-old virgin who knew nothing about men and didn't want to learn, she scolded herself. Luke's a good man, he's let me set the pace for our relationship; I think we'll just let things take their course.

386

'Oh, my thoughts aren't worth a penny,' she said aloud, meeting his eyes and seeing the quizzical gleam in them. 'Hasn't it been a lovely holiday, Luke? I don't mind admitting that I'm going to miss you almost as much as I miss the girls.'

Luke's eyebrows shot up and he slowed the car in order to reach across and pat her knee. 'That's the nicest thing you could have said,' he told her. 'I shall miss you horribly but we must meet whenever we get the opportunity. After all, I'd say we were more than just friendly acquaintances now, wouldn't you?'

Rose, agreeing, suddenly noticed that many of the sheep in the field past which they were driving had lambs beside them. 'Oh, Luke, pull into that gateway so we can have a proper look,' she said eagerly. 'Auntie Blod said that lambs in the Lowlands district came earlier than in the hills . . . oh, aren't they sweet?'

Luke complied, and Rose was able to steer the conversation back to farming. In discussing such matters, she was able to put out of her mind how they would spend the coming night.

As they drove away from the fascinating lambs, Luke could not help glancing quizzically at Rose but her face was still averted as she enjoyed the countryside, drowsing in the early April sunlight. He wondered what she had been thinking to bring such a burning blush to her cheeks when he had offered her a penny for her thoughts. He himself had been wondering whether it would completely spoil their relationship if he suggested that they might share a bed. The maddening thing was, he could not think of a way to ask her which would leave him an escape route if she refused – an escape route which would mean he could say, *No, you misunderstood me; as if I would make a suggestion like that!* He glanced across at Rose again and battled with an almost irresistible urge to stop the car, slide his hand round the back of her neck and pull her gently towards him. Then he would kiss her flushed cheek, the line of her jaw, the firm white skin of her neck. He would cuddle her, tell her how beautiful she was, explain that he had never felt like this about anyone . . . oh, oh, oh, it had been dreadfully hard at the farm, to keep his kisses gentle, to see her disappear into the room she shared with Dilys whilst he made his way to his own bed.

Not that he would have missed the days he had spent at the farm, not for anything. The more he knew of her, the more he loved her and he found her daughters delightful, even though, at times, he could not help wishing them elsewhere, because he realised that kissing and cuddling Rose was not possible when the girls were present. He had no wish to alienate them and knew that a show of the sort of affection he felt would probably both annoy and embarrass them. So, enjoyable though their stay at the farm had been, it had also been frustrating. And now that he and Rose were alone, he realised he was afraid of letting her see how he felt in case she honestly could not share his feelings. Perhaps a woman needs more time than a man to make up her mind, he told himself. If only it were possible to explain that he loved her unconditionally, but somehow he did not seem able to find the words.

He drove on. Sometimes they talked, commenting on the scene through which they passed, sometimes they were companionably silent, and presently Luke told Rose to keep an eye open for a comfortable-looking inn or public house. 'We'll need a meal and it would be nice to stay the night in a village, or perhaps by a river, so we can have a walk, stretch our legs, before bed,' he said. 'Um, Rosie . . .'

'Yes?' Rose said, as the silence lengthened. 'What were you going to say, Luke?'

'Um . . . there's a pleasant-looking pub; the one with the thatch, by that little stone bridge. See it? Shall we stop there? We'd get the best of both worlds. That bridge must cross a river, yet it's only fifty yards or so from the village itself.'

Rose looked across at him, raised her eyebrows, began to speak and then seemed to change her mind. 'It looks lovely,' she said briskly. 'I wonder if the land-lady makes home-made pickles?'

Luke drove the car in under an arch leading into a small courtyard, slowed to a stop, applied the hand-brake and turned off the engine. He got out but left their suitcases locked in the boot. 'Better make sure they've a room – rooms, I mean – for us before we march in with our luggage,' he said. He could have kicked himself for not being bolder, but it was no good now; he would ask for two single rooms and then, when they had eaten and were taking the walk he had promised himself, he would tell her how he felt about her.

They went into the inn through the back door, along a corridor and into a pleasant little hall. There was a bell on the counter and Luke rang it and, almost imme-diately, an elderly woman appeared. She was wearing a fold-over floral apron and there was a smudge of flour on her nose, and she carried with her, as she approached them, the comfortable smell of food cooking. 'Glad you rang the bell 'cos I'm cooking the evening meal and I'm by meself this evening till the village girl comes in to help serve, and me husband gets back from visiting his old mother,' she said, beaming at them. 'Now what can I do for you, my dears? Is it a room you're wanting? I thought I heard a car drive into the courtyard, a few minutes since, but Mr Symes – he's a travelling salesman and a reg'lar – is stayin' here a couple of days so it might of been him.'

Luke opened his mouth to speak but Rose forestalled him. She put her left hand on the counter, smiled at the landlady and said: 'Yes, we would like a room. We didn't bring our luggage out of the car in case you were full, but if you have a room free, my husband can fetch it in right now. Oh, I didn't ask your terms.'

'Ten bob for me best double what overlooks the river, seven and six for the others, and I'm Mrs Rogers.'

'Nice to meet you, Mrs Rogers. Luke, darling, shall we spoil ourselves and have the best room?'

Luke was so astonished that he could only open and close his mouth and Mrs Rogers, plainly interpreting this as horror over her high prices, said quickly: 'The ten bob includes your breakfasts, o' course, and I does a grand breakfast: eggs from me own hens, a pile of fried potatoes, toast and home-made marmalade, o' course, and as much tea as you can drink.'

Luke pulled himself together. 'That sounds just fine and dandy,' he said. 'And we'd like dinner tonight, please.' He turned to smile down at Rose. 'It certainly smells delicious, doesn't it, honey?'

'It's onion soup, followed by steak an' kidney pudding, mashed potatoes and peas, with an egg custard or apple snow for afters,' Mrs Rogers told them. While she spoke, she had been fishing under the counter and now produced a large, leather-bound book. 'If you wouldn't mind signin' in, sir . . . at one time, no one ever bothered, but it's different now. Just your name . . .' Her eyes travelled over their uniforms. 'And where you're stationed, o' course.' She chuckled richly. 'Your home address wouldn't be no manner o' use since I can tell from your voice you're an American, though you're wearin' our uniform and not theirs.'

'I joined your air force before America came into the war,' Luke said, well used to answering this particular question. 'I'll just fetch our luggage in. Rose, will you sign in, honey?'

He left Rose filling in the visitors' book and returned, presently, a bag in either hand. Then he and Rose followed the landlady up the creaking oak staircase, along an uncarpeted corridor and into a delightful, low-ceilinged bedroom, whose window overlooked fields and meadows as well as the willow-girt river. There was a washstand, a square of carpet and a large, brass bedstead, as well as a couple of easy chairs and, of course, a dressing table.

Luke glanced towards the bed, then quickly away, but Rose walked calmly across to it and examined the number of blankets before turning to thank the landlady. 'It's a lovely room,' she said sincerely. 'We'll settle ourselves in, have a wash and brush up, and then come downstairs. When do you serve dinner, Mrs Rogers?'

Mrs Rogers told them, adding that there was a bathroom at the end of the corridor. 'The water's always hot because it's fed by the Aga and we never let that go out,' she told them. 'See you in a moment, then.'

She went out, closing the door behind her, and Luke turned and lifted Rose into his arms in one swift, exuberant movement. 'Rose Nadolski, I love you more than I've ever loved anyone in my entire life and I want to marry you just as soon as it can be arranged,' he said huskily. 'I was standing there wondering why you'd put your left hand on the counter . . . oh, Rosie, Rosie, Rosie!'

*   *   *

Rose had expected to feel shy and awkward when she and Luke made their way up to their room after they had had an excellent dinner and a long, meandering walk through the soft April evening. The river smells had been sweet and in the comforting darkness, under the willow trees, they had kissed and cuddled passionately so that, in the end, going to their room seemed both easy and a natural thing to do. Once there, Luke's matter-of-fact, loving attitude made shyness seem both foolish and unnecessary.

They went to the bathroom separately, to change into their night things, clean their teeth and wash. Rose got into bed first, and when Luke came in he turned off the light and fumbled his way across the room in the darkness, cursing as he cannoned into one of the chairs, so that they were both laughing when he joined her under the blankets.

'It's all very well for you to laugh but I might have broken my toe,' Luke said ruefully, trying to rub the injured member and making Rose gasp as his knee struck hers sharply. This set them off laughing again until Luke put a stop to such nonsense by kissing her.

Looking back on it afterwards, Rose could only marvel at how sweet love could be with the right person. She and Luke, she decided, were made for each other. Next morning, as they got themselves ready for the day ahead, she told Luke, shyly, that she had never known, had never guessed, that loving could be so sweet.

Luke, carefully shaving in front of the small mirror on the washstand, turned to smile at her. 'It was the same for me,' he told her. 'Oh, Rosie, we're so lucky to have found one another! Let's make a vow never to lose our way again.'

Chapter Fifteen

Luke dropped Rose off at the gates, waved a quick farewell, and turned the car about. They had said their proper farewells parked on the side of the lane which led to the airfield and Luke was glad they had done so. It would not have been the thing for two people in uniform to start exchanging fond farewells where anyone might see them.

Luke drove back to his own station noticing, with some alarm, that he was having to fight to keep the car on the road. The wind had been getting up all day and now it was really bad; he pitied whoever was flying tonight. If this wind kept up, taking off – and landing again – could be a tricky business. However, he told himself as he went to park the car, since his leave did not end until midnight he, at least, would be safely out of it.

The thought had scarcely formed in his mind when he heard himself hailed. It was Fred, his squadron leader, walking rapidly across the hard standing towards him, a grin almost splitting his good-natured face. 'Thank God you're back, Luke,' he said as soon as Luke had alighted from the car and dragged out his grip. 'Your crew have agreed to just one more sortie tonight to help out, and since you were supposed to be on leave we'd put young Masters down to pilot Bouncing Betty, but he's not really experienced enough for this kind of weather.'

'But my leave doesn't finish till midnight,' Luke

pointed out. 'Still an' all, I guess I don't want to see Bouncing Betty slammed into the runway or shot up over the target, if I can help it. What'll y' do with young Masters, though?'

'Oh, he can go with you as second pilot; he'll learn a thing or two just watching you,' Fred said breezily, twirling the waxed ends of his moustache. It was the largest moustache on the station and Fred was always playing with it; Luke knew the other man was proud of it, despite the jokes which abounded, the men referring to it as 'Fred's spare propeller' and daring him to shave it off so that they could see whether he really had teeth.

'Okay, he's welcome to travel as supercargo; if I'm hit, he could come in useful,' Luke said jokingly, then wished he hadn't. He had never considered himself superstitious but since flying the Wellington he had noticed that none of the crews liked going on a sortie on their birthdays or special anniversaries, and no one liked being put in at the last minute, in case the vengeful god who watched over aircrews decided to pick on someone who should not have been in the air at all on that day. But you couldn't let superstition dictate your movements, so he gave Fred a big grin and reminded him that they would be a pack of sandwiches short, since he could scarcely take over young Masters's grub if he was actually going to fly with them. Fred frowned thoughtfully, then said he would consult Masters, see how he felt.

Luke made his way to his room, where he undressed and got into bed, after a glance at his watch. It was barely two o'clock; he could sleep for four hours and still be in plenty of time for the briefing.

He awoke to find that the wind still howled around the hut, if anything noisier than before, though fortunately it had not woken him. He got up, padded along to the bathroom for a wash, then went back and dressed himself in his flying gear. Another glance at his watch told him that he should go down to the anteroom for a cup of char and a bun before the briefing, especially as, if Masters was coming with them, he would have to plead with the head cook for extra rations for the flight.

However, as he emerged from his room, he met young Masters coming towards him, holding out a packet of sandwiches and a bottle of cold tea which the cookhouse had provided. He grinned cheerfully at Luke, handing him the food and drink with a flourish. 'Fred explained that you were back early and going to fly Bouncing Betty yourself, so I've got a night off since my own kite isn't scheduled to go on this raid,' he said. 'It was quite a relief; no one likes taking another feller's place.'

'Thanks,' Luke said, taking the sandwiches and bottle of tea. He did not remind Masters that any sort of last minute change was also considered unlucky. What was the point? The younger man was clearly relieved to be let off the hook; it was both cruel and unnecessary to mention that Luke himself was now in the invidious position of actually flying the kite when he should have been sleeping soundly in his own bed.

However, it was a blessing that he and Rosie had decided to break the back of the journey the previous day! At least it had given him time for four hours' solid rest, which meant that he was not starting off tired and stale. On the other hand, of course, had he been later arriving, Fred might not have spotted him, might not have suggested he should fly Bouncing Betty tonight. Still, he was truly fond of his crew and knew they would be a good deal happier with himself in charge than with the young, and relatively untried, Masters.

'By Jupiter, am I glad it's you handling the old girl and not that young feller,' Phil, the wireless operator, bawled in Luke's ear as the heavy plane left the ground. It had been a fearful take-off with the wind now gusting, now dropping, now coming at them from the wrong angle; Bouncing Betty had not been the only bird to have to make several attempts before she became airborne. Now, however, Luke eased back the stick, pulling her nose up into a steep climb to get above the clouds – say five thousand feet. They knew their target was the factories which abounded along the Rhine and that these were always well defended, not only by gunners on the ground but by every fighter the Nazis could put up. Still, if he kept as high as possible until they were right over the target, then laid their eggs quickly and turned for home, they should be all right.

The plane droned on and the men became absorbed in keeping themselves warm and alert, for it was extremely cold. They had to keep radio silence so could not chat over the intercom, but when it was time for Luke to eat his sandwiches and drink his tea, he had a few murmured words with Phil. Phil slid into the co-pilot's seat, checked the instruments, then bawled above the noise of the engines: 'How did your leave go?'

Luke smiled reminiscently. 'It couldn't have been better,' he said dreamily. 'We're going to get married, Rosie and me.' He shoved a sandwich into his mouth, noticing it was bloody Spam again, and spoke rather thickly through it. 'Damn, I told her I'd ring her tonight. I wonder if she'll guess I'm flying? I told her I wasn't, but I'll ring her tomorrow, first thing, before breakfast – hers, I mean, not ours.'

Phil nodded. 'Well, that's just great, skip,' he said. 'Tell you what, though, I'm damn glad it'll be you and not me who has to land if the wind stays at gale force. You'll be fishtailing all over the runway, trying to put her down without losing a wing or smashing the undercarriage.'

Luke nodded grimly. 'It was hard enough getting her up,' he reminded the wireless operator. 'If the Met boys knew about this hurricane, I'd have thought we'd have been grounded. But there you are, they'll be full of it tomorrow morning when it'll probably be dying down.' He took a swig of cold tea, then belched. 'I almost envy young Masters, snug in his bed.'

'Almost? I envy anyone who's asleep in their bed,' Phil said frankly. 'Not long to go now though; another hour and we'll be over the target.'

When they reached the target, there could be no doubt that it was the right one. Throughout the flight, they had been aware of the dark shadows of the rest of the squadron, and as soon as they saw the moonlit river below them, and the enormous flat-roofed factories on either bank, the quiet night became a very noisy night indeed. The flares which lit up the scene below them so that they could drop their bombs accurately were joined by the bursting shells of flak some of which came near enough to Bouncing Betty to make her name seem entirely appropriate as she rocked about the sky. Below them, they could see the fires caused by the first bombs to drop, and all too soon they saw the leading Wellington go down in a mass of screaming flame, whilst a Ju88 followed her, machine guns blazing as she sought to slaughter the crew. Not that the crew had had a chance, Luke thought grimly, fighting to keep Bouncing Betty steady as they approached their particular target. Below them, several factories were on fire, but one large one seemed undamaged and it was for this that Luke was heading. He tried to ignore the attentions of the German fighter planes, only jinking from time to time when it became a matter of survival to do so, but mostly he held the great plane steady. He knew that Neville, the bomb aimer, was waiting for exactly the right moment and swept a little lower, reducing speed and, because of the extra drag, having to fight the kite like a recalcitrant horse as her nose dipped and she seemed about to stall.

But it was all right. From behind him he heard the cry, 'Bombs away!' and hastily reached across to increase engine power and pull her nose up. Even as he did so, he heard Neville shout, 'Let's go, let's go, let's go!' and knew that their task was accomplished; knew it even more satisfyingly as the plane banked in a turn and he caught a glimpse of the huge factory, with smoke and flames pouring through three enormous holes in its roof.

All around him, chaos still reigned. It was a clear night but the smoke and the flak and the constant attacks from the German fighters turned the sky into bedlam. Luke felt profoundly grateful that their job was done; now all they had to do was get home safe and face the difficulties of trying to land, without mishap, in a hurricane.

All around them, the shapes of other bombers heading for home could be seen, but he knew the German fighters would follow them as far as they dared and hoped that the Spitfires and Hurricanes would soon appear to harass the Luftwaffe.

Behind him, the men were settling down, beginning to discuss the raid, wondering what the weather would be like in four or five hours' time when they reached Norfolk. The fires and confusion of the Rhine were far behind them now, the great planes droning quietly on beneath the stars. When a Ju88 suddenly flashed in front of Bouncing Betty, Luke was so surprised that, for a fatal instant, he did not jerk the stick into immediate avoidance, and in that moment the two planes actually collided. Luke heard himself scream at the chaps, telling them to get out, as the plane began to lose height. Then he was battling to tighten his own parachute straps, which he always loosened before climbing into his seat, and following the crew out through the hatch.

One moment it was all noise, bright lights, fear and confusion. Then there was rushing air, ice-cold against his face, and the certainty that this was the prelude to dying. Frantically, his fingers felt for the ripcord, found it, tugged gently, then a good deal harder, and he felt the shock in every part of his body as the 'chute opened and jerked his mad downward career to a painful, blessed stop.

Luke glanced around him and felt an almost crazy relief flood through him as he counted the opening 'chutes. They were all there, floating downwards as he was, some ahead of him, looking like pale mushrooms against the dark of the ground beneath, others to his left or right . . . but all there, all apparently in one piece. He had been last out and had noticed, with what small, cool part of his mind had been noticing anything but the danger, the kite's doomed glide earthwards. Luke thought that his crew were a pretty cool bunch. They had answered his urgent shout to bale out in a sensible and orderly fashion; grabbing for their parachutes and jumping as soon as they were able to do so . . . and it could be the saving of them. For one moment – a horrid one – it occurred to him that they might not all have got out after all; that one or two, or maybe more, of the parachutes he had seen might belong to the crew of the Ju88 which had crashed into them. Then he dismissed the thought with a shudder. Poor devils, they hadn't had a chance. The collision had simply annihilated their craft; what was left of it had gone down in flames, falling faster than the Wellington . . .

His thoughts were interrupted. From below them came an almightly crash, then he saw the flames and knew it was Betty's funeral pyre. That would give their position away all right, he told himself, but found that he could not worry overmuch about what lay ahead. It was so strange, so peaceful, floating gently earthwards, with the sky above them dark as the stars began to dim, and the earth beneath them totally black apart from the flames from the aircraft. Luke found himself relishing the silence; quiet was something totally absent from the experience of flying a Wimpey, particularly once they drew near their target, and as he looked down once more it occurred to him for one horrifying moment that all that blackness might be sea.

Then he chided himself for an idiot; had poor Betty plunged into the sea she would scarcely still be burning, and besides, they had had hours to go before they would have been over water. Gently descending, he realised that the moon had disappeared, perhaps behind a mountain top, and the starlight was not strong enough to show the ground beneath in much detail, but he remembered that one could steer a parachute to a certain extent, and hoped to be able to keep clear of any trees. He could see no lights and hoped they were in open country – moorland for preference – but was still too high to be able to make even an informed guess. They had been extremely lucky, he reminded himself, that the fighter which had collided with them had been by itself, not accompanied by other aircraft which might have followed them down, machine-gunning both men and 'chutes as they descended. He knew it happened sometimes, had seen it himself, and thanked God for their own escape from such a fate. What was more, because they had flown some distance from their target before the accident happened, there was a strong chance that they would be captured and imprisoned and not quietly killed as had happened to many an airman parachuting down amongst the houses and factories he had just bombed. If he'd been able to choose, it would have been better to parachute into France, but choice, unfortunately, was seldom available, and life as a prisoner of war would be infinitely preferable to death by howling mob.

So when the ground grew close enough to identify what was beneath, Luke felt he could not complain when he saw that it was forest, stretching as far as the eye could reach. He stared over to his left, where Betty had burst into flames, but could no longer see even smoke. Either she had not flamed for long or the wind was stronger than he had thought and had carried him well away from the crash, he told himself, even as he became entangled in an extremely tall beech tree and heard at least one of his crew crashing into a similar specimen, though at some distance. Fate had dealt pretty kindly with them, he thought, as he began, as speedily as he could, to unbuckle himself from his harness. In a way, it was the most hazardous act he could have contemplated, since he was pretty near the top of the tree and might easily plunge to earth without the parachute to hold him up, but he did not intend to simply swing here, like a damn fool butterfly caught in a spider's web, until some German or other came to cut him down. No siree, he would take his chance on a speedy – but not too speedy – descent to the forest floor.

One glance at the parachute itself told him that he was unlikely to be able to disentangle it. He knew he was supposed to bury the 'chute, though no one had ever explained how one dug a fairly long and deep hole in the unyielding ground beneath large trees without so much as a teaspoon to help. Still, the question was academic and did not trouble Luke at all. Looking around him – for he was still in the upper branches of the tree – he realised that he, and at least one of his crew, had landed in a very extensive forest, most of which was still leafless, though the buds would be bursting in a few days. By screwing up his eyes and staring in all directions, he thought he could make out another 'chute in the branches to his left, and presently, as the light grew stronger, he was sure of it. Gingerly, he began to descend from his lofty perch, wondering as he did so at his own calm acceptance of the situation and concluding that, after the hell of the bombing raid, almost anything else would seem positively pleasant. It was the first time he had descended by parachute – the first time he had ever been so high in a tree, come to that – and because the night was balmy and there had been no enemy fighters to shoot him up, he had rather enjoyed the experience. The peace of the forest could not but affect him and he remembered, gratefully, a childhood spent scrambling up and down trees as he began the long descent. Had he been able to see just exactly how high he was, he might have panicked, for several times he missed his footing in the dimming starlight and once he seized upon a branch too thin to bear his weight and crashed ten feet before landing, far too abruptly, upon a wide and spreading branch.

He told himself, afterwards, that he might have got down uninjured, had it not been for the voice which hailed him from below. 'Hey, skip! Is that you?' Luke gave an almighty start, lost his hold on the branch, and crashed some fifteen feet to the ground, his fall only partially broken by landing on the crew member who had shouted to him. Cursing, he got to his feet, only then discovering that his left ankle would not support him and seemed to be at a very odd angle.

The man who had called him proved to be Neville, the bomb aimer, and Luke addressed him crossly as the other man scrambled to his feet: 'You bloody fool, you scared the life out of me shouting like that. I wouldn't be surprised if I've busted my ankle.'

'Well, you knocked all the breath out of me, and I wouldn't be surprised if you've broken a couple of my ribs,' Neville grumbled, but he grinned as he did so. Luke saw the flash of his teeth in the grey dawn light. 'What'll we do now, skip? Where's the rest of 'em, d'you think?'

'Dunno,' Luke said shortly. His ankle was beginning to hurt like hell and even the thought of putting it to the ground made him wince. 'I'm gonna sit here, see if the pain goes off if I stay still for a moment. You go and see if you can find the others, only don't lose me, for God's sake, because with this ankle I'm goin' no place, not without help.'

'Right, skip, and I'll see if I can find you a couple of stout branches to use like crutches,' Neville said. He fished a penknife from the pocket of his flying suit. 'I'll blaze a trail so I get back to you. Sure you're all right to be left? You're beginning to look pretty green.'

'It's the pain, and shock I suppose,' Luke said, as laconically as he could. 'Off with you, Nev.'

For a while after Neville had left, Luke simply sat and surveyed his foot. He knew he ought to take his boot off in case the ankle swelled, but he found he was not at all keen to so much as touch it. However, it had to be faced, so he began to draw his foot up, the breath hissing between his teeth at the sheer agony of even such a small movement. When he could reach his boot, he untied his laces and began to try to get it off, but already his whole foot, and the lower half of his leg, was swollen and shiny, as well as turning an increasingly deep purple. Luke groaned aloud and retied the lace, though loosely. He imagined that if Neville could find the other crew members, they might somehow manage to get him to the edge of the forest. They would have to leave him then because they would want to try to reach France, and must know they could scarcely do so while burdened with an injured man. All right, so he was clearly destined to spend the rest of the war as a prisoner – for you, the war is over – but that did not mean his entire crew must suffer.

Presently, Neville returned. He was alone but he carried what looked like two stout cudgels, one under each arm, and announced proudly that his trusty knife had come in useful for stripping the branches from a couple of young saplings to make the skipper a pair of crutches.

'Well, I dunno,' Luke said doubtfully. 'If there were a few more of us . . . but with only us two, and me with only one foot . . .'

'P'raps I ought to take your boot off,' Neville said doubtfully. 'I wish Brendan were here. He's done a

First Aid course – he'd know what's best to do. If I tried taking your boot off, I might be doing more harm than good without knowing it.'

'I've already tried; it won't come off. My foot's already too swollen, and anyway, the boot sort of contains it – if you know what I mean. Without the boot, it would flop around too much. So you didn't see any of the others? How far did you go?'

'Not very far,' Neville said, rather evasively. 'To tell the truth, I was afraid of getting lost and not being able to find you again.' He grinned deprecatingly at his skipper. 'I know I blazed a trail but a penknife doesn't leave a huge mark and, of course, I only marked one side of each tree. If I'd walked past a marked tree on the wrong side, it would have been all up with me; real babes in the wood stuff.'

'And you didn't come across a road, or the end of the trees, or any sign of habitation?' Luke asked, rather helplessly. He remembered stories of the enormous German forests which stretched for mile after mile, without so much as a track between the trees. It was all very well talking about escaping to free France, or even trying to make their way back to England, but that would mean living on the country, and since they had no gun with which to shoot squirrels, and the forest seemed to consist mainly of beeches and oaks, they could scarcely survive on acorns and beech mast, even had such things been available in April.

Neville shook his head. 'Nothing but trees,' he said gloomily. 'Look, skipper, are you up to trying to move, because I've a nasty sort of feeling that if we just stay here, it's only our bones that the searchers will find. I've got my compass so we shan't walk round in circles, but we'd better move on while you've still got the strength.'

The light was getting stronger all the time, though

it still came dimly to them beneath the almost leaf-less branches. Luke looked doubtfully at his bomb aimer's rough crutches and then at his horribly swollen and painful foot. 'I'll have a go . . .' he was beginning, when a thought struck him. He had no idea where Neville had landed after leaving the plane, but doubted that he had been at the very top of any of the surrounding trees, since he seemed to have escaped without any obvious bruises or abrasions. He said as much and Neville replied, cheerfully, that he had been lucky; he had come down in a clearing, had shed his parachute, buried it, sketchily, in leaf mould, and had then walked towards the sounds of crashing which had been, he realised now, his skipper's far from effortless descent. 'But first, old feller, I think you should shin up one of these trees – go as high as you can without risking a fall – and see what you can see from up there,' Luke said. 'When I was at the top of my beech, it was still pretty dark so I couldn't see much, but you might be able to pick out some sort of landmark, or even a thinning of the trees. Why, you might even see other parachutes, because I'm sure I can't be the only one who got tangled in branches. Then we could meet up; we'd have a much better chance of finding civilisation if we were all together.'

'Right, I'll have a go,' Neville said, though his voice was doubtful. 'Whilst I'm doing it, skip, do you want to have a go on the crutches? A sort of practice, like?'

By now, Luke's foot was on fire with pain and his ankle sheer agony. He only had to make the tiniest movement for bone to grate against bone, and even the thought of trying out the crutches brought drops of sweat standing out on his forehead. 'I'll wait till you come back, if it's all the same to you, Nev,' he said hoarsely. 'I wouldn't dare try alone in case I fell.

And if I fell, I don't think I'd ever manage to get up.'

'Right you are; stay put until I get back,' Neville said breezily, but Luke could see that his bomb aimer was worried. Neville was a short, stocky man, which might make it difficult for him to assist his much taller skipper if they had to walk further than a few paces. But it was no use worrying over what might never happen, so Luke leaned back against the trunk of the beech, closed his eyes and tried to think calming thoughts whilst listening to Neville grunting with effort as he began to scramble up a big old elm tree, with branches spaced a good deal closer than those of the beech through which Luke himself had descended.

Presently, he opened his eyes and saw that Neville was out of sight, though the movement of the upper branches showed that he must be nearing the top of the tall elm. Luke felt rather guilty; it had been his idea for Neville to climb a tree and he had not thought to suggest a beech, an oak or a sycamore, but now he remembered that elms were tricky, that their branches could appear stout but break off easily, earning them the nickname of coffin wood.

However, ten minutes or so later, he felt the ground shudder slightly as Neville jumped down from the lowest branch. His face wore a beam. 'There's a 'chute in a tree and someone tugging at it no more than a hundred yards off,' he said gleefully. 'Don't worry, I noted the direction, and whoever it is, I'll have him back here before you can say knife. With two of us, one each side, we can move you to a better spot in no time. Oh, and I forgot to mention, I've seen a road and the trees on the other side of it are definitely more sparse. Skip? You all right?'

Luke had closed his eyes again as soon as he saw his friend was safe, but now he opened them, trying to fight off a feeling of total weariness. 'I'll live; I never heard of anyone dying of a broken ankle,' he said weakly. 'I'll just rest for a moment while you go and find the owner of that 'chute.'

Luke must have dozed, for he awoke to the sound of voices and saw, with real pleasure, Brendan accompanying Neville across the short distance to the foot of the great beech. 'I've bust my damned ankle,' he said wearily. 'I tried to get my boot off, but no luck. Still, if you and Neville can help me to the road . . .'

They got him there. It took them two full hours and if the journey was tedious for them, it was sheer agony for Luke. When they reached the road, and propped him against a convenient tree, he told them they must begin to make their way towards the French border if they meant to try to escape.

'We can't leave you here alone,' Neville said firmly. 'God knows when you'd be found, if at all. Besides, we're miles and miles from the border, so I think we'd best stick together. We can try to take you a bit further . . .'

'You'll leave me here,' Luke said, with all the firmness he could muster. 'Let's face it, I'm no use to anyone with a busted ankle, I'd only hold you back. Someone's bound to come along and I'll end up in hospital. We're always being told how efficient the Jerries are, so I guess they can set an ankle as well as any Yank or Limey.' He grinned at them. 'Good luck, fellers, see you back in Blighty when the war's over. Oh, and can you get the news to my girl? I don't want her thinking . . . thinking . . .'

He was looking at his crew as he spoke and suddenly realised he was seeing them as though through water. Brendan was speaking, asking him which girl, but he was no longer capable of replying. He was descending a long slope which ended in darkness, and he was glad to enter it.

Luke came round with a shout of pain and a jerk which, he thought afterwards, might very well have been the last move he ever made, for when he managed to focus his eyes he saw that he was looking down the barrel of a rifle. He realised that the throbbing pain in his forehead must mean that the owner of the rifle had jabbed him there, quite viciously, to bring him round; he could feel a trickle of blood running down the side of his face.

The man standing in front of him spoke, but since it was in German, Luke could not understand a word. He was an old man, wearing breeches, long leather boots laced up to the knee, a faded shirt and an ancient tweed jacket. He wore a pair of tiny, much mended spectacles behind which his eyes glared, the whites showing all round the irises and proving, to Luke's secret dismay, that his questioner was scared out of his mind and might easily decide that shooting someone as dangerous as himself was his best option.

The man butted him with the rifle again, this time in the chest, and Luke groaned and tried to pull himself upright, then gave a shout of pain as the movement disturbed his ankle. Hastily, the old man levelled his rifle once more, this time pointing it at Luke's head. He heard the safety catch click off, saw the old man's finger tighten on the trigger, and gave himself up for lost.

Despite the fact that she was very tired, Rose got little sleep that night. The wind increased to such an extent that all hands were called out to either hold the aircraft down or get them into hangars, if there was sufficient room. Rose, with her companions, battled across the airfield, trying to keep their eyes half closed, for a veritable dust storm had arisen to make things even harder for the would-be rescuers. Whilst out there, they saw two pines and a sturdy elm tree come crashing to earth, and one of the storage huts simply blew away, leaving the cardboard boxes of supplies to bowl merrily across grass and runways, with anyone who could be spared from the aircraft in hot pursuit.

'How on earth will the kites get down safely in this?' Kate asked Rose, as they staggered to the cookhouse, bearing a large cardboard box full of cornflakes between them. 'Our fighters didn't go up, did they – too light, I suppose – but I bet the big bombers, the Wimpeys and Lancs, took off on their raids.' They had reached the cookhouse by now and dumped their burden amongst the other assorted boxes and bundles which had been brought into the shelter of the brick building. 'You'll be wanting to ring East Wretham in the morning to make sure your Luke got down safely.'

'Luke wasn't flying tonight; he was still on leave until midnight,' Rose explained. She pushed the damp hair off her forehead and whistled: 'Phew! I doubt the poor bloke has had much sleep though, because they'll turn everyone out, even the officers, to save as much as possible from being smashed to bits by the wind. Have you ever seen anything like it, Kate?'

Kate shook her head, then chuckled. 'Did you see ACW Franklyn, though? She's only a little thing, she can't weigh more than six stone, and the wind picked her up as though she was a feather, bowled her six feet along the ground, and might have taken her further if LAC Roberts hadn't grabbed her as she passed. I've never seen a girl so furious. She was weeping with temper.'

'Who can blame her?' Rose said, as the two of them

emerged from the cookhouse. The wind seized Rose's once neat brown hair and flung it across her face so that she was forced to stop, gather it up and hold it back with one hand. 'What'll we do next? I'm dead tired and we seem to have done all we can do to help but, to tell you the truth, I'm scared our hut will blow away, taking us and our beds with it, like Dorothy in *The Wizard of Oz*!'

Kate had opened her mouth to answer when a voice came booming and crackling over the tannoy. 'All personnel to take themselves to the cookhouse, for tea and a wad,' it announced. 'The Met Office tell us that the gusts should die down by evening.'

Kate and Rose turned with one accord, and made their way back to the cookhouse, relieved to be out of the wind and in a solid building, though the roof, Rose supposed, was as liable to blow away as anything else on the airfield.

Across the room, Jen and Mo hailed them. It appeared that they had been working in the cookhouse helping to get the tea brewed and the wads on the go, so were comfortably ensconced at a table for four by the time the other two entered. They greeted the newcomers cheerfully, and for some moments the talk was all of the destruction the storm was wreaking on their airfield and what must be happening on other stations.

'We saw a barrage balloon going past at one hell of a speed; it took the chimneys clean off Grundy's farm as it went and is probably halfway to France by now,' Mo said cheerfully. 'And Bates had washed a pair of stockings and some knickers and hung them on that bit of a line behind the hut. She said even the line's gone and God alone knows if she'll ever see her knickers again.'

'Was your chap flying tonight, Rosie?' Jen asked,

taking a large bite out of her bun and speaking, rather thickly, through it. 'If so, landing will be pretty dicey, won't it?'

'No, he's not flying, he's still on leave,' Rose told her. 'But I'll ring first thing in the morning because no doubt he'll have been up most of the night, like us, and with a bit of luck he'll know when he's flying again so we might have a chance to meet.'

Jen waggled her eyebrows. 'How a week's leave can change a person,' she remarked. 'Before you went, you even objected to Luke being spoken of as "your feller" but now, you're actually talking . . . well, like the rest of us.'

'He's asked me to marry him,' Rose said proudly. 'I think I must have been mad not to realise that life with Luke would be totally different – wonderfully different – from life with Steve. Oh, I know it's wrong to speak ill of the dead, and I don't meant to do so, and besides, it's all over; Steve is a part of my pre-war past that I want to forget, and Luke, believe me, is my future.'

The three girls nodded, clearly impressed. 'Lucky old Rose,' Kate murmured. 'I hope and pray that one day I'll meet someone who can mean as much to me as Bobby did. As for you two . . .' she pointed a derisive finger at Mo and Jen, 'it's about time you settled down and made the current flame the happiest man on earth. Who are the current flames, by the way?'

Jen giggled. She was notoriously free with her affections but had been going out with the same mechanic for five months, and this time seemed to have no urge to move on. Mo, on the other hand, was true to her peacetime boyfriend, who had joined the army and been sent to Burma. They exchanged letters, but many months elapsed before such letters arrived and lately Mo had had a couple of dates with a Hurricane pilot, though she assured her friends that Joe and herself were simply marking time until her Norman and his Mandy were back in England; for Mandy was a Wren up at Scapa Flow and her leaves were never long enough to allow her to come this far south.

'When we're as old and withered as you two, we'll probably marry and have kids and that,' Jen said airily, and seeing the wistful look in Mo's eyes, Rose felt guilty. She was so lucky to have Luke close at hand; poor Mo must have heard about the terrible fighting in Burma, where the troops were using jungle warfare against the Japanese, whilst the Burmese did their best to avoid both combatants. She must know that, even as they spoke, her Norman might be dead, or in a Japanese prisoner of war camp, which would be almost as bad. It wasn't fair to tease her when her future was so uncertain.

Rose was still congratulating herself on her luck when she went to the mess immediately before breakfast next morning, hoping to be able to get to the telephone before others had the same idea. She was lucky and the voice at the other end of the line informed her, crisply, that she had reached East Wretham and asked her to whom she wished to speak.

'Flying Officer Nadolski, please.'

There was a short, awkward silence, then the voice at the other end said, cautiously: 'I'm sorry, who is that speaking?'

Rose's heart plummeted. Why had he asked who she was? Why had he not just gone and fetched Luke? Of course, it would be better if he told Luke who was calling, but the chaps usually simply sang out that so and so was wanted on the phone.

However . . . she cleared her throat. 'I'm Corporal Rose McAllister, ringing from Coltishall airfield,' she said, as crisply as she could. 'Luke and I only came back from leave yesterday, so I know he wasn't flying, but I thought I'd have a word . . .' Her voice tailed off.

The voice the other end cleared its throat in its turn. 'Sorry, corp, thought I'd better ask,' he said. 'Flying Officer Nadolski took his Wimpey over Germany last night; he went as a favour to the CO really, because the only pilot spare, so to speak, was a youngster, three months out of training school.'

'Oh, I see,' Rose said, with a most uncomfortable feeling beginning to tie her stomach into knots. 'Have they got down yet? Is . . . is he safe?'

'It's been a wild night and the wind's been gusting at well over eighty mph,' the voice said evasively. 'Several of the kites haven't come in yet, but at least one was blown far enough off course to end up in Kent, so no need to worry too much yet. Give it a go later, corp.'

Rose put the receiver down slowly and walked back across the mess, heading for the cookhouse. She told herself that it was too much to assimilate in one go, that she must sit down and think about what she had been told. Oddly, there was anger mixed with her anguish. How could he have agreed to fly when he had no need to do so, was officially on leave? How could he risk his life which, she now realised, was as precious to her as her own? But by the time she reached the cookhouse, her common sense had begun to reassert itself. His crew meant a great deal to him, perhaps more than they would have meant to someone who had been born and brought up in Britain. Luke was not a loner from choice and his crew had taken him to their hearts, realising, as Rose had only just begun to do, how solitary he was, without so much as an old school friend, let alone a relative, for thousands of miles. So naturally, when the chips were down, his crew would come first; he would never willingly leave them in the hands of a stranger.

In the cookhouse she gravitated, like a pin to a magnet, towards the table where Kate, Mo and Jen sat. She gave them what she thought was a cheerful smile, but there must have been something in her face which told its own story, for as she sat down Kate spoke at once, her eyes anxious. 'What's up? I thought you said Luke wasn't flying last night? God, girl, you're white as a sheet. Has he landed yet?'

'He flew last night and no, he hasn't landed yet,' she said wearily. 'I spoke to some chap . . . I didn't recognise the voice . . . who said that they'd put a young fellow on to fly Bouncing Betty, a young fellow who'd only had three months' experience. So when Luke turned up, all bright-eyed and bushy-tailed from his leave, his squadron leader asked him if he'd fly Betty instead of the new chap. And – and he'd not landed when I rang, or not at East Wretham at any rate. The bloke I talked to said another bomber had landed in Kent, so I suppose . . .' Her voice trailed away.

Jen leaned over and gave Rose's shoulder a comforting squeeze. 'Think of the gale. It's enough to blow anyone off course,' she said briskly. 'You stay where you are and I'll fetch you some brekker; got your irons?'

Dumbly, Rose handed her cutlery over, though she said that she knew she would be unable to eat a thing. 'Still, tea would be nice,' she admitted. And presently, with a large pile of scrambled egg and a small piece of bacon before her, she found that she was ravenously hungry and cleared the plate, as well as drinking two cups of tea.

While she ate the girls chatted, making suggestions as to how Luke might have got down perfectly safely, either on another airfield, or possibly on his own, though since her phone call, of course. Rose knew that this was an attempt to keep her spirits up, but she appreciated it none the less and went out to work still feeling worried, but determined to put a good face on it. Today she was driving the Winco up to Lincolnshire where he would be part of a large group watching an experimental aircraft giving a display of its powers. She might ring East Wretham from there, because she would not be wanted whilst the trials were being performed. Usually the Winco, a pleasant fair-haired man in his forties, with a neat little toothbrush moustache and humorous grey eyes, told her to go to the cookhouse for a meal and then to take a good book into the mess and amuse herself until he called for her, but today, Rose thought, she would simply have to keep telephoning East Wretham until someone could give her news. That it might be bad news, she did not dare contemplate.

By four o'clock that afternoon, Rose imagined that every officer on East Wretham airfield must be heartily sick of the sound of her voice. She contemplated going for a walk along the perimeter but knew, the moment she did so, that she would be called on the tannoy to take the Winco home, so stayed where she was. I'll have one last go, she told herself, as the clock hands crept slowly round to half past four. The wind had died down earlier than the Met Office had anticipated, but there were stories coming in from all over East Anglia – barns, sheds and even roofs blown away, trees uprooted and hedges battered, crops ruined and telephone wires torn down – so Rose convinced herself that there was still a chance that Luke, and Bouncing Betty, had landed safely somewhere in England. Because of the chaotic conditions, he might be unable to get in touch with his own station, might even now be crossing the country on public transport, not dreaming that she even knew he had been flying because, after all, he had still been on leave and she might have been too busy to telephone his mess until quite late that evening.

But at half past four, the phone was answered by Chubby Davies, who flew a Wellington bomber, and was a member of Luke's squadron. Rose had met him a couple of times and greeted him as cheerfully as she could, asking for news of Luke. If he had known her better, if he had realised that the relationship between herself and Luke had deepened into something more than casual friendship, he might have answered her less frankly. As it was, he said quite breezily: 'Shot down I'm afraid, old girl; saw it myself. But they all got out – I counted the parachutes – and they were over open country, so they ought to be okay.'

'Shot down?' Rose quavered, her voice rising, despite her determination to stay calm. 'Oh, Chubby, was anyone injured? Did you . . . did you . . .'

'Well, they weren't really shot down; a Ju88 came at them but what went wrong I don't know, because he crashed straight into them. We hung about to make sure no one tried to shoot them up and we saw the kite hit the ground and burst into flames some way from where the crew baled out. They were lucky really,' he added, in a ruminative tone. 'Bouncing Betty was a goner from the time the Junkers hit her, but she didn't burst into flame, or break up, until she hit the ground, so the crew were able to bale out all right. And I think her engines couldn't have packed up either, because she went down in a long glide and that means that the Germans will look for them a good few miles from where they'll actually have landed. So maybe, even now, they're making their way back to England. England, home and beauty,' he added, sounding almost envious, as though he himself would have enjoyed such a trek.

For Rose, however, it was a different matter. She tried to tell herself that since there had apparently been no exchange of fire, Luke would have landed safely, unwounded and perhaps even eager to pit his wits against the enemy and get home – or at least to a neutral country – before he was captured, but it was uphill work. Hideous pictures kept appearing before her inner eye. Stories of English bomber crews parachuting safely to earth only to be torn to pieces by an angry mob, or of men landing in icy seas or lakes and dying of exposure, filled her mind. When she was called over the tannoy, and drove her staff car across to where the Winco waited, her mind was so full of horrors that she could scarcely answer his cheerful questions as to how she had spent the day, and very soon began answering so completely at random that the Wing Commander guessed something was up.

'I'm afraid you've had bad news, corporal,' he said quietly, after they had travelled a dozen miles in almost complete silence. 'Do you want to talk about it? Is it your young man?'

'Yes,' Rose said, after a moment. 'He flies a Wimpey – a Wellington, I mean – from East Wretham airfield. He was over Germany last night and had turned for home when a Ju88 flew into him. Flight Lieutenant Davies watched them all bale out and said all the 'chutes opened, so he hung round to make sure they weren't shot up, and said they all got safely to the ground. Only – only I can't help worrying. You hear such awful stories and – and Luke was on leave, he shouldn't have been flying at all . . .'

Despite her resolve, Rose's eyes had filled with tears, blurring her vision of the road ahead. The Winco obviously realised this for he told her to pull in at the next gateway, and when the car was stationary he produced a large, pale blue handkerchief and handed it to her, telling her to have a good cry and then to mop her eyes and blow her nose, and remind herself that her young man had been most awfully lucky to get down safely and would undoubtedly return to her as soon as he was able. 'And you can't spend the rest of the war worrying about what might never happen,' he told her, 'because I remember you telling me, when you first started driving me, that you had been making uniforms for the forces but decided that that was not sufficient, so in order to help the war effort even more you joined the WAAF.' He grinned across at her, his funny little moustache tilted up at the corners. 'So you see, you must put your worries to the back of your mind, say a prayer for him night and morning, and in between, concentrate on your job. It'll be hard, I know that, but you're a brave young woman, and a darned good driver and I don't mean to lose you. All right?'

Rose gave a watery sniff, put the handkerchief away in her pocket, promising to let him have it back when she had laundered it, and started the car. 'I know you're right,' she said in a subdued tone. 'Other girls have worse problems, but they keep cheerful. And – and thank you, sir, for being so – so understanding. I'll remember what you've said.'

The watery-eyed peasant did not shoot Luke, largely because the rifle was not loaded, but also because before he could do anything, Neville had burst out from the covering trees, causing the old man to drop his gun from fright. At this very moment, a lorry had come careering along the road, driven by a hard-faced young soldier. He saw the small drama being enacted by the roadside and pulled up with much dust and a screech of brakes and jumped down, calling something to the slightly older soldier in the passenger seat.

Neither had a word of English, but said: 'Engländer? Sprechen sie Deutsch?' and upon nods to the first question and head shakings to the second, promptly loaded both men into the back of the truck. The merest movement hurt Luke so much that he was unable to stifle a yelp of pain and then a great many groans, but this was all to the good, as it turned out, since the soldiers took them straight to the nearest civilian hospital, where, to Luke's amazement, he was greeted by a doctor who spoke excellent English, though with a strong Scottish accent.

'I took my medical degree in Edinburgh in 1936,' he said briefly. 'We're going to have to set that ankle before you can go on to a prisoner of war camp, but your friend has no business here. We will dispatch him as soon as we can find transport.'

Luke, lying on a stretcher, trying not to move a muscle, had a word with Neville before his friend was taken away. 'Get a message to Corporal Rose McAllister – she's based at Coltishall – and tell her I'm alive and in hospital; say I'll write just as soon as I'm able,' he said urgently. 'Tell her not to worry; I'll be just fine.'

Neville agreed to do so and shortly after that Luke was taken to the operating theatre and anaesthetised, coming round some time later to find his left leg in plaster from toes to knee and his right arm in a similar condition.

'You cracked the radius in your right forearm when you broke your ankle,' the doctor told him. 'But you're lucky, both injuries should mend without leaving you unduly incapacitated. And as soon as you're out of plaster you'll be joining your friend in the nearest POW camp.'

After that, there were all the formalities of being

taken prisoner, the filling in of forms, and so on. And a few weeks later, he was hustled from the hospital to an ancient army lorry and taken to the prisoner of war camp, where he found Neville, Phil and rear gunner Toby already gloomily ensconced, though they told him, as soon as they got him alone, that Brendan had not been taken so far as they knew. 'Lucky beggar will be back in England in a few weeks,' Neville said enviously. 'Oh well, I suppose the worst we'll have to suffer now is boredom. Unless we can think of a plan to break out, of course. There's an escape committee, but they haven't managed to spring anyone yet.'

'Well they aren't going to start with me,' Luke said firmly. 'My ankle still won't bear my weight and I don't imagine I'd get far on two sticks. What's the food like?'

'Basic,' Neville grunted, 'but there's Red Cross parcels; they're all right. And you can write home, of course.'

'Great! I wrote to my folks, and to Rose, from hospital, but God alone knows if the letters even got posted. Not one of the nurses spoke a word of English and they just said jah, jah, jah, and bustled off whenever I asked a question. So I'll write straight away; anyone got a sheet of paper and a pencil?'

'Hello, Rose, what's up?' Jen had intercepted Rose as she shot out of the mess, her face pink with excitement. Rose skidded to a halt and flung both arms round her friend, giving her a hard squeeze.

'He's alive! I've just had a letter from him,' she squeaked. 'He broke his ankle when he parachuted down, and they put him in a civilian hospital, which is why he wasn't reported as being a POW. But now his ankle is mended, and he's at the same camp as the rest of his crew. Oh, Jen, I'm so *happy*!'

Chapter Sixteen
1945

'Petal, Daisy! If you two girls don't get a move on, we're going to miss your mam's train. Well, I declare, anyone would think you didn't like parties.' Auntie Blodwen was shouting up the stairs and was presently rewarded by the sight of Petal and Daisy, in their best summer dresses, beginning to descend the flight. Blodwen noticed, with a little stab of anxiety, that both girls' faces wore that 'contained and sulky' look which seemed to come over them whenever their return to Liverpool was mentioned. She could understand it in a way – she loved the children as much as if they'd been her own, and knew she would miss them dreadfully when they went – but, as she frequently reminded them, Liverpool was only a few hours away on the train, and even if their mother was too busy to bring them to Wales, their Auntie Blod and Uncle Gwil would be quite happy to do the journey in reverse, to find out how they were.

It was now September, and though one could scarcely say things were returning to normal, everyone was getting used to the thought of living in a country at peace. There had been celebrations when the war in Europe had ended in May, more celebrations when the Japanese had accepted defeat on 14 August. The girls might have expected to go home then, except that they had no home to go to and their mother was still in the WAAF. But now she had said, in her last letter to the Williamses, that it was time for her small family to be together once more. She had been 'demobbed', as they called it, a couple of weeks ago and had found herself a job in an office in Liverpool's Renshaw Street, though what she did there she had not fully explained. Apparently, however, she was earning sufficient money to rent a tiny, tumbledown terraced house, not too far from her work, and thought that this would do for the family for the time being, at least.

The last time she had visited the farm had been in early August, when she had been full of excitement because Luke Nadolski had been told he would be repatriated to England, where he would be officially demobbed from the Royal Air Force. Rose had explained that the two of them meant to marry, but that Luke would probably go home first to see his parents and his brother, before returning to claim his bride.

Blodwen had felt a little doubtful when Rose had outlined this plan because she had heard of several cases where American servicemen had left British girlfriends, or even wives, behind whilst they returned to the States to be demobbed there. The wives and girlfriends had never heard from them again, and the United States Army had proved to be exceedingly tight-lipped over the whereabouts of such men. However, Rose had seemed so happy and confident that she had not voiced her fears, and now it appeared they had been groundless. Luke had come back and he and Rose meant to marry by special licence in St Peter's church in Ruthin, with the girls as bridesmaids, and Uncle Gwil to give her away.

Blodwen straightened the large ribbon bows in each girl's hair and checked their appearance. Yes, they looked neat and very pretty. Petal's hair was naturally wavy, but Blodwen had rolled up Daisy's darker locks in pipe cleaners the night before, and now curls bobbed on her shoulders.

Blodwen reached her own coat down from the back of the door and ushered the children into the yard where Dilys was waiting with the pony trap. Today was Tuesday and the wedding was fixed for Saturday so, in the time-honoured manner, Luke was to stay at the Castle Hotel, in the Square, until then. This delighted him, for he was intrigued by the old half-timbered houses, the narrow streets and the ambience of the small Welsh town. Luke had only returned to Britain a couple of days earlier, but Blodwen remembered him from his previous visits as a pleasant, easy-going young man and thought the children liked him, so why were they showing such glum faces? Blodwen had moved heaven and earth to produce pretty brides-maid's dresses and had managed to acquire some para-chute silk, which she had dyed to a beautiful shade of pale blue. The village dressmaker had made it up into two delightful dresses, but even that had not brought genuine smiles of pleasure to the children's faces. Blodwen felt a little impatient with them, had lectured them on how their mother deserved some happiness, had reminded them that they liked Luke, that they had been happy in Liverpool before the war and would undoubtedly be happy there again.

'Only once Luke has got a good job, I dare say you'll move into the country, or at least into the suburbs,' she had said comfortingly. 'Last time your mam came to stay, she was asking me about rearing chickens and pigs . . . all sorts. Just you wait, you'll find yourselves having a whale of a time and hardly missing the farm at all.'

Daisy had spoken then. 'It – it isn't just the farm,

or you, Auntie Blod,' she had mumbled. 'It's all our pals. People like my friend Phoebe, and – and Nicky. People who are staying here.'

'I've told you before, Liverpool isn't a million miles away,' Auntie Blod had said. 'You'll come back regular, I'm sure of it. Why, your mam knows how much you mean to us; she isn't going to take you away for ever.'

The girls had exchanged glances which Blodwen had been unable to interpret, but then Daisy had murmured that she was probably right and changed the subject.

Now, however, Blodwen hustled the girls into the pony trap and asked Dilys to have dinner on the table in an hour. 'Unless the train's very late we'll be back by then, and though Luke is staying in Ruthin I'm sure he'll come back here and have a meal with us,' she told her daughter. 'Still, perhaps it might be better if you stood the spuds to one side of the stove and moved the casserole from the main oven to the side one, because there's no denying that trains are a bit unreliable.' She beamed at her daughter. 'Oh, I do love a wedding, and since they're having the reception at the hotel, I'll be able to sit back and enjoy myself without having to worry about the food.'

''Bye, Mam, and don't worry about the dinner, I'll see to it,' Dilys called, as the trap rattled out of the yard.

Making their way along the lane, where already the nuts on the hazel trees were beginning to turn brown and the hedges were starred with hips and haws, Blodwen chatted to the girls about the wedding. Receiving only monosyllabic responses, she felt her annoyance returning. What was the matter with them? Could they possibly resent their mother's marriage? After all, they had had to live without her for the past few years, and had seemed to understand that she was doing her bit for her country but still loved them dearly. Blodwen glanced across at them and made a sudden decision. She pulled the pony trap on to the verge, slowed and stopped, then turned to stare accusingly at her passengers. 'Just what is the matter?' she demanded baldly. 'If you show your mam and Luke those long faces, you're going to make them very unhappy and I'm going to feel ashamed. It might seem to them as though I've tried to take your mam's place, and that I would never do. So far as you're concerned, I know your mam must always come first and that's fine by me. Now come along, and tell Auntie Blod why you're not even happy about being bridesmaids.'

Once more, the two girls exchanged glances, and rather to Blodwen's amusement first Petal and then Daisy gave a little nod before Daisy began to speak. 'Auntie Blod, they aren't just going to take us to Liverpool; it's only a rented house and Mam's giving it up at the end of the month. They're going to America, to the little town where Luke was brought up, and Mam says we've got to go with them, because we're only kids. Last time she came to stay, we begged and begged to be left behind, but she got so upset – she *cried*, Auntie Blod – that we had to give in and say we'd go, only – only we don't want to, not one bit. It's – it's such a long way, and so different! Oh, I know they speak the same language, but it truly is different. So you see, you won't be able to pop on the train to come and visit us, and we shan't be able to visit you. It may not be so bad for Petal because she's younger, but I'll be in a class with girls and boys of fifteen . . . oh, can't you understand? They'll have made all their friends and they'll only be in school for another year so they're not likely to accept me, a stranger . . . *can*

426

you understand, Auntie Blod? Mam couldn't – or wouldn't – she said I was being foolish and would soon have a heap of friends, and probably an interesting job as well. Only – only it's not what I want! I shall hate it, I know I will!'

Auntie Blodwen stared from face to face, feeling the heat creep up into her cheeks. I must have been mad not to have realised, she thought. Of course he'll want to take them back to his own place, his own country, and Rose will want it too. She had a pretty hard life before the war, what with that bully of a husband and that dreadful damp little house, and no job worth speaking of until the war came along. But it's different for the girls; they've had a wonderful country childhood, and they've made a good life for themselves. Of course they love their mother and want to be with her, but they're torn. I wonder why Rose never said that they would be going to the States? But of course, she took it for granted that I would guess the farm she talked about couldn't possibly be in Liverpool. And the girls said nothing because they knew that Gwil and I would be upset, because there's no denying, we're mortal fond of them and not getting any younger. In fact, we'll probably never see them again, as they'll be starting new lives and, whether they know it or not, we'll simply become a part of their past, as they will become a part of ours.

But she could not say this to the children, of course. For a moment, she wondered how she could make it more bearable for them, then decided the honest approach was best, though she chose her words with great care. 'I expect you must have guessed, my loves, that I had no idea your mam was going to take you so far away,' she said, trying to keep the quiver out of her voice. 'But I suppose I didn't want to face up to losing you quite so soon. It *is* hard on you, but just think for a moment; think what life has been like for your mam, not just during the war, not just while Luke was a POW, but for many years before that. When she was little more than a girl herself, she married a man who – who turned out to be thoroughly unsuitable; isn't that right now?'

Both girls nodded vehemently. 'He were a beast and a bully,' Daisy said forthrightly. 'He hit our mam – oh, often and often. We hated him, didn't we, Petal?'

Petal nodded until her curls bobbed, but both children kept their eyes fixed on Blodwen's face.

'Right. So your mam had to set out to bring her children up, not just without any help from her husband, but with actual hindrance. He drank the money she earned when he was on leave – and towards the end he attacked you, didn't he, Daisy?'

More nods, and Blodwen saw, with some distress, that Petal's eyes had filled with tears. 'Yes, he pulled Daisy's hair out by the roots and smacked her about, and I wanted to kill him,' she said, in a small, choking voice. 'I prayed to God to get him killed, and when He did – get him killed, I mean – I wished I'd just prayed to gerr'im sent away. I didn't *mean* him to be dead, but I were too little to protect Mam and Daisy, so I guess God did the right thing, after all.'

Blodwen was appalled by the weight of guilt which Petal must have carried, but realised that the child had very sensibly decided that her father's death had been God's decision, not her own. So she smiled at Petal and patted her hand before resuming. 'Well, what I'm trying to say is that your mam has walked a long and lonely road for a great many years but now she's going to have a loving partner to walk with her. Luke is a good man, gentle, generous and full of humour. He'll make her very happy and take from her shoulders the burdens which must have seemed so heavy. But, fynwy fechan i, your mam couldn't be happy in America, knowing that you had been left behind in Britain; you are her real family, the only family she's got, apart from Aunt Selina, since Uncle Frank died. So you see, for your mam's sake, you've got to make the best of America. They call it the land of opportunity and I'm sure it is; you'll have chances there that you'd never have here because we're struggling just to keep our chins above the flood, whereas over there, the war didn't touch them. They know nothing about rationing, or air raids, or being homeless.' She smiled brightly at them. 'So now, my dear ones, you have a choice. You can give something back to your mother for all that she's done for you; you can show her happy, glowing faces and be sweet to Luke and look forward, and not back. Or you can be mean and miserable and ruin her wedding day, and go to America complaining every inch of the way. Which is it to be?'

The girls once more exchanged glances, but this time, to Blodwen's relief, smiles hovered on their mouths. 'We'll be happy and make Mam happy – and Luke,' Petal said.

'Yes, we'll do that. And when we get there, we'll make the best of it,' Daisy added, with decision. 'Luke *is* nice and we don't really want to make anyone unhappy. But I'm telling you, Auntie Blod, the moment I'm old enough, I'm going to come back. Don't you think I shan't, because I shall. You haven't seen the last of me and nor has Ty Siriol.'

Auntie Blod leaned forward and gathered both girls in her arms, and there was a lot of hugging and kissing, and a little bit of crying, before she set the pony in motion once more.

'You are both good and loving girls,' Auntie Blod told them fondly, as she steered the pony out of the lane and on to the main road. 'I'm truly proud of you and I'm sure you will come back one day.'

It was now June 1946 and Daisy stood in the window of the small bedroom she shared with Petal, looking out over the endless acres of waving corn. She had had eight months to grow used to her new life but was finding it harder with each day that passed. Her bedroom faced what the Nadolskis called a back yard and the McAllisters called a garden, which was fortunate really, because the bedroom Rose and Luke shared faced the front, which overlooked the main road. What Daisy called the garage – and the other kids called the filling station – was to the left of the house, and the General Store, where Rose now worked, was to the right. Consequently, the front bedrooms were quite noisy for there was a good deal of traffic on the road and, of course, the garage was a noisy place in itself. Cars came in and out for repairs and bodywork to be done, and the mechanics shouted to one another, revved engines, hammered out dents in mudguards and fenders, and generally made a great deal of noise.

The new car showroom which Mr Nadolski had started shortly before Luke left was on the far side of the garage. Luke's brother Max had been in charge of it ever since its inception and was, Daisy thought, rather resentful than otherwise of his brother's joining the firm. Daisy knew that Luke and her mother were eager to move on, to start a business of their own which would pay them sufficiently well to rent a place of their own, too. The Nadolski house had never been intended for occupancy by so many people.

Luke's parents had been welcoming enough when the McAllisters had first arrived, had begged Daisy and Petal to call them Gran and Grandpop, as Max's children did, but Daisy knew that such tolerance could not last. The strain of having four extra bodies in a house which already contained the old couple, Max and his wife Bonnie, and their sons Dexter and Joel – stupid names – would have tried the patience of a saint, for though the house was roomy enough for the six people who had inhabited it, it was definitely cramped for ten. Upstairs, there were four bedrooms and a boxroom; one for old Mr and Mrs Nadolski, one for Max and Bonnie, one for Rose and Luke and one for Dexter and Joel. That left the boxroom for Daisy and Petal, which suited them well enough. No, the trouble came downstairs, where there was a large kitchen, a parlour which was seldom used, a small and functional bathroom and what Bonnie and Max referred to as 'our livin' room'. When Luke, Rose and the girls had first moved in, they had been told to consider the parlour as their own, but soon realised that this plan would simply never work. Mrs Nadolski had spent much time and thought on the furnishing and decorations in the parlour and the room was crowded with knick-knacks, ornaments, fancy furniture and many pictures. Because of this, Luke and Rose usually sat in the kitchen, as did everyone else in the family, for Bonnie and Max had formed the habit of letting Dexter and Joel and their schoolfriends use the living room whilst they themselves joined their parents in the kitchen. Often, the boys wandered into the kitchen as well, in search of food and a chat, or simply drawn by a need for company.

Daisy sometimes felt as if the house was pressing

in on her, as if she had no individual identity any more. Life had been so different at Ty Siriol, yet when she thought about it, the Williamses had mostly lived in the kitchen, where the farmhands had joined them at mealtimes. Thinking it over, she decided that it was the unspoken criticism from Max, Bonnie, and Gran and Grandpop which made her feel constantly unwanted. She did not blame them for this; ten people into one house simply would not go – she remembered Auntie Blod's saying about quarts into pint pots – and hard though everyone tried to give each other space, it was impossible.

Daisy sighed and sat down on the bed, getting out her pencil and the block of writing paper, and preparing to start her letters home. She wrote to Auntie Blod and Uncle Gwil once a month, and Nicky Bostock every week. In the early days, she had settled down at the kitchen table to write her letters, but the snide remarks passed by Max and his wife, and the fact that Luke's parents constantly peered over her shoulder and actually read bits of her letters aloud to one another, had speedily driven her to seek refuge in her own tiny room. There was no space for a table or a chair up here, but she preferred writing in peace to the relative comfort of the kitchen. What was more, though her letters to the Williamses were as cheerful as she could make them, she was completely frank with Nick. She told him that the lessons at school were so different that she was constantly made to look foolish, that the other pupils had formed friendships and alliances at an early age and had no interest in her, an outsider, and that to top it all she did not like the food, which was so different from the sorts of things they ate back home. She was being made to have the rest of this year in school, but even when she left, things would not be very much better since it was taken for granted that she would work in the General Store, releasing Rose either to take a job in the small town or to help her husband and brother-in-law in the new car showroom.

Auntie Blod was a good correspondent and wrote regularly – long, interesting letters, full of details about the farm, the countryside and the friends Daisy and Petal had made, but unfortunately Nick, who was so loquacious in person, hardly seemed able to string a dozen words together on paper and despite Daisy's weekly letters to him, she had only received three replies in six months.

It was a pity, of course, because Daisy longed to know every detail of Nick's life in Ruthin for, during her last months at the farm, she and Nick had grown closer and closer. Nick was eighteen now and a deep and loving friendship had grown between them. They had planned all sorts of things, had been so sure of their shared future, that Daisy had actually applied for a summer job in Ruthin, at a shop only a few doors away from Foley's.

When she had at last admitted to herself that Rose would go to America, and take her children with her, Daisy had also had to tell Nick and thought she would never forget the stricken look in his eyes, nor the way the colour had drained from his face.

'But she can't do that,' he had muttered. 'You and me, Daisy, we – we're going to be together, ain't we? I mean, when we're grown up – really grown up – we'll probably get married, won't we? If you get that job in the flower shop, we'll be able to see each other whilst we're working, as well as in the evenings. Oh, Daisy, she can't take you away from me!'

But she had, of course. Children have no rights,

Daisy told herself bitterly now, painstakingly beginning to write to the Williamses, telling them all the small events which had happened over the past month. Petal was doing well in school and had made several friends, though she missed her own place just as badly as Daisy did. But she was lucky in that Dexter was in her class at school and championed her when the others mocked her British accent, or thought her stupid because she knew nothing of American history or literature.

Daisy was still at it when she heard the thump of footsteps on the stairs and the door burst open. Daisy automatically turned her notepaper face down but she need not have worried. It was Rose, looking flushed and excited. She swooped on Daisy, giving her a big hug and half lifting her off the bed. 'It's happened at last, Daisy darling! Luke's got a job – nothing to do with car showrooms – it's the sort of job he's always wanted, and the money's awfully good; we shall be able to rent a decent place of our own. It's a fair way from here, of course, which will mean poor Petal will have to change schools, but you're almost at the end of your time in education and we'll be living pretty near a big city, so you'll have a much wider choice of jobs.'

Daisy responded to her mother with a beam and a hard hug, but said cautiously: 'Is it a flying job, Mam? I know he said that America is full of commercial airports, but I didn't know there was one near here.'

'It isn't near here; I told you, it's a hundred miles or more away,' Rose said. 'But more 'n' more towns and cities over here are taking to commercial airways and Luke's had so much experience, both as a pilot and in training others, that I was sure he'd find something – and he has. Oh, Daisy, darling, we're so happy; can you be happy for us?'

'I'm happy for me as well,' Daisy said fervently. 'And you'll be making a lot of other people happy too, Mam, because no matter how much they pretend, Max and Bonnie are dying to see the back of us.' She did not add that old Mr and Mrs Nadolski would feel the same, because it seemed unkind, though she knew it was true. Luke's parents were old, and old people don't like the even tenor of their lives disturbed. And we have disturbed them, just by being here, even though we've done our best to fit in, Daisy told herself. Of course they had done their best, particularly Mam and Luke, but the truth was, a quart into a pint pot doesn't go. 'When do we leave?'

Rose gave her another hug. 'In a fortnight,' she said exuberantly. 'Luke's already got us temporary accommodation – a flat over a greengrocer's shop – just until we find somewhere better. But oh, Daisy love, it will be all ours! We'll make our own meals and have baths whenever we want to, and come and go as we like. As I said, Luke's salary will be princely compared with . . .' she looked guilty and lowered her voice to a conspiratorial whisper, 'compared with what Max pays him now, I mean – but I'll get a job as soon as we're settled in, and you'll be in work as well, before we know it. Oh, my love, I know how hard it's been for you, how hard it's been for all of us, but that's all over now. Life is going to be so good.'

Daisy returned her mother's beaming smile. 'Have you told Petal yet?' she asked. 'She won't mind about changing school again, Mam – you know Petal, she loves change, and new people, new places. And I'll get a job just as soon as I can, because . . . well, because there are things I want to save up for, and I can't do that – save, I mean – on the money Luke's mam pays me for working at the store weekends.'

'No, I haven't told Petal yet because she's gone off somewhere with Dexter, but I thought you might tell her for me.' She pulled a face, though her eyes were still shining. 'Luke's asked me to break the news to his mum and dad – he's telling Max and Bonnie – but I wanted you to be the first to know.'

'They'll pretend to be awfully sad and complain about us leaving,' Daisy said wisely. 'They'll say you're taking their boy away before they've had a chance to get to know him again – and their grandchildren, of course. But they won't mean it; it'll be . . . what's it called . . . lip service. In their hearts, they'll be glad as glad.'

'And so they should be, because Luke isn't happy working for Max or dealing with new cars, and they both know it,' Rose said, with her hand already on the doorknob. 'You go and find Petal, darling, and by the time you get back, everyone will know.'

'Well, Rose, honey, it's all very well to say Luke hankers after flying, but he come back here willin' enough, he's settled in nicely, he and his brother is good friends . . . I guess it's kinda hard on you not having a place of your own but it's kinda hard on Father and me. You're an ambitious woman – I dare say there's nothing wrong in that – but Father and me ain't gettin' no younger and you're tekkin' our boy away after only eight months. I'm sure Father feels, same as I do, that we were just gettin' to know our Luke after all them years when he were fightin' for your country, an' now you're tekkin' him away.'

Rose suppressed a smile; Daisy was a bright kid and had anticipated exactly what old Mrs Nadolski would say, but it would never do to let her amusement show, so she said gently: 'I'm so sorry, Mother, but it's only a hundred miles away and Luke will come home often, I'm sure he will. And you know Max has said, several times, that he managed the showroom alone without any trouble during the war, so though he may miss Luke as a brother, I don't think he'll miss him in the saleroom. Luke has often told me how good Max is with customers and added that he himself simply doesn't have the same . . . knack as Max for picking out the right vehicle for each person. But he's an excellent pilot, Mother, and isn't it better that he should be in a job he loves and excels at rather than one he doesn't really enjoy?'

But Mrs Nadolski could not agree and continued to clutch her grievance to her bosom, and to blame Rose – though obliquely – for the forthcoming change, despite the bright smiles on the faces of Max and Bonnie, and her own husband's oft repeated remark that it waren't right to stand in the way of young folks, even if it did seem that their boy had changed and grown to think less of his family whilst in England.

Rose longed to point out that Luke's family now consisted of herself and her daughters, but did not do so. In a fortnight, you'll be away from them and in your own place, she reminded herself. You'll never again have to put up with Bonnie's covert jealousy and spiteful remarks, or your mother-in-law's whining, or Max's patronising air when he talks to Luke as though he were the wiser brother, when he, Max, never even went to High School. Only another fortnight and we'll be free as birds; I can put up with anything for two little weeks.

When Luke came home that evening, they took themselves off for a long walk so that Luke might tell her all about his new job and the city which the airport served. He made no pretence of being anything but jubilant over leaving his parents' house, though he admitted it had been good of them to take the family in. 'The whole thing's been my fault, in a way,' he said, as they turned for home once more. 'I meant to come home for a couple of weeks, just to see how things stood, and then I meant to get a job – any job – in another town, so that we could start our new lives as a family. But I kinda got drawn into the car business and Max was so reluctant when I wanted time off for interviews . . .' He sighed and bent his head to kiss Rose's neck, just beneath her ear. 'But it's almost over now and I guess having us at home for eight months means my parents have got to know you and the girls in a way which wouldn't have been possible if we'd only stayed a fortnight.'

Rose agreed, though she added with a chuckle that, possibly, this had not done much to improve relations between the parties concerned. 'But it doesn't matter, because when we really do have a place of our own, we can invite them over and I can cook a proper meal and serve it nicely, and show your mam that the English are just as domesticated as the Americans,' she told him. 'And there's one other good thing; even if the walls in the apartment over the greengrocer's shop are as thin as the ones in your parents' house, it won't be as – as embarrassing to have a little cuddle, as it has been these last eight months.'

Luke put both arms round her and gave her an enormous hug. 'Once we're settled, I'd like us to have at least one baby which is part of both of us,' he said, almost tentatively. 'I've never mentioned it before, because to add another soul to my parents' house would have been unthinkable, but . . . well, how do you feel, Rosie? Do you hate the thought of starting all over again with diapers and bottles and baby gear? Only the girls are growing up; Daisy wil be out in the big world before you know it. And I really like kids.'

'I like them too and I'd love to make a baby with you, darling Luke,' Rose said, carrying his hand to her lips and planting a kiss on the palm. 'As soon as we're settled, we'll make it our first priority.' She twinkled up at him. 'I'll put it in my diary when I get back tonight. One baby for Mr and Mrs Luke Nadolski; shall I order a boy or a girl?'

Laughing, and still entwined, they entered the house and shut the door behind them.

Daisy sat in the window seat of her very own bedroom, looking out at the wintry scene in the garden below. They had been in their new home for nearly two months now, for they had left the apartment over the greengrocer's shop as soon as Luke had seen the pleasant old timber house on the outskirts of the city and had managed to arrange a bank loan. It was a big, old house, and for the first time in her life, Daisy had a room of her own. She also had a job in the offices of a large department store in the city and was beginning, though cautiously, to make friends. And today she had had a letter from Nick, a proper letter with proper news, and though ill-spelt and badly written, it had brought back to Daisy's mind once more how much she longed to be back in Britain and how desperately she missed Nick.

She had always meant to go home but had never really considered how she would do so. Buses, trains, ships, planes – she guessed she would need to employ most of them to get back to Ruthin and Nick. But now that she had a job, all things were possible. She would save up, she vowed, putting away every spare cent, and perhaps by as early as the following summer she would be able to begin to plan her journey. Sitting on the window seat she could see, by craning her neck, the long, winding road which would be the first step towards home and Nicky, for she still thought of Britain as her home and America merely as a staging post.

Now, in her mind's eye, she seemed to hover above the road and to see, trudging along it, her own small figure. What was it Auntie Blod had said when she had talked to them about Rose's life? She had said that Rose had walked a long and lonely road but that in Luke she had found the perfect partner to walk with her . . . something like that, anyway. Well, she, Daisy, would soon be setting out on a long road, and maybe it would be a lonely one, but at the end of it there would be Nick. In her mind, she saw the little grey town nestling in the soft Welsh hills, as an eagle or a bird of prey would see it, and her imagination circled and dropped lower, lower, lower, until she could see St Peter's Square and Nick with his arms held out to her, and the familiar, crooked grin on his face.

Sighing, she turned back into her room once more. She thought of the miles and miles which separated her from New York, where she could perhaps get a job on a liner bound for Liverpool; then there were the miles and miles of ocean to be crossed, and more miles before she arrived at her destination. Yes, indeed, it would be a long and lonely road, but she would do it. Nick would wait.

Daisy smiled to herself and turned to go downstairs to help Rose prepare the evening meal.